By Christopher Bramley

World of Kuln
The Serpent Calls
Tides of Chaos

World of Kuln Expanded
Notes on Dragons
The First Vampire

Humour
The Lordt's Quest

Children's
The Snaggetty-Boggitt

Non-Fiction
Involve Me

THE SERPENT CALLS

CHRISTOPHER BRAMLEY

A World of Kuln novel

SANCTUM

First published in the United Kingdom in 2014 by Sanctum Publishing
This hardback edition published 2022 in the United Kingdom by Sanctum Publishing

A CIP catalogue record for this book is available from the British Library

ISBN 978-0-9931273-6-6

Published, Designed and Set by Sanctum Publishing
Set using Pfeffer Mediæval/Cinzel Decorative &
Adobe Garamond Pro 10.5/13
www.sanctumpublishing.com
All images, maps, and other media Copyright © Christopher Bramley

Foreword and Acknowledgement

This first book in the world of Kuln is a culmination of years of writer's block, being lost in a *slightly* overly complex and huge first book, the sheer task of creating a huge world and universe before the story was ever done, and dreams and ideas that began at around age thirteen. It has only been within the last five years that I actually sat down and managed to construct the basics (working in IT and never thinking of using spreadsheets is shameful), but a significant portion of this novel and the things that happen within it wrote themselves as I went. I had a plan, a structure; the book apparently had other ideas, and some of them could not be changed.

It has been tiring, frustrating, and utterly worthwhile. I am glad to finally share this with people, and I hope the characters who live and breathe herein are loved by as many others as I. The story you read here is the paint on the canvas of that universe, whose texture shows through and will continue to do so in future books.

I would like to thank first editor John Jarrold for extremely constructive and solid advice on the first draft edit; Karen Traviss for her excellent advice and precious time; Trudi Canavan for encouragement and insight at the WFC; Patrick Rothfuss for a brief but very helpful conversation on POV at the WFC, and for his most excellent beard; Ben Stevens for his advice, reviews, friendship and encouragement; second editor Tiffany Stoneman, who not only gave me friendship and peer review but excellent editing, advice and a uniquely non-fantasy viewpoint; Matt Cook, Sarah Keogh, Mike Bridge, and a fair few others who gave me peer reviews, encouragement or friendship during a behemoth of a novel; my family for encouraging me to write when I was young; Geoff Daniel, my English teacher at school, who was the single most important person to catalyse my writing through his support and belief in me at a tender age, and for whom Chapter 1 is left relatively untouched in homage (from my submittal at 13! A few less Cyclopes now); and finally my beautiful partner Grace, for her support and prayers and belief in me.

I also remember my close friend Michael Green, who always promised he would read this book and now never will. His encouragement, intellect, capabilities and inspiration in all things he did were shining examples of how we can live our lives fully every minute and truly Get Shit Done.

Miss you, man. Rast would have respected you.

- CB, 2014 (edited 2021)

ANARIA

~100 Miles

LODNOR

UNITED TERRITORIES OF MEYAR (FORMERLY HANÁ)

NASSMOOR

ARKON M

TERENDON

FOOTHILLS OF NARIE

FOOTHILLS OF RIE

EYOTSBURG

LAKE MERIMAKEA

SOLTSVAR MTS.

KIRHOLDING

RELDENHORT PLAIN (ORK TERRITORY)

STORAKTAR RIVER

PUNS

CAPSUM

THE PITS OF BLAKE

SKYBREACH MTS.

EYDA

SERGOTH PLAINS (HUMAN BARBARIAN TERRITORY)

DARKENSPIRE (DWARF TERR

GORBINOR

IGNATE

SKYREACH MTS.

NOVIN

ACHENOR

BANISTARI EMPIRE

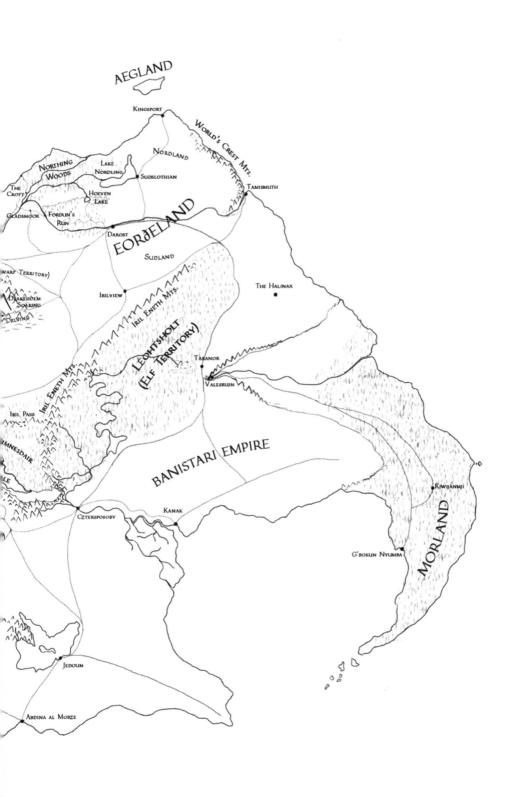

AEGLAND

KINGSPORT

WORLD'S CREST MTS.

NORDLAND

NORTHING WOODS

LAKE NORDLING

SUDSLOTHIAN

TAMISMUTH

THE CROFT

HOEVEN LAKE

GEADSMOOR

FORDLIN'S RUN

DAROST

EORÐELAND

SUDLAND

(...WARF TERRITORY)

THE HALINAX

DRAKEHOLM SOARING

IRILVIEW

IRIL ENETH MTS.

...DELVING

LÉOHTSHOLT (ELF TERRITORY)

TARANOR

VALESRIIN

IRIL ENETH MTS.

IRIL PASS

...IMNESDAIR

BANISTARI EMPIRE

...LE

KIWIJANMJI

MORLAND

KANAK

CZTERSPOSOBY

G'BOKUN NYUMBA

JEDOUM

ABDINA AL MORZE

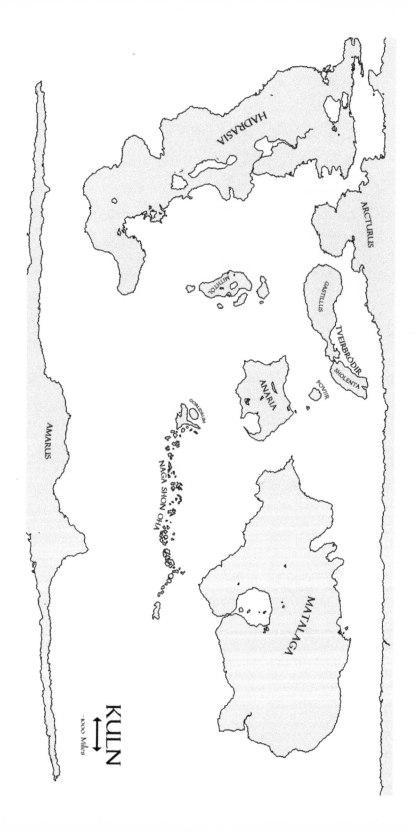

Dedicated to the memory
of Michael Green

'Thus it was that the natural powers of Universe were overwhelmed by the turmoil of Outer Chaos in an attempt to destroy Kuln, and, failing that, implant agents to ensure its fall. The Chaotic gods saw a chance and exerted all of their power. Bracing against dark strands of matter and energy, they forcefully violated natural order in a blaze of destruction.

The lesser gods of Kuln, forgotten by all, awoke in fury and rose to meet this threat. By supreme efforts they thwarted it. But an Evil had come to their world, and they were unable to stop it entering. Chaos was kept at bay. The Twelve awaited the next move in this endgame, and all living gave praise that they were spared.

Thus Universe continued in its dance... and Chaos waited.'

- Excerpt from the ancient scrolls of Za'Amon, Seeker of the order of Illuminus

ONE

He shouldn't have been out this late, certainly not alone.

He had discovered several alarming facts about the Prime Alderman and his council that he needed to tell his colleagues, and was distracted by both what he had learned and the missive he had sent only yesterday with the key. The key to survival; the key they had sought for a long time.

He shouldn't have investigated the sobbing which had cut off so abruptly, but it had pierced his contemplation. With bile rising in his throat, frozen in shock as he looked at what was left of the butchered woman, he heard the cruel laugh behind him, between him and safety. The voice came, low and merciless.

'Give me your pendant, *old man.*'

Turning, he saw the murky silhouette of a man lick the black wetness off his knife blade deliberately, horribly, and panicked. As he ran from the demon clothed in flesh before him, he heard running footfalls following. For the first time he could remember in a long life dedicated to thinking, he acted without thought. He simply ran for his life.

He paid no heed to the buried realisation that he ran into the darkness of Crowden where thieves and cut-throats lurked, away from the pools of light marking the main thoroughfare. He ran from the laughing figure, fear lending him movements that stiff joints and a plump midsection hadn't had for years, but he knew it was not enough.

The younger man moved like the wind, like a cat, and seemed to be toying with his quarry. Several times the wheezing scholar stumbled in his panic, yet he survived to run on. Frantic glances over his shoulder showed him his pursuer keeping easy pace with him.

Finally he turned into a dead-end alley. At the end he turned, backing against the wall, his heart drumming and his breath ragged. The sheer sides of the houses rose windowless to each side, too high to scale. The man in front of him stank with the metallic tang of fresh blood. Half of his face was lit by a slice of moonlight, the eye glinting with feral delight, the rest lost in the sharp and deep shadows cutting across rough cobbles.

The moons are bright, thought the old man distractedly. *Strange that I should be thinking of that.*

Time was running very slowly; the clouds clutching at silver Lunis like fingers were frozen in place, rimmed with stars.

Deeper than the sea, he thought. *Drowning in shadow.*

Panic welled up anew, the first fast occurrence since he had run down this alley. He knew few would hear, and none would care.

A slow flash caught his eye, as the pale light reflected off the knife blade diving slowly towards his throat. Anticipation and fear had stretched this moment in a way he'd never believed possible.

Uh...

His eyes now locked on the bright blade, fascinated, unable to look away or feel the wall pressed to his back. He was unable even to get his hands up to try and ward it off.

MOVE! his mind screamed. His body refused.

The light... so beautiful...

He couldn't take his eyes off the glint of the blade. It glowed with poisonous spite, tinged with the green light of Xoth as it hovered opposite Lunis. It mesmerized him and promised deliverance from his fear... his age... his responsibilities... Peace from pain, darkness from light.

His attacker was now just a dark shape before him as the slow slice of the knife finally reached the end of its arc. The sharpened edge of the blade touched the side of his neck, caressing the skin and parting it like a maid peeling a silk sheet off a bed. The blade slid on, feeling foreign yet as unstoppable as the rising of the sun.

At first there was no pain, just a sudden sense of gushing release as his carotid artery was severed. Blood ran in sudden sheets down his chest, warming it. He couldn't swallow. From the sudden whistle of breath it was obvious his windpipe had also been pierced. Darkness rimmed his vision, and his thinking grew fuzzy.

Keep a clear head, he thought crazily. *I gave my life to thinking...*

Images flashed randomly through his mind. The pictures were so clear! His work, his love, his life. Memories of a sister, long dead, and the path to his learning. The years passing by. The making of an old man.

Old, yes, but he didn't want to die. A tiny spark of defiance flared in his heart for a fraction of a second. An animal instinct for life, deeply buried for years, reared its head. Too late it tried to get him to fight, to run, to scream for help – then sank back quietly, as if understanding that it could do nothing more.

He felt mortally weary. Dizziness washed over him, and he struggled to fill his lungs. His breathing grew thick with bubbles, and he was vaguely aware of drowning on his own blood. Now there was pain, but it was a distant bright nova in peaceful darkness.

As his head grew lighter, he thought triumphantly, *He will not find it!* For a second more he knew everything with crystalline clarity, and then he was no longer sure what the other would not find. It didn't really matter.

The alley tilted, and kept going. Darkness descended faster now, and closed over the sight of the grinning devil before him holding up a knife dark with liquid.

My blood, he thought. Then a feeling of mixed anguish and joy swept through him as his eyes ceased working.

Mother! he cried. Blackness took him.

ભ   જ

Ventran knelt quickly next to the body of the scholar. The sightless eyes stared upwards as he lay in the pool of blood draining from his neck, the edges congealing. Grinning, he considered his quarry. It had been a good chase, for an old man. Good fun.

Checking around his victim's ruined throat he was unsurprised to find nothing of value. As he rifled through the clothes, he felt a spark of pleasure as he considered the girl as well. It was a last-minute idea to drag her off the road, and he hadn't been able to help himself. Gods knew what she had been doing out alone... but she wouldn't make that mistake again. It hadn't taken much to reduce her to mindless fear, her sobbing luring the old man away into the darkness. From there cutting off his escape had been easy.

With a scowl, he snapped his attention back to the task at hand. The man had nothing on him but a money pouch, a third full of copper penants and a few silver lunes. He rechecked every inch of clothing, rudely dealing with the cooling flesh.

Rising in fury he kicked the corpse, flopping the head back into a puddle of moonlight. He glared at the glazing eyes above the button nose and short white beard. The face was old if not deeply lined, and a fresh splash of blood lined one cheek, dark in the silver-green light.

Damn him, he thought. *All the way back into Crowden for nothing.*

It had been a good chase though. He'd almost been able to breathe his victim's fear, and at least he was halfway back to safety. He considered mutilating the body in revenge then rejected it. Wary by nature, he knew that either of the missing people might already have others seeking them.

The girl had been obviously rich, and important enough for someone to go to the expense of tracking her and trying to identify her killer. Although the chances were slim that anyone knew who he was or that he'd been there, he really didn't want to have to avoid city hitters - best to not get caught at all. He would treasure that kill for a while though; her skin soft from lack of work and eyes wide, any beauty she had possessed marred by stark terror. He had not laid his hands on a noble girl before, even a low ranking one, and had found her reactions much different to the others. It had been as if she could not believe it was happening right up until the last, when animal panic overcame her.

Ventran sheathed his weapon and turned to run further into the darkness of the poor quarter. His eyes swept the shadows around him, and he bared his teeth; his reputation and blood-spattered clothes would keep him free of most cut-throats, and any that stopped him would learn their mistake swiftly.

Sweeping through the narrow streets of Crowden, Ventran headed towards his safe house, stumbling once and cursing as he slipped in excrement lying in the street. He bit off the words as the rattle of guardsmen alerted him, unusual in this part of town. Without a backwards glance he disappeared into the shadows.

Skirting several alleyways that he knew contained thief gangs, he made his way to a narrow passage nearby. Unlike some of the older cities like Terendon, Lodnor had no organised thieves to speak of. Meyar and its disparate states were in constant upheaval, and most of the guilds were either not able or not willing to expend the effort to maintain stability in the country. It certainly wasn't as profitable here as in other nations, unless you were one of the elite or catered to their tastes. It made life unpredictable, and anyone foolish enough to be ambushed by an entire gang had little hope of escaping unscathed. Wiping his mouth, he sauntered down another alley and then out onto a quiet cobbled street adjacent to it. There he looked around, and darted into a doorway.

Vague whispering sounds were his only clue to his being watched from a crack in the door. He showed no sign of hearing them as he knocked twice and rattled the handle. Pausing for a count of twenty, he had the countersign on the tip of his tongue.

Silence.

He waited impatiently. The door didn't open, and no one looked out or asked him for the rehearsed entry code.

Glancing around in irritation, he repeated the procedure. Finally he leaned in close to the door and whispered urgently.

'Let me in, you bastard, or I'll rip your eyes out and bowl your head into the river!'

The door spy opened a crack, and the doorman looked out. He was a large man named Gort, and he had made it clear he did not like the slight man, or his standing in their leader's eyes. He grinned at Ventran evilly.

'Bugger off!'

The spyhole slid shut and Ventran swore sharply.

'Let me in!' he growled frantically. Although Crowden was rarely ventured into by the law, when watchmen entered it was in large squads. He had already seen one patrol, and there would be more after the brutal work he had done, likely soon. His tone rasped out in angry promise.

'*I'll wear your guts for this.*'

The door opened slowly, the keeper looking around it in mock surprise. 'Aw, Ventran, I didn't see you there. You shoulda knocked with the password.' He hocked and spat deliberately in the doorway. Ventran darted inside. As the doorkeeper closed the door, he glared at him.

'*Pifing* idiot. That was shit-brained.'

The doorkeeper stared back, and then smiled derisively. 'Yer not as special as yer think, Ventran. Does yer good to wait.' His smile dropped. 'And I don't like you, *boy.*' He turned his back deliberately on Ventran, who snarled in fury. His hand dropped to his knife, teeth baring.

'Ventran.' The voice came, pitched low and powerful. The massive dark-skinned form of Hallar moved out from the shadowed stairwell. 'He will see you now. You are late.' The Morlandish accent was heavy.

Gort laughed harshly, chewing a sliver of wood, his stubble greasy. He didn't even look around as Ventran climbed the stairs quickly.

Stopping at the second door he took a deep breath to calm himself, pushing his anger away with an effort, and knocked.

'Enter.'

The voice was like listening to hinges creak, old and drier than dust, yet compelling and powerful. Ventran turned the handle and pushed at the thick oak.

'Ah, Ventran. And do you have it?'

The voice belonged to a small man with a ring of thinning blond hair from his temples to the back of his head. He sat hunched over a desk in very dim light. Gaunt and pale, his red-rimmed eyes pierced the gloom.

Teeth clenched in anger, Ventran shook his head. 'No.'

'And were you seen?'

Ventran shrugged. 'Yes. A girl and the old man. It's taken care of.'

Sontles grinned at him and Ventran felt nervous. The figure in front of him might be frail-looking, but it projected a force of will that was almost a physical blow. This was someone used to dealing death, and being obeyed. He had killed many more than Ventran.

'There was supposed to be one, Ventran. You have an unwholesome appetite for carnage. I do not like unknown factors. Who else?'

'A minor noblewoman. Out, alone. She worked well to set a trap for the old man.'

Sontles' eyes flared.

'A noble? Do you not think that was unwise? Now we will have to be much more careful if we are to avoid discovery. The city will be in an uproar, whether she was the lowest daughter of a merchant noble or the Lady Kelnar herself. *There are no murders in the Glades.* This could expose us. So, why should I be pleased at this?'

Ventran shrugged, unapologetic but wary. He had no more been able to help killing the woman than he could stop breathing.

Sontles let the silence grow, and then spoke again. 'You revel in slaughter, and you have a certain… artistry about you with it. This, I think, is one reason I like you. I think I need to find a way to channel these urges. It can be done. You are not stupid.' He shook his head.

'We will not speak of this again… if nothing comes of it. But you *will* learn to curb your impulses.' The note of warning was unmistakable. Ventran let out a small breath of relief and nodded his acceptance.

'So,' Sontles breathed. 'We were wrong. The old fool did not have it.' He sat hunched in thought, the air around him dark with his mood.

Ventran watched him, and said abruptly, 'That doorman is a lackwit. He kept me waiting for no better reason than his dislike of me, and endangered us all. I want his guts.'

'Hmm,' said Sontles, delicately drawing a fingernail down the table, leaving a shallow furrow in the hard varnish. 'He needs discipline, it would seem. I think I should summon him up here for a… discussion. Explain some things to him. He is not a Teromen, so he does not understand.'

'Needs more than that,' muttered Ventran inaudibly. The small man heard him anyway, and smiled. He changed the subject, throwing a piercing stare at Ventran.

'Ventran, we must settle this. I have left the Church of Terome at a critical time. The new Holy Voice is an unknown, and may prove troublesome. I do not know how his church ballot won over our candidate.'

Popularity, thought Ventran sourly. Sontles had nearly controlled the entire church before this new man had been elected. He was proving to be both moral and admired, and very politically astute.

'Teromants would have caused notice if they had been sent. The Darostim are not without resources. Now I fear they will hide what we seek even further away. *I want that pendant!'*

Ventran squirmed uncomfortably. Details of politics bored him, and he already knew all this.

'So, I came myself, and I brought you with me. I wanted this business over with quickly and quietly. Something that seems to be... regrettably beyond us now. Happily, luck may be with us. Your manner of killing the woman as well as the old fool may be seen as simple murder, as long as you did not defile the bodies...?' Ventran shook his head. 'Good. It may be that the kills will be linked, and that might distract from our true motives.'

Ventran was glad his caution had won out over his temper and he had not given in to his urges. The old man would likely be seen as just another victim, with nothing to tie his murder to the Teromens, the devout worshippers of the god Terome. He was not one of them, but was wary of their military arm, the Teromants, who were a law unto themselves. 'I don't understand why this pendant is so important,' he muttered.

Sontles shot a scathing glance at him, shrugging his neat light grey and black robe back.

'I will tell you when - and if - I think you are ready for it. You have much to learn, Ventran. You can think of it for now as...a key to power.'

'Power?' asked Ventran curiously.

Sontles did not answer. His eyes were hooded as he stared into the distance.

'It is time,' he hissed to himself. 'Balance tilts, the Darostim are exposed, and the key is nearly within our reach.' Looking back down at the text before him, Sontles grinned wider than before, his teeth gleaming. He swung his glance to the steadily burning candle at his elbow and lifted his hand.

'You are excused. Deal with the lookout as you must.'

Ventran smiled lazily and bowed. He rose and opened the door as Sontles spoke again.

'So it begins.'

Darkness descended.

TWO

It was Karland's birthday. He struggled through the sparse undergrowth, muttering to himself angrily. The day had dawned heavy and grey, sporadic bursts of thin cold rain whipping The Croft. This was the first birthday without his best friend Seom since his fifth. They had always celebrated together, and he had spent it listlessly, barely acknowledging the wishes from his family. The day had started badly and quickly worsened; his father Brin had not slept well the night before, and seemed annoyed at his son's lethargy. Eventually, unable to bear more confrontations, Karland simply left for his and Seom's favourite spot to spend the day brooding. By the time he returned home, his father had been furious.

'Where in all the hells have you been, boy?'

'Out,' Karland said in surprise.

Brin glared at him. 'Didn't occur to you to tell us? Your mother cooked you a meal. The food is hours cold!'

Karland snapped, 'Well, I didn't know, did I? You've spent the day being angry with me. I didn't want to fight any mor-'

'Well, you have failed in *that*, boy.'

Becka ran in, hearing the raised voices. Karland noticed his younger sister Gail peering around the door, her eyes wide.

'Brin, it doesn't matter. Leave it. Can't you see he's miserable?'

'Not as miserable as he's going to be,' retorted Brin. The usually placid man was very angry for once, and Karland was choosing a bad day to become rebellious.

'Come on, Brin. Come to the kitchen,' she said, looking at Karland in sympathy. Karland shut his eyes, feeling a deep emptiness in his gut, and heard his father leave.

Not today, he said silently in desperation. *Please. Not all this today.* With few friends, he felt the absence of Seom keenly, knowing he would probably never see him again. He was interrupted by his sister's voice.

'You *ruined* today,' Gail said obnoxiously. 'I wanted cake and nice treats, but mother wouldn't even let me eat your food. You *wasted* it. I wanted a fun day today.' She pouted. 'You are so *selfish.*'

Karland felt the unfairness of her words bubble up inside. Suddenly he snapped.

'*I'm* selfish? You are the most selfish person I know. I don't care what you want. It was *my* birthday. You're just upset because you want the attention from everyone all the time, you spoilt little brat. I *hate* you.'

As her eyes widened in hurt he regretted his words. Gail might be spoilt, and she was being unfair, but she was too young to fully understand. It was just that everything in Karland's recent life had gone wrong. Seom, Ben Arflun's continued harassment, his growing sense of not fitting in, all of it was too much.

Tears welled up in Gail's eyes and she started crying huge, racking bawling sobs as only a wronged child could produce. There was a momentary silence from the kitchen, and then Brin burst back in, his fury reignited. Becka was behind him, crying now.

'What have you done now, you bad tempered little bastard?' he shouted.

Karland opened his mouth, but Brin cut in. 'You do nothing but cause trouble, you worthless *waste of space!*' he roared. Karland, shocked by words he had never heard before, stared at his father, and then his anger ignited.

'*FINE!*' he yelled, the unfairness and anger tearing through him. He ran for the door and slammed it shut behind him in fury, hearing a shout of anger from his father over the cries from Gail, now in tears from all the shouting.

Karland ran to escape what he could not bear.

Not on my birthday.

ભ   ૪૦

Wrapping his small thick cloak around him, he had hurried out of town. The tall, rangy smith had waved as he passed, but Karland hadn't seen much else except the road through the angry tears.

The Croft was too confining, the site of all his misery. A hot need to get away from his father, his family, and his empty-feeling life burned within him. He had never had an argument with his father like this before, and couldn't understand the cause. Brin was usually placid and practical, although he did not fully understand his often lonely son.

Karland spied the far distant Northing Woods as he left town. Always forbidden by his parents to go there, a newly-woken rebellious worm flashed a fang in his heart, and he set out for the dark green patch on the horizon, ignoring the trees closest to town where men worked. Miles later, he turned from the road to cut across several fields to the hedged borders of the town's farmland, heading towards them.

Unlike the friendly copses and small woodlands surrounding the peaceful town of The Croft, the forest was a wild and dark place, with rumours of outlaws and dangerous animals. Even the rough farm hands in the outlying areas of the town rarely went far into the woods. Every year there were rumours of people going missing there, and old tales retold of bears and wolves in winter. Wild hogs often ventured out warily in search of crops to spoil, and were devils for getting through the fences erected to keep them out.

From time to time he spoke to the hunters and trappers that came to the town. They were strange, often wild-seeming men who went into the forest alone or in small groups. His father sometimes bought furs for orders to complement fabrics, and the men seemed rough but generally pleasant. They spoke occasionally after a drink or two of the silence, the peace – and the loneliness.

Gruff and capable, many treated hunting as an art, revering the chase and outwitting of their prey, but all of them treated the meats and furs that made their livelihood with great respect. He learned that they were careful of where they hunted or trapped. It was dangerous work, and they had to skirt the timber workers on the western edges of the Northing Wood. Karland loved imagining himself running a deer to ground with bow and arrow, his skill against its natural talents, but the work after that sounded hot and unpleasant.

Several miles later he had picked his way through the fields and entered the fringes of the great Northing Woods. He headed into the trees and worked through the underbrush for an hour until he found a small clearing. Pausing, he became aware of the furtive sounds of the woods. This was very different from anywhere he had been before. The silence was intense, broken only by the whispers of wind in the trees and the rustling of undergrowth. The woods were gloomy and ominous. The trees grew thickly and had an intertwining canopy, and unlike the copses closer to The Croft these woods were wild and close, strewn with all manner of ferns and bushes hampering visibility.

His emotions and his exertions had tired him thoroughly and he had not eaten for hours. His parents would be worried now, and serve them right. He would go home and apologise to his mother, and maybe things would be all right again. The woods were foreboding, and suddenly home seemed more bearable than the intense silence.

Moving to the point in the clearing that he thought he had emerged from, he realised with a sinking heart that his heedless run into the woods had left him without his bearings. There was little light under the thick canopy. Deep down he was beginning to think he had made a bad mistake. He walked through the woods in the direction he thought the town was, but found only endless trees. After a time dusk began to settle and Karland began to panic, stumbling in his weariness. All the stories of bears, packs of wolves, wood spirits, and boar with tusks like spears began to seep into his mind. He started to run, then gave up quickly; the undergrowth snagged at him regularly as the light decreased, he was stung repeatedly by nettles, and brambles scratched him and tripped him more and more frequently.

He felt the emptiness in his stomach and realised that he was very hungry, and not only that - he just wanted to be home, safe. Not even punishment from his father was unappealing at that moment. It was obvious that he was stuck here at least until morning, and he had a horrible feeling that the deeper he went in to the wood, the less likely it would be that he would ever wake if he slept.

An idea surfaced in his mind, and he started looking for a suitable tree. Before long he found one and after a few false starts pulled himself carefully up, finding wide limbs that had interlocking smaller branches through a good solid fork about twenty feet up. It bounced under his weight, but felt sturdy. Too tired for once to worry about the height, he settled in.

Pragmatically, he used his soft belt to lash himself to the tree, afraid he would fall in his sleep. As comfortable as he could expect to make himself, he sighed, huddled in his cloak. This was a far cry from the stories of adventure he loved being told; he was hungry, cold, miserable, afraid and alone, and being prodded in the back however he lay. Uncomfortable as he was, once he closed his eyes he fell quickly asleep, exhausted.

He snapped awake once with a jolt as a large dark form snuffled below him, and then fell back into slumber. Finally he awoke, exhausted, stiff and numb, with a gnawing hunger and even greater thirst. He was also wheezing from the exposure all night, even though it was summer.

Climbing stiffly down, he nearly fell twice as nerveless fingers and legs refused to work. He cursed, frightened at the realisation that he could easily vanish here, to die of hunger and thirst. Forcing himself to action, Karland decided his first priority was to find water.

As he moved off through the woods, he spied a few nuts and brambleberries. It was not enough though, and he wept with relief later on in the morning when he stumbled across a small brook. Without pause for thought, he ran to it and dropped to his knees, cupping his hands and liberally splashing great handfuls to his mouth. The water was cold and sweet, and the best drink he had ever had in his life.

Reasoning that the brook would lead to the river, he followed it for several hours. There was no end to the trees, and Karland was morosely wondering if he would truly ever escape from this place alive when a faint smell of smoke brought him up short.

Following his nose, he moved at an angle away from the brook, and not far away found a high, heavy screen of brush. Following it to a break, he lurched into a small clearing with a dying fire at the centre. A low tent was slung at one end of it, and there were bundles heaped around the edges. The clearing was littered with wood, fabric and the cast-offs of meals, messy and unkept. It wasn't until he moved into the middle of the campsite that he realised that the bundles were skinned and semi-skinned animals; behind the pile of skins was a grisly mound of dirty pink shapes. Animal carcasses, some whole, some dismembered, lay with muscle and bone naked to the air, flies and maggots crawling on them. Beheaded deer lay next to boar, squirrel lay next to bear cub, rabbit lay splayed next to badger, no rhyme or reason to it.

The sight was sickening in its carnage. Half the pelts were rotten or badly removed and many seemed to have been too much effort to cure. Although some meat had obviously been taken for food, the rest was hacked and spoiling. The campsite stank of decomposition underneath the smell of smoke.

Staring at the appalling sight, a sound made him look up. Karland saw a shape appear out of the trees at the far edge of the clearing. Alarmed, he stood, feeling his pocket for his little knife. The shape resolved to a tall lean man, rough looking with sharp grey eyes which darted constantly; stubble and dirt lined his face in equal quantities. A bow was slung over his shoulder and he had a shortsword and a knife on his belt, both looking dull with use.

The man looked around, and then dropped his gaze on Karland.

'Hello, boy,' he said in a smoother voice than his looks suggested. Karland stammered a greeting, his own voice sounding odd in his ears after so long silent.

'Whatcha doing here?' asked the man intently. 'This is my camp. Are you with others? Your father, perhaps?'

'No,' said Karland. 'I ran away.'

'Not wise, boy,' remarked the man, a feral gleam in his eyes. 'These woods are dangerous. Animals, other things… evil spirits. Voices. I wouldn't be here, in your place.'

'I am lost,' confessed Karland. 'Please, sir, can you help me find the town again?'

The man looked at him as if he was a fool.

'*Please, sir, I'm lost,*' he mocked, squeaking his voice in parody. 'You townsfolk, coming out here, not knowin' the woods. *Idiots*, all of you. And you pifing sneer at me when I bring my trade to town, like I'm one of these soulless beasts.' He glared at Karland and moved into the campsite.

Karland shifted uncomfortably, unsure of his response. The man seemed volatile and angry, different to those hunters he had met before.

'I am hunting,' said the man. 'I have been following a bear, boy. A great mother of a bear. What a pelt. What a head! She killed my dog, but I will have her hide stretched out soon. I don't have time or care to hold the hand of a young fool.' He smiled condescendingly. 'Have *you* seen her?'

He barked a laugh at his own wit, showing teeth that were a grubby yellow, and then the smile dropped from his face again. Karland wondered if he was entirely sane.

'She's somewhere around here, boy. I've bin following her for *days*. Her trail vanished. She's a sly one. Woods hold other dangers, too. They grow darker every year, yus; they do.' He laughed nastily. 'If she finds you, you'll be dead, boy. Naw, you best stay here for now, if you don't want to end up having her crack your skull open. Now, you got food? I haven't foraged.'

Karland glanced towards the hideous pile without meaning to look at it.

'I have some nuts left sir, but I was hoping you had some food-', he began, and was then rudely brushed aside as the man pushed past him. He looked at the rotting flesh as if he'd never seen it before and then rounded on Karland, his face twisting.

'Think I should eat rotten meat, worm? I got no food for you. I had the good bits off this maggot feed days ago. Give me the nuts.'

Karland gasped as the man bunched a hard fist into his jerkin and searched the pockets roughly until he found the meagre supply. He began stuffing them in his mouth immediately, and then stopped mid-chew and looked more closely at the dirty cloak Karland wore. It was good quality cloth, a gift from his father.

'Give me that,' he said, spraying nut fragments. Karland shook his head. The man jerked the ties open and pulled it off Karland, and slung it round his shoulders. It was too small, but he didn't seem to care. Karland, about to protest, bit his tongue, frightened of the reaction.

'Better get more food,' the dirty hunter remarked around a mouthful, bits of nut in his foul teeth. He dug around his waist and found a flask. Karland found it thrust in his direction.

'Fill it.'

Cowed, Karland took it and moved to the brook, looking around for the wounded bear. The flask smelt of spirits, strong and raw. He dipped it hurriedly and returned. He was scared now; he had never met anyone like this before.

'So, um, why did this bear kill your dog?' he asked nervously, trying to strike up a conversation in the hope that he could get the man in a good mood.

'Bitch was somewhere away and I tracked her filthy cubs, two of them,' said the man around the last mouth full of food. He spat into the low fire, a chunk of chestnut flying out.

'I skinned 'em good, haha. Still wriggling! Squalling and crying like stuck pigs, they was.' His speech relaxed into more colloquial cadence. 'Was getting them ready and she came back. Set Drogar on her and went for my bow. Pifing bear broke his back with her paw. I shot her twice clean, broad blade! And she still ran. Damn dog cost me money and time. Had to raise it, train it, feed it. Bah! Idiot mutt. If he'd distracted her right, she would have been easy pickings. Now I hafta follow her and find her. I will. I will! Filthy whore. When she's dead, I'll take her cubs' skins back as well. Wish I'd had more time to make them suffer for all the trouble she's caused me.' By this point he sounded like he was rambling more to himself than Karland.

Karland pulled back, his disgust overriding his caution at the cruelty. 'You killed her young and now you are hunting her down to torture her?' It sounded horrific.

The man looked up, volatile anger twisting his face. Karland stammered, but the damage was done. The man jumped up and his arm blurred. Suddenly Karland was face down in the dirt, his cheek stinging. He flipped over and scrambled backwards, panting in fear.

'You dare judge me, boy?' shouted the man. 'I'm worth more than a mangy dog, I'm worth more than some fat bear and her disgusting cubs, and I'm fucking well worth more than town scum like you! You're lucky I don't like little boys, or I'd make you pay in ways that unman you!'

He drew a well-worn knife from his belt. The pitted blade was slightly curved inwards from repeated honing and the back was roughly serrated, but the blade was sharp, if ragged.

'You got a clever mouth that needs to be shut. I don't take lip from no one.' He spat at his feet, a great gobbet of green and white, then cocked his head and grinned cruelly.

'I think I'll make you a new one, one that doesn't have anything clever to say. Then I can use you to lure the bitch. Yes, I think so. Let's see you judge me when that mangy bear dies gnawing on your cold guts.'

He advanced towards Karland, who turned to flee and tripped, landing heavily. As he got up again, a terrifyingly strong hand grabbed his throat and turned him to face his attacker.

'You're not going anywhere but hell, boy,' breathed the man in his face, his breath rancid.

Karland couldn't breathe, couldn't scream. Panicked, he flailed with his limbs. A shin crashed up into the man's crotch through sheer luck, and he swore in pain and threw Karland down hard.

'That's earned you a slower death,' he rasped, glowering in hatred.

As the man straightened, the forest behind him burst asunder and a gigantic form exploded out, brown and furious. It hit the man at an angle from behind, and he flew forwards into the tent, snapping the hang rope and collapsing it. Karland caught a glimpse of a red-on-brown hulk as high as him at the shoulder thundering past with a rasping roar, and then an enormous paw much bigger than his head slammed down on the cloak covering the man's lower back with a horrific crack, holding him crookedly in place. He yelled once in fright and despair, and then the huge head tore down, and the yell cut off in a momentary bloody gurgling choke as the teeth ripped through his spine and neck with a snapping, tearing noise.

The great bear raised its head and roared in triumph, pumping blood sprayed on her teeth and muzzle. Broken arrows jutted from her shoulder and ribs. She dipped her head and tore a chunk of flesh from the dead man's shoulder, and turned her head to regard Karland. The flap of flesh hung from her jaw.

His paralysis broke and he shrieked in terror. Leaping to his feet, he ran mindlessly, away from the horror that had just occurred, not knowing if the bear was even now chasing to rip him apart too. He stumbled in a blind panic through the underbrush and trees without any sense of time, and finally crashed into a huge clearing filled with vine-covered edifices near a rocky outcrop.

Staggering into the clearing, and into afternoon sunshine, he collapsed on the outskirts of the structures, weeping and unable to move any further.

THREE

Karland gradually calmed down, realising that he was safe for the moment, if still lost. Trying to forget the horror he had witnessed, he moved to the forms. They looked strangely angular, too much to be natural; ruins that probably no one else knew about, they offered refuge. One big building seemed fairly intact. It butted up against the large stone outcrop that rose from the forest floor, developing into a series of small hills going further back. The dark interior of the ruin made Karland wary, and he decided to climb up to the hill and view the land around him.

Heartened for the first time, he nimbly climbed the pitted outside of the wall, using vines and holes to get to the top. The building angled up fairly steeply to the rock face, which rose higher but didn't look too hard to climb. Looking up at the small escarpment, he moved several steps towards it.

Karland's right foot came down on roof which was solid for a fraction of a second, and then vanished. His foot followed the stone and found nothing, and he fell forwards, his other foot catching in the ivy and his hands finding the edge of a hole. The lip crumbled slowly and he clutched desperately at the vines around it, his foot slipping free and dangling his body over the drop, his breathing panicked. He snorted determinedly through his nose, nostrils flaring and eyes wide in shock. He had another second to wonder how deep the building went, and then with a tearing snap the thin stems he held gave way at one end.

He yelled and fell through the ivy, long climbers ripping from the walls as he frantically clutched at them. Spinning, he fell and hit the floor with a thump. A few seconds later his shock and disorientation lessened enough for him to realise his right arm was numb, and he was lying on his back.

The arm didn't seem to want to move properly and, lifting his head dizzily, he saw that there was already a huge painful lump just below the elbow. Trying to straighten the arm didn't work and seemed to make him feel like throwing up, so he stopped and waited for his head to clear.

It seemed that he lay there for a while. Through his dizziness a sound intruded, slowly. At first he didn't register it, and it wasn't until he heard the words that he consciously realised someone was there.

'Greetings, young man,' said a querulous voice. Karland tried to turn towards the owner, and twisted, instinctively trying to put his arms down on the floor to balance. The hurt arm refused to respond, and instead of grounding himself he pitched sideways face first into the floor with a muffled yelp.

'Mmm, oh dear,' said the voice, and a gnarled hand dropped to his shoulder. It was stronger than it looked, and helped him upright, another hand on his back. The stabbing pain of his arm receded long enough to allow the person helping him to distract him, and he looked around into the bright eyes of an old man peering at him over strange round glass spectacles that rested on a slightly beaky nose. His face was seamed and his hair was erratic and white, and overall he was skinny.

'Bit of a fall - you are lucky you didn't hurt yourself badly. It could have been quite nasty.'

While Karland stared at him dully, the old man looked intently at his arm, and ran a hand lightly over the area. It burned like fire and the puffy flesh felt strange, and he started to pull back, but as quickly as he did it the old man stopped.

'I believe you may have fractured the ulna, given point of impact and distension of tissue along the outside of the forearm,' he confided severely. 'I need to look in further detail, so I can treat it. You may have concussion from the drop you took as well. I had best examine you further. You are very lucky you didn't land on any of this stone.' He indicated lumps, some quite large, that had likely fallen from the hole above. 'If you had impacted your cranium at a severely perpendicular angle, you might well have been killed.'

Karland drew back from the stream of incomprehensible words and found his tongue.

'I'm all right.' He winced at the agonising pain, sweating as his arm moved and sent jolts through the constant burning sensation. Looking down he could see his flesh was straining against his normal arm, and it looked as if he had grown a large purple egg under the skin. His vision was a little blurred, and he felt sick.

'Are you, indeed?' the old man smiled. 'You have no reason to be afraid of me. In fact, mm, it is most fortuitous that you landed here of all places, outside my door. Gods help you if you'd wound up with one of your idiot town healers.'

'What?' said Karland. It all seemed surreal to be sitting here talking to some strange old man. He noticed that the odd fellow appeared to be wearing some kind of flat slippers, open at the heels, which flapped on his feet as he shuffled around.

'Why, I am intimately studied in the intricacies of anatomy and bio-mechanics, and I am well versed in the theory and practice of biological healing by the Daktarim themselves!' beamed the old man. 'I can set your bone and have your arm on the way to being stronger than ever. I wouldn't trust half these rural healers, although,' he lowered his voice conspiratorially, 'some of them have remarkable wisdom. Remarkable!'

He frowned, lost in thought, and Karland bit his lip. The pain was increasing steadily and his hands were trembling. 'Thanks,' he said vaguely.

The old man frowned at him and suddenly concern set his features. 'Of course, the first stages of shock will be passing, and the numbness will be wearing off. Come, the entrance to my dwelling is just over here. You quite literally landed on my doorstep.'

He helped Karland to his feet and supported the boy as they moved towards his door. It was an ancient looking wooden door, solid and set firmly into a stone archway; if it had been closed Karland would have thought it was part of the edifice. As they passed through there was the distinct shape of a huge bolt the other side.

'Mmm, ironwood,' remarked the old man cryptically. He helped Karland onto a bench and closed the door. The room inside was small, framed with stone which blended skilfully into natural rock. There was a strange lantern in the corner, which gave off a very bright white unwavering light with no smoke. The back of the room faded into darkness, although there was an orange glow and warmth from coals in a small alcove to the side.

'Now, my intrepid explorer, if I am not mistaken you are Karland, mmm?' asked the old man. 'The son of the cloth merchant?'

'Yes,' said Karland, feeling a little bit sicker, and trying to focus. He wondered how the old man knew who he was.

The old man leaned in closer, peering at Karland intently. Bright eyes looked at him from under a high brow, with slightly bushy eyebrows and an aquiline nose, wrinkles creasing the forehead and around the eyes.

'I am Aldwyn.'

He turned and moved to a cupboard, opening the door and rustling around inside. Glass clinked, and several times he turned something around and looked at it closely before thrusting it back. Eventually he brought some vials over to the table.

'I'll make you a tisane,' he said, 'and a compress. We'll take the swelling down and ease the pain, and then I can look at resetting it. Hmmm… alas, I don't think it would be wise to use alcohol as a soporific in this case…' The rest faded into muttering.

Karland looked at the old face and slightly furrowed brow and nodded, feeling strangely comforted. Aldwyn looked at the break site, pulling the sleeve short of the elbow while Karland glanced at the jars on the table. He could see the word 'Feverfew' on one, and what looked like dried sticks in another, and yet another filled with murky honey.

Aldwyn picked up a sandy box from the table and extracted an enormous twisting root, which he snapped a few pieces off and then re-seated it under the sand.

'Ginger,' he confided. 'From the south! Quite hard to get, but it is very good for all manner of things.' Deftly Aldwyn made the compress and looped a thick bandage around the break.

'It will soak through, but just leave it,' he said. 'Keep it on the table, above your heart.' He turned and pulled the pot off the embers, producing a little clay mug from somewhere. He opened the jars and dropped pinches of herbs into the mug, muttering absent-mindedly as he did so.

'Feverfew to take the pain, hmm, motherwort I think to quiet the nerves, enough to partially sedate, that will help when it re-sets… Pity there is no ramor-clay in this part of the world. Liquorice! Yes, that will help.'

He pulled a large jar of what looked suspiciously like cloudy horse urine to Karland out from under the table with a flourish, and produced a mug. He poured a measured dose of the yellow liquid in, dropped a huge dollop of honey into the mug and then added the hot water and herbs.

Karland eyed the mug askance. Whether it helped his arm or not, he wasn't too keen on drinking whatever it was. Aldwyn frowned and then waved the mug at him.

'For goodness' sake, boy, it will help the pain and nausea. Drink it!'

Mixed with the smell of herbs and honey from the cup came the strong smell of cider vinegar. Relieved, Karland drank the goopy mixture down. Shortly afterwards, he felt detached, and grinned foolishly.

Aldwyn nodded and unwrapped his arm gently. The swelling had diminished and the flesh was a little less purple, although it still looked puffy and bruised. Karland was mildly interested to note that the arm looked… wrong. It almost looked as if he had a second elbow, and there was a definite tear in his skin along the break.

Supporting it carefully, Aldwyn raised the arm, sending a twinge along it which was annoying but easy to ignore. He felt carefully along the bone, noting where it was jutting up and had broken the skin slightly, and tutted.

'A clean break.'

Holding the elbow firmly, with two fingers running up the broken bone, he made sure of his grip, muttering indecipherable words that tugged at Karland's consciousness oddly. Suddenly he pushed hard, guiding the broken end with his fingertips and firmly levering the arm straight again as he spoke strange words.

Karland yelled, the intense burst of pain overwhelming his sedation, and his vision went black with white flashes for a long moment. When his vision cleared, his fingers trembling, he could see Aldwyn holding his arm, which looked a lot more normal, and winding a thick, solid-looking bandage around it. He could feel pressure along the outside of the arm, and when the old man removed his hand, saw the end of a straight, wrapped piece of wood poking out from the edge of the bandage.

'Splint,' said Aldwyn. 'It will keep the bone straight and help it heal true. I've matched it well. Luckily it was a clean break. You need to rest it for a good couple of weeks. Holding it above your head won't hurt, either. Well, it probably will, but I mean, mm, the healing process.'

Karland felt unsteady and exhausted, and thought he'd misheard. *Must mean months.*

The old man noticed his head nodding and smiled.

'Well done. I'll prepare a bed for you.'

Dreamily Karland let Aldwyn take him through to a warm spot, and as he lay down he dropped straight into a deep sleep.

CR   SO

Karland woke, a dull ache in his arm reminding him of his fall. The fingers were puffy and swollen, and the elbow was managing to emanate a constant low level background pain which was just enough to be noticeable, interspersed with jagged shards throbbing sharply along to armpit and fingers. He waved it experimentally over his supine body. It didn't hurt particularly until he tried to rotate his hand; after the first wave of agony he decided to leave it alone.

There was a large cup of water nearby, and he struggled upright and then grabbed it, draining it thirstily. There was no sign of Aldwyn in the little cavern. Over the occasional low ashy shift of the embers, Karland thought he could hear snoring and the odd snort.

He sat upright and then carefully got up, feeling strange. His arm still felt lifeless. Staggering over to the fire, he sank into the big padded chair and looked up at the shelves, glancing at titles randomly.

Human Anatomy, he read, assembling the long and unfamiliar word slowly. *Gods and Religions. Dragons. Orks – Creatures or Men? Mysteries: The False Sciences. Sword Forms. Aprolistic Trancendentalism. Topography of Anaria. Map of the Known World. Ocean Creatures. Treatise on the Philosophies of Acum.* Half of the words were indecipherable to him. He marvelled at the sheer number. There were books there he couldn't read at all, titled in other languages, some monstrously thick. More populous than the books were the scrolls, hidden in their own slots.

Karland sat there for a time in a semi-doze, warm and comfortable, the frights of yesterday pleasantly hazy. Eventually the sound of movement alerted him. The same peculiar bright light beamed out and Aldwyn shuffled into view, wrapped in a heavy old robe and blinking.

'Hello, ah, Karland,' he said, stifling a yawn. 'How is the arm?' He placed the lantern on the table, where it shimmered and ebbed strangely. Karland waved the appendage at him morosely.

'Better thank you, but I feel like I'll never use it again.'

'It will be as good as ever, never fear,' said Aldwyn. He moved to the damped fire and fed it, putting the pot with water still left in it from the tea back on. 'A cup of tisane, and then we must think what to do with you, heh,' he chuckled.

'What is this place?' asked Karland as Aldwyn busied himself

'This is an ancient place, full of memories and forgotten knowledge,' said Aldwyn. 'It used to be a place of learning, hundreds of years ago. A sect of scholars led by a loremaster called Thingos lived here and collected knowledge of any kind so that it would never be lost. They came from all walks of life, all religions. In its time it was known as one of the greatest centres of understanding.' He sighed, and placed two steaming cups on the table.

'Something bad happened here – quite what is not clear. But they were all killed, the pedestal of wisdom cast down. This place where I live was a storage chamber in looks, but was a library in truth, used to store rare books by one of the highest of the brothers. The door is ironwood, as strong as any iron weapons. It was never broken, and fits so tightly to the stone around it was likely never even seen. There are many such alcoves against the rocks in these rooms, but only this one is a safe house.'

He sipped his tea noisily, pulling air through to cool the liquid.

'I study here and gather my own knowledge for it. It is a blessedly quiet place of learning.' He peered at Karland, over his glasses. 'Now, we must work out, mmm, what to do with you. You will heal quickly, and though I have never seen this man you spoke of he clearly meant you ill. I don't espouse, mmm, death, but that he died is quite fortuitous in the circumstances. I will need to charge hunters to deal with the bear, mmm, to my regret. You are very lucky to be alive.'

Karland nodded tiredly, remembering the evil buried in the man and his violent death.

'I will visit town for supplies in the morning. There is a relatively safe road very near here I use that leads to the main road in. And I will talk to your father... and explain a few things. He may not be as angry as you fear, mmm, I think.'

Karland smiled gratefully. 'Thank you. I hope so. This place is wonderful.' He glanced around wistfully. 'May I visit sometimes?' He was keen to investigate the books and strange corners here, and talk to Aldwyn more.

'We shall see,' smiled Aldwyn, following his glance with approving eyes.

They ate a fulfilling if plain breakfast and then went outside into sunlight and a small courtyard. A small dray with large brown eyes trotted over to snuffle at them in a friendly fashion. Aldwyn patted him fondly on the nose.

'Come, Hjarta. It is town for us, today, hmm?' he said, producing a collar that he fitted to a small cart. It looked old but serviceable. Aldwyn didn't take long to hook Hjarta in to the traces and collar, and shut the large wooden courtyard doors after them. Covered in ivy, Karland could barely see them.

As they travelled Karland glanced at the woods from time to time and shivered. There was no sign of the bear. He hoped it didn't find them, or anyone else, but also felt strangely sad for it.

He understood its pain and rage. The dead man had been evil in a great many ways. He would never forget the shocking events of two days before, and he realised something a little saddening: the sedate life of the little town would never seem quite the same again.

FOUR

The old woman entered her house in the outskirts of Eyotsburg, thoughts on her last patient. The man should recover in a few days, and his family were grateful. Ginel shut the door and moved towards the ladder to the roof, wondering if a new bird had arrived yet.

She failed to notice the feathers and blood until she was at the foot of the ladder, and gasped in shock. Tiny limp forms were everywhere, and none had any tags.

A low laugh chilled her and she turned to see a young man with a feral grin beside the door she had just closed. She had not even seen him as she entered. Something about him terrified her.

Ginel cowered away from him. She had been jumpy for days, feeling eyes on her. Dismissing it as imagination, concentrating on her studies and herbs, too late she realised she had ignored the signs. She was thankful she had sent the last package by hand, trusting only one person to deliver it to Greck.

She had one last duty to discharge, although she had never really believed it would be necessary. Her shaking hand darted to a pocket. Tearing the wrapping off the compact white pill she removed, she forced it into her mouth and bit. The acrid taste of cyanide burned her tongue, and she moved to swallow.

Suddenly he was there, a vice-like hand gripping her throat under the chin. A fist thundered into her gut and breath exploded from her mouth, carrying her death with it. Fingers rammed down her throat and she vomited hard, shaking, her mouth burning agony from poison and stomach acids.

'Not yet,' came a mocking voice. 'No easy way for you, bitch.' Her head swam. Despite the brief contact, the poison had begun its work, but for now she lived. Somehow her terror was stronger than her pain; she could bear death, but she didn't know what this man would do to her first.

She stared at him in fright, struggling to breathe, and he grinned at her.

'You *will* die. But you can choose if you die fast, or slow… and if everyone you have healed in the last few days also dies. Men, women, children.' He leaned closer. 'All I need is information about your friends. Let's begin.'

ભ   જ

To his astonishment, Karland's parents were not as angry as he had expected. Brin had been slightly shamefaced and Becka had been tearful, not knowing what had happened to him. Karland had apologised, equally ashamed at the worry he had caused.

After they reconciled, the old man talked to his parents. Karland was taken aback by the seemingly sudden offer to take him on as an apprentice that Aldwyn made. He didn't hear the reasons given to his parents, but they reluctantly agreed that Karland needed to engage himself with more than working for Brin.

And so for the first time in his life Karland found an outlet for his thirst for knowledge. Aldwyn fielded every question, and would often answer in so much detail that Karland quickly learned to only ask what he really wished to know. What the old man didn't have in his head was readily available in a book or scroll, and he had an almost eidetic memory for what he had read. To the obvious amazement of his parents, Karland became focused and dedicated on his work.

His arm healed very quickly. He had not misheard; within two weeks only faint bruising showed any sign of the injury, and the bone was as solid as ever. When he asked Aldwyn about the unnatural speed of the healing, the old man muttered and then gave him basic exercises to do every day to ensure he regained full strength. Karland was not fooled. Aldwyn could do something incredible, and it was one of the few things he was reticent about.

As the months passed he received the occasional letter from Seom, the letters shaky and unpracticed. Karland always replied quickly in far more detail than his friend, looking forward to those precious moments of contact. His Darum became excellent, and Aldwyn started him on Old Darum, which many of the texts were written in.

Alongside language, politics, and history, Karland also discovered an entire world through maps and stories. The continent of Anaria, three thousand miles end to end, held a fascinating variety of lands and races. To the south lay the tropics of Morland and the sands of the Banistari Empire, and rumours of the pale fey folk in the vast forest of Léohtsholt, far greater than the Northing Woods near The Croft. To the west lay the Nassmoors, and beyond that the United Territories of Meyar, the city-states in constant upheaval. Karland found this hard to imagine against the slow pace of rural Eordeland.

To the south west lay the Arkons, the highest mountains on Kuln, looming over the great plains and the tribes of nomadic orks and barbarians they held. These were bordered more than a thousand miles west by mountains that hid the secretive realm of Ignat, and beyond that the coastal monarchy of Novin. It was sobering to learn that Eordeland was but a small part in the north east, and the only non-monarchy, but it was the most enlightened in the world according to Aldwyn.

Karland had never been that popular with the youths in the town after Seom had left. They did not understand him or his studies, but apart from Ben Arflun - who took particular delight in making his life miserable at every opportunity - he was generally ignored. As a result, he threw himself even more into his studies.

For his fourteenth birthday Karland received a letter from Seom, who said his father's business grew well and invited Karland to see him one day. He missed his friend greatly at times; one of the few who backed him up when Ben decided to use him as a punching sack, and a constant companion in mischief. The boys had even sworn as blood brothers in youthful seriousness, slicing their palms to clasp. He grinned, remembering Seom's panic when he cut too deeply; his friend wasn't good with blood at all. One day, perhaps, he would see him again. Aldwyn was a good companion, but he was not Seom.

He was old enough now to visit Aldwyn on his own when he wished, but he rarely travelled so far alone. Over the last few years, the lands around The Croft had become more dangerous. Strange shadows were seen sometimes in and around the woods. More and more often men did not return. Odd, rough folk from other places drifted through the town, causing unrest and sometimes real problems. Murders - once unheard of – had become a sporadic crime, and a gallows grew up at the gate.

Even the sparser southerly woods around the library of Thingos grew darker. More than once, something had tried to enter the door at night, and tracks had shown that it had prowled around the gates to the courtyard where Hjarta grazed; the little horse was now firmly locked away each night.

Whispers of glimpsed creatures from myth and legend grew. Week by week, month by month, a quiet dread was creeping over the town, punctuated by an occasional loss of sanity. It was as if the world itself was not right any more. Karland touched on these things in his letters to Seom, and was depressed to learn that Seom had noticed the same when he received the replies.

Eventually, he mentioned it to Aldwyn.

'There are omens all around us that the world is changing, Karland,' said the old man thoughtfully. 'I have found this of concern for twenty years now, and everything I have seen and learned tells me that the world is no longer running smoothly. Nature grows strange. Men grow strange. People tut and shake their heads when I ask of new darkness creeping at the borders, worse deeds than ever before known here, but they do not listen. Even nature is not as it was. Why, this year alone, how many more storms have we had? How many crops are failing? We have had word of new troubles elsewhere, mmm. Earth-shakes, giant waves, storms that level entire towns – and they dismiss them as stories!' He sighed. 'Something is not right in the world, I fear. But then great changes always seem dire to those in their midst. Look at the Kharkistani Empire.'

'The what?' asked Karland.

'Four and a half thousand years ago, mm, a great warlord united the tribes across the east of the great continent of Matalaga, east of Anaria. The Kharkistani Empire spanned the known world for hundreds of years, and the core still exists today, but it fell, as all Empires must. Here.' Aldwyn pulled a huge volume down from a shelf with a grunt. 'You know about Anaria now. I think it's high time we added Hadrasia, Matalaga, Naga Shon Oha, and the rest of the world.'

ভ৯ ৪৩

Several weeks later, a roaring yowl unlike anything Karland had ever had heard woke them during the night. They could faintly hear terrified whinnies from Hjarta; the sound had come from the courtyard door. Aldwyn rushed about in his nightclothes, collecting several pouches and delving into a deep chest that Karland was forbidden to investigate. Karland, his heart in his mouth, followed Aldwyn down the corridor, clutching a small dagger.

Aldwyn opened the door slowly and carefully, trying not to make a sound with the key. A dark, semi-upright form prowled the courtyard, bathed in shadows. Karland could not imagine how it had climbed in. Hjarta was neighing in fear inside his enclosure, the thick wooden door not as solid as ironwood. Even as they watched, the form threw itself against the door, snarling in fury and hunger. Karland jumped.

Aldwyn peered at something in his hand, and then whispered to Karland, 'I don't have many of these left. Close your eyes as soon as I throw this, boy, and then throw this.' He handed Karland a paper-wrapped sack the size of a large stone. It was quite heavy. 'Don't squeeze it, don't drop it! It will take your hand off. Try to hit the creature. *Now!*'

He threw something at the shape. A blinding white light exploded out with a bang, bathing the courtyard. Through purpled afterimages, he caught an indistinct impression of a half-jellied hairy nightmare face filled with ragged fangs, a long pointed tongue, and a whitened eye, the other jet black and glistening. The body was hunched and twisted. The shape shrieked as it blinked pained eyes, pawing at its head. Karland flung the package.

There was a deafening crack, like thunder. Agonised screams erupted, and the blinded and deafened shape fled, scrambling up the walls. They heard it fleeing clumsily through the ruins. Aldwyn hurriedly shut the door; neither of them slept that night.

The next morning, a long dark trail of blood was all that was left, and a few long toes. They had wicked claws and a slimy look.

'What *was* that?' asked Karland nervously.

Aldwyn shook his head. 'I do not know, boy. I do not know.'

'What was that you threw?'

'Ah. I had a tube with a mix of, aha, potassium perchlorate and magnesium, which-'

'All right, it made sudden light,' said Karland, sensing a lecture. 'Please, my head hurts. No long names today. What about mine?'

'I call it Aldwyn's Mixture, aha,' said the old man, grinning proudly. 'It's a mixture of red phosphorus and potassium chlorate and-' he caught Karland's long-suffering look, '-other things. Very explosive. It had to be carefully prepared and cushioned to be handled. Enough impact and, bang!'

He chuckled, and then whispered, 'Actually, another fellow found it in ancient times. I just researched the ingredients. I was working on Banistari Fire too, an old weapon, but no one recalls the composition of that.' He stretched. 'We must visit The Croft today. Come, let us get ready.'

Things did not improve when they reached town. They travelled to the general store to receive messages and pick up supplies, and were told that now all outsiders were being treated with suspicion, or turned away. One of the townsfolk had been raped and beaten last night, a girl his age - the third this year – and they did not know who had done it.

Aldwyn was resigned at the news, but when he heard that there had also been several men in the last few days asking about him specifically, he grew very quiet. Karland thought he looked frightened, although he relaxed when he heard that the wary townsfolk had not given the men answers. They had left to the southeast two days ago. Aldwyn brought out his ever-present inkpot and short quill, and penned a hurried message.

'Can you get this to Gladsmoor? To the Peddler's Respite? A man will be there in the next week. His name is Rast. He *must* get this, Jack. This is urgent.'

The storekeeper nodded. 'I never let you down before, Master Varelin,' he said. 'And this sounds important. Tell you what. I got more supplies needs getting from there in a few days, dried meats and the like. I'll drop it meself.'

'May the gods bless you, Jack,' said Aldwyn. 'It is urgent.'

As they left the store, Karland looked at his teacher's pensive expression.

'Who were the men Jack mentioned?' he asked. Aldwyn shook his head.

'I don't know… no one but Rast should know that I am here. It does not bode well.' Karland shrugged; he plainly wasn't going to get answers. 'Let us visit your parents.'

They made their way to the shop where Brin was at work. Aldwyn was muttering to himself distractedly as they pulled up.

'Go in then, and tell them we are here,' he said, flapping his hand. 'I'll see to Hjarta.' Karland slid down and moved for the door. Entering, he found his father bent over the counter, making notes in his precise hand. He paused for a second, looking at the work-worn face fondly. His father seemed to have accepted that he was not really cut out for cloth, and since Karland had demonstrably shown his knowledge and put his intellect to use, their relationship had eased considerably. Whilst Brin still never complimented Karland, he heard from his mother of his father's occasional pride. It was not the same as hearing it himself, however, and he hoped that one day they would breach the remaining awkwardness between them. Brin still found it hard to show emotion with his children, especially his teen son.

'Good morning, father,' he began, and then heard the rattle of the cart outside. Somehow he knew Aldwyn was leaving, and without a word he tore out of the door. Hjarta was already part of the way down the street. He cursed, and cut sideways between the houses, rounding the tavern nearest the edge of town, and skidded out in front of the surprised horse.

Aldwyn reined Hjarta to a stop, and Karland stumbled over, panting heavily. He grabbed the little horse's collar, and stood glaring at his friend. Aldwyn sat there looking miserable, an ashamed expression on his face.

'Listen, lad. I need to travel quickly. Something urgent has, ah, arisen-'

'You're running away,' said Karland bluntly, breathing hard. 'You're going to just leave me here alone again, trapped in a life I don't want. What is going on?'

Aldwyn sighed. 'I am deeply concerned, my boy. Deeply. Come on. Let's see your parents and then get back to the library. I'll tell you there.'

Aldwyn approached the ruins of Thingos warily, something Karland had never seen before. He peered around cautiously, motioning Karland inside quickly. Once inside, he locked the door and held up the lamp.

'Are you going to tell me what is going on?' Karland asked, troubled.

Aldwyn sighed and motioned him to the fireplace to sit, falling heavily into his high-backed chair.

'Karland, I have been a fool. I have spent much time telling you about the dark times I fear may be coming upon this world, and I cannot even see the obvious under my nose.' He shook his head. 'These strange happenings… murders, creatures, now people asking around… I may be putting this entire town in danger.'

'What? From who?'

'Karland, listen. There are many forces at work in this world.' He took a deep breath. 'I am part of a group of scholars that… stay in contact. One by one, they have spoken of rumours… then dark tidings. Then lately of people searching for them. Many have now gone silent… fled, or worse. I am starting to fear that I too am being hunted.' He pinched his nose, eyes shut.

'I must leave here. Tomorrow. I was due to meet this friend of mine here a month hence; he has been travelling, seeking to verify our suspicions. If there *are* men searching for me he may be too late.'

Karland shivered. Aldwyn sounded scared.

'So, I leave tomorrow for Gladsmoor, and hope he is there… and that I do not meet these men. He will take me to Darost, to other friends. I tried to leave because I did not want you to be a part of this.'

Karland sat back, angry with his friend for the first time. 'And you couldn't say anything?' he said. 'You believe they won't know I have been your student? What if they find me instead, or my family? Or they catch you alone?'

Aldwyn looked ashamed.

'You are right, mm, of course. I did not think. I panicked.' He sighed again. 'I am not sure what to do. You still have much to learn, and leaving you like this is not fair either. You are talented, mm, and need to continue your studies. I know you never felt as if you belonged in The Croft.'

He said no more, and after a moment Karland had a wild thought.

'Can I come with you?'

Aldwyn looked at him in disbelief. 'No! It is far too dangerous-'

'I can be useful,' argued Karland, hardly daring to believe what he was suggesting. 'I need to study more and you know I don't belong here. I still have so much to learn! And you should have company. You said I should see Darost – well, why not now? You may need my help, as well, and-'

'Wait! Wait,' interrupted Aldwyn, breaking in. 'Perhaps you are right. It may be safer for you if we both leave for a while, and perhaps… it might do you good. It makes sense not to travel alone… Ah! This is all so sudden.' He shook his head as if arguing with himself and then surrendered, standing and pacing in front of the fireplace.

'I will take you, mm, if your parents agree. But Karland… it may be dangerous. I hope it will not be, but it may. You must do as I tell you, and we must be cautious. Let us sleep. Tomorrow, we will revisit your parents. Do not speak of all this! We are simply… going to Darost. Travelling to the centre of learning. It is not far from the truth of things. So, pack what you need tonight, and be ready. We leave before dawn.'

Karland sat quietly after the old man left. His mind was whirling; he would leave The Croft to journey to one of the greatest cities in the eastern realms. He felt as if he was being set free. It would be an *adventure.*

ʕ ʖ

Ventran felt fierce delight as the young woman whimpered mindlessly. His dominance over first her flesh, and then her mind, gave him an electric thrill. Terror had cowed her; rape had torn her defences down; and then torture had cut her mind free from its bonds, one strand at a time.

His years of training in the arts of death had given him new perspective, new ways of applying suffering, but he rarely became distracted from the true goal. Sontles had taught him that lesson well more than once.

He moved towards the woman – no more than a girl, really – and whispered softly in the dimness next to her sightless sockets, the ragged bloody holes gleaming in the single candle.

'Hurts, doesn't it?' he said. 'The pain… can go. Any time you wish it.' She shook her head feebly, more in response to a voice than to his words. Her mouth opened spasmodically, the only untouched part in her ruined face.

'Tell me the names of the others, and I will take away your pain,' he promised.

Ventran had worked on hundreds of victims in hundreds of ways in the last few years. He had become expert in the arts of torture, and knew that while a few rare people could withstand it until death, most could not. Many spoke from fear, or to salvage as much of themselves as they could. Life to many as a cripple was better than death. But some… some would not speak until he had stripped them of hope, of all but a spark of life, and left them with nothing but the pain.

These could never live for long, never heal… but he was adept at keeping them alive, and they would do anything for the promise of release from their torment, if their minds were still intact.

This girl had surprised him greatly when he had eventually tracked her down. Betrayed by an old woman she had never met, he knew she was no mere scholar. Finally, he sensed, he had what he was looking for.

Taking her by force had broken her in many ways, but she had kept her secrets until now, despite the pain and the terror. Her mind was barely cohesive, and he had played her body with great skill to keep the breath in her.

This was her last day, he knew. All she knew was the agony. She was failing. In a twisted way he respected her inner strength far more than the old woman.

Her head turned as she sought him, and he bent close.

'Fr… free. You will… free me?'

'But tell me their names, and I will end your torment,' he promised. To his surprise he meant it. The girl sighed, her will gone and her body struggling. She began to recite names, barely intelligible, and he noted everything quickly. Eventually her voice began to die and her words to wander, and he knew she was of little further use. He drew a shiv and slashed her across the throat, ending her quickly as promised, and stepped back to her last gurgles. He would leave her here as a message to those she had betrayed. He chuckled in glee to himself. Their turn would come; finally, he had what he needed, what Terome needed – names of Darostim.

Sontles would be pleased.

FIVE

K arland was taken aback with how little his parents argued. They accepted
Aldwyn's explanation that he had been called away urgently to Darost
despite having been woken earlier than usual. The village was still, with most still
abed, and as Becka handed them some food for a moving breakfast, Brin smiled
up at Karland.

'So, you go to see The Sanctum,' he said. 'I studied there when I was young,
too.' Karland blinked in astonishment. 'I hope it offers you more than I chose in
the end... I took a different path.' He shrugged and laughed a little sadly. 'Good
luck, my son. I should have known you weren't cut out to be a cloth merchant.'

'Thanks,' said Karland, clasping his father's hand and smiling at the poor
attempt at humour. He had never known his father studied in the great
University of Eordeland, but now he understood why his parents had acquiesced
so easily. One day he resolved to ask his father more. He turned to his mother to
find her eyes brimming with tears.

'My son,' she smiled, her lips quivering. Karland surprisingly felt his own eyes
sting a little. She hugged him fiercely and he felt his neck grow wet. Finally,
Becka released him and turned to Gail. Beckoning the girl, she pushed her
towards her brother.

'Give him a hug and kiss goodbye, Gail,' she said. Gail shook her head.

'No! Yuck. Where is he going?'

'He is going travelling, Gail,' she said gently. 'To learn new things and see
great cities. You might not see him again for a long time.'

Gail looked at her brother sceptically, and then relented.

'Ohhhkaaaaay,' she said, and gave him a loose hug, a sister's mild distaste on
her face. When he squeezed her however, she suddenly squeezed back. She
stamped her foot, nearly catching his toe, and she whispered, 'You'd better come
back sometime. And I want a present from far away!'

He nodded, and let go. She moved back, watching him, and he realised that he would miss her.

'Karland,' called Aldwyn softly from the cart. 'We must go.'

Karland waved to him and then turned back and smiled at his family.

'I'll come back,' he said. 'And maybe you will be proud of me.'

His father coughed, his voice rough.

'I'm proud of you anyway, son. I know you will do great things.' Karland nodded, unable to speak past the lump in his throat. He turned and mounted the cart, and his mother called to Aldwyn.

'Keep him safe, Master Varelin.'

'As safe as I can, mm,' the old man promised. He clicked his tongue and slapped the reins, and his young dray flicked its ears and trotted off, the cart creaking behind. The town was grey and quiet, the only real bustle coming from the far-off stream bank and the craft holds that lined it. Strands of mist wafted through the air, and Karland felt them chill on his skin.

He looked back as they passed the outskirts. The gentle pace of life here would be missed. Feeling a little adrift, he turned back and sat, thinking, as Aldwyn patiently drove his dray along the main road southwest. His thoughts turned to his family, and those few friends he left behind; they were content with their lives in the town, but he was not. Ben Arflun at least he would likely not see again, but where once he would have been joyous, now he was strangely indifferent. Years of taunts and hits seemed somehow so minor now.

After a while, he looked over.

'So what now?'

The old man laughed, genuinely amused. 'My boy, we have barely managed two hours yet. Another hour and we will stop to rest the horse and have a bite to eat. As to Darost... mm. Well, it is about two-hundred and thirty-five miles away as the corva flies. But the road has to bypass the edge of the Northing Woods, and then it turns west to cross the river. From there it goes south, then east again, so we will travel, ah, perhaps just over one hundred leagues, or three hundred and ten miles or more before we reach Darost. '

'Corva?

'Sorry, mmm. Crow.'

'Why so long? I mean, can't we just go straight there?'

Aldwyn sighed. 'Hmm. Not really. There is a lot of wild country and arable land, crossed by waterways in between. It would be longer, harder, and probably more dangerous, if it could be done at all. If we are very lucky we might make Gladsmoor before dark tonight, but it is around forty miles so we need to keep the pace reasonable and, hmm, rest for my poor horse's sake.' He smiled over, his eyes peering over the tops of his odd glasses.

'We should be safe for now – there is only one stretch of real wilds between us and Darost, and even that is relatively safe. Almost all of Eordeland is tamed. There are some parts of the northeast and to the south that are still wild, but this is a realm of men, governed by the Council of Twelve in Darost – the most learned scholars in the lands. Of anywhere in Eordeland, perhaps even Anaria itself, I would say The Croft is one of the more idyllic places I have seen. But we must maintain caution… even here you have begun to have troubles.'

Thoughts of the insane hunter resurfaced in Karland's mind, along with other happenings that had marred the peace of his home in recent years. Aldwyn was right.

'I hope they will all be all right,' he said. The Croft was all he had ever known until the day he had met first the bear, then Aldwyn. He wondered briefly what had happened to that bear, and thought, too, of Seom. He had written a hasty letter explaining that he was travelling, and hoped to one day meet him again, but until then to be patient for word. Like his friend before him, he had left The Croft behind.

CR   SO

Whenever they stopped Karland surreptitiously tried to rub some life back into his buttocks, numbed from the bouncing on the hard seat. By the time the sun was well up the country was moving to low rolling hills that the road wound between. Shortly after entering the hills they passed a camp a hundred feet from the road. Horses were tied in a row, and five men rested around a pot bubbling on the fire. They were heavily armed but not uniformed, and Aldwyn did not slow. The men ignored them except for one who stood and shaded his eyes to watch them pass.

'Mercenaries,' muttered Aldwyn. 'It is unusual to see them in Eordeland. I will tell the next outpost that they are here.'

A little after noon rain began to fall and they hastily pulled off the road into a nearby copse for shelter and food. Aldwyn rummaged for the cloaks he had packed away while Karland rubbed the little dray down and fed him. Hjarta snuffled wetly at his hand, grateful for the attention.

They got under way again, Aldwyn hunched over the reins like a gaunt bird, his gnarled hands poking out of wide sleeves. Karland's cloak was even bigger on him, so he bundled himself up in it miserably and tried to sleep. At least the thick wool cushioned his rear.

In the late afternoon dark began to set in early, helped by the heavy clouds. As the light faded Karland wondered if they would be admitted to their destination. Finally the trees thinned and before them lay Gladsmoor, a glowing dot out on the open grass. Not long afterwards the guards waved them through the gate so they could close it for the night.

Gladsmoor was a large trading town perhaps four times the size of The Croft, famed for its sprawling cattle market and beef trade, the largest in the east. The town was a sprawling heap of houses surrounded by a sturdy fence, the roads that wound through the outlying steadings meeting in the centre in a large marketplace. To one side of the square an occupied gibbet swung in the rain, warning that Gladsmoor did not tolerate criminals lightly.

Karland stared, wondering what the man had done wrong.

Aldwyn peered short-sightedly around, and then asked Karland to help him find the Peddler's Respite. After some searching, and eventually asking a miserable-looking patrolman, they found the tavern. Karland unhitched Hjarta and curried him while Aldwyn argued the price of lodging and stowage of his cart and horse in the barn.

The common room was fairly well kept, with old but swept wooden floors and scarred tables. The inn was heaving with men and women drinking wine, ale, and mead. Loud laughter and shouting filled the air, along with the trilling of barmaids and the thump of tankards. A group of women were cackling over something in one corner, and a dark figure nearby was unconscious in a pool of what he hoped was red wine. Men were shouting orders at the barmen, and Karland caught voices raised in anger.

Aldwyn seemed not to notice any of this. Clutching his precious bundle of books to his chest, he told Karland to wait for him while he took them to the room, peering around him.

Karland watched him stagger up the stairs with his load and realised a golden opportunity to try his luck. Edging through the boisterous crowd he fetched up against the bar and found himself facing the innkeeper, who smiled at him kindly.

'A cup of wine, please.' He tried to make it sound casual; he was only allowed a sip of wine to celebrate Solsistere. The innkeeper, his eyes sparkling with amusement, handed him a large wooden goblet. Karland thanked him, hardly believing his luck. His face fell as he raised it to his lips and found that it was so weak that it was essentially water. The innkeeper chuckled and moved on, leaving Karland a little embarrassed. He pushed his way back through the crowd to find a table, noticing that several figures were watching him with interest. He decided to follow Aldwyn up the stairs instead.

As he changed direction in the crowd an arm knocked him, nearly sending him over. He caught his balance but his drink did not fare so well. It jarred from his hand and splashed over him, the floor, and the owner of the arm. As the cup hit the floor there was a good-natured mindless cheer from some nearby men at the mishap.

Karland blinked through the wine splashed on his face as two large grubby hands grabbed him and dragged him towards a pugnacious stubbled face. Wild hairs stuck from his nose and his breath stank through missing teeth. The man looked angry, but there was something else there too, a look that reminded him of Ben Arflun.

'You little shit!' he said, shaking Karland like a terrier with a rat. 'Cover me in your piss, will you?'

'I'm sorry,' managed Karland, twisting to get free. The man sneered.

'You'll be more than sorry, whelp!'

Struggling, Karland panicked. He tried to shout for help, but his voice would not work.

The man turned to drag him outside and then gasped as a massive cloaked form loomed over him. A huge hand that made his own scarred knuckles look like a child's inexorably clamped on his wrist and lifted it from Karland, who stared up at this new apparition in fright.

'This little one is not worth it, *friend*. He did not mean to disturb you.' The man drew in a breath to retaliate, and the huge cloaked man added, 'Come. Let me buy you a drink and put this behind us.'

The man hesitated, staring up, and then seemed to deflate.

'Fine. Stupid little bastard should watch where he is going.'

'I am certain he will do so more in future, though the fault was shared. No insult was intended, I am sure.' The shadowed face turned to Karland. 'Boy, go and sit by that wall behind you until I return. Do not try to leave. I will find you.' He turned to the man and pulled out a pouch that clinked.

Karland was terrified. He wished Aldwyn would reappear. He stood a moment, and then his nerve snapped and he bolted towards the stairs. He heard the deep voice of the giant shout, 'Boy!' after him, and frantically increased his pace.

Down the corridor at the top of the flight to the left was an open door with a light, and he heard the voice of an old man. He sprinted through it, heart hammering, and turned and slammed it behind him. He sank to the floor beside the door, his heart beating in his chest like a bird fluttering to escape, and sucked huge panicked breaths in, his eyes shut.

'Um… can I help you?' said a querulous voice. Karland's eyes flew open to find himself sitting across from an old man and his wife, who were looking at him in surprise. He was standing behind a chair, where she sat bundled up with embroidery in her lap. They wore good clothes, better than his family could afford, and appeared to have been mid-conversation.

He gasped, 'I- wrong room. Sorry. Someone is chasing me!' The old man goggled at him, and his wife smiled kindly, her old face crinkling.

'I am sorry young man, but we cannot help. Better to tell the innkeeper to call the guardsmen,' she said apologetically. 'There is nowhere to hide in here.' She did not sound overly concerned, perhaps thinking that he was involved in a childhood game.

Karland heard a creak in the corridor. He backed away from the door, waving at the couple to keep quiet. They watched him, puzzled.

The door swung inwards, revealing a gigantic dark form. The couple gasped along with Karland, who felt the strength drain from his limbs. There was no escape.

'Come along, boy,' said the figure softly. 'Let us leave this couple be.'

Karland felt trapped, numb. He moved towards the door mechanically and stepped out, oblivious to the concerned looks of the couple. As they emerged a door three down opened and Aldwyn stepped out. He peered towards them.

'Karland?'

'Aldwyn! Help me!' sobbed Karland, the fright too much to bear any more. The old man frowned and peered up at the huge form behind him.

'Get in here, Karland,' he said, staring at the man. Karland scrambled into the room and collapsed on the bed, where he lay panting. He heard Aldwyn come in behind him, and turned over.

With a screech, he sat up, banging his head on the wall. The giant was ducking his head into the room behind Aldwyn. Next to the old scholar he looked at least seven feet tall and as wide as three of the old man. His face and form were still shadowed.

'Oh, do stop that, Karland,' said Aldwyn irritably. He turned to the figure. 'So you found the boy, Rast.' The figure reached up for the clasp to his cloak.

'Yes. One of the local bullies was picking on him.' He pulled the cloak from his shoulders, and Karland got his first look at him.

Rast was the biggest man Karland had ever seen, bigger than any of the large farmer's sons around The Croft or the woodsmen who supplied the town with timber. Nearly six and a half feet tall, he looked like he could carry their dray on his back without much effort. His waist was solid but narrow compared to his broad chest and shoulders. Every muscle was leanly outlined under his close-fitting tunic, hinting at great strength.

He was a towering statue of a man's figure, everything in proportion. The impression was offset by his face. Rugged, with deep set grey eyes, he had a medium, very slightly hawk nose that overshadowed a mouth set grimly. A pronounced line ran from the edge of each nostril down past each side of his mouth, heightening the forbidding demeanour, and crow's feet were faintly visible at each eye. His hair was very dark and fairly short, shot through with a sprinkling of silver. There was a faint scar on his forehead, and his ears were slightly smaller than expected.

'Not so frightening, am I boy?' he said gently with a faint smile. 'I greet you, Karland.'

'He travels with me to Darost,' said Aldwyn. 'Karland, this is Rast Tal'Orien. Rast, this young fellow is Karland Dresin.'

Karland felt his cheeks heat in embarrassment. 'Thank you for helping me downstairs.' He hesitated. 'Sorry for running away.'

The big man waved a hand.

'No matter. Best to run away from people who threaten you until you can defend yourself. That fool was spoiling for a fight, although it seems only with someone smaller than him.'

Aldwyn said, 'Rast, we need to get to Darost soon. I have discovered some alarming things.'

'Yes,' said Rast. 'The world is changing for the worse. When last I sent word I had travelled west through the Reldenhort plains and down through the Sergoth. Barbarians grow less tolerant of the weak merchants from other nations. Novin is trying to annex Ignat again, after decades of peace. I eventually moved north through Eyotsburg into the Meyar Territories before the borders shut, and it is far quieter than usual. I think that worries me the most... their Prime Alderman is always looking to expand his borders, and the Hanári rebels are laying low.'

'Rebels?' asked Karland in interest. Rast glanced at him.

'Yes, boy. Haná was a kingdom until the king was murdered ten years ago; in the chaos following his regicide, his family vanished too. A council of Aldermen arose under the orders of one man, the Prime, and the kingdom split into territories and became Meyar. It has not been a good time for the people there, and there are still many who wish things to be as they were before.' He shook his head. 'And now problems seem to be everywhere else, too. There are rumours of people missing, superstition made flesh, political tensions and rioting where before there was no unrest. This goes beyond bickering nations. The trade from Deep Delving has dropped from a flood to a trickle, and they turn strangers away forcefully. The Barbarians of the plains are snapping at the Orkish tribes for the first time in generations, and in turn the Orks grow more resentful of humans by the week. No one has seen the elder race for many years, and there is even talk of Druids roaming the lands openly.' Aldwyn raised his eyebrows at that. 'More than one hundred years of balance are slowly breaking down. Treaties with Eordeland are becoming less heeded. Something will give if the Council does not act.'

Karland's head whirled with the information; he knew the names from his studies, but then it had all seemed so unreal. Hearing of rebels and war coming was difficult to imagine – it was all so far away.

To break the mood, they went downstairs to get food. Aldwyn ordered wine for himself, watered wine for Karland, and water for Rast. They were served a decent roast meal with generous potatoes, which was surprisingly good. As they ate the old couple came into the room, and smiled at Karland when they saw him at ease with the others. He grinned sheepishly back. At one point he saw the man who had threatened him sitting near the bar. The man's back was pointedly towards them.

After the meal they returned to the room. There were only two beds, but Rast sat himself in a chair with his back to the wall, facing the door and window equally.

'Sleep easy, my friends,' he said, the chair creaking gently under his weight. 'I will keep watch tonight.'

Karland found the big man oddly reassuring now that his forbidding aspect was tempered. He fell asleep quickly to the familiar sound of Aldwyn snoring like he was sawing an old log in half.

୧ ୨

Karland stirred in his bed as the first light of morning crept between his eyelids. He felt well rested, and stretched, yawning. Opening his eyes, he turned his head and saw Rast standing at the window, watching the day unfold.

'Good morning, Karland,' the big man said quietly.

'Morning,' yawned Karland. 'Did you sleep? You were awake when I rose last night, too.'

'I don't find I need to sleep much. Our friend may require something cataclysmic to wake him, however.'

Karland looked over at Aldwyn's bed, which was heaped in a strange position and oddly quiet. The occasional sudden grunt and drawn out snore erupted from it. He knew from experience how hard it was to wake his mentor. Unlike most people, Aldwyn rarely woke in the night to eat or talk and then sleep again; he tended to slumber all the way through.

Leaving him in the room, Karland dressed and ventured to the common room with Rast, and shortly there were two steaming plates of food in front of them. Hot green cha was put down with a small pot of honey to sweeten, and Karland exclaimed in delight at the traditional spread of Eordelander mushrooms, tumbled eggs, tomatoes and a heap of crisped bacon. It was a hearty meal. Rast requested a huge plate of tumbled eggs placed in front of him on some rough dark bread, generously covered in black pepper. He brought a mouthful to his lips, sniffed it deeply and contentedly, and then began to eat, glancing around the room as he did so.

As they were finishing their meal, Aldwyn stumbled down the stairs, blinking sleep from his eyes, his hair dishevelled. He made his way to them, waving the one morning server over, and requested porridge. Rast spoke up and asked for the same. In answer to the boy's astonishment he said, 'Enough oats and eggs will keep you going all day.'

Aldwyn cackled suddenly. 'Enough oats will, Rast!'

Rast ignored him. 'We should travel soon. The streets will not be too busy, and we should get as much distance under our belts as we can. The innkeeper told me that last night there were men asking after a traveller fitting your description. An honest man, I think; he told them that guests under his roof were not to be discussed.'

'Men?' said Aldwyn, waking up a bit. 'What sort of men?'

'Couldn't say,' said the big man. 'But since I received your message, and you mentioned your concerns, attracting less attention would be a sensible idea. Is there any reason that there would be men searching for you?'

'There are many reasons that men may be looking for me, but none that I welcome. We must make haste to Darost…mmm, via Fordun's Run. It is only forty miles east or so, and it is a shorter route than the cattle drives.'

'Let us not attract too much attention,' advised Rast. 'None will be expecting me to accompany you. Let us move slowly with the herds first and then take this indirect route. But you owe me explanations; there is much I do not know here.'

'Of course. We can talk on the road, away from… other ears.'

The porridge arrived then, cutting off the conversation, and Rast and Aldwyn fell to. Rast ate his plain, while Aldwyn salted his.

Karland asked, 'So, how far is it to Darost?'

Rast shook his head, swallowed and said, 'Best not announce our destination any more in public, boy. But by the roads we will take, a good few days travel, perhaps two hundred and thirty miles. Your little fellow is not conditioned for speed. Let us finish up here and go.'

They packed hurriedly, and then followed Rast into the stable. Karland dropped his bundle in the back of the cart. Turning to see where Rast was, he was confronted by a huge stallion's head that seemed to dip from the roof to eyeball him. The startlingly blue eye seemed to accept him as safe, and a warm snort erupted from the nose below it. The horse moved forward, a magnificent creature, well-muscled and lean.

Rast appeared from the other side, trailing his hand on the muscular neck, and said, 'This is Stryke. Be careful of him. He is war-trained and will not tolerate you unless I am near. He is not to be fooled with.'

Karland swallowed and shrank back a little. His experience with horses was limited to the dray and farm horses, which were placid and slow. This horse looked dangerous, and it was huge – a good seventeen hands, big enough to carry Rast's weight easily. Large hooves spread the weight of the powerful body, and muscle rippled under the darkish creamy skin. The mane was flaxen and long, and the horse seemed to glow slightly in the interior of the stable. Karland could not help staring. The horse was striking, as the name suggested.

'What kind of horse is he?' he asked as Rast lead him out. A small pack and a second rolled cloak were slung on a thin saddle that ran to a breastplate over the horse's chest, and there was a lightweight bridle in black over the stallion's head with reins coming off the sides.

'He is what the Ignathians call a *cremlo*,' said Rast. 'He is a little bit of a destrier, but also something of a courser. Powerful, strong and agile, though he will not have the endurance of Hjarta there. He is also remarkably intelligent for a horse, and understands some spoken words and commands. Stryke comes from a distinguished line.'

The stable hand, following hopefully, spoke up. 'Here, mister. If he hadn't sat so quiet all night I'da wondered if he was broken. Aintcha going to fit a bit on that bridle?'

Rast smiled slightly. 'Stryke does not need a bit, Master Ostler. We understand each other very well. I often ride with no tackle at all.'

The man shrugged. 'Your funeral, then.' He coughed tactfully.

Rast tossed him a few coins, obviously more than the man expected, and said, 'My thanks for the care. You have fed and dressed them well.' Out in the small courtyard, he mounted Stryke, and then looked at Karland. 'Are you coming, boy?'

Karland broke his gaze from the pale horse, which out in the grey light of day seemed a little less white and a little more of a dark cream. He jogged to the cart, where Hjarta was patiently standing in his traces, seeming not to feel the solid collar around his neck. Aldwyn was fussing with the reins, and looked down impatiently.

'Well? Hmm? Come on then.'

Karland jumped up, and they set off. Rast hardly touched the reins, Karland noted. The big horse moved fluidly for its size.

They passed quickly along the road, onto the packed mud which had not fully dried from the rain the day before. As they passed the east gate, Aldwyn snapped his fingers and reined in. At the quizzical expression of the morning guards, he described the men that they had encountered many miles back in the peaceful farming country. They nodded and told him it would be investigated.

The wide road stretched out in a straight line across the open grassland in front of them, with few settlements. The soil was too poor for anything except for grazing cattle. In the distance moving specks suggested cattle herds. To the south there was already a slowly building stream of traffic coming to the town. Before long the road would be packed with traders and cattlemen coming to the Market, arranging the transport of herds to the cities where they would be slaughtered or sold. There were far fewer drovers along their road, apparently moving between settlements.

The day remained grey and cheerless. Karland could not stop watching the plain unfold around them; he had never moved across such a large flat expanse before.

Eventually he turned to Aldwyn, and said, 'That's weird.'

'Mm?' said Aldwyn, not paying much attention. 'What's that? What is weird?' He peered around.

Karland gestured. 'Well, I just thought: we are on a plain here, and we can see a long way each side, and if you look as we go, after a bit it looks like we are balanced on the edge of two giant plates that meet where we are.'

Aldwyn looked at him askance, and Rast glanced over. Karland caught the looks and hurriedly tried to explain.

'And, as we move, the world to either side revolves as if on these huge plates that stretch into the distance, with the pieces on the edge next to you flying past, and the places further away revolving more slowly, like on a flat wheel? Um. If you watch long enough, you realise that the trees and animals and stuff don't even notice. All they see is us pass. But to us, we are the little cart on the meeting bits of two halves of the world, and they revolve to each side of us -'

'I can't say that I have, no,' replied Aldwyn, looking at him very peculiarly. 'But then, everything around us is subject to a certain amount of, ah, personal interpretation.' He blinked at Karland, and then looked at Rast, who almost smiled. 'I must say, though, you certainly have a curious mind at times.'

Karland opened his mouth to explain further, and then gave up. *He* knew what he meant. He watched the giant plates of the world spin towards him on each side, and the cattle on them didn't notice a thing.

SIX

Aldwyn seemed to be getting grumpier as the miles rolled by. 'Gods,' he eventually muttered in irritation. Rast quirked an eyebrow in question at the imprecation.

'What's wrong?' Karland asked.

'Ever since you told me, I can't see myself anywhere except at the middle of two platters,' Aldwyn snapped. 'I never used to notice!' He looked peeved, and stared ahead with a frown. Rast smiled slightly and carried on riding. Karland laughed, and Aldwyn's irritated glare did nothing to stop him.

The trio pulled into Fordun's Run late enough in the day that dusk was not long off. They had taken a very leisurely pace east, trying to seem part of the general plains traffic. Karland could see that the town was smaller than Gladsmoor, but with the heavy waterside trade and the ford it was old, and they passed many small streets and alleys.

They chose the largest of the three inns in the big village along the main road that ran through the centre of town. The Run Wash was cleaner than the other two, and Aldwyn insisted that he preferred to spend a little more for more comfort and a large room to study in. Karland was simply happy to stop. Rast made no comment, merely guiding the cart to the stables and flipping a copper digit to the stablehand.

Inside, the common room was shadowed in parts and bright in others, with wooden pillars adjoining thick beams overhead. Solid tables lined the walls, and smaller tables for those standing were scattered in the central space in front of a heavy wooden bar lined with kegs. To Karland this place was clean, wondrously organised and comforting.

A few workers were at tables, and one man sat at a table a little way from the bar, glancing around occasionally. He was thin with wild hair and a toothy smile, looking a little like a fox, his age hard to guess. As they looked around he rose and moved over, bowing very slightly.

'Greetings, gentles. I am Glab, and I welcome you to my home, the Run Wash. May I be of service?' He looked at them enquiringly.

'Ah, hello,' beamed Aldwyn. 'What a lovely looking establishment, young, mm, man. Very clean. Spacious! We have just arrived and would like a large room, if you would be so kind.'

'Of course,' said Glab, looking at them and taking in their state. Politely refraining from asking to see money first, he said, 'A room that would suit to fit all of you will be fifty decs for the night.'

Karland stared. Fifty decs was a fortune for a small place like this. The Croft's main inn cost ten silver for the biggest room. Glab caught his look and smiled.

'Ah, you think my prices high?' He chuckled. 'Well, perhaps they are, young master, but consider this: I have no rats or vermin here. My house is clean, and I look after my staff. Included is a decent meal, and I take pride in making sure my customers are happy. Surely that is worth something?' His eyes glinted with humour.

'I think it worth the price, friend,' said Rast, startling them. He had come in silently. 'I have heard tell of the hospitality of the Run Wash, and I see it was not wrong.' He opened his pouch and handed over the coins, clinking them one by one into Glab's hand.

'My thanks,' smiled Glab. 'I get many strangers through here at times, as this is the biggest ford on the Run – but at the moment it is quiet, most here will be townsfolk. I tell you what – for this same price you can have a room each, if you wish. I am no more than a quarter full, and the rooms are for genuine travellers, not, ah, laygirls.'

Aldwyn smiled back at the very generous offer. 'Thank you, Glab. We appreciate the generosity, but we have things to discuss, and this young one-', he gestured to Karland, '-needs to learn his books.'

Glab glanced at the big chest held immobile in Rast's huge arms and nodded. 'Fair enough,' he conceded. 'Will you be in the commons tonight? We usually have a goodly crowd in, and they like news from afar… although I advise you to go upstairs if anyone rough comes in. We've had trouble with some men in the last few months.'

'Men?' asked Aldwyn warily.

'Mercenaries, they struck me, perhaps out of contracts or too lazy to find real work. They crippled my doorkeeper a short while back, nearly killed him. Poor Lar never recovered fully. They are fighting men and we can't match them, so they do as they please and more arrive every month. We find it best not to confront them. They usually leave after some swagger when there is a crowd. I think they have formed a gang of sorts here. There is a lot more crime now in Fordun's Run... even a death or two now and again, and we are a peaceful folk.' Glab was unknowingly wringing his hands in distress now. Aldwyn smiled at him.

'I'm sure, ah, we will be fine.'

'Your rooms, then. Follow me.'

Glab led the way up the solidly set steps with little creaky give in them and directed them to a large room near the stairs.

'This is one of the bigger rooms,' he said, opening the door. 'There are two beds big enough even for your silent friend here,' he glanced at Rast, 'and a lounge-couch that is comfortable enough for your young friend.'

'This will do nicely,' said Aldwyn, waving Rast to put the chest down. The room was fresh, the floor was treated and covered in part with a plain heavy rug, and the beds looked soft and clean. The table had a small plant in a pot on it, and heavy curtains were bunched at the windows, the red matching the red trim on the cream beds and rug.

Glab opened the door and turned back to them.

'If you care to come and share your news, I will stand you a draught of ale each for the trouble. It will be quiet enough until tonight.'

'Thank you, mmm, but I will read,' said Aldwyn. 'Can I trouble you for my dinner to be brought up here?'

'Of course,' said Glab, smiling. 'I will have one of the serving girls bring it up later.' He exited and shut the door.

'There goes an honest man,' mused Aldwyn. 'He values customers and genuinely wants to give them good service - a rare thing in these times! A shame such a good man is beset, mm, with ruffians.'

Rast grunted, and then addressed Karland. 'I think it best if I start giving you some training; you must learn how to defend yourself. Tonight I will go over finger, hand, wrist and elbow locks. Close in work, since we are limited on room. Sealing, breaking, separating, tearing, locking; all useful to you. You need to learn which to use and when, and how to escape them.'

'Yes, and I will study whilst you do this,' said Aldwyn. 'Then before dinner I will teach Karland some of the history of this place whilst he recovers.'

'Do I get any say in this?' asked Karland, annoyed. He wilted when they both turned their eyes on him.

'You wanted to *learn*,' remarked the old man. 'Mmm? Well, you shall. But it requires dedication, mm, and whatever you learn, you must practice, be it books or practicality from Rast.'

'Yes, yes, all right,' Karland mumbled.

Rast beckoned to him.

'Come. Let *me* see what you can learn.'

⁎ ⁎

Aldwyn stayed upstairs as Karland and Rast moved downstairs into the common rooms later to get a meal. Glab welcomed them and motioned them to a table against the wall. The room was almost full, and loud.

Rast told Karland to remain at the table and moved off to talk to a large man, although with much of his size gone to fat. He sat at a booth nursing a large tankard with his left hand; his right arm and hand were badly misshapen, the shoulder canted, and his face was warped, a welter of red scars and lumps with half his left ear missing. He stared miserably at the table and barely responded to Rast at first, but eventually showed a spark of interest and replied.

The big man nodded and gently shook the mangled right hand of the other man with no apparent distaste. He detoured to the bar and motioned, handing over some coinage. Glab smiled and clapped him on the shoulder, and then left with another large tankard of ale for the man in the booth.

Rast returned with water for himself and Karland, his expression sombre. Karland, curious, was about to ask who the man was, but then Glab appeared with a thick stew, coarse wholemeal bread and slices of chicken next to it on a platter. He said to Rast, 'Lar has difficulties with life now, but I give him free ale and feed him. You didn't need to pay for a tankard.'

'He deserves it,' returned Rast. 'Aldwyn is a healer. Tomorrow we will ask him to perhaps reset his arm and hand, help him regain mobility. I can give exercises that will help him regain some use of his arm and hand, too. Looks to me like he should have died from those wounds. He was badly hurt.'

Sorrow crossed Glab's face as he leaned forward. 'Anything you can do is appreciated. One of the men I told you of was free to the point of being dangerous with one of my girls. Lar went to throw him out, but the thug had friends here. They dragged him outside and beat him… and worse. By the time the watch arrived they had gone. We thought he was dead.'

He shook his head sadly.

'This town has always been peaceful, but in recent years things have become tense. Our watch is not trained to stop soldiers, and there are many of them. Unless the watch catch them in the act, they can do little, and we cannot stand up as we would like - we are farmers and merchants, not warriors.'

Rast spoke firmly. 'This town will one day find that someone will stand up for them. I think these men will find it a hard lesson when it happens.'

Glab smiled, shaking his head. 'I wish I could believe you.' He turned and left. Karland and Rast looked over at Lar, who saw them and smiled horribly with his warped face, lifting his good hand in gratitude. They returned the salute and began to eat.

CR   SO

They ate slowly, watching the room fill as it got later. Rast spoke little, mainly keeping watch and sipping his water. As they sat finishing their meal, the merriment and level of sound dropped rapidly. Karland glanced over to the bar and saw Glab, white-faced, furiously polishing tankards. Several smirking men had come in and were insulting the common folk of the inn. One or two were pushed roughly, and not a few hurriedly finished their drinks and left the room. One of the men looked over and nudged his companion, and he started towards Rast and Karland. Karland saw Rast glance up then continue with his meal.

A solid shadow fell across the table, flickering slightly in the light from the lamp in front of them on the ceiling. Karland looked up, directly into the pitted, unpleasant features of a big man who had a look of general contempt on his face and a dangerous air about him. His clothes were of no particular note, and he didn't appear to have washed recently. Whilst he had some bulk to him, a lot of it appeared to be fat. The face had a slightly prominent nose, and more dirt than most would wish for. He had rough stubble; through it his mouth was twisted into a sneer.

'Newuns. Strangers. Never seenya here before. Pricey place to stay, this dump. You got money.' It wasn't a question.

'Not much,' said Karland, nervously. He was aware of the drop in the hum of the common room, and realised everyone was watching.

The man leaned forwards and produced a long, slightly curved knife with a sharp edge all the way down one side. It looked stained and pitted with rust - or dried blood - but was held in a manner that suggested he had used it often and readily.

'Well, thinks I should have it anyways.' He looked at Rast and glanced down to the pouch that slumped to the side, hanging off Rast's belt. Rast didn't look up, finishing another spoonful contemplatively.

The grin vanished. 'I'm talking to you, *big man*. Hand it over quick or your young play-lad gets a new breather in the throat. Now.'

He brought the sharp edge uncomfortably close to Karland, who shrank into the bench back in alarm.

Rast swallowed the last spoonful and continued to ignore the man. The ruffian snarled, his patience gone. He reached for Karland, murder in his eyes, and then his hand fell short as the heavy table was slammed into his midsection in a sudden blur of movement from Rast. Punching straight out with his palms in front, his back braced against the wall behind him, his massive arms swept the heavy table back as if it were a stool, the bowls jolting off it and smashing on the floor.

The knife vanished from near Karland's right ear as the man was driven back several paces and toppled, gasping and clutching his gut. The table landed on his sizeable stomach, driving even more wind from him.

Without seeming to have moved, Rast was abruptly between Karland and the man, who struggled to get the table off him and rise, his knife lying off to the side. The room was deadly silent apart from the attacker heaving the table off and gasping, everyone stunned by the suddenness of the events.

His two companions loomed. Pushing through the farmers to the table, they made for Rast. Before they got there, the first man rose, anger darkening his face, made his move. He flourished the dagger and twirled it in his right hand in the manner of a seasoned knife fighter, scowling.

'Big mistake,' he snarled, hate in his eyes.

His anger overcame his wariness of the size of the man in front of him. He lunged for Rast's stomach with unexpected quickness. As Karland gasped in shock, the man changed his thrust and suddenly sliced upwards towards his throat. The speed and movement left no doubt that he was very good with a knife, and had probably used this tactic well before.

To Karland it appeared that Rast's eyes stayed almost unfocused. He seemed, in that split second, to be relaxed and ready for death. The knife shot for his throat, his attacker's face set in a triumphant grin, the foregone knowledge of the kill in his eyes.

And then the huge man was somehow out of the path of the knife. The blade slid past his neck, the assailant's eyes beginning to widen in surprise at the lack of contact, and Rast grabbed him by the wrist with his right hand, his fingers wrapping around and digging into the joint with crushing force. He slammed his left forearm against the extended elbow of the thug's knife arm and simultaneously swivelled, using the natural leverage of the straightened arm to spin his attacker face first into a nearby pillar of wood with terrible power. The man's scream was muffled as his face impacted upon the hard oak full force, his nose snapping at the collision, front teeth cracking and knocking loose, one cheekbone breaking. The scream rose as his face was dragged roughly down the wood as his arm was pulled up and rotated, forcing his head down, then held and twisted up straight to his side to the point of breaking.

Extending his grip slightly, Rast almost gently rocked the arm to each side and down as he pulled and levered, braced against the man's head and neck on the pillar. With an audible pop the knife wielder's arm disengaged from the socket of his shoulder. The long knife dropped from suddenly nerveless fingers and he collapsed as Rast freed his grip, his face streaming blood, his right arm limply akimbo at a strange angle on the floor, his face vacant in shock.

Seconds had passed since the man had attacked. Karland was as astonished as everyone else. The rest of the room was frozen in disbelief, most of the patrons having been unable to understand exactly what had happened in the blur of motion. A man had pulled a knife, and almost immediately he was on the floor moaning in pain and covered in blood.

The other two attackers forced their way free of the farmers, bellowing in rage, murder in their eyes. Rast spun and dipped, flicking the knife off the floor with his fingers, the handle slapping over into his palm in an almost negligent manner. As quickly as it had landed, it was flicked out with sinister fluidity as he whirled to face them. Too fast to follow the knife left his fingers with a whir and buried itself solidly in the forearm of one of the men. He yelled loudly, his arm flying back, the point of the knife sticking through his forearm. His companion cursed as he stumbled into him, moaning in pain, and then came in warily. He transferred a wicked looking poniard to a reverse grip in his other hand and circled around his accomplice. A few of the patrons began to move in, and Rast's soft voice cut into them.

'Stay back.'

Rast kept his focus on the third man. He waited, watching for the man's inevitable lunge. The attacker knew knife fighting as well as the first had, the weaving patterns of the blade looking well-trained to Karland.

The man darted forwards, swinging his free hand over and down to slap Rast's leading arm out of the way, the other poised to thrust through once the way was clear. Rast's face was calm in the split second of the strike, and then his arm shot forwards, palm open and up. It was so fast it passed over the assailant's deflecting hand and then his wrist connected with the inside of the wrist of the knife hand. As the knife arm was knocked aside Rast's arm seemed to somehow rebound off it and slam stiff fingers into the attacker's throat with crushing force.

A horrible compacting-gristle noise followed and the third man was suddenly choking in panic, unable to breathe. Rast followed his strike through, turning his hand and sliding his arm around the man's neck, stepping in next to him and then moving around him and spinning backwards. Karland had never seen such a high or fast kick before. Rast's left foot shot up and out sideways through the arc of the spin and slammed into the temple of the man with the knife through his arm, snapping his head round. He appeared to have used the third man for balance until his arm whipped out in the direction of momentum as his foot completed its arc, and the damaged man fell away, collapsing in a heap further back at about the same time the second man's eyes rolled up in his head and he dropped like a sack of potatoes. Karland was astonished; Rast had used the choking man to start the kick and then used the spin to strike and throw in equilibrium, dispensing of two opponents in one movement. Start to end, it had been like watching a perfect, violent dance. None of the attackers rose, and the one who was writhing on the floor was purple in the face.

In the ensuing silence, one of the farmers near him plucked up the courage to stammer out a question.

'Who *are* you?'

'My name is Rast Tal'Orien,' Rast said quietly. He didn't even appear to be breathing hard.

A mutter swept the crowd like a wind. Karland heard the name repeated.

'Thank you, sir,' the farmer said. 'I don't rightly think I ever saw anything like that. You have our thanks. Will they live?'

'Yes,' said Rast bluntly. 'But two of them will be crippled if they don't get those wounds seen to.' He left Karland little doubt that he could have killed the men had he chosen, although the man struggling to breathe on the floor seemed to deny Rast's words.

Noticing Karland's, gaze, Rast said, 'He will recover too, but he'll think twice before attacking anyone needlessly again. His voice should return in time. They will keep some damage from this night for the rest of their lives. Not as much as they deserved.' He glanced towards Lar, who was watching with a peculiar triumph on his damaged face.

Rast nodded to Glab. 'I think it time we retired for the night. I apologise for the damage.' He glanced at the bloody pillar, the shards of crockery dotted around the overturned oak table, and the ruined thugs being propped up and searched by helping hands and then none too carefully dragged out the door.

Glab waved his hands. 'They tried to kill you. It is to my shame we had not the courage to interfere. I never thought they would be so bold in my inn. A fight with a tavern brawler is one thing. A sitting patron in full view is quite another!' He smiled faintly. 'Anyway, I'm sure the worth of the damage will be covered by their purses before our watch haul them off.'

Rast nodded, and moved for the stairs without looking back. Karland trailed after him, seeing gratitude in the faces of the locals.

'They shoulda ben killed!' one field worker called from the middle of the room.

Karland heard Glab tut as they ascended.

'If they were dead, we'd have had many more to deal with, with vengeance on their minds. Rast Tal'Orien takes the onus of the actions, and keeps us clear. He did the right thing.'

Karland wondered what that meant for him and Aldwyn.

SEVEN

The woman screamed in fear as Rey grabbed her arm and twisted it. 'Hurry up!' his accomplice hissed, leaning out into the light from the nearby alleyway. Night had fallen, but the streetlights shed enough light to show the struggle to anyone investigating the noise.

Rey clapped his dirty hand over the woman's open mouth, nearly stifling her, and wrestled her into the narrow opening. He had made sure she was alone and that the town watch were nowhere near, but that would change soon – it was a risk mugging someone this close to the main thoroughfare. He could be jailed, even lose a hand.

The woman was a little taller than him, and big boned. Whilst she couldn't match the little thief's wiry strength, she was being inconvenient, and if she didn't have enough money to compensate for the impromptu attack - the guild's rates were steep for ad-hoc work - the watch would be the least of their worries. The thieves' guild only had a relative finger here instead of an arm like the main cities, but the finger was sharp and cruel, and didn't take kindly to freelancing.

His fellow thief appeared and helped him drag the woman back. Not uncomely, her blonde hair was as wild as her eyes as she stared in shock and fright over his hand.

Rey wondered what she was doing out alone at this time. *Pretty stupid*, he thought. It didn't matter; he was only interested in her purse. Anything more would carry a far worse sentence from the watch, and the guild frowned upon that kind of attention. Doncan grinned at him, face pale in the shadows. He wasn't as circumspect as Rey and had a libido that would see him dead one day if he didn't rein it in.

Rey threw her on a pile of refuse and quickly stuffed a rag in her mouth. Tying it around her head, he pulled her upright by her hair.

'I want your money, nothing more,' he said roughly. 'Give it up quickly, and your jewels, and you'll not be harmed.'

'Aw, come on Rey,' whined Doncan. 'Only money? She's cute enough…' he broke off as Rey wheeled to him in anger at his colleague's stupidity.

'You *idiot!*' he hissed. 'She's heard my name! And I am sure she saw your face out there. We'll have to kill her – she could recognise us! You've ruined everything. This should have been simple.'

The woman moaned around the rag and shook her head in panicked denial, her eyes wide and nostrils flaring. She was trapped against the wall with them between her and freedom, and she knew it.

Doncan leered at her. 'Well, I may's well be more friendlier first then,' he began, and broke off at the look on Rey's face.

'We kill her quickly, take the money, and get the hells out of here,' snapped Rey. 'This place is too close to the road. I shouldn't have fucking listened to you in the first place, and I won't be here when the watch catch you with your pole out.'

Doncan grumbled and unsheathed his knife. Rey turned to look down the alley to keep watch, so he had an excellent view when the enormous shape dropped soundlessly to the ground out of nowhere, right in the middle of it.

He blinked.

'Doncan!' he hissed, not sure if he was seeing things correctly.

The shapeless shadow rose slowly from its crouched pose, foreboding and huge, and Rey got the distressing feeling it was staring at them as it stood halfway between him and Doncan. Then a head rose from it and the shape billowed out to each side, looking like nothing so much as a huge bat unfolding its wings.

'*Doncan!*'

The other thief turned irritably to snap, and yelped as the shape suddenly launched forwards at him, unfurling like some flying nightmare to engulf him. Rey heard a brief squeak from the bound woman, and then it slammed into his companion, sweeping him into the shadows.

Rey stared in shock. The speed of the thing was inhuman. Doncan was a strong man with a temper to match. Now he had simply… vanished.

He turned and ran out of the alleyway, ignoring the girl, just trying to get away from the nightmare that had taken his partner without leaving a trace. He glanced wildly behind him, and saw nothing at the alley mouth. Nevertheless, he darted between streetlamps and wove down several more alleys.

A minute later he stood gasping, hand on a wall for support. He could see the stars outlined against the buildings to either side when he looked up, and as his heart slowed he wondered what the creature had been. No doubt the woman was dead, his partner too. He shivered. The guild needed to know of this, and he wanted nothing more to do with freelancing.

A slight whisper of noise disturbed him, and he looked up again. The stars vanished as a huge black shape blotted them out and dropped towards him. He leaped back and pulled his knife as it thumped softly in front of him, right where he had stood. His head rocked back with his knife half drawn, and suddenly he was seeing inner stars. Rey was tougher than his stature gave him credit for, however. No stranger to night time scuffles, he shook the glancing blow off. Knife held low, the cry trapped behind thinned lips, he feinted and then thrust towards the shape's upper half. His hands were quick and, with the confidence of a man with many years with short blades, he knew the knife would strike the creature.

The shape seemed to shift around the path of the thrust and what felt like an iron bar slammed inside his wrist, the knife falling from numb fingers, causing him to gasp in pain and shock. He had barely a second to register the pain before his feet were swept from under him. He flipped in mid-air and landed on his shoulder and neck, nearly breaking his collarbone. A grip that felt like it was grinding the bones in his wrist to powder wrapped around his arm and there was a twisting feeling as weight slammed onto his chest. He screamed as his arm pulled straight then hyperextended. His elbow snapped backwards, and then his air was cut off. Rey's feet drummed the floor in spasm. His arm felt on fire. Caught in an unbreakable force, his last shreds of consciousness waned as he lay broken, gibbering inside at the demon that had come for them all, and then he knew no more.

෴ ෴

Jorna overcame her fright and ripped the filthy gag off. Her mouth tasted horrible, and she spat until she was dry to rid herself of the taste. She tried to work out what had happened. One second she had been sure she would die, and the next... something had swooped at the thief like a demon, and he had vanished. The other one – Rey? – had turned and run, and somehow the thing was halfway up the nearest wall, moving swiftly up and vanishing onto the roof.

The most disturbing thing had been the lack of noise – deep breathing, slight scuffling, and the soft but solid thump as it hit the thief, and the horrible crack a second later. It had all happened so quickly.

She stood unsteadily, and then shrieked as a whisper of movement beside her resolved into the hulking shape from earlier. As far as she knew this thing had eaten the two attackers and come back for her.

She stood there trembling, incapable of moving, and the shape reached for her... and took her hand. Numbly, she let it lead her to the mouth of the alley. It bowed its head and vanished back into the shadows. Her hand dropped to her side and she ran out to the streetlight, where a squad of guards found her a few minutes later staring wildly at the shadows around her.

Jorna resolved that meeting her lover in the centre of the town might need to stop. Perhaps this was a sign that her husband deserved her full attention. Fervently, she swore to herself not to leave at night again.

It was definitely an omen.

ؒ   ࡊ

Karland woke with a start. It was still dark. He glanced around the room blearily, trying to see what had woken him. Rast's voice came back reassuringly out of the shadows, where Karland could just make him out, alert and watchful as he always seemed to be.

'There is a disturbance in town. Don't worry. It doesn't seem to be too nearby, and I can hear the watch, so it is likely being dealt with. Go back to sleep. I will make sure we are left alone.'

Tired from the day's ride, Karland needed no more urging, and closed his eyes again. Through the rapidly descending blanket of placidity, he could hear Aldwyn's dry snores, soft and regular, and felt comforted. He was with his friends and safe.

When he awoke, the window was light. Both Aldwyn and Rast were nowhere to be seen, and he could hear his stomach grumbling. Throwing off the blanket, he quickly dressed and moved downstairs. As he descended, he became aware of a murmur from the common room that swelled as he walked into the room. He stopped, surprised.

The room was at least as full as the night before, and full of excited chatter from farmers normally away working their fields. Glab was deep in conversation with a group of burly young men near the bar, and Rast was nowhere that Karland could see. Snatches of conversation and shocked faces caught his notice as he weaved through the room.

Aldwyn was at a table in the corner near a window, a pot of steaming tisane in front of him, and a board with bread and cheese. Light shone through the panes, brightening the room. It was a pleasant day outside.

He beckoned Karland over and called a young lad for more food. The boy nodded and disappeared, returning with food and a cup a few minutes later. Karland sat and started eating wolfishly. The bread was rough brown and fresh, the cheese very strong.

'Fresh, mm, today, so I am told,' said Aldwyn. 'Farmers tend to, mm, eat well when their crops are good. They control the product at its source, as it were.' His eyes crinkled under his white brows. Karland grinned at him between bites, but kept eating steadily. 'Well, Karland. You haven't had good experiences with inns thus far, eh?' He smiled in sympathy. 'Times are getting rougher, lad. It only used to be like this in the big cities, never in towns in the country.'

Karland shrugged. 'Well, both times Rast was there, though the first time I did think he was after me. I'm fine.'

Aldwyn chuckled around a mouthful. Karland looked up to see Glab moving towards them. The crowd was dissipating, the farmers very late to their fields, leaving merchants to chatter. Lar was sitting by the bar, his face pale. His right arm was heavily bandaged from fingertips to shoulder, and a steady supply of ale cups lined the counter, even at this early hour. A large pouch of something sat next to him on the bar.

'Good morning, young master,' he greeted Karland. 'And to you again, sir. I would like to thank you for what you have done for Lar. The healing will be hard, but with luck he will use his arm again in time. It is much straighter.'

Aldwyn waved his hand peremptorily at the formality and said 'Mmm, Master Glab, really, I must insist. I am simply Aldwyn. Yes, I am pleased. Most of the use may return, although it will not be perfect, especially his hand. I did what I could. Just ensure he takes the herbs as instructed – not with the ale! - drinks plenty of milk, eats lots of cheese, and that he does the exercises Rast gave him. Perhaps in two or three months he will find himself able again. I would, ah, suggest that you tone down the ale after a week or so.'

Glab nodded.

'Well, sir, you have our gratitude. And what a to-do today has brought! Ever since last night when your giant friend humbled some of our troublemakers, the town has been a-stir. Last night was a bad time. Has Master Aldwyn told you what happened?' he asked Karland.

Karland shook his head, remembering the faces and conversations he'd caught in the room. Glab's face brightened. The innkeeper was quite obviously a gossip. He settled himself on the bench across from Karland and signalled for a fresh pot of tisane.

'All over town last night, young master, something attacked people. A demon of darkness that came from nowhere to strike men down. The watch were overwhelmed – we are a small town and there are only perhaps eighteen of them all told, and half that on duty last night. The rest were called in on emergency, but even that was not enough. This creature struck all over the town.' Karland was fascinated, and Aldwyn also looked keenly interested.

'Every time the guards arrived they found nothing but the maimed or unconscious. All the victims were men of ill repute or mercenaries like the ones who attacked you here yesterday. The watch eventually stopped investigating – they saw nothing and were too frightened to continue. They ringed the main square with torches, sending out a call to people to gather. Most stayed in their houses and barred their doors and windows. People were terrified last night, but it luckily seems not one honest person was hurt by this demon, though several saw it. Those who could describe it said it was like a giant bat that flew out of the night and took people suddenly.' He shuddered.

'It actually killed no one, although there are a few men who may yet die of their wounds. Two ruffians who waylaid a local hussy were hurt, one very badly – he may never speak or eat properly again, if he lives. One group of five men were breaking into the Blake warehouse on the western side of town, and had attacked the nightman when he found them.' Glab's face fell in sorrow. 'Danrel was a good man. They broke his skull. Master Varelin looked but said there was nothing we could do but make him comfortable. He died this morning.' He sighed.

'The gravest casualties were in the group that attacked Danrel. The only one who has woken up is gibbering. We think his mind has snapped, but from what we can make out this demon dropped into the middle of all of them as they entered the warehouse and maimed them all horribly. Half their wounds were from their fellows, I think – no one else attacked had cuts. Few will walk again if they live. I cannot understand how five armed men could not strike one creature. Maybe it isn't even flesh.'

'What about the men?' asked Karland.

'They are doomed to lives as beggars now. The town is meeting later to work out what we can do with them. Folk here are decent, and we cannot just leave them to die. Your friend Rast showed little sympathy but suggested that they keep the streets clean for a pittance, or do basic work. Most of them are worse off than old Lar now. There are a lot less bad men capable of being bad this morning, if you take my meaning. It has given us some hope in an odd way, despite the fright of this creature loose at night. We had a town council meet, early on, and we will be stopping any more ruffians coming in to town. We will make our watch bigger, and round up the other troublemakers, and honest folk maybe can then start to feel safe here again. Whatever this demon is, I hope it leaves. Then we can feel truly safe.'

'What do you suppose it is?' asked Aldywn.

'I don't rightly know, Master Varelin. Stories are already being told that it craves blood, and last night was just a warming up, so to speak. A priest of Delmatra has been consulted to see if it can be barred from town, although some people are hailing the demon as a saviour. People are more frightened of this thing than the thugs that were taking our town from us, but it has not attacked any but dishonest folk – yet. Well, I must get back to work – I think today and tonight will be very busy for us all. Please come to see me before you leave. I have a parting gift for Rast for the service he rendered last night.' He stood. 'Enjoy your breakfast, on me.'

He walked away to the bar, leaving Karland's mind filled with alarming images of a giant bat-like demon that swept silently out of the night to take grown men. The morning seemed less bright somehow, and he shivered, thinking of how he and Rast had been disturbed by the commotion last night.

Both of them jumped badly when the light was suddenly blocked by a massive cloaked form. Karland looked up into the faintly amused face of Rast, his heart hammering.

'You're both nervous this morning,' the big man remarked, a slight smile on his face. Aldwyn looked annoyed.

'I simply was not expecting a great lout to suddenly block the light out, thank you, ah, Rast,' he snapped. Karland flushed.

'I was thinking about the demon they say was out there last night,' he said.

'Well, it is bright morning, and I went out to search with the others. I could find no traces of this demon, only men. Whatever it is, it is gone for now.' He paused reflectively. 'I think it is a good idea to move on soon though. From what I have heard I think it is not a danger to the goodly folk of Fordun's Run, but I would rather be safe and leave the area quickly. It has not been seen here before, but that does not mean it will not be again.'

'What do you think it is?' said Karland.

'The descriptions are not detailed,' admitted Rast. 'It could be anything. There are many strange creatures in this world.'

'I do not like the sound of this demon. It sounds like no natural creature I know of,' said Aldwyn. 'I hope no one thinks it connected with our arrival. The folk here are honest and fair, but I think we should leave soon.'

Rast nodded. 'People already remember that I was involved in a fight last night, before the attacks. If you are finished eating, we should go.'

'Oh, Glab said for you to see him before we went,' remembered Karland. 'He said he has something for you.' Rast nodded and moved towards the bar where the serving boy was polishing and stacking tankards to call through the door to the kitchen. As Glab emerged, Karland and Aldwyn headed for the stairs to get their things.

CR   SO

Sontles grinned sharply when the note and the bloody package arrived. He opened it to find a heart within, cut from one of Ventran's victims. The note held priceless information. Now they could act. Ventran had learned well.

Perhaps one day he would even ordain him into his own order as a reward.

EIGHT

Their horses were well rested and curried and Hjarta was already harnessed to the cart. Rast's destrier tossed his head, muscles bunching, but calmed at his master's sure touch. Turning, Rast stashed the large basket he was carrying in the rear of the small wain under the low peaked canvas, and then mounted Stryke.

Karland and Aldwyn mounted the wain and Aldwyn clucked at Hjarta. The cart moved off, Stryke trotting sedately alongside it, the bunching of his shoulders and hindquarters suggesting he would prefer to be running. The horses trotted down the wide main street from the Run Wash, parallel to the river. Not long after this they reached the ford itself. Upriver all the way to the Run Wash, the shallow ford and the large gravel lining it turned the river into a clear, white-tipped leaping stream that gave the inn its name. Downriver it dropped into murky depths abruptly, the fast water looking deceptively slow. Splashing through the shallows, they crossed over. The sun sparkled in the water and the shallow's tinkling song filled the air.

Karland glanced back at the roofs of the settlement watching for movement, until he caught Rast's impassive eye and swivelled around again, pretending he hadn't been looking. A few miles further on, he looked back once more to find Fordun's Run an anthill in the distance. As they entered the lowlands forest the Run coursed through, Aldwyn seemed to come out of his reverie.

'Rast, mm, what did the excellent Glabrin gift you in that basket?'

Rast smiled slightly, looking ahead, his eyes scanning the land.

'Cured meat, and a great deal of it. That strong cheese as well. We will eat well for many nights. He would not hear of refusal or payment.'

'Ah!' said Aldwyn, his eyes gleaming. 'The cheese? Eh? Good. Good.' He looked inordinately pleased with himself. Karland smirked. He was beginning to suspect that his elderly friend had a particular weakness for cheese. Then a more sober thought occurred to him.

'Rast, can I ask about the fight?'

'If you wish,' said Rast.

Karland frowned at the noncommittal response.

'I never saw anything like that. Do you often do that? I mean, kick in a fight?'

Rast shook his head. 'Usually, no. If you are confident of the outcome, it can be devastating. It was also the last thing he expected, and gave me extra reach. For me it was a valid risk. *You* should not kick in a fight. Not without a lot of practice.'

'But-'

'Believe me, boy. Don't kick.'

Karland's face fell. Aldwyn chuckled in sympathy. 'Never mind him, Karland. He is just feeling sore that, heh, he will have to share his new-found cheese with us tonight.' He winked, and Karland had to smile.

'Well, all right. But it was so shocking. It all happened so quickly – how did you know what to do, what they were going to do?'

Rast was silent a minute, swaying with the movements of his horse. 'It is like anything, Karland. You learn the ebb and flow of battle, the types of opponents you face, what you can do or not. There are different ways of fighting against single opponents, armed opponents, or multiple opponents. Bigger, stronger, faster enemies; singly or in great numbers, everyone faces them eventually. You learn in time how to read and react.

'It is not perfect. It is impossible to completely predict another unless you know them well. But I knew the leader was looking for real trouble, not just words. It was in the way he moved, the air about him. The crowd were scared of these men, and with good reason, if they and their comrades are quick to maim or kill.

'Other than that, I can only say there is a peculiar timing to fighting, and you learn to move with it. The only thing that teaches you this is constant practice. You will learn not to freeze, not to panic. You learn to relax, to read an opponent, but it takes time.'

Karland considered this. He had not realised how much work being a mighty warrior would take. Soon, however, his thoughts invariably turned to the mystery of the demon from last night. The bright sunshine and the blue sky, tufted with clouds, seemed to mock his fears of this morning when Glab had told him about the creature, but it was too tantalising a mystery for a young boy to ignore. He wondered idly if Rast would have defeated it had he found it that morning, secreted away in some lair. In Karland's mind, it was a dark thing with bat wings and menacing fangs, eyes like pits and muscles like steel.

They camped that night in a small hollow set back a little way from the road, surrounded by trees. The clouds hid the stars and only a faint dissipated glow in the sky spoke of the prime moon. Xoth was too weak to pierce the cover with its greenish tint.

Rast used deadwood for fire, and two old logs to reflect heat as the night was cold. Warmed from the front, they cooked a light meal, sitting the other side of the fire under the spreading boughs of a tree for shelter. The horses had been watered at a small brook that trickled through the hollow, and the food was cooked on flat stones taken from nearby. Karland had brought some nicely worn ones back from the brook, but was warned that wet rocks could explode in sudden heat, sending out dangerous fragments. After drying for a while on the side of the fire, they were pushed gradually close enough to heat sufficiently.

Karland rolled himself into his bedroll after eating, tired from the travel, but he could not sleep. Gradually the ground stole his heat, and so he lay there, listening to the night and wondering how people could stand camping out as they travelled. Used to the quiet of rooms, the snuffling of Hjarta and the snorting of Stryke as they stood nearby was distracting, as were the subtle noises of the wilds.

He missed his family and his own bed for the first time, and wondered if he should have done things differently. Running a trading business had seemed awfully boring back then, but right now the dullness – and accompanying comfort – appealed strongly. His mother's upset had been obvious, and he was feeling homesick. Travelling to new places was not the fun he had assumed it would be. It was hard, tiring and disorienting, and nowhere was a sense of familiarity. His only link back to his previous life was Aldwyn, and even he seemed different here. More focused, more realistic, perhaps more fatalistic.

Rast was a mystery to him as well. He was calm, mysterious and a little frightening in his focus. Although he fought like a hero of legend, Karland wondered what use he would be in a fight with well-armed foes. An unseasoned boy of fourteen years and a skinny old scholar were unlikely to provide much threat to anyone wishing to harm them, and he was no longer sure that he was so safe. Rast was their only protection.

He fell to thinking about Aldwyn's belief that things were growing darker every year. Forest animals were more likely to attack and men fought more; barely a week went past without a fight – or worse – even in a peaceful town like The Croft. People vanished, running away or found dead, or did terrible things.

With a shudder, he recalled how, one day over a year ago, the miller had placed his infant son casually on the crown wheel of his millstone and watched as the boy was ground into the grooves by the cogs. The neighbours had come running at the horrified screams of his wife, walking in to find the son she bore crushed to an unrecognisable pulp, and arrived in time to see him strangling her with a look of feral delight on his face.

They pulled him off her, but were unprepared for his savage rage. He fought with the strength of two men, biting two fingers off one man and clawing the eye from another, and leapt through the open door. Running from the building laughing insanely, he vanished into the river that flowed into the woods. By the time the shocked populace had searched for him, he was gone. His wife had recovered, but as soon as she was left alone she had tied a millstone to herself and somehow summoned the strength to throw it – and herself – into the waters.

For a quiet town like The Croft, this was unspeakable tragedy. Sadly, this was no longer an isolated occurrence. Now no one left their doors open, and the watch kept a careful eye on the borders of the town at night. Children were watched closely and avoided strangers.

Karland tried to turn his thoughts from these depressing matters and his home in general. He tried to be positive about the city that lay before him – usually resplendent in his mind with potential adventure – but failed, downcast. As he lay there feeling truly miserable, rain began to fall. It was not a hard rain, but it was cold and depressing.

The tree sheltered them from the fall, and the sound of his shivering was lost in the quiet rhythm. Just as he was about to shift, he caught Rast and Aldwyn's voices as they sat nearer the fire, at the edge of the shelter. Karland strained his ears, and forgot about the cold and feeling sorry for himself. Behind the hiss of drops in the fire, and the patter on the leaves, he could hear the two speaking, and they plainly thought he was asleep.

CR   SO

'The rain,' Aldwyn said softly. 'It falls like the tears of a god. Sadly, wetly, as if to gently wash away all that was done wrong. Weeping in sorrow that this world may end, and all else along with it.'

'Do you really believe that?' asked Rast quietly.

'I know what we may face, better than perhaps any other, but, mm, deep down? I don't know. I think perhaps, looking out on this night... yes. Yes, I believe it. Can you not feel it?'

Rast was quiet for a while. He did feel it, in a way. There was a disquiet growing in the world, a subtle imbalance that spoke of change.

'But you are a man of science,' he said at last. 'You are not religious. I've heard you cursing religious doctrines as mindless countless times.'

'I may not be religious,' said Aldwyn seriously, 'but I know the gods exist, and much more besides them. Religion is not the same thing as belief, Rast. And I believe in higher things than just the gods of this world... or outside it.' Rast threw him a puzzled look. 'Perhaps if we manage to survive, there will be a cleansing rain to wash away the sins of all of us,' continued the old man. 'Or perhaps we will all be washed away instead. Who can tell? I, ah, may be a man of science, as you say, but I have to accept the realities of this existence, and gods are undeniably one of them. No, my friend. I am not religious – but I have a belief in what is real, and some gods are real.' He smiled and glanced over. 'I just don't believe in bending one knee – or the other – to prove it.'

The two figures, one massive, one old and bent, sat staring for a time into the fire. Eventually Aldwyn looked at Rast.

'What about you?'

'What do I believe?' Rast shook his head. 'I have never seen a god. I have no time for religion. Some things cannot be explained, even by your studies, but I believe in what I can see, what I can feel, what I can fight. I believe in my own strength, and the certainty that one day it will not be enough. Yet on that day, still will I fight.' He smiled grimly. 'But what you say has merit. I, too, have noticed that the world is changing. I have heard the tales of the strange happenings hereabouts, but it is happening everywhere that I have been, and it grows worse the closer you get to wild places like the Dimnesdair. Even the Barbarians will not go near there now, and people say the lands around there are becoming dangerous.'

Aldwyn considered the words. 'If even you are concerned then things are worse than I had dared fear, my friend. The end of times could be realised in our lifetimes.' He sighed. 'It is past time to return to Darost, and this time I will find a way to make the Council listen. Do you think we face war?'

Rast's face was grim.

'Perhaps. But I could not say involving who.'

'Mm, whom,' corrected Aldwyn absent-mindedly. Rast smiled and shook his head, then got up and moved to just past the edge of the shelter, the fire to his back. He closed his eyes for a moment to restore his night vision, and then peered out into the darkness, senses alert.

'Tell me more about these people who have been trying to find you,' he said after a while. There was no answer. Just as Rast wondered whether the old man had fallen asleep, Aldwyn spoke.

'I don't know. I have... suspicions. What I do know is that, one by one, my colleagues spread throughout the world have stopped responding to me. They have just – vanished. I worry I may be the only one left.' His voice quavered. 'Some of them were old friends. Some were worthy adversaries. Many did not agree with me, but we were united in our drive to learn more… especially about the future. We may not all agree on the cause, or the timeframe, but more than a few of the scholars of Darost see disaster ahead. I fear we are being silenced for something one of us has learned.'

Rast turned to look at him.

'Rast, I am terribly frightened. I think I am in danger, and I have put you and the boy in danger too. I must speak with the Council of Twelve. Anaria stands in peril, and you may be my only hope of reaching Darost alive.' He sighed. 'I should never have brought Karland, but he may be important. I did not know what else to do.' He stood, and moved to his blankets.

Rast grunted. He didn't truly believe in guesses and prophecies. He believed in cold hard facts and experiences. But the old man was truly frightened, and not just for his own life. Aldwyn was right – a darkness was growing in the world. For the first time in memory, creatures of legend were reported coming out of the depths of the Dimnesdair, both the forest and the huge dark valley beyond. Creatures that most had thought fanciful were proving a bloody reality. Remote places were becoming less safe than civilised places, and even some of those seemed to be slowly rotting from within.

The old man was right about something else, too. They were being followed, and his intuition told him that their intentions were not friendly.

A slight noise behind him caused him to focus, and he turned, staring at the bundle where Karland lay. With a sigh, he realised the boy was awake and had probably heard much of their conversation. With a final check around him, he moved over and found Karland shivering violently with cold, teeth chattering. The boy was of average size for his age, with reasonable tone and build, but he often seemed smaller and younger due to his lack of confidence. Dark brown hair swept his forehead as he looked up at Rast, his grey-blue eyes full of questions, but he could only manage one.

'Why-y-y am I so-o-o-o c-c-c-old?'

'We need to work on your campcraft, boy,' said Rast. 'Never sleep directly on the ground. Roll your blankets under yourself as well as over. The ground will steal your heat far faster than cold air. Conserve energy until you need it. Don't waste it.' He helped Karland sit up and wrap himself properly. A few minutes later the boy stopped shivering as his bedding warmed, and colour came back to his face. He opened his mouth to ask the rest of his questions, and Rast forestalled him.

'Another time, Karland. Sleep.' His expression brooked no argument, and Karland wisely chose to follow his advice. Rast settled to watch his charges and think on what Aldwyn had said.

ᚱ   ᛋᛟ

The next morning showed signs of sky through the cloud. The rain had stopped during the night. Karland woke warmed and thankful for Rast's advice. Not far away was a bundle that was making the most astonishing snorting noises. He sat up and looked for Rast's bed, but there was no third bundle.

He eventually found Rast, standing quietly at the edge of the cover. His form was hard to pick out, covered as it was in the dull grey cloak. The hood was thrown back, showing that dark hair shot with iron grey. Karland watched him, wondering when he had slept. He was content to lie in the warmth and observe the big man, who was obviously at home in the woods. Rast stayed almost motionless, moving only every few minutes to a new spot, flowing silently like a large cat.

Karland was fascinated. There was something visceral about the way Rast moved. He played a game, trying to keep the big man's outline in view when he paused, but even when he had seen Rast travelling it was not always easy to pick him out when he stopped.

Growing hungry, Karland sat up. The campfire was low but glowing, indicating it had been fed during the night, and there was fresh water in the pot next to it. The next time he looked up, there was no sign of Rast at all. He carried on making tea, and got the fire started again. Moving down to the brook while the water heated, he found a softwood twig and chewed the end lightly, and then cleaned his teeth with it. The fibrous ends felt good against his gums and between his teeth, and he felt a lot cleaner for it.

By the time he returned, Aldwyn was peering blearily around the clearing, blinking. As Karland moved over to the fire, Aldwyn spotted the pot beginning to bubble.

'Bless you, young man,' he croaked. 'The black tisane, if you would.'

Thirty minutes later, they were packed away and settled after a light snack. Stryke and Hjarta were still standing in the morning light, and patches of sky were becoming more frequent, yet Rast was not back from wherever he had gone. Karland left Aldwyn sitting on a log and untied Hjarta, leading the stout little dray to the traces of the small cart and beginning to position him.

He nearly shrieked when a calm voice directly behind him said, 'Pay attention to what goes on around you, boy.'

He jerked round to see Rast standing uncloaked behind him, within arm's reach. His heart hammered; he had not heard the slightest sound. Rast looked faintly amused.

'I could have been anyone with a little woodsmanship, Karland. You heard enough last night to know that we may be followed, so I would suggest you stay alert.'

'Where did you vanish off to?' demanded Karland angrily, red faced. 'You left us alon-'

'I left you awake,' Rast cut in, 'and went to investigate something. We were followed by a group of men, but they passed us by in the night. It seems they broke from the road a mile or so further up and continued cross-country, perhaps in an attempt to catch us – or head us off. The road loops back up ahead, but I think we are moving slower than they expected.'

'Who are they?' asked Karland, his ire forgotten in a wash of fright.

Rast shrugged heavy shoulders. 'I have no way to tell who they are, or their intentions... but I do not think they are good. Come, I need to talk to Aldwyn. Finish up with Hjarta.'

By the time Karland had finished hooking the horse into the traces, Rast had broken the news to Aldwyn, whose face was white.

'Are you sure they were looking for us?'

'They were stopping every mile or so to scout, which means they were searching for something. Given what you told me last night, I don't want to leave anything to chance. We need a new route.'

'I always intended to stop by a small tun up towards Hoeven Lake,' considered Aldwyn. 'It's through a heavy tract of forest and out of the way, but hidden. There is a turn-off near here.'

'A bit out of the way,' remarked Rast off-handedly. The old man shifted, glancing at Karland.

'I have an old friend there. Besides, we could use supplies.'

They broke camp quickly, and moved out onto the road. Rast ranged ahead on Stryke, leaving the cart to follow, returning often and suddenly. After a few miles of this, he came back and reined in alongside Aldwyn.

'This turning had best be soon,' he murmured. 'I don't like this road. I feel an ambush up ahead. If we cannot follow the track off soon, we will need to move cross country ourselves – and that means no cart. Either way stands us in good stead of being caught if we are being hunted.'

Aldwyn peered ahead. 'A mile, no more.' Rast nodded, his face blank, and moved out in front again, senses alert.

A little under three quarters of a mile later Aldwyn slowed. Rast was waiting by a tiny, partially overgrown track, all but invisible. Rarely travelled, it led – according to Aldwyn – to a secluded series of small villages and tuns surrounded by grass and farmland, connected by a larger, more frequently travelled road up ahead where traffic to and from Darost moved.

Slowly and carefully they moved off the road. Rast kept back to hide their passage. It was peaceful in the woods. The thick undergrowth and less crowded trees were unlike the clearer forest floor of the Northing Woods near The Croft. The sun had finally fought its way clear of the clouds of the morning, and the odd lance of sunlight pierced the canopy.

After a few hours of travel, they passed the fringes of the woodland onto a small strip of grass preceding a shallow valley that enclosed a small lake. Nestled within it, writhing pillars of smoke reached intermittently for the sky.

Several small farms were clustered in the sheltered vale, each a few miles apart from the next. Aldwyn moved across the grass and headed for the southern tuns, driving straight despite the vanished trail. It seemed clear that he had been here before. Karland tried to ignore his stomach and watched the farms grow slowly, the creeping cart creaking and bouncing more than usual on the rough ground.

NINE

Aldwyn pulled the cart up before the wooden gate of the smallest of the three southerly tuns. The little farmstead was homely, with a barn, several pastures, and a sprawling bungalow surrounded by a fence. It was neat and tidy, but looked well used. Cattle moved placidly in the distance, and chickens clucked and scratched in the yard around the house. It was a peaceful scene, and the first time Karland had felt more at home since leaving The Croft. Gladsmoor had been a busy town, not a welcoming community such as he was used to.

They reined in outside the gate, Rast leaning forwards to whisper in Stryke's ear. The horse flicked it irritably back into Rast's face. Rast dismounted, and hobbled Hjarta while Karland and Aldwyn climbed down. As they opened the gate, Karland saw a flicker of movement from the side of the house, but it was gone too fast to decipher. The trio moved towards the door of the low house through the gate. As they approached the front door opened.

A plain-faced but pleasant-looking man stepped out, with the solid build of a farmer who had spent his life at honest toil. His arms and shoulders and neck were heavy, as was his midsection, but he did not look fat, and he was not very old. He nodded politely to them, eyes flicking to each only long enough to take them in without offence. When he smiled, his large teeth were even and strong, and he looked suddenly less plain.

Reaching out to clasp their hands, he bade them good day. Introducing himself as Jon, he asked what he could do for them. It was clear that neighbours visited often here and that there was little trouble. Karland caught another flicker behind them at the edge of the house, and was sure that Rast's sharp eyes had seen it too.

'I am Master Varelin, a scholar,' said Aldwyn. 'Karland is my student and Master Tal'Orien travels with me. If you can spare it, mm, we can pay for a night's lodgings and some food?'

Jon shook Karland's hand, absent-mindedly squeezing it in his powerful grip.

His face quirked when he shook hands with Rast, as if his grip was harder than expected.

'Of course - if you don't mind a tight squeeze and my being out in the fields mostly,' he said. 'We get a fair few visits here, though most don't stay the night. We have a big barn, and plenty o' space for your little wain and the horses.' He ran an admiring eye over Stryke, standing still at the gate. 'He's a beauty, mister. Cremlo, is he? Biggest one I ever saw. Trained, too. You catch any of ourn standing still there with the free fields at their back!' He chuckled, and Rast smiled.

'Yes, he's trained. I should see to him myself, as he can get irritable if he doesn't know the currier.'

Jon grinned his easy grin. 'Oh, no arguments there, Master Tal'Orien. I would like to keep my fingers, if it's all the same to you.' Behind him a young woman came out, and he spoke in her ear. She smiled and moved forward to greet them.

'Welcome, travellers. My name is Talas.' Peering at her guests, it was clear the young woman's vision was not very good, but her smile was welcoming until she turned to face Aldwyn. Her smile gradually faded and she frowned.

'I know you,' she whispered, looking troubled. Light dawned in her eyes. '*Master Varelin?*' Karland shot a look at Aldwyn in surprise.

'It has been a very long time, mm, has it not, Talas?' said Aldwyn.

Jon shifted behind her, surprised. 'Talas, love, you know this gent?' he said taken aback.

'Well,' said Talas, recovering. 'Partly. I met him when I was much younger. He helped me when- when I needed looking after.' Her face was troubled, and Aldwyn smiled sadly.

'My dear Talas,' he said, 'I am sorry to suddenly appear again and shock you, mm, in such a terrible fashion. Come, I would love for you to tell me how you have fared. My, but you have grown! His smile grew happier. 'Why, look at you! Married. And with a farm, still so young, mm?'

Jon smiled, more at ease, and Talas found a little more colour and managed a smile as well. 'I am so sorry,' she said, and then her cheeks reddened further. 'I must confess I have not thought of you for some time! And now I leave you standing here on my doorstep. Please, come in. Jon, they are doubly welcome. Master Varelin came with Greck when he brought me to this farmstead.'

Greck? thought Karland, strangely affronted that these strangers knew his teacher.

Jon nodded. 'Well, guess I should thank him then,' he said. 'You never told me about him, love.'

'Later,' she said, shooting him an indecipherable glance.

'Of course, my angel,' he said, half-mockingly. She stamped her foot and pushed him, but she was smiling.

Karland was boiling with questions for Aldwyn, but he bit his tongue as Rast excused himself and went to see to the horses. Jon took them through to their kitchen where they sat; a plate was set aside for Rast, piled with cut tomatoes, thick sliced salted ham, coarse brown rustic bread, and hot farm mustard.

Aldwyn and Karland tucked in with gusto, needing no further prodding. Halfway through the meal, an older couple came in from the rear door and were introduced to them as Talas's parents, Hendal and Marta. They remembered Aldwyn, and greeted him warmly.

'Goodman Hendal,' said Aldwyn, 'I am very glad to see, ah, how well young Talas has done! Indeed. And your other young charge? I hope she is likewise doing well.'

'Oh, yes,' said Marta for her husband. 'Talas and Xhera have been dutiful daughters. We have never needed any others.' She looked at her husband fondly.

Seeing Karland's confusion, Hendal said, 'We could not have children, you see. So when word came of two men looking to foster young orphan girls, well, Marta jumped at the chance like a chicken on a worm.' She looked at him indignantly and Karland laughed at the image. Hendal chuckled.

'The farm has been in our family for some generations now, lad, so I am glad we can keep it in the family. We added Jon some time back, didn't we Jon?'

'Yes,' smiled Jon, ever placid, 'and it's very hard work, but rewarding.' He looked slyly at Talas. 'And so is the farm.'

She threw a tea towel at him. 'You!'

'Ah, mm, and how is my friend Greck? I have not heard from him for many a year,' said Aldwyn.

'Did you not know? I am hearty sorry,' Hendal said, his lined face sad. 'Greck Hordane died of fever near two years gone now.'

Aldwyn looked shocked, and the farmer shook his head. 'He had things he said were yours - mostly messages and papers and such - but he never got to telling us where you went. We kept them for you in case you ever came by.'

Aldwyn sighed sadly and nodded. Karland could see it was a blow to him. Jon hastily turned the conversation to lighter matters, speaking of the recent bad weather, their good crops, and the healthy livestock. There seemed nothing untoward here in this valley, which was refreshingly untouched by the outside world.

Hendal turned to Karland and said, 'You've not seen Xhera yet then? She's of an age with you, might be happy to have some company. She's off doing some chores. Should be back soon for lunch. That is, if she ha'nt been distracted by her books again.' He rolled his eyes.

Talas laughed. 'She was the one who told us that we had visitors, pa,' she said. 'You'll be lucky if the chickens were fed right today. She's very curious. I think she's just being shy.'

For a minute Hendal looked annoyed, and then Marta elbowed him in the ribs and his breath exploded out with a whoosh. Marta said, 'Oh, come, dear. Those chickens are fat enough to miss one feed.'

The look of mock outrage that the old man assumed dropped from his face as Rast ducked into the kitchen. Hendal looked alarmed for a second, and then grinned. 'My pardon, mister. I thought the sun went in right there when you blocked the doorway!' Karland grinned to himself, remembering his first meeting with Rast.

Rast bowed fluidly at the introductions and said, 'I greet you, Goodman, Goodwife. I am honoured by your hospitality.' Talas pointed him at the table, and he sat next to Hendal and began to eat, pausing long enough to murmur in the Goodman's ear.

Hendal laughed quietly and then called loudly.

'Xhera! Get in here, girl. I know you are out by the woodpile, listening in.' He winked at Rast. There was a pause and then a girl walked in, blushing slightly and looking annoyed. Karland stared. She was very different to the girls he had grown up with.

'How did you know I was there?' she demanded.

'I know everything that happens on this farm, girl,' he said airily. 'Get over here and greet our guests. And eat!'

The girl came over to the table, looking at the guests curiously. She had fair skin, with a faint dusting of freckles over her nose and cheeks; a few carried over to her top lip. Bright blue eyes the colour of a spring sky peered from a finely boned face, under a fringe of very dark hair which was wound up on the back of her head and secured. Her figure was on the cusp of womanhood, but she would probably never be much bigger. A small chest and toned body spoke of constant farm work, and she had a toiler's hands. She looked somewhat like a smaller version of Talas, but Talas had much lighter hair, and was not quite so fine boned; nor did she have Xhera's piercing gaze.

Karland could not look away from her, his heart beating harder in his chest. He thought she was very pretty.

'Hello,' she said seriously, eyeing them with interest. 'I am pleased to meet you.' Karland noticed that her accent was as educated as her sister's. Neither of them spoke like the farmers, and he wondered where they came from. Their names were certainly not local.

She sat and pulled over a plate of food, thanking her sister. As she ate, she felt Karland's eyes on her, and looked up directly at him. He immediately looked down, fighting to keep from blushing, suddenly unsure what to do or say in case he seemed like an idiot.

As he ate, his ears pricked up when he heard Aldwyn talking to Hendal. He was asking how things had gone with Greck after he had left, and how the last ten and more years had been. Apparently he had been some kind of distant cousin.

Rast was explaining news from other lands to Jon, who kept looking surprised and saying, 'Never did! Well, mister.' He shook his head at the tales of general unrest. 'I just don't understand why people don't just leave each other be. Get on with their lives and try not to cause a fuss. There's enough to be done without causing troubles on top!'

Catching Karland's eye as she ate, Xhera smiled at him shyly, their amusement of their older companions shared unspoken. She had, he noticed, very nice, sharp-looking teeth, which gave her an interesting smile. His heart jumped every time he saw it.

To Karland's surprise Aldwyn suggested they take several days to rest, as he had some reading to do before they reached Darost. The family refused payment for the meal, saying they had enough food to accommodate even a big man like Rast, and if he didn't like it he could sleep in the barn. Hendal clearly felt in Aldwyn's debt, and his hard farmer's voice overrode Aldwyn's feeble protests.

Excusing themselves, one by one the family left to finish farm chores, leaving Talas to tidy the kitchen and show the guests to the spare rooms. Rast moved out to help Jon and Hendal with any heavy work they might have. After being shooed out when Aldwyn was unpacking his precious books, Karland lay on his own bed in a room stacked with wicker boxes. His stomach was full of good honest food, and his thoughts were of a serious-looking dark-haired girl with light freckles.

Today, he thought, had been a good day, all in all.

CR   SO

The next morning, Aldwyn rose late. He refused to be bothered with questions and insisted on studying the messages and documents left by Greck. Karland quickly realised that he was best left alone. He spent the morning eating breakfast and investigating the farmhouse. Rast was out helping Jon and Hendal, and Marta was involved in pottering around doing the many small things a farm requires on a daily basis, and Talas was busy tidying and preparing meals. It seemed her poor eyesight made it difficult for her to work on many parts of the farm, but there was plenty she could do in the farmhouse.

Talas eventually suggested he go and find Xhera, who was feeding livestock, as she was sure she would like the company. Karland got the polite hint, realising she would prefer him out from under her feet while she worked.

He left through the kitchen door, and saw a small cluster of kittens in the longer weeds to the left, playing amongst the piles of wood and old cart wheels that were stacked there. He crouched and held his hands out, making a kissing noise, and their heads snapped round, ears twitching. Swaying on their feet, they were tiny, and regarded him solemnly. As soon as he moved closer, they staggered off quickly into the nooks nearby, vanishing. Their mother lay further back in the grass, relaxed but watching him. The cats were apparently semi-feral, and were not really interested in tolerating human company.

He shrugged, feeling foolish, and stood. Beyond the small fence encircling the house was the trail to the barn and outlying buildings. Not bothering to open the gate, he hopped over it. The sun was warm on his face.

He wanted to talk to Xhera more than anything, but was nervous and unsure what to say. Telling himself he was being foolish, he prevaricated, walking along the stone wall that held the sheep towards the barn. The day was warm, and he quickly removed his heavy woollen jerkin to wear only his light linen tunic.

At the door to the barn, he paused. It was open a crack and he peered in, his eyes unable to see far. The space was warm, noisy and full of heavy smells. The interior was very pungent, and faintly unsettling.

'Hello?' he called, moving in cautiously. His voice was answered by snorts, disparate clucks, and a deep lowing. A huge white horse's head rose over a stall front and descended to regard him, reminding him of when he had first seen Stryke.

He jumped and whirled at a tap on the shoulder to see Xhera looking at him curiously.

'Are you all right?'

Trying to cover his embarrassment, Karland stammered, 'Well, um. Haha. Erm.' He tried again. 'Ah, Talas actually asked if I could help you.'

Xhera looked at him for a second, considering, and then nodded, a small smile on her lips. 'Thank you. That would be nice. And maybe you can tell me about your journeys? While we work?' She sounded a little wistful.

'Of course, he said.

Xhera gestured to the two heavy wooden buckets she was carrying, one full of grain and the other full of something that looked like refuse. Seeing his glance, she said, 'Feed for pigs and chickens. I've done the rest already.' There was a faint hint of reproach that he had risen so late and lounged around most of the morning.

'Let me help with those,' Karland said, eager to help.

'All right,' she said gladly. 'You take the slop. I'll take the grain.' Karland lifted the bucket, nearly grunting at the uncomfortable weight. He was a little disheartened at how easily Xhera handled hers.

She led him around the barn to the sties at the rear to feed the pigs. Walking behind her, he could not help noticing her figure. She had a slender form, but it was more muscular than the girls from The Croft. Her shoulders were broader than on most girls he had seen, and her arms slender with no excess on them. She seemed to have no difficulty in picking up the heavy wooden buckets, and her hands had far more calluses than his.

She evidently took pride in her appearance. Today in the warm sun she was wearing a light calf-length tunic, and he could see quite a lot of her neck and shoulders. Despite her outdoors work she had very fair skin, and there was a faint dusting of freckles across what he could see of her shoulders. The slender neck under the loosely tied up hair fascinated him. He found himself yearning to stroke the smooth skin, and blinked.

Arriving at the hogs, which squealed in delight when they saw the buckets, Karland poured out the mess of food into the pen where directed. The pigs were large and pink with stiff light grey bristles, and they snuffled delightedly at the scraps.

'We don't allow them to forage,' she said, looking at the biggest pig fondly and scratching its back as it ate. This elicited a head jerk and deep squeals of enjoyment. 'Old Ruf here would be off like a shot, and if he didn't vanish off into the woods to be a nightmare to truffles and rabbits, he'd be in our vegetable garden ruining it.'

'Do pigs do that a lot?' said Karland, eyeing the big form.

'Swine are very smart,' said Xhera. 'These three know if the buckets are full or empty from the way they are carried. They could easily plan the invasion of our precious food garden.'

'Ah,' said Karland, hoping he sounded knowledgeable. 'Back home they have fences that have to be patrolled. Wild hogs get in all the time and eat what they like.'

She nodded, and then said, 'Will you tell me about your home?'

Karland described what it was like growing up in The Croft. To him the town and the places sounded boring, but Xhera drank it in. When he mentioned Aldwyn and his library, she became animated. Before he knew it, he found himself telling her about the bear. Xhera listened, mouth and eyes wide.

'What a horrible man! It must have been very frightening. Nothing like that ever happens around here. The most that has happened has been a few cattle vanishing. It must be amazing, travelling,' she said. 'Never knowing where you will end up, seeing different things, learning different things...'

'Haven't you ever travelled?'

'Not apart from coming here, and I don't really remember that. I was very young. I've asked and asked, but Talas has never told me anything. For years I thought Hendal and Marta were my parents. It's not something I like to talk about.' She sighed. 'But I think of it sometimes. I haven't got many people to talk to here, so I think and read a lot.'

'There must be other youths around,' said Karland.

'I have some friends, but they are only interested in cows, and chickens, and-' her cheeks reddened, '-haylofts. They don't care about learning. Most of them can't read, and none of them care about the world outside this little valley. I don't see them much anyway – all I do is work on the farm. It's so *boring*.'

Karland nodded in understanding. 'I felt the same about my father's business. He trades in cloths and fabrics, and I can't think of much more boring than cloth. At least you have different things to do here every day, feeding and things.'

Xhera shook her head morosely. 'You'd think so, but every day is the same routine.' Then her lips parting in a smile that made him weak at the knees. 'But you got out and travelled! I would love to do the same. I just... I just don't feel that this is where I should be. There must be more out there for me.'

Karland stared at her, realising that her thoughts echoed his. Xhera tentatively put a hand out and took his, and he started.

'I am glad you came, Karland. You aren't like the others. I like talking to you... I feel like you really understand what I mean. Will you help me feed the chickens? They are up near the house. And you can tell me more about Aldwyn's books.'

'Of course.' Karland managed to keep his voice steady, and was very proud.

⊰ ⊱

Over the next few days Karland and Xhera spent virtually all their time together, and it was clear that they had found a real connection between them, something he had not had since his best friend left. Karland realised that he may have found a friend as true as Seom.

Rast helped on the farm, and followed it with training every day. When Karland asked him why, Rast told him that if he did not keep his conditioning when he could, it could mean their lives. Moving large objects, running, and climbing around the barn were followed by hitting a wooden beam repeatedly. Palms, fists, forearms, elbows, feet, shins, knees, heels, even fingertips were all slammed into the wood.

Hendal shook his head in wonder. He couldn't bear to watch, he said, but in all his years he had never seen a man do such things without damage.

Rast would finish by performing a series of movements in the air like a dance. He flowed gracefully from step to step, his arms spinning and chopping deceptively fast, his legs planting solidly or sweeping up and out. It was impossible to work out what many were for. When Xhera asked in amusement why he chopped his upright arms together in front of his face, she was taken aback at his reply that it was for breaking an arm and didn't ask again.

Aldwyn looked less rested and more worried every day, avoiding questions and staying in his room. Left to his own devices, Karland grew closer to Xhera during the days at the farm, and refused to think of their rapidly approaching departure.

One evening she showed Karland her collection of texts. 'There are more books here than in the whole rest of the valley,' she told him proudly. Karland realised that Xhera had been taught equally well for her whole childhood, and she probably knew as much as he did about many subjects. He realised the trust it took to show him her collection.

The mild discomfiture did not stop him sneaking out that night with her to gaze up at the stars that glinted through wisps of cloud from the roof of the house. They pointed out the constellations they knew and discussed the stories surrounding them in whispers. The night was quiet, with only faint murmurs of sound in the distance. As they lay there staring upwards Karland was acutely aware of the slight form next to him. She shuffled over a little to share his warmth, and his heart felt like it would start shaking the roof as her hand stole out to take his.

'It's really strange. It's like I've known you years, Karland. You're so different from the boys around here. But… I have only just met you, and you will be gone again, leaving me to a life that constricts me. What will I do when you leave?'

He didn't know how to answer the thoughts and questions echoed in his own heart, and eventually turned his head to look at her. 'I feel it too. Like we will be the best of friends, I mean, meant to know each other, um. Like a sort of connection. I was trying not to think of leaving... but.' His voice grew serious, and he looked directly into her eyes.

'Xhera. Whatever happens, I will see you again. There is no way I will lose your friendship now I have met you.' He sighed at her expression. 'Do you really hate it here so much?'

'I want to see the world!' she said, fiercely. 'I am so much more than all *this*! This small valley, the people who live in a happy bubble here, never seeing the greater world around them. *Farming*. I want to learn, study, teach, not feed chickens! I wish I could visit Darost, the Library of Thingos, The Croft, meet Seom... but more than anything I want to know more about my life, find out what my sister will not tell me from when I was young.'

'Your sister?' he said. She did not reply. 'Well, anyway... I will come back. I promise.'

Before he could react she kissed his cheek and rolled away shyly to look upwards once more. 'Oh look! Behind that cloud... the Great Dragon!'

The constellation she pointed out just looked like a cluster of stars, but it swept across half the sky, majestic. They spent the next half hour so wrapped up in conversation that they jumped when the window below them thumped open and a rough voice enquired acidly if they planned on going to bed any time soon. Hearts thumping, they slid off the side of the roof and ran grinning to their beds, leaving Hendal muttering to himself.

ଔ   ຽ

The next morning, when Karland rose and went to the kitchen, everyone except Rast was gathered. Even Aldwyn was there, and Hendal looked grim. With a sinking feeling in his stomach, Karland sat down next to Xhera, who was looking pale. Hendal glanced at him.

'Last night, lad. When you were on the roof, talking. Did you hear anything strange?'

Karland was taken aback. He shook his head. 'Not really. I mean, there were faint noises, wind... maybe I heard a few animals-'

Hendal broke in. 'Far-off noises?'

Karland nodded. He looked around and asked, 'Why?'

Hendal sighed. 'Word came this morning. Two of the farms further north... something was there in the night. One family heard something but didn't go out to look, lucky for them. Found half their sheep dead. The second? Some... thing... killed stock and two hands that went out to look. Some kind of beast, mayhap, but there's never been anything dangerous in these hills.'

Karland's jaw dropped. 'Does anyone know what?'

Hendal shook his head. 'Your big friend is out looking now. By his self, though I spoke agin it. All right, everyone. The work won't do itself. We'll hear more later.'

Karland met Xhera's eyes for a minute and she nodded to the table, her face sombre, and left. He ate breakfast reflectively, and was about to go and find Xhera when Rast ducked in, still wearing his cloak. Talas sent Karland to find Hendal, who sent him to collect the rest. By the time they returned, Rast was finishing a quick meal.

His answers were short. 'I did not find it, and I do not know what it was. It was large in size, and ate meat – that is certain. The tracks were similar to a cockindrill of the southern swamps; it certainly likes water. The beast entered the lake from the south west, and it left heading east. The creature killed wantonly. One farm hand is missing entirely, the other died from blood loss, and they lost cows and sheep. That is all I know.'

The creature sounded like nothing on earth to all present. Karland couldn't think of anything large enough to kill a cow apart from bears or wolves, but Aldwyn said they were rare outside the deep Northing Woods. He fervently hoped it was long gone, but when he looked at the farmers he realised that these were people they had known. Talas and Xhera were grey, and Marta simply stared at the floor, her face drawn.

Rast suggested the farmsteads keep a closer watch from now on, and perhaps erect community encirclements. Hendal didn't look happy, but he said he would discuss it with the other farmers, and sat with his thoughts.

Into the silence, Aldwyn spoke, his face still drawn. 'I think we have stayed long enough, in any case, mm, Rast. I have found... distressing tidings in the information left for me. I needed to study it, but now more than ever we must get to Darost.'

At this, Xhera's eyes flew to Karland and she spoke quickly. 'Talas... I want to go with them to Darost.' He stared at her in shock. The room was silent for a second, filled with incredulous looks.

'Leave?' Talas gaped at her sister. Her voice rose, and Jon put a hand on her shoulder. 'With who knows what out there? Why would you want to leave? You are safe here, and have everything you need! Where did this foolishness come from?' Her blazing gaze swung to Karland, but Xhera spoke first.

'Everything I need? I don't fit in. I don't know who I am. I don't even know where I came from because you won't tell me!' Her eyes filled with angry tears. 'Karland is the only friend I have found that understands me and I'll never see him again! You never let me do anything, or leave the farm. There is more for my life and I can't find it here!'

Talas stared at her sister, her mouth open. Jon squeezed her shoulder.

'Beloved. You can't say you haven't noticed as how Xhera doesn't always fit in here. She does a grand job, but she would rather read than feed the chickens. You should know. You taught her.'

Talas shrugged his hand off, and ignored the sympathetic looks from her parents. Karland's cheeks were hot with chagrin for his friend, and he was unsure if he should say something.

'No. *No!* I'll not hear of it. You're all I have left, and you are too young to be off on your own. You are not going with them, and that is final!'

Xhera glared at her sister and then fled through the kitchen door, sobbing bitterly. Karland spent the rest of the day looking for her, but she was nowhere to be found.

TEN

The party did not set out until early in the afternoon the following day. Xhera had vanished, and Karland was annoyed and upset that their friendship had been thrust aside by her anger to the extent that she did not even bother to say goodbye. He was outright angry with Talas; he thought she had been very unfair to her sister, and did not forget she had blamed him. Xhera had not been seen since the day before, and he was keenly disappointed that she had avoided them. He searched all the places they had frequented, but her chores remained undone and she remained unseen.

He could tell that Rast was not pleased at the delay in leaving, although the big man showed no obvious signs of it. His original plan had been to leave in the morning, but despite his plans Aldwyn had slept late and then spent a long time fussing over his documents. After the old man had snapped at them for the third time, they left him alone.

At midday, Talas fed them lunch. Karland tried to be polite, as she had apologised profusely for the argument. Rast offered to help Jon affix a new wheel on his farm cart while they waited. Talas watched the pair of them rinse themselves off at the yard in cold water when she brought them out some fruit, and Karland saw her looking at Rast's upper torso in something akin to awe.

There was little trace of excess fat on him, and his massive back and arms rippled under the cold that sluiced over them, turning his many scars silver as they caught the light. Few were on his back.

She peered with undisguised delight at the magnificent form before her until an amused throat clearing from her husband turned her cheeks pink. She stammered, and he threw his head back and laughed. He himself was by no means unsightly compared to Rast, but could not match his physique. Karland thought how rare it was for a man to be so secure that he felt no jealousy, but his thoughts quickly soured again. Xhera had not appeared for lunch either.

Finally, Aldwyn seemed satisfied he had found what he was looking for, and proclaimed that they needed to leave immediately.

Their supplies were packed with Talas and Jon's blessings. Hendal and Marta gathered to see them all off, and would not hear of payment for the food. The party readied the small wagon that held Aldwyn's books, and eventually Karland could not restrain himself any more.

'Is Xhera not coming to say goodbye?' he asked, accusation in his tone. Talas looked uncomfortable. Sighing, she shook her head.

'Apparently not. I don't think she is happy with me, or anyone at the moment. I will say goodbye for you. You may meet one day again – you are always welcome back.' Karland bit his tongue as she smiled a little hopefully. 'Safe journey, Master Varelin. You are always welcome here.'

Jon stepped up as well. 'Take care, Master Tal'Orien. The roads through the woods int as safe as they were, and we're still waiting for aid from Darost.'

Rast nodded and nudged Stryke with his heels. Aldwyn flapped the reins with a gentle *thwap*. The dray trotted out of the steading gate after Rast.

In irritation Karland hunkered down next to Aldwyn. He'd thought Xhera would at least come to say goodbye, and would not readily forgive Talas the obvious hurt she had caused her sister.

They followed the south-westerly trail through the trees, keeping a steady pace. It gradually turned south, and ran to a wide road through thick trees either side. After a couple of hours of silence, Rast spoke.

'We should reach the main road which leads to Darost before dark. If our luck holds, we will have lost any-'

He broke off abruptly and motioned Aldwyn to halt. Karland shivered as Rast slid off his horse and murmured 'Stand ready,' into Stryke's ear. The war-trained stallion rolled his eyes, flicking the ear and stamping a front hoof. Rast scanned the left forest edge, and then stepped back towards Aldwyn. Moving close along the right side of the cart, he spoke in a low voice.

'We are being watched. The trail ahead is trapped with rope we might not have seen before it fouled the horses. Best we deal with this now.'

Turning his head, he called out across the cart, 'I know you are there. Come forward. We have nothing for you to take, see for yourselves.'

There was a moment of silence, and then two men slipped from the woods to stand halfway between the cart and Stryke. The horse grunted in a very unfriendly manner and showed his large teeth, and the men gave him a respectful distance. The leader was a wiry man with a nasty grin and one ear that stuck out. His smirk grew as he took in the cart.

'Well now, weary travellers. You spotted us, so you did,' he remarked casually, giving no indication of annoyance that his ambush was spoiled. His tone was careful as he attempted to gauge the party. Warily eying the cloaked bulk of Rast as he moved around the cart to place himself between them, he continued.

'There is a new tax on the road, see. A toll or levy,' and he rolled his eyes to his companion in sarcastic amusement. 'We are poor honest folk just trying to collect as is our duty, so if you would hand over the horses and your goods, we will make sure you do not regret it.'

Rast held up a hand. 'Let me stop you there,' he said. 'The third of your company in the woods-' his arm swung to point without taking his eyes from the leader '-will regret using his rather shabby bow if he tries to. We do not have much except food, and that we need. Let us pass in peace.'

His voice held a tone of calm that seemed more threatening than bluster would have been. He threw back his cloak and tilted his head back on his strong neck, piercing the leader with a discomforting gaze, and motioned Aldwyn and Karland to duck down into the cart.

The leader began to speak, and hesitated. He peered at Rast and frowned. Karland could see that he was cautious of the warrior. He shushed his companion, who was whispering to him, and motioned to him to walk around the cart to peer in. Rast shifted slightly, and the reluctant approach faltered.

'Do we look like we carry anything of value?' asked Rast. 'We came from a farm. What you see is what we own... but I assure you we intend to keep that little.' His gaze did not waver, and he uncrossed his arms. His heavy shoulders heaved under his tunic.

At the unnerving sight of his huge limbs, the leader smiled as pleasantly as possible. 'Well, now,' he said. 'Mebbe you's what we would describe as not taxable.' He flapped his hand at his companions, and the third came to the tree's edge, bow in hand. His hand flapped further until the man shouldered it. It was obvious that he was unhappy with his proximity to Rast. They all stood for a moment, staring at each other. Hunkered in the cart, Karland watched with bated breath.

'Hoge won't be liking that,' muttered the other one.

'Better that he don't like it than we get creamed,' the first snarled back in a low tone. 'I think at least one of use wulnt make it back if we attack him. You want to be that one?'

'Nah!' said the other bandit. 'Don't like the looks of this one.'

The lead bandit thumbed his protruding ear and grinned again, this time at Aldwyn and Karland. 'You may pass,' he announced grandly, gesturing.

Rast waved to Aldwyn. 'Get going, old man,' he said. 'I will stay here to make sure our nervous friend doesn't have a change of heart.'

He moved closer to the two, who shrank back, intimidated. They were clearly used to attacking folk from ambush, not confronting battle-ready giants. Karland noticed a greenish rope lying across the path as they rumbled over it, barely ten feet ahead of where they had stopped, and turned to watch as Rast got on his horse. The big man casually mounted, turning to look at the outlaws one last time before digging his heels in to catch up and get out of range of the bow.

The men made no move to attack. Even as his horse gained momentum, they were melting back into the trees. Rast set the pace and the cart rattled quickly along.

൪   �

Eventually Karland could contain himself no longer.

'Why didn't we fight them?' he burst out. 'You could have beaten them all!'

Rast glanced at him. 'With a bowman in the trees? I doubt it would have released true, but a solid hit would still kill. Besides, I do not think they were alone. I suspect that not far away is a camp full of them. Would you have liked to have fought five? Ten? Twenty? Their ambush failed. Had they judged me correctly before coming forth, they would have tried to kill me first, leaving you two defenceless. It was luck that they came from one side only, so I could use the cart as cover. Luck they came too close. Still further luck that they were easily intimidated. They like easy prey.'

'Then why didn't they shoot you when you got on your horse?' said Karland.

Rast shrugged.

'I knew they likely would not,' he said. 'It was not a great gamble. Men like these are often cowards. The fear of trying and failing can be greater than doing nothing. Nevertheless, my paramount obligation is to Aldwyn - and to you. When you have the luxury of choosing your fights, do so carefully.' He turned to Aldwyn.

'We have moved too fast for men afoot, but I am wary of another ambush up ahead. I will check. Keep to this pace and call out if you need me. I will be back soon.' He heeled Stryke and galloped up the road, vanishing quickly.

Aldwyn looked over at Karland, slumped on the seat next to him.

'Mmm, tiring, isn't it?' he said pleasantly, looking back at the road. 'All this excitement, worry… gets the heart and, hehe, glands pumping. Tires you out. I'm lucky, my boy. I'm old enough that by the time I realise I should be shocked, hmm, it's generally over.' He chuckled.

They travelled on for several minutes, hearing only the creak of the cart and the thump of the horse's hooves. Karland was about to speak again when he heard a thin high sound from the direction they had come. Something in it chilled him, and he started and looked at Aldwyn. The old man was focused on the road ahead, and had not heard.

'Aldwyn! Did you hear that?' The scholar turned to look at him.

'Hmm?'

'A sound, like a cry. There it is again!' The scholar shook his head.

'Are you sure, my boy? Perhaps the wind... I heard nothing. Mmm?'

He jumped as Karland suddenly grabbed the reins from him and reined Hjarta to a stop. Aldwyn looked about to protest in annoyance, but he obviously saw the look of intense alarm on the boy's face, which dissolved into horror.

'It's a girl!' he gasped. 'I'm sure it is. We must help her!'

Aldwyn shook his head. 'Karland, it could be anything, mmm. Why would there be a girl here, away from any settlements? It makes no sense. Highly unlikely. Come, we should follow Rast. We must reach Darost soon.'

Karland looked at him anxiously for several seconds, and then another faint scream reached him and he made his decision. He dropped from the cart and sprinted into the woods in the direction of the sounds, convinced that something terrible was happening.

'Karland!' called Aldwyn desperately behind him. '*Karland!*' And then in surprising fear: '*Rast! I need you!*'

క   ɕ

The calls faded as Karland ran, stumbling through the low brush. The canopy here was heavier than at home, so there was less underbrush under the trees. Aldwyn's old voice was not very powerful, and after several hundred feet the calls grew much fainter.

He kept barely enough sense to keep the road more or less visible. These were wild woods, like the deep Northing Woods near The Croft. He shied away from those memories and concentrated on moving. A sick feeling sat in his gut, and he hoped he was wrong.

Focused on finding the owner of the terrified cries, he stumbled onwards through the brush and trees, unconcerned with how much noise he was making. After what may have been several miles of scrambling, he fell to his knees, his heart hammering in his ears, panting. His shoulders felt like a spike had been driven through from one to the other with every breath, and his legs trembled.

As he gasped for breath, he heard a sharp sob from his right. It was faint and distant, and he gradually became aware of low laughter as well. Controlling his breathing with a heroic effort, he crept forwards, trying his hardest not to step on any twigs. A whiff of smoke reached his nose, and the light grew slightly as a clearing in the trees came into view.

The rough circle was probably one hundred feet at its widest and big enough to house the semi-permanent shelters of the eleven rough-looking men crowded to Karland's left. Among them he recognised the three ambushers from the road.

They were gathered around something on the moss, laughing. A big man was in the middle of them, crouched next to a bundle. He pulled at it and was shaken off.

Growling, he swung his arm in a slap that knocked the hunched shape sprawling. Another terrified sob tore out and Karland froze in shock, heart hammering. It *was* a girl, and he knew her.

Through the ringing in his ears he heard the crouching man speak. 'If you ain't offerin' it up, slattern, we're goin'ta take it the hard way. Everyone pays a price goin' through 'ere.' He dropped an ungentle hand on a knee.

Xhera exploded into furious thrashing, shrieking through her sobs. One foot caught the man hard on a cheekbone, and he shook his head, wiping the loose dirt from the red mark it left.

'Bitch. We done NOTHIN' yet, not like you'll be getting' now. You 'ad yer chance. Spread her out, lads. Let's see what she got for us.'

A raucous cheer erupted from the grinning men, and one knelt to pull her arms above her head as one each took a leg and pulled them uncomfortably apart. Karland could see into the circle of men with their movement, but he still could not move, frozen by what he saw. The girl's struggles were futile and she wept and pleaded, her voice ragged.

The big man, obviously the leader, casually leaned down and tore her blouse open, exposing small breasts to the cool air. The others cheered, offering lewd comments.

The big man laughed, squeezing one painfully hard, and then forcefully pulled the long skirt up, tearing the waistline. Xhera's body bucked as he exposed her most sacred parts, and a couple of whistles erupted from his men. She was barely flowering as a woman, and the thought of her tender unwilling flesh being defiled beat against the prison of Karland's immobility like a caged bird, frantic to get through.

The leader held up a finger, and then stuck it in his mouth to wet it, prompting harsh laughter. With horrible intent, he roughly probed her genitals, found the entrance to her, and rammed his finger in, twisting it hard. The men howled at the resulting gush of blood that signified her virginity as Xhera screamed mindlessly in pain and hopeless denial of her violation.

Something in the scream snapped the paralysis Karland had been locked in, and he bolted towards the outlaws. Nothing was in his mind but anger, and the reverberations of the scream.

Yelling in fury, he charged the nearest man, flailing. At his emergence the men wheeled, alarmed. The nearest, wiry and not much bigger than Karland himself, swung a fist and missed. Through sheer luck Karland's flailing fist caught him on the bridge of the nose, not breaking it but making his eyes water enough that he didn't see the next blow which caught him square in the groin as Karland barrelled into him. With a yelp, the man dropped to his knees in pain.

The next outlaw was ready and backhanded Karland so hard across the face that the boy was sent spinning head over heels sideways, blacking out for a split second. His jaw was popping as he worked it, trying to stop the world revolving. He felt sick and one eye was swelling shut already from the massive blow. He lay there unable to move, listening to the muted mix of laughter and angry shouting from the men through a surging in his ears. He managed to turn onto his stomach and raise his head, which sent darkness crowding around the edges of his vision.

A few of the bandits were looking around warily for others. Most were laughing or shouting. The leader was standing next to Xhera, roaring with laughter through his beard. The small man whom Karland had knocked over was on his feet, his face twisted with rage and pain. He started gingerly toward Karland with a knife in his fist, stepping carefully.

'Leave 'im,' shouted the leader. 'He ain't goin' nowhere. I said *leave* 'im, Jimil. Little runt'll get what's coming, but if yer kill 'im now he won't 'ave the pleasure of seeing what we do to his little friend.'

The small man stopped, a vicious look on his face. It twisted into a cruel smile.

'Stay where you are, you pifing little shit,' he snarled at Karland. 'Friend of yours? Sister? She'll love what we give her, till the end leastways. I'll go last, see, and get some practice in with the blade while I plough.' He called out to the leader.

'Hoge! Do her then, and make her sing!'

The large man with the beard chuckled and held up his finger again, still lubricated in blood. The men crowded round the writhing, sobbing form, some undoing their leggings in preparation for the fun.

Karland managed to focus on Jimil. The dirty little man was sneering at him, his eyes promising death. He turned his head to glance at the rest, and then something huge and solid whipped around his windpipe and he was dragged back out of view with a gurgle.

Karland turned his aching head in astonishment to see the small man struggling with the giant shape of Rast. Jimil's right arm shot up with the knife, trying to stab. Rast had his right arm locked around the small man's throat, his right hand clamped on his left bicep and his left hand tight to his own ear.

He responded to the attack with lightning and brutal efficiency, clamping the left hand down on Jimil's left wrist and jerking it to the side of the man's neck. The knife scored Jimil's own shoulder and dropped from nerveless fingers as the huge hand tightened to the bone's breaking point.

Rast changed his grip and squeezed powerfully. The wiry man was jerked sideways, his arteries cut off by two big forearms and his own arm so quickly that he did not even have time to call out. His face quickly went red, and then took on a blackish hue. Bulging panic glazed to incomprehension, and then nothing, one eye blood-red from ruptured capillaries.

Rast held him there until his struggles had stopped, his massive back tensed, then he let the limp form drop. The whole fight had taken less than fifteen seconds. Without a backward glance at Karland, he started towards the outlaws, who hadn't noticed the brief struggle.

A moment later Rast slid up behind the bowman from the road, whose rough laughter cut off as he gasped sagging and white-faced; Rast's powerful grip clamped down onto his shoulder, the fingers digging agonisingly deep into the muscles and pressure point below, numbing his whole arm. His bow dropped from fingers that refused to hold it.

'Let the girl go,' said Rast clearly, his tone cold and dangerous with the first anger Karland had ever heard from him, 'and I will spare you.'

His voice cut through the anticipatory cheer of the men and they quietened in surprise, turning to see who had spoken. The leader looked up from his undressing, his jaw dropping in disbelief that quickly turned to rage.

'*Kill that fucker now!*' he roared in fury, hopping with his feet entangled as some of his men likewise tried to tuck themselves away. Others ran for Rast, pulling weapons, one bandit holding Xhera dropping her arms to run for a bow.

Karland rose shakily to one knee, watching with his heart in his mouth. Rast spun the bowman by the shoulder and whipped his left arm around, elbow first.

It cracked into the man's temple, snapping his head to the side, and he went down in a heap.

Three men rushed him in the same instant. Two held knives and the other was struggling to draw a sword; one was the leader of the ambush, thumbing his protruding ear. Emboldened by numbers, he shouted in glee.

'Nice to see you agin, me de-'

Without hesitation Rast leapt at them, bearing all three to the ground. Behind him Karland saw another bowman curse and start circling, an arrow nocked but now with no clear shot.

The wiry man screamed and dropped his knife as Rast's knee smashed into his face. Another found mighty legs locked inexorably around his neck as they fell. Rast hooked his left arm under the neck of the last, using his whole body to drive his right fist downwards brutally into the man's face again and again as the second made horrible strangling noises. The man kept enough wits to try to drive his dagger into one of the legs throttling him, but the blade was turned by a leather boot. Rast responded by rolling violently to the side. There was a wet crack and the knife dropped from spasming fingers as the dead man voided himself.

One final punch to the devastated face of the last man left him bubbling through his ruined mouth, motionless. Moving incredibly quickly for his size, Rast rolled backwards onto his hands and sprang to his feet, blocking another knife with one hand and chopping his straight hand hard into the man's neck. The man dropped like a puppet with its strings cut. In the background the man with the bow called for a clear shot.

Ignoring him, two more men jumped at Rast. He started to evade, and then rocked on his feet as the wiry man who had been kneed in the face cannoned into his back and wrapped his arms around his neck, yelling in hatred.

One of the men in front lunged for Rast's solar plexus with his hunting knife. Rast swayed to avoid it, the knife lightly scoring his tunic. The other man, big and solid with sunken knuckles, swung a heavy blow at his face. Rast twisted and ducked, and the blow cracked into the already damaged face of the man on his back, who screamed.

Karland watched in fright, trying to get up on legs that would not obey him. He still felt very sick, but watched in awe. He had never seen such power and speed before. As quick in reflex as any of the legendary barbarians, Rast's balance was superb as he avoided the simultaneous blows.

Face calm, blood running down his neck from his passenger, Rast turned his chin into the crook of the elbow choking him. He wrenched the arm off him with an explosive surge of his arms and broke it sharply over his shoulder. This movement became a fast throw, wheeling the shrieking man over in an arc to hammer into the attacker to the right, who was lunging again with his knife.

The swung man cried out in agony as the knife lodged in his body, and they both fell, leaving Rast facing the big fighter. The brawler swung his arms up to guard, obviously trained in fist fighting, then jumped as an arrow streaked past, nearly hitting him. He roared in anger at his companion, his eyes not leaving Rast, but was still unprepared for the heavy stomp to the outside of his left knee which snapped the joint inwards. As he fell Rast delivered a powerful uppercut to his head, cutting off his grunt of pain sharply.

Two men who had not been fully dressed arrived, one holding a short sword, with a third close behind. Rast stepped smoothly away from the heap of men, one of whom was cursing and trying to climb out from under his dying comrade.

Wary, they spread out around him to take him all at once, but were unprepared for his speed as he closed with them, keeping them between him and the circling archer. The nearest barely had time to gasp before rigid fingers smashed into his throat. His trachea gave with a crack, and he dropped to the ground, choking horribly. The sword swung for Rast, who whirled under it and extended a leg, taking the man's feet out. The man fell, gashing his own leg badly with his sword blade. Rast came back up with his hands ready as the other man ran in with a cestus and launched his weighted hand at Rast's face.

Rast's hands were a blur as he blocked and diverted the punches. It was obvious his opponent knew how to use the weapon well. Barely a second later the other knifeman arrived, having fought free of the dying man who had landed on him. The huge man's arms moved so fast Karland couldn't see them, and then stopped abruptly.

Somehow the knife was sticking out of the cestus wielder's chest with the outlaw looking at it in surprise, still holding the hilt. White faced and gasping, a faint whistling accompanying it, the man with the cestus sank down clutching at the dagger as a front kick from Rast slammed into the other man's sternum, cracking the ribs and driving him backwards like a child.

Breathing deeply, but not heavily, Rast stepped over the intervening forms to stand in front of Hoge and his last outlaw. Finally with a clear shot, the man holding the bow released, his aim true. Rast kept his gaze on the man and moved as soon as the arrow left the string. With almost contemptuous ease he angled sinuously out of the path of the arrow, which would have hit him in the shoulder, and then moved towards him implacably.

The bowman stared in shock at the advancing giant. He took one more look at the broken men that had been so quickly dispatched, and abruptly ran, throwing his bow to the side.

Hoge, his clothes once more intact, roared in fury at the coward. He turned back, putting a heavy boot on the moaning girl's neck as she tried to crawl away. He stared at Rast in hate. Disbelief and rage at the decimation of his men warred on his face.

'Let her go,' said Rast softly.

'One more step, laddio, and she's dead,' hissed Hoge.

'It's me you want. Let her go. You don't need the girl, not now.' Rast held his hands out. 'Don't you want revenge? To put your knife in me, look into my eyes when I die? I have no weapon.'

Hoge bared his teeth.

'I can kill yer', he snarled. 'These pissants are nothing. You've had training, but I was a Walker. You ain't so special.'

'Then let us see how good the Walkers are,' said Rast.

Hoge growled and cruelly ground Xhera's face into the mossy dirt as he stepped towards Rast. He held his knife in an underhand grip along his forearm and crouched low, studying his opponent, his other arm extended in front of him. Rast stood ready, balanced, eyes on Hoge's face.

With no warning Hoge attacked, sweeping the knife in a slicing arc. It somehow flipped over in his hand as he abruptly swum his arm through at a different angle and lunged straight ahead. Rast's arms jerked up in front of him, and they collided hard. Even as Karland gasped, Hoge threw his head back as if to shout in triumph over Rast's shoulder.

He remained there staring for a few frozen seconds, mouth closed, neither he nor Rast moving. The anger had drained from his face, leaving it blank. A bright rivulet of blood flowed from his left nostril.

Rast moved, breaking the tableau, and the bearded man fell sideways like a tree, oddly rigid. His own knife was lodged vertically under his jaw, piercing his brain.

⌒ ∞

Silence descended on the clearing, broken only by the moans of the maimed and dying and the occasional sob from Xhera, who was curled up and shaking, making no attempt to cover herself. Rast stepped forward and took off his cloak, using it to cover her. Xhera didn't move from her foetal curl as Rast picked her up with exceptional gentleness. He turned his head to look at Karland.

'Are you able to follow me?'

Karland nodded carefully, his head feeling like it would fall off.

'Come, then.' He moved off into the trees at a different point to where they had both come from, leaving the clearing littered with dead and unconscious bodies. Karland walked carefully after him, the sickness slowly subsiding.

He couldn't see out of his left eye, and a splitting headache throbbed solidly with each step. It seemed a long time before they were at the road. They moved out near the point of the first ambush and found Aldwyn's cart and Rast's horse pulled up under the trees, the old man peering around nervously. His gaze fixed on Karland and worry vied with anger in his expression. As he opened his mouth, he saw Xhera in Rast's arms and gasped in dismay, all chastisement forgotten.

'Gather blankets, Karland,' said Rast quietly. Karland moved to the back of the cart, his thoughts wooden. Aldwyn hastened to help, but was brought up short as Xhera began to cry out, kicking. Rast placed her in the cart hurriedly and backed away from her as she shrank away from him. Her face was streaked and dirty, twisted in fear, and she huddled in her torn clothes. 'Karland – see if you can help her. I think she needs to be kept distant from grown men for now.' He moved quickly away towards his horse, his face grim.

Karland carefully approached the cart. Xhera's eyes darted to him, and she opened her mouth.

'It's all right, Xhera,' he said thickly, his swollen face making it hard to speak. 'We will take you home. Rast dealt with those men.' Her shivering lessened as he continued to speak gently, his voice full of the friendship they had begun. Her eyes seemed to clear, and she blinked. A wracking sob escaped her.

'Oh, Karland!' she said, and then she lost control. The sobs that came now were not of fear, but of release, and he moved to her, climbing into the cart and holding her hand awkwardly. She gripped so hard the blood left his fingers, and then with a wail she threw her arms around him and clung tightly. He felt tears prick his eyes as he hugged her back.

'You are safe now,' he whispered into her ear. 'I promise I'll look after you.' He hardly felt the cart begin to move as Aldwyn began heading back for the farm, his eyes clouded with sadness behind his glasses.

Ș ș

Ventran felt buoyed up by bloodlust. He had hardly stopped travelling in the last few months, but he felt innervated, powerful. Every one of the wandering scholars he tracked down and killed was like another brutal orgasm, each one different. Some he simply killed without questioning, allowing his bestial side to take over. Many of the farther victims he had dispatched mercenaries to kill, but they had proved unreliable.

One name stood out in particular; it was as if the old man was prescient. Either by luck or skill, he had evaded everyone.

Aldwyn Varelin, he said to himself. *Where do you hide?*

A thousand miles and more away, Ventran would send word to his contacts in Eordeland to watch for him. The planning of years was coming into play now, and soon the Darostim even in the heart of The Sanctum would know the wrath of Terome. The church had grown much in the last hundred years, from a gentle unfocused religion to a militant and feared organisation. He didn't care about the god at the heart of it, but it allowed him freedom to do as he wished.

The source Meyar had placed within Darost would soon be ready to act, and the allies they sought would carve their way through the realms in blood and war when the time was right. Eordeland would fall, and the most powerful of Meyar's opponents would be lost to chaos.

ELEVEN

I t was full evening before the cart arrived back at the tun. As they pulled up, Jon came out, his honest face set in a worried frown, and hurried down the path to the gate. Throwing it open, he saw Xhera in the back of the cart with Karland's arm around her, sitting in silence and staring. As he started forward in alarm, Rast intercepted him and motioned for him to be calm. Jon nodded.

'Xhera,' he called. 'We have been so worried! Come up, all of you. Master Tal'Orien, can I ask you to stable the horses? I don't want to get bit or kicked.'

'Of course,' said Rast. 'I will join you shortly. Be easy with her, Goodman. She has had a rough day.' Sliding off Stryke, he helped Aldwyn down and then climbed onto the cart, calling a sharp command to Stryke to follow. At his name the stallion's ears pricked. Jon went to help Xhera down and looked dismayed when she shrank from him.

'I'll help her, Goodman,' said Karland. Jon glanced at him and then narrowed his eyes as he took in Karland's swollen face. He now couldn't see out of one eye, which was dark and puffy, and he still didn't feel steady.

As soon as they were off the cart, Rast set off for the barn, his large destrier following obediently. As they neared the house Hendal stepped out and called gruffly. Jon motioned him back. As they entered, he looked at his daughter with concern, seeing the change in her.

Karland led Xhera to the kitchen where Talas and Marta sat. He could see that Tala's eyes were red from weeping. As soon as Xhera came in, she shrieked, '*Xhera!*' and leapt out of her chair.

Running over, she threw her arms around her sister, and as if pressure was suddenly released Xhera began to cry – not the hysterical weeping of before, but a cathartic vent of her emotions. For a few minutes Talas held her, and Karland retreated to a chair where he sat wearily.

Finally she pulled back, her frown deepening, and spoke more sharply. 'What in the *hells* do you think you were do-'

'*Talas.*'

Jon's strong voice cut her off, his tone sounding odd compared to his usual soft speech. She blinked in surprise. Before she could argue, he spoke again.

'Sit down, and leave Xhera alone. She needs your comfort, not your anger.' Looking closely at her sister, she swallowed her next words with some effort and sat.

'I thought I had lost you,' she said. 'The horrible stories of some beast killing people, and then you were gone... none of the other farms had seen you, and I just thought-' she broke off, and hugged her sister tightly.

No one spoke for a moment, and then Marta said, 'Well. It's well that she is back. I'll make tisane for all. I didn't expect to see you again so soon, Master Varelin.'

'Mmm,' said Aldwyn. 'I, ah, confess, I hadn't expected it either. Both our youngsters have a story to tell... and Xhera's will be the harder.'

'But tell it she should,' said Rast's voice from the doorway. He moved into the room. 'This wound runs deep, Xhera. Do not let it fester inside you.'

Xhera nodded weakly after a moment. 'You may be right. I feel better now I am home.'

Marta flapped her hands. 'Everyone: *sit*. I will get tisane. Karland, what happened to your face?' Talas gasped as she noticed his injuries, and Aldwyn moved towards him.

'I will tend to him, mm, while we talk.'

Marta nodded. She bustled around the kitchen, and everyone sat in silence, waiting. Xhera's eyes returned several times to Karland's face, her expression mortified. He returned her look and smiled slightly, painful though it was. A few minutes later, they had hot tea, and Xhera sat with her hands around her mug, staring at nothing.

She was still very pretty, even bruised and dirty. The memory of her body was imprinted in his mind; not in the manner he had wished, but as a horrible violation. She looked much younger now than she had yesterday.

Xhera took a deep breath.

'Well... I was so upset, I went to read my books... but they didn't help like they usually do. I just wanted to get away – to be free. I feel so trapped. More than ever, I need to... I don't know. Be someone.' She pointed to Karland. '*He* understands. When I met Karland I realised that my friends here are not really friends, not like he is. I couldn't bear meeting someone who finally understood me to lose them again just like that.' At this Karland felt a sharp pang; any warmth at her admission was buried in guilt that he had caused this. He listened lifelessly.

'I had thought, well. If I left and travelled towards Darost, I could get there, or maybe find them on the way-' her voice rose to a squeak of anguish and she closed her eyes, tears brimming again. 'So then they would have to take me. So, I, I, didn't really think, I just took some food and walked into the woods. It was lovely and peaceful. And I got less angry, and even missed the farm a bit, but I knew I was doing the right thing.'

'And you didn't think about us, what we would think?' demanded her sister. Jon put a soothing hand on her arm. Xhera bit her lip.

'You were so unfair. You wouldn't even listen to me! I would have come back, I swear. I didn't consider you might think me dead. I forgot about those attacks until I was a long way into the forest. I was close to the road though, and the woods don't have many big animals here. You said so yourself many times.'

Talas opened her mouth again, and Aldwyn caught her eye and shook his head. She closed it, and Xhera carried on.

'I walked for hours and hours, got a little bit lost once. Sometimes I walked on the road and sometimes I was in the trees. I tried to keep an ear out for Master Varelin's cart, but I was worried it would be one of you to take me back. Better if – if it had.' Karland closed his eyes, his guilt intensifying, then forced them open again.

'I was thinking of Darost and the libraries there, and the next thing I knew a dirty hand was over my mouth. I tried to bite, and all I saw was an ugly man leering at me. He dragged me to some others and they laughed, and said I would have to pay a toll. I told them I didn't have anything but food and they had better let me go or a patrol would have words with them. They laughed more.' Her eyes filled with tears. 'Then the first one slapped me hard. I couldn't think, and then their hands were on me. I didn't know what to do, and I just st-st-started screaming. I couldn't stop.' Her shoulders shook, and she carried on through her tears.

'They grabbed at me a bit, and then one said something about sharing the wealth or someone called Oje or something would be having words. They dragged me a long way, poking at me and saying the most horrible things.

'We came to a big clearing full of men, I don't know how many. I was pushed out in front of this big bearded man, who said I had to pay them all the toll, and then I could leave. I started saying again I had nothing and he grabbed my hair and laughed at me. I was terrified. He forced me down and said I gave it up freely or they would take it, and the taking would b-b-be worse.'

She shut her eyes tightly for a second. Karland didn't think he could bear any more. His eyes were pricking and all he could think was *it's your fault, it's your fault.* If not for him Xhera would never have left the farm. He tore his eyes away and looked at the others. Talas's face was drained of colour, and Jon's was filled with surprising fury. Hendal and Marta both had faces lined with sorrow. He shook his head and tried to calm himself.

Xhera swallowed thickly and carried on.

'I kept screaming and struggling, and after he demanded a few times he said they were *all* going to take payment. I knew what he meant.' She gulped a few times and visibly braced herself. 'So he threw me down and two men held me, and he p-p-p-ulled up my sk-k-k-irts and-' she shook her head, not wanting to look at anyone. She coughed for a few moments, half sobbed, and continued.

'He did something with his finger that hurt, really hurt. I started to panic so much I didn't know what was going on. I remember them all laughing... and then I saw Karland.' All eyes swivelled to look at him, although he hardly noticed in his misery for his friend and his guilt.

'I was all alone, and then he was there. He was so brave! He ran right in and knocked one man over, but the next knocked him flying.'

Karland bowed his head. 'I'm so sorry,' he said. 'I was useless.' He felt like crying. 'It was my fault you followed me.'

Xhera smiled through her tears at her friend. 'It wasn't your fault, Karland. I chose to follow you. You never hesitated, just ran in - like my protector,' she said, hiccoughing with a little laugh.

Rast spoke up. 'It was bravely done, Karland. I might have arrived too late otherwise.'

Her smile faded. 'And he was struck down. I thought we were both dead. And then the big man over me looked up and started to shout and swear. It was all so confusing. I heard yelling and fighting, and when I looked up, none of them were standing. None! But I remember nothing else – save Karland.' She took a deep breath, closed her eyes, and then opened them again. 'Your voice brought me back when I felt lost inside.' She lapsed into silence.

Hendal was the first to speak. 'That could have been much worse, child. I han't heard of highwaymen here, especially this close to Darost. That's bad. Praise the Gods you are safe.'

'I'm going to take Xhera to wash and bed,' said Talas, with a look that brooked no argument on her drawn face. 'We can talk more tomorrow.'

Marta nodded. 'I will come too, dear,' she said to Xhera, who sniffed and nodded. 'You have had a day I wouldn't have wished on anyone. Come.' The girls rose and followed her, hand in hand. Xhera looked back at Karland once as she left.

Hendal pondered for a moment in silence.

'Last time I went that road, it was harvest,' he said. 'Been more'n half a year now. Was a safe road, once. I best tell people it's not any more.' He sighed heavily.

'Wise,' said Rast. 'Any produce carting or travel should be done in groups. Armed. Travel is more dangerous recently, even here. But I do not think you need fear that particular group again.'

'No need to fear?' asked Jon. 'How many were there? How did you get the children away? Do you think they will reband? I mean, are we in danger here?'

Rast shook his head. 'There were eleven of them. Their leader was a very dangerous man, a Plains Walker out of Novin. They are highly trained – elite mercenaries. I do not know what one was doing here. Most of the rest were common outlaws, I think. But no, they will not reband.'

Hendal snorted. 'How can you be sure, Master Tal'Orien?'

'Six are dead and four are likely crippled; they may not survive without healing. Only one escaped clean, but the Walker is dead. Believe me, Goodman. They are no longer a threat. Still, it would be wise to raise a group of armed hands and clear any survivors out of there.'

The men stared at Rast.

'Wait, Master Tal'Orien. I feel I missed summin' there,' said Jon. 'Xhera spoke true? You fought them all on your own... without hurt?' His tone was incredulous.

Rast shrugged. 'I took them unawares. The Walker was very well trained, but he was complacent. The rest were common thugs, although a couple had weapons training. Only two had bows, and had little opportunity to use them.'

Karland knew how they felt. He wasn't sure he believed it, and he had watched the whole fight. Aldwyn was the only one to show no surprise, intoning words quietly and applying strange smelling tinctures. Karland's face tingled, feeling better already.

Rast returned the farmers' looks with a slight smile. 'I am trained to fight, and I have been tutored my whole life in battle. It is what I know best. Most of the time they were more danger to each other than me, although-' he fingered his rent tunic consideringly, '-one or two knew their work well enough. I would not normally choose those odds, but I had no real choice. It was a calculated risk. I could not leave Karland and Xhera in their hands.'

Hendal's rough voice was thick. 'Well, then, I bless and thank you, Master Tal'Orien. Thank you, for saving my daughter... and her innocence.'

Rast shook his head. 'You have no need to thank me, my friend. I did what needed doing.'

Hendal exhaled heavily. After a moment, he said, 'Rape is not something that is known around here. We've had, what, Jon – three fist-fights in the last two years? None of them sober. We are simple folk, and understand hardship, but we have not dealt with this before. I thank the Gods she was not badly abused.'

Karland spoke up tiredly.

'But she *was* abused, Goodman. It was horrible. I am glad Rast killed the man who did it.' He didn't add the shame in his heart, that he hadn't been able to prevent it.

Hendal accepted Karland's words with a nod. 'A spiritual violation, if not a fully physical one.'

Rast shook his head, eyes hard. 'Rape is rape. You violate someone against their will, however you do it.'

After a pause, Jon spoke.

'Come, law-father. It's done, and ended better than it could have. I think with a little time, Xhera will recover.' Turning to Rast, he said, 'We can never repay you, sir. But know you're welcome at my stead forever.'

Hendal nodded, and added, 'Anything we can give you to help you back on your way, Master Tal'Orien. Anything we have.'

'I think it's high time you called me Rast,' said the big man. 'And our thanks. I do have one request – should anyone ask after us, anyone at all, I'd appreciate it if you have never heard of us. Aldwyn is required in Darost, and we have been followed for part of our journey by men I suspect mean us no good will.'

'Never heard of who?' said Hendal, straight-faced.

Karland started nodding, staring at the floor, and then looked up as a big hand fell on his shoulder. He shrank back a little. It was the same hand that had brutally destroyed men, broken bones, and ended lives not a few hours back.

If Rast noticed, he gave no sign. 'Come, lad. We forget you have had a rough day too. You need to sleep. We leave in the morning.'

꙰   ꙩ

Early the next morning, in the pale light of dawn, they readied to set out again. Aldwyn was busy repacking his books as Rast readied Stryke. Karland sat apart on a low stone wall. His face was less swollen but still sore, and he was miserable, the grey misty morning suiting his mood perfectly. He heard a light step, and felt a comforting slim hand rest on his shoulder.

'What's wrong?' asked Xhera.

He didn't answer for a long minute, and then looked up at her. 'I failed you. You shouldn't have thanked me. I was useless.'

Xhera slid her arm around him and sat next to him.

'Don't be an idiot,' she said softly. 'You were so brave! You and Rast are my saviours both, but *you* were the brave one. You tried even knowing you could not win.'

He looked at her serious little face, then shook his head in denial. 'But-'

'Stop it!' she said, slapping his shoulder in frustration. 'There were eleven of them! By all rights all three of us should have been killed.'

He was quiet for a few minutes, thinking about what she had said, and felt new determination. He could not make up for failing to protect her, but he grimly resolved that he would never fail her again. It was a mystery how they had grown so close so quickly. The connection he felt was deep, but concealed within it there was a hint of yearning to be perhaps more. Karland managed to smile at her.

'Are you all right?'

Her face twitched but she smiled weakly. 'I will be, I think. I need some time.'

'Still want to see the outside world?'

'Yes! But... not now. I need to talk to Talas about things. She told me last night she has thought of sending me to Darost many times, as I would be better there studying, but she has always been afraid of losing her only sister. I think she needs me as much as I needed her. I guess I am all she has from when we were young.' She shrugged. 'She also said she was sorry.'

They sat quietly for a little while, holding hands. Then Xhera leaned over, turned his head, and kissed him gently on the lips.

At his astonished look, she said, 'That is for fighting to protect me. And for being my friend.' She looked shy. 'You're the first boy I ever kissed like that, so I hope that means something.'

Karland smiled at her. It gladdened him, made his heart sing, and simultaneously confused him a hundred times as much as before. He summed it up.

'Um.'

She looked amused, and he cleared his throat and tried again.

'Just try not to be in danger any more, because I will always try to save you.'

'I haven't forgotten your promise, you know,' she said after a moment. 'You will come back to see me? And take me away with you?'

'I swear it, with everything I have,' promised Karland.

Xhera threw her arms round him. 'Thank you,' she whispered. 'I will count the days until you return.'

A call reached them. Jon was waving, and the dim bulk of Rast loomed behind him, holding Stryke by the reins. They slipped off the stone wall Karland had been sitting on, and walked over reluctantly. The farmers clasped hands with Karland, and waved to Aldwyn, who was already mounted, peering myopically through his spectacles.

Rast grasped hands with the farmers and bowed to the women. Xhera showed no reluctance in Rast's presence now, Karland saw. He wondered if that would be the case if she had seen what he had. Uneasily he regarded the big man, then mounted next to Aldwyn. He turned to look at his friend.

As the cart left, Xhera called out, 'Don't forget me!'

'Never, I promise!' he called back. He watched her until they vanished behind them, and then settled into his seat, his thoughts on a dark haired girl with serious eyes.

They passed back down the road and out of the sleepy little valley. The sky grew lighter, and the mist began to wisp away. It promised to be a beautiful day, and travelling down the road in the woods was much more pleasant this time, with the strong morning sun lighting the trees to either side. Rast kept a wary eye out, often riding ahead as usual. By mid-morning they had reached the spot where Karland had run off into the woods. There was no sign of any of the outlaws.

During one of the forays by Rast, Aldwyn turned to Karland.

'What's, mm, wrong with you, Karland? You've hardly spoken to us since we left.'

Karland shrugged. 'I feel bad about Xhera, trapped there. And, you know. What happened.'

'Ah,' said Aldwyn. He shifted uncomfortably on the wooden seat. 'Well, mm. Not your fault. You were very brave. And you may well see her again. Try and see the positive side.'

They rode on for a short while, and then Karland spoke hesitantly.

'There's something else,' he confessed. 'Rast.'

Aldwyn's eyebrows rose in surprise, but he said nothing. Karland tried to find words to explain.

'I never saw anything like it, Aldwyn. It was like... like a puzzle, and he fitted himself into it. Wherever he was, their weapons weren't. I didn't know a man could be so, well. Agile. But at the same time, he was so brutal.' He remembered the blank look on Hoge's face, dead before he even knew it, and shivered.

'I was frightened when I met him, and I thought that was how he avoided fights. Then in Fordun's Run, I saw him defeat three men. It was amazing. But what I saw yesterday was so different... he was utterly merciless. He killed, crippled, and did it as if he didn't care. I don't know what to think of it all. I liked him, but now I am-' he let the last out in a rush, '-frightened of him.'

Aldwyn looked at him sternly for a long minute.

'My boy, you listen to me. Life is not always easy, or safe. Rast protected you with his life. Even the best warrior can be killed by chance, and that fight jeopardised everything we are trying to achieve.' Aldwyn was actually frowning at Karland. Puzzled, he opened his mouth but Aldwyn overrode him.

'Rast is an honourable man and will give his life for us if he must. I have read many of the old texts of ancient warriors, legends in their time, and Rast naturally embodies the same principles. No truer and stronger ally could we wish on our journey. But you must learn that when there is no alternative you must cut, commit, drive with every fibre to complete the task, because there is no room for doubt when you have no choice left. I believe you quickly learn to either act, or die. Rast is alive precisely because he understands these things. He is a supremely skilled fighter; in all my years I have never seen his equal.

'So realise this, lad. He prefers not to kill. However right they were, *your* actions forced him to do so. So, mm, be a little less judgemental, if you please.'

Karland felt his cheeks redden with shame. He hadn't considered that his deed had forced Rast into the fight. He bit his lip to stop the words that wanted to be shouted childishly back at his mentor to evade the blame; words that – even a week ago – he would have voiced. He forced himself to face the fact that he had been unfair to his friend, and nodded reluctantly.

Aldwyn watched his reaction and smiled, his face crinkling.

'You're a good lad, Karland, and you are growing up,' he said fondly. 'Rather than hate what Rast did, why not learn how to protect yourself so next time it may not be necessary, hmm?'

Karland swallowed this bitter pill and decided that it was a good idea. He remembered his promise that he would protect Xhera, and excitement began to stir. If he could do what Rast could do, he would be able to keep her safe.

Another mile saw them joining the main road to Darost. Rast waited for them to the side. He said, 'I think the fact we are days behind our previous travel should mean we have lost any pursuers, but care is needed. Darost is still more than a day hence.'

They proceeded carefully, but met no one. That night they camped back from the road again. Rast said they were not far from the crossing over the river Run, and if they pushed ahead they might reach Darost not long after noon. The night was uneventful apart from Aldwyn's snorting, which woke Karland twice. Each time, Rast was watching.

When, thought Karland sleepily, *does the man ever rest?*

He woke again the next morning to find he had somehow managed to roll twigs into his hair and blanket during the night. His face was still bruised but only a little sore now, and he enjoyed his light breakfast.

They travelled and camped uneventfully for a few more days before

Rast hurried them now; noon was a busy time at the gates of Darost, and the greater the crowds going in and out, the greater the chance they could get into the city without being detected. He did not consider their pursuers would have given up, saying they were likely waiting ahead in Darost.

The woods were thinning as they came to the bridge over the Run. The sun shone steadily through them, and the morning was rife with a multitude of birdsong. Spring was here, and the birds knew it.

Where the Run Wash reached Darost, it fed into the Eaofer, which little resembled the river crossed at Fordun's Run. The bridge was an arched stone affair with detailed architecture and a high arch, very unlike the functional bridges Karland was used to and more than wide enough for the little cart. They rattled over its apex and he looked down to see the sun sparkle in the waters. Looking up and following the river east he caught his first glimpse of the fabled city, according to Aldwyn one of the oldest in Anaria. It gleamed stony beige in the distance, peaks and towers visible, and seemed to stretch out leagues to either side.

A few miles further on the road joined the Greatway, the main route into Darost. Running west it split, going up toward Meyar and down toward Novin and the plains. East from Darost, it curled down around the Léohtsholt and south to Valesruin and the borders of the Banistari Empire. The road was filled with traders and travellers, and they blended with them, feeling secure anonymity for the first time in many days.

Gardens, fields, and small houses dotted the land south of the wide road. To the north, huts with small boats pulled up to the shore were clumped along the river almost as far as the bridge they had crossed. It was very picturesque in the sunshine. For many centuries this land had been at peace, and the people had prospered.

The throng moved inexorably towards the city. To the left of the gate the wall ran towards the river, curving around out of sight, and to the right the wall stretched out onto a grassy plain that surrounded the city. A quarter of a mile immediately surrounding the walls and gate was packed earth from countless travellers and campers, with a small settlement permanently outside the gates themselves.

Rast had suggested that Aldwyn remove his spectacles and allow Karland to drive in the hopes that any searching eyes would only be looking for an old scholar alone. Karland inexpertly took the reins and directed Hjarta towards the great gate in the walls, which loomed over them. Solid stone, they were fifty feet high and fifteen feet thick.

The gates themselves were a good thirty feet high, fifteen wide, and made from cross-bound ironwood, nearly as hard as the stone around them. They stood open to allow passage in and out of the city. Karland couldn't see how they could be shut; they looked far too heavy to move. To either side of the gate, massive square gatehouses reared up.

The cart passed through under the disinterested eyes of city guards in green tabards with a white twelve-pointed star on the chest. They moved up the main thoroughfare towards the spires in the centre of the city. A low sprawling dome was visible between the buildings. Karland drank it all in; the city looked as if it went on forever.

They were in Darost, the heart of learning in Anaria.

TWELVE

K arland could see Aldwyn come alive as they moved into the city. He looked around, his usual vague manner becoming more authoritative and a smile on his face. He didn't stop talking, explaining significant structures and areas as they passed them to Karland.

He crowed with delight at the Tower of Jehennah looming in the midday sun to their right, high above the city. As the road weaved towards the river, he pointed at a stately river barge, ornate and flat bottomed, ferrying a hundred people to the smaller northern portion of the city on the opposite bank, where the legal and financial institutions built their many-columned houses of money.

Karland listened to the stream of information, bemused. He was dumbfounded by the sheer scale of the city. Reading about it had not prepared him for this, the bustle of the biggest city on the northern continent.

Aldwyn didn't notice his charge's wide-eyed stare as he relived his memories. Karland only turned to look at him when he ceased talking. The old man had seen the low dome of the Sanctum, surrounded by its spires, and stared with a deep longing in his face, a quiet joy, as if he had come home. Karland felt his heart go out to his friend.

Aldwyn did not take long to find his voice again, telling Karland that the sprawling building was actually a collection of buildings built from a honey-coloured stone found downriver, and occupied nearly a sixth of the ground space on the south bank of the city. It was surrounded by a green ring of parkland, and the low dome was actually twelve segments, connected by walkways and doors up to the sixth story. On the sides facing each other, the outer dome's curve and the inner segment ends, balconies opened out. Each segment had its corresponding tower, every one uniformly two hundred feet high, rising straight from the rear where the dome met the outer grounds and topped by a different architectural spire. The tallest by far was in the centre, a twelve-sided tower with each side meeting a segment at its point. Under these were arches, leaving a wide walking space in a small ring around the tower, and between each corner well-tended gardens flourished. The tower rose from a thick stem to a narrow rounded top, faintly domed around a high copper-sheathed spike, with broad windows spaced evenly around it, one to a side. Its windows were nearly three hundred and seventy feet above the ground.

Only the square Tower of Jehennah and the two cathedral spires – of Delmatra, God of Erudition and the main god of Eordeland, and Isha, child Goddess of Life – topped it. It gave unparalleled views of the city, and the plains and forests beyond. The entire campus held accommodation and learning for twenty thousand - twelve thousand scholars alone, not counting administrative and household staff - and was far bigger than The Croft. Karland had never even dreamed something like this might exist.

'It's amazing!' he said in awe.

Rast shrugged, inscrutable as ever. 'It's a big building. Prettier than most.' Karland felt a little offended that his companion was not impressed. The dark green flag of Eordeland snapped from the towers, an open book with twelve pages that reared into stylised flames around the same star the guards wore emblazoned on it in white.

'That symbolises the flame of knowledge, mm. Eordeland's role for more than a thousand years, my boy,' said Aldwyn, following his gaze.

They followed the main road through the city to the square before the Sanctum. The wide gates had a constant stream of people going in and out. Guards in different livery to the ones at the city entrance stopped everyone entering, some briefly and others for detailed explanations. They watched a grey-templed man with a hawk face sweep through without looking at anyone. The guards ignored him and his entourage.

'Mm,' said Aldwyn. 'The Sanctum is not just for scholars, lad. It is where the Council of Twelve hold sway over this land. Petitioners, businessmen, ambassadors, scholars, scientists, practitioners, guildsmen. All pass, ah, within. It is where we too are headed.'

Karland had assumed that they would be staying in another inn, but it was obvious Aldwyn expected to stay in the vast structure before him. They approached the gates and joined a long line of people waiting. Karland found it extremely annoying that self-important looking people seemed to ignore the queue and walk past to push in further up, or argue their way through. After half an hour they reached the busy-looking official, who glanced at them briefly.

'State your business, please,' he said brusquely. Aldwyn fiddled with his glasses and put them back on his nose.

'Ah, I am a registered Scholar of the Sanctum. I am here to discuss urgent matters with the Council of Twelve,' he said.

The official's mouth quirked.

'You and everyone else, friend. It's a two-day wait currently. There has been a crisis involving Meyar, from what I understand. You say you're Papered?' He sounded disbelieving.

'Yes. And it is precisely that crisis which I wish to discuss, young man,' said Aldwyn severely. He twiddled his fingers. With a start Karland realised he was wearing the ridiculously large flat engraved ring he usually kept around his neck. The official frowned at him and shrugged dismissively.

'Well, there's little accommodation free. Perhaps you should book in now and come back in two days. There are some nice inns along the waterfront. You might be seen if you are lucky.' His tone was faintly condescending, and Aldwyn's face flushed.

'Perhaps, hmm, *perhaps,* you should ask the Welcomer Captain why a scholastic member isn't recognised or, mm, welcomed. Welcomer *Sergeant.* We will wait.' He glared at the man, who was staring at him suspiciously. He waved over a guard and whispered in his ear, and the guard moved off at a brisk pace.

'If you will just wait to the side there please, sir,' said the Welcomer Sergeant. He promptly ignored them and carried on with the flow of people as soon as the cart had moved to the side, watched closely by the attentive squads that lurked to either side of the gate.

'Bloody paper pushers,' muttered Aldwyn. Karland laughed in surprise. Aldwyn rarely swore about anything.

Rast grinned at Karland. 'I think he has annoyed our esteemed companion.'

'You could be right,' agreed Karland.

'*Well,* really,' snapped Aldwyn. 'It seems courtesy is lacking nowadays!'

Twenty minutes later the guard returned with a decorated official. The man was tall, broad shouldered, and blond, approaching his thirties, with blue eyes and a clean-shaven face. He looked at Aldwyn closely for a minute, and then at his ring.

'Councillor Varelin?' he ventured uncertainly. Karland turned to stare at his teacher. *Councillor?*

Aldwyn smiled. 'Captain Robertus, I believe. I am glad to see you again! Mmm, I trust you are well. It has been quite some time. Would you be so kind as to explain to the Sergeant here that I am, in fact, a Papered Scholar of the Sanctum?'

'Of course, sir,' said the captain, saluting. Turning, he barked in a far more clipped tone, 'Jonus! Get over here!'

'Sir!' saluted the official, waving a guard over to take his place. He trotted over, looking slightly nervous. Robertus glared at him.

'Can you please explain, Jonus, why you chose to ignore this man's ring? It seems plain enough to me.'

The Sergeant swallowed at the acidic tone, and said, 'Well. Sir. There has been a recent spate of fakes on the black market, and I didn't recognise him-'

'This here, *Sergeant,* is *Councillor* Aldwyn Varelin.' Aldwyn made quieting motions, which were ignored.

The man stared at Aldwyn, stammered, and settled for, 'Ah.'

'Yeeeeees,' continued the Captain. He caught Karland's eye and winked. 'Should have checked, my son. Should have noted the *finer* details here. You've been briefed on the bogus rings.'

Aldwyn waved the ringed hand hurriedly. 'It's all right, Captain, really. Just as long as it's, aha, cleared up. Can we just get inside?'

'Sir.' The Captain turned back to his wilting subordinate. 'Jonus, what should be the correct procedure in this instance?'

The Sergeant rolled his eyes upward. He knew what was coming and was obviously hoping to get through it as lightly as possible.

'Sir! In moments of doubt such as this, sir, I closely examine and cross-check the ring with another official! I also ask visitors to state name and rank if no paperwork is presented! In extreme doubt I escalate to a designated official such as yourself! Sir!'

'And did you do all of this?' persisted Robertus. Jonus closed his eyes.

'No sir! I found myself busy and suggested the gentleman go away, sir! I did however escalate, sir!'

The Captain grunted. 'Not very clearly, Sergeant. The message I received was... ambiguous. However, we will consider this matter closed if the Councillor wishes it. Please ensure he is recognised – along with companions – forthwith. I don't want to hear of deviance from procedure again. Am I clear, Jonus?'

'Yes sir!'

'Carry on.' He turned back to the three before him, carefully waiting until Jonus had walked away and his back was to the gate before smiling. 'Good lad there. Bit too serious, too liable to get flustered. That should buck him up a bit. There's been a spate of forgeries recently, and the thieves' guild is causing all kinds of havoc with them. May I ask why you waited in line?'

'I was trying to keep my presence, mm, low profile for the moment. Sadly, I fear that is undone. Besides, we are all here to see someone,' said Aldwyn equably.

'I despise busybodies who push through with no good reason.'

'Sorry, sir,' said Captain Robertus. 'I apologise for the misunderstanding.' He waved them after him and set off towards the Sanctum stables on the right.

'You are also, of course, aware that I am not a Councillor in actuality,' said Aldwyn. Robertus shrugged as he gestured over stable hands.

'You hold the same rank, sir. The fact you don't sit in the Bulb-' he indicated the twelve-sided chamber high above them on the central spire, '-makes no difference to me.'

'You're a *Councillor?*' asked Karland finally, unable to hold his peace. 'As in, one the people in charge of *Eordeland?*'

Aldwyn scowled at him over his spectacles. 'No!' He squinted at Karland's dubious face and snapped, 'Oh for the love of the gods! I'm just a scholar.'

'Mind this horse,' said Rast to the stable hand. 'He's war trained. Don't touch him – just feed. And don't make threatening movements.' He pointed. 'Stryke! *Hastus verin.*'

The horse looked at him flatly, and then moved forward into an empty stall and turned. The stable hand looked surprised, then nodded and carefully shut the gate. Rast collected Aldwyn's valuable books without comment when the old man looked a little wild at the suggestion a porter take them and carefully hoisted the sealed box to his broad shoulder.

They left Hjarta with his eyes closed in enjoyment, unhitched and being rubbed down, and walked with Robertus toward the Sanctum. The wide path was clear of stones, and the grass was capped by heavy, tall hedges which shut off the grounds from casual visitors. Guards stood every fifty feet and saluted the Captain as he passed. He returned them absent-mindedly.

'So… you are in charge of the guards?' ventured Karland. Robertus smiled.

'The Welcomer Guards, yes,' he said. 'We are not city guards, who defend Eordeland from military attack; we are trained in different ways, and protect the council and scholars here in The Sanctum. Above all we must keep the knowledge of Eordeland safe; so where the city guards would have normal ranks, we also have Ministrators to aid the council, Council Guardians, and many others. We are expected to be as able to understand a scroll or political nuance as swing a sword.'

'It sounds hard work,' said Karland dubiously. 'So you knew Aldwyn before, then?'

The captain smiled.

'Councillor Varelin is a notorious name here, lad,' he said to Karland. 'He famously disagreed with the Council in a closed meeting. No one is sure what it was about, even now. That was years ago.' He eyed Aldwyn, who was muttering to himself, and leaned down to whisper.

'Rumour has it that he was even asked to lead the Council of Twelve and he told them to stuff their request where the light of the sun never reaches. He left to work as one of the University's travelling scholars instead. Caused a right uproar.' Rast's mouth quirked, his sharp hearing picking up the conversation.

'Wow,' whispered Karland back. 'They must have really annoyed him-'

'What are you whispering about?' demanded Aldwyn suspiciously. Captain Robertus snapped upright.

'Nothing, sir!'

'Hmm,' grunted Aldwyn. Karland grinned at the man and received another quick wink in reply.

೦೩   ೪೦

They walked through the high arch between the nearest sections of the Sanctum. Each passage was known as a Port, for no obvious reason, and the main one lay to their left. The Captain called over a household official and muttered to him. The man ran off, and the Captain beckoned them after him. Aldwyn moved forward to question Robertus about the changes in the city, and Karland took the opportunity to talk to Rast.

'Did you know? About Aldwyn, I mean.'

Rast looked down and shook his head.

'I knew there was more to him than met the eye, but I had never guessed his status. Strange that he refused the leadership. He has always told me what he would do for learning if he had the chance.'

'I don't really know him at all,' Karland said mournfully. He felt a little lost finding that his old friend was someone else. Rast smiled and shook his head.

'Don't be foolish. He is still, *ah*, Aldwyn. I am sure he has his reasons. He may even tell you what they were. Don't rely on everything scuttlebutt-' he nodded to Robertus '-tells you.'

'Why do you call him scuttlebutt? That sounds fairly rude,' said Karland.

Rast laughed quietly. 'It means 'rumour'.'

'Oh,' said Karland, feeling foolish.

They walked for nearly ten minutes, taking in the sights around them. Rast had been to Darost many times, he said in his usual equitable manner, but this was his first inside the Sanctum. Karland had never seen architecture like this; it didn't seem possible that human beings could build such an edifice.

They had walked along many corridors, climbed several sets of stairs, and walked across a walkway to the next segment by the time their guide slowed and turned to them.

'It is too late to see the Council now. Unless it's an emergency, they need to finish today's backlog of meets,' said Robertus. 'They break for lunch in an hour, and then resume an hour after that-' he ignored the disbelieving snort from Aldwyn, '-and then they finish around four of the clock. I can't see you having any problems seeing them tomorrow morning, but I'd advise starting early so that nothing is too likely to interrupt.' He grinned. 'The self-important rarely roll out of bed before ten of the clock, and then they have to break their fast and journey here.'

'Thank you Captain - for all you have done. You needn't have accompanied us all this way,' said Rast.

'On the contrary,' smiled Robertus, 'a Councillor warrants a ranked guide. These rooms are in one of the Pinnacles facing the tower, as merited by visitors of import. The tops of all twelve arches have a narrow walkway from Pinnacle to tower doors which lead up to the Dodecagon. They can only be accessed from a stairway in each Pinnacle which leads to Council chambers like this. Thus, it will not be such a chore to see them tomorrow.'

They arrived at a set of ornate doors, where they were met by a gaunt man in fine clothes flanked by chambermaids and a porter. He nodded impassively at the Captain. Robertus introduced him as Castellan James, and, saluting, left them in his capable hands.

'If the Lords will come this way,' the acerbic-looking man said softly. He clicked his fingers and the porter opened the door quickly. Preceded by the chamber maids, he entered the room, and stood deferentially to the side, looking around sharply to ensure all was in order as they disappeared through the bedroom doors one by one. Rast carefully deposited Aldwyn's box on the floor inside the door as Karland looked around.

The room was marble-floored and square. Opposite the entrance glass paned doors led to a wide private balcony. In one corner a spiral staircase climbed to the high ceiling, ending in a door. On the far right eight white steps led down into a depression in the floor with a fireplace set into the wall, a low fire already lit.

The rest of the room was sparsely furnished. On the left wall, a series of high-backed chairs sat facing the wall with desks in front of them holding rolled scrolls of varying types, an inkpot and quill, and red sealing wax.

'Sirs,' said Castellan James, 'Here you will find rest and refreshment. I will have the maids bring up fruit for you. If you require luncheon we can serve it here.' He indicated the dining table.

'There are three rooms in this Council Suite. The largest is to your left, and the others are either side of the fireplace. Tomorrow-' he indicated the spiral stairs '-you may utilise the direct route to the Dodecagon. I will prepare breakfast and wake you at seven of the morning clock precisely.' No one doubted him. 'If you require anything further, please do not hesitate to contact the staff.' He indicated a purple rope pull to the right of the door, hanging from the ceiling, as the maids returned.

Aldwyn smiled. 'You have outdone yourself, Castellan,' he said. 'Thank you, mm, for your care. It is good to be back in the Sanctum. May I ask... were you the Reeve before?'

The man's lips twitched slightly. Karland thought that was the closest he ever likely came to a full smile. 'I was indeed, Councillor Varelin, for many years. I still am, in point of fact. I found neither job was being done efficiently enough when I took on the role from Castellan Marston, so I oversee both. Efficiency is up fifteen percent in household duties now.'

Rast nodded gravely, and Aldwyn looked startled.

'Oh, ah. Um, good. Well done. Well, thank you for your care, Castellan. We shall see you tomorrow.'

The Castellan bowed and left, taking the maids with him. Rast closed the door and turned, his face solemn.

'Fifteen percent. That *is* impressive.'

Karland started laughing, and Aldwyn scowled momentarily before bursting into a cackle. 'He always did take his role seriously. Still, hehe, I bet he does a good job. This place seems more organised than when I left. James came from the Mathematica Academia, I believe. Very orderly lot, mostly.'

Karland remembered something. 'Robertus called this the University. What did he mean? I thought this was called the Sanctum.'

'The Sanctum is the collective term for all areas within these grounds. The grounds themselves, the Academia and their towers, the Dodecagon-'

'The what?' interrupted Karland.

'The Council Tower, boy, named for its sides,' snapped Aldwyn. 'Where was I? Oh, Sanctum. So: and the Librarium, which lies under our feet, and so forth. But this is a place of learning, and contains as close as we can come to the sum of all our knowledge. Thus we name it the University, a little arrogantly if you ask me; as if any one place could house all information everywhere! We've barely begun, and it's been here almost two thousand years. Repaired a lot, too. Seems very pretty at first glance, but if you look hard enough you can see the cracks.'

'I think this place is amazing,' protested Karland.

Aldwyn laughed. 'Oh, it is, Karland. Few rate this much – I think our good Captain decided to upgrade us in importance. I'm not going to object. These lodgings are usually only for visiting dignitaries and *actual* Councillors. Whatever he told you, hehe, I am not one.'

'So, what is the tale there, old friend?' asked Rast. 'I confess I had no idea you were so exalted.'

'I'm not! I'm not,' said Aldwyn, and sighed. 'Ah, mm. Look, I'll explain something about the Sanctum, and perhaps, mm, you will understand... and I think it is time for other truths as well.'

He moved to sit in front of the low fire. The others followed him, Rast swiftly crossing to each bedroom and the balcony to ensure they were alone. Light streamed in through the closed windows as Aldwyn began.

'The City, the Sanctum, Eordeland itself is headed by the Council of Twelve. They are the ultimate heads of the twelve houses of Academia here in the Sanctum, which in turn have their own sub-academia. They accept responsibility for governing the Sanctum and this entire nation.

'They head an overseeing body known as the Universalia Communia, which oversees the twelve houses. To even join, you must prove yourself over many years before the rest may elect you, whereupon you must pass four core examinations and eight electives, showing demonstrable prowess in every major Academia. These are the most learned people in the lands; to be a member is to be part of the elite. The Council of Twelve is elected from here. They are supposed to impartially champion Eordeland and the learning of knowledge.'

He sighed heavily for a long moment. 'This is all common knowledge here, more or less, but what I now tell you must never be repeated.' He waited for their nods, and leaned forward to speak softly. 'A few of the Universalia Communia are also *Darostim*.'

'Darostim?' Rast's breath whistled between his teeth. 'I thought them a legend.'

'I'm hardly legendary,' was Aldwyn's wry response.

Rast, for the first time in Karland's memory of him, looked truly surprised. 'You are among the Darostim?'

Karland looked between his friends, bursting with questions, and Aldwyn glanced at him solemnly. 'Yes. But the questions will have to wait, mm. The maids will return soon and this is for your ears alone.

'I have been a member of the Darostim for nearly forty years. Not all of us are

Universalia Communia by any means, but we are all dedicated to preserving the knowledge of this world and keeping the greater balance. This University holds great knowledge, and this is what the Sanctum protects. It is the shining hope of the world should darkness ever fall. The information here goes back millennia, and the most precious is hidden in the Combic Libraries under the Librarium.

'A decade ago, some of us realised that unrest has been building across Anaria for decades, centuries. It was predicted in some frighteningly accurate writings, and they hold true. This is no brief darkness, Rast. We slide down a slope undercut by chaos, and there may be no recovery. The more alarming say that it could be the end of all things.'

'Apocalypse?' suggested Rast.

Aldwyn's face was haggard. 'Perhaps. Certainly of all the nations, through war or disaster. But there are hints that it might go beyond petty wars and nations. It may mean the whole world; all worlds, perhaps. The unravelling of existence. I have been desperately searching for answers, but I find only portents and meaningless riddles. This is what the Darostim arose for. We pick our unseen path through the swirls of chaos for fear we will all be lost, as if nothing had never existed.'

They sat in silence, listening to the faint hubbub of noon filtering through the glass. The sunshine seemed so cheerful that it was impossible to believe what had just been said.

'Do we have no chance?' Karland finally said, and shivered.

Aldwyn shrugged. 'It seems there have been many chances that have gone unfulfilled for various reasons. Chaos grows strong. Evil deeds grow, and the world shifts. Dark things stir, nightmares are made flesh. Nature warps, and the very planet shudders in its journey. It was this I brought before the council nearly ten years ago, thinking their request I be Arbitrator would make them listen. Instead, I was laughed at. We argued, and they called my theories rubbish from old books. They! The leaders of a nation of scholars that collect those books! I declined to formally take my place, mmm. Every four years one of the Twelve is voted by the others to be the Arbitrator, the first among equals. It is the highest honour. I told them to choose another.

'Two of the Twelve were Darostim. They believed me. But the rest – ha! Too, mm, comfortable to want change. Too scornful of non-scientific sources – and even science they dismissed. Too reliant on only what their own eyes and, mm, dubiously rooted logic tells them. Not all mysteries are myth! I told them they were fools and left to seek what could be done to avert this rising catastrophe. One particularly obscure text I referenced, the Book of Sarthos, hinted that something integral to this last chance would appear one day. I gleaned a date, finally; a date and a chance, a hint. I needed more.

'I found much in the ruined Library of Thingos, thought lost for years. So I settled near to you, Karland, and continued my studies. Imagine my surprise when you, mm, dropped into my lap. Ahaha.' His eyes crinkled with a smile for the first time since he had begun.

Karland's mind was swimming from this information. Aldwyn looked deadly serious, and after that strange beast had visited them he was less likely to dismiss stories. Another voice broke into his thoughts.

'Some of this I knew,' mused Rast, 'from what you told me before. Prophecies and whispers are not something I trust, but you have shown me too much to be easily dismissed. And now I find you are Darostim! How well you hid that, old friend.'

He cocked his head and held up a hand. At a knock on the door, Rast rose and opened it to find maids bobbing with trays of fruit, water and wine in decanters, and cotton napkins. They placed them on the dining table and asked if the guests would like luncheon.

'Aldwyn?' called Rast. 'Shall we eat?'

'Yes – we can finish our little chat, hehe, over food, and then I think we should take advantage of free time to explore the Sanctum. It has been many years, and I would like to see how much has changed.' He looked at Karland, who was nearly hopping. 'And the young man appears, ahaha, to have contracted ants in his undergarments,' he added.

One of the maids swallowed a laugh, and the other grinned. The one smiling was attractive and not that much older than him, and Karland scowled at being taunted in front of women – women, he noticed, that seemed to be well endowed in the hip and chest departments. There was a noticeable swishing as they moved.

One maid rattled off a list of foods, which were airily chosen by Aldwyn. Karland eyed the prettier one sideways, and saw her covertly eyeing Rast's oak-like frame. Swallowing a pang of annoyance, he sat at the table without waiting for the others and started on the fruit. He was starving.

છ   જ

A fine meal was freshly prepared by one of the many Sanctum kitchens, and Aldwyn resumed his tale as they ate, peering over his spectacles at his friends.

'For almost two thousand years the Darostim have guarded knowledge and truth, using their knowledge to bring balance where needed. We know that Order and Chaos are the two sides of a coin often confused with Good and Evil. Sometimes they are the same, but sometimes they are on unexpected faces. There are members from every nation, every class. But the Darostim have their heart *here,* in Darost.' He slapped his knife down flat on the table, producing a ringing crack.

'We must persuade the Council that balance is tipping, and that times grow bleak. That, I fear, will be the hard part. With so much responsibility and focus comes much-narrowed vision. At the same time we must seek aid from my fellow Darostim. There are other forces at work we do not understand, and I tell you both what I have told no one else because I trust you as I trust few others.'

He speared a thin slice of sun-dried ham and a few roundsprouts on his two-tined fork, and ate them slowly.

'I think it is a blessing in disguise, our being here too late for the Council today,' said Rast. 'We can explore this afternoon, gauge how things lie in the city. I will move about the grounds, see if I can pick up any trace of our pursuers... perhaps talk to the guards.'

Aldwyn nodded. 'Yes. Let us finish, hmm, this lovely repast, hehe, and venture out into the sunshine, no?' He smiled at Karland, who nodded. The prospect of exploring this vast place banished all questions from his mind. So eager was he to explore that he barely heard Aldwyn's call to remember the floor and Academy number, and he didn't wait for Rast.

രു   ഇ

Karland crossed several balconies, pausing to stare around him at the architecture. The ceilings were high and soaring, and the materials were like their room – expensive sandstone and marble, yet clean and simple in design.

In some ways, the Sanctum made him feel that it was like a temple of some kind. It was solidly built, yet it seemed to be remarkably light and airy – probably something to do with the amount of arches and windows built into each wall. It held the same reverent hush in many areas of people concentrating carefully on things of great importance. In contrast other areas were as noisy as a town market, with the masses of people bickering and moving to and from the Council chambers, or on the way to one of the communal food halls. Welcomer Guards were surprisingly unobtrusive, sticking mainly to the more populated areas, and were unfailingly polite and helpful.

After some time wandering, Karland found himself on the ground floor at the edge of a garden. An arch rose several stories to each side, and in front of him, springing from the shrubbery, was one of the twelve corners of the great central spire. He looked up, blinking. It seemed to reach for the clouds. The sun turned the garden into a lovely place, with soft green grass and people lounging or standing talking softly, or moving along the perimeter. Birds sang, and butterflies flitted from flower to flower.

Entranced by the sudden beauty amidst the hard stone, he moved out onto an empty patch of grass and sat, the sun warm on his side and face. He breathed a deep sigh, knowing that summer was on its way. For the first time since he had left his home, he felt fully relaxed. Even the farm hadn't been so peaceful. His belly was full of very good food, and he had a few hours to himself. What more could a fourteen year old boy ask for? He felt his eyes drifting shut.

'I wish more people were so at peace with nature.'

His eyes snapped open, and he looked around. The nearest people were a group of younger scholars having an enervated discussion about something. It certainly wasn't them; they appeared to be arguing theories of mental manipulation of the ether-flux, whatever that meant.

The voice spoke again, softly, 'Although I would hardly class this as true nature.'

He looked over to his right and saw a shape standing at the edge of the bushes. It had been easy to miss; the robe it wore was light, but of a green-brown hue that fitted well with the colours of the bush behind it. Beneath the robe a filmy white garment hung, cut off high at forearms and knees so that there was less chance of it becoming dirty. Both layers clung to a form that was slightly hourglass shaped, but tall and slender. At the same time there was an impression of capability, maturity, wisdom, although she barely looked past twenty.

The woman smiled at him. Golden hair framed the face, glowing in the sunlight, casting a slight shadow on her features from which two startlingly green eyes with a gold sheen glowed. The face itself was handsome, strongly boned but with a hint of delicacy about it. Her teeth were sharp and even between full lips, and she had a light cudgel at her waist, the wood lovingly polished by the wear of her hands.

'What do you mean? Why wouldn't I like this garden? It's peaceful,' he said.

She shook her head. 'No. I mean you appreciate this better than many others. You are feeling the place, moving with it, being a part. Those-' her eyes flicked to the discussion, '-are arguing about silly matters, matters of the mind, hypothetical, not real. *This* is real.' She said it with quiet satisfaction in her voice.

Karland looked at her, struck by how unblemished her features were. She was standing peacefully but with poise in the garden, and he realised she was barefoot and flexing her toes in the grass. Rather than enjoying it, she seemed to be *experiencing* the garden moment to moment, fitting here in some indefinable way.

'I was born in a village,' he confessed, her eyes boring into him, feeling like he should justify himself in some way. 'But I have always felt at home outside. It's peaceful, sometimes exciting. I like trees, I like animals-' he tried not to think of bears '-and I love thunderstorms. I don't like deep woods though.' He shivered at old memories.

'A pity,' she remarked in her soft voice. 'They are very peaceful. Patient and deep. I like to run in them, to feel the slow heartbeat of the forest.'

Karland thought that an odd remark. Now he came to think about it the woman looked a little wild. He wondered where she was from, but before he could ask she cocked her head in a peculiar manner at a call from the far arch.

'I would like to talk more some time, young one. Perhaps we will meet again here. But for now, I bid you farewell.' The intense light green eyes with that strange sheen to them looked down at him, and then they were gone as she moved gracefully away.

Karland spent the rest of the afternoon lying on the grass, watching people pass and relaxing in the warm sun. He considered the strange woman and decided that he would like to talk to her again. Perhaps she would understand if he told her the story of his experience with the woods; she seemed to know them well.

As dusk fell he wandered back to the room. It took him nearly an hour to find it, and by then he was hungry and thirsty. He finally remembered that the Academia were split into numbered segments, and the floors were likewise listed, and ended up outside their suite on four-three.

Aldwyn looked up from near the fire in surprise as he burst in. Karland waved, shut the door and fell on the fruit and water on the table. Rast moved in from the balcony, and Karland found himself telling them about the woman and the garden.

'Ah yes,' said Aldwyn. 'The Gardens are lovely. Little slices of heaven, each different. They are frightfully expensive to maintain, but the sub-college of Botany seem to enjoy it. I am unsure about the woman though. Could be from a strange sect, mm, perhaps.'

'She sounds like a nature priest to me,' said Rast.

Aldwyn nodded thoughtfully. 'You could be right. Ah well. I think we should probably retire for the evening. We have to be ready for the Council.' He picked up a strip of leather and placed it in his book. 'Let us go to our rooms, heh.' He yawned. 'Been a busy day.'

They bade goodnight to each other, Rast moving back out onto the balcony. Karland opened his door and was stunned by the size of the room. Two large cabinets and a dresser lined the walls, and the floor was a layer of rich golden wood, polished until it glowed. It was bigger than his family's dining room by far, and had a huge bed in it that could have fitted four people. The pillows were plumped to an unlikely degree, and after undressing and laying on them, he stacked three to stop his head sinking down through their vast softness.

Images flew through his mind from the day alongside darker, half-forgotten images from the deep woods. He dozed uneasily, walking them again, but this time he calmed as he dreamed of the tall woman walking with him in the darkest places.

Somehow it made him feel better.

THIRTEEN

Karland woke the next morning and stretched luxuriously. The room around him was well lit with the light of dawn. From his bed, he could see the top of the balcony running along outside the window. His brain slyly informed him that he could steal another twenty minutes of sleep at least. He knew he should get up, but somehow just didn't care enough, so he lay there dozing.

He sat up abruptly at a hammering at his door.

'Karland! For goodness's sake, boy, wake up!' Aldwyn's voice sounded peeved, and Karland realised he must have dropped back off. Wiping sleep from his eyes, he rose and fumbled for his clothes.

Dressing slowly, he yawned, thankful for the rich wood covering the floor. Marble would have been cold. His dreams from last night were muddled, and he wondered if that was why he was so tired. Shuffling from the room, he found Castellan James standing attentively next to the main doors, hands clasped in front of his waist. Rast was talking to him in low tones, and Aldwyn was moving around the table to sit and eat. The old man waved Karland over. A large bowl in the middle held a hot pile of egg, and each plate held a slice of smoked and salted streamrunner and grilled tomatoes.

Karland woke up a little at the sight, his stomach rumbling. A metal pot had steam rising from a funnel, and each place held an ornate fine china cup and saucer, luxuries virtually unheard of when mugs were standard fare for tea throughout Eordeland. The cups were thin enough for some light to filter through them, and decorated in blue on white patterns.

'Mm, from the Banistari Empire,' Aldwyn informed him. 'Much of their culture is uncouth, and away from the cities the desert people can be quite savage… but they have many surprises to them like these. Very profound and artistic people.'

'May I provide anything else, sirs?' enquired Castellan James politely.

'Do you have Kaf, Castellan?' asked Rast.

James looked puzzled. 'Kaf?'

'Dark, bitter-'

The Castellan's face lit up. 'Ah! *Kohfee*. Yes, we do. We have a mountain roast imported from Banistari. It is renowned for its vigour. Some of our scholars find it helps them to... stay alert.' The thin lips twitched in that near smile again. 'Or to become alert. I will order some up. If you need anything else please use the pull cord.' He bowed slightly and left the room.

Rast looked satisfied. 'Fresh Kaf! A rare treat. It is very expensive outside Banistari.'

Aldwyn swallowed his tea. 'Too, mm, bitter for me, Rast. It also has, ah, profound effects on blood pressure and metabolism in high quantities. Maybe your trained body can take that, but my old bones might have a bit of a shock.'

The Kaf arrived ten minutes later, a curiously designed pot pouring out a dark, rich smelling liquid. Rast sipped it with evident enjoyment. Karland emptied his tea quickly and cocked the cup at Rast.

'Can I try some?'

'Only a little,' warned Rast. 'You might not enjoy it. It is a very intense aroma and taste.'

Karland shrugged, confident the drink would be fine. The first sip didn't taste quite how it smelled and he screwed his face up at the strong bitter taste, smacking his lips desperately. Aldwyn nearly choked on his eggs laughing as Karland tried to pretend he was enjoying it, but in the end he gave up ruefully and pushed the cup away.

'It's an acquired taste,' said Rast, sipping again. 'It will wake you up, if nothing else.'

'Let us make ready,' said Aldwyn. 'It is nearly eight of the clock. I want to catch the Council as early as possible. Unless they have had their *kohfee* as well-' he cast a wicked glance at Rast '-we may catch them somewhat, heh, torpid this morning. And we have important matters to discuss. You too, Karland.'

Karland nodded in surprise. He had assumed that he would be left to his own devices.

They finished their food and rose to prepare. Karland tidied himself up as best he could, and sat in the fireplace recess on the thick cushions to wait. Rast joined him, wearing a dark tunic with long sleeves and loose leggings. More than twenty minutes later, Aldwyn stepped from his room.

He wore a light cream-coloured toga picta, bordered in a vivid dark blue with interlocking squares along the hem embroidered in gold, and his feet were in lambskin slippers. Karland, accustomed to seeing his friend in varying states of dishevelment, could not believe how suddenly stately Aldwyn looked. For the first time, he understood how he might have been a representative for the council of a nation.

Noticing their looks, he shrugged ruefully and adjusted his spectacles. 'Well, if I want them to take me seriously, I should climb the whole elephant, so to speak,' he said defensively. 'I may not officially be a Councillor any more, but as far as I am aware, the status was never, ah, officially revoked.' He blinked at them, and then slung a long white wool top cloak around his shoulders.

'Shall we?' He lifted a pouch full of scrolls and books to his shoulder and led them up to the bolted door. He opened it and stepped out onto a larger staircase, which led up past several other doors to a larger portal. They emerged into the cool morning air, the heat of the sun through the clouds not having removed the moisture from the night yet. The day was warm and grey, with the sun a milky yellow orb through the clouds, diffusing the light and heat. If it rained later, it would be muggy.

The exit was at the foot of a two-man wide curving slope with high walls dropping to chest height. It led off across the span of an arch to the tower beyond. To the left and right, other arches with similar walkways likewise led from communal doors to the tower, hidden from view from the ground by their walls. The tower loomed over them in the crisp morning air, shadowing one of the arches. As they walked across the span, Karland felt solemn. He knew that today would be a day of important decisions.

The arch was very solid, and on one of the other arches he could faintly see other figures moving towards the tower. Most were empty. The small party reached the other end and found a door with a round handle in the middle, which Rast reached out and turned.

It turned smoothly and opened into a small chamber where a Welcomer Guard stood in front of another door, locked with a strange three-cogged tumbler with symbols on it. He was next to a chair and table where it was obvious he could relax in between visits, and wore the bars of a lieutenant.

The Guard stood to attention and saluted. 'Good morning, Councillor Varelin,' he said respectfully. 'Please give me a moment.' He turned to the tumbler, hiding it slightly with his body. Karland watched, interested.

'If you wouldn't mind stepping back a touch, young sir,' the guard said politely. He waited until he was certain Karland was not able to see what he was doing. A few clicks later he snapped the tumbler to the side and opened the door.

'Sorry,' mumbled Karland as they filed through. The guard smiled.

'Everyone is curious, young sir.'

They emerged onto a wide balcony that ran around the tower almost entirely, dropping near the middle to a seating area perhaps ten feet below the rest of the balcony with a low railing so spectators could look out. Nearly opposite where the balcony began was a wide staircase exit that descended six storeys to the ground floor, guarded both top and bottom. Suppliants had to walk around the perimeter of the tower to ascend the next staircase which rose another dizzying two hundred and forty feet, narrowing as it went. In the centre of the tower was the longest and most ornate chandelier that Karland had ever imagined.

Waiting for them was Captain Robertus. Rast nodded and clasped his hand, and the younger man saluted Aldwyn and grinned at Karland. He gestured them towards the high staircase rising to their left.

'Councillor Aldwyn. It has been decreed that this morning you be met in the Council Chambers themselves, rather than in the Tower Hall below. I have been asked to guide you.'

Aldwyn looked surprised. 'Not the Hall?'

'No, sir. I believe they felt you accorded some honour, and it is far less public. I impressed upon them your desire for secrecy, and the request you asked me to convey last night must have intrigued them.'

They followed him to the staircase. An Eordelander wearing ornate uniform similar to Robertus but more functional was coming down the steps, a Captain's Seal on his shoulder. He was brown-haired and lean, with dark eyes and a square jaw.

'Captain Robertus,' nodded the City Guard Captain.

Robertus grinned. 'Captain Dorn.' He turned to the others. 'Captain Dorn is the commander of the militia city-wide and the Council Champion-at-Arms – a largely honorary title. He is the one you must speak with regarding anything outside the Sanctum. My authority is only absolute within it.' His face held a wry smile that Dorn returned. It was obvious to Karland that the two professional soldiers got on well. Dorn saluted them all in greeting.

'Are we still on for *Vingitunis* tomorrow night?' Robertus asked.

Dorn nodded. 'Indeed, Captain. I will enjoy our rematch.'

'I look forward to it.' Robertus saluted, smiling briefly, and Dorn returned it casually, continuing along the balcony.

Robertus watched him go. 'That is a good man,' he said. 'I would have him at my side over any one squad in the city.'

'His skill with blades is renowned,' remarked Rast.

Robertus nodded. 'It is well-deserved. Come, we should continue.'

Karland asked, '*Vingitunis?*'

Captain Robertus shrugged. 'A card game that requires little thought and much luck. Good to pass the time.'

'Oh.' He looked around. 'May I look over the balcony? What is below? The Tower Hall?'

'If you are quick, lad. The Council is not to be kept waiting, but I can understand your curiosity. It is quite impressive. Go on.'

'Don't worry,' called Aldwyn as Karland ran off the go down the steps into the seating area. 'My old knees won't enjoy these stairs anyway.' He tailed off into mumbling. Robertus leaned down to him to enquire something, gesturing towards a curious flat platform with small chairs on it against the wall on the stairs. He received a flapping hand in response.

Karland reached the edge and looked out over the balcony. The sight was breathtaking. Spiralled by the descending staircase, which ended up wide on the floor seventy feet below him, the Tower Hall held a crescent table with high backed chairs, almost thrones, but padded with red leather and all equal in stature and spacing. Inside this was another, lower set of chairs, luxurious but plain. The table was a dark and solid wood, and looked old. There were a few cleaners at work, preparing the gigantic room for the day; a little to the right he could see the tall double doors to the tower, one currently open, and the small shadows of guards around them. This, then, was the Hall where the common folk saw the Council.

At a call from above, Karland turned and ran up the stairs to the others, who were climbing slowly. Breathless, he caught them up, and said, 'That is pretty amazing. Do people normally get seen there?'

'Mostly, replied the Captain. 'Only private or extremely important matters get seen up in the Dodecagon, which of course gives the tower its name.'

'Of course,' murmured Rast.

'Do you mind stopping all this, ah, natter?' snapped Aldwyn, wheezing. He was a little red in the face, and seemed to be moving quite slowly.

Robertus looked at him in concern.

'Sir! I respectfully request that you allow us to call the lift-rail. All the council members use it, and you yourself spoke of urgency.'

'It is foolish to tire yourself needlessly,' remarked Rast.

'Fine!' puffed Aldwyn. 'Bring it then, Captain. Silly business. I am sure these steps were, mm, not as steep last time I was here.'

Robertus nodded, and Karland saw him hide a smile as he called down. Karland was grateful that he was careful of Aldwyn's pride; his friend did not like to be seen as feeble. The guard standing next to the lift-rail looked up. He nodded and called through the wall. After an initial jerk the platform ascended to their level with a smooth motion, stopping roughly where they were.

They stepped on the lift-rail and sat on the solid seats. With a whirring clanking, the lift-rail spiralled upwards at slightly more than walking speed, the arm it sat on following a slot in the wall that ran parallel to the staircase. Aldwyn sat frowning, thinking.

Karland whispered to Rast, 'How is this going up?'

Rast shrugged. 'No idea.'

They reached the top, rising to sit next to the stairway which had narrowed to an open portal. A small antechamber held an ornate door with two more guards in front of it, and several unguarded plainer doors to the side. The guards saluted the Captain.

'Pro-Tem Councillor Aldwyn Varelin, to see the Council,' reported Robertus formally. The guards saluted Aldwyn.

'Sir... They are already in session, and requested you go directly in.' They opened the door and the party entered the Dodecagon.

'Behold, the heart of Wisdom in Eordeland,' Captain Robertus said formally.

CS   SO

Twelve chairs lined the far wall of the chamber, much less ornate and far more comfortable looking than the ones below. They were close together, almost within touching distance, and all were occupied. In the centre of the room sat a simple round table.

Seven men and five women sat, dressed in similar garb to Aldwyn. There were different colours, but the style was identical, down to the pattern on the hems. None of the chairs held young faces; many looked near to Aldwyn in age, and one looked positively ancient. There was a momentary silence, and then this last man stood, a broad smile on his face.

'Aldwyn Varelin! So it is true. You have returned. It is good to see you.'

Aldwyn smiled and bowed. 'Councillor Tarqas. I am glad to see you, mm, in good health still. It is good to return. Yes, good to return.'

'Not such good health, these days.' Tarqas waved over at the side, where a Welcomer Ministrator stood. 'Please. Bring chairs. We may be some time, and it is hardly meet that an old colleague must stand to talk to us.'

Robertus left them to speak in the ear of a burly council member, and the travellers sat.

'My thanks, Brandwyn,' said Aldwyn in relief. 'I will admit it is more tiring climbing here than I remember, even with that blasted contraption.'

Tarqas smiled, sitting, but before he could continue, a skinny man with very short receding hair leaned forward and interjected.

'Yes, indeed, Master Varelin. It has been many a year since you vexed us. Might I hazard a guess that you have returned to air your tired stories again?'

Councillor Tarqas coughed.

'Please, Councillor Novas. For your information, I sent word asking him to advise us.' The rest of the Council looked at him in some surprise. 'We need all our assets in these troubled times. We should allow our old friend to speak. He has earned that right, I think, and we have matters to discuss with him too.'

One of the younger Councillors, a sour-looking woman with a pinched face, grunted, her face twisted as if she could smell something bad.

'Personally, I think *Master* Varelin gave up any right to speak here when he left so precipitously.' She looked like she would go on, but the woman to her right held up her hand and spoke sharply. She had a strong square jaw, and iron grey hair.

'Advisor Interjectory, Councillor Eremus. Aldwyn Varelin never had his Councillorship revoked or contested. He has simply held it *in absentia*. He holds the right to speak.'

Eremus subsided, muttering.

'Allow me to introduce our current Arbitrator, Councillor Mira Lyss,' said Tarqas. Aldwyn nodded to her, smiling. A slight smile touched her lips as she nodded back.

'Draef Novas and Brandwyn Tarqas are already known to you, Aldwyn, as are Ulric Drostaca, Nessa Contemus, and Aurelia Brókova. The faces you may not know are Councillors Jamus Holmson, Joy Eremus, Whyll Regus, Marcus Andragostin, Augusta Andragostin, and Daffydd Gusta.'

Ulric was the large man Robertus had spoken too, Karland noted. The Councillors nodded one by one, all except Councillor Novas and Councillor Eremus; he snorted and she stared at Aldwyn with open hostility. The male Councillor Andragostin saw the curious looks of the company and remarked, 'We are brother and sister. The first on the Council, if memory serves.'

'It does,' Augusta said, amused. 'Since you came from the Memoria Academia.' They were the two youngest on the Council by quite a few years.

'May I introduce Rast Tal'Orien, and my apprentice, Karland Dresin,' Aldwyn said. Rast rose, bowed fluidly and sat again. Karland stood, banged his knee painfully on a table leg, and bowed with a red face, sitting again to try and rub it surreptitiously under the table.

'Rast Tal'Orien is a name that I have heard,' said Councillor Holmson. A few other heads nodded.

'Then perhaps what I have come to tell you will bear some weight, if my word is not enough,' said Aldwyn. 'Master Tal'Orien concurs with me. In fact if it were not for his protection, I may not have made it here at all.'

Many faces showed surprise, and Tarqas gestured. 'Please, my friend. Speak.'

'I said this a decade ago, in this very room, and now I will, mm. Say it again. I believe a storm has been building for centuries, and it will get worse. We have seen evidence of societies in decline, and I have spoken of portents that foretold disasters. I told you Haná might fall; I told you that the peace between the realms was at risk. You would not listen then. I pray you will now.' He pinched the bridge of his nose. 'You must have seen signs of things being other than they always have been. Troubled times come, and we do nothing to forestall them.'

There was a moment of silence, and then Tarqas spoke.

'Aldwyn... many who sat here before did not believe you. I remember well the day you left us; I felt that perhaps what you said bore investigation, but not enough of us agreed. Since that time others have also noticed that things are slowly changing. Crime is rising even in this orderly city, and rumours of strange happenings are reported across Eordeland.

'You are not the first to come warning of rising chaos. Khazâ-dí Djûpur is shutting its borders as we speak. Ignat is doing the same, and Novin is collecting mercenaries as if they were gold. The Léohtsholt woods have to all intents and purposes been barred to men, and we have been visited by a Druid warning that even the natural world is showing ominous signs of change for the worse. This last was dismissed at first... but tales are growing that support her claim.

'Barely a month gone, Banistari lost a whole fleet of ships in the Bay of Nestus. A wave tore them apart on a clear day, and went on to decimate several coastal towns. There was no warning, and this is not a single incident. Natural disasters appear to have been occurring more often, in a manner that has infuriated – and baffled – the predictions of the Academia Meteorologica.' He looked uncomfortable. 'Matters you spoke of ten years gone made little sense to us then, but I do not think your warnings so wild now. Your words have become fact, and thus I called for your advice.'

'Absolute rubbish,' protested Novas. 'Things always seem bad, but are rarely better or worse than before. To suggest you can pull a prediction from a book and apply it to future demographics is inaccurate at best-'

'The method may seem inaccurate,' interrupted the quiet, deep voice of Ulric, 'but whichever way you read it, Novas, I agree with Tarqas and Varelin. Things *are* changing, by the year. Barely a week goes by without an increased count of rapes or murders, let alone minor crimes, or some disaster that needs our attention. Our Judgementus Legalis and Guards are overwhelmed.'

He turned to Aldwyn.

'I don't think any of us cared for what you told us when we met last,' he said. 'None of us connected the fall of Haná with your warning. We respect you greatly - yet with little evidence but patchy data and theories of some of the more... esoteric... of the Universalia Communia, what were we to do?'

Aldwyn spoke quietly. 'You were supposed to listen, Ulric. I was never given to alarmist statements. I thought that some of you would at least enquire further, would trust me, having known me so long.'

Ulric shrugged heavy shoulders. He obviously had Poviiri blood, and looked like he should be wearing a spiked helmet instead of sitting in a toga, despite advanced middle years.

'Perhaps we suffer the curse of scientists and scholars. Without overwhelming demonstrable evidence, we see only conjecture.'

Aldwyn shook his head, and unrolled several scrolls from his pouch.

'Councillors. I gave you multiple examples of predictions made by many texts, including the Book of Sarthos, all of which were proved startlingly accurate against official records. I showed you trends of social stagnation and breakdown across multiple cultures, mm, *directly related* to the problems we began to face. I thought you would listen. Instead, I was ridiculed and ignored so greatly that I felt the request at the time that I be Arbitrator hollow and worthless. What use was my advice if it was already not being heeded? That is why I left to search on my own.'

'The Book of Sarthos? A pointless piece of drivel. The man was mad,' snapped Novas.

'Perhaps not as mad as you think,' Aldwyn said. 'He clearly predicted the collapse of the kingdom of Haná, and we watched it disintegrate into the United Territories of Meyar. He also stated *to the day* when Gorudrum, the greatest volcano known, would erupt again – and many lives were lost because he went unheeded. There are many such examples. I, mm, admit it is not easy to decipher; there are related sequences in it I do not understand. Nevertheless, the few events deciphered are predicted with astonishing accuracy over almost fifteen hundred years. How can that fact be so trivialised?'

'There is nothing clear about that book,' said Councillor Eremus acidly. 'It can be interpreted in many ways to best find what you wish to hear. A common star reader can do as much on any back street. It is hardly *scientific*.'

Aldwyn opened his mouth to protest, and Councillor Lyss held up her hand, speaking loudly.

'Councillors. Advisor Interjectory.' She looked around. 'We are not achieving anything with this debate. It is clear to us now that there is more truth here than was thought ten years ago. May I suggest that we request Councillor Varelin validate his statements, *without* interruption? Then I feel we can better judge what our decision must be. The Council must not be divided. Today, it is a simple fact that currently there is unrest in *all* nations, ours included, and we must act soon.'

Councillor Eremus snorted in a very unladylike fashion. 'Aldwyn Varelin's advice was not sought at the behest of this Council. A few members took *that* upon themselves.' Karland was really beginning to dislike her. She was utterly disdainful of his teacher, and clearly thought little of him. His glare went unnoticed.

'Nevertheless, he is here, and it was the right of those Councillors to ask,' Mira Lyss said sharply. 'We are struggling to comprehend the cause of events. Do we wait until desperation, past the point of return, before we act? If he can help us understand our path, however unlikely the source of the information, then we should listen.'

Nods and disparate small noises greeted this, but no one disagreed. She nodded at Aldwyn.

'If you please, Councillor.'

'Madam.' Aldwyn gravely inclined his head. He thought a moment, and then lifted his face. Karland expected to see him angry, resolute, but he looked old and tired, and frightened.

'Councillors. Consider what is happening. Chaos is creeping across the lands of Anaria, and the realms are unstable, many on the brink of war. People everywhere are losing their minds and their lives. Myths come forth again. Nature itself is not acting as we have come to expect. People are frightened. Trust, communities, civilisation even here in Eordeland trembles. Our land here is awash with outlaws, and other, darker things roam free – I have seen both with my own eyes travelling here.

'I have read texts that tell of a time when the world will break apart, when darkness will cover it before it ultimately ceases to be. Some correspond alarmingly with the events of the last few decades. Every passing year has convinced me more that I was not mistaken. I have not been idle, Councillors. I kept contact with much of the scattered Universalia Communia, men and women who believed - at least in part - as I did. I had messages passed to me for years from an old friend, one of the few who knew where I was. On the way here I stopped to collect the rest, and the news is dire.

'One by one, they have begun to go silent, and their information has dried up without trace. Many were in fear of their lives. From their messages it seems someone is trying to prevent us, um, learning something. That *something* must be important. I have collected the hard-earned knowledge of the secrets of the Arcanum Academia from colleagues who no longer answer me. I think our whole world stands in grave danger of a growing anarchy, and I have come to believe this chaos is directed, that there is a restless malice at work in this world. I urge you, I *beg* you to listen, to try and find the source of these problems before it is too late. Because I believe there *is* a source.'

He sighed, and pinched the bridge of his nose, squeezing his eyes shut. When he spoke again, his voice quavered, and his words sent a fresh chill up Karland's spine.

'I think... I dread... that I am also now hunted. I was followed here, that much is certain. I do not know which frightens me more – my own fate, or the future of this world.' His gaze took in the silent Councillors. 'This is more than unrest in one nation, of natural disasters, of spreading madness. We may be coming to the end of things as we know them. A terrible dark storm gathers. It is violent, almighty, and one which may sweep this world away in its passing.'

◌   ◌

There was a long silence after this proclamation. Not even Novas spoke, instead chewing his lip and staring at the floor. Karland tore his gaze from Aldwyn and looked around at the Councillors, expecting them to speak out as they had earlier, but none did. Finally, Brandwyn sighed.

'Dramatic though it sounds, I fear you may be right. What you say worries me, more than I can possibly tell you.'

Ulric sat up. 'You say there are problems in the hinterlands? We have been receiving increasing reports from all regions of outlaws, ruffians, bands of men. As recently as a week ago, a large war party of men was reported two hundred miles northeast of Darost, in the heart of east Norland.' He glanced around. 'We were not sure where they came from, or their purpose. They have not yet moved toward Darost, but we have begun evacuating people from nearby steads as a precaution. I am awaiting the return of our main forces from a routine border patrol mobilisation.' There was a silence as he spoke. Councillor Ulric seemed about to add something, and instead, to Karland's surprise, Councillor Novas leaned forward.

'Councillor Varelin. You speak of other scholars going quiet, vanishing. I can shed some light on this, for all of us. I am currently the point of contact for most-' his eyes glittered at Aldwyn '-of our roving scholars, and receive reports sent from across Anaria. You are unfortunately correct. Of our scattered colleagues, there are few left hiding; almost every ranking scholar outside Darost is dead.'

Aldwyn closed his eyes, his face paling. Novas continued grimly.

'Someone is shutting down our eyes and ears. Some deaths have seemed happenstance, but there has been no question of murder in others. Slowly but surely, deliberately, we are being crippled, irreplaceable knowledge lost with each death. I am in no doubt that, in this at least, you are correct.'

Aldwyn swallowed. Karland felt a chill at the thought of the unseen men who had followed them.

Eremus snorted scathingly, 'Come, Varelin. As if anyone could reach you here, if indeed you are followed. We are in the guarded heart of The Sanctum.' She sounded impatient, her disbelief evident.

'There is yet another problem,' Councillor Brókova said quietly. 'If you meant to show us your findings from the Book of Sarthos, I fear you will not do so here. Our copy was destroyed by fire.'

'What?' cried Aldwyn, opening his eyes. 'But, but, the old texts are kept safe under the Librarium-'

'Yes,' she said. 'We do not know what happened. But there was a fire in that section of the Combic Library. Many books and scrolls were destroyed. One of our most revered Librarians died in the blaze. It seems incongruous that he could have caused it after so many decades of service. A flame in the Library? It is unheard of.'

For the first time, Rast spoke.

'Do you think it deliberate?'

Councillor Regus answered. 'We do not know. No one has said it was other than an accident, but many of us held suspicions. He would never have used naked flame there; it is forbidden.'

'This is ludicrous,' snapped Councillor Eremus. 'A doddering old fool dropped a candle in a protected part of our library and took himself and some old texts with him. Ascribing other motives to it is guesswork, and distracting. We should be looking at our civil unrest, which, whatever *Councillor* Varelin says, is all we have here. Why should the state of other lands concern us? Some of us are not so old and foolish as to believe any outlandish conclusion because it can be fitted to a situation.' She paused, abruptly aware of the furious glares from her peers, who had stiffened in affront.

'Elder Librarian Sampas was Tertius in the Order of the Scrolls,' said Councillor Lyss coldly. 'He had tended the Combic Library for more than half a century, and his knowledge of the Arcanum scripts was unmatched. He had never before used other than the lambent jars, as decreed in Library edict, and his mind was as sharp as the day he began here. If you cannot show the respect due a great man, then be silent, Councillor Eremus. You know not of what you speak.'

An uncomfortable silence followed. Even Novas was looking at his colleague with distaste. She refused to meet anyone's eyes, colour high on her cheeks. Karland grinned to himself at her discomfort.

The silence was broken by Councillor Gusta, who had not yet spoken. His dry reedy voice cut through the stillness like a weak flute.

'Our course is clear. We must cease our bickering and decide on what we *can* do, now, today. That the world is changing, and that it is for the worst, none of us can contest. The question then remains what we are to do about it.'

ଓ   ଧ

They broke for lunch at noon and were shown back to their quarters by Robertus. Karland felt that Aldwyn was finally getting heard, and was eager to see what the Council would do next.

'When do we hear the decision?' he asked Robertus. The Captain glanced down and smiled.

'Don't tell them I said this, lad, but the Council is in some ways a glorified committee. You won't see them until tomorrow at earliest, if not the day after. They have many other things to attend to, and they will need to discuss this internally. I would take the chance to rest and relax, explore the University.'

Karland was surprised, but he couldn't deny he wanted to see more of The Sanctum. He nodded, resolving to explore while he could.

FOURTEEN

It was two days before they were summoned again. Karland had spent most of his time getting lost, bored with Aldwyn revising his notes. Rast had vanished on his own errands.

Robertus met them again, but he seemed distracted, some of his usual affability absent. 'I have just had an urgent despatch. I am afraid your talk will have to wait,' he said as they ascended. He entered before them and swiftly spoke to Ulric, who grunted.

'Before we begin,' said Ulric after they had all seated themselves, 'Welcomer Captain Robertus has urgent news. He has been working closely with Guard Captain Dorn on the matter of these mercenary troops in the absence of General Colcos.'

Robertus nodded, and stepped forward at attention. 'Esteemed Council members, I bring troubling tidings. Merchants returning from Novin, Meyar and Ignat bring word of squads of mercenaries spread throughout the western plains and up to the very borders of Eordeland. Captain Dorn and I feel it is wise to assume those men we now find within our borders may also be mercenaries rather than simple groups of outlaws. Reports hinted at scattered groups of five to thirty men with military training, slowly congregating in the north east. Under orders from Councillor Ulric, Captain Dorn and I sent a battalion to investigate this small army as a precaution.

'Battalion Commander Pollard was ordered to discover what the band intends and to direct it peacefully out of our lands. As they travelled he sought information about these groups of men that are appearing - they are springing up like weeds after rain. What we have discovered is that they are slowly moving towards this growing army. It is small yet, but we are alarmed at any foreign army within our borders. If it is left unchecked, we cannot guess how it might grow – it is already far larger than we thought.'

'How large?' asked Councillor Regus.

'Initial reports several thousand now, and growing.' The Council murmured, taken aback. 'Many of our patrols are late reporting in or missing altogether, and we have had no word from several entire provinces for some time. We assume they are cut off from Darost, or worse. The battalion commander that made contact reported that the leaders of the group were cooperative but sly, as if they humoured him, and claim that they are protecting the smaller communities 'from evil that is stalking all the realms'. They avoided all requests to leave, and the commander insists that the men are a cohesive military unit.'

'That is a dire insult,' breathed Councillor Holmson. 'A suggestion our troops cannot protect their own people, thrown in his teeth! I am surprised he did not reciprocate.'

'Battalion Commander Pollard is a professional man, sir,' said Robertus. 'He feared to upset a tense situation, and as they outnumbered him three to one, he felt it wiser to return with a full detachment of soldiers to escort them from our lands. He stands ready to drive them from our nation, forcibly if need be. These men are too well trained to be drifters. There is another motive here. We must discover what it is, and how so many men got past our borders. He also reported that he saw a lot of Meyari weapons… and some evidence of Hanári surcoats. The blue on purple is unmistakeable.'

'*Hanári?*' said Ulric, startled. 'Those standards have not existed for nearly ten years, since the monarchy was overthrown.'

Karland looked at Aldwyn, who shook his head wearily. It was a lot to take in – everything Aldwyn had told him, and now this. Even Rast looked perturbed. The Council talked excitedly until Councillor Lyss brought them to order.

'Captain. There is more?'

'Yes, Councillor. This morning word came from two survivors of a large squad of Eordeland Guards. The squad was heading to east Norland on a routine patrol from General Colcos. They were ambushed by a band of men twice their size, and were decimated almost to a man. One of them has since died, but both believe that they were attacked by Meyari. This is the first confirmed attack we have had reports of. I believe these men are infiltrating us in preparation for a military strike.'

'Are you telling me that the United Territories of Meyar may have a hostile army inside our borders?' demanded Ulric. 'That the Prime Alderman is attacking Eordeland? This is lunacy. Their ambassador is under our roof at this very moment for trade concessions!'

'Sir. A small army perhaps, and well hidden, but military intelligence estimates they have been gathering for the better part of two months. They must have been passing the border in small groups in the hopes of remaining undetected.'

'Is that so?' Ulric's face was grim. He looked around the chamber and spoke formally. 'I request of the Council that we investigate forthwith, with all action necessary to secure Eordeland. I am prepared to take responsibility for all proceedings myself and represent the Council in this case, if that is the wish of the Twelve.'

There was no dissent. Ulric turned back and gestured one of the Welcomer Guards over. The man approached next to Robertus and saluted smartly.

'Please inform the Politikus of Meyar that his urgent and immediate presence is required in the Dodecagon,' said Ulric. 'Phrase it as a request. Politely ensure he realises it is not. Escort him here, as is due his rank.'

'Councillor.' The man saluted and left hurriedly.

Councillor Regus stared at nothing. 'Something must be done about these men immediately Colcos returns.'

Mira Lyss nodded. 'Thank you, Captain Robertus. Our apologies, Councillor Varelin, but your matter will have to be tabled until we have talked to the Politikus.'

Aldwyn nodded. 'We will wait outside, then.'

'No, I request you stay,' contradicted Brandwyn, 'if it please the Council. This matter is part of what we called you here for, and it would be foolish to exclude you. Whether you sit amongst us or not, you are a Councillor, and one of the Universalia Communia.'

In deference to the Politikus, Karland, Rast and Aldwyn stood as the table and chairs were moved off to the side, clearing the floor. The room thrummed with tension as the Councillors talked to each other in low tones.

'This is very serious,' muttered Aldwyn. 'I suspect that Meyar is heavily involved here, but this makes no sense. We live in a powerful nation at the far end of Anaria. This could mean war, and I cannot think Meyar would challenge Eordeland.'

'So why would they do it, then?' asked Karland. Rast shrugged.

'They would only do it if they had a clear advantage, but I can see none. They have tried to cross the Northern Stonestride to take the city-island of Eyotsburg many times in the last few years and been rebuffed each time. Now the borders of Meyar are closely guarded on both sides. Within Meyar foreign merchants are closely regulated and watched, but still they bring back rumours of atrocities within some of the Territories. The Prime Alderman holds more power now than the king he overthrew. But even with forced conscription, they could not hold the field against the roused forces of Eordeland. There is something else here.'

ભ   ૪

Barely twenty minutes later, there were voices outside the door, and then they were flung open. Forcing his way rudely past the guards, a small man in bright purple satin stepped through, a thick stole on his shoulders. His face was shrewd, with a wide nose that looked incongruous with his close set eyes, and his hair was combed back in oiled waves.

His face was red and his breathing heavy from a mixture of outrage and haste. Before anyone could greet him he glared around the room and then spoke acidly.

'This... *cretin-*' he glanced at the guard, who stared forwards impassively, '- dared to haul me here from my fast-breaking. I *demand* he is flogged for his insolence, and I will accept the apologies of the Council once it is done.' He had a faint accent that Karland could not place.

Twelve Councillors watched him coolly. Karland was surprised, after witnessing the bickering earlier. He had expected them to argue, but now he understood why this Council was one of the most influential powers in Anaria. What had happened earlier was a closed discussion involving a long-absent member. This was international politics. The Council, internal strife set aside, was an implacable machine, intelligent and unified.

'Politikus Belen,' said Councillor Mira Lyss formally. 'Your presence was requested by decree of the Council of Twelve. We have a very serious matter that has come to our attention and find that we must, regrettably, engage you immediately to resolve it.'

Belen opened his mouth to continue protesting. Before the Politikus could respond, Councillor Ulric leaned forward with a glance at Mira Lyss and continued.

'My lord. We have received some puzzling, even troubling news. It appears a large party of armed men have somehow slipped inside our borders, and lie no more than three hundred miles from this very city.'

'Councillor Ulric,' the Politikus said smoothly, 'this is regrettable news, but I hardly think it worth interrupting my morning meal for! I cannot see how this involves me. Are you requesting aid from Meyar?'

There was a faint smirk on his face. Karland found himself intensely disliking the oily little man. As he glanced around the room, the ambassador's eyes fell on the small group to the side. The smirk dropped from his face, and he stared at them with a hint of surprise.

'Not officially,' said Ulric, a look of faint distaste on his face. He was a direct man and clearly did not like Belen's verbal fencing. 'But perhaps in a manner. We have reason to believe that the men are, in fact, Meyari.'

'Preposterous!' sputtered Belen, his attention snapping back to Ulric. 'You cannot prove that! Why should they be Meyari? On behalf of my nation, I am offended by the very suggestion. I intend to press for a full apology.'

'Please, Politikus Belen. I did not accuse Meyar of anything, merely stated the believed origin of the majority of these men. It is not just this one army that concerns us, although it is the largest. Our countryside appears to be awash with armed men, and now it seems people have gone missing, even been killed. Am I to assume you know nothing about this?'

Belen glared at him.

'Of course not. It is not the policy of Meyar to interfere with other nations. It is also not our fault if mercenaries have been allowed inside your borders due to your own laxity. The implication they are Meyari is insulting and disruptive to our diplomatic relationship.'

Ulric shook his head.

'My lord. Our delegation reports that these men wear Hanári surcoats, bear Meyari weapons, and indeed speak Hanár. Is it not natural to assume that they are Meyari? We were hoping you could shed light on this. It is obviously of great concern to us.'

'Anyone could wear Hanári battle dress. It is ten years unused, and could have come from anywhere. Meyar has her own uniform, as well you know!' Belen seemed agitated, eyes flicking distractedly back to the three to the side. Karland thought it odd that he kept staring at Aldwyn.

'I object strenuously to all your allegations. Even if they were Meyari, how dare they be blamed for any deaths? You have no evidence your patrol was destroyed by them.'

There was a sudden intake of breath from some of the Council, and Belen's face was abruptly wary. He looked like he was rapidly reviewing his protests internally to find his misstep.

'I never said that we had lost an entire patrol, Politikus,' said Ulric quietly. 'How did you know that?'

'You clearly said-'

Ulric cut him off. 'I never mentioned the patrol. It was large and all but two were slain. This was the first battle inside Eordeland in three generations.'

'Well, there you are,' said Belen, his face relaxing. 'News like that would spread fast. I cannot recall where I heard it. I obviously overheard one of your guards, perhaps yesterday.' His tone was airy.

'My Lord.' Robertus stepped forward, his voice quiet. 'I myself only received this news not an hour ago, and relayed it to the Council immediately. It is not common knowledge.'

'Well, someone with less discipline must have passed rumour then, Captain,' Belen said, smiling nastily. Robertus shook his head in polite disagreement.

'Only Captain Gardenson of the City Guard knew of this, my Lord. None of the guards you have had contact with could have known. I am the only Welcomer Guard with this knowledge.' His voice was faintly apologetic.

A faint flush appeared on the neck of the Politikus. He sputtered, and then turned quickly to the Council. 'This impertinence is outrageous!' His protest rang out in a silent room. The Council of Twelve watched him carefully. The silence stretched, and then Ulric spoke formally.

'Politikus Belen. It is the decree of the Council of Twelve that both you and this army of so-called mercenaries be removed from our borders within two days. After this time, any Meyari in Eordeland not already registered as a Scholar or trading merchant will be either ejected or detained, depending on circumstance.'

Belen's eyes bulged slightly.

'You have no right! There is no evidence that I am involved in this farce! What fault of mine if your army cannot protect your own country?' he shouted, his face ugly.

'Other than Captain Robertus, who is above your accusations, the knowledge can only have come from this force of Meyari themselves, Politikus. I believe you have confirmed for us both their origin and their intentions. Our ruling stands. Within forty eight hours you will be stripped of diplomatic status if you remain in Darost.'

No one said a word. The only sound was the heavy, shocked breathing from Belen. His face contorted as if he did not know what to say, and then he hissed with surprising venom.

'You will regret this. Meyar's friendship is not lightly cast aside!'

He turned on his heel and stalked from the room. Ulric nodded at the guard that had brought him, and he followed.

No one spoke for a long minute, and then Councillor Contemus spoke up, a frail old lady with a clear strong voice.

'So. We have entered a new time of upheaval. We may not be opening hostilities, but to other realms it will appear that we are now at the brink of war with Meyar. We must ensure we are not left defenceless.'

'What I do not understand is what Meyar hoped to accomplish. They must know they do not have a military advantage against us, and there has been no cause for hostilities,' remarked Councillor Holmson.

'It was strange,' said Augusta softly. 'He seemed distracted. I would not have expected one as slippery as he to make such a mistake.'

'He seemed very interested in Councillor Varelin,' agreed Councillor Regus, drawing muttered agreement from the whole council. 'Something is not right here.' He turned back to Aldwyn, who had sat at the table again off to the side. 'Councillor Varelin. What are your thoughts? This seems to mesh all too well with what you said.'

'There is something behind all this,' responded Aldwyn. 'If we look at Meyar, chaotic and full of internal unrest since the fall of the monarchy, it makes no sense. There is no reason for them to launch an offensive against a much more powerful nation. I have long thought there to be more to Meyar's meteoric rise than meets the eye.'

'Eordeland is the symbol of freedom and liberty in the East,' said Contemus. 'Gaining control of our land or even simply weakening us would demoralise the stronger realms, and we have fertile arable land and organised society, with great knowledge hidden in the University. There is knowledge here that must never fall into the hands of those who would misuse it.'

'It cannot be expansion,' remarked Ulric. 'They have the whole of Nassmoor just beyond their borders, and Meyar itself is not small. But the Territories are not as united as they like others to think. It all comes back to what they hope to gain by staging an unsustainable attack over a thousand miles away, and that I cannot guess.'

'Is there any chance this army might have succeeded in overthrowing Darost if all these 'mercenaries' joined forces?' asked Rast.

Robertus shook his head. 'Not in a hundred years. A third of our military could destroy the entire Meyari army, and most of the reserves live in and around Darost. It is the best-defended city in the East, even with the army elsewhere, and that doesn't take into account its strategic defences.'

Eremus stirred, a frown on her face. 'So... if they are not here to attack, what was their purpose? To prevent other aid from coming?'

'From east Norland?' asked Holmson. 'There is nothing larger than towns and forts all the way to the coast, bordered by wild trees and mountains.'

'Or, mm, is there?' said Aldwyn. He blinked and looked around the council. 'That squad, the only one attacked... was it heading to east Norland?'

Councillor Lyss sat upright. 'Perhaps it is not aid they seek to block. You are suggesting that there is more to this? Something they wish to hide? They cannot possibly have secreted an entire army there.'

'It does seem that they don't wish us to go there,' reasoned Aldwyn.

Gusta stroked his chin thoughtfully. 'The reports of homesteads going quiet... and the patrols late reporting in. What regions are they from?'

Captain Robertus looked grim. 'Mainly the northeast, Councillor. They are coming in from all directions, but most are from the northeast. We had not realised.'

Ulric thumped his large fist onto the arm of his chair. 'Captain Robertus! I want you to brief Captain Dorn and help him to assemble two regiments of Eordeland Guard to reinforce Battalion Commander Pollard and sweep the area. Bring in reserves if you must. They are to remove those Meyari with deadly force if they are not gone within two days, and then they are to continue into east Norland and report back. I want another regiment on standby for reinforcements.' Rast nodded to himself, and Karland felt a thrill of excitement.

'In the meantime I want all our military on full alert. Border patrols are to be brought to full strength, and this city must be secured. And someone get me General Colcos!'

œ ঝ

Karland watched Robertus salute and leave at speed. Morning seemed years ago now. So many things he had never suspected were not only real but being discussed by the people in charge of the entire nation, and somehow he was in the middle of it. He was also unsure how to feel about Aldwyn – his friend had so much to him never suspected that in some ways he was like a different person.

Novas spoke first.

'We must find the cause of all this. If this is happening in every realm as we believe, Anaria will be torn apart.'

Marcus Andragostin spoke. 'We should analyse the problems by severity and locations. We should be able to pinpoint the major problem areas.'

'How about Meyar?' snorted Novas. Marcus flushed.

Aldwyn spoke before they could bicker further. 'Councillors. You requested that I, mm, advise you.' He looked around them. 'It is true that troubled times seem widespread, but the first major omen of something wrong was the dissolution of Haná, a hitherto stable and productive realm. Of all our neighbours, Meyar is now the only one truly closed to us. With their illicit foray into our lands, I would suggest we look there first.'

'And how do you propose we do that?' said Regus. 'We have just evicted their representative!'

Augusta raised a palm. 'Do we not have a scholar there? I thought there was one assigned to the old King?'

'Kelpas Withy was found murdered with his throat cut in an alley far from his room in the Palace nearly two years ago,' said Novas bitterly. 'One of the first killings. The Prime Alderman's clerk expressed his 'shock, grief, and regret'.'

Aldwyn closed his eyes in dismay.

'He was a good friend,' he said quietly. 'One of the messages was his. He said what he sent me was being sought, but not by whom, or for what. He also mentioned something of importance regarding the Prime Alderman and the Church of Terome, the main religion in Meyar, and a name: Sontles. I believe Kelpas was on the verge of returning to Darost.'

Heads shook. The name meant nothing to them.

'He died before he could tell *us* anything,' said Novas, slightly accusing.

Ulric rumbled, 'The more I hear, the less I like! Terome may be involved? We do not need to add religion to this mess. What did he send you?'

Aldwyn hesitated, and then reached into his tunic. His hand pulled out a pendant on a slender thong. Shaped like a long teardrop with a blunted six pointed star at the narrowed top, it had symbols carved on it under the grime of years in a peculiar-looking metal.

'This.'

He pulled it off and handed it to the nearest guard, who passed it up to Councillor Gusta. The pendant was passed slowly down the line, each looking at it carefully. All shook their heads.

'None of us know what this means,' said Contemus, 'and it's not a language I have ever seen.'

'I have,' said Aldwyn, 'but it makes even less sense. I believe it to be a dialect called *Naga-tō*.'

Augusta laughed. 'It is a matter of debate as to whether Dragon-kind *have* a language, let alone a humanised dialect, Councillor Varelin. Most believe them to merely be mythical and destructive beasts.'

'It is unusual to find it written in human form,' agreed Aldwyn, 'but it *does* exist. Look at our older records. They speak of the Drake Years as a time of terror when Dragons killed mortals as a direct response to the actions of men. It was a simultaneous reaction from the species as a whole, which denotes communicative language. It was not the response of mindless creatures.

'I know a little of the tongue from our oldest records, as much as any human is likely to know, but I do not know what the pendant says. Kelpas believed it to be linked to something that granted the bearer vast power, but I cannot say if is it real or what it is. He said it was 'a key to a power locked away which might restore the greater balance.' I am not sure what he meant.'

'A weapon of some kind, perhaps,' remarked Novas.

There was a long pause, and a steward brought out glasses and pitchers of water. Karland finished his quickly and asked for another. He was parched, and famished; noon was approaching rapidly. Just when he thought he had accepted one surprise, another appeared – now the council spoke of legends alongside war and murder. He had never realised that being in the middle of great events would be so tiring, or confusing, but he now felt a keener sympathy for Aldwyn. It must have been a heavy burden to bear.

Ulric drank his glass in one draught, wiped his mouth with the back of his hand, and spoke.

'We must decide where to go from here,' he remarked, 'and soon. This afternoon must be spent in war council with our military leaders if we are to act quickly enough.'

'This morning's discussions have equal weight, I think. We must find an origin to these happenings and an answer, that much is obvious, but Eordeland cannot be directly involved,' said Lyss. 'We are now formally at odds with the United Territories of Meyar. If we are seen to be sending spies after we have closed diplomatic relations, there *will* be war.'

'But we *must* discover the cause of the upheaval affecting all the lands,' protested Aldwyn. 'Or there will be war anyway, and it will entangle us all.'

Marcus Andragostin was looking keenly at Rast.

'Master Tal'Orien. I understand you are well travelled, and I believe that you are not an Eordelander.'

'You are correct on both counts,' said Rast, no expression on his face. Karland could see what was coming. 'Am I to guess that you are going to request that I involve myself in this excursion?'

'You *would* be a logical choice,' admitted Novas. 'You are not an official – or unofficial – representative of Eordeland. We need to find answers quickly. If Councillor Varelin is correct, and much as I hate to say it, I think he may be-' his face was rueful, '-this chaos, this unrest, is slowly growing and will inevitably involve us all. If you were able to find out what we need to know – the source of these problems, and how to combat them – we could attempt to resolve them.'

'I am certainly capable of slipping into Meyar,' agreed Rast, 'but I would not know where to begin. I am not one of your scholars. I am a simple man. My best skill is staying alive. Even that may be sorely tested if I agree to your request, and slipping back out again would be far more difficult; yet I cannot deny the need. I have seen firsthand the rot that is creeping into the lands. Perhaps if I had one of you with me, with the authority and knowledge to decipher the situation, something might be done.'

Karland held his breath, not daring to break the silence.

'Can we send Dorn?' asked Tarqas. Ulric shook his head.

'We need him here. Robertus too. We are limited to the few people we can trust, and all of us are needed here if we are to avert this crisis.'

'Perhaps... there is a way,' said Regus. 'Aldwyn Varelin both is and is not a member of this Council. He is the one we have – grudgingly in part – turned to for advice. His studies and predictions are the basis of our discussions today. I would say he is uniquely suited to finding the cause of this widespread chaos, if Rast Tal'Orien will go with him.'

'What?' protested Aldwyn. 'Wait one, mm, minute! I am older than anyone here except Nessa! The journey here was hard enough. You expect me to travel into the heart of danger, where my colleagues have been murdered, and find what we need?'

His fright was almost palpable. Karland suddenly realised that behind all the myriad things his friend was, he was an old man in fear of his life.

Ulric rumbled back to life. 'You must admit, Councillor Varelin, that it is your information we are deciding to base our survival on, which you have so strongly advocated and proved us wrong with. You yourself have said that you required us to make a decision on these matters. Our decision is to depend on you. Are we wrong after all?'

'No! No,' said Aldwyn desperately, 'but please. You must understand. I am old, weary. Such a journey will be perhaps harder than I can bear. I have given so much already, and the likelihood of my success is miniscule!'

'I think we have no other choice, old friend,' said Brandwyn Tarqas, regret heavy in his voice. 'If we are to survive, you and Master Tal'Orien offer us the best chance we have – however slim. This involves you more than anyone else. The pendant, your research... you are focal to them all. There are no other logical options; we must prepare for war.'

Aldwyn opened his mouth, but nothing came out. The denial was plain to see on his face.

Councillor Contemus smiled sadly at her old colleague's anguish.

'Dear Aldwyn. You are the only one qualified that can be trusted to do what must be done. Who would guess your motives? A simple travelling scholar, with a fighter for protection - merely an extension of the last decade and, indeed, your journey here. Travelling as such, who would notice or suspect you?'

Eremus smiled spitefully.

'I think Councillor Varelin is caught between the Mountain and the Valley,' she said. 'If he truly believes in everything he has said, why, he should be pleased to do all he can to prove it and to avert disaster.'

Several of the others shot her disgusted glances, but no one could gainsay the truth, however ill-put. Aldwyn sat silent, his face pale, staring at the table.

'Aldwyn Varelin. Will you take up the quest that this council lays upon you, under the protection of Rast Tal'Orien?' said Mira Lyss formally. 'It is the view of this council that you are the best suited to perform the task ahead – perhaps the only one who might guide us through this peril. No one knows more about this turmoil than you. You have warned us of it and now must work with us to divert it before it destroys us. If there is any source to this unrest, any weapon or aid linked to this talisman, anything that can preserve us, you are most likely to find it. Can you deny us in our hour of need?'

Karland felt sorry for Aldwyn. Rast was as inscrutable as always, but Aldwyn looked as if he were gripped in the throes of panic. Finally, he looked up at the council.

'I cannot do this,' he whispered. 'I am sorry.'

FIFTEEN

With General Colcos sent for and the defences of a nation to organise, the Council broke for the afternoon; Tarqas proposed meeting again the next morning to try and find another way. The councillors watched with a mixture of pity, sadness, frustration and in one case contempt as Aldwyn walked out silently.

Karland's heart went out to his old friend. It was a hard price to ask after all he had already endured. Rast said little, but it was clear he expected no one to replace Aldwyn.

There was a brooding air of inevitability hanging over them all. Aldwyn was unresponsive as they rode back down, and once back in their quarters he shut himself in his room without touching the lunch laid out. After eating, Karland and Rast stood on the balcony, talking quietly.

'Will he be all right?' Karland asked Rast, worried.

Rast shrugged. 'They ask much of him. He is an old man, and from disbelieving him they suddenly demand that he risk his life for them. He has given much of his life already, but they ask more. It is a hard choice.' He sighed. 'Aldwyn is a brilliant scholar - one of the most intelligent people in Anaria perhaps. But he is also a frail old man at the mercy of events he has spent his life warning others of. I am the only protection he has, and if he is right he truly needs me.' He shrugged heavy shoulders. 'But I also think the Council is correct. He is our best chance to do what needs to be done. He has the knowledge and the skills to seek out the heart of the maelstrom we head into, and perhaps discover how we can avoid it. Who on the Council can replace him? No one who knows enough; no one that can avoid implicating Eordeland in spying. One wrong step here, Karland, and we will be in the midst of a full-scale war.'

'But... Captain Robertus said Meyar would be crushed!'

'Nothing is certain in war, and strength may fall to cunning. Something is not right. Too much is unknown, and that makes me wary.' His face didn't show his concern, but his words were unsettling.

'So... if Aldwyn went with you to Meyar, what would happen to me?' Karland said, unsure what he wanted the answer to be. Rast turned to look at him.

'I do not know,' he said finally. 'I would leave you safely here, if I could.'

Karland considered this gravely, feeling strangely uprooted as important matters he did not understand caught him up in their wake. He watched the bustle below.

'They mentioned a Druid,' he said finally. 'I wonder if it was that woman I met.'

Rast shrugged. 'Could be.'

'She seemed a bit strange. Who are the Druids?'

'A religious sect,' said Rast. 'They don't adhere to one god or another. Instead, they revere an entity they call... Gìa, I think. It is meant to represent all of nature, or the world as a whole, more of a vast spirit or collection of spirits than a god. They name themselves protectors of nature, and it is said they have strange affinities with trees and beasts. I know the Elves are known to consider them friends.'

'Elves?' laughed Karland. 'Aren't they just tales, children's stories? Faeries that steal milk and babies, beguile humans, play tricks?'

Rast smiled faintly. 'They are real enough. They are a joyful people, and love to laugh, but they are hardly milk stealers. I cannot think of any Elf I have met that would willingly take on the task of rearing a grubby and intolerant human child.'

'You have met Elves?' said Karland, his eyes wide.

Rast smiled in genuine amusement.

'Your life in The Croft has been sheltered, Karland. There is much in the world people believe to exist that does not, and much else they dismiss that is real.'

'So what are they really like?'

'Oh, they can be entrancing. They are very beautiful. Many think them close to perfection. But they are wise, and intelligent, and kind, yet terrible in anger too. They move like quicksilver, and have senses humans cannot match. They dance and laugh readily, and are very close to this world. The Elves are an ancient race, and know much that other races have forgotten, or never knew. They were patient with me, but I think humans frustrate them at times. They can be very distant.'

'Oh.' There didn't really seem much more to say. 'I would like to meet one, one day.'

Rast laughed quietly. 'Everyone says that about Elves.'

'I don't think Aldwyn is coming out of his room,' said Karland mournfully after a few minutes. 'I was thinking of going to the Gardens again today. Want to come?'

'Why not,' agreed Rast. 'The Council will not call us again until tomorrow.'

Karland scribbled a note for Aldwyn and they left the room. He tried to follow the route he had taken yesterday, but lost his way again. Rast eventually took the lead and unerringly found his way down and out, to Karland's annoyance.

They soon found the garden he was in before. There were not as many people here now, and the sun was a white hot ghost-orb through the clouds. Rast seemed to appreciate the garden, moving with his typical controlled flowing gait across the grass. When he suggested they look at the other gardens, Karland readily agreed. Aldwyn's descriptions had interested him.

They moved unhurriedly from arch to arch. Each garden had different and yet complementary plants. One was filled with heavy orchids, their cloying scent hanging over the compound. A faint mist came down from outlets in the walls above them. Interspersed with these were strange bell-shaped cups and gaping, fleshy flowers. It wasn't until Karland saw one of these snap shut on a wasp that he realised some of these strange flowers ate meat. He shuddered and moved on.

Arid, spiky plants filled another, and thick creeping shrubs the next, each a different world. The twelfth garden was simply a lawn leading up to the huge tower doors, bordered by two curving strips of the flowers he was used to seeing in spring. Several leisurely hours later they were back where they had begun.

'Interesting,' said Rast. 'It must take constant effort to keep some of these alive. Many of these plants I have never seen.' He looked at Karland reflectively. 'We have also been followed for some time.'

'What?' Karland started and looked hurriedly around.

Rast rolled his eyes. 'Try not to make it *too* obvious that we are aware of it, boy.' He sat on the grass back in the original garden they had started in. Karland sat with him, eyes darting. He saw nothing.

A minute later, Rast spoke again loudly. 'You might as well step forward. You have been following us since the fifth garden we visited.'

A slender figure seemed to appear from the bushes, and Karland recognised the tall beautiful woman who had spoken to him yesterday. She was still wearing her clothes of natural hue, and her piercing yellow-green eyes were fixed on Rast in surprise. 'I am impressed. Most people would never have known I was trailing them. I have, however, been following you since the fourth garden you passed through.'

Rast nodded in acknowledgement with a slightly rueful grin, and stood. 'Can I assume you are the nature priest we heard the Council speak of?'

'I am a Druid, yes,' she said softly, stressing the word. Her eyes hardly blinked, never left Rast. 'I am Leona. And you?'

'I am Rast Tal'Orien,' he said. 'This is Karland Dresin.' Her eyes moved to Karland, and she smiled, her face pretty.

'Yes. The young one who likes nature but fears deep woods,' she said. 'We meet again, Karland.' He nodded, uncomfortable at her intense demeanour and her sharp gaze.

Her eyes returned to Rast. 'You move proudly, smoothly, like you are part of the world,' she said. 'As a wolf, a tiger. Like the earth is your ally and your subject. You are a warrior, a hunter? The name seems familiar to me.'

'I have trained in many arts,' said Rast. He changed subjects. 'The Council said you came with a warning.'

'Yes,' said Leona. She looked troubled. 'They would not listen. I can feel the balance of things shifting. The course of the world changes, and *Gaia* is unable to keep equilibrium.' The name sounded different to Karland from when Rast had said it. 'Dark creatures stir, and we cannot speak to them or see their minds. Nameless dreads drag themselves into the light. We are unable to find the source of all this evil, but we have felt it building for many years. I came here to find answers from the so-called seat of wisdom, but I have found nothing but derision and laughter – apart from a few kindly souls that allowed me access to some of their precious library. There were no answers there either. It would take me a lifetime to find any.' She sounded weary. 'To them I am merely a nature priest, a tree-loving fool following a hollow religion. Arrogance! They do not understand. They will not until it is too late.'

'They might listen now,' said Karland, feeling annoyed that this serious woman was so dismissed here. 'We were talking about that-'

'Karland!' said Rast sharply. Karland shut his mouth quickly. Rast smiled at Leona in apology. 'My apologies, Druid. We are not supposed to speak of our meetings with the Council.'

She nodded in understanding, although she was plainly curious. '*You* are not laughing at me, Rast Tal'Orien,' she said thoughtfully.

Rast returned her look impassively.

'No, lady. I am not. You are not the only one to warn the Council of growing dangers. More than that, I cannot say. But I think they are fools to dismiss you so lightly.' Leona smiled at this, her face transformed once more. Karland felt his heart beat a little faster. The stare she was giving Rast was almost uncomfortably direct.

'You are both bound up in this,' she said. 'I feel it. I will not ask further, but perhaps it is worth my requesting to see the Council again. Heed my warning: this darkness is not without direction. Sooner or later, these creatures will come forth in strength, and may all the gods have mercy on those they encounter.'

'I wish you luck, lady,' said Rast. 'I think they will be busy for some time to come. But I hope they listen. I do not think your warnings are insignificant, and they may be related to our own.'

She inclined her head. 'I thank you, Rast Tal'Orien.' Her gaze switched to Karland. 'We may meet again yet, Karland,' she said. 'Perhaps one day I will teach you the peace of the deep woods.' He nodded. Every time she smiled a dimple appeared on her left cheek and he rather liked it.

Without another word she turned and moved off into the next Garden. Karland watched her leave, noticing how smooth her movement was. Remarkably like Rast's, in a way.

Rast bent down towards his ear. 'It is impolite to stare at the motion of a lady's hips, boy.'

'I wasn't!' hissed Karland, his face scarlet.

Rast chuckled. 'Come. Let us go and see if Aldwyn has emerged from his room.'

ର   ഇ

The sky was darkening as they arrived, guards at each end of the hall. Entering the room they found Aldwyn sitting in the sunken fireplace with two of the Council. All the doors were shut, and they were speaking in low tones.

They stood in alarm as they entered. One was Brandwyn Tarqas, and to Karland's surprise the other was Draef Novas. They moved to go, but Aldwyn stopped them.

'Rast. Karland. Please, secure the door.' He turned to the councillors. 'These two may be fully trusted,' he said. 'They know who I really am, and of us. What we say involves them too.'

Tarqas nodded after a brief pause. Novas considered them sharply before he, too, finally nodded and sat. Aldwyn turned to Rast and Karland.

'Draef and Brandwyn are Darostim as well,' he said. Karland was truly surprised. He had thought Novas to be opposed to Aldwyn. They were like chalk and cheese, although the skinny man seemed to have lost a lot of his irritation in private. 'Draef has news that has put a new and, um, worse light on all the scholars that have vanished or turned up... dead.'

Novas sighed heavily.

'Almost all were Darostim. Worse, the deaths are not limited to the Universalia Communia either. All across Anaria, we have been slaughtered, regardless of station. There is no question that we have been compromised, although I do not understand how or why.'

'Whatever this unknown group are trying to prevent us learning, they know we work to uncover the truth,' said Tarqas. 'They are well organised, and must have many members. These deaths have happened across the continent, sometimes within days of each other.

'The Darostim have stood on the brink of the darkness and the light for over a thousand years, but we cannot be the only scholars of ancient knowledge. Gentlemen, I think we must face the possibility that we now face a gathering of those directly opposite to us – a dark brotherhood.'

'But how can they know so much?' asked Rast. 'If what you say is true-'

He paused at a knocking at the door. Holding up one hand, he slid up the steps and across to the door, a dangerous tension in him. Opening the door, he relaxed a little.

'Who is it?' Aldwyn called.

'Captain Robertus.'

'Let him in, Rast.' Rast nodded at the guard captain, who entered grim-faced and crossed to the top of the steps. He showed no great surprise at seeing Tarqas and Novas there.

'Councillor Varelin,' he said, saluting. 'I come to report personally to you, as I have all other council members. Little more than an hour ago Politikus Belen managed to get several of his personal servants out of his quarters. It was a dangerous attempt. We were not expecting them to jump from the balconies on knotted sheets. One fell and broke his skull, and one was caught when he landed badly and snapped his ankle. Two vanished. We searched for them, but failed to find them.

'We can only guess what their motives were. The Politikus cannot be held for questioning, and the time limit Councillor Ulric gave him means we are bound to allow him to continue to prepare to leave. He is due to set out tomorrow at noon with an armed escort to the border. When questioned, he said he did not know why his servants ran, then demanded the release of the injured one into his care for 'questioning'. I have complied, but I do not trust him. I have alerted the rest of the Council; they have asked me to arrange a city wide search with Captain

Dorn. I suggested martial law for the duration, but the council felt it was an overreaction.'

'If anything, it's not reaction enough,' snapped Novas. He turned to Tarqas. 'We should go.'

Tarqas nodded, coughing. Captain Robertus regarded the old man fondly.

'Come, Councillor. I will walk you back to your chambers.' He helped Tarqas out of the door, nodding goodnight to those inside, and shut it. Novas remained standing.

'I had best go as well. There will be another early start tomorrow, and we need rest to make the right choices.' He shot a glance at Aldwyn at that, but said nothing else, then smiled faintly and hugged Aldwyn briefly.

'I am glad you returned, Aldwyn. We may not agree on everything, but you are still my friend. We will find who did this to Kelpas and the rest. You may be sure of that.' Stepping back, he bade them goodnight and left.

Aldwyn caught the look of surprise on Karland's face. 'Draef is a good man,' he said. 'In public he nearly always disagrees with me to ensure no one connects us. It makes it harder to mark us both Darostim... though,' and he chuckled, 'he does often disagree spiritedly with me anyway. Draef doesn't suffer fools lightly.'

'We are no nearer an answer from the Darostim than the Council, it would seem,' remarked Rast. Aldwyn scowled.

Karland changed the subject. 'We met the Druid,' he said hurriedly. 'It *was* the lady I met yesterday.'

Aldwyn's eyes lit up with interest. He looked at Rast, who nodded. 'A real Druid,' he breathed. 'Interesting, mm. What did she say?'

'She spoke of growing chaos and its effects on nature, and a balance tipping, and dark things stirring,' Karland said. Rast laughed quietly.

'There was a little more to it than that, but the boy has captured the essence quite well. She is very good. I did not even know she was tracking us at first in the Gardens. She has spoken before to the Council, but from what she said her warnings went unheeded.'

'She seemed very interested in Rast,' said Karland off-handedly. Rast blinked.

'I seem to remember someone nearly mentioning all the council secrets of the morning to her,' he retaliated. Karland muttered to himself and drifted over to the writing desks.

'You could have told her, I think,' Aldwyn said. 'Druids are not just 'nature priests' as even some of our Council presume. They take their roles very seriously, and evidence suggests they are not just totally dedicated to the natural order of things, but that some of the rumours about their powers are true. As far as a human can be one with nature, they are, and anything unnatural or evil they will attack single-mindedly. Perhaps I should speak to her.'

'Maybe we will see her again tomorrow at some point. In the meantime, I think we should prepare for bed. It will be an early start, another long day... and a critical one for decisions,' said Rast gently.

Aldwyn looked stricken, swallowing hard. He seemed humbled and sad for a moment, and then abruptly this seemed to vanish as he looked up and saw Karland fiddling with a candle on a writing desk out of boredom.

'Karland! What are you doing?' barked Aldwyn.

'Um... seeing what this wax is like, Aldwyn,' Karland said uncertainly. He waved a dripping stick of the red sealing wax that he had been curiously melting over one of the candles while listening.

'Gods! Do you know how much that stuff costs? Leave it alone. Have you got any on the floor?' He squinted at the marble. Karland stepped sideways onto a bright red splotch and shook his head guilelessly.

'Hmm,' muttered Aldwyn. Rast made a noise, but his face was blank when Aldwyn looked at him.

Aldwyn waved his arms at their rooms, a disgusted look on his face.

'I think we had better get to, ah, bed. Before Karland decides to see how much costly vellum he can scribble on.'

⋘　　⋙

Karland slept, dreaming of a small, dark-haired girl whose company he missed. Aldwyn's shut door thankfully blocked his titanic snores; Rast's room was as silent as the grave in contrast.

The night wind blew, gently caressing the dark corners of the balcony. There was a pregnant silence, a pause in the quiet of the night, and then a faint sound came from one of the panes of glass on the balcony door. A gooey mass was smeared softly across the glass, followed by a faint wet crack from a quick blow. The pane fractured, but no shards fell to the floor; whatever was on the pane held it all in place. A carefully gloved hand came through the edge of the shattered mess, seeking the latch, and found it. Gently it clicked it lightly upwards and withdrew.

A faint swirl of wind announced the opening of the door, dying slightly as a shape filled the doorway. A shadow moved forward into the room, carefully sliding its feet along the marble, oddly soundless. It passed over the threshold and moved unerringly towards the room where Aldwyn slept.

Suddenly, it was yanked sideways as a grip like iron clamped on its left forearm. With a shocked hiss of breath, the shape slashed out, raking a curved hand at the attacker. It caught nothing but cloth, which tore as if the fingertips were razors. The figure found its arm and shoulder reversed sharply at an unbearable angle in what it recognised as a keylock.

A split second later, a sharp crack from its shoulder and a gasp announced a broken shoulder blade, and the shape sagged slightly. Recovering quickly, it slid a slim curved blade free from a waist sheath with the other hand, the blade sheathed edge-outwards and following the virtually flat waistline. The figure moved like a striking snake, yet it was nowhere near fast enough.

A blow to the elbow numbed the whole hand. The intruder caught only a glimpse of a huge shape moving incredibly fast directly in front of it in the darkness, and then a crushing blow slammed into its solar plexus, lifting it clean off the ground and straight through the unopened half of the door. Glass shattered with a hundred tinkling reports in the quiet night, and the door split as if made from twigs. Several large pieces of glass embedded themselves in the form, another slicing across the inside of the right bicep, deep enough to release a massive spray of blood that hit the wall as a black curve in the dim moonlight.

A severed artery was the least of its problems; the tumbling shape struck the top of the balcony railing with the back of its knees. A horrified cry burst forth, and it flipped over backwards, smashing its head on the stone as it fell, wheeling off the balcony. Two seconds later there was a solid thud as it met the stone floor four stories below.

Rast slid out onto the balcony, his face grim. He would have preferred to take the intruder alive, but in the dark he had only been able to react to the sudden reach for a *shirka* by instinct. He couldn't risk closing; the assassin had been using a *lovar,* tipping the fingers of one hand with steel claws for grip and attack that were more than likely carrying poison. The weapons marked the man as Ignathian, not Meyari.

His eyes darted left and right, looking for other attackers. There was no one. He looked quickly over the railing at the shape sprawled below at a curt angle, a pool of blood mixing from a broken head and the arm.

He was definitely dead.

Rast heard Karland's door crack open and moved back in. The boy was looking at him sleepily.

'What was that noise?' His eyes popped to wakefulness as he took in the shattered door and the glass everywhere. Rast motioned him back from the destruction and moved to him, murmuring softly.

'Get your things, Karland. I want you to do it quickly and quietly, and then get into Aldwyn's room. Wake him and wait for me. I will be surprised if there is only one.'

Even as he spoke his ears detected a quiet scraping at the main doors. He had barred them last night as usual, but there should be two guards outside in the corridor. He jerked his head at Karland. The boy gave a start and hurried off.

Rast moved away from the window and crossed lightly to the door. He heard muffled swearing on the other side, and the door creaked as someone tried to quietly open it. Behind him Karland scampered across the room to Aldwyn's door.

He tried to make his voice a touch higher.

'Is that you?' he hissed through the door furtively.

The noises stopped, and then someone whispered, 'Open the door, assassin! Welcomers are coming. You made too much bloody noise.'

Rast moved away from the door, backing towards Aldwyn's room, his suspicions confirmed. The assassin had backup to finish the job in a more traditional manner should he fail. He looked up and around the room, thinking quickly.

'Assassin?' the voice hissed. There was a pause, then a curse, and someone hit the doors a heavy blow, realising that something was wrong. The sound of heavy chopping started, the door shuddering from axe blows. Although they were barred, two doors were weaker than one would have been, and they cracked and split after a few more strikes from each axe. Several shapes hurled themselves against them and they burst open.

Figures poured into the room, grey cloaks covering a mix of attire. In the light from the hall which dimly lit the chamber there were flashes of City and Welcomer guard uniforms under a few of the cloaks. Nearly twenty of them rushed through the opening, weapons drawn, and halted. The room was empty, and they took in the damage to the balcony doors.

One moved to the side of the entrance and gestured at all the far rooms and the balcony. Men moved to check as he turned towards the room holding the scholar and beckoned the remaining six men and women to follow.

They were totally unprepared for the huge form that hurtled into their midst from its perch over the entrance where it had been holding on to the ornamental niches and corbels in the wall. The whole group collapsed into each other, one woman yelling in shock. The shape lashed out precisely with elbows, feet and hands, and three were down before the rest recovered and attacked.

One man lunged at the broad shape, which somehow ducked and flowed away, leaving his sword standing from the chest of the leader. The man coughed in shock and sank twitching, his eyes disbelieving the sight of his chest laid open through to his lungs.

Rast came out of his crouch with one big fist braced in the other in front of his chest, his extended elbow sweeping upward with unstoppable force as he twisted round. The elbow shattered another man's jaw, nearly severing his tongue with his own teeth.

The man next to him swung an overhead chop with his axe and watched in disbelief as the huge man seemed to fall over backwards away from the strike. He did not see the foot which snapped upwards and sideways as a counterbalance, slamming into his neck below the ear. It hit so hard that he flipped over in mid-air, landing in an unconscious heap, his clavicle snapping at an awkward angle. A man and woman that had fallen were up again, groggy, and Rast exploded into motion, slamming blows alternately into one then the other, ducking under arms, cracking ribs, and jamming stiff fingers into necks. Choking and bruised, they collapsed after a few seconds of the disorientating barrage without even managing a defence.

Already the other men were streaming back into the room from the balcony and the other two quarters. Unable to make out exactly what was going on in the dimly lit flurry, they approached cautiously. As the last two men fell, they saw a lone figure standing and roared in rage, secrecy forgotten, racing to engage.

Rast ducked, scooping up the fallen axe. As the first man reached him, he swept the axe in an underhand sweep as if he was knocking a stone along the floor. The unorthodox move confused the slight swordsman, his sword raised to ward off a chopping blow, and the axe head swept up and took him under the sternum so hard that he left the floor.

Rast grunted in effort and continued the sweep upwards, his muscles bulging as he twisted. The swordsman jerked into the air, his eyes already glazing in death. Swept overhead as Rast dropped to a knee, the inert form flew off the axe to slam into the wall even as his killer spun back around on one knee, the axe chopping out sideways. It took the next man in the right knee, tearing his lower leg half off and sending him tumbling. Several more men tripped over him, falling in a pained heap and stabbing each other with drawn weapons.

Rast whirled upright, ducked under a sword that would have beheaded him and continued the spin, jerking an elbow up into the back of the swordsman's head. The stunned man flew forward, poking himself in the shin with his own weapon and howling in anger, his vision bursting with white. The next woman didn't even have time to get her knife up before a solid oak haft cracked into her temple, dropping her like a stone. Rast moved so fast that the attackers were unable to strike him. A few blows sliced into his cloak, but none connected.

The other axeman swung his weapon up, tightening his stomach. He was well trained and knew how to fight axe-to-axe. He swung down hard, ready to curve the trajectory sideways when the big man swung to block, and blinked when Rast dropped his axe completely.

Two iron hands shot up and stopped the axe mid-strike as if it had hit a tree trunk. Barely did the axeman register this than a foot hit him in the testicles so hard it lifted him two inches from the floor. He came down in a knock-kneed foetal position; the only thing that stopped him falling was the rising knee that hit him like granite in the face, breaking his nose and knocking him over backwards unconscious.

There was a rising sound in the corridor as more armed men raced towards the room. Rast scooped up the other axe, and ran with one in each huge hand directly towards the pile of men that were scrambling towards him in rage. Surprised, they braced for the attack, but at the last second he veered towards the door of the scholar instead and burst through it, the men on his heels.

The door slammed shut again, and there was the sound of something heavy falling across it. Two distant chunking sounds rang out as the axes bit into wooden floor. The assailants shouted in anger as they realised that the figure had taken the only two axes that they had. Calling into the corridor, they attacked the door with vigour.

Within minutes their numbers had multiplied threefold, and they attacked in desperation. They were long past stealth, and they could hear fighting nearby as their comrades were overwhelmed by the now-alerted Welcomer Guard.

More axes were brought forward and they bit into the door. Most of the men were more eager to kill their recent foe who had killed and maimed over a third of their party than they were for the death of the scholar. He was just business.

'Come on!' roared one of the attackers, as they shouted and slammed axes into the doors. 'Kill them *now*!'

The axes hacked a final hole in the door to show a dark room with a large cabinet on its side across the door. 'Force that door!' commanded the attacker, waving his arm. Two men threw themselves at the door but it didn't move an inch. 'Again!' he yelled. The door still didn't give, although there was an ominous creak the other side as the cabinet flexed under the blow.

He opened his mouth again, and a knot of Welcomer guards erupted through the ruined doors. Robertus was at their head, driving into the side of the milling mass of attackers.

Well trained, armed, and armoured, they hacked their way through the attackers, who suddenly realised they were cut off from escape. Nearly half broke and ran for the balcony, looking for a way out. Two tried to climb down and got stuck, clinging precariously. One hooked an elbow around a railing and called for help. The other scrabbled for a moment and then fell with a despairing scream.

Still others threw their weapons down or over the edge and stood with their hands up in surrender. The rest fought on grimly. All of the attackers with guard uniforms under their cloaks realised that, for them, there was no way back. Several times a Welcomer was shocked to recognise a face; several were hewn down as they tried to recover from their surprise.

The end was inevitable. Shortly the last attacker was down or captured, and the rest were forced to their knees with hands on heads. It took three guards to haul the wailing man on the balcony back to safety. As the other Welcomers began the grim task of lining up the dead and collecting the wounded, a guard wearing the bars of a lieutenant called through the door to Aldwyn.

'Councillor Varelin! Are you all right?'

'Unharmed,' came the querulous reply. There were squeaky-pull sounds of blades being levered out of wood followed by a dragging sound marking the removal of the heavy cabinet. The door opened and Aldwyn shuffled out, fright and exhaustion rimming his eyes. The guard saw that both axes had been slammed deep into the floor right behind the toppled cabinet, preventing it from moving and probably saving their lives.

Karland came out next, as pale as a bed sheet. Rast stepped out last, poised as always despite being covered in blood. His cloak was soaked and sliced beyond repair, but he appeared unharmed. He stared at the bodies and prisoners without emotion, and then turned to the guard.

'They were specifically after the Councillor, Lieutenant. These attacked after I killed an assassin.' He gestured at the balcony and the lieutenant nodded. Rast looked around.

'Where is Captain Robertus?'

The lieutenant sighed heavily and pointed to the lines of dead and wounded near the door, his face twisted in anger and sorrow.

'No,' whispered Karland.

SIXTEEN

Captain Robertus was lying near the door. His youthful face was calm, with no hint of anger, fear, or the ever-present grin that Karland liked so much about him. His complexion was pale, and a smear of blood marred his left cheek. Someone had closed his eyes.

Captain Dorn stood looking at him, his jaw clenching. Blood-stained hands rested on the twin shortswords at his waist.

'He was returning from walking Councillor Tarqas back,' he said, biting his words off bitterly. 'Unarmed, apart from a dagger. Must have stayed to talk. He always did like to spend time with his uncle.'

'His uncle?' said Aldwyn, dismayed.

'Yes. Jerome Robertus worked his way up the ranks and proved himself every step of the way so he would never be accused of special treatment. Brandwyn Tarqas never gave it, either, but he always had a special place for Jerome. He was a popular man, and the only relative left to him.'

'I never knew,' said Aldwyn.

Dorn shook his head wearily.

'I was meant to meet him tonight. The lieutenant reported that Robertus heard a disturbance – probably your dispatching of the assassin, Master Tal'Orien – and was heading this way when he happened to see several suspicious men heading for his uncle's room. He followed, and managed to prevent them from killing Councillor Tarqas, but was wounded in the fight. Still, he collected a squad and came here. I met him on the way as I looked for him, and joined their ranks. We met resistance several times, and were separated; we had not expected three separate battles. A lot of traitors were involved tonight, perhaps a hundred all told, and all within the Sanctum.' His eyes flashed. 'Some were ours, for Delmatra's sake! I myself cut down a man I have known for five years.' This betrayal seemed to fuel his anger. 'Jerome was so worried about Councillor Aldwyn that he charged straight in, and was stabbed from behind as he fought by one of his own guards – one he mistook for a friend. He never stood a chance.'

'You lost more than one good man tonight,' said Rast, looking at the dead Welcomers.

The lieutenant next to them bared his teeth.

'Curse them! May maggots fester and eat their guts from the inside out!' he spat, looking at the prisoners.

Karland nodded numb agreement. He felt like throwing up. Robertus looked as if he were sleeping, apart from his unnatural limpness, pallor and the large dark ragged hole they had seen under his right armpit before his hands were folded serenely on his chest.

Dorn continued. 'The Welcomers have been fully mobilised, and my own Guard is locking down the city. Even now we are checking all Council members and the Universalia Communia. There may have been other attempts. One of the guards of your level was in with these filth, and he murdered his colleague to allow them to your door unchallenged. It was him I killed, after he stabbed his Captain. I will find the people behind this, and they will pay.' There was no outrage in his voice, just a statement of fact. He turned to the lieutenant.

'In the absence of a Welcomer Captain, I'm assuming command. Keep the prisoners here, unharmed. They need to be questioned, but the Council can decide what to do with them. They directly attacked two Council members! Ensure they are guarded closely. I am going to escort Councillor Varelin to Councillor Tarqas. Despatch guards to escort the rest of the Council to those quarters as well, and send a full squad to take Politikus Belen into custody immediately; this follows the escape of his men too closely to be mere coincidence. And find your ranking officer under Captain Robertus and brief him. I want him fully up to date.' Karland barely heard the words. He could not even shiver at the thought that there had been an assassin in their room; instead the grey numbness blocked all else out. He could not stop looking at Robertus. It was hard to believe he was gone.

'Get me General Colcos as well. He will need to be present. If anything critical comes up, find me. I will return shortly.'

He turned on his heel. 'Please follow me, Councillor.'

They exited the room as the lieutenant began calling orders. The commotion had roused two whole Academia from slumber, and the curious were clustered at the edge of a blockade of guards and on balconies opposite. Welcomer guards lined every corridor in force, with more arriving as they travelled.

'Get these people back!' ordered Captain Dorn. 'And clear the path to Level Six, Mathematica Academia.'

'Sir!' shouted one of the guards, another lieutenant.

Their progress was rapid. Barely ten minutes later, they climbed a set of stairs to the sixth level where Tarqas had his residence. There was a squad of guards outside his door, and voices were coming from within.

Without pause Dorn saluted the Welcomers and opened the doors. His rank gave him equal status to Robertus, and he was not questioned, although the guards noted Rast's blood-covered form with wary eyes. They moved inside to find Tarqas flanked by Mira Lyss and Nessa Contemus. Guards stood on the balcony, watchful. The room was more ornate than the one they had, and smaller, but retained its functional design.

'Aldwyn! Thank the gods you are all right,' quavered Tarqas. He glanced at Karland and Rast, and then looked enquiringly at Captain Dorn. 'Captain, thank you for your help tonight. It was fortunate that you were here. When will Captain Robertus join us?'

Dorn stood fully at attention, his face pale but resolute. 'Councillor Tarqas,' he said formally. 'It is with the greatest regret and sadness that I must report that Captain Jerome Robertus fell in combat, performing his duty to the Council. He protected Councillor Varelin unto death.' He held the old man's eyes, desperately trying to convey his condolences.

Brandwyn Tarqas breathed deeply, looking at him, and then tried to speak. His face was grey.

'Wha-... what?'

'I am deeply sorrowful, Councillor. Captain Robertus was one of the casualties of the attack tonight.' Dorn's face was sad, his jaw set.

'No,' whispered Tarqas. 'Jerome.'

He covered his eyes with a shaking hand, and then turned away. His shoulders shook, and he seemed to wilt. Councillor Lyss put a hand to her mouth, and tears filled her eyes. She looked at Contemus, who stood, hardly breathing, her head bent and her eyes staring at the floor. Nessa looked up and shook her head sadly. She motioned to Lyss and then walked slowly to Tarqas. Her hand touched his shoulder, but he did not respond. Slowly she drew him to her and moved towards the bedroom. He moved with her, leaning on her as if his legs could not support him. Karland felt the first pangs of sorrow and wondered how much worse for his uncle it must be.

As they went in and the door shut, Lyss wiped her eyes quickly. She sniffed, and then spoke, steel in her voice.

'Captain. What exactly happened tonight?'

'We are uncertain as yet, Councillor. It appears that a renegade strike of more than one hundred, including some of the Welcomers and City Guard, attacked with the sole intent of killing Councillors Tarqas and Aldwyn.' Her face registered shock. 'Captain Robertus killed those that came for Councillor Tarqas, and then fought his way with a squad to the main attack, which was aimed precisely at Councillor Varelin.'

'There was an assassin,' interjected Rast softly. 'Ignathian, I believe. He broke in with poisoned weapons. The other attack came after he failed; I did not manage to capture him alive.' His tone held regret. 'He was well trained and swift. I am sorry.'

'That you countered him at all is something to be thankful for,' remarked Lyss. 'Assassins! Traitors! Here! Never in the history of the Sanctum has this happened. How many were captured?'

'Upwards of twenty,' responded Dorn. 'I ordered them detained in the room until you can decide the best course of action.'

'How many did we lose?'

Dorn closed his eyes; there had been no way to avoid this question.

'Of the defenders, we lost fourteen Welcomers including Captain Robertus. We need to urgently review checks on our guards; I counted seven Welcomers amongst the attackers. All but one are dead, and I do not think he will survive long.'

'See that he talks before he passes,' was her unemotional response. She looked at Aldwyn. 'Councillor Varelin... Aldwyn. I am glad you are unharmed. This is the worst time to reiterate it, but now more than ever I must stress the importance of our request of you. It is abundantly clear that you are far more important than we realised.'

Aldwyn held up a trembling hand.

'Madam Arbitrator, there is no need to persuade me. I am not safe anywhere, mm, it seems. I cannot believe someone struck here, in the heart of the Sanctum. It is obvious that they try to silence me. I fear the hunters have caught up.' He bit his lip. 'There is more you must know before others arrive. Captain, you are under strictest oath to not repeat this. Councillor, I will accept your word as well.' Dorn saluted Aldwyn, his face grave. Mira Lyss took no offense at Aldwyn's tone and nodded.

'Just before the attack, Brandwyn and Draef were in my room. We... we are Darostim, all three.'

Lyss's eyes widened. 'Darostim!' she breathed. 'I thought that an old myth.'

'It is not,' said Aldwyn. 'We work to keep the balance and knowledge of this world. Draef told me that nearly every scholar that has died recently has been

Darostim. Worse, even outside the Universalia Communia there are also members of the Darostim being murdered one by one. We have been discovered, targeted. I believe that was the focus of the attack tonight.'

Councillor Lyss shook her head. She seemed to be accepting the news better than Karland had. 'I cannot believe what I am hearing, but neither can I deny it. Darostim! Why would you be the targets?'

'Because we have discovered something they wish us not to pass on, perhaps. We are some of the most learned beings in the lands, from all races and backgrounds. It is we who stand watchful between the light of truth and knowledge, and the agents of chaos and evil,' answered Aldwyn. 'If we are removed, who will be able to use the information we have gained? Who will warn the world of the darkness which threatens?'

Several guards entered the room, followed by council members, and one crossed to murmur to Dorn. The incoming Councillors moved to Lyss, demanding to know what was happening. Aldywn fell silent.

Karland was thinking hard. Something that Aldwyn had said poked at his mind repeatedly, and he tried to concentrate on it. It was hard; his mind was whirling from this evening, and he kept seeing Robertus's pale face.

'Aldwyn,' he said, frowning, pinning down his nagging though. He was ignored. He tried again.

'Aldwyn.'

Rast nudged Aldwyn, who turned. 'Mm?'

'You said Councillor Novas was one of you, and you and Councillor Tarqas were attacked-'

'Gods!' Aldwyn stiffened in alarm, even as Captain Dorn waved the guard away.

'Councillor Lyss. I regret to inform that Councillor Draef Novas has been found dead in his quarters.' Dorn looked utterly frustrated, impotent and furious. 'He was discovered with his throat cut.'

Aldwyn stumbled to a nearby seat, the second shock too much to take. Lyss stared at Dorn.

'No sign of the murderer?' she asked woodenly.

Dorn shook his head.

Lyss gestured to the rest of the council, who were staring at Dorn in shock. 'I must inform you all of what has happened,' she said. 'A moment, please, Captain.' Dorn saluted and moved to the guards at the door.

Off to one side, Rast stood with a hand on Aldwyn's shoulders. 'I am sorry, old friend,' he said. Aldwyn had tears in his eyes.

'B-but – Draef! And Robertus. Ahh, Brandwyn.' He shook his head wearily.

'I know this is hard, but we must make our decision quickly,' said Rast softly. 'We are a sitting target here. They know where you are, and if we do not move soon, they will try again. If they succeed all this becomes irrelevant.'

Karland held his breath. He sensed a tipping point for Aldwyn. There was a long pause, and then the old man gulped and nodded.

'I place myself entirely in your hands, Rast. Let us see what we can do to thwart our enemies. If you had left on your own, I would be dead now, and I am tired of losing friends. Tired of being scared.'

Karland felt both relief and fright. They could have been dead tonight. He had never seen his friend look so – so *old*.

Rast nodded and turned to the Council, who wore mixed expressions of shock, disbelief, and anger. 'We will do what you ask, but we must leave tonight. *Now*. We cannot lose pursuers if we can be predicted.'

Captain Dorn turned from the guard at the door, raising his hands. 'Councillors!' he called. 'Meyari Politikus Belen is gone.'

'Gone?' demanded Ulric. His big hands twitched.

'Does the ill news not end?' breathed Mira Lyss.

'We think he used the attack as a diversion – possibly he even ordered it. The guards left his quarters to investigate the commotion and he slipped out. He is nowhere in the Sanctum that we can find, and every Meyari he had with him is also gone. I ordered a city-wide lockdown alert as soon as the attack was over. He may still be here.'

'*I want him found*,' snarled Ulric. 'And someone clap the bastard in irons this time! Where in the hells is Colcos?'

'En route, sir. Once here he will take command of the Welcomer Guard from me.'

'Good. I want that Meyari army destroyed. Belen just forfeited his time limit.' The big man was grinding his teeth in anger. Karland almost wanted to be with the army, to strike at the people that had killed Robertus and tried to kill Aldwyn.

Mira Lyss spoke to Aurelia Brókova, who moved to the room where Tarqas and Contemus were shut away. Knocking quietly, she opened the door and slipped inside. A minute later, she reappeared, followed by Brandwyn Tarqas, red eyed and haggard, and Nessa Contemus. They both moved slowly, as if they had greatly aged in the last few minutes.

They reached the rest, and Mira Lyss spoke decisively, her control returned in full.

'We have a decision to make, here and now. We have been attacked at our heart. This strike should never have been possible! Never have we been compromised this way, in the heart of liberty in Anaria. Instead, we have fifteen brave men dead, traitors in our midst, and we must ballot war with Meyar. This madness cannot be excused. Councillor Novas is dead. Captain Robertus is dead. Assassins struck at Aldwyn and Brandwyn. The rest of us were unharmed this night, but for how long? Now more than ever, we need to find the heart of this chaos. Aldwyn Varelin... I humbly apologise. We should have listened, but we were all wrong. We have paid dearly.'

Aldwyn looked around at them all, his eyes falling on his old friend last and holding his red-eyed gaze. 'The thrust of this attack was mainly aimed at me. I endanger you all by staying. What matter if I die here or on the road? At least I might accomplish something first. I will go.' He looked sick, but spoke firmly. 'I will go because I am needed to, but I will also go for the memory of those who died to protect me tonight. Can I be any less courageous?

'Vote on a war if you must, but you know deep inside that as of this moment Eordeland is already at war, and I fear things will get worse. I intend to be on my way within the hour with Rast. Karland...'

Karland's heart hammered suddenly. He wasn't sure what he wanted the decision to be.

Rast interjected. 'Karland should come as well.'

'Is that wise?' said Councillor Holmson.

'Is he safer here?' countered Rast. 'He has been seen with Aldwyn. If we go, I will not be here to protect him. We can educate him – in survival as well as lore. He will be as safe with us as any are in these times. Besides, with him along we can allay suspicions. He is the right age for late apprenticeship, and is already a student of ours.'

'He is part of this,' agreed Aldwyn reluctantly.

'But he's just a boy!' said Augusta Andragostin, and several others shook their heads at this new folly. Karland felt the frustration at the last few days boil up, and before he realised what he was doing, he had spoken.

'You didn't listen to Aldwyn before and look what happened. I don't want to be left alone here. I want to help, and I want to stay alive. Will I live longer with Rast, or you?'

He glowered, and then realised whom he had spoken to. His mouth seemed to weld itself shut, and he scuttled back towards Rast under the glares of several of the leaders of Eordeland.

'The boy is right,' said the huge man quietly, putting his hand on Karland's shoulder. Karland relaxed. Rast was like a rock in the confusion and upheaval of the last few weeks. 'How many of you paid heed to our warnings? How many dismissed the Druid, too? I think we have all become too steadfast in our beliefs. It is time to open our eyes.'

Eremus snapped, 'Listen-', but before she got any further, she was cut short by a tired voice from the side.

'They are both right,' said Tarqas. He straightened, and spoke more forcefully. 'They are both right. If we had listened, been prepared... maybe Jerome would not be dead. Maybe the Darostim would not be being hunted down. Maybe chaos would not have found a hold in the greedy hearts and minds of our people, even here where we are so proud of our democracy.'

Alarm appeared on Aldwyn's face, and whispers of surprise sprang up from the Council. *Darostim* was repeated with varying degrees of belief.

'The time for secrets is past, Aldwyn,' said the old man, his face drawn. 'If we do not share what we know, we are doomed. The Darostim may already be doomed. If we cannot trust the people in this room now, whom can we trust?'

Aldwyn nodded reluctantly. 'I am so sorry, Brandwyn.'

'I do not blame you, old friend,' said Tarqas softly. 'Your decision to go or stay would not have affected tonight, and you tried to tell us. You tried. They did not entirely succeed; had they killed us all, the rest would have never known the truth. This goes far beyond Meyar.'

Aldwyn took off his spectacles and pinched his nose, closing his eyes wearily. 'Can I request just one thing? Can this Leona be found and brought here?'

Mira Lyss nodded to a guard, who left to bring the Druid. 'What will you need?' she asked. Rast shook his head.

'Not much. Supplies. Food. If you can make our horses ready, we will leave immediately. There will be no more sleep tonight for anyone, I think.'

'You are right about that, Tal'Orien,' rumbled the large form of Ulric. He looked more normal next to Rast. It wasn't until you saw him next to a guard or councillor that his bear-like frame stood out. 'The Council will not sleep for a long time. We must vote on war, and sweep the Sanctum clean of these traitors. We must also fulfil our ancient edicts and lock down the Combic Libraries. Already too much has been lost, and I suspect now that fire was not a mistake.'

Karland wondered how the people in the Croft would feel about war, imagined his father with a weapon. It was a grim thought, and must have shown on his face. Ulric smiled.

'It is what we exist for,' he said. 'To preserve the freedom and knowledge of humanity against disaster.' He lowered his voice so that only Karland and Aldwyn heard. 'And it may be that you are not the only Darostim on the Council.' His eyes glittered from beneath bushy brows, and then he called a guard over to collect their belongings from their ruined quarters. As he left, another entered and reported to Mira Lyss.

'Councillor. The surviving traitor is dying, but we extracted information from him before he lost consciousness. He spoke the name Ventran, and of a cleansing army. He was also branded with the symbol of Terome.'

'Terome,' Councillor Lyss muttered. She shook her head. 'And two names: Sontles and Ventran. Maybe one of these is responsible. Thank you. Interrogate the others… and arrange physical inspections of everyone within The Sanctum for brands. We will have to seek what connections we can.' The guard saluted and left.

Barely twenty minutes later the Druid arrived in the chamber. She came into the room like a cat, graceful and lithe under her cloak. Casting her hood back, her strange eyes regarded Rast, and her delicate nostrils flared.

'You have sown much death tonight, Rast Tal'Orien,' she said. 'Many fell. I smell their defeat on you, *Banidróttin.*' The last word was almost purred, a low growl in her throat, yet she did not look contemptuous. Admiration was closer to it. Karland wondered what she meant.

'An interesting name,' remarked Ulric cryptically. 'I'd agree, having heard how many fell. Mistress Leona, you are here at the request of Aldwyn Varelin.' He indicated the old man, who fiddled with his spectacles and peered at Leona.

'Oh, mm, my,' he said. 'I had no idea Druids were so pretty.'

She looked at him politely, although a faint flush tinged her cheeks. 'Master Varelin,' she said with a small smile. Her eyes turned to Karland, who felt his ears heat and redden. 'Karland,' she greeted him gravely.

'Hello, Leona.'

'Aldwyn, please, Leona-?' asked Aldwyn, with a tilt of his head. Leona smiled.

'We have little need of other names in our circle, Master Varelin. We know who we are. Tell me, why have you called for me?'

'Leona, I know that you have spoken to Karland and Rast. I know of some of your warnings. I also know you are a Druid, and I realise what that means more profoundly than they do. Can you tell me how long you have known of this imbalance you mentioned?'

'We have felt it growing for years, Aldwyn. Remote places are becoming abundant with things that nature has rejected. The great woods you call the Dimnesdair are no longer trodden with impunity, even by my people. Creatures and evil men spread everywhere. It is not just in the towns of men that darkness stirs.'

'Years,' muttered Aldwyn. 'It took me years of study to see even part of a pattern, and only because I was, ah, pointed in that direction by vague portents in old tomes. You could have saved me a lot of effort.'

'At first we did not know how widespread it was,' responded Leona. 'When it was so obvious it fairly screamed to every living thing, we decided we could wait no longer for help. Our efforts to stem the tide were in vain, and we needed aid.' Her voice took on a tone of reproof. 'So I came here for wisdom and was dismissed as a fool. I only hope it is not past time to do anything.'

'Yes, well,' said Whyll Regus, looking uncomfortable. 'As to that: on behalf of the Council of Twelve, please accept our sincere apologies. You were not the only one to have been ignored.' He glanced at Aldwyn. 'Wisdom brings its own fetters, it seems. The broader our learning, the narrower our view becomes.'

'Mm,' muttered Aldwyn.

Tarqas had also moved over, and he added, 'For what it is worth, Madam, I tried to give you what help I could. I am sorry it was not enough.' Leona looked at him intently, and then smiled her sharp smile.

'I remember you, Councillor Tarqas. You gave me access to the Archives.'

'What is done is done,' said Aldwyn. 'Leona, I called you here to ask for your company. We are journeying to find the cause of this chaos and see how it can be averted – if it can. The realms are on the brink of war and now you say nature is out of balance too. You could help us greatly.'

The thought of Leona helping them on their quest relieved Karland more than he would admit. She was deep and gentle, wild and alluring, and reassuring in a totally different way from Rast or Aldwyn.

'Are you sure this is wise?' broke in Councillor Regus. 'You are already taking a child with you. She is an unknown.' Karland bristled at being called a child again.

'A Druid is above reproach, Regus,' snapped Tarqas. 'You obviously know little of them. Leona may sense things we could not, and a Druid will fight chaos to the death with more powers than just mere flesh. I would have thought anything that increased the chances of success would be welcomed!' The old man glared at the younger Councillor. Regus raised his hands placatingly.

'I merely ask, Councillor. I meant no disrespect.' He bowed slightly to the Druid.

'Leona.' Rast broke in, his deep voice urgent. 'We need to leave, tonight. Will you come with us?'

She nodded. 'There is little for me here. We will find this evil together, Rast Tal'Orien.' She turned to Aldwyn. 'I will come with you, and your cub, and the

Banidróttin. I will await you by the stable. Come soon.' She left the room as gracefully as she had entered it.

SEVENTEEN

'Where will you go first?' asked Tarqas as they walked down to the stables. He seemed reluctant to say goodbye to his old friend. Aldwyn looked at him and blew his breath out.

'I need the Book of Sarthos,' he said. 'Without it, we have few clues. I never expected to find it gone here. That was a copy derived directly from the scrolls themselves.'

'It is a heavy blow,' said Tarqas wearily. 'We have... all lost much recently.' His face was sad. Aldwyn gripped his shoulder briefly, and continued.

'There is yet hope. The library of Thingos was thought lost, but much of it still lies safe. That is where I have been, studying.' He looked over at Karland, who wasn't listening, and added quietly, 'And more. The boy may be as much a target as I am.'

'Really?' Tarqas looked at the boy, who was staring at the gates ahead. 'Thingos? But his sect was destroyed. I thought their library burned to the ground.'

'Oh, the main one was, mm. But many of the older scrolls and books were securely stored in a hidden library, and that was safe. It took me years to find but it was beyond my expectations when I finally located it. There is a copy of the Book of Sarthos there, amongst other things.'

Tarqas looked almost happy for the first time. 'Delmatra be praised! Normally I would say those books should be moved here but with recent events maybe they are safer there. So you go there to collect it? Then where?'

'Hmm. Meyar, I suspect. The less anyone knows of my path, the better protected I am.' For a moment his fear nearly broke through again. 'I am frightened, old friend. I may not return. But I will not let war or worse take us if it can be helped.'

Tarqas nodded. 'You have Rast. I would rather him than a platoon of our best guards. His name is whispered amongst them now. Even before tonight his deeds were renowned.'

They reached the stables to find Rast ready to mount. Aldwyn's small but sturdy chest was already loaded and Hjarta was in his collar, reflectively chewing at something. Stryke stamped further back in the gloom next to a beautiful chestnut palfrey with no tack or saddle. Leona stood beside it, her green eyes glinting in the flickering light from the stable lamps.

Aldwyn turned to Tarqas as Karland scrambled into the cart.

'Brandwyn. I am truly sorry for your loss. I never knew.'

The other returned a small smile. 'You were never meant to. He was a good man, my sister's son. His parents would have been as proud as I was. As I *still* am.'

Aldwyn embraced his friend briefly. 'He achieved great things, all on his own merit from what I understood. You should be proud.' He sighed. 'If I find a source to all of this, if I find out what this key is and why Kelpas sent it to me, I will send word.'

Tarqas raised his hand to stop him. 'Go with Delmatra, old friend. I have faith in you. You have been the only one to suspect danger all along. If you fail, be sure of one thing: no one else could have done more. While you are gone, we will also search here. This reference to an army – perhaps it means the Meyari? And this name, Ventran... is he behind all this? Why? We must find answers.' He shook his head, and then turned as Captain Dorn appeared. 'Ah, Captain. Come to see our little fellowship off?' he asked.

The Captain returned a small smile. 'Sir.' He nodded to the group, and held out a small scroll tube. 'Councillor Varelin. The Eordeland Guard and the Council extend you this writ, which will commandeer without question any Eordeland unit not engaged in combat. It is merely a precaution.' He handed it to Aldwyn, and then sighed. 'I wish I could send troops with you, but until General Colcos returns and we are back at full strength, I can spare not even one squad.' He glanced at Rast, and then Leona. 'But you should be in safe hands.'

Rast nodded, and clasped Dorn's hand. 'Captain. Thank you. I hope we meet again in better times.'

The Captain smiled. 'Indeed. And if war does come... it would at least be my honour to fight beside you, Master Tal'Orien.'

Rast also smiled.

'Likewise. Your bladework is famed.' He swung himself onto Stryke. 'Until we meet again.'

Aldwyn had heard of guard Captain Dorn's skill. He was rumoured to be one of the finest swordsmen alive and was one of the few who could wield two swords perfectly. He imagined the two fighting together would be quite a sight to behold.

He flapped the reins and followed Stryke as Leona swung smoothly up onto her horse behind them. As they passed, Tarqas raised his hand in farewell, Dorn standing tall beside him.

They trotted down the cobbles toward the gate. Now, it was shut with a thick contingent of guards surrounding it. One swung the gate open and saluted as Rast guided Stryke out onto the main thoroughfare and headed west.

The city was quiet, although in some areas it was never truly asleep. Guards were in evidence everywhere, and some sections were in uproar as the guards swept for the missing Politikus. When they arrived at the western gate, towering in the middle of the fifty foot walls, they found a full three squads of guards turning people back as they tried to exit. The sergeant peered at them and sighed.

'Councillor?' Aldwyn nodded. 'This is going to raise merry hell, pardon my Kharkistani. Captain Dorn sent word. I hope he sends reinforcements as well; this lot could turn ugly.' He motioned to a squad, which surrounded the cart and the horses, and they walked forward through the crowd. Even at this time people were expecting to come and go, and seeing the cart allowed through brought angry questions from traders and public alike. Perhaps a border fort would expect to have the gates shut at night, but Darost was the hub of eastern trade in a peaceful land, and the gates had not been barred in his memory.

The other side they found another crowd with several more squads holding them back. The gate shut solidly, cutting off the uproar from inside. Rast heeled Stryke for the opening the guards made, and the crowd fell back. Hjarta gamely followed behind, the cart creaking and rattling, and Aldwyn caught glimpses of wild eyed men and women glaring at them as they galloped past, the cart jouncing slightly on its thick leather straps.

Rast kept the pace as high as it was safe to in the dark all the way to the bridge leading to the northern farmsteads. They turned once more across the river Run into the trees towards Hoeven Lake and set off at a trot.

'Are we visiting the farm again?' Karland asked in surprise.

Aldwyn nodded, thinking of how the next few weeks would unfold. 'It seems we retrace our steps, and I need somewhere safe and quiet to think, away from Darost... then, mm, on to the library of Thingos before heading north and then west across the Nassmoors. I need the extant copy of Sarthos' book!' His attention drifted again. He was still frightened, but a sense of inevitability had come over him, and he still had many secrets he had not told the others. Karland was not destined to be a bystander in events.

He was brought back to the present as Karland turned to the shadow of their silent companion, trotting alongside the left of the cart. 'You will get to meet my friend Xhera, Leona.'

She smiled slightly. 'Is she your mate? You seem unsure.' Karland stammered, and Aldwyn chuckled for the first time since the events of the night.

'I am sorry,' laughed Leona. 'I tease you, perhaps unfairly. Youth is an uncertain time. I would be honoured to meet your friend.' Aldwyn took pity on Karland and intervened.

'You have a lovely horse, mm, Leona. A mare?'

'Yes.'

'She seems well bred, although I am no expert. What is her name?'

Leona laughed quietly. 'She has her own, yet none I have given her. What need has she of a human name? She is a palfrey, and from a long line of good breeding. We have access to excellent stock, and they usually agree to bear us.'

'Agree?' asked Karland.

'Of course. I would not ask her to bear me if she did not wish to do so. That would be unfair.'

Karland shook his head. He was quiet for a moment, and then turned to Aldwyn.

'Will it be long before we are there?'

'Gods preserve us!' said Aldwyn in despair. 'We have only just set out! Patience, boy, patience. Before sunset tomorrow, with any luck. We will be camping soon enough, I'll wager.'

Perhaps half an hour later, Rast pulled them over into some trees and settled the horses in the darkness.

'No fire tonight,' he said. 'We need only sleep. Tomorrow we will reach the farm.'

൦ଃ   ෨

Karland dreamed fuzzy, half-remembered dreams that night. When he awoke well after dawn, he couldn't remember any of them beyond a disquieting sense of loss. He lay there, feeling rapturous. Today he would see Xhera again! He wondered how she was faring. When they arrived, it would be barely two weeks since he had left her. And yet so much had happened since then – earth-changing events. Councils, Druids, traitors, assassins, legends, keys to hidden power… and overshadowing it all, the loss of someone he admired.

He thought of all the things he would tell her, and then a sudden thought struck him like a lead club. What if he had misunderstood their friendship? Suddenly he was nervous. Infused by a burst of energy he sat up and struggled free of his blankets to find Rast sitting on a nearby log, watching him in amusement.

'Bad dreams?' he said over the ever-present rasping of Aldwyn. Leona was nowhere in sight. Karland shook his head.

'Do you think... do you think that Xhera still likes me?'

Rast laughed quietly. 'Karland, it has hardly been twelve days. You have a deep bond, and leaped to her defence uncaring of your own life. She is unlikely to forget you.'

Karland could not help the beaming grin that broke over his face. The big man laughed again, and picked up a long stick lying nearby. He looked at Karland gravely, leaned out and prodded the bundle with Aldwyn in the centre. It heaved sideways, the snores interrupted, and a bizarre lip-smacking came from it. Rast prodded again, and the scholar flailed at the irritation, waking up in the process.

'What? Eh?' he scrabbled for his spectacles, so unlike the others in evidence in the Sanctum which were designed to sit only on the nose. His hooked over the ears on a frame – his own modification, as he had proudly told Karland more than once.

Jamming them on, he glared suspiciously at them. Karland was laughing, and Rast sat stone-faced, looking in another direction.

'Impudent boy,' he muttered, glaring at him.

Karland's laugh sputtered out. 'What?' he demanded, disbelieving. Aldwyn scowled and rolled out of bed, stumbling off to the bushes.

Karland looked at Rast. 'You deliberately let me take the blame for that,' he accused. Rast shrugged.

They were eating breakfast when Leona stepped into the camp. She nodded to them all. 'The trees whisper freely. These woods are not so wild, but it is good to be back among the trees.' She smiled and breathed in deeply through her nose. 'There is no one nearby.' Karland saw the slight dimple again on her cheek again.

She looks happier, he thought. The city hadn't seemed to be a good place for her.

Leona glanced at him and saw him watching her. 'You seem at ease in *these* woods, at least,' she remarked with a smile.

They packed and hitched the dray to the cart, and set out again. Hours passed. They turned up towards the lakeside tuns, watchful, but there were no signs of bandits this time around. Leona looked into the woods as they passed the site of the fight, and shook her head.

'Something happened in there. Much blood was spilled recently.'

'Rast fought bandits there,' said Karland, interested. 'Many days ago. How can you tell something happened?'

She glanced at him with her strange eyes. 'Druids have senses for wild places,' she said ambiguously. 'I just know that something happened. It's... like a smell.'

They made good time, and around late afternoon they came in sight of the farmhouse. Karland silently cheered. The thought that he would see Xhera had eclipsed all else, and he had been driving Aldwyn silently mad for the last hour with his nervous energy.

It seemed that Rast's advice had been heeded. The beginnings of a wall ran around the farmhouse and the immediate surrounds. Apart from the wall, the tun was much as Karland remembered it. It felt good to be back in this homely place.

No one came out to greet them, so Rast knocked at the door. It was opened by Talas, holding a wooden spoon. She gasped in surprise, and then smiled.

'Aldwyn! Rast! Karland! You return already!' She held the door wide. 'Come in, please. I confess I thought we would not see you again for a very long time, if ever.'

'Talas,' nodded the imperturbable Rast. Aldwyn kissed her on the cheek, and then introduced Leona. Talas peered at her curiously, and smiled in greeting. Then she looked at Karland, a mixture of emotions on her face.

'I am not sure if I'm delighted or downcast to see you,' she said in mock severity, a small smile still there. 'After what happened, and your leaving... Xhera has been impossible, and inconsolable.'

He beamed at her, his hope rekindled. 'It is good to see you, Talas! Where is she?'

Talas laughed. 'Patience, young man. She will be back any minute for food, which I was making. Sit! Please. Be welcome here. I have some cold food to share.' She glared at Rast. 'If you even think about trying to pay for it, I shall smack you.'

Rast held up his big hands in submission, and Karland nearly burst out laughing at the mental image of the small woman beating the giant warrior with a wooden spoon.

They sat and were provided with cold salted meats, fresh bread, butter and eggs. There were only a few slices of cheese left. 'We are a week away from the next matured batch,' she apologised.

Marta joined them, coming in early, and greeted them warmly. They were halfway through their meal, chatting quietly as Talas bustled around the kitchen, when the back door opened.

'Talas, I thought I saw horses in our-' began Xhera, and then her eyes lit on the crowd at the table. Karland was smiling hopefully.

'*Karland!*' she shrieked, dropping her pail with a clatter and running across the room. She cannoned into him so hard he nearly came off his chair, and then he was lost in her hug and the smell of her. He closed his eyes tightly, breathing deeply, all his fears and doubts vanished. He was with his friend again, and nothing else mattered.

A light cough intruded.

'Well! I certainly can't wait for *my* greeting, if it will be like this,' remarked Aldwyn slyly. Xhera bounced up and laughed, and then ran to the old man and hugged him tightly. As she turned to Rast, Karland saw in amusement that Aldwyn's spectacles were now hanging from one ear.

Rast looked at Xhera with a faint smile and hugged her briefly. Then she turned to the new member of their group, curiosity on her small face.

'I am Leona,' said the Druid, rising and bowing.

Xhera studied her seriously, and then smiled.

'I am Xhera. It is good to meet you,' she said politely. She swung back to Karland. 'I *never* thought you would return so soon. You must tell me everything! What was Darost like?'

A cleared throat interrupted her. 'Xhera,' said Talas reprovingly. 'We need to clear the table for Hendal and Jon. You can spend time with Karland later.'

Xhera nodded glumly, and moved to help. Karland joined her, and she brightened.

Not long afterwards, Jon and Hendal returned, and were delighted to see them. They sat to eat, Karland taking his place next to Xhera. Hendal was so eager to talk to Rast about what had happened that he nearly choked several times. Karland watched a little anxiously as Marta sat next to him, resignedly ready to thump him on his back.

'Things were right stirred up here after you left, Rast, and no mistake,' Hendal said. 'Most tuns have a good wall base round them now. We're getting there with ours, slowly. Bit of a chore but worth it in the long run, I reckon.' He chewed some ham reflectively. 'Sent some lads down the road to those bandits you spoke of. They took as much as they could in the way of weaponry, though it were more like pitchforks and the like.

'They found no one alive. Plenty of dead, though, nine I think. You surely took them apart.' His face was full of respect. 'Never seen anything like it, they said. We've got together a patrol o' sorts now. Just around the tuns, like, but the farmhands stick in a good bunch and make sure what's what. I'm sure it ain't anything much by you, but it's what we got. No one is complaining about it since they saw them bodies... and since that thing killed its way through here.'

'That is wise,' said Rast. 'Any show of alertness will help ward off trouble.'

'So how long are you here for this time? I'm guessing you did your business in Darost. Heading home?'

Rast shook his head. 'Not for long. We have greater travels ahead. We can stay tonight, if we may, and won't need much in the way of supplies.'

Aldwyn held up his hand. 'Well. Perhaps, mm, we can stay a day longer. We could use a good rest before we begin our true journey.' The look he gave Rast was unreadable. Rast shrugged. Karland looked at him curiously; he thought they were in a hurry.

Hendal nodded. 'Fair enough. Well, let's finish up here and to bed then. I got an early start. If you've no objections, we could use your legs and back tomorrow, Rast. Broken axle on a wagon.'

Rast smiled. 'Of course.'

'Plenty of time to talk tomorrow, then,' said Hendal with a twinkle in his eye at the identical downcast expressions of Karland and Xhera.

Karland resolved to tell Xhera a few things tonight before he burst, whatever Hendal said. He slipped out of his room into the dark hallway, debating whether he should try and find which room was hers to haul her out of bed. As he stood there deliberating, a door two down from him opened and Xhera herself slid out. She jumped when she saw him, and then smiled. Beckoning him, they crept to the kitchen, treading with care on the wooden flooring.

Entering the kitchen, she closed the door, and then gave him another hug.

'It's so good to see you again,' she said quietly. 'Tell me what happened to you in Darost! You seem different.'

Karland outlined what had happened. She gasped when he told her that Aldwyn was a Councillor.

'He's one of the people in charge of the *country?*' she said, looking shocked.

'Sort of. He's a bit retired I guess. But there is more.' He went on to tell her of the meetings. She was amazed that he had met the whole Council. He started skipping over the details of their quest and the background to it, thinking that she would be uninterested, but she noticed and demanded to know everything. Unable to refuse his friend, he told her about the killings and warnings of Aldwyn, all the problems in the land, his meeting with Leona, and the request from the Council. The embers died as he told the tale, but he could see that her mouth was constantly open. Now he heard it told, some of it sounded far-fetched. When he told her about the attack she was horrified, her hand going to her mouth when she heard of the death of Robertus. She could see it had affected Karland deeply. Finally, she sat back and shook her head. 'It is unbelievable, Karland. But as bad as it was… I wish I had been there.' She yawned and then looked around. 'It is so late! We need to sleep. I need to talk to you tomorrow about something important, but… well. Tomorrow.' He nodded and they slipped back to their rooms.

ભ જી

Karland woke very early the next morning, and bounded out of bed despite the late night. He was keen to find Xhera and finish their talk while they had the chance.

Aldwyn's snores were deafening from the next room; he shut the door carefully, and sneaked down the corridor to the kitchen, pausing at the end. Xhera was already there.

'Morning,' she said. 'I didn't sleep much… I have been thinking about what to tell you. Things have not been the same since I came back. I feel different.' Her expression was very serious, and Karland patted her hand. Her experience had been horrifying, and it would take a long time for her to get over it.

'Let's get some tea, and you can tell me what is wrong,' said Karland. Xhera nodded, setting a large pot to boil over the low fire. She came and sat next to him, and Karland once again experienced the slightly light-headed mixture of pain and bliss at her presence. He supposed he would never stop feeling confused where she was concerned.

She was quiet for a moment, and then looked at the pot, bubbling away, her eyes unfocused.

'Since you came here… I have felt different. This doesn't feel like my place, my home any more. I mean, it does, but it never felt quite right to me… and when I met all of you, I knew I belong somewhere else.' She bit her lip between her teeth delightfully. Karland couldn't help but stare. 'But I don't know where. And since, since what happened, I just… I don't feel safe. I can't think of what I am doing, I can't make myself care about this- this *farm* stuff, when there are books, other places, things to learn and see... I just need to be away from here. *Really* need to.' She looked so forlorn. Karland reached out and took her hand.

She squeezed it sadly with a small smile. 'No one understood me much before you came. When you leave again, what becomes of me?'

Karland didn't know what to say.

She was about to say more when Rast ducked into the kitchen door from outside. Karland shook his head. Would he ever get up before the huge man?

'Do you plan on boiling that dry?' he said, looking at the bubbling pot. With red cheeks Xhera jumped up to make tea. 'I have been fixing that wagon with Jon. We rose early so breakfast would be welcome.'

Even as he spoke, Hendal stomped into the kitchen, alert and smiling.

'Mornin'!' he said cheerily. Karland and Xhera glanced at each other, knowing they would have no more time to talk.

After breakfast, everyone went separate ways. Karland helped Xhera with her chores, but she was quiet. Lunch came and went in relative silence, with Rast and Aldwyn talking to Hendal and Jon. Leona stayed polite and withdrawn, despite Talas' attempts to draw her out.

Finally, in the late afternoon, Xhera and Karland found themselves returning to the farmhouse. She paused, and when he did the same she drew a breath to speak, looking pale, resolute and frightened all at once.

'Do you remember when I said I wasn't ready to leave?' she asked softly, not looking at him.

'Yes, I remember.' He wondered where she was going with this.

'Well, I changed my mind. I have been able to think of nothing else. Every minute weighs on me here; every day I want to get away more and see what I can, find my place in the world.' She glanced up at him. 'I want to come with you.'

Karland shook his head, the warm thought of travelling with her buried by alarm. 'I'm not sure, Xhera – look how Talas reacted last time. It's only been two weeks! You still need time to recover-'

'I don't need *time*.' Her eyes flashed at him. 'I need *space*. My own life.'

'Our journey may be very dangerous.'

'*You* are going.' Her stare was challenging, and he couldn't answer that without insulting her. Karland sighed doubtfully. He was not looking forward to the renewed argument, but he knew he could not dissuade her... and part of him did not want to.

'I will ask Aldwyn,' he said finally. 'I can see how unhappy you are here, but I worry for your safety if you come.'

'Worry for me more if I remain,' she said. 'I do not know how long I can live like this any more.' She sounded alarmingly matter of fact. 'My life here does not feel worth living, and it holds bad memories now. I feel trapped.' She looked so miserable that Karland's heart went out to her.

'We'll ask tonight,' he promised.

'Thank you,' she smiled at him, her eyes full of hope.

೧ ೧

'My thanks, Talas,' said Aldwyn. 'A most *excellent* repast.' He pushed his plate away.

'When do you leave?' asked Hendal.

'First light tomorrow,' Rast answered. Karland tensed. It was the start of their real journey, and he felt a cold certainty of what was about to happen before he had even managed to ask Aldwyn quietly.

Xhera's voice was thin but clear. 'I want to go with them.' Silence fell and she raised her chin in defiance, glaring at her family. 'I mean it.'

Talas' face flushed again. It was obvious that she had feared this, but that wasn't stopping her quick temper from rising.

'Seems to me we had this discussion once before,' said Jon quietly. 'And look what happened.' If he was trying to scare her, it wasn't working. Xhera turned her glance to him.

'And would that have happened if I had been with them?' she challenged. 'I don't fit here! I never did. I want to go with them.'

'Are you *quite* finished?' asked Talas in a dangerously low voice. 'They are leaving without you, and that is final.' Karland looked to Rast, and the big man nodded agreement.

'But-' was all he got out before Talas' glare affixed him in his seat.

'And I suppose that this is your doing, Karland? Didn't you get her into enough trouble last time-'

'*Talas,*' rumbled Jon warningly, his relaxed demeanour vanishing. 'Do not lay blame or insult our guests. We cannot blame Karland for what happened, or who she is.' His wife turned her glare on him, her chest heaving in ire.

'Karland. She cannot come,' broke in Rast's voice. 'I know you both wish it, but think, boy. You know what we ride into.'

Aldwyn looked between them, saying nothing.

Talas returned her gaze to Xhera. 'You are not going. It is final, as it was before,' she declared. 'I will not have my only sister in danger!'

Xhera slammed her chair back, eyes blazing. '*You are SUCH a selfish coward!*' she screamed.

The whole room went silent. Hendal and Marta looked astonished and upset. Jon was looking at the floor, and Talas was so angry that she was losing control even with guests there.

Xhera continued, tears leaking down her cheeks. 'You want *only* what is best for you! *If I stay here, I will die!* Is that plain enough for you? I will rot inside, lose myself. *You* fit here, and you know who you are. *I do not!*'

The last shriek rent the air, and Talas shot to her own feet, ready to forget guests and screech back.

Karland leapt up instead.

'*Enough!*' he yelled, taking everyone by surprise including himself, his voice cracking between full manliness and youth. Talas opened her mouth, but he cut her off. 'Listen! Talas, why can't you see how unhappy she is? I know exactly how it feels. I faced the same at my home. She needs you to set her free!' Talas's gaze bored into him, and he hurried on. 'No! Wait! *Listen.* She would be in no more danger than I. In fact, she is as well read and as capable as me in pretty much everything – she could study with Aldwyn as I do. I have no reason to be travelling either, is what I mean. If she should not go, neither should I.'

'Don't be a fool, boy,' said Rast.

To everyone's astonishment including his own, Karland glared at the big man.

'In this, it is *you* who is the fool, Rast. If she does not come, neither do I.' He sat again, face red with fright and anger. The big man looked at him without expression.

A noise from Talas brought his gaze back. To his astonishment her eyes were tearing, her lip trembling. 'None of you understand,' she said brokenly. 'Xhera is all I have left of our family. I can't lose her.'

'If I might add to this discussion,' came Aldwyn's calm voice. Jon's arm dropped to Talas's in comfort, and Xhera was looking at her sister defiantly, but with a realisation in her eyes. The old man removed his spectacles and pinched the bridge of his nose briefly.

'I think,' he said regretfully, 'that she should come with us.'

Talas shook her head mutely. Karland looked at Xhera, his eyes mirroring utter surprise; he had not expected Aldwyn to back him up. Aldwyn held up his hands.

'She is not happy here, you cannot deny that. For all the wrong reasons these two are correct. She does not belong here, and could be in more danger here than you realise. You have always known she was not meant for a farmer's life.'

Talas stared at him, her face gradually paling.

'I know better than any, mm, what happened to you. I understand why you protect her. But why did you never tell her of what happened?'

Xhera was looking at her sister accusingly, and Talas shrank back. She finally spoke.

'I… I didn't want to lose her. I lost everyone else. And I didn't want her to think it was my f-f-faulllt-' she broke down completely, and Jon's arms went around her. Xhera shook her head, fresh tears in her eyes. She reached out to her sister, and Jon stood.

'I think mebbe you two should talk,' he said gently, leading them to the door. Talas gulped and nodded, and they left the room.

಍   ಹ

Rast looked at Karland as they all sat there in silence.

'You are growing up, boy,' he said. 'All too quickly, perhaps, and you grow teeth too. It is good that you are learning to make your own decisions, as long as you think them through. I cannot deny that Xhera is as capable as you, but I still do not think this wise.'

Hendal sighed. 'I knew she would leave here one day, Master Tal'Orien,' he said. 'I guess I would rather she left with you than most anyone else, if she has to go.'

'Always a little quiet and fey, that one,' said Marta. 'Talas has stifled her a bit, but you shoulda seen them when Aldwyn and Greck brought them. We found out some of the story over the years – Greck told us here and there – but Talas made us promise not to tell Xhera. That girl has always carried the guilt of what happened.'

Jon nodded. 'She still wakes sometimes with the same nightmare. Never tells me what it was.'

'What did happen?' asked Karland.

'There was some kind of disaster, and most everyone in their town was killed. Not many survivors. Talas was off with her sister out of the town at night without permission, looking for something; all they would have done at home was died, but logic ain't worked well for Talas there. She thinks if she hadn't run off it wouldn't have happened, like it were some kind of punishment,' said Hendal.

Marta shook her head sadly. 'Never really let go of the thought, poor girl. We thought she'd heal over time… thought she had, was happy, until Master Varelin came back. Seems she never really did.'

Karland sat silently, digesting this. How frustrating for Xhera to know only that her real family were gone apart from her sister, who would not speak about it. And now he understood Talas a little better, too, and felt sorry for her. What must it be like to blame yourself for something like that?

The door opened and both girls came back in, eyes red and puffy, but they were holding hands and trying to smile.

'I think I understand a bit more now,' said Xhera, coming back to sit next to Karland. 'I just wish you had told me before, Talas. Of course it was not your fault. You saved us both.'

'Only by mistake,' said Talas, but she looked more at peace, as if telling had finally lanced the guilt. 'I still don't want you to go... but it is *your* life. Deep down, I know how much you need to be somewhere else. I just didn't want to see it. I just want you to be safe.'

'If she don't go with these people we trust, then sooner or later she will go with others, or alone. Better this than that,' suggested Hendal gruffly.

'It is not that I don't want to stay,' said Xhera quietly. 'You are my family. I just... cannot. I need to find my own way. If not now, then when?'

Karland squeezed her hand. Talas smiled querulously.

'I fear you may be caught up in events. Look what happened to us. We came here from tragedy, and the few memories I have are terrible. But *that* is why I am so scared to lose you.' She took a deep shuddering breath. 'I am sorry.'

Xhera smiled at her sister. 'I understand,' she said quietly. 'And... thank you for telling me. I feel better knowing.'

Silent until now and virtually forgotten by everyone, Leona leaned forwards and placed a comforting hand on the woman's forearm.

'Take heart, Talas. Cubs must leave their home one day, or you deny them the chance to become more than just cubs, and that is what our role is. We allow them to do just this; to find their own way for themselves.'

Talas nodded, and then sighed, her breath trembling out.

'I know. Just... come back safely, Xhera.' She looked at Karland and smiled, a little. 'And that *is* down to you, Karland.'

He nodded seriously. Somehow, it was all right, and Xhera would be free to find her own life. And he would be there for her whatever happened.

EIGHTEEN

The goodbyes were tearful, but Talas seemed more content than before once she had accepted that she had to let Xhera find her own way. Karland guessed that it had been a long conflict for her. Until last night none of them had perhaps understood the depth of Xhera's loneliness and desire to be free.

They set out in late morning, farm duties delayed to say farewell. Xhera waved one last time as the cart rattled out of the tuns. Rast led them across the grass, back the way they had originally come, and they took the small woodland path through the trees. There was sunlight enough to bathe them in a soft gold-green glow, and the woods buzzed with activity in the warmth.

Xhera looked a little nervous. Karland understood after her last foray into woodland, but soon she relaxed and began to enjoy the journey.

'Talas was sad at your parting, of course,' said Aldwyn as they rode, 'but she should be happier now. I think she has long needed, ah, closure on what happened. For better or worse, it is out of her hands, and your life is your own.'

Xhera nodded, her little face as serious as usual. 'Thank you, Aldwyn. I am not sure what would have happened had you not spoken up.'

'She needed to let go,' he said simply. 'You are a young woman. Better she bear the pain of letting go now than you grow to hate her.' He smiled. 'It is easy for age and experience to forget how fast children become, mm, young men and women. But one of the conditions of your accompanying us was that I teach you as I do Karland.' Karland groaned in mock sympathy, but Xhera's eyes were bright and she nodded eagerly.

'Looks like you have competition, my boy,' cackled the old man. Karland hoped she didn't make him look like an idiot.

Leona rode alongside them, eyes mostly shut, enjoying the woodland. Karland had told Xhera that she was a Druid, and that she held an indefinable kinship with nature. Without tack or saddle, her horse deftly picked her way along the path. Leona paid no attention to riding other than balance, and it was a little odd to watch. When they rejoined the main road and turned northwest on it, Leona opened her eyes and smiled at them.

'That was peaceful,' she said softly. 'A welcome return from the bustling world of men.'

They travelled north for the rest of the day. Pulling off the road, Rast found them a small hollow that was ideal for a camp. Karland and Xhera complained when, after they had finished setting up their blankets, he told them that they had an hour of training with him to complete before they could eat.

'The days of rest are over,' he said firmly. 'Given everything that you have been through, I thought you would welcome training that could save your lives. Karland, I thought you wanted to keep Xhera safe?'

'Of course,' Karland said firmly, glancing at her.

'And how will you do that if you know nothing about fighting? I have taught you but a few tricks. Now you learn in earnest, every day. Tired or not, morning or evening, you will train. You sit in a cart all day, so you must work harder. At times, you will run alongside it. You will practice combat, run, and lift heavy things, push your limits. These will make you strong and capable.' Xhera snickered, and his eyes flicked to her. 'You, too. You need to learn to defend yourself since you are likely too curious and wilful to stay out of trouble. Now come, strip to light tunics.' He took them to the side and gave them exercises to do, most of them seemingly having nothing to do with fighting. None were easy. Throughout it all, Karland noticed that Leona's eyes were on the big man, approving.

When he allowed them to stumble to the fire, trembling and sweating, they were handed food and drink. Gasping, Karland nearly choked trying to get it down his throat.

'Did... you... train like... this?' he puffed at Rast.

'No.' The big man smiled. 'My training was hard.'

Karland glared at him, and Rast shrugged.

'I have trained for hours almost every day of my life, and had to stay alive even when I was too tired to think. In one month, you will look back and understand how easy this has been.'

Leona laughed softly.

'You prepare them for life well, warrior.' She glanced at Karland. 'Realise, Karland, that outside cities – and inside them, too, deep within people – nature is red, raw and deadly. Most things exist at war with other life, although there is a certain harmony to it. The world is like this. Progression, evolution, betterment only comes through struggle. What you learn here will keep you alive.' She looked at Aldwyn. 'And what do you teach, scholar?'

Aldwyn regarded her thoughtfully.

'Everything else, Leona. Everything else. Art, philosophy, mathematics, healing... the wisdom of ages, and so forth. There are some few things you do not directly learn from, aha, strife.'

She bowed her head, smiling acquiescence to his logic as Xhera possessively patted her pack, which held her precious books. 'Then perhaps I should also teach the ways of nature,' returned the Druid. 'Between all three, it may be they might be able to learn something of value.'

'Oh, I wouldn't go that far,' grinned Aldwyn, glancing slyly at the two young people.

෬ ෨

The party made good time the next morning and entered Fordun's Run by late afternoon the next day. Glab welcomed them back. Rast received countless offers of drinks from men who passed through the bar - it seemed that the town was virtually free of ruffians. Most had left, and those remaining were still afraid of the demon that had stalked them. In addition, the watch was four times larger now, and with many younger men. Volunteers all, they had established a grim, no-nonsense attitude towards trouble.

It was strange, Glab said. No priests had found any signs of a demon, and the townsfolk were hailing it as a saviour rather than a devil, although it had not struck again. Karland wondered if it was another creature passing through a town. He tried to scare Xhera later with tales of the demon, but was met with frankly disbelieving looks and gave up.

They spent a comfortable night. This time Karland better appreciated that for a country inn the Run Wash was very good, and Glab refused payment for the rooms.

The common room was full of cheer that night. Karland managed to sneak half a pint of ale, much to Xhera's delight, but they both thought it horrible and it was quickly abandoned to its fate. Lar was in evidence, his arm still bound. Excitedly, he told Aldwyn that it was already beginning to itch - a sign of rapid healing, Karland told Xhera - and could even move his fingers a little. Xhera looked at his scars with dismay, but the others smiled at him warmly.

Leaving with many good wishes the next morning, they set out. The road was clear into Gladsmoor, the main traffic having gone through earlier. They rode right through. Rast stopped only to talk to the guards, whose numbers had tripled. Some people had been robbed and killed by mercenaries. They had fled northeast pursued by a squadron of Eordeland guards. The guards had not returned, nor had any travellers come from that direction apart from a few traders, who had fled west in the distance. Few had stopped to talk and those that did spoke of trouble.

Rast was clearly perturbed by this news. Karland asked if it was the Meyari force moving west. Rast shook his head in uncertainty and suggested they hurry on to the library. They rode through dusk, and continued more carefully that night, although the moon was out and there was little cloud. The road was a white slash in the darkness, and they followed it through the low hills until they dropped away into countryside. Karland was sure if it was daylight that he would be able to soon recognise the land.

They turned off east into the woods before The Croft along a path that led along the border of the woods themselves. After a time they turned off north towards the Library, and Leona sniffed in appreciation.

'*These* woods are wild,' she said with approval. 'Old and wild. I can feel their heart.' Then she stiffened and her head swivelled back to the main path. Seconds later hoofbeats were heard from the east, and a rider shot past in the gloom. Karland caught a glimpse of the rider hanging oddly over the panicked horse's shoulder before they were gone towards The Croft.

'He was running sorely wounded from something,' she said, her tone worried. 'Let us hurry and reach sanctuary.'

Troubled, they pressed on. Under the trees, it was nearly pitch black, and Karland wondered the wisdom of riding horses even this slowly in the dark. Leona however was whispering quietly to herself, and the horses were following hers without misstep.

Eventually they emerged into the clearing with the ruins. In the moonlight, they looked ancient and foreboding, but Aldwyn sighed happily. In some ways this was as much his home as The Sanctum. It held many of his own works alongside many more precious books, scrolls, and scripts housing wisdom of the ages.

Rast took the horses through to the courtyard and stabled them. Aldwyn produced a massive iron key and opened the hidden ironwood door, humming happily to himself.

They walked along the corridor nearly in total darkness until Aldwyn crowed in quiet delight and they were suddenly bathed in a pure white light. He handed his lambent jar to Karland and shuffled past them to close and lock the door.

Inside the cave itself Aldwyn bade them make themselves at home. He had much to gather, he said, and dragged out a sturdy wooden chest, bound with brass at the corners and bearing a solid iron lock. Rast dropped the small trunk and moved to light a fire in the fireplace. As he did so, he reassured Leona, who seemed a little uneasy shut away underground behind man-made doors. Aldwyn noticed the two youngsters clustered around the fireplace, poking at shelves of jars.

'Here, here,' he muttered distractedly, pulling out and uncovering the other white lamp. 'Karland, show this little scholar around. Replace what you look at, and remember: do not touch the older scrolls, as usual.'

Karland nodded, taking the lamp, and Aldwyn bustled away ahead of them. Rast had flames going in the fireplace now, and with it once more in use the cave took on the homely feel Karland was used to. The deep shelves of jars nearby threw back reflections from the dancing flames, and it was almost as if he had not left.

Karland beckoned Xhera to follow as Rast sat on Karland's stool and leaned forward to talk to Leona, whose eyes shone strangely from the depths of Aldwyn's chair. They followed the wall around to the left, passing the passage to the courtyard on the right, and then Aldwyn's alcove. A deeper darkness opened to the left, slanting downwards for hundreds of feet. The floor was surprisingly smooth as it dropped. He guided her until she was used to the deceptively shallow long steps which were easy to stumble on if you didn't know they were there. They travelled downwards in a slow spiral, the air cool and dry, and then spied another light far ahead. Rounding a corner, they found Aldwyn poring over shelves, many of which Karland had been instructed under no circumstances to ever touch or remove scripts from. When she saw the full library, stretching back into the darkness, Xhera gasped. This was a treasure trove for any scholar. The library was not big, but it housed more than two thousand works. Aldwyn had a whole section of his own amongst the forbidden section, but there were plenty of other authors to read. Xhera was fascinated by the diversity and age of some of the books.

When they returned to the living rooms, they found the old scholar arguing with Rast, a mutinous expression on his face. Rast was implacable, and Aldwyn was waving his skinny wrists excitedly.

'I *need* all these volumes, I tell you,' he snapped. 'I require them to study what is happening correctly!'

'There are too many,' said Rast. 'If you travel with a veritable library, it will cause notice, as well as slow us. Most people do not have access to this many books, and they will not all fit in the chest.'

'We could get another one,' said Aldwyn, scowling. Rast shook his head.

'No. We cannot. Understand, Aldwyn: we take only what we need beyond doubt. If we take what we *might* need on this quest, we should return to Darost for a train of coaches and an army. Take only what you can fit within that chest.'

Xhera grinned, and then thought of something. 'What about *my* books?' she said, worried.

'Better leave them here,' Karland said. He sighed at her mutinous expression. 'Well, whatever. Argue it out with Rast if you like. But if Aldwyn can't take his, I bet you can't take yours.'

A few afternoons later Rast bade them make ready to leave. Leona had seemed restive all day and had spoken to Rast more than once, a troubled look on her face. Aldwyn had only a few precious books and a few flashes and phosphorus bombs packed. He flew into a flapping panic the instant anyone set foot near the padded bag that held them.

'I want to get to The Croft before sundown if possible,' he said firmly. 'I am increasingly worried about the stories we heard in Gladsmoor, and Leona senses something very amiss. We would be wise to listen to the words of a Druid.'

Leona stopped her restless prowling. 'There is a… feeling around us that grows sharp today, a foul wind that blows to the west. I felt it in the courtyard earlier. The forest is restless. Something here is worrying at my mind, like a darkness that creeps upon us.'

As he lifted his belongings, Karland wondered what Leona could have detected that unnerved her so much. She didn't seem to know herself, but if it upset someone as capable as her he was not really sure he wanted to find out what it was.

CR   SO

It was after dark when they finally stopped in view of The Croft. Something was wrong; lights shone over a fresh high wooden palisade topped with sharpened ends. As they slowly approached, they were challenged.

'Halt! Who goes in the night?'

Before Rast could respond, Karland indignantly shouted back, 'Who are *you*?'

There was a moment's silence. The voice seemed taken aback. Finally it responded, 'Janos. Apprentice to the Smith.'

'Janos! It's Karland. Let us in!'

'Karland? Karland who?' Janos replied. Karland cursed.

'Karland Dresin, son of the Cloth-Trader. Remember?'

After a moment, the voice called back in surprise. '*Karland?* Well, uh. I remember you. You really back? Hold on.' Muffled discussions drifted over the wall.

'We will open the gates, but you must enter quickly,' came a new voice. The gates cracked just wide enough to allow the cart, and they entered the town. Karland gasped as he saw just how many of the men in the town bore new-forged arms. Janos, his big face creased with worry, came towards them accompanied by the mayor, of all people. His face relaxed in relief.

'It *is* you, Karland,' he said.

'What's going on?' Karland said, looking around. 'Who are all these people?'

The Mayor, Thomas Bedwin, stepped forward. 'A lot has happened since you left, lad. A lot.' He looked at Rast, and the same relief that Janos had shown crossed his face. 'Sir – you look like a fighter, a warrior. May I have a word?'

Rast motioned the others down. 'Our errand is urgent,' he said. 'We cannot stay.'

Mayor Bedwin looked distressed at the words. 'Sir – I do not know what to do. We have seen nothing but peace here until recent times, and now everyone here faces even graver danger. The only guards here are wounded. We need help.'

Rast looked around him and saw fear and desperation on many faces. As he turned, he saw Karland's face, and sighed inwardly. The boy's family was here, and it seemed they were in peril. He looked at Aldwyn, who nodded tiredly.

'Let us speak,' he said as he led Stryke to a clear spot near the wall. 'Hastus, Stryke. Hastus verin,' he said, looking into the stallion's eyes. An ear twitched as the only response. He gave the usual warning, and turned to the mayor.

'Where is my father?' asked Karland.

Mayor Bedwin shook his head. 'Later, lad. Your father is busy helping the smith make brigandines for us. Come with me.'

☙ ❧

They followed him to the nearest large building, the Crafter's tavern, now surrounded by rough wooden structures and tents. Moving inside, they found the common room crowded with men, their faces bleak. The Mayor moved to the fireplace, and then turned to them. Karland recognised some of the town elders.

'From where did you journey?' asked one. His tone was abrupt, perhaps even desperate. 'How came you all here without harm?'

Rast glanced at the others, sensing something amiss. 'We came from Darost. Our last stop was Gladsmoor. We turned off to the Northing Woods where Master Varelin has his living, as you may know.'

'Yes. Most odd,' cut in the Mayor. 'We always thought that most odd. But Gladsmoor, you say – when were you there last?'

'Maybe four days past. Why? Karland tells me that this town has changed since he left – and that little more than a month ago.'

'Gladsmoor has fallen,' was the grim reply. 'Two nights gone. People fled north and south both and some ended here, in our town. We're the most northern of the trading stops until you hit the coast, and people were hoping maybe that we would be out of the way.' He shook his head. 'I'm getting muddled. Let me start at the beginning.'

Karland stared. *Fallen?* What was he talking about?

'Not a month past, we had a rough-looking group of men here asking after Master Varelin. They were rude and seemed up to no good so we told them that there was no man of that name in the village and to leave. They tried to threaten and bribe information from us, but they put backs up. Eventually they left, but things got stranger. There have been rumours from eastern towns of people fleeing west. Townsfolk started seeing strange things at night, close to the village. One night a man was killed in the town itself by something that had come from the forest. People are frightened; too many are missing, and some have even gone mad. We set up patrols. Everyone took a turn. Seemed to make a difference, and people slept better.

'Then the first refugees arrived from the east. Two men and a woman were all that was left of a large merchant's train. They were slaughtered by a horde of creatures, they said. No one believed their tales. Two have died from their wounds, and since then we've had more people in every day - until three days back. Then they just stopped coming, except from Gladsmoor. My guess is there was no one left. They all bring the same tales: fell creatures in the east that have been killing and ravaging steads, farms and towns across the north of Eordeland. No one knows where our own army is. We fear they come this way.'

A tired voice broke in from the side. 'Orcs. I already told you, Bedwin. They are orcs.' A scarred trapper sat there. He was wounded, with bright eyes. 'They come from the east at night, following the line of the woods, killing all unwary in their path. Men, women, children: all slaughtered. Gladsmoor would be a pretty prize with all those cattle, and is the only reason you have not seen them yet. When it fell, we were cut off.'

'Excuse our guest,' said Bedwin, troubled. 'He still has fever from the attack. The weapon used was unclean in some way.' He turned to the trapper. 'Kel, you are unwell; I hope the fever breaks soon. It must have been all those mercenaries that have been around of late.' Others nodded.

'He may speak truth,' said Rast.

Everyone stopped talking. In the sudden hush, Aldwyn stepped forward with his pack to look at the injured man.

'Orcs are real,' Rast continued. 'And his story rings true. I do not understand where an army of them could come from here of all places, but I tell you this: I have faced them, and they are a vicious foe. They hate the sun, and will attack at night. You have seen strange things and creatures of legend come back to life in your woods, and yet you do not believe in orcs? You will not listen to a man wounded by them?'

'But- well, we thought they were old stories,' Bedwin said. 'We thought maybe that he was hallucinating from the fever.'

Rast shook his head in frustration. 'He is lucid enough,' he said. 'This is grim news. Did anyone else speak of this?'

'No-'

Another man with a blue laced tunic cleared his throat. 'Thomas. You know today, those last refugees from Gladsmoor? A lot of them are guards. They said it was horrible creatures that came in the night... not men. Many are wounded and still resting, and we thought they were in shock from the attack-'

'And no one told me,' said the Mayor in despair.

'What happened in Gladsmoor?' asked Rast.

The man in the blue tunic answered. 'It's a big place, but pretty open. Easy pickings for an attack I guess. Hundreds of these things attacked in the dark – barely managed to get people out. Many are dead and the herds are slaughtered or scattered. We sent for aid south with most of the refugees, but we were cut off and came north. I don't know if any got through to Darost.'

Bedwin sighed. 'We held an emergency moot and built a palisade in the last week or so. It's why we've been so busy. Every spare supply went into it, all the wood we had for building and shipping to the coast. We strengthened it as we could and posted lookouts. Your arrival caused no small alarm.' He paused, and beckoned for a cup of water. Taking a sip, he made a face.

'So there you have it. It is too late to run and we face an attack any time. None of us are fighting men, sir, apart from the guards from Gladsmoor, and they are fair exhausted. We need help. The highest ranked guard here is a young corporal.'

Rast nodded, thinking.

'You have made a start,' he said. 'But what I have seen so far has been barely sufficient. The wall is strong, and well wrought for quick work. But you must strengthen the gates and plan your defences – you have limited resources and no path of escape. Cycle watchmen on walls every few hours to prevent them becoming too tired, and ensure that there are more at night. That is when an attack will come. Do you have anything that will help make your wall retardant to flame?'

'I am not sure.'

'Find out, Mayor Bedwin. The wall does you no good if it becomes a burning trap. How many men do you have here? Do you have weapons for them all? Are any trained in combat?'

One of the other men answered. 'There are perhaps two hundred and fifty able men and women. Of that I'd say no more than sixty have fought before in some fashion, old timers or guards or the like. People here are crafters and farmers. The smith is working night and day to make basic arms, but even with that over half will be armed with either old family weapons or makeshift.'

'They must start drilling immediately,' said Rast. He glimpsed Karland's face, full of trust, and knew they could not be left to their fate. He turned his resolve to the battle ahead. 'There is little point in just giving them weapons they do not know how to wield. They should be learning fighting, teamwork, and how to take orders right now – not just sitting around waiting for their turn at watch! If you are to have any chance of survival, you must be an army too. I can help you prepare, but know that if we do not prevail the survivors will be tortured, raped, and killed.'

'You are hard,' accused one of the men around them. Rast turned to him, looming in the firelight.

'I am *alive*,' he corrected. 'Orcs will not stay long in one place, not in Eordeland. The risk is too great. They will destroy what they can, kill all they can, and move on. Darost is mobilising against other threats, and it must know of them by now if survivors went south. The army will arrive; we just need to hold out a few days.' He looked at the Mayor. 'I will do what I can.'

The Mayor nodded and exited. Rast turned to the others. Aldwyn looked anxious.

'It seems your instincts were right, Leona. We must now do what we can to survive.' He turned and followed Mayor Bedwin outside.

The Mayor called out loudly for all the men not on duty to gather. They came forward slowly, tired but curious. 'This is Rast Tal'Orien,' called Bedwin. 'He is in charge of the defence.'

Rast stepped forward. 'There is no time to waste. We face a foe we know little of, and there is much to be done.'

One man called out, 'Why should we do what you say?'

'Because I assume you do not want your guts sliced out before your family are defiled by the enemy,' said Rast coldly. 'You all have much to fight for, but none of you will survive if we do not defend this town together. I offer you the chance to save your loved ones, and perhaps take some of them with you. I want anyone with any combat training to gather ten to fifteen and train them in the basics of weapons as a squad. Nothing pretty, just useful and functional. Slice, cut, stab, club, whatever it takes. You are to kill two orcs each before you are permitted to take a wound. Is that clear?' A few grins sprang up, and he nodded to himself, seeing hope rising on some of their faces.

'You fight for more than just your lives; you fight for your families,' he said. 'We do not face men. We face orcs. They may be savage, but I tell you this: I have fought them before, and I have killed them. We will *not* let them cross that wall. I will stand with you in the teeth of the enemy, and we *will* endure.'

They shouted back in defiance, and he knew that for many, their fate was now sealed.

ର   ଛ

Karland looked at Xhera's pale face as they followed Rast out. He had feared they would leave his family here at first, but even Rast's decision to stay was cold comfort.

'It seems like everywhere I go, we end up in a battle,' he said morosely. 'Nowhere is safe. I guess sooner or later we would have to fight. Better with people you know than trapped and alone.'

She shrugged, worry in her eyes, and he knew she thought of her farm and cursed inwardly. 'Your family are well out of the way,' he said comfortingly, and she nodded.

'From what Aldwyn said, this is spreading; there is fighting everywhere,' she said softly.

Around them Karland saw townsfolk that he had known his whole life shout challenges to the attackers. A cold feeling settled in his gut.

How many would die?

NINETEEN

R ast and Aldwyn stayed at the tavern to discuss the defences with the Mayor and the town council. It would be a sleepless night for them all.

Karland took the opportunity to go to his family's house, taking Xhera and Leona with him. It seemed like the population of the town had tripled since he was last here. People rushed to and fro with weapons, shields, water casks, bundles of food, firewood, and other supplies. He waved at a few people he knew, but did not stop. It seemed like years since he had left. So much had happened in so little time.

He threaded his way through the random tents that had sprung up in every available nook, and found himself outside his father's shop. It was quite late now and he had thought that they would be asleep, so Karland was surprised to see light from within.

He took a breath and knocked on the door. A muffled query came from within, and then a bolt was drawn back. The door opened and Karland saw his father standing there, his eyes tired. They widened, and then he laughed.

'*Karland!*'

He bounded through the door, energy restored, and wrapped his son in a fierce hug. Karland hugged him back.

'I thought we would not be seeing you for a long, long time, yet here you are not two months later!' He looked up questioningly at his companions. 'And with ladies in tow.' His eyes took in Xhera, and then he looked at Leona's strange eyes and fierce beauty. He stared before shaking his head. 'Ah – come in. Come in! Come and sit at the table. Your mother just went to bed – let me get her.'

'No, it's all right-' began Karland, but his father was gone. Shrugging, he moved through the littered garments covered in metal plates and leather. They passed into the dining area where Karland sat them at the table. 'I'll see if there is anything to drink,' he said, and moved to the kitchen. As he collected cups and filled them from the water cask, he heard footsteps on the stairs, and walked out.

'*Karland!*' Becka cried softly, enveloping him in a hug.

'Wait-' he said, and water slopped all over him. He rolled his eyes and hugged her back. Xhera began giggling silently at the large stain on his tunic as he brought her cup. He ignored her and introduced them both. His parents greeted the girl and the Druid politely, and then turned back to him.

His mother leaned over and murmured in his ear, 'She's very pretty. Where did you find her?'

Karland felt his cheeks redden and he glanced at Xhera's expression. 'She can *hear* you,' he protested in a pained voice. His mother yawned and grinned sheepishly.

'Well, she is. Sorry.'

'So, anyway, tell me. What have you been up to? A lot has happened since you left. Master Varelin looking after you well?' his father asked, taking pity on him.

'Well enough,' answered Karland. He told his parents a quick version of recent events, omitting the assassination and a few other points.

'So you two and Master Varelin and this – Rast? – and Leona here are on your way through in search of the source of the troubles?' his father asked. 'My son, on an important quest. I am impressed, Karland. Talking with the Council indeed!' He sighed. 'You picked a bad time to visit. I am glad to see you, but things are not good here. Everything has changed. We expect to be attacked soon, as Gladsmoor has been. Trade has stopped. I have been trying to use what cloth I have to clothe those that survived the attacks further east and help build what armour we can.'

'Rast is a warrior,' said Karland, 'and I have never seen his equal. He is our best chance.'

His father grunted in surprise. 'Really?' He looked unsure. Karland knew that look – as if he were still a child, unable to understand harsh realities - but he knew he was not the same boy who had left here. He was older now than a month or so would suggest, and he met his father with a steady gaze. 'We would not leave you to fight alone,' he said. After a moment his father nodded.

'I heard him speak. He is no great orator, but people listen to him. He is a capable man, and we can see it.'

They talked for a short while, his parents interested in their travels and the fact that Leona was a Druid, although Karland could tell they didn't really understand what it meant. They finally excused themselves, saying they had to be up early. Karland asked if they could stay, and Becka looked offended.

'Of course! Where else would you stay?'

'Listen to your mother,' said Brin.

Karland smiled at them both. It was good to be back.

໔   ๖

Karland was rudely awoken the next morning by a shriek that jerked him awake, and then something hit him in the testicles. He doubled over at the sudden attack with a heartfelt groan, and managed to move the offending weight. Looking up, he found his younger sister bouncing on him, demanding he get up and tell her about his trip.

'Get *off*, Gail!'

With a pout she slid off, and then noticed the sleepy form of Xhera nearby, woken by the noise. Suddenly shy, she whispered, 'Who is *that?*'

'Xhera, Gail. Gail, Xhera,' he said in muffled tones as he pulled himself out of bed.

Xhera smiled sleepily. 'Hello, Gail.'

' 'Lo,' said Gail, suddenly tongue-tied. She studied Xhera, and then announced loudly to Karland, 'She's very pretty. Why is she with *you?*'

'Thanks,' he muttered, yawning. 'She's a very good friend. She is travelling with us.' He had a sudden brainwave and dived for his bag, coming back with a blank scroll of vellum in a red ribbon purloined from The Sanctum.

'This a special vellum scroll for very important things to be written on, so don't ruin it.'

Gail grinned, and then took it carefully from his hands. '*Fankyou*,' she said quickly, and ran out of the room beaming.

Xhera laughed. 'Is she always like that?'

Karland sighed. 'Pretty much.'

They went downstairs to find Leona talking seriously to his mother. His father was nowhere to be seen. Greeting the others, they had breakfast, and then Karland joined his mother in the kitchen, carrying the plates. She smiled her thanks.

'What a beautiful young woman Leona is,' she said. 'Very nice, but a little… different.'

'She's a Druid, mother. She's very close to nature. Look, I should eat then see if I can help today. Rast said we could be attacked any time.' Becka nodded.

After eating he looked for his father but Brin had left the shop, so he went to the tavern with Xhera. Aldwyn was asleep in a chair in the common room, snorting so loudly on occasion that he drowned out the people talking around a rough map on the main table. They were giving him looks of mixed annoyance and amusement. Rast was there, talking to some of the Gladsmoor guard. He turned as they came in.

'Karland. Good. I am glad you saw your family. I fear today will be our last free of enemies. Movement to the southeast was seen before sunup, and Leona has said they close in faster than we expected. If the day had no sun, I fear we would be feeling their charge already.'

'Are we ready?' Karland asked apprehensively.

Rast shook his head. 'In one night? No. But we are preparing what we can. Your father actually has something that can prevent flame on cloth, and we are coating what we can of the walls in it. With luck we may hold, but we must move those who cannot fight into the middle of the town and barricade them. You and the other young ones must help them there and protect them. Xhera, you too. Leona-'

'My place is out there,' she replied. 'I will scout the hills.'

'That is too dangerous,' Rast said.

'I tracked even the mighty Rast Tal'Orien for a time without his notice,' she said, 'In broad daylight and tame gardens. Can you doubt me in the wilds? Even you would not find me there – of that you can be certain. And I do not recall offering you a choice.'

Rast studied her and then shrugged, with a slight bow. 'My apologies. No doubt you can take care of yourself,' he said.

She nodded and vanished through the doorway. One of the councilmen glanced at Rast. 'The gates are sealed. How will she get out of town?'

Rast shrugged again. 'She is a Druid.' He turned to Karland. 'Wake this old timber saw here and take him with you to the centre. The girls and boys will defend outside the hall, the girls inside as last defence for mothers with young. If they break through, you must do everything possible to prevent them reaching the infirm and children.' He indicated the town hall, right in the centre of town. 'This is the best building to defend. It has a basement, I am told. I am relying on you do get this done; if anyone doubts your authority, tell them to speak to me.' He turned away, already busy with other things.

Xhera grinned at Karland. 'In charge of inner defences?'

He grimaced, remembering the disdain many of the others had for him. 'Half those boys used to... Never mind. They won't do what I say.' She glanced at him, her grin dropping.

They took Aldwyn to the town hall, blinking sleep from his eyes, and then searched out the youths to defend the town hall. As it turned out, he was pleasantly surprised; Janos had spread word of their return, and few of them questioned Rast's word. He felt more confident until he ran across Ben Arflun. The larger boy laughed and all the old fears resurfaced.

'You? You are too weak to be in charge. *I* will take over.' He pushed Karland hard and he nearly fell. 'Cry off back to your old lover, paly-boy,' sneered Ben, 'and leave this cute arse with a real man.' He leered at Xhera's body as she gaped in affront, laughing and as confident as ever of his power over the other boy. Karland shook his head, cowed, and turned away, heart racing. He felt as powerless as he ever had, but this time there was a difference. Ben's eyes on Xhera stuck in his mind. His anger mounted and the hate of years surged behind it. He had always avoided fights, usually ending up the victim. Not half a year ago Ben had forced Karland under water in a trough without reprisal, and the shame still burned. He heard Xhera say something to Ben, and then heard a slap and a cry.

Something snapped inside him. He whipped around and launched himself past Xhera, who was holding a red cheek. Karland slammed several solid punches into the bigger boy's face, even though his muscles felt like water as they landed purely through instinct.

The attack was greeted with shocked astonishment. Ben dropped on his behind, stunned and dizzied with a black eye and a split lip. The punches had been harder than he would have said Karland could ever hit. The faces around them reflected his disbelief.

'If you don't want more of that, do as you are told,' Karland said, his heart hammering in reaction and his voice shaking. He couldn't believe what he had just done. Each punch had flowed like Rast had shown him, and he still trembled with rage at Ben's treatment of Xhera. *He dared touch her!* 'If you won't listen to me, maybe you will listen to Rast Tal'Orien. I'm pretty sure punches from him will *kill* you.' He walked up to the boy on the ground. 'Now apologise.'

'Fuck off!' snarled Ben, glaring up, still shocked. Karland's foot caught him on the chest, pitching him backwards hard.

'This isn't a game anymore, *shithead*,' he said quietly. 'Apologise now, or I will fucking hurt you. *Badly.*'

He meant every word. Trembling with reaction, he knew Ben's power over him was forever ended. It seemed surreal, but his head was clear and for the first time he was not afraid. Ben clamped his mouth shut, and Karland drew his foot back grimly, staring at the boy's mouth.

'*I'm sorry!*' burst out Ben in panic, reading Karland's intent. 'Sorry! Just leave me alone!' Karland stared at him, and then around at the shocked expressions of the other boys. He turned away in the silence, leaving Ben with blood streaming from his lips. Suddenly he heard bawling behind him, and could not help laughing in shock. Ben was crying!

'Get up and do what you are told,' he said emotionlessly, and walked away.

Xhera walked with him. 'You seemed to enjoy that,' she half-accused.

Karland stopped and stared at her. 'He has beaten me black and blue since I was eight years old. Today I finally stood up to him, because he *hit* you, and this is your reaction?' he said in disbelief. 'Perhaps a *friend* shouldn't judge so quickly.' His victory ashes in his mouth, he walked away.

Steps followed him.

'Karland?' He kept walking. 'Karland, I'm sorry.'

'Once, he kicked Gail so hard she limped for a week, and I was blamed for it. I tried to stand up to him and hurt me so much I couldn't see straight for two days. After everything that has happened… after my promise to you… ' he ran out of words.

'I *said* I was sorry. Really. I shouldn't have jumped to a conclusion. You are right. I just, I just didn't expect any of that. I've never seen you angry before. And - thank you. He didn't hit me hard, really, but thank you. It seems you are still my protector.' She smiled hopefully.

He blew his breath out. 'Forget it. You have no idea how good that felt, though. I don't think he will bother me again.' She hugged him and he felt his anger fade as he hugged her back.

They rounded up the rest of the youngsters, and went door to door, explaining carefully the orders that they had been given. Few people refused to leave their houses; there was comfort and safety in numbers, and the town hall would provide both. He hoped for the sake of those who did stay that no orcs broke through.

Eventually he found himself back with Rast. The big man moved to the wall to look over and then returned. With a few minutes to himself now and Xhera in tow Karland spoke to him.

'So, what do we face?'

'It may be a thousand orcs. They have lost maybe half their number by my estimation from garrison strikes… and passing into the woods. Leona says the old wild places do not tolerate their presence. They differ greatly from those living on the plains.'

'What is the difference?' asked Karland. He had read of the tribes of men and green-skinned Orks that roamed the great central plains.

'The Urukin are the tribes of the plains, nomads and warriors all. They are fair in their way and revel in their free life. They are like us in many ways, but physically stronger and more powerful, although they live less years. But those facing us are different creatures that live under the mountains, loving the dark, hating the light. They are twisted and cunning, and can live centuries.'

'That long? It seems so… unfair.'

'Do not envy them an increased span,' said Rast. 'Rather pity them. They are miserable creatures, hideous and dirty and hating everything including themselves. They live to hurt and desecrate, and find pleasure only in death and pain and ill fortune. Orcs will fight anyone – each other included – for sport or food, but above all others they hate Dwarves and the plains Orks, and they fear the Elves terribly.'

'Why?' asked Karland.

Rast shrugged. 'Dwarves and orcs are bitter foes. Dwarves hoard underground territory and treasures jealously and orcs desire both. There are many more orcs in the world than Dwarves; they breed more quickly and live a similar span, so they often find themselves in battle. If orcs can kill a dwarf, they will do so with glee.'

'What about the plains tribes? The, uh, Urukin?'

'There is a different tale that is not told swiftly. Orks hold the rune for *K* as sacred, a sign of honour. They refer to their fallen kin as *orcs* as a deathly insult. Uruks are strong, proud warriors. They are everything the orcs are not, and the creatures hate them and desire them both. Even stronger than for the Dwarves is their hatred of the tribes.'

'They sound horrible,' said Karland.

'They are. They will follow only those they fear and desire nothing more than to kill or enslave all others. You will rarely find many together, as they are rowdy and argue easily, but do not underestimate them. They may lack the brute power of the Urukin, but they are fierce, and delight in killing.'

'As to, mm, what we call an Orc,' broke in Aldwyn, who had come up and been listening in, 'Whichever name you give them – Orc, Goblin – they are the same creatures. Fascinating race. Can see a little into the infra-red spectrum. Heat, you know.' He paused thoughtfully, and then to Karland's surprise, continued, 'But I will not say that without doubt all orcs are inherently evil. Perhaps some are not so afraid, misguided, full of hate, and chaotic… a product of their race, mm.'

Rast shrugged. 'It is hard to find redeemable qualities in them, and no orc is likely to give you the chance, but I have met men as bad as any orc in my time.'

Leona appeared on the walls with them, returned from her scouting.

'The hills are teeming with the vermin,' she interrupted. 'They seem spread in groups – there are some on the fringes of the woods, but they will not enter of their own free will. I sense their fear of the wild places and the woods hate them in turn – destroyers, desecrators all! If they go too far in the trees will not allow them to leave.'

Rast shook his head. 'Perhaps a thousand,' he grunted. 'We have two hundred and fifty to hold for maybe a week. Behind makeshift palisades with green unseasoned farmers, this will take some doing.'

          CR   SO

It was late afternoon when all of the defenders assembled, apart from a skeleton force on the walls keeping watch. Faint movement was reported in the hills far away. Rast gathered the men and women defending the walls and spoke to them briefly. He knew that they were tired, but reminded them of how much they had accomplished. He also told them to be wary of the unclean arrows and blades of orcs, which often caused festering wounds. The orcs would come tonight, and try to overwhelm the walls. Every available man was to sleep now, ready for battle. Rast gave them no illusions; they faced an army four times their size and would receive no quarter.

'Be steadfast, and we will yet weather the storm,' he said, seeing the remnants of the Gladsmoor garrison look grimly at each other, knowing what they would be up against. 'Get what rest you can. It will be a long night. They will come with the dusk.'

TWENTY

I t was not yet twilight when clouds drifted in to cover the sun. As they grew thicker and the light grew dimmer Rast called for the defenders to prepare. They assembled, each having spent the last night and day training with, working with, and sleeping alongside their squad mates under the watchful eye of a more experienced guard.

Five of the farmers had flat-out refused to trade in their scythes for more usual weapons, protesting that they were experienced at harvest and felt comfortable with their dangerous weapons. Rast had watched them wield the implements and nodded grimly. He planned to use them as an internal shock squad, spread out and ready to react if any orcs broke through. With their reach and large blades the scythes would make bloody work of any foes. Karland fervently hoped that they struck fear into the attacking orcs; they scared the hells out of him, and he was hoping to be a long way from them when the attack began.

Two hundred and fifty men and women coalesced on the walls on a thick plank walkway above head height. Some faced the woods, but most clustered either side of the gate at the southwest. That was where the attack would come – from the direction of Gladsmoor. They were pale and quiet now; last night there had been countless whispers of orcs and their ferocity.

Now the guards leading each squad provided more than just drills, buoying their squad's spirits in low tones. There was nowhere to go. They would fight, or die.

A call went up from a lookout who thought he saw movement in the hills beyond the orchards and fields to the south. From this distance, it was hard to see anything clearly.

'Steady,' called Rast. 'Wait for my call to loose, and keep watch east and west as well. And remember: if the call *flash* goes up, avert your eyes or be blinded.'

They had thirty bows between them, ranging in age and size. The oft-used ones were held by competent bowmen, mainly hunters. One old refugee farmer proudly waved an ancient crossbow, lubricated and restrung, which looked as if it could cause horrific damage.

Karland stood among them next to Rast with his heart in his mouth. He should have been back at the town hall along with the others but they had all crept forward to see the enemy.

He heard a shout and saw a single figure crest a rise on the road in the open. Slightly stooped and broad, it looked up under shading hands at the sky. It was growing late and would be dusk soon. The clouds were very heavy and spoke with finality that there would be no more sun today. He shivered, and saw others around him swallow in fear, some with trembling hands clutching weapons in a sweaty grasp. Several men and women wore odd smiles, more a baring of teeth than anything else; others were yelling in open defiance. Only Rast watched without expression.

The figure looked around, and then pointed at the town. A faint snarling shout echoed out. As if summoned, a host broke over the hill behind it, swarming hundreds strong, and raced across the fields. Seconds later Karland heard the cries of the orcs, and he felt a keen stab of paralysing terror. The enemy was come.

They ignored the farms and houses that stood obviously empty and raced for the log palisade, knowing that their victims lay within. Fields full of food for the harvest were trampled flat as they poured forwards, tumbling and snarling in a wave. The attackers were mainly squat and broad, a little smaller than men, their skin ranging from a green so dark as to be almost black to a pale, sallow green-yellow. Slanted yellow eyes peered from bony faces, their ears pointed on heads crowned with stringy, greasy hair, and sharp, yellow-stained teeth gleamed with saliva, the bottom two canines much longer and peering over the bottom lip as they screeched and roared in bloodlust. The men on the wall quailed. These were monsters of legend, brought to life, the bogeymen of stories made flesh. At the noise Karland drew hastily back, knowing he needed to fall back to the town centre but unable to leave.

'Steady!' called Rast. 'Release at forty yards! Aim high!'

The bowmen drew and waited, arms trembling. The rest gripped their weapons tightly.

'Steady!'

The orcs were closer now, their eyes gleaming in hunger. Karland began to make out individual features.

'Steady!'

The impact of nearly two thousand feet could be heard as they slapped down on the earth. The jingling of armour and clashing of weapons grew, and the roaring was becoming deafening. Men blanched and squad leaders shouted encouragement.

'*Loose!*' shouted Rast, and thirty bows and a crossbow released their arrows. They hissed out into the dark mass, and almost all found their mark. More than twenty orcs fell, some screaming in pain. The men on the wall roared with one voice; their nightmare foe was proved mortal, and they had struck the first blow. Excitement mounted. A second volley shot out, dropping more orcs, which caused those behind to stumble or fall in turn.

Rast turned his head to Karland. 'Get your squad to the inner defences, boy! *Now!*' He turned back and called to the men on the wall. 'Be prepared. They must not breach the wall!'

The defenders roared. Karland scrambled down, calling to those boys he saw. The word spread and boys and girls streamed towards the centre. A deafening crash sounded as orcs slammed into the palisade and gates, testing their strength. Karland ran with the others towards the barricades around the town hall and the horses.

Slipping through narrow gaps in the barricade they took up places around the building. Karland counted heads through the door; everyone was there who was coming. He called for the doorway to be blocked and guarded, joining the others out in front. Clutching short and quickly-forged swords in frightened hands they were the last defence of the defenceless.

His gut was heavy with the responsibility. Looking back through the doorway as it closed, he caught a glimpse of Xhera's frightened face along with that of his mother and his terrified sister.

He would not fail, he swore silently.

CR   SO

The orcs hit the wall below Rast and to each side, counting on overwhelming the wall at the weakest point as fast as possible. The heavy gate shivered as the larger orcs at the fore slammed into it, testing its strength. Several tried to climb it but had little luck on the vertical logs. Those that made it off the ground were slashed at from above, forcing them to drop again.

The attack took a new direction as orcs below hoisted some of their fellows onto their shoulders. From there they could almost reach the top of the logs, and they slashed wickedly at the defenders, hissing. Further back, a huge orc was bellowing orders in a mixture of Orkish, Darum, and the dark dialect of the orcs which Rast did not speak. A good hundred orcs broke free of the mass and moved back, unstringing their own bows. With their first attempt to swarm the walls thwarted, they moved to siege tactics instead.

'Take cover!' shouted Rast, hearing the returning whine of orc arrows as they released. The arrow flew at the top of the wall, many arching higher to fall inside. The defenders ducked, but several were struck to collapse and fall from the wall. One screamed as he toppled forward into the yelling faces of the goblinoids to be hacked apart.

It was worse inside the compound. Arrows buzzed in, sending people scurrying for cover. Many were wounded and several were killed, one woman dropping as she ran to the wall holding quivers of arrows. More arrows than she had carried pierced her body. Rast caught a glimpse of Brin dragging himself under cover with an arrow through his thigh, clutching his sword and wearing his own armour. He couldn't spare him more than a quick thought.

'Aim for the archers!' he shouted. He expected the orcs to draw back from the wall and gate, but they were so eager to breach the wall they continued lifting their fellows up as high as they could. Defenders were slashed and stabbed horribly as orc heads and shoulders appeared over the tops of the walls, yet more orcs fell dead back on their companions.

A cry to the left turned him around. Several orcs had gained the top of the wall, and stood over the cooling, hacked bodies of defenders, one of them a councilman. More defenders were down than orcs. The remaining squad leader engaged them, hewing into an arm before stabbing through a ribcage. Her sword caught in ribs, and as she desperately tried to free it a spiked mace tore half her face off.

Rast ran for them. More orcs were rising behind them and the farmers were falling back too fast, their courage gone. It would only be seconds before they fled.

He smashed into the orcs, evading their strikes with the ease of long practice. Slamming his shoulder into the wounded one, he sent it head over heels off the wall onto its fellows below. The bloodied mace swung in, and he ducked, then trapped the arm across the orc's body. At the same time he kicked hard backwards, hitting the orc behind hard in the gut, then slammed an elbow into the trapped orc's eye. The cheekbone gave way with a crack and the creature yelled. The orc behind him forced itself painfully upright to plunge a jagged sword into his back, and found the weapon torn suddenly from its grasp. An iron hard grip latched onto its throat around the windpipe. The orc in front of Rast, blind with pain, lifted its mace only to have a foot slam into its chest and throw it far out from the wall. The mace fell into the orcs below, hitting one in its upturned face and dropping it like a stone.

Even as he kicked, he tightened his grip and yanked as hard as he could. With a wet tearing crunch, he tore the throat from the choking orc as it swung a sword up. It staggered, jetting blood from the ragged wound in its neck as it fell backwards into the enclosure. He flicked the gobbet of flesh over the wall, then whipped his arm overhead in a glittering arc. The sword left his hand in a spinning blur, hurtling end over end until it cleaved blade-first through the face and head of an orc being raised up a little way away. It bent as it dented and tore the iron helm, and the creature slumped with brains and blood leaking out from the massive wound.

His instincts took over. Rast leaned suddenly sideways, his right arm coming up, and a thrown spear aimed at his chest instead slapped into his hand. The farmers were bug-eyed as he turned to them.

'They can be killed as easily as men. Do not let them gain the wall!' he shouted. Heartened by his skill, they replied with a renewed shout and surged back around him, laughing. He turned and hurled the spear high out over the battle. It fell, lodging in the shoulder of a large dark skinned orc which dropped snapping and squealing in pain.

The bowmen continued to pick the more exposed orcish archers as their targets and whittled the attackers down, although they lost more than a few of their own. The rest of the defenders fought on bravely, and Rast moved among them. Everywhere he walked orcs fell, maimed or dead. His presence rallied them hugely, and they shouted his name when he came among them.

'*Rast! Rast! Tal'Orien is come!*' Everywhere the cry went up orcs learned to flee or die. He was like a flowing machine sowing death in the heart of the struggle, and he took no visible wound.

After two hours of struggle, the orcs began to lose heart. They had lost more than twice the number of each fallen defender, and a demon strode the walls that they dared not face. They withdrew without warning, moving beyond bowshot. The sky was dark and torches were being lit by the defenders; they had done well, but now both sides knew that they would face their foe in the dark.

Rast set men along all the walls, knowing that with the first attempt to breach the walls failed orcs might try to slip over the walls unseen in the night. The humans lacked their ability to see in the dark, and theirs would be the advantage now. The wounded were carried to the tavern nearby where Aldwyn and those others who knew healing tended them.

The mood was strange. Tension was high, and men were weary and frightened, but there was a sense of triumph. They had faced a foe from the worst tales and held. Many of them had killed more than one, and the surviving Guards kept the morale high, knowing they would need all their confidence this night. Rast walked among them, congratulating them quietly on their courage. Everywhere he went, his name was whispered. He heard them saying that he had performed impossible feats like the old legends come again, and that he could not be touched by enemy weapons.

Leona moved with him, whispering her report. Somehow able to scout and report on the movements of the orcs without being seen, she left to do so at regular intervals. She apparently saw at least as well as they in the dark, and Rast was now fully trusting of her abilities. From her came the name she had given him in Darost, repeated among the men until it became his new title: Lord of Death.

Banidróttin.

The orcs watched the walls, their eyes gleaming yellow in the darkness. The scales tipped in their favour now, and they waited.

ℝ   ⅀

Three hours later, they attacked without warning. Arrows whistled in from the darkness, felling a few unwary defenders, and then the orcs struck with snarls and shouts. It was harder to see them now, despite the torches, and the defenders found them gaining the walls far more easily. Three times the walls were almost breached, and three times the defenders managed to throw them back.

Rast moved where the battle was most frenzied, bringing cries of '*Banidróttin! Banidróttin!*' The orcs quickly learned his new name, and snarled it with hate and fear. They swarmed to his location, trying desperately to kill him, but Rast took only scratches and left dead and dying orcs in his wake, hurling them broken from the walls. The orcs cursed in superstitious fright. The human bore no arms, and yet was a living weapon.

Where the orcs were thickest, cries of '*Flash! Ware the Flash!*' went up every so often, followed by a bright searing flash and thump erupting from groups of the attackers. Burned and shrieking in agony, their eyes were seared by the light. Painful for humans, it was physically damaging for the far more light-sensitive vision of the orcs. However, it was not long before they were all used up, apart from one that Rast kept along with the remaining phosphorus bombs. He knew he would need to make them count.

෬   ෪

At the height of the attack a group of twenty orcs managed to slip over the north wall unseen. They swiftly killed any that they found; several unprepared wounded farmers, craftsmen and others alone in tents and houses were butchered. The orcs followed the paths until they found the town hall barricades and swiftly realised that this must be where the helpless were kept. Hungrily, they found the narrow passages and began to weave their way through the barriers, skinny spindly-armed goblins creeping in front of solid squat orcs. The lust of killing innocents glinted in their eyes.

Half were within the barricade when a cry went up from outside and the remainder turned to face a small squad of farmers that had appeared without warning, on patrol. Outnumbering them two to one, the orcs laughed nastily. The farmers carried nothing but some form of strange stick, and there were only five, thinly spread out.

The first goblin dashed forwards with a shriek and the nearest defender spun his arms in a complicated motion. To the astonishment of the others the goblin screamed as its entire arm sprang away to hit the ground, twitching. The stick came back around and they saw the gleam of a huge dark crescent blade before the scythe opened the goblin up to the throat.

With a roar, the orcs charged, realising this was a real threat. The defenders retreated in a loose group, scythes curving around them in dangerous arcs. The orcs kept a respectful distance, but the scythes were deceptively fast, and shortly there were only three orcs to four farmers left standing. The rest of the creatures were dismembered and dying, and soaked the ground black with their dark blood for many yards. As one, the remaining orcs scrambled for the barriers. Only one of them made it.

The scythe wielders paused, frustrated. There was no way they could safely wield their weapons in the confines inside. There were twenty-six boys in there with weapons, and they had to hold until more help arrived. One man dropped his scythe and ran desperately for help, and the other three stood with despair etched on their faces as they listened to the battle within.

෬   ෪

It was exhausting standing defence within the barricade. Nerves were frayed to breaking point. The youngsters could hear the fighting and the screams of dying men and women – men and women they knew – and many faces ran with tears of fright. Karland himself was shaking so hard his teeth chattered, and he was not the only one. Ben Arflun had stopped trying to give orders. His face had worn stark terror until it went eventually blank and he had simply thrown down his spear and shield and refused to move. He sat muttering quietly to himself, eyes tightly shut as if to deny what was happening.

All of the boys had dreamed of battle, had played at being warriors, heroes, adventurers, but this was terrifying reality. They and the four girls that had refused to be shut in the town hall ranged between ten and fifteen years of age - a hard age to face the stark truth of mortality.

Furtive movement and the sound of flapping feet and wicked laughter from the barricade brought gasps and panicked breathing. As the first dark form moved into view of the torches, a cry from outside the barrier challenged the intruders, and the sounds of battle echoed. The orcs safely inside approached slowly, knowing that their opponents were inexperienced, enjoying their fear.

'We's gonna gut you lads,' snarled one of the orcs. 'All of yer. Slowly. And for the girlies…' It grinned, showing ragged pointed teeth and two long lower canines. There was a pause, punctuated by shrieks from outside the barrier. Time seemed to slow as the orcs snarled, laughing horribly. The defenders all gripped their weapons – except Ben, who was still sitting as if he was not there.

Karland suddenly found his mind was clear, and his trembling had stopped as his training with Rast and his calm from defeating Ben all snapped into place. One of the orcs charged, roaring with bloodlust, and he steeled himself and leapt forward. Three other boys yelled and ran to meet it too, and the sides clashed.

The orcs carved through their opponents horribly. Youths Karland had known his entire life were disembowelled in front of him, impaled through the guts to scream in terror and pain, knowing their short lives were over as their innards were torn to ragged shreds. Karl Dowerson staggered back, spraying several of his horrified friends with the hot blood pumping from his throat, his face twisted in gasping panic with a profound resignation for one so young. The orc sword that had ripped his throat and artery open swung back, flinging blood, and decapitated him. The torso fell with a bloody ragged stump next to the rolling head. A girl he didn't know went down choking under a hacking dagger.

Many died in the first few seconds, frozen in horror or simply outclassed in combat; yet most fought tooth and nail for the children and mothers behind them, and several orcs fell to their combined numbers. It was not enough.

Karland ducked a blow from a broad, curved blade and stabbed wildly, scoring the orc in the thigh. It shouted in rage, and twisted to run him through, its face evil and full of lust. As he twisted desperately, a fist crashed into his face and he fell backwards, scrabbling to retreat, his sword lost.

Karland fancied he could hear his heart thumping as time seemed to slow even further. He heard the screams and panicked choking of boys who would never become men, the few girls who would never be married, the squealing snarls of the orcs tearing them apart. He heard the panicked whinnying of the horses, milling within the makeshift corral to the side. They could smell the horrible stench of the orcs, the blood and death. The creatures struck a deep fear into the horses, for they loved horse flesh, and there was no escape for them. If there had been room to run, they would have trampled everyone in their panic.

Then one deeper angry whinny cut through the rest. Stryke was not in the corral, by design or by chance, and instead of retreating the huge horse whirled and barrelled full into the orcs from the side as they charged, bowling several over and scattering the rest. The giant cremello reared, screaming in anger, and lashed sharp fore-hooves at the attackers remaining in front. They fell back as Stryke crashed through them to Karland.

The stallion turned its head slightly, eyes wide, and then bucked, slamming both feet over Karland's unprotected head into the face and chest of the orc as he lunged. The orc's body flew back to slam into his comrades as if launched from a catapult, its face a bloody mess, neck broken.

Karland leapt to his feet, yelling, and snatched the first weapon he found – something that looked like a cleaver. He had found a place of calm acceptance bordered by hatred and rage and ran at the nearest orc, which was clambering to its feet. Putting every fibre of his being into his strike, he swung.

The orc raised its shield to cover its head, but guessed wrong. The cleaver bit deep into its side, curving up and sticking as the weight of the body held it. Karland let go, still yelling –now in triumph – and the orc staggered back looking astonished before it fell. The other boys screamed and shouted in a mixture of fear and excitement, running towards their foes. Stryke was lashing out in utter fury, and suddenly the orcs were trying to escape him with desperation on their bestial faces. He had killed several more of their number, and there were now only three orcs left. They were joined by a fourth which had come from outside and looked dismayed at a second battle. One orc dodged past a boy and girl and ran at Ben, who still had not moved. Karland ran after it, grabbing a fallen short sword as he ran.

A tiny voice in the back of his mind asked, *Is it worth saving him?*

Yes, he replied so fiercely that the shameful part quailed. The orc reared up to cut the sitting boy down with a horrible-looking blade, and Karland shouted at it.

'Try *me*, you *bastard!*'

The orc turned, and Karland's sword took it in the left arm instead of the kidney. It snarled in rage and struck at him; Karland managed to block inexpertly, knowing he was doomed, but he didn't care anymore. He was full of rage at this thing that dared defile his world.

The orc jerked suddenly, snapping its teeth at Karland, and then fell to the side, kicking feebly. Behind it stood Ben, his eyes clearing and his spear in its back. He raised his tear-stained face to Karland, his expression blank, and nodded. They looked at each other for a second in understanding and mutual thanks and then turned to the battle to find it over. The last orc fell under the weapons of a dozen screaming youngsters, stabbing and thrusting in hatred and fear until it didn't resemble an orc anymore. As their fury was spent they stopped one by one, breathing heavily, some weeping.

Then there was silence, and Karland looked around, disbelieving of the last few minutes. He saw eleven orcs dead, Stryke trembling in rage, and twelve boys and two girls, ragged, weary, blood-stained and wounded. He also saw many still forms that he would never forget. Boys and girls he had known, had seen die in a horrible manner. A few were moving, however, and that was some hope.

To one side, Ben suddenly threw back his head and let out a cathartic scream of triumph, a release of the paralysing fear they had felt. The others were suddenly cheering and screaming in reaction as well and to his astonishment Karland found he had joined them. He turned to see townsfolk emerge fearfully from the town hall, shock on their faces, and he knew then that they had survived.

TWENTY-ONE

The orcs finally broke off their second attack, their diversion failed, and did not come again that night. It was clear that a push at the walls was not working, and they left hundreds dead behind them.

Rast remained vigilant and gave orders without ceasing. He listened without expression to the report of the intruders and commended the scythe carriers and the survivors. Leona paced inside the walls tirelessly, watching for a second infiltration, but none came. They had lost half the first defenders on the wall to wounds or death.

At some time between midnight and dawn, Rast vanished with Leona. The town council members looked unhappy, but refused to answer any questions. As dawn broke, Leona and Rast reappeared, looking tired but happy, reporting that they had seen the orcs break for the distant woods to hide from the day and followed them without being detected. Using stealth and skill they had killed many orcs, and frightened many more into thinking the woods meant instant death.

Weary, they went to their beds. Rast said he would be up in one hour, and refused to listen to talk of sleeping any longer.

Karland spent that day being tended and sleeping the sleep of exhaustion. The morning dawned fine and bright, which seemed almost an insult to those that had died in darkness and death.

The world had changed for him again. It had begun when he had met the trapper that had been killed by the bear, and the innocence that had begun dimming had finished burning free last night. Everything looked grimmer, clearer to him now. The parents who had lost children were inconsolable, especially given the brutal manner of their death, but the townsfolk were proud. Their sons and daughters had died defending those they loved.

He moved to the walls to stand amongst the tired survivors keeping watch. There was no movement from the orcs, who had seemingly vanished. Leona spoke to him once after returning from scouting, her cudgel stained, and said that she had found them hiding in the fringes of the woods in the low hills to the south. They were afraid of the deeper woods and were not resting well. They had lost a good number, although they still had many archers.

The townsfolk mourned the dead and moved them to the houses nearest the gates. Karland moved to help Aldwyn and his healers as they tirelessly attended the wounded, cleaning wounds that would otherwise fester from the foul blades of the orcs and making comfortable those that were badly hurt. The fifth scythe wielder was back on his feet at least, and three more of the wounded boys might survive.

He found his father, limping with a blood stained bandage on his leg and a determined look on his face, and was thankful that he was safe. Xhera took the news to his family in the town hall, bringing back news of their joy; not everyone had been so lucky.

Dusk approached, and he watched the townsfolk grew nervous, talking amongst themselves.

ଓ   ଚ

Shortly after dark the orcs gathered in the fields, determined to raze the town tonight. The moon was bright, and they were apparent as a dark, seething mass.

Leona pointed and muttered to Rast who looked around the field. He could just make out the dark forms of a group of orcs carrying a large tree trunk towards the palisade from the eastern forest edge. He cursed quietly. If the orcs smashed the gate open they would be quickly overrun.

As if the thought had triggered them the orcs attacked, howling in frenzy. The wearying dance began again, and the defenders threw wave after wave off the walls. To Rast's right, the lean smith was blasting orcs backwards of the wall tirelessly with a large maul. To his left, Gladsmoor guards shouted encouragement to the farmers under their leadership as they fought.

Protected by the wall, the defending archers were accounting for themselves better than the orcs. A few early volleys left most of the remaining orc archers dead or unable to release further. Only seven defending archers had fallen, but that was a higher number than they could afford to lose. One was the old farmer with the crossbow, struck in the eye by a filthy point to tumble from the wall.

Rast himself took the crossbow. It was a horribly clunky ancient thing but it had a strong draw and the farmer had not been using it to its full range. Rast sighted on the foremost orc carrying the tree, just visible in the darkness, and let fly. The crossbow's sights were off and the bolt sliced down to vanish into the ribcage of the orc behind. It fell forward, tripping the orcs behind it.

With a crash, the tree dropped, crushing two legs and a chest and wounding several others. Screeches of anger drifted from that direction and he smiled grimly. It had been a lucky shot in the dark, but anything that slowed them was welcome.

He had no time to crank the mechanism again. A fresh wave of orcs was at the wall and this time they were hacking at the wood itself, covered by shields. The defenders dropped what they could on the attackers.

Rast called for what spare oil they had, and had them try and pour it outwards from the wall. He prayed that the retardant chemicals used would protect the wood, and dropped a flaming brand. The sudden shrieks of burning orcs leapt skywards with the flames, and they scattered in mindless agony, beating at their bodies. Tens of orcs roasted to death, and their charred corpses blocked their companions from the wall. With relief, he saw that the wall was merely scorched apart from two tracks of flame which were doused quickly, but the relief was short-lived. The orcs bearing the trunk arrived, and manoeuvred it to the gate.

'Stand ready!' Rast shouted. 'They must not breach the gate!'

The defenders rushed to attack the ram-bearers, but were driven back by a hail of arrows. The gate shuddered at blow after heavy blow. One defender leaned out with a phosphorus bomb and was struck in the temple, the arrow lodging deep in his brain. He fell, dropping the bomb, and it exploded with concussive force next to the trunk. The blast took several orc legs out, and cracked the bark, splintering the wood. It did not significantly damage the ram, but several orcs dropped dead. More ran up from the dark mass, lifting the ram and hammering it home again. Suddenly there was no more time; the unseasoned beam holding the gates shut snapped as one gate tore off the new hinges and fell at an angle.

Rast played his last trick as the gates smashed and orcs leapt into the opening. In the middle of the enclosure was a huge bonfire, covered in oil, and as the orcs poured into the enclosure, flaming brands were hurled onto it from all sides. The light dimmed for a moment on the walls, and then the last phosphorus bomb was hurled into its midst.

There was a crack like thunder and the whole pile caught with a thumping whoosh. A year's supply of oil flared up dazzlingly. The defenders, prepared, covered their eyes, but the orcs were blinded painfully and screeched.

The defenders fell upon them and drove them back. At their head was Rast, striking quickly and powerfully, knocking orcs aside like children. He twirled and ducked as he struck, leaving the defenders behind him to finish his disabled opponents. Leading them out into darkness teeming with orcs, he hurled the last phosphorus bomb. It exploded, driving the surviving orcs back shrieking in blinking terror.

'To me!' he cried. 'Drive them back! Defend the gate!'

The defenders broke through the unprepared ranks of the orcs in a wedge, Rast beyond the tip. They stopped at the gates, but he dove forward seemingly to his death in the ragged ranks facing him. He did not move without purpose, however. Almost directly in front of the gates was the great orc that had directed the attack, come in closer to watch the slaughter in glee. Fat and bloated, it was heavy with muscle, one great chipped fang standing up. Seeing him coming, it roared in fury, spittle flying from its ragged teeth.

'Kill the *Banidróttin!*'

Several massive orcs moved into Rast's way. They looked heavier than a normal human, and more followed. They stood ready to slice at him with strange, angular thick-ended swords. Rast put his head down and sprinted, and then crouched at the last second. They sliced down at him, and he leapt, uncoiling like a spring. Tucking his head down, he flipped over their heads with remarkable grace, one sword missing by a finger's width. At the apex of his arc he hurled the last flasher behind him, and landed behind the three orcs at the rear.

The flasher exploded as he landed, orcs shrieked in agony. The three nearest swung blindly, blinking afterimages of the leaping man from their eyes.

The great orc's eyes bulged in shock as the human landed lightly in front of him. Rast turned in place and grabbed an orc by the head, wrenching it up and left powerfully. As its neck broke, he caught the sword it dropped, and whirled into a dazzling attack. The orcs either side of him turned and chopped, and his sword weaved over and down diagonally, deflecting one sword. He immediately snapped it up and around his back, stopping the other with a clang where it would have cleaved his spine. Sliding the sword along so the hilt lay close to the other blade, Rast chopped down overhead, yanking the other blade over and down. He sliced sideways along the blade and up, cutting through the throat of the orc attacking him, and then rotated as it dropped choking to deflect three quick strikes from the next before slicing down and almost taking one of its legs off.

As the orc fell, he whirled in place with the sword straight out and decapitated the frozen huge fat orc with a single blow. The corpse of the chieftain slumped, spewing thick blood to the floor. Completing the move, the sword arced in a figure of eight blur around him, ending up hilt-first, the blade along his arm. He crouched low over the body with one leg extended and a hand out in warning, staring at the approaching orcs.

They stopped in their tracks. Mutters sprang up around him. One goblin chanced its luck, springing from behind, and he turned and jumped. Spinning almost horizontally with the sword held out, he met it in mid-air. There was a scream, and the goblin fell in a welter of blood, two halves loosely attached by spine and guts.

Rast landed and crouched again, daring any to approach.

The orcs facing him backed away in panic from the demon before them covered in their dark blood. Panicked shouts of '*Banidróttin! The Banidróttin! Lurtz-ha! Flee!*' erupted, and the orcs retreated in fear. It could not last long, he knew. They would overwhelm him when they found their courage.

Without warning a horn sounded from the south. With a resounding crash a second army of men hit the orcs with military precision. Shouting in triumph, the defenders renewed their waning attack, and the remaining orcs broke and ran. Rast struck down any that came near him, and they streamed around him.

Most fled northwest, silently and swiftly, only a few fleeing east. All were quickly lost in the darkness. Rast took a deep breath, moving towards the town and the defenders as the reinforcements merged around them.

Into the broken gates, triumphant, marched the men and guards of Eordeland and the survivors from The Croft. The cheers were deafening. One by one, the rest came forth, not daring to believe it was over. Rast smiled grimly at the victory as he joined them, weary and stinking of orc blood. He did not think they would return.

Bolstered by the fresh men, he arranged a watch on the walls and gate, and then ordered the survivors to find rest. The fight was finally over. They had survived.

છ   જ

Xhera picked her way through the survivors, looking for Karland. A full third of the town's farmers and crafters had died in its defence, along with nearly half the refugees. Several council members had survived, the Mayor among them. She passed the smith in his forge, dour as ever, the hammer he had used to break orcish heads back to work. Janos, his apprentice, was not so lucky. He had lost his left arm below the elbow, although he would live.

Nearly one hundred and thirty men and women had died on the walls, and another forty inside the town itself. Some had died in their homes, refusing to leave and butchered by the orcs that had infiltrated. The townsfolk and refugees had begun the daunting and gruesome task of collecting and burying the dead and building a pyre for their dead foes. She tried to imagine how it would feel if it had been her farmstead, and could not. Karland was uninjured, but not unaffected. She thanked Isha that he had trained with Rast and survived.

Everything mercifully smelt of smoke, so the tang of blood and the stench of the orcs was somewhat muffled. The huge bonfire was still smouldering, and another even greater would be built outside town to burn the orcs that had fallen. Of those, there were well over five hundred. They had paid dearly for their attack, and lost their archers and captain. She had seen boys and men moving among them, ensuring that they were all dead.

The reinforcements were a mixture of guards and men from several towns, responding to the requests for help. They had been alarmed and astounded to find they fought orcs from the stories, and impressed that the defenders had held. They also brought word of the other Gladsmoor survivors - there were more than hoped for, as most had escaped south. They, too, had rebuilding to do, in addition to the tedious job of rounding up thousands of cattle from the moors.

The orcs had apparently crossed the Norlands from the eastern mountains and run along the southern edges of the great Northing Woods. To Xhera's relief, the natural break running east to west in the trees had kept them well north of Hoeven Lake, which bordered the southern stretch of trees. They had run west and crossed the shallows well north of Fordun's Run, but been balked by deepening waters and woods to the north.

Gladsmoor had been directly in their path, but the guards had been alert enough to evacuate many, warned by several stampedes of cattle from the east. Losing some of their number to the forest, the orcs had pushed north, stymied by wide deep rivers to the west. South were heavily guarded borders, and annihilation. Turning north through the hills, they had moved to strike west nearer the coast, and Rast had said that The Croft had presented an easy target on the way through – or so they had thought. Other towns had apparently not been so lucky. Slow to respond to the tales of *myths*, more than a few had been decimated by roving bands of orcs on their way west. Xhera had felt before as if trouble followed them; now she realised it was spreading everywhere.

She finally found Karland at his parent's house. His mother had wept with relief when she had found that her son lived; his father walked stiffly, but was otherwise fine, and had killed two orcs. It seemed even Gail had learnt that life was not always pleasant, and she was silent. The price of that learning had been high.

Karland himself was quiet, and the stories were already growing. Alone of all of the boys, he had killed an orc single-handedly, face to face, leading their attack and breaking them out of their paralysis. He had also saved someone he had once considered his worst enemy; the orcs had put that former childishness into real perspective. She sighed to herself. In more ways than one, this would never be the same home he remembered, and she felt it keenly for him.

Last night the Mayor had spoken passionately, solemnly swearing to erect two memorials to the battle. One was to honour the brave defenders just inside the gates which were to be rebuilt and strengthened along with a new wall. The other was to be at the town hall itself in memory of the terrified youths that had died to protect their families. 'We will never forget,' he told the gathered townspeople, a huge silent crowd. 'But we will recover.'

Above all he had hailed Rast as their saviour. When the cheers had finally died, the big man had shaken his head and spoken firmly and briefly.

'It needed to be done.'

He had refused all payments and gifts; the town would need everything it owned to repair and rebuild. Leona likewise shied from the gratitude, content to help where she could.

'Karland,' Xhera said, touching his arm gently. He looked at her with troubled eyes and she felt for him again. 'Rast wishes to speak with Aldwyn… and us.' He shrugged, and called to his father, who was working with Aldwyn to fashion more fabric into bandages.

When they reached the town hall, the Mayor, the relief guard, and the council were there with Rast and Leona. A guard lieutenant was giving word on the fleeing orcs, which were apparently trying to push on through the day. Aldwyn said this would leave them dizzy and weak, and it meant they must be desperate.

'So, the orcs have fled north and west,' Rast mused. 'They *must* be what Meyar was protecting in east Norland, but why?'

'These creatures were protected by *humans*?' asked the lieutenant, his face disbelieving.

Aldwyn nodded. 'Meyari assassins struck at the Council of Twelve in Darost while their army apparently protected the orcs all the way from the World's Crest mountains. Trust not the Meyari! They are at, mm, war with us now. You must send word of what has happened here to Darost. Eordeland must guard well her borders. I am charged to find out how Meyar is involved in current chaos pervading all the lands. Mmm, *orcs* in Eordeland! Rast, I suspect they will head directly across the Nassmoor. There *must* be a link to Meyar.'

Rast's face was grim as he nodded. He turned to the Mayor. 'It is to my regret that we must leave so soon, but this is of great importance. We are charged by the Council of Twelve themselves to investigate. Aldwyn Varelin is a Councillor, though not fully seated.' This produced murmurs of surprise.

The Mayor nodded. 'We can ask no more – what remains is for us to rebuild anyway. You have done everything that you could – and more. I have never seen such prowess in battle! You saved us, Master Tal'Orien.'

Rast smiled. 'I merely gave you the spark to save yourselves, Thomas Bedwin. I seem to recall you knocking orcs flying with a large club over the course of several hours.'

The Mayor blushed. 'Yes, well.' Already popular, he was now becoming a local legend, a leader willing to take the vanguard. 'Anything we can spare is yours. What troops will you take?'

'None,' replied Rast. Confronted by shocked stares, he laughed. 'I do not intend to fight! We will stay far behind. Orcs move at an incredible pace when roused. We could not catch them if we tried; we merely track them, nothing more. If they run during daylight, they are desperate indeed. They are vulnerable now, very much so.' He turned to his party. 'We will leave tomorrow morning, early.' Catching Karland's gaze, he added, 'If you still wish to come?'

Karland barely hesitated. 'I am part of this, remember? My family is safe because of you. The least I can do is follow and do what I can.' He smiled, and looked at Xhera. She smiled back and nodded agreement.

'Jolly good,' beamed Aldwyn. Xhera would not have blamed Karland for staying with his family, but then in his position she would have followed as well. The last few nights had reinforced to them all that nowhere was safe now – not even The Croft.

'It is agreed then,' said Rast. 'We leave on the morrow.'

 co   so

Morning proved cloudy, with brief sunny patches piercing through. Aldwyn, fidgeting impatiently, muttered that the orcs would move quicker now.

Rast glanced at him sideways. 'Do you suppose I can track five hundred orcs in broad daylight?' he asked mildly. Aldwyn glared at him, but stopped complaining.

They readied the horses as the town bustled around them. Rast had been the only one able to approach his angry horse after the fight at the town hall, although since then Stryke had decided Karland was acceptable. As he helped ready the giant cremello, Karland laughed nervously. He still hadn't forgotten the feeling of the plate-sized hooves whistling over his head to kill the orc, and said as much to Rast. The big man, soothing his steed, glanced over at the boy.

'Don't worry, Karland. Stryke is trained in warfare much as I am, but he sees you as part of my herd, which makes you part of his.'

'Well, I can see why he is called Stryke,' said Karland lamely, not sure how he felt to be part of a herd. 'He was very accurate. I never realise how dangerous a horse can be.'

Rast shook his head in amusement.

'Ask any farm hand. They are a hundred times stronger than a human and many times heavier. Of course, he also dislikes orcs. Horses are usually nervous and use their speed as their best defence, but Stryke is different – most warhorses are, especially chargers. But that is not why he is named Stryke. His name means 'Iron' in Poviiri. He will protect his herd to the death.'

Casually, Karland asked, 'So... *he* leads the herd?' Xhera's lips quirked.

Rast refused to be drawn. 'Stryke and I are equal partners. We protect each other and the herd. He is intelligent enough to know that I am not to be challenged. Most horses would not understand this – but then again, even Stryke had to be broken.' He patted the horse's neck fondly.

They were ready to go by mid-morning. Aldwyn had left what supplies and instructions he could, and taken longer doing so than he had wanted, but nobody begrudged him the extra time. Even with his expertise in healing, many had died of their wounds; the weapons of orcs were not forgiving.

Karland's family came to see them off, along with half the town. They all had to decline money, extra supplies and even requests to journey with them, the latter mainly from the boys who envied Karland his minor celebrity and relationship with the great *Banidróttin*. Rast had, however, accepted several hastily tailored cloaks from Brin to replace his old one, which was irreparable.

'I must admit, son, you were right in what you told me. And you're caught up in this whole thing,' his father said, shaking his head in wonder. 'Master Aldwyn, Master Tal'Orien. Thank you, truly, for looking after my son. And... I hope he makes you as proud as he has made me.'

Karland found a slight lump in his throat. He had never thought to hear that from his father.

Aldwyn smiled. 'Be assured, he already has, mm, Brin,' he said.

Becka cried a little, and hugged him goodbye again. He even had a fierce hug from Gail; she had been terrified by the battle and knew her brother had fought for her.

Rast called to the Mayor to remember to keep watchful, and Thomas nodded. They rattled through the gate in the cart accompanied by the horses to the cries of *'Banidróttin! Rast Tal'Orien! May you live long!',* and to his surprise, a few shouting *'Karland! Karland!'* One of those was Ben Arflun, grinning ear to ear and pumping a big fist in the air. After a moment of astonishment, Karland grinned back.

They turned north out of the gate, and followed the trail. Nearly five hundred hurrying feet – bare and rough-shod both – had made a mess of the fields, making a beeline for the trail to the northwest rather than following the road. As they rounded the bend, Karland looked back. The Croft had changed, and although it would be forever in his heart he knew it would never be the same for him.

The road curved west then southwest alongside the river. The skies stayed cloudy, and they passed out of Eordeland altogether a little before dark two days later. Neither Karland nor Xhera had ever left their country before and both were a little disappointed that it felt no different. The party camped that night next to the river and quickly fell asleep.

The orcs were plainly trying to find a way across the river. Near the end of the next day of travel they arrived at the Nassing Bridge, which showed signs of their passing. Crossing over they camped a little south of it to await the morning. They had made almost fifty miles, to Aldwyn's surprise. Hjarta was full of more energy than usual; Aldwyn suspected it was something to do with Leona, who tended every horse briefly when they camped. Even Stryke liked her, and set aside his usual suspicions. As always, Rast sat up late, this time murmuring in conversation with Leona until Karland's eyes shut of their own accord.

The next morning after some study into the distance Rast grunted, looking down across the plains. 'They do not move west towards Meyar, but south. Perhaps they plan to go to ground in the foothills of the Arkons.'

'Near to the dwarves?' questioned Aldwyn. 'That is close to Deep Delving.'

Rast nodded. 'The Arkons are hardly small; they might avoid the dwarves. But wherever they go, they head there with all speed.'

Aldwyn looked thoughtful. 'I have been too busy the last few days to think on it, but something has been prodding my mind for some time. Something Sarthos said, buried in his ramblings. I thought Meyar was where we must go but I am unsure, now you mention mountains.' He grimaced. 'Let me think on it. Mayhap the answer will, aha, spring to the fore.'

'The Arkons?' enquired Xhera. Karland knew the answer, and spoke before

Aldwyn.

'The highest mountain range in Anaria,' he said. 'West of Eordeland, at the top of the great plains. That's where the main dwarven city is, Deep Delving.'

Xhera looked surprised. 'A city of Dwarves?'

'Come,' broke in Rast. 'We have no time to lose. Mount up.'

They pushed on early. Rast followed the tracks with puzzlement plain on his face. They had now turned southeast as if to approach the Eordeland border again and neither he nor Aldwyn could understand it.

They passed a grim reminder of the orcs later that day; a large merchant train lay silent and still on the road. Everyone was dead, the horses too, and not all of the remains were whole. The orcs had found fresh meat for their cookpots, and Karland felt sick. It seemed they did not just eat horseflesh.

Two days later the puzzle cleared somewhat, although it introduced another. They were now east of the Arkons themselves, the massive peaks rising forbidding from the plains, but to Rast's long vision the trail of the orcs now plainly curved southwest, away from the Darost border.

'They are bypassing the Arkons!' he said in surprise. 'This becomes stranger and stranger. This leads them away from Eordeland and reprisals; they look to be heading southwest of the Arkons and into the Reldenhort Plains. That is dangerous for them - they must be weakened harshly in the day. They cut directly across the lands of the Ork tribes, and run high risk of being caught. There will be no mercy for them if that happens.'

As they lay down to sleep that night, the scholar abruptly jumped up, talking excitedly, and it took Rast several minutes to calm him down and make sense of what he was saying. The others sat up, interested.

'I remembered!' Aldwyn said. 'There is a phrase in the Book of Sarthos. That is why I thought of mountains. It is roughly translated as '*Great power unlocked by key, within deep hollow of the mountain lies*'. It means nothing to me, but it suggests, ah, that we will find it somewhere in mountains.' He grabbed the pendant hidden around his neck. 'Kelpas didn't say what it was, if he even knew.' He sighed. 'That was why I thought it interesting the orcs headed for the Arkons! Because, you see, it would all fit. They must have had *some* reason for moving across Eordeland. It was incredibly dangerous for them. Indeed, without Meyar's intervention they would had never got so far. Actually… it just means we have to find a 'hollow in the mountains' that may hold some great power.' He shrugged, making a moue with his lips as his excitement waned. 'Maybe it is all just a reach of imagination.'

'Keep thinking, scholar,' said Rast with a small smile. 'You have done well so far. I am sure in time this will fall to your magnificent brain as well.'

'Ah, well, yes, but time is the one thing we are, aha, short on.'

The next few days saw the trail turn away from the road. Rast spoke to Aldwyn and they turned off to follow the trail across the plains; the going was slow as Aldwyn wanted his little cart to keep its axle and wheels unbroken. The ground where the orcs had passed was trampled flat, which helped, and the grass stretched before them like an ocean.

On the eighteenth day after they had left The Croft they spied a dot of fire in the distance on a grey afternoon. Rast estimated that they might reach it before they camped that night; it could be anything, but if it was a campfire at least it meant a hot meal. The plains tribes were honourable, he said, and if it was a merchant, so much the better, although few visited the Orks. Few could find them on the plains.

It grew dark as they travelled, and still it burned. Rast frowned, but they did not stop their slow approach. The fire grew larger and larger.

Eventually Rast swore softly.

'That is no camp fire,' he said. It was clear that the fire was huge, a beacon burning on the plains for hours. It had died somewhat now, but would likely burn into the next day. When the wind blew toward them, a foul burning stench filled their noses. They pulled up and hobbled Hjarta. Leaving the nervous horses well back they approached on foot. Drawn towards it, no one spoke until they were as close as was sensible in the smoke and heat.

'We have found the orcs,' Rast said bleakly.

TWENTY-TWO

O rc bodies were piled ten, fifteen high. The fire lit the night and foul smoke rolled off it, blowing every which way as the wind moved about the grassland. There must have been nearly five hundred orcs on the pyre.

On these open plains, there was little chance any could have escaped. The ground was churned up into mud and dirt, the grass torn up by the ferocity of the fight. Rast scanned the tracks. 'It looks as if many large beasts and heavy beings attacked them. Probably an Ork tribe.'

They stood well back, looking at the burning corpses for a while, their mouths and noses covered. Even through the thick cloth Karland could smell the stench of orc bodies and charring flesh, a sickly-sweet combination. Leona looked as if the smell was a physical assault. She was wincing, her nose covered and her face pale. Rast supposed the combination of odours was the last thing a protector of nature with heightened senses would wish to smell. Xhera looked at the death, her face unreadable, and then she turned away and closed her eyes. Karland's face was pale in the light, and was Aldwyn cursing softly at the sudden end of their chase. Whatever the orcs' connection to Meyar, it might only be found there now, if at all.

Leona's head lifted warily. 'We are surrounded,' she said quietly.

'Orcs?' said Aldwyn in alarm.

'The tribes,' corrected Rast.

Shapes began to fade out of the night. They were large, most as big as Rast, some even bigger. Karland couldn't see many details in the shadows, but made out eyes gleaming in the firelight – as, disconcertingly, did tusks. He glanced around to find a wall of green clad in leather and fur closing around them from all sides. There seemed to be few swords in evidence. The preference ran towards heavy hammers, axes, and clubs, with more than a few large spears pointed at them as well. The eyes were dark and intent, studying him more closely than he could their owners.

The highlights on their green skins gleamed yellow-white in the orange firelight, and the massive muscles underneath bunched. The orks were built very solidly, and looked ferocious and tense. It would not take much for them to explode into violence.

When they saw their quarry were all humans they paused, muttering in surprise. One stepped forward, gripping a massive morningstar. He was bald, with pointed ears that stood out in contrast to his smooth scalp framing a broad-nosed rugged face with two large tusks rising from the bottom jaw. They poked from between the lips to lie against the cheeks level with his nostrils along slight grooves in the flesh. A sleeveless open fur jerkin hung from the shoulders, and his waist down was covered in a rough kilt. From one ear a black collection of feathers and thread hung in a knot.

In a rough voice that sounded slightly strange as it spoke around the huge teeth, the ork spoke, almost spitting the words in disgust.

'Humans! What you want here?'

Rast held up his hand to the others, indicating he would respond, and addressed the ork calmly, holding his eyes.

'Greetings, *Urukin*. This band of orcs marauded in Eordeland. We followed, but it seems your tribes found them first.'

Low angry mutters met this, and the big ork squinted at them suspiciously.

'We slew them all. Why you follow these *Goruc'cha,* these fallen? You maybe their allies?' A keen look appeared on several tusked faces, and Karland heard the sounds of weapons being hefted.

'*Allies?* To this filth? Are you witless goblins?' snarled Leona. Karland saw Rast wince. Several orks roared in anger, and she threw back her hood. 'Do none of you recognise a Druid anymore? Is the land so closed to you that you listen only to bloodlust? We fought these off at great cost. Do not insult us.'

The bald ork stared at her, and then raised his hands and snarled something loudly. The anger around him subsided a little. He looked carefully at her, noting her robes, her eyes, and her bearing. Grudgingly, he nodded.

'Druid, maybe. You welcome to our plains if so. Others are not.'

'Yet I travel with them,' she replied.

He stared at her and then made up his mind. 'We take you to camp. *Urukin* tribes are at war with all now. Many bad thing happen in recent days. Over-Chief says kill any human found off roads, but Druid not expected. So we go to Brukk. *He* decide.'

It was clear to Karland that things would be unpleasant if they did not go with the orks. At least a hundred stayed with them and the rest faded back into the night, some moving to huge dim shapes which moved off slowly. The orks moved on foot at a pace matching the horses, and once they started moving it did not seem that they would ever need to stop. They moved over the plains for more than an hour at a high pace, the little cart rattling over the uneven ground and Hjarta blowing hard through his nose, his eyes wild. Aldwyn was concerned that he would break an axle, and even more concerned his little dray would overreach his reserves on the rough ground before they stopped.

Eventually Karland asked in a low tone, 'Where are they taking us?'

Aldwyn shook his head. 'I do not know. They are nomadic so their camp may be nearby. This Brukk, their Over-Chieftain, is like a king – but he will have earned his name and rank by the strength of his arms. The orks are a violent and powerful race, although they have been at peace with humans for years - mainly the human barbarians who share their lifestyle - but it seems that has changed. If they think us allies of the orcs we followed, they will kill us.'

'Oh.' Karland didn't know what to say. 'But they seem to trust Leona?'

'So far. Druids are revered by orks and barbarians alike. We shall see what this leader says. Orks are savage, brutal, and not very civilised, but they are not stupid.'

Leona said nothing from her plain palfrey, her eyes burning green-gold in the darkness.

'Where are they from?' said Xhera. 'I have only heard stories before. I thought them more like animals.' A large ork snorted and glared up at her as it ran beside the cart. She added hastily, 'Clearly they were wrong!'

Rast answered from the side where he rode Stryke. 'No one is sure. These plains have always held orks. Humans have often avoided them, or looked down on them, but they are cautious of warring with them. You interfere with an ork at your peril. They have far more stamina and are much stronger than most men, and have better night vision – and sense of smell.' He grinned tightly. 'Excellent strike troops.'

Another ork running with them laughed harshly. 'Orks are strong!' he shouted in surprisingly good Darum. '*Urukin vah varsi, hai!*'

'*Hai!*' roared the orks around them as they ran, laughing. Karland stared at Rast questioningly.

'It means roughly 'the strength of Orks is in their arms',' the big man said. 'They are a fierce, proud people. They are warriors.'

A dot of light came into view on the rolling plains, bright in the darkness. Not long afterwards they could see it was a collection of fires, looking as if several tribes were gathered.

They moved into the camp past lines of lookouts who called a greeting to their kin which was returned by their captors. There must have been over two thousand in the camp including the hundreds that had escorted their party in.

The cart came to a stop with a big ork fist on Hjarta's collar. Leona's palfrey was likewise halted, although after a snap of large teeth the suddenly cautious ork next to Stryke let Rast stop the war horse. A clear space was indicated by the bald ork, who had run close to their cart on the way back. He was breathing deeply but steadily from his exertions, though a heavy sheen of sweat dotted his head.

'Camp here, humans. You will be watched. See Brukk tomorrow, decide your fate.' An ork reached into the cart and grabbed the packs with the blankets, tossing them into the open area. Another picked up the chest with Aldwyn's books in it and appeared about to do the same, prompting an outraged screech from him. Rast stepped forward and held out his arms.

'Our thanks. I will take it.'

The ork stared for a second, and then shrugged, tossing it to Rast as lightly as if it was empty. Rast caught it with equal ease, and carried it to Aldwyn, who muttered to himself and fussed over it.

Looking around as he laid out his blankets, Karland could only see a few orks watching them. 'Aren't they being a bit relaxed with us?' he asked Rast.

Rast shook his head. 'There are far more watching than you think, and they can see us very clearly. You note they did not allow us wood for a fire. Orks have far superior night vision to humans, and we have no real weapons apart from Leona's club.'

'Orks can see traces of, mm, *heat,* so their vision is augmented well past ours,' broke in Aldwyn from the side. He had recovered from his annoyance at the treatment of his books by reminding himself that orks had little use for them. 'All their senses are keen. Their biology is fascinating! Unfortunately the fallen orcs retain a lot of the benefits-'

He cut off at Rast's quickly chopped hand and harsh whisper. 'Aldwyn, if one single ork hears you draw a parallel between them and those foul creatures, we are all dead. Do you understand?'

Aldwyn nodded and swallowed. 'Ah, yes. Yes.'

'Why do they hate orcs so much? And why would it be bad that we don't have weapons?' Karland wanted to know. 'Doesn't that mean we are not a threat?'

'The first is... a story for another time, boy. The second? It may mean we are not the threat they expect, but if they see us as weak they may kill us anyway,' said Rast. 'Orks respect strength. I only hope they can respect logic as well. They barely tolerate human merchants – they rarely trade – but merchants don't follow their sworn enemies as we did, and things seem unlike they were. We should get what rest we can. The morning will decide our fate.'

☙ ❧

Barely past dawn they were roused, shaken roughly awake by the orks – apart from Rast, who appeared to already be on his feet.

'Come,' said one of the orks shortly, and turned. The others closed in around them and they followed, leaving their possessions on the ground behind them. Aldwyn looked like he would protest but a look from Rast warned him to be silent. Xhera cast Karland a fearful glance and he squeezed her hand.

They trooped through the early morning camp site. It was dark enough that there were still some torches, although the sky was rapidly lightening to the east. Eventually they were brought to a halt in front of a wooden dais decorated with bone and furs. Dawn was grey around them now, yet there was a throng of orks there already, men and women both. The women had heavy breasts, their tusks barely came above their lips, and their features were somehow softer, but nevertheless in their feminine way they were every bit as muscular and powerful-looking as the males. Few of the orks carried much fat.

A huge chair on the dais resolved as thick bones tied together, the seat being a great skull with a long nose. The back arched up high, and the tassels of a dark thickly furred cushion could be seen. No more than that was apparent, as the chair's occupant filled it completely. A huge ork with bristling eyebrows and a wide face glared down at them, his dark eyes shadowed. One of his tusks was severely chipped, and he had thick arms knotted with veins under broad sloped shoulders. He was the first truly fat ork Karland had seen. His waist bulged but it was evident there was still great power in his wide frame, and few of the other orks had his stature. He wore a helm on his head with two horns. One was steel but the other seemed made of a thick brown horn, polished and solid.

'Show respect to Brukk Ogrefist, humans,' barked the ork that had brought them. Rast received a shove in his back, as did Karland. Leona was not touched, but glared instead at the ork behind Aldwyn and Xhera, who dropped his hands uncomfortably and left them alone. Rast cast a glance behind him and then faced the chieftain.

He bowed low, and called, 'Brukk Ogrefist, I greet you. May we be faced one day in fair battle.'

Silence stretched out, and Karland realised this was a ritual greeting that was being ignored by the big ork. The light grew and still he studied them. Suddenly, he spoke in perfect Darum with only a faint accent.

'What do you want, humans?'

'Only to continue our journey,' replied Rast.

Brukk laughed harshly. 'Human, you were caught following *Goruc'cha*. No crime can equal this apart from killing an ork in cold blood. The only reason you yet live is her.' He jutted his chin at Leona. 'Tell me why you followed the fallen filth and perhaps you will persuade me this should continue to be the case.'

'The girl is from a farm near Darost,' said Rast. 'The boy from a town in North Eordeland. Barely three weeks past the town was attacked by nearly a thousand orcs in a place they have never been seen before. Eordeland itself already prepares for war with another realm.'

'So you followed such fell creatures - just you?' said Brukk acidly.

'At a distance. They failed to take the town and we killed many, but they would have prevailed had the Guard not come to our aid. Outnumbered and leaderless they broke. Some fled into the Northing Woods but the core struck out west then south. We followed in the hope they provide some clue to the source of the unrest. There is much we do not understand; they were protected by Meyari as they crossed Eordeland. That army was crushed, but not before these creatures escaped. We expected them to head toward Meyar.'

A low angry murmur susurrated through the crowd.

'We know of Meyar,' snarled Brukk. 'There have been human mercenary groups throughout our plains for months. Much trouble has been caused. Many orks have died. We gathered the tribes, and cleared the plains at cost of much *Urukin* blood. Now we deny our plains to all humans. Stick to your pathetic roads if you wish to see your journey's end.'

Rast bowed. 'With our foe dead we have no further purpose here. If you will let us pass, we will move to the nearest road.'

The great ork regarded them coldly.

'I don't think so,' he said at length. 'There is more to this.' He looked at Leona. 'And you. What is your part in this?'

'I believe the source of unrest and the imbalance in nature are the same,' she said smoothly. 'Surely you have felt this? The world is not right.'

'The only things that seem *not right* are held in your story,' snapped Brukk. 'I am not sure I believe these explanations. Humans lie too easily. They have little honour.'

'I am a Druid! A protector of this land. How dare you doubt my devotion,' she snapped right back, her eyes flashing. Brukk gazed at her levelly.

'So,' he said. 'Maybe. You are free to go, Druid. I recognise the signs of your calling, but you are not welcome. I would prefer you left our plains.' His eyes turned to the others. 'We had merchants here not long ago,' he said softly. 'They said they were not like the mercenaries. They were not like the bad humans, they said. I caught them stealing from me, spreading rumours, trying to break the tribes from each other. Human games.' His eyes glittered.

'None of them were good with an axe. It bothers me that you were following the fallen, the *Goruc'cha urch*. You say you seek the heart of this danger? Pah! I see no weapons. An old man, a girl, and a boy… and a weaponless warrior.' He looked at Rast's frame approvingly. 'You at least are not weak. Who are you?'

Rast chose to answer as if the question had included them all. 'This is Aldwyn Varelin, of the Council of Twelve of Eordeland. You harm him at the peril of all of your tribes.' The orks muttered, but Brukk sneered.

'What use have I of a human council of weaklings? And this girl? What about the skinny boy? Are they also on this Council?'

Rast ignored the sarcasm. 'She is Xhera. His name is Karland. Students. They have proved their bravery.' Karland did not feel brave at that moment. 'The boy is *kap*-runed.' Karland remembered Rast telling him the orks held a K in names sacred. Why was Rast telling them this now?

A buzz of talking went through the crowd. A multitude of large ork eyes turned on him, weighing, assessing. Brukk eyed Karland closely and then burst out laughing.

'*He?* He has earned his *kap*-rune? He looks weaker than a ten year old goblin!'

'Karland has survived assassins, orcs and chaos all untrained,' said Rast quietly. 'Do not doubt his courage.'

'And what of you?' said Brukk, wiping his eyes and chuckling. 'Who are you?'

'I am Rast Tal'Orien,' said Rast. A few orks muttered the name, but Brukk looked unimpressed.

'Another overblown human fighter who has survived long enough to have his name spread,' he snorted. 'Well, *Tal'Orien*. I do not like humans. I said that any found should be killed honourably and quickly. Since that has not happened with you, I now must decide your fate.'

The big ork sat forward, looking around the crowd, and then glanced to his right at an even bigger ork, who sat quietly. Unlike Brukk, he showed no fat at all, and looked as if his body had been sculpted. The striations of his muscles rippled cleanly through his green skin, and he was handsome. Numerous scars crossed his broad chest, one long and jagged. Another ran down across his top lip to his chin between his tusks. His black hair was pulled back in a top knot, the rest free down his neck and shoulders. An ornate gold ring stood in his ragged left ear, and a wide leather baldric crossed down over his left shoulder to his waist. Other than that, he was bare-chested with furred leggings and bare feet. Noticeably bigger than Rast, he looked even stronger, and his big dark eyes watched the group calmly.

Brukk grinned nastily, his lower lip peeling away from his tusks to reveal their full length, and his other teeth, which were surprisingly similar to those of a human.

'I see a Druid and a Warrior,' he said, 'burdened by three weaklings. Weaklings do not deserve to live. Either they fight to prove themselves, or one of you champions them. I will name a challenger. The fight is to defeat, blood, or death.'

Aldwyn went pale, and Karland felt dizzy. It was obvious which challenger Brukk had in mind. The other ork looked like a mountain.

Leona spoke, her tone full of anger. 'This is beneath a leader of the orks,' she said. 'Where has the fabled honour of your tribes gone?'

Brukk glared at her.

'This does not concern you, Druid!' he retorted. 'You are free to go, but they must prove themselves or die honourably. You speak of honour? I do not consider humans to have *honour.*'

'This is madness,' said Rast. 'We mean no harm. Why can you not allow us to go on our way?'

'Listen to the coward!' shouted Brukk. '*Draga sanoa muk Urukin viguk!* If you will not fight, you will die. I do not trust you, human.'

Some of the orks shouted, and it seemed to Karland that not all of them were enjoying this as much as Brukk. The massive ork was still sitting to the side, watching events, his face devoid of emotion.

Rast held up his hand. 'I will fight,' he said coldly, 'But even you must see this is foolishness. We should be fighting those who threaten us, not each other. There will be enough blood for us all before this is over.'

Brukk ignored him and rubbed his big hands gleefully.

'So, the human warrior will fight for the weaklings. In honour of your *reputation* I call on the champion of our tribes. Grukust! You will fight for the orks.'

The quiet giant sighed slightly and looked at Brukk as the chieftain gestured. '*Viguk, Grukust. Urukin vah varsi!*'

Grukust reached behind him, and produced a mammoth axe. Standing, he hefted it. Almost five feet long, it had a twin head with ornate and intricate runes set on a thick, solid haft. The blades swept outward from the top, each rising very slightly before reaching a tip, and then each blade's cutting edge swept downwards in a slight arc to a long point. These curved back up to near the head of the thick haft again, giving a large light blade with long points for hooking over shields. Despite this design the axe still looked weighty. Karland doubted he could lift it easily.

The ork was every bit as impressive as his axe. He topped Rast's height by a good half foot, and was definitely heavier. Rast was leaner and did not have his huge bulk, but they were strikingly similar in form.

Grukust moved down the steps, not as graceful as Rast. His muscles twitched unconsciously, and Karland suddenly realised that he might see a companion die in front of him. He remembered Robertus, and felt sick again, groping for Xhera's hand. She squeezed it hard, her face intent and her breathing fast.

Rast took off his cloak and tunic and folded them. He drew a murmur of appreciation from the crowd for his heavily-muscled figure, more like their own than most humans. Grukust stopped opposite him, and planted his axe head downward, watching his opponent quietly.

'May we be faced one day in *fair* battle,' said Rast, bowing to Grukust. He stood back, poised and ready. Grukust looked at him then back at Brukk.

'Begin!' shouted Brukk, watching intently.

Grukust swept his axe up, and looked at it, then at Rast. The seconds stretched out. Abruptly he shook his head and spoke in broken Darum.

'This battle not *fair*. You have honour, human.' The crowd gasped.

Brukk looked as if he had been struck. 'What?' he bellowed.

Grukust looked at his angry chieftain. 'The human not even have weapon. There is no honour in fight him.'

'Then someone give him a weapon!' shouted Brukk.

'*Drog!*' Grukust roared back. Xhera jumped and Karland barely managed not to do the same. 'They are with Druid. They fought *Goruc'cha urch* – I can see it in eyes. They show honour. One has earned *kap*-rune. It not matter if not same meaning as *Urukin*, all races not same. They greet in manner of tribes! This not our way.' He drew himself up in front of his furious chieftain. 'I will not fight them. For *our* honour.'

Brukk looked as if his eyes would pop out of their sockets. '*Grukust!*' he yelled, spittle flying everywhere.

The humans were taken aback at the unexpected turn of events, but it was nothing to the astonishment of the orks. Words were lost in general uproar. Some of the crowd was roaring in rage at Grukust and the rest were snarling at them in turn, apparently agreeing with his choice. As tribe champion it seemed the matter of his bravery was unquestioned and they seemed more divided over whether it was a greater dishonour to fight the humans or not.

Through all of this, Brukk sat staring daggers at Grukust, who stood like a stone with the sea breaking over him. It was obvious this was the last response he had expected. He finally stood and bellowed repeatedly until the throng was more or less quiet, then in a dangerous voice addressed Grukust.

'If you will not fight, then leave the circle, *pelkuri*,' he said. Grukust snarled at the insult, his teeth peeling back from his tusks. With difficulty, breathing hard through his nose, he regained control and turned to Rast.

'May we be faced one day in fair battle, human.'

Rast smiled slightly. 'But not this day.'

Grukust nodded and stepped to the side to face his chieftain, stone-faced against his wrath. Brukk ignored him, pointing to another big ork with a low mohawk who was missing an ear and a tusk.

'Niruk! Fight this human. Kill him quickly. We will show them some of us are not *cowards*.'

The new challenger spat on the ground. It was clear that for Niruk the fight was to death. Rast watched him warily. The craggy ork picked up a morningstar adorned with spikes long enough to reach Rast's heart and stepped forward. He was grinning in anticipation, sneering at the human.

Rast stood ready, watching. The ork seemed to be busy enjoying the prospect of battle; all of a sudden he charged, swinging the weapon back for a devastating blow that would kill the human in one hit. The crowd screamed in general bloodlust, men and women both. Xhera gasped and closed her eyes. Karland watched in horror.

Rast waited until the ork was within ten feet and then sprinted forward. His left hand closed on the right hand of Niruk in a crushing grip as it held the haft to the side. The right slid up over the ork's thick neck, and then Rast snapped his body double, jerking the ork's head down as he drove his forward knee up. Niruk's momentum pulled him off balance straight into Rast's knee. Augmented by his own speed and weight, the blow hit him with stunning impact, breaking his nose and dazing him. Rast twisted to the side, jerking the morningstar from the stunned ork's grip and yanking his arm. Niruk plunged forward and slid past him, ploughing a foot along the ground on his face.

The cheering died in astonishment. Rast held out a hand and dropped the morningstar with a thud to the grass in the sudden silence. The fight had taken seconds.

Brukk looked as if he was denying what his eyes had just seen. Niruk was groaning and trying to get up. Rast looked at Brukk for a moment, and then turned.

'Come,' he said 'We are leaving.' The guards backed away slightly, unsure if they were free to go, and Rast looked to the others to make sure they were all right.

Leona smiled at him, and then her eyes darted away and she cried, 'Rast!'

At the same time, there was a shout behind him. Rast whirled to find the dirty blood-spattered face of Niruk halted a few feet away, rage fading to surprise at the thick arm around his neck. He began to struggle. Grukust stood looking over Niruk's shoulder at Rast, calmly choking his thrashing comrade. Abruptly, he let go and then slammed a thundering hook into Niruk's temple. The other ork dropped as if poleaxed, his eyes rolling up in his head. Grukust turned to his chieftain.

'Brukk.' His voice was low. 'This not how orks have honour.'

Brukk appeared on the edge of apoplexy, and was actually quivering with rage. Grukust held his eyes.

'Human won fight, fair. Honour says they go. Are they free?'

'No!' yelled Brukk. 'The fight was not over! YOU prevented them losing, *pelkuri! Drogo viguk-*'

'*DROG!*' yelled Grukust, cutting him off. Brukk looked astounded. 'YOU are coward, not me! I am *proved* not coward; I am champion of chieftain of all *Urukin* tribes! I proved honour with blood and bone. Any ork wish to fight without honour, they fight *me.*' He glared around him. No one looked keen.

'Brukk Ogrefist, *he* is *pelkuri*. Scared of *urch*. Scared of world. Scared of losing what he has. Not enough orks to fight whole world, but still he tries make them – to protect himself. Does not act like leader of orks any more. *Has lost honour.* If Brukk will not lead with honour then Grukust will not follow.' The big ork reached to his belt and tore off a collection of feathers and strings, intricately bound in a totem, and threw it on the floor.

Every ork was watching breathlessly. The tension was palpable. Brukk somehow managed to master himself partially after a few purple-faced moments, his temper driving him through witless anger into the calm waters of deadly intent beyond.

'Do I take your *kapanim* from you then?' he asked, dangerously quiet. 'Do you become Gruust again?'

Every ork seemed to freeze. Karland guessed that, of everything he had seen and heard this morning, this was the deadliest insult by far. Grukust was quiet for a long moment, apparently trying to control himself. He breathed heavily, staring at his hands which clenched and unclenched in gigantic fists in front of him. Finally, he looked up.

'Even you not able to do that, father-brother,' he said, his voice filled with conflicting emotions. Karland stared at the big ork. *Uncle!*

Grukust still held Brukk's gaze. 'Do I challenge for tribe? Here, now? Brukk knows Grukust will not lose.'

Brukk looked as if he had been struck. It was obvious he had never considered such a thing. Shock warred with his temper, and then inevitably his pride won. 'Take these humans, and get out, *hylcio*', he said hatefully. 'You are not of this tribe from this moment on. Take your new *friends* and leave.'

For a moment Karland thought that Grukust would challenge, as he had threatened, but then he spoke.

'*Hai.*' Grukust's face was stone. 'For honour of our people.'

He collected his axe and turned his back on his uncle, on his people, who watched with expressionless faces. Without another word, he walked back towards the compound where the humans had left their belongings. Brukk watched him go, his eyes unreadable.

ଔ ஐ

Karland packed the last of their things on the back of the cart. In the morning light they could see that further back the ground they had slept on was ringed by huge beasts, many times bigger than Rast's charger. Built like orks, they had no finesse but massive strength and muscle under a light short pelt that varied from grey to brown. A long head swept down to a square muzzle for cropping grass, and above their nostrils a great horn swept upwards, with a smaller one behind and horny plates running up the forehead like armour. Karland had never seen anything so big.

'*Rinoks*,' Aldwyn answered his question. 'The barbarians have aurochs bulls that are about as big. Both keep them for, mm, meat, milk and war. Perfect nomadic creatures.'

He was rechecking his books, fussing over them to make sure none were damaged from the rough treatment last night. Rast moved over.

'Hurry. We had best be gone as quickly as we can. The happenings of this morning have upset the orks greatly.'

'What do you make of our, mm, new companion?' asked Aldwyn.

Rast shrugged. 'He is the epitome of an orkish warrior. Proud, strong, brave, honourable, and likely difficult to control or reason with. But Grukust broke his own clan loyalty rather than go against his honour, and he will travel with us whether we like it or not. We may find a strong ally in him, and we can trust him... in some things. He will not go against his honour or his clan though, and it will make it hard to go anywhere human. We are barely tolerant of each other at the best of times. If the orks are killing humans now, things could get very unpleasant.'

'Is he dangerous?' asked Karland.

'He is the champion of all the tribes of a whole race of warriors, which I suspect is the only reason he wasn't called out as a coward by the crowd and killed. Just remember, orks are very short tempered. Try not to annoy him.'

Karland nodded, eyeing the huge ork cautiously. He helped carry the last of the gear to the cart where Xhera and Leona were sitting. They were watching Grukust carefully placing things in a pack that looked as if it had a giant log bound to it.

'Look,' said Xhera quietly to Karland. 'They don't want him to go.' Her voice was soft and sad. He turned to see a crowd gathering. Some orks had walked with them as they returned to get their things but now many more were there, watching. A few spoke to Grukust, some urgently, but most stood silent. Grukust calmly listened to everything every ork said to him, then shook his head at each and continued packing, his face like stone.

One ork woman came forward to talk to him quietly. After he repeatedly refused whatever she had said, she grabbed him gently by the back of the neck and leaned her forehead against his, looking into his eyes. It was a very intimate gesture, and Karland looked away after a second. When he looked back, she was gone into the impassive crowd.

Eventually a younger ork who looked much like Grukust pushed out from the gathering, and spoke at great length. When Grukust finally spoke, he did so loudly in his broken Darum rather than orkish, his words for all those gathered.

'Darus, our uncle wrong, acting with no honour. Today was great sorrow for us. If I stay, maybe tribes not be united any more. If I leave, maybe Brukk realise mistake. I can not follow him any more. I refused to fight - for honour of *Urukin* - and now I not part of tribe.'

'Brother, you know Brukk will not change his mind,' replied Darus in Darum at least as good as his uncle's. 'He showed poor judgement, perhaps, but his honour to the tribes goes back many years. He looks out for us all.'

'Brukk was once powerful, good man,' said Grukust, 'Earned great honour.

But he old now. His fear speak for him. He will not listen. Grukust knows not all power is in axe, in arm. *Listen* to the humans, Darus. They right. Things not good here now, maybe anywhere. Many orks dead, ork tribes nearly at war with humans. Humans already at war with humans. Maybe whole world at war soon. To fight for honour one thing; this maybe battle for survival. I want fight *right* enemy.' He held his brother's eyes intently. 'Rast Tal'Orien is not enemy. He believe this too. Brukk shame himself and all *Urukin* today. When he do thing wrong, he speak for ALL of us.'

He was struggling, and switched to his native tongue, speaking rapidly to get his point across. Darus grimaced but nodded. There were some grunts from the crowd, whether in agreement or not it was unclear.

Darus waved his hands to quiet them, and replied in Darum.

'Know that most of us disagree with our uncle. His judgement on the humans was... ambiguous... but his treatment of you was not forgivable. The tribes may drift despite your leaving; Brukk may be challenged. Just know that *we* do not consider you outcast, or coward.' His voice dropped. 'I don't believe he truly does, either.'

'We all judged by our action, our words, not what we thinking,' said Grukust sadly, clapping his hand on his brother's shoulder. 'Include me too. I am glad you not think badly of me, brother. Now I go, and maybe an ork can help find what trouble us all, restore honour. Look after Dellus... and my *rinok. Touk okuu mai olka band lona band aina aika kotna, Velki.'* Karland guessed Dellus was the woman that had parted from him.

'And may we prevail,' said Darus softly. He gripped his brother's forearm tightly, and then turned to the humans. 'I am sorry for any dishonour in your treatment. We face hard times. Our uncle is making hard choices.'

Rast nodded. 'I hold no ill will. Perhaps in time Brukk will realise not all humans are the same... as not all orks are, either.' He looked at Grukust. 'There are dark times ahead, and we will need to fight together.'

'It may be you are right, human.' Darus watched him closely, and then smiled slightly. 'I am... glad... you were not killed without honour. You are a strong warrior, and I think you have honour of your own. I hope you *honour* the choice my brother made.' With one last look at Grukust, he stepped back.

'Niruk WILL hold ill will, human,' snorted Grukust to Rast as Rast mounted. 'He only care about killing. Strong warrior, but no honour, not clever.' He shrugged, and pulled the drawstrings tight on his pack. 'We go.'

Under the watchful eyes of the orks, the party moved back out onto the plains. None of the watchers spoke. The horses rode freely, and Grukust ran alongside Hjarta at a steady pace. He did not look back. As they passed the last of the guards, a shout came from a lone throat behind them.

'*Grukust-a vah varsi, hai!*'

'*HAI!*' roared hundreds of voices in a great shout.

Grukust stopped and turned. After a moment, he unhooked his great axe. With one arm he lifted it over his head in salute, the twin blades black against the horizon. Then he turned back to his lonely path with his new comrades.

TWENTY-THREE

With the orcs defeated there was no reason to travel cross-plains, so they moved southwest towards the nearest road. Rast's concern for Aldwyn's cart on the rough ground was only outweighed by the teeth-clattering sickness of the three occupants, and they travelled slowly to spare the cart axle and the dray.

Grukust did not speak much to his companions and barely acknowledged their existence, appearing lost in thought. When they stopped for food in the late afternoon he did not seem overly tired from his running. Karland found it hard to believe his stamina, and mentioned it to Rast.

'Orks are a hardy race,' the big man replied. 'Grukust could run from dawn to dusk and eat on the way without needing rest, but he could not do it too fast. Humans have different biologies. We are not as strong, not as powerful… but we are faster, more agile, more adaptable, and live longer. We are also more physically diverse - compare me to Aldwyn.' He watched the massive ork reflectively.

'Orks overheat quickly,' he said. 'They have fast metabolisms geared towards muscle. I have rarely seen a small ork, and Brukk is one of the few fat orks I have seen. He must eat well. Their stamina is vast as long as they are not overtaxed; make Grukust work too hard, and he will burn out fast. But if you ever have to fight a berserk ork, don't. They can tear people apart and will shrug off mortal wounds.'

Karland's eyes turned back to the huge green form sitting quietly slightly apart, his axe across his lap and his legs crossed. He watched Grukust take a handful of rations from Xhera and nod to her. As he ate, his eyes returned to the ground.

Karland was fascinated by him. Grukust showed no signs of imminently tearing anyone apart, and eventually curiosity won out over wariness and he summed up the courage to approach. He stood nearby and when Grukust did not move, he spoke.

'Hi. My name is Karland. Well, I suppose you have already heard that. Um.' He waited, and still nothing. 'Would you mind if I sat?'

Grukust shrugged. Karland took that nervously as a tentative acceptance and sat to the side.

'I wanted to thank you for what you did. You saved us.' There was a long pause. Just when Karland thought that was it, the ork replied.

'Your thanks not needed. It nothing. Did it for honour of my people, not for humans,' said Grukust shortly.

Karland shifted uncomfortably. 'I didn't mean to intrude.' He began to rise, and Grukust looked at him for the first time. Karland noticed that his dark eyes appeared over-large for his face. It seemed to be an ork trait.

'Sit,' Grukust said, motioning. 'I just not in good mood. Glad that you not dishonoured, glad you alive. You are Karland, with *kap*-rune?'

'You mean my name?' asked Karland, sitting again.

'Yes, young one. Orks have sacred *kap*-rune. When earn adulthood from Age Quest, *kap* added to name. Gruust became Grukust.' He thumped himself on his chest.

'How did you earn it?' asked Karland, interested. The big ork grinned tuskily.

'Killed Wyvern.' His tone was proud.

That didn't mean much to Karland, but he nodded. 'I haven't killed anything, really. Well... actually, I did. I killed an orc. Maybe two.'

'*Goruc'cha?* Ha! Knew Brukk wrong,' snapped Grukust, his eyes flaring. He relaxed almost immediately, to Karland's relief. He was a little alarmed at how quickly the ork's temper flared, but the volatile being seemed to calm down just as quickly. 'What about rest of Rast Tal'Orien words? Assassins, other fights?'

'I cannot fight very well,' admitted Karland ruefully. 'I've just been lucky to survive. We all have. Many bad things have happened since Aldwyn and I left The Croft.' He thought of Xhera. 'And some good things.'

Grukust snorted. 'Luck three parts in ten, in fight,' he said. It took Karland a few seconds to work out what he meant.

A shy voice behind them startled him. 'He attacked more than ten armed outlaws to rescue me, without a weapon.'

Karland jumped and felt his cheeks warm as Xhera appeared and sat. 'I failed. Rast had to rescue us. Pretty stupid, huh,' he said. Grukust chuckled for the first time and shook his head.

'Stupid. But brave. I think maybe you earn *kapanim*. You still alive.' His eyes, hitherto only expressionless or angry, sparkled with unexpected humour. Karland realised that his new companion had unsuspected depths. The ork felt a little less strange to him, and he smiled. Grukust nodded back, and spoke again with conviction.

'I made right choice, human. Your deaths would have dishonoured whole tribe. All tribes.'

Karland agreed wholeheartedly.

CR   SO

Aldwyn peered at the little group. 'Our young companion has managed to engage our new, ah, friend,' he remarked to Rast. 'Remarkable. I was unsure he wanted anything to do with us.'

'I think Grukust will prove to be more than he appears,' said Rast. 'Karland is a friendly lad, and the fact I named him *kap*-runed will be of interest. I could not believe Brukk threatened to remove his champion's rune name. Grukust seems to be intelligent, and well controlled for an ork. That slur would normally earn swift death.'

'Well, mm, it also came from his uncle,' said Aldwyn. 'Perhaps that stopped him. In any event, Brukk had no power to do that, mm, from what I understand.'

'Quite handsome, for an ork,' broke in Leona off-handedly, her sharp ears picking up the conversation from where she sat ten feet away. Aldwyn blinked. He always forgot how sharp her senses were. She laughed at his reaction, then turned serious.

'The orks will be trouble if they have declared war,' she said. 'Even I was barely tolerated in their camp. Never has a shepherd of the land been treated so before by them. They used to revere the plains, but Brukk spoke of them only as a place of battle. It seems this unrest has pervaded the orks, too – and if them, how many others?'

Rast sighed. 'It is ill news, indeed. Perhaps we should join the youngsters and talk to our new comrade now he is being responsive.'

The three of them drifted over, and Aldwyn heard Karland telling the ork about the attack in the Sanctum. Grukust was listening with amusement at how many Rast fought. Seeing the big man approach, he said, 'Rast Tal'Orien! Your manling telling me very good stories. It good you kill assassin,' he sneered at the thought of someone so dishonourable, 'but then you attack whole room? Maybe you and Karland the same. Brave but stupid.' He was obviously enjoying himself. 'How many you really kill?'

Rast, as usual, waved a hand to avoid the question, disliking talking about himself. Aldwyn answered for him, eager to talk to the quiet being.

'They came when the assassin failed. I shut the door to my room, Karland my only defence.' Karland puffed up a little. 'Rast came through the door shortly afterwards and barricaded us in. I think the guards that saved us in the end said that at least seven were dead or wounded when they arrived, perhaps more. Not bad for an unarmed man, eh?' He elbowed Rast in the ribs. It was like hitting rock.

The big man scowled at him. 'I do not take life lightly, Aldwyn. You know that.'

Grukust looked impressed. 'Seven? Unarmed? Ha! Well, I saw Niruk defeated like baby goblin. Maybe it good I not fight you.' He chuckled, although an expression of interest passed over his face at the thought. He settled back, more at ease with his companions. 'So why you follow *urch*?' He said the word as if it was distasteful.

Karland and Xhera opened their mouths, but Aldwyn overrode them.

'We were trying to see where they were headed, mm. They had a purpose, one important enough to risk crossing your territory. The orcs appeared where they have never been seen before, having travelled the breadth of Eordeland protected by a small army of humans.' Grukust shook his head in disbelief.

'The orcs killed many, laid waste to many homesteads and doing, ah, unspeakable things. We need to find the link between them and Meyar. It is of great worry that a human realm has allied with such foul creatures, especially one that tried to murder some of the Council of Twelve. We thought they would turn northwest to Meyar, but they were heading southwest until they were slaughtered. Now we are unsure where to go next. If we go to Meyar we risk losing the trail.'

Grukust pondered for a few minutes, and then turned large dark eyes on him.

'I know where they going,' he said. 'Not Meyar. *Ankealaak-so*. Rumours of great many *urch* there. Have fought many in recent months, all going same place. Evil comes from that valley. *Urch* gather there too. Woods there full of *Goruc'cha*, ogres, other things. Dark place. Orks not go there.'

'*Ankealaak-so*? asked Leona.

Grukust waved his hand vaguely southwest. 'Great dark place of trees behind mountains. Dangerous, full of bad things.'

'The Dimnesdair?' said Aldwyn. It was the only place that dark and unnatural, and was in a direct line from where the orcs were going.

Grukust shrugged. 'Maybe?'

'I wonder why they headed there,' mused Rast. 'That is far from Meyar. This gets more confusing.'

'If that is where they travelled perhaps we should follow,' said Aldwyn. 'There may be some clue there.' Then his eyes widened. '*A Hollow in Mountains!* Of course! A valley... The Dimnesvale! It all makes sense, Rast. There are legends of great power hidden in the deepest recesses; it may be what we seek.'

'Old man, of all the places you did *not* want to go, the Dimnesdair is the worst,' said Rast grimly. 'Strange twisted creatures roam freely there. Even in the woods around the valley there is danger, and in the valley itself... it is perilous.' Aldwyn blinked, his excitement dying, but Leona's reaction sent fear through him once more.

'Chaotic. Unnatural. Unholy,' Leona said fiercely. 'There are many orcs and their kin in those woods. It is the one place in Anaria where they abide the trees and we do not. Those woods are not like others – they do not welcome my feet and their heart does not welcome order. Druids do not go there often. The valley itself is an abhorrence full of abominations. No god envisaged *that* demon-spawned pit.'

Aldwyn closed his eyes, his excitement gone. He opened his mouth and forced himself to speak. 'So you-' he swallowed. 'You think this the source of all this chaos?'

'We have two paths, and a choice to make,' said Rast after a long pause. 'Here and now. Do we journey to Meyar with few clues, and lose time we do not have if we are wrong? Or do we walk the darker path and follow it into the Dimnesdair where other answers may lie?' His words gave Aldwyn hope. Perhaps they would find answers in Meyar after all.

'I do not wish to walk those woods,' said Leona. 'But it *feels*... likely, a place of unrest growing in the land. This could be a place where the evil is spreading from. And your theory makes sense – a hollow in mountains, a power to be used. It all fits. Perhaps we can enter without being detected – much of the deadlier life lives within the valley itself, and even the orcs will not venture far in there. If we do not enter the valley we have a good chance of avoiding most of the danger; the fringes are just woods. We may be able to find answers and escape if we are careful.'

'I don't think I want to go there,' said Xhera, looking frightened.

Karland was plainly nervous too. 'Not unless we have to,' he agreed.

'I fear treading there,' said Aldwyn flatly. He held a deep fear in his gut that they would not return. 'I will be of little help. What use will I be in the woods? Perhaps Meyar should be our goal, mm, after all.'

'You hold the knowledge of what we face and the expertise to glean answers,' said Rast firmly. 'Only you can read the pendant and decipher this power. You cannot shy away now, old friend. There is danger anywhere we go, and at least here is it direct, something I can protect you from. Skill in battle is less use against subterfuge and politics, so you will be in as much danger in Meyar. It will just be a different kind.'

'I also not want to go to woods,' said Grukust, 'but you right, old man. Danger, change, chaos everywhere. I worried about tribes. We are strong, but cannot fight whole world, cannot live on plains ruined by war. If we may find what you seek in *Ankealaak-so*, we should look. It nearer than Meyar.' He chuckled harshly, without humour this time. 'And I too also protect you there. If you go to Meyar, I not able to come.'

Aldwyn pinched his nose, giving in.

'Curse you all. You are right. I am only one frightened old man. This is more important.' His voice shook a little, but his resolve held. 'Let us look there first. It may be we find nothing; it has long been a place of fear and myth and wild tale.'

Rast nodded. 'The Dimnesdair it is then. We will scout the woods at the pass and look for signs of orcs gathering. If any exist, clues as to why must be sought. If there is nothing, we will look deeper – or leave. Leona – we will count on your guidance in the woods.'

She smiled at him, her strange eyes seeming to reflect the light. 'I will guide your feet, Rast Tal'Orien. And it *will* be your feet; we will need to leave the horses before the Pass.'

'*Ankealaak-so*,' growled Grukust resignedly. 'At least there *Goruc'cha* in there. I will oil *snagka*.' He shrugged his heavy shoulders, hefting the huge axe.

Leona's answering grin was sharp.

ର   ରୀ

They stopped again at dusk. The plains still seemed to stretch forever against the two opposing mountain ranges of the Arkons behind them to the north and the distant Iril Eneth to the south. Grukust untied the huge log that was attached to his pack and used his axe to cut several disks off the end. He cut a square of turf out and lifted it, building a small crosswise platform from the twigs in the cart, and placing the disks on top. Satisfied, he concentrated on coaxing a flame with tinder and flint.

'What is that?' asked Karland. Xhera watched curiously.

'*Rinok paska,*' the ork grunted. Karland picked up the log, which was lighter than it looked.

'*Paska?*'

'Dung,' said Rast, looking amused. Karland dropped the log hurriedly.

Xhera watched him wave his hands for a few seconds and then fixed him with a level glare. 'Don't you *dare* come near me with those hands.'

Eventually Karland settled for spitting on them and wiping them on the grass. He scowled at Aldwyn, who was cackling with laughter. Grukust was watching him in puzzlement.

'It dry?' he said in confusion. This set off another gale of laughter from Aldwyn. The ork glared at the old man, who didn't notice. The hunched ork stared at him, frowning, and then looked again at Karland. Abruptly his teeth bared in a wide grin, visible between his tusks.

'Ha!' he said, laughing. 'You think this *wood*! Where from?'

Shaking his head, still grinning, he gestured at the flat plains around them and then carried on with his task. Aldwyn chuckled again, and Xhera breathed a quiet sigh of relief. The big ork had not taken offence, but it was still hard to gauge their new companion.

They settled in, the light fading. The fire burned surprisingly brightly, and they set about cooking a meal. Grukust sat slightly apart again, staring into the fire with lidded eyes and chewing his food slowly.

Eventually Xhera got up and moved over to him, standing to the side and watching compassionately. After a while she said in a small voice, 'It must have been a hard thing to do. Leaving everyone behind.'

Grukust nodded distractedly. '*Hai.*' He replied in Orkish.

Xhera put her small hand on his shoulder. He tensed slightly, surprised by the contact. To her surprise his skin felt like hot human skin; only the hue and thickness said it was otherwise. Her heart went out to him.

'I am also alone.' She paused, a sadness born of companionship welling up. The ork looked up at her curiously. 'I only have my sister in the world. There was a disaster… everyone in my town died, nearly. My parents are kind and caring, but they are not my real parents. I worked on a farm, but felt trapped my whole life.' The grief was still fresh, but lessened by the catharsis she had shared with Talas. She realised she was pouring her heart out to this strange being, but he was listening carefully.

'Until I met Karland, I was stuck in a life not knowing where I came from. It was safe, secure, loving, but killing me slowly. He made me realise that it would be bearable if I had someone who was there for me through all the bad times.' She smiled. 'He is the closest friend I have. I gave up my life there to come with him, to help Aldwyn. They are worthy friends.'

She sighed. Grukust was looking at her, his face unreadable. 'I guess what I am trying to say is, well. Being alone, losing your old life, it can't be changed, but with a friend it can be borne. So, um... if you need a friend, maybe I can be one. I know I am not strong, or even an ork, but you need not feel alone.'

The ork was silent for a long minute, surprised by her words. He looked genuinely touched by her offer. It was obvious he had never expected to find acceptance outside the tribes and had prepared for long lonely travels.

He smiled at her. 'Thank you, Xhera.' Her name was hard to say with tusks. 'I am honoured by offer. You have true heart. I happy to be your friend. You humans... different from others I met. I swear protect you from all harm.' He thumped his chest. 'We not be lonely any more together, neh?'

She smiled back at him. 'We will all be your friends,' she said.

Karland broke in from a little way away. 'Like a new tribe!' The boy grinned.

Grukust chuckled, and carried on eating. To Xhera, he looked like his heart had been warmed by the unexpected companionship, and she was glad. Perhaps his future was not so bleak after all.

꒰   ꒱

Leona was standing slightly apart away from the smoke with her eyes closed, letting the wind blow her hair. She looked very much at home on the plains to Karland, despite her professed love of woodland.

'Someone comes,' she announced, turning her head west before opening her eyes. Rast stood. Grukust and the others looked up curiously, but the ork did not stop eating.

'Who?' asked Rast.

She shook her head. 'There are many, with great beasts.'

'Other tribes?' muttered Rast. 'Or barbarians? I cannot think it would be goblins coming from the west.'

Karland watched as moving dark dots resolved in the fading light. They would arrive by the time it was dark, and were plainly heading for them; the light from their fire would be seen for miles.

Stars were beginning to glimmer overhead and the moon was rising by the time the newcomers arrived. In the light from the fire, Karland saw four massive creatures, nearly as big as the *rinoks* the orks kept. Gigantic bulls with huge upswept four-foot horns from either side of their skulls over big liquid bovine eyes, they had large humps on their powerful shoulders, broad hooves like small shields, and at the shoulder they were higher than even Grukust was tall. These must be the aurochs that Aldwyn had mentioned, as different to a normal cow as a goose was to a chicken.

Between the lead two a low platform was slung on six rawhide cords from special harnesses. It was bound firmly to beams in front of and behind the huge shoulders on each bull and again at the rear. The platform held what seemed to be a pointed tent big enough for a large man to sit in, but nothing could be seen of what was inside. The rear two bulls carried only possessions and packs.

Twenty men and women accompanied the bulls. Tall and well formed, most of them had dark hair, square cut or bound back from their faces. In the fore was a man wearing a leather baldric similar to Grukust's but with a small spaulder topped with sharp metal studs. He wore calf-length leather boots bound upwards in a crossways pattern to just below the knee. His hair was long and dark, hanging to his nipples and braided at the temples. The face was grim and lined, but his body was powerfully muscled and he was nearly as big as Rast. There was a striking similarity in physique between these humans and the orks that they had seen. Karland guessed that these were the barbarians of the plains. All of them were armed; one man bore a sword that looked heavier than Grukust's axe. It must have been over six feet long. Karland wondered how he wielded it.

The leader held up a hand to halt his people, and appraised Leona and Rast. He took in the massive man in front of him with no expression, but when he looked at Leona closely, his eyes widened.

'*Ahtolk!*' he exclaimed, bowing.

Leona smiled and inclined her head. 'I greet you, Chieftain. May you walk far.'

'My thanks,' he replied in rough Darum. He looked as if he would say more, but Grukust chose that moment to stand and come forward and his grim expression dissolved in a look of astonishment.

'You travel with an *Orok!*'

Mutters of surprise were heard through the barbarians.

Grukust grunted. 'Greeting, Chieftain. I not expect to see barbarian here in our land. Where you travel?'

'*Mai johtua jotta koruta,*' said the barbarian in what sounded like fairly good Orkish. 'I would talk with Brukk Ogrefist. Strange and deadly beasts roam our lands. Many battles have been fought, both with men and foul *orch,* and the tribes must decide to fight singly or gather. We come for peace and advice, not for war.'

'Tread carefully, Chieftain,' said Rast. 'Brukk Ogrefist is less fond of humans these days, as we found to our woe.'

Grukust remained silent.

'Always before has he received us,' said the big barbarian. 'We are not weakling merchants! We are allies. But you, what do you do here?' The question was curious, not aggressive.

'We followed a large band of *orch* that struck in Eordeland itself. Unrest is everywhere. Many nations verge on war. We followed to seek answers. The ork tribes found them first and the orcs were slaughtered. We were captured and brought before Brukk. He was... not sympathetic to our story. Grukust risked his honour for us.'

Under the curious stares of the barbarians, Grukust grimaced.

'Take care, human. Brukk not as reasonable as once was. *Urukin* facing same as you, but he not listen. Instead he order all humans apart from Druid killed, and make honour of all *Urukin* less-'

'*Impugned,*' muttered Aldwyn.

'- and when I question honour of Brukk's decision, he declare me *hylcio*.' Grukust continued, oblivious.

There were a couple of gasps.

'*Outcast?*' said the leader is a disbelieving tone. 'Why did you not challenge?' Grukust shrugged.

'Did they not think you a coward?' The tone of voice suggested that he was unsure if he should think the same. Grukust shrugged again and levelled a challenging stare down at him.

After a moment the man smiled slightly. 'A mistake, I think. Our thanks – we will be careful. The plains are vast, but this night we can rest with you.' There was a question in the tone, the words sounding ritualistic.

Grukust nodded. 'Our campsite welcome you. I am Grukust.' He struck his chest.

'Nilthar.' The human smacked his fist onto an open palm in front of his sternum and bowed slightly. The barbarians all followed suit. Rast bowed back.

'I am Rast. Please, join us.'

Nilthar nodded, and walked forward to sit at the fire. The barbarians moved to their tasks efficiently and with no need for conversation. Several moved to look after the aurochs, others unhooking the strange platform and carrying it carefully to sit slightly back from the fire. They produced a large sack and fed the fire with compact pellets until it was big enough for all of them. Karland sourly guessed that from the look of it they also used dung.

The rest of the parties were introduced, and Karland found himself fascinated with the barbarian women. One in particular was pretty in a wild way with brown hair tied back from a small oval face. Her slender neck was complemented by piercing blue eyes and tanned skin, and her midriff was bare above long and well-muscled legs. Blue swirls decorated her left temple and ran down her neck to her chest and back. Many of the barbarians had similar markings.

Xhera elbowed Karland as he stared at the woman. 'Pervert!' she hissed fiercely at him, half-joking. He blushed and shot a glare at his friend, who sniffed.

Lean and sinewy, the barbarians moved like prowling cats. Karland realised that it was also how Rast moved – raw, natural, but controlled, hinting at supremely fast reflexes. Not a few of the barbarians were also watching the big man closely. Had Rast dressed in like fashion, Karland might have thought him one of them.

Leona sat quietly, watching the barbarians intently. Her eyes often drifted back to Rast. It seemed she too had noticed the similarities. They gave her a respectful distance for the most part, although several stopped and offered her food or drink. To all these she smiled and shook her head, her wavy golden hair bobbing.

As the night grew more chill Karland and Xhera wrapped up, as did Aldwyn. Leona, Rast, Grukust and the barbarians seemed not to notice the cold, though none of them wore much.

Karland wondered what the aloof barbarians kept in the strange tent. Aldwyn had only shrugged when he asked him and went back to flipping through one of his books, squinting through his spectacles in the dim light. Xhera had said she thought it to be a treasure, but Karland argued that surely a box would be better than a fabric cone.

Several of the barbarians sat near the tent, guarding it. As he watched, one of them raised her head and she moved to the tent to unlace it. Karland caught a brief glance of a hunched form inside and then the flap came down. She spoke to one of the men before sitting back next to the entrance as the man made his way towards Nilthar. He turned his attention to the chieftain.

The stern man and Grukust were speaking at length in a mixture of Orkish and Darum. The barbarian looked perturbed at the news he was receiving; it seemed Nilthar had not realised he spoke with the champion of the combined tribes. Dismay laced his stern features.

Rast joined the conversation and added what they had found in Darost, and the three warriors fell to speculations about possible battle. One thing seemed clear: none of the tribes stood to gain in any upcoming war – human or ork.

Nilthar spoke, troubled. 'I need guidance. This goes beyond one tribe. After we return, we will call a tundra moot.' His face creased in thought, but he was interrupted by the warrior from the tent, who whispered in his ear. Nilthar blinked and called something in his own language to the woman, who bent to the tent and spoke. She straightened and nodded, her face surprised. As one, the barbarians stopped whatever they were doing and turned to sit cross legged, facing the tent. Their faces were relaxed, but there was a subtle tension. No one spoke, and Karland motioned to Xhera to get her attention.

'We are honoured,' said Nilthar into the silence, looking stunned. 'Our shaman wishes to see the stars and be among us... among *all* of us. *Aikileik!* This has never before been done with outsiders present. Please – I ask you to not interfere.'

Karland felt an odd sense of foreboding at these words. Breathlessly he shuffled on his backside over to Xhera, who was watching avidly. He opened his mouth to whisper, and without looking she clapped a hand over it. She shook her head and he subsided, annoyed.

Nothing happened for a further minute or so. Just as Karland was beginning to wonder if he could speak, a vulture-like head speared through the tent flaps and sat motionless in the firelight, perhaps the head of a strange staff.

Aldwyn spoke to them softly. 'What a curious headdress! The barbarian tribes are, aha, highly superstitious. They believe everything can be killed, but are wary of the supernatural. They have a spiritual guide, that they believe grants them supernatural power and a way to commune with that which they dread. This must be their shaman - supposedly not the same as other men. It is not known if they are a separate breed that has formed, mm, a symbiotic relationship with the barbarians, but they believe all the power of a tribe flows through the shaman. This is a rare sight. It has only ever been conjectured, to my knowledge- *Oh!*'

His exclamation came as the flaps parted further and the head came out on the end of a bent neck. With a thrill Karland realised that it was an actual head, not a staff. A three-fingered taloned hand on a stick-thin arm with a strange curve to it came out under the head, propped on a gnarled staff. The figure exited the tent and stood. It would be a little over six feet tall were it not so hunched at the shoulders, making it look even more vulture-like. The head was large, but not as large as a man's, and the strange creature was clad in a dull red-brown robe that was open to the waist, showing a scrawny frame. The chest and neck were covered in what looked like small blue feathers, layered like scales, which petered out leaving wrinkled skin of the same hue.

The whole creature was blue, the same colour as the blue-copper markings the tundra tribes wore. The talons on the hands were black and sharp, the finger joints knobbly, and the edge of the hand starting from the last finger had more feathers, starting small and running up the underside of the arm in a fringe as if they were the faint vestiges of wings.

The beak on the head was black and hooked like a bird of prey, but longer than expected. It looked cruel. Black expressionless eyes glinted like beads of obsidian in the flickering firelight and under each eye a startlingly red whorl spiralled out from a dot on each cheek. At odds with the strange mix of man and bird was the short black crest of stiff hair bordered with small black feathers. The light robe trailed on the ground, worn and tattered. Karland couldn't see the feet.

The peculiar being moved strangely, an old man's shuffling gait combined with quick, predatory birdlike moves of the head. When it stopped moving it was like a statue, not even blinking. It was a disturbing sight, especially as it seemed that the huge hunch to the shoulders was both physical and the result of a structure under the robe giving a peaked hump which rose high behind the head.

Xhera whispered to him, breathing in his ear so the tundra people would not hear. 'I don't like it.' Her tone conveyed her unease and Karland was inclined to agree with her. The bizarre thing was almost a mockery.

Aldwyn leaned forward, his eyes intent. 'My, my,' he muttered. 'So *that* is a Sergoth Shaman.'

The creature shuffled forward toward the fire, and stopped a little way from it. The head darted around, and then it jerked up, looking at the sky. It lifted its staff, gripping it under the head, and pointing swept it in a semicircle over the whole camp including the barbarians. They all moaned in unison, even Nilthar, their superstitious dread obvious.

The shaman peered at everyone in turn, and shook its staff three times in the direction of Karland's party. Something in the gesture made Karland shiver.

It turned and shambled out to the fringe of the firelight and sat with its back to the light looking out onto the plain. The shaman didn't move, looking like a withered hummock on the grass. Nilthar moved over without a word to join all of the Sergoth people in a ring around it. They sat and bowed their heads with closed eyes, and fell silent.

After a few minutes Karland looked at Aldwyn in query. The old man shrugged. After eating and setting bedding they all sat to talk quietly.

'I have never heard of this before,' said Rast. 'The barbarians guard their spiritual guides closely. They are shy and leery of others. I do not know why this one chose to come among us.'

'Everything changing,' said Grukust. 'Orks know of shaman, but never see. Barbarians sometimes bring on important visit, but that happen three times in my life only. Must be very serious to bring here again.'

'The old scrolls make sense!' said Aldwyn eagerly. 'I thought they wore trappings, but they are a whole separate species. Amazing! Whatever happened in the ancient past, these creatures are now revered as the source of power in the tribes. They have a strong hold over them.'

'No hold, I think,' said Rast. 'There are tales of powerful rites among the barbarians. I think these bird-men are the link to their spiritual side.'

'I don't like it,' said Xhera fiercely, prompting several shushing motions. She continued in a lower voice. 'Well, look at it! It looks cruel, horrible. It frightens me.' Karland nodded. The creature was unnerving.

To their surprise Leona disagreed. 'I have felt the presence of these creatures before. They are emotionless, not natural... but neither are they unnatural. They belong on these plains under the stars – I cannot explain it. Maybe they are chaos finding order in this world; not evil, nor good, but *right*. There are whispers of strange rites performed with strange powers, but one thing is clear: they guide the tribes, and this one said something about our party. I am concerned more with what was said than with speculation of what it is. It is said that they can dimly see the future paths of men.'

After making ready their beds Karland watched the silent ring of people for a while. Occasionally one of them shifted, but none opened their eyes. The bird man in their centre remained a statue.

Eventually Rast spoke. 'Karland, Xhera – you will train for an hour with me.' Karland opened his mouth to object and Rast pinned him with a glance. 'No arguments. You need to work every moment you can.'

Aldwyn flapped his hands at the youngsters, who grimaced, but followed Rast. Grukust watched them with interest, nodding approval at the hard training. They were set striking and blocking with their hands, followed by kicking exercises. Eventually Rast allowed them to stop, sweating and weak with exertion. Karland moved tiredly to his blankets near the fire. A little way away, one of the aurochs looked at him, grinding a mouthful of grass. It burbled a snort from its nose, spraying dripping mucus from wide nostrils, and flicked its tail. The huge beast didn't look aggressive, but Karland supposed that seeing one eating quietly at night was different from facing an enraged one in battle. The bull would go through a line of men on foot like a boulder rolled through a field of corn.

Karland fell asleep with difficulty, his mind flickering over events of the last day or so. His mind drifted into dream where a giant grey bird man with blood dripping from his serrated beak pronounced death on him, pointing a staff which writhed horribly. Xhera called his name as he slowly sank into a mindless pinkish goo, unable to struggle. Suddenly the dream moved on, and he dreamed instead of rows of silent, beautiful barbarian women with blue whorls on their faces, his to command and rule the world with. With a small smile, he sat back in a wooden throne and watched them marching past until morning.

ᘉ   ᘒ

A deep lowing sound woke him, the noise rumbling through him rather than going via his ears. Blearily he rolled over, peering into the sky that was only just being touched by the light of dawn. It seemed that the barbarians were leaving; the shaman's tent was once again laced and being lifted to rest between the two lead aurochs.

He dragged himself out of his blankets stiffly, yawning. He ached all over. Several barbarians nodded to him. The pretty woman that he had been unable to take his eyes off the night before passed, and to his chagrin returned a direct stare. He blushed as she smiled in amusement at his reaction and carried on with her duties, leaving him with a strange feeling in the pit of his stomach. A cough brought him around in time to see Xhera emerging from her blankets with puffy eyes. He left her to reach full wakefulness and moved over to where Rast was talking quietly to Nilthar and Grukust.

'He spoke words of doom,' Nilthar was saying quietly, his face as somber as ever. 'He said that many of you may fall before you finish your journey. Your quest hangs in the balance. He cannot see if it will succeed, but it is of the utmost importance.'

'For the sake of us all, don't let Aldwyn hear you say that,' muttered Rast. He paused for a moment, reassured by the rasping snores that were still erupting from a pile of clothes near the fire. 'We all know the dangers of this quest, but he is terrified. He is hunted and he knows he cannot defend himself. Worse, he believes that the fate of this whole world may hinge on what we find. If he is reminded of the dangers every step of the way he may not be able to carry on. He is old and frail and his might lies in his mind, not his arms.'

'Weak old man,' snorted Grukust derisively. 'Orks go on death-walk when they get too old, too sick. Keep might in body. What use is might in mind if you have none in body?'

'That's your culture talking, not you,' said Rast, showing a little irritation. 'You are intelligent enough, Grukust, so understand: the might in his mind is far greater than either of us carry in our bodies.'

The ork grunted sourly. For a moment Karland thought his temper and pride would break free, but then he shrugged his heavy shoulders. 'Maybe might in body not enough if none in mind either,' he admitted grudgingly.

Rast nodded, and smiled at the ork. 'That is true. And you do well to disprove what many humans think of your people, my friend.'

'We also know orks are not stupid,' said Nilthar. Then he actually smiled slightly. 'But they are so strong in body that they often need heed little else.' A shout from a companion reached him and he signalled with his hand. 'The guidance we took last night showed dire things on the grass horizon. We must forge a strong bond with the orks – a pledge of mutual support – or a time will come when perhaps neither will survive. Should you meet my people in the future, give them the words of Nilthar: you were shaman-met, and judged as worthy. They will help you, if they value their honour.'

'You have our thanks. May your tribes prosper,' said Rast. He clasped forearms with Nilthar. To Karland, they almost looked like cousins in the morning light. Grukust grasped Nilthar's hand in the way of men and the barbarians left, heading northeast at their deliberate pace.

Leona moved to them, her feet bare as usual, and motioned to the snoring scholar. 'We had best wake him from hibernation and continue.' They all looked with amusement at the pile of blankets, complete with a tuft of white hair at the top.

'I think,' said Grukust to Rast, rumbling in laughter, 'his snores mightier than his mind *and* our arms.'

Rast smiled.

TWENTY-FOUR

The journey became easier when they finally hit the great western road that ran along the line of the Iril Eneth. Five days later the squat shape of Punslon came into view at the base of a sheer rocky outcrop. The large town sprawled along the base of the overhanging rocks, with the minority of buildings on the plains side of the road. Karland noticed that more of the town lay further back in a recess between two sections of the cliff.

There was only one main road that ran through the town, and all of the stores and taverns were strung along it and its side roads. Behind them were houses and a large structure of wood and stone which was apparently the town hall. On the north side of the road, the buildings faded roughly in the middle to a large open space for a market. Rast said that this was where they held the famous Plains Trade festival twice a year, and people from many nations came. The plains barbarians came in numbers, and it was not unheard of for even orks to come, although the townspeople were barely tolerant of them. Barbarian savages were more or less acceptable, Rast said dryly, but non-humans apparently were not.

There was never a day without a few stalls or wagons, but it was a small affair for travelling traders to buy and sell stock compared to the festival. Being the biggest trade settlement in the centre of the continent, the people of Punslon boasted that their town was the hub of all Anaria.

They passed into the edges of town. The wide road held no gates, and there was a low fence that did little more than delineate town limits running either side of the road. The first buildings were poorly built and simple; the true town started a little further in, where the taverns began on the south side of the road.

Barely had they passed the limits when a squad of guards came into the road from a large building set to the south side and blocked the way. The leader called out peremptorily.

'You can't bring *that* in here.'

Karland looked in the direction the man stared, and saw Grukust. The ork stood impassively. He glared at the guard.

'Are you referring to my companion?' Rast asked pointedly.

'Yeah. Town rules. Orks stay market-side. Not having their sort causing problems.'

'I think I am beginning to see why orks don't like humans much,' murmured Aldwyn. 'These are their closest civilised neighbours and they are treated like beasts.'

Rast smiled disarmingly. 'Oh, I am sure that is true for a Plains Trade festival, but surely one ork, spoken for and in the company of humans, is not a problem.'

The guard shrugged. 'Listen. I don't make the rules. I just enforce 'em. No point getting your codpiece in a clove hitch over it – way it is. You want to stay the night, you get either a nice tavern south-side, greenless, or a shitty one north-side with a barn for your... friend.' The squad looked ready to argue the point; one had a whistle raised to his lips.

'Your manners and your attitudes are poor,' said Rast. 'We will find a tavern on the north side.'

The man nodded, uncaring. 'Whatever. Just realise there is a hefty fine and punishment if he is caught south-side. We're not stupid, mind. If we have to evict this snotrag-' Grukust growled involuntarily '- we know damn well half of us won't make it unscathed. So what we do, see, is we come and find you instead. Be warned.'

Rast nodded. 'You've made your hospitality perfectly clear, *friend*.' He turned to Grukust. 'You have my apologies for this. I did not expect such treatment. Let us find a tavern that will take us all.' The ork shrugged noncommittally. Karland noticed that Grukust was very stoic when he kept his temper under control.

They passed the line of guards, who stood back and lined the south side of the road, watching them. Nearly to the marketplace, they found a tavern set a little way back down a slight side-road. A weathered sign marked it the Inn of Cards. As they drew up outside a stable appeared and whistled. Another virtually identical boy popped out of the straw.

Rast dismounted and turned to the door as it opened. The innkeeper himself stood there. He had bushy black moustaches which went up each cheek from the lip, making it look like the wind had blown them horizontally and left them there at points. He welcomed them effusively but paused when he saw Grukust. Rast noticed and directed a challenging look at him.

'I hope our friend isn't going to be a problem.'

The innkeeper sighed and shook his head. 'I got nothin' against his kind, sir,' he said. 'Just surprised is all. We only see orks normally in festival time.' He turned to Grukust. 'Master Ork, you been here before I reckon. People in this town, well... they don't like outsiders, or things out of the ordinary, or things that ain't as good as what they think, or... well. You know what they are like. I mean no offence.'

Grukust nodded. 'I know.' His tone was neutral.

The innkeeper nodded. 'Welcome, all of you. My name is Geraldt. I only ask that Master Ork here kindly try not to lose his temper in my establishment. Folks here are a bit uppish at times – bad enough with the likes of north-siders like me, worse with them of the Sergoth, and if you ain't human... well, that's a whole 'nother level. It should be quiet enough that I don't get much grief for having an ork in the tavern, no disrespect to you Master Ork, but I can do without expensive renovations. With any luck for you, but none for me o' course, it will be a quiet commons tonight. Are you staying long?' His tone hinted it was not a good idea.

'One night,' said Rast.

'For the best, sir. Hopefully no one causes trouble. Some people here ain't too bright none either, and that's a bad mix when you think you're better'n everyone else.' He sounded a little bitter. Being a north-sider was obviously just as subject to snobbery as living on the plains. He beckoned them through the door. 'Come in. Come in. Will you need supplies?'

'One moment, innkeep.' Rast waved the stable boy down as he hoisted the chest off the cart . 'I'll come back out in a moment and settle him, lad,' he said. 'My horse is battle trained. I would not approach him.'

He lugged the chest through the door after the others. The common room was clean, if not particularly well lit. 'We require supplies, and advice,' he said placing the chest on the floor inside. 'Does anyone know the best trail east into the Iril Pass?'

Geraldt stared at him as if he were mad. 'Is that where you're headed? You got a death wish?' He shook his head. 'I were you, I wouldn't go near the place. There's a path near town sure enough, and even a road of sorts that leads there. Lumber teams work the edges, but it is the very edges. They work trees at their camp, team the wood back here. There was another camp through the pass for the ironwood, but not any more. Strange things live deep in those woods. Orcs, not the plains kind.' He nodded at Grukust. 'Ogres, some say. Horrible beasts. Men get killed, or just vanish. It's always been a dark place. Got worse of late, and then there's the witch.' He shuddered. 'Why would you need to go there?'

'Witch?' asked Karland, eyes gleaming. Geraldt opened his mouth to explain, and was cut off by Rast.

'We search for something.'

'You're mental.' Geraldt shook his head. 'The lot of you. No disrespect. All you'll find there is death if you go too deep. Oh, the edges are fairly safe in the day this side o' the pass, but deeper in, at night? The lumber crews deserted the far camp. A shift went all the way out there and found it destroyed, everyone dead. Torn apart, eaten, you name it. They came back right quick. A few people here lost their minds too, run off to the plains or the woods. None of 'em came back. We've stepped up border patrols here since, though I reckon we are safe enough in town.'

'We intend to be careful,' said Rast. 'We have a Druid with us to walk the safe paths.' He indicated Leona. Karland hoped she would be enough; Geraldt's dread was clear.

'Your funerals, sir. Just warnin' you. You seem friendly enough. Your Master Ork there should know all this, though. I'm surprised he ain't spoke up.'

Grukust shrugged. 'I have axe,' he said phlegmatically. 'Anything attack me in woods, I hit it.'

After a moment the innkeeper grinned weakly. 'I suppose that might help right enough,' he agreed.

'What market news?' asked Rast, changing subjects.

'The Banistari trader is late this season, and the Meyari ha'nt come at all, but we've had good traffic from Novin, even some from Ignat. I hear tell there is some dried fish coming from Eyotsburg too, but that isn't in yet.'

'No thanks,' muttered Karland.

Xhera leaned over. 'Is it that bad?' she whispered.

'Like rancid death,' he whispered back. She crinkled her nose.

'My thanks,' said Rast. 'Come on. Let's find supplies.'

಄   ಞ

They emerged into a bright cold late afternoon that looked as if it should be hotter than it was. The odd large clouded scudded across the sun, dropping shadows across the plains as they stepped onto the road. Forward and right, the Town Hall loomed four storeys over the other buildings, and to its right a rocky column rose even higher in the centre of the town. Further back into the cleft between the huge cliffs behind the town hall were the richer houses, mostly hidden from view and protected from the elements.

'Don't wander south of the road,' Rast warned. 'People here are not friendly.

If you are lost, head for that rocky spire and you should reach the road. Be careful in the market. There will be thieves aplenty.' He pointed out the market to their right, with an intermittent posted fence running along the edges next to the houses and workplaces. The stalls were clustered along the road and houses, leaving a large open space where it bordered the plains. 'This spills right out on to the plains when it is time for the festival. More than forty thousand people come together to trade. Many of those living here are businessmen, not mere traders.'

The voice of the market was loud. As they approached, it resolved into traders shouting their wares, trying to outdo each other in description and volume. Some of the stalls were very impressive; one merchant was selling high quality burnished wooden furniture at an exorbitant price, and his stall was larger than the Inn of Cards itself. The furniture was beautiful, but it was also heavy and more costly than any team and wagon used to carry it. Karland wondered who bought it and how they took it away.

There were wares from all over Anaria. Another stall held weapons from the smithies of several realms. Rast had to drag Karland away from some unusual knives, telling him it was better to get one good knife he knew how to use than an exotic one that he didn't. Karland protested and they finally compromised on a straight single-edged dagger with a long but broad blade – a good all-rounder, Rast said. He examined the steel closely and discarded several blades before he accepted one for Karland. Karland was entranced by his shiny new blade, and paid little attention as Rast quietly haggled over some odd looking knives with the merchant. He managed a full five minutes before he sliced his finger with the edge. Rast shook his head. Leona looked amused, and Xhera rolled her eyes.

Further through the twisting stalls they found one with big metal-sheathed trays which looked very heavy. They were made from stone of some sort to keep the produce in them cool. Rast ignored it all, saying that they needed travelling rations. Food that needed keeping cool was not suitable, however nice it looked. Aldwyn irritably insisted that he at least buy some fruit, and Rast shrugged.

Everywhere they went, Grukust drew stares and whispered comments. Some of the merchants refused to even acknowledge him, although others greeted him as they would any customer, one even calling a welcome in rough orkish. Grukust was surprised and replied in Darum, regretfully moving on after it turned out the man was selling *rinok* leather – Grukust had no need for more. Wherever they went, Karland heard whispers follow them.

They collected dried meats and hard cheeses as well as trail bread. Rast stuck to long-lasting nutritious food, most of which was boring as far as Karland was concerned. He also bought a costly rope, heavy and solid.

The party spread out a little. Karland found himself walking some way behind the ork. He had stopped enjoying the market now, despite all the strange nick-nacks and interesting items. Instead he worried about the amount of glances towards the ork. He was becoming aware of the negative attention, and had a sinking feeling in the pit of his stomach. It was only a matter of time before Grukust noticed, although for the moment he seemed oblivious. Karland guessed people were more polite when there was an entire ork tribe among them.

He was staring at a stall of cloaks, trying to see if they resembled anything his father would trade in, when he heard voices behind him. Grukust was off to his left, the main hubbub of the market in front of them. He turned his head and saw two men staring at the ork. The fatter of the two was not too well dressed, but the other would have been considered smart were it not for the tattered sleeves and the lightly-stubbled face set in a permanent expression of pomposity.

'Look at 'im,' muttered the fat man. 'Filthy scum. One of them evil orcs that prey on people. Cowards. They eat human flesh.'

'Naw,' drawled his companion. 'Yer wrong, Kildan. Ain't like you say. They don't do nowt too bad at the market come festival time. They's just like beasts. A dog can't help biting you no more than an ork can help hitting you.'

'So where do the legends come from, eh?' snapped the other man, wiping his jowls. He had a profusion of flesh-tags around the folds on his neck, and his breathing was laboured. Obesely fat, he sweated even in the mild heat.

'Mebbe there are some bad ones,' conceded the other, 'Like there are bad dogs. But most of 'em are just dumb savages. Them Sergoth Barbarians are like, whatcha call 'em, litrey geniuses compared to these. But I reckon they are all right long as they stay away from us.' He announced everything loudly and nasally in a manner that suggested he was always correct, the words spilling offensively from a pinched mouth under a thin nose with long nostrils. His large companion glared at him in distaste.

Rast's voice in his ear made Karland jump.

'We need to leave before Grukust hears these fools-' the big man began. A bellow split the air even as he spoke. They turned to see Grukust looming one stall away, his gigantic hands clenching and unclenching in fury.

'*Animal?*' he shouted. '*Dumb savage?* Pathetic weaklings! You know nothing. Orks have more honour than most *humans*. I done nothing wrong.' Rast moved over quickly to intercept the two men, noticing a crowd gathering around them.

'Listen to 'im, he can't even speak proper,' sneered the long-nosed one. The fat man laughed unpleasantly. They seemed unconcerned by Grukust's deepening breathing and tensed muscles, confident that he wouldn't dare harm them.

'Shuln't even be in town. Cryin' shame that the watch let any sorts in now. See what I mean though? He don't *look* evil. Just big and dumb.'

Rast interrupted forcefully. 'I suggest you both leave. We have done you no harm, so do everyone a favour and shut your mouths.' His tone was flat.

Neither man seemed alarmed. 'Ooh, look at that. He's got a friend,' said the smaller man, moving away from his friend as if to get around Rast to Grukust. Rast moved with him, blocking his way. Karland was worried; this was getting ugly, and there were guards in the crowd. For now they seemed to be enjoying the spectacle. A quick glance showed the others in a group with Aldwyn, Xhera's face angry.

'Ah, cowshit. He's behavin' cos he's around real people. Pifin' orc. Can't eat any of our babies 'ere, eh? Not under our watchful eyes,' leered Kildan.

Grukust's eyes bulged in disbelief at what he had just heard. Kildan continued smugly, 'Betcha he'd be after any small children left alone-'

The ork roared in fury and leapt at him. Kildan squeaked hoarsely and tried to run, but only succeeded in tripping over his own feet to crash into a stall of jars and oils, just missing a large collection of cushions in the next stall. Rast jumped to intercept Grukust, who swung a huge fist in rage. Rast ducked fluidly. The fist knocked a supporting corner of another stall over, bringing the stall down beside them.

Karland couldn't understand why the ork had tried to hit Rast, until he caught a glimpse of the ork's face and the terrifying sight of the berserk rage on it. The fat man was scrabbling away in fear through broken glass and cushions, moaning and leaving a trail of blood and urine behind him. Rast blocked Grukust's path to him and spoke loudly to the enraged ork.

'Grukust! Calm down. This fool is not worth being lynched over!'

Grukust ignored him and tried to get past, slamming an open right palm onto Rast's chest hard to thrust him out of the way. Even as it landed, Rast's right hand came over the top to grip the edge opposite the thumb. He twisted the arm powerfully, his other arm sliding over the locked elbow and controlling Grukust's arm. Grukust roared in rage and jerked against the pressure. Rast thrust downwards with his left and pulled the ork's hand up with his right, forcing him off balance. Grukust fell to one knee then was pulled flat, ending with his face pressed hard to the floor.

Karland watched in despair, worried Rast might have to seriously hurt him to disable him, or be injured himself. Grukust was monstrously strong, and he was fully immersed in the berserk rage that orks were prone to, hardly even registering pain.

Letting go of the arm, Rast moved to mount the prone body to apply a choke from the rear, but the huge axe strapped to the ork's back denied him. Even as he hesitated, Grukust rolled underneath him quicker than expected, nearly slashing his leg, and scythed a fist around. Rast jumped back, and the ork scrambled to his feet. From the corner of his eyes Karland could see the guards approaching; their weapons were out, including a crossbow, and they looked like they were in no mood to argue. So far Grukust had not touched his axe, but the instant he saw weapons someone would die.

'Grukust, I need you to calm down,' Rast said into a mask of fury. The ork was not listening. Froth dripped from the ork's mouth next to a tusk, and he growled incoherently.

Karland was astonished when Xhera suddenly stepped in front of him to face Grukust. She looked up at the towering figure, and called softly.

'Grukust.'

He growled, staring at Rast over her small form.

'Grukust, look at me.'

The ork's glaring eyes flicked down, and he hesitated.

႙   Ⴍ

Eating children! Nothing was more sacred to the orks than their young. He wanted to destroy, to hurt, to kill. How dare the fat human accuse him of killing children!

But here was a young human – no threat, although blocking him from continuing his assault. His thoughts were clearing and his rage was draining. A throb was making itself felt in his right wrist and elbow. He shook his head and snarled, the anger not wanting to let go.

'Grukust.'

He looked down again to find the small human girl right in front of him. He recognised her. She smiled up at him under clear blue eyes. 'It's me, Xhera. We are your friends.'

Friends. A sense of sadness at the loss of his tribe shot through him, buffered by the acceptance he had shared with these people over the last few days. Instead of judging him they had defended him, turning his view on most humans upside down. This girl in particular lent meaning to the word *friend.*

Abruptly Grukust sensed movement behind him, and whirled. The girl gasped. A rat-faced man with a long nose holding a savage-looking dirk in his hand was backpedalling frantically from an aborted lunge, dismayed by the failure of his attack. Grukust swept his hand up and slapped the knife from the man's hand.

He moaned and wrung stinging fingers, and then the backhand returned like the fist of a god, carrying all the ork's strength and anger. It caught him full-force across the face and he flew pinwheeling to the side a good ten feet into a so-far untouched stall of wicker baskets, which collapsed in a cascade over him.

There was a moment's silence. Grukust shook his head, breathing heavily. A headache was starting, as it always did after he went *baresark*, but he was becoming aware of things around him again, slipping out of that pure state where the simple choice was to fight and prevail. He looked around to see Xhera with her hands in front of her mouth in shock, and behind her the rest of his friends, Rast looking grim. Shame washed through him, and some chagrin at the blurred memory of how easily this big human had deflected his attacks.

'*Paska*,' he muttered to himself.

Xhera was pale. She looked at the feet sticking out from the mountain of wicker. 'Are you all right?' she asked the ork.

Grukust nodded, and looked at Rast. 'Sorry, Rast Tal'Orien.' Now the rage was past he felt guilt that he had caused his new friends problems.

The big man shook his head. 'We'll talk later. We have bigger problems right now.'

Grukust turned to see a semicircle of sharpened steel approaching. Behind the guards the crowd grew thicker, with curses and shouts heard. Several stall keepers had emerged from the ruins and were yelling; one was standing staring at his bloodied cushions, shaking his head in despair.

'Come quietly, ork. You're under arrest. Public unrest, property and goods damage, assaulting a human. Possibly murder,' a guard commanded. He looked over at the wicker stall and seemed disappointed to see a leg twitch.

Rast held up his hand. 'You all saw that he was intentionally provoked and then attacked with a knife. He only defended himself.'

'Call it what you want, matey,' said the guard nastily. 'I saw a dangerous savage attack humans and badly hurt one of them when he drew a knife to protect hisself. He comes with us. He is now bound by law.'

Xhera moved in front of the ork, between him and the steel. After a moment, Karland followed, as did Leona. Rast and Aldwyn moved to the fore, the old man muttering to himself distractedly.

Rast looked back, and then said conversationally, 'I don't think so. Unless you fancy carving your way through paying *humans* in front of a hundred witnesses to take him. This old man here is also a high-ranking scholar of Darost. I'm sure you would look good with that on your career, *corporal*. If you are so worried for the welfare of the man who drew the dirk, perhaps you should see to him.'

The guard pursed his lips in indecision. Grukust's head thumped.

Aldwyn refocused. He glanced up through his spectacles and added, 'Mm, I believe that under section, three, or is it four? Of Punslon law, article two, it states that self-defence is a legitimate reason for bodily harm as long as a weapon is not used. If I recall, isn't that to ensure that Market Disputes are allowed to vent without getting too serious? Ah, my, it's been a long while since I was here last.' This was incomprehensible to Grukust; ork tribal law was uncomplicated.

Rast smiled. 'I recall that Punslon law is strictly adhered to for trade reasons. Shall we raise this officially with your Mayor as Darost representatives? I'm sure he would be delighted at this waste of his time.'

The corporal stared at them coldly. 'Squad dismissed,' he snapped after a long moment, and turned to the crowd, who were muttering. 'Get back to your business!' A few voices shouted imprecations, some shouting encouragement for Grukust, others for the ork to be taken.

'Shut it! Move along. Someone clean this mess up. These two can pay for damages.' He waved at the broken stalls, and left without a backward glance, his men trooping away to various points in the market. The crowd looked ugly.

'We leave *now*,' said Rast. 'Officially they cannot do much, but they won't help us if we are attacked by a mob.'

Ten minutes later, they were out on the road. Grukust muttered to himself at the indignity of running away. Rast caught his eye but said nothing. Grukust bit his tongue.

They moved rapidly along the road, afternoon winding down into hints of dusk. Turning left towards their inn, they entered it with relief. Not many were in the common room, although there were a few men sitting drinking. Several cast suspicious glances at the ork, but most ignored them.

'We must talk,' said Rast. He waved over Geraldt, who came forward with a smile. 'Ale, please. Three.' He glanced at Grukust, who nodded glumly. A drink would be welcome.

'Water,' said Leona.

'Wine,' said Karland casually, sneaking a glance at Rast. Xhera echoed it after a moment. Geraldt looked at Rast in amusement.

'Three parts water,' amended Rast. When Karland sighed, he said, 'Do you want wine at all?' Karland nodded glumly. 'So.' Geraldt smiled and left to get the drinks.

There was a moment's silence, and then Grukust spoke in a low voice.

'My temper cause us problem. Sorry.' It was not in orkish nature to apologise often, but he knew his companions would have trouble from this.

Rast sighed. 'You were provoked, deliberately and strongly, but if you travel with us you must learn control, Grukust. Unlike *Urukin*, humans can be very different. Some are honourable, some are not – and many will say things designed to demean or degrade others. Especially in this town, with its prejudice, you must learn to ignore insults.'

'They insult my honour-' began Grukust, feeling anger again.

Rast interrupted him.

'They were not *worthy* of your honour. Try considering the words of such men as... unequal.'

'Sort of like a lower level,' said Karland. 'They can't insult your honour, because they are beneath you.'

Grukust rumbled. It sounded suspiciously like cowardice to him.

Xhera joined in. 'Would you consider the words of a small child the same as an adult?' He shook his head. 'So... think of them as rude children. Their words are not worth your anger.'

'I think, mm, the problem is that if you lose your temper, you fall *baresark*,' said Aldwyn, using the Orkish word. 'So it is simple! Don't lose your temper.' He beamed happily, his eyes crinkling. Xhera rolled her eyes, Leona looking with frank amusement at the old man.

Grukust thought about this. The words were direct and simple, and spoke to him.

'Yes. You right, old man. It simple. I just keep temper. Anger like pain; just let it go through, disappear.'

He saw Rast and Karland swap doubtful glances, but resolved to prove them wrong. It *was* that simple; he could show these humans that an ork had as much control as any of them! With new resolve Grukust downed his ale. The taste was strange and there was not much alcohol. His face twisted. 'What this made from? You need try proper ork ale. Make you strong.'

'Make you drunk,' whispered Aldwyn to Karland.

'Probably made from *rinok paska*,' whispered back Karland. Aldwyn choked with laughter.

Grukust felt a second of anger, then laughed. 'I hear that.' Karland went red, a curious thing he had noticed with humans. 'Xhera right. You all friends. I listen to advice. And I tell you all: I made right choice. Brukk was wrong! I restore his honour. But I am glad to do in company of you.' He thumped his empty tankard on the table and smiled. 'I behave.'

Rast nodded to him. 'Let's eat.'

The common room filled a little more as talk turned to their destination. As food arrived, Leona fell silent. Grukust's eyes turned to her. She was sitting up straight, casting her strange glance around the room. It was obvious she sensed something. Closing her eyes, she lifted her head almost like a questing hound.

'My pardon,' she said, rising swiftly. 'I will return soon.'

'What is wrong?' asked Rast. She ignored him and left quickly and gracefully. The others looked at each other.

'Druids have, mm, odd senses, do they not?' said Aldwyn reflectively.

'Leona can deal with problem. We should eat,' said Grukust. He felt their stares. 'What? She powerful Druid! And food is here. She ask if she need us with her. I think she want be alone.' He eyed the food again and tucked in, unconcerned. After a few moments the others followed suite, but he noticed Rast sitting facing the door, his back to a wall as usual. He was half-listening to the others, his eyes on the door she had left through.

∞

Leona stepped outside, and moved towards the lamp-lit shadows opposite the stable, stopping in near-total darkness down an alley. Her eyes shone like lamps.

'I know you are there,' she said. 'Quite a distinctive musk. It has been a long time.' Her vision pierced the shadows around her, and she saw a neat, compact shape step forward.

'Leona.' The voice was level and mid-range.

'*Erus Ex Noct Noctis,*' she greeted him formally. 'It is good to see you again. What are you doing here?' It was unlikely to be a casual visit, but she hoped.

'Looking for you, dear lady. Looking for you.'

'Well, with your usual efficiency, you have found me, old friend. Why do you seek me?'

The small man moved forward and studied her with startlingly blue-grey irises. He sighed slightly, and shook his head. 'I come as a favour, the bearer of ill news. *Vir prodigium en vastatio.'*

Leona stared at him in disbelief. What he said was impossible. The horrors the Druids sought to contain had never broken free like this before. 'You are sure?' she said.

The small man nodded. 'In great number. Greater than counted for millennia.'

'Where? How could this have happened?'

'More than one place. Entire villages have been slaughtered, people killed or worse across western Anaria. The biggest concentration appears to be in the north of Novin currently but I fear they are on the move.' His pale face was expressionless. 'This is grave. It could be the worst uprising in memory. Something stirs, something comes, something happens that should not be. Almost all of your brethren have journeyed to contain them; I hope there are enough. For the first time in millennia the Druids may be unable to hold the balance.'

Leona bowed her head and sighed heavily. This tore her loyalties unbearably. 'The quest I am on is critical,' she said. 'We seek the very source of the unrest, and answers. I searched long to get here. But this other news is dire indeed. What matter the evil we uncover if another evil destroys the living first? Am I to abandon this quest when I am needed the most?'

'That I cannot answer, my friend. I cannot even offer my aid. As it is, I am sorely needed elsewhere. It may be, though, that our quests are not so different. I seek an... aberration of my own that I believe to be near the heart of this chaos. All of this may be related. It stretches coincidence too far that this should all happen at once.'

'Ai! You are like a storm front, always bearing the worst of news. I should have known when I sensed you.' The small man didn't say anything, and after a moment Leona shook her head. 'I am sorry. That was unfair of me.'

He smiled slightly. 'Well. I do have a habit of bearing bad news. But that is not the only reason I am here, Druid. Your companions are of... interest.'

She shot him a glance. His plain features below his brown ill-cut hair were expressionless. 'How do you know of them?'

'I have been keeping an eye on the affairs of men, of late.'

'I think it best in that case if you come and meet them. This will all take explaining anyway. They will think I desert them.'

The small man offered her a slender arm. 'Let us then go inside and clarify. This world enters a time of testing, and even the Gods may not survive it.'

TWENTY-FIVE

A s Leona re-entered the common room, Rast's eyebrows rose at the sight of her new companion. Small and neat, he was a touch under average height, and slender. His face was plain and calm, framed by untidy short brown hair, and he wore a thin grey cloak over dark, archaic looking clothes. In fact, he was utterly nondescript until you saw his eyes. They blazed from his face with astonishing intensity, the irises a piercing blue-grey that spoke of ice and sun and sky and a strange hint to the pupil. Rast suspected he was another Druid.

It was hard to meet the intense gaze, but the small man acted as if he was unaware of it. Leona brought him to the table, where he bowed low to them all.

'This is an old friend of mine,' she said. 'He has sought me out with grave tidings. His name is-'

'-far too formal and foreign for this meeting,' he interjected smoothly in a mild tone. His voice was not very deep, but he pronounced his words beautifully. In fact, he sounded like Aldwyn, albeit much younger. 'You may all call me Night.'

'Night?' echoed Xhera. 'That's a strange name. I mean, um. Different.' She reddened.

The little man smiled without rancour. 'I am sure your names are as strange to me. Where I was born, we are often given such names. It is a crude translation from my language, but it is primal and powerful, as many of our names are. Might I know yours?'

They introduced themselves and the small man greeted each quite formally, even speaking flawless orkish to Grukust who was visibly impressed.

'So what are these grave tidings you bring, Night?' asked Rast cautiously.

Night smiled slightly, his lips not quite parting. 'There are actually several reasons for my coming here this night. One regards the tidings I brought Leona, but I must confess I also know a little of your quest.'

'Eh? What do you mean?' demanded Aldwyn warily.

'I am a...scholar,' said the small man. 'I collect knowledge.'

His tone was light, but Aldwyn frowned suspiciously. 'Which Academia?'

'Ah. I am a student more of life. I have never enrolled in your University, Aldwyn Varelin, although I have visited. The Sanctum with its Combic Libraries is most impressive, and your name is well known there. You are considered one of the most learned of the Universalia Communia.'

'You seem to know much about me, ah, Night,' said Aldwyn nervously. Night smiled his thin smile again, but his eyes smiled with his lips.

'Like you, I study many things,' he replied. 'And like you, I am also seeking causes of recent ... upheavals. Evil has awoken. Which, as we both know, is in reality more attributable to root influences of chaos than a true meta-ethical dichotomy, although it has certainly allowed evil itself to flourish.'

Aldwyn's eyes glinted and he opened his mouth, but Night held up a hand to forestall him. 'Normally I would love to talk in detail with you, Aldwyn Varelin – it is rare I get the chance for long discussions with the erudite! – but here and now we have no time. I also come to warn you. There is talk in this town tonight both sides of the road of you and your *Urukin* companion. The townspeople drink and reflect on the injuries of the day. There may be trouble. The guards are doing nothing to dampen this feeling – on the contrary, many appear to be fanning it, and you are not well hidden here. The innkeeper is honest enough, but his patrons are not necessarily so. I think you should leave before anyone decides to come here for retribution, ill-deserved or not. You may have little time, so I propose that we hasten and you leave town as quietly as possible.'

Rast pursed his lips. 'We thank you for the warning, Night. Tell us what news you bring and why you know so much about us.'

Night nodded. 'As to the first... perhaps Leona should tell you, since the news was for her.' All eyes turned to Leona. She returned them boldly until she came to Rast, and then looked away.

'Every Druid has been recalled on a matter of grave urgency,' she said softly. 'Unnatural aberrations stir, beasts that revel in mindless slaughter. For centuries we have held them in check, but they have risen again.'

'Are you serious?' Xhera asked.

Leona nodded. 'These creatures are one of the more dangerous of the children of chaos. Unchecked, an army of them could decimate everything except the largest cities – those too, in time. They are monsters; evil, aware, and living to slaughter. Those victims that survive being attacked often face worse than death.'

Night coughed. 'More or less. So: you can see how even a small army of these would be a problem, and we face a horde. I do not know how they have grown to be so many so quickly. The Druids keep careful watch on these monsters, as they do all unnatural beasts.'

'We kill them when we find them,' hissed Leona, hate in her eyes. Rast glanced at her, surprised. 'The Druids have means of combating these monsters, but there are not many of us. We will need our full strength to deal with this host before it increases beyond control.'

'So you must leave us,' said Rast in a neutral tone.

Leona would not meet his level gaze. 'I am sorry,' she whispered.

Karland looked at her in alarm. 'But-'

Rast interrupted. 'She has no choice, Karland. Try not to make this hard on her.' His tone held no note of the disappointment he felt. Leona looked at him gratefully.

'Thank you,' she said. 'I will find you all again, I swear. Our quest is of the greatest importance, but this threat is immediate and lethal. Unchecked, it could swing the greater balance towards what we seek to prevent... a spiral into chaos.'

'We understand,' said Aldwyn a little sadly. 'Truly. But, mm, we will miss you.'

Grukust leaned forward. 'You make sure you kill some for Grukust,' he said, and grinned. A small laugh burst from Leona, and she leaned over and hugged the huge ork in a rare expression of friendship. His eyes popped in surprise, and Karland and Xhera grinned at his expression. Rast smiled inwardly.

'Watch for me in the coming months,' she said, her eyes straying back to him. 'I will find you.'

'When will you leave?' he asked softly.

'Tonight. Later. I will ensure you leave here safely and part when we are outside town. I can move faster on my own anyway.' She smiled.

'Leona is not the only one to hunt,' remarked Night. 'I am a student of men, of politics, among many other things, and one problem with governing bodies is that there is a massive potential for subterfuge and immorality which is open to exploitation by corrupt men.' He looked at them all in turn. 'And others. In recent years the church of Terome has shown signs of massive internal upheaval. They are becoming the true power in-'

'*Meyar!*' shouted Aldwyn excitedly. Several heads turned at other tables, but he didn't seem to notice. 'I *knew* it! That explains much. Of course, we have had little, ah, information. Someone has been killing scholars.'

'Name them Darostim,' said Night quietly. 'I am well aware of the organisation. I was one myself, once.'

Aldwyn was mute with astonishment. He opened his mouth but Night waved a hand at him. 'Aldwyn, I am with you in this battle. I fight for stability, for peace in this land. I do not answer to your council, or the Darostim, but believe me when I say that I will do what I can in my own fashion. There is one I have been seeking – powerful, evil. I have finally traced him to the Teromens. Dark times come to the loosely affiliated Territories of Meyar; the rich grow too powerful and the poor edge toward slavery. In outlying areas there are tales of torture in the name of Terome, and curfews and new laws are growing more commonplace. People are turning on their neighbours, spying is encouraged... even the big cities are feeling the changes now. At the centre of it all, Terome spreads like a cancer, and not just in Meyar. The temples are rising everywhere.'

'Meyar and Terome are involved in Eordeland's unrest too, and allied with orcs within our borders,' said Aldwyn. 'They hunt both me and an artefact I seek. I have been seeing glimpses of these happenings for ten years, and only now others see – perhaps too late. War now seems inevitable. But it may be that we search for the same, um, answers.'

'Mayhap,' agreed Night. 'But Meyar is not alone in this trouble. It is widespread, and there is more. Many travellers have disappeared in Anaria these last years; traders are frightened and reluctant to travel. Inter-realm economies will eventually collapse if this continues. I fear the festival here will be poor this year. Something stirs in the pit of the Dimnesvale and unseemly things come forth from the Dimnesdair. Now orcs connect the dark valley here with Meyar.' He shook his head. 'It is sad that Haná fell. It was a fair kingdom once.'

'It was.'

The two scholars fell silent for a moment.

'This knowledge is hard-won for us both,' mused Night. 'How did you learn of all this?'

'I correlated my own studies with the Book of Sarthos,' replied Aldwyn.

'Of course!' Night enthused. 'I have read Sarthos' work. Fool, for not considering it before! I was so busy with my own observations.' He grimaced. 'We have been working from different ends of the same equation. But my time here grows short, as does yours.' He glanced at Rast, who nodded agreement. 'I propose a concord. I will hunt in Meyar and find any references to an artefact of power or an alliance with chaos while you trace the origin of these orcs.'

'There was mention of a 'hollow in mountains',' mused Aldwyn. 'And a name: *Sontles*. I will seek answers where the orcs headed – and where perhaps this great power we seek to unlock may lie.'

Night nodded. 'The name means nothing to me, but the phrase would fit the Dimnesvale, and the only power in the Vale is reputedly in the Pit of Kharkis, the

crevasse in the north end. Discover what you can. We can meet in, say...
Eyotsburg. Together we may find the answers we seek.'

'That is an excellent proposal,' said Aldwyn, beaming. He looked at Rast, who
nodded agreement, and then a thought struck him. 'What about Grukust? Can
he enter their city with us?'

'I think you will find Eyotsburg less judgemental on the whole than a
provincial self-inflated town like Punslon,' said Night flatly. 'It is a port. I'll wager
that stranger than our green friend here has been seen there. Meyar however
would be another matter. That is one advantage I have over all of you: I hardly
stand out in a crowd.'

'How do we find you?' asked Rast.

The cryptic little man shook his head. 'I will find you. Have no doubt of that.'
He glanced around. 'You should go. Already we have delayed too long.'

'I will speak to Geraldt,' said Rast.

Night nodded. 'I will meet you outside.'

The party gathered their belongings, and Rast made his way to the bar to get
their chest.

'Can we trust the men at the logging camp?' he asked.

The innkeeper nodded. 'Oh, yes, sir. As it goes, I know a few of the wood
cutters. My cousin works the trees, and he's a good man – one of the veterans in
camp. I will give you a message for him. He will be able to help you. Will you go
now?'

'Yes,' said Rast quietly. 'There was trouble today in the marketplace. My
friend was provoked. For your trouble, and a favour, keep the payments for the
rooms; if you can tell everyone who asks that we are elsewhere in town, it will not
be stretching the truth too much.'

'Of course,' said the innkeeper.

'You have our thanks,' Rast said, and grasped the innkeeper's hand. 'It has
been a pleasure to find one honest man in this place.'

Geraldt shook firmly, and sighed. 'There used to be more, sir. Still are some.
But largely, this place is gettin' worse. If it weren't for my grandfather's inn here,
I'd be leaving right quick. If you go out through the back door mebbe you won't
be noted.'

Rast nodded. He lifted the chest and stepped through the kitchen door.
Karland followed him out. The cook was absent, although there was food spread
everywhere.

They stepped out the back door to find him sprawled on a stool against the
wall, smoking a strange coiled leaf. His skin was much darker than theirs and he

had a thin gold ring through his eyebrow. White teeth stood out as he grinned at them mysteriously, and then he went back to his quiet contemplations.

⋘ ⋙

They entered the stables from the rear to find the others grouped around the cart and the horses. Night was nowhere to be seen. To the delight of the hastily roused stable lads Rast flipped them a half-silver each.

'Let's get moving,' he said to the others. They saddled up and moved out of the stable, the cart rattling loudly in the night air. Karland turned to look behind him, and when he turned back he found a slender form next to him on the cart. He jumped, and then recognised Night and sighed in relief. The man moved more like Leona than Aldwyn, however much of a scholar he was.

'You suit your name,' he muttered, heart fluttering. The little man grinned disconcertingly in the darkness.

'I like to think so.'

Geraldt appeared in the doorway and hurried over to Rast. 'Here,' he said, thrusting a hurriedly scrawled note to him. 'Give this to Danial.'

Leona lifted her head, and then cursed softly. 'I hear a number of people approaching.' Even as she said it, the sound of shouts became apparent to all of them.

Geraldt swore. 'Luck be with you,' he called, and ran back inside.

'That is not a few people,' muttered Rast. '*That* is a mob.'

He spurred his horse to the end of the short street and turned left, eastwards towards the Pass. A shout went up, and Karland saw a large mass of townsfolk approaching from the west, many bearing torches and weapons. The obese Kildan was limping at the fore with no evidence of his scrawny friend. His hands were bandaged heavily, as was one arm.

'*There! There!* The snotrag is right there! Look what 'e did to me!' he roared. 'Baby killin' foul orc attacked me, no reason, nearly killed me! Josh Barquin can't eat neither with a broke face. Nearly broke his neck. Kill the stinkin' orc!'

The crowd roared, mindless and mostly drunk; there must have been nearly a hundred men and women, more than a few in guard uniforms.

Grukust stopped dead, his teeth baring. His hand crept towards his axe.

'If you do that, half of us die,' said Rast coldly. 'You have a responsibility to us. A promise to Xhera. *Where is your honour, Ork?*'

Grukust whirled with a snarl, and glared at Rast. As if it pained him, he turned his back on the mob. Grabbing Hjarta's collar he moved forward in a run, nearly dragging the little dray with him. The mob broke into a stumbling run.

'*He's getting away! The coward is getting away!*'

'*Move!*' shouted Rast. They galloped down the street, and the crowd fell behind quickly, yelling in disappointment and unsated blood lust.

'Cretins,' said Night disgustedly. 'I am sure our fat friend there would not have been the first in line when it came to the fight. Nevertheless, it is lucky we were not caught in the inn.'

'Without your warning, ah, Night, we might well have been,' said Aldwyn. 'Thank you.'

The little man waved a negligent hand. 'My pleasure.'

The hooves of their steeds mingled with the rattling creak of the cart as they thundered down the road. A squad of guardsmen poured out of their building, but they were looking the wrong way, and shouted in surprise as they swept past them. They were out of town in a few minutes and a short while later they reached a fork where a faint trail led south towards the woods, unseen in the night. There they paused, and Leona moved to speak quietly to Night.

'This has all happened so fast,' said Xhera softly. 'Do you think we will see Leona again?'

'I hope so,' said Karland. 'I like her. Aldwyn says she is a powerful Druid. If she can make it back, I think she will. Besides,' he said thoughtfully, 'I think she is too interested in Rast to stay away.'

Xhera giggled. 'You noticed too?'

'I should keep such speculations to yourself,' said Aldwyn drily. 'The hearing of Druids is excellent. Fear not for her. I am more worried what we shall do without her guidance in the woods.'

They moved over to the Druid. She was watching Rast talking to Grukust; the ork was apparently still angry, but Rast spoke calmly, and he reluctantly nodded.

'Interesting,' said Night. 'Your *Urukin* friend willingly listens to a human. That *is* unusual.'

'How do you know? I can't hear what they are saying,' said Xhera.

Night grinned tightly.

'Oh, I can tell,' he said. 'Your green friend is angry he ran from a fight. That is the way of orks. But he must consider which is more honourable – a fight he cannot win, or keeping his obligations to his friends.' He raised his voice. 'Rast Tal'Orien. I must take my leave of you here. Leona, I will journey with you as far as the North Plains Road.'

She nodded. 'We will head out north and bypass the town.' Her eyes turned to them all, and lastly to Rast. 'We will meet again. Stay safe, all of you. May you be blessed by *Gaia*.' Then she paused, concentrating and talking in low tones that Karland could not understand. Hjarta's ears flickered, as did Stryke's. She motioned with her hand.

'Your horses will guide you well until we meet again.'

Karland threw a glance at Xhera. She shrugged.

'Be safe, Leona,' said Rast softly. 'Come back to us.'

'We'll miss you,' said Xhera. Grukust nodded.

Karland looked at her gravely. 'You still have to walk in the woods with me.'

'I will,' she said. 'I promise.'

She pulled her chestnut horse up next to the cart. Night climbed lightly up behind her and held on. She started moving away, and then cast a last glance over her shoulder. Her eyes reflected a green-gold flash in the darkness, and then they were gone, hoof beats fading into the night.

Rast's face was expressionless. 'Let's move out. If we follow this trail we should reach the wood cutter's camp in a few hours. Stay alert.'

They turned off the main road, and moved at a steady pace down the trail. The moon was dark but Xoth was high, and the night was clear, so it was not too hard to navigate. Karland shivered in apprehension as all the evil creatures Geraldt had mentioned came back to his mind, gathered in the darkness. He tried to think of something else.

A few hours later they had reached a dark, looming tree line. The trees ran off to the left in shadows and were lost in the night, and to the right they ran up to the rocky cliff that ran round to the edge of Punslon. They were cleared in a wide arc from either side of the road for a good half a mile, but then they closed in around them, and the party found themselves hemmed in, the horses slowed to a crawl. They could not afford to injure them in the darkness. The woods had a strange feel to them, wild and ominous, but this side of the pass at least they were merely woods. According to Aldwyn, the trees on the other side reputedly stretched away in a heavy and increasingly strange forest for many miles before dropping away into a vast and deep valley.

'I'm frightened.' whispered Xhera. Karland took her hand, and her grateful look made him sit up straighter.

More than an hour later, Rast held up his hand, and they halted. The night was quiet. Gradually they realised there was a glow off to the right in front of them, and they moved down the trail towards it.

'This is the camp,' said Rast softly. 'They will have sentries.'

Suddenly the trail broke through the edge of a wide clearing. The trees were gone in a large circle around the trail, and right in the middle was a large camp, brightly lit. It sprawled behind sharp wooden pickets, a small village in its own right, with a tower on each corner of a high wooden wall lighting the ground for hundreds of feet.

A call came out when they were still a few hundred yards away. Rast replied, saying they were in from Punslon and were told to speak to Danial. The sentry who had challenged them sounded suspicious, but told them to pull up to the heavy gate and wait. Aware that they were under close scrutiny, Rast did so, and told the others quietly to sit still.

Another voice rang out again from the palisade. 'Who told you to seek Danial? It is late, stranger. The gates are closed.'

'An innkeeper in Punslon, Geraldt. I have a written message from him for Danial.'

There was some conferring, and then the voice called out reluctantly. 'Approach the gate. Mind you get inside fast. Night ain't no time to be out in these woods.'

Even as he spoke, the gate of thick cross-mounted timbers swung in. The small group moved inside quickly, pleased to be free from the sombre woods around the clearing. Inside they were met by a rough-looking man with a small beard and a solid build, rubbing tired eyes.

'What brings you 'ere so late?' he asked brusquely.

Rast replied levelly, 'We are travellers from Punslon. We had not intended on being out so late in these woods.'

'Damn strange, if you ask me.' Then he saw Grukust and stared, his suspicious face relaxing a little. 'Mebbe not so strange. What did Geraldt say about Danial?'

'That he was an honest man and could provide us some help,' said Rast, his expression blank.

The man snorted. 'Ha! Did he now.'

'Can you take us to him?'

'I *am* 'im, as you have likely guessed. Come, let's see about stabling your horses.' He led them to the right, where there was a large communal stable. Rast stepped down from Stryke and turned to Danial.

'We may need to leave them here a time. Just be careful of my horse.' He drew the scrawled note from his pocket. 'This is for you.'

Danial glanced at it.

'Well, that's 'is writing, sure enough,' he laughed roughly. 'I got a cabin here. You can stay there tonight. Should be room for all of you, but it will be cosy.

Used to be a bit fuller.' His face was unreadable. 'We best get your friend out of sight. *We* don't care so much out here, but Feller's Camp's got several squads of Punslon Guard these days to look after the lumber comin' to town. Not so much a camp now; got two hundred men on and off.'

They left the horses settled and followed him through the outskirts of the camp to a large cabin. He entered first, lighting a lamp and then gesturing them inside. The interior was sparse – a bedroom, a table, three small chairs, a small chest and a lot of swept floor. Rast put down Aldwyn's chest and held his hand out.

'Our thanks for this. You have been more cordial than I had hoped.'

'Ah,' Danial shook his hand, 'if Geraldt speaks for you then I am glad to help. Gets damn borin' out here. Besides, you likely upset a fair few people neither of us care for.' He grinned suddenly. In the warm light, it was easier to see his resemblance to his cousin. They both had broad faces and a slight gap in their front teeth, but Danial sported a short full beard and had bigger shoulders, less of a plump midsection. He waved them to sit. 'Lemme look at this note.'

He sat and read, his lips moving slowly. Either he was not good at reading, thought Karland with the easy disdain of someone who did it without thinking, or his cousin was bad at writing. *Probably both.*

Danial's face grew more sober as he read, and at the end he grimaced and stretched, rubbing his face wearily. 'This note from Geraldt seems odd,' he said. 'Ain't a good reader – one o' three in the camp! – but he said some right queer things. Seems like I am to help you in any way, and he'll make the difference up if I am outta pocket.' His brows drew down. 'You ain't threatened him? He sounds, well… worried.'

'My word on it,' said Rast.

Aldwyn looked indignant. 'Certainly not!' he protested, his hair slightly wild.

Danial chuckled. 'All right, old father. It just reads weird is all. And he says you are travelling *into* the woods, is that right?' He shook his head when they all nodded. 'You must be insane. Out here they are woods, mebbe a bit darker'n normal. Further in? There's all sorts. Good place to vanish.'

'We have heard the warnings, Danial,' said Rast. 'We have no choice. We have been sent from Darost seeking answers, and we think some lie inside the Dimnesdair. We don't like it any more than you.'

The wood cutter stared at him. 'Ha. Well, I *don't* like it. Seen too many go into the woods and not come back. Our other camp lost damn near thirty men. We don't have the grit to go for the big ironwoods through the Pass any more; hard enough to cut the damn things in the first place without murdering beasts around. It's allus been sorta *dark* here, but now it's more than that. Evil, murky, horrible. This life is all I have though – I can't leave any more than Geraldt can, for all our drunken promises to.'

'What, ah, do we *really* need to be careful of?' asked Aldwyn. 'We've heard a lot of stories. We would like to know the, aha, real facts. I assure you, we wish to stay as safe as we can.'

'You must be jokin',' sighed Danial. He shook his head in disbelief. 'Right. This side of the Pass, there's a few bears, wolves, bandits, forest cats, the usual. Not much comes through it. It's a narrow steep windin' trail that was a demon's work to get trees up. Somethin' comes through sometimes though, and your guess is as good as mine for what it might be. We stay in 'ere at night.

'There's a lot of paths in these woods. *Somethin'* made all them trails. I ain't sayin what but I has suspicions, and we guard this camp at all times. It's far down the trails towards town, so we don't get bothered much, but we see weird things here and there. Once in a while men go missing. Don't allus find 'em. You don't go alone out here is the rule. Found foul prints of late that have most here demanding we leave the woods. Men whisperin' of goblins an' ogres. Some of the newer ones laughed till we caught an orc near the camp a while back. We killed it quick, but it worries me. We never saw 'em Plains-side before.

'Then there is the woods witch. Round here she is known as *Jetzibabah*. I know men who swear they seen her, but I never have. Mebbe she's just a crazy forest lady, mebbe she ain't even real, but there are stories going back a long way about her in all the plains towns.

'In some she's a misunderstood old lady. In others she's a hag that eats children. When men goes missin', people say say she took 'em. Heh. But all that together is a damn fine set of reasons to turn around and go back.'

'You would also be wise to leave, my friend,' said Rast grimly. 'If what you say is true, your camp is in real danger. Witch and devils aside, we followed almost half a thousand orcs through the plains, and they were heading right for this Pass. You may be out of the way for a small band, but if there are more? The world is getting more dangerous, especially in areas such as this. You should leave this place.'

'Brilliant. That is just what I needed to 'ear.' Danial's face was a mix of worry and frustration. He sighed heavily. 'Look, I'll tell the others. Mebbe we can fortify, or even leave, but I doubt it will be the second. This is our life here. I put everything I had into it. My years, my back... my family. I lost them all to fever, nearly died meself. This cabin, it's all I got left to remind me I ever had 'em.'

Xhera's eyes were bright with tears. Karland didn't know what to say, but Rast spoke compassionately. 'Would it not be better to stay alive and honour your memories of them than die here?'

'Mebbe you're right,' said Danial. 'It were a while ago.' He shrugged.

'You and your cousin have been of great help. We still need to leave our horses here. We cannot take them deeper into this forest, especially if this Pass is so hard to travel.'

Danial grinned. 'You'd do well to get a horse through there without injury,' he snorted. 'It's passable, but it's a chore. If you can leave me money for feed, I can look after them. How long will you be gone?' He left the obvious 'if you come back' out, but they all heard it nonetheless.

Aldwyn looked at Rast. 'Hmm. Hard to say. A few weeks at most. Less, I hope.' His voice held a faint quaver. 'We will start tomorrow morning, early.' He glanced at the impassive Grukust, who had not spoken throughout all this. 'Best if we are not noticed too much.'

'Yeah,' said Danial. 'Most of us are too busy with the trees to pay much mind to snobbery, but idiots is like mushrooms – they sprout up in any shitty place, like it or not.' His eyes darted to Xhera. 'Um, pardon my Banistari.'

'Grukust, can you unload the main pack? We'll eat, and then sleep,' said Rast. The ork nodded. 'Danial. Your cousin was right. You are a good man. You have our thanks, and this. There is more than enough for feed in there, and some more besides.' He held out a small pouch, which clinked.

Danial took it and nodded. 'I'll help because me cousin asked, but I won't say no to a little extra. It's a hard life we got 'ere.'

TWENTY-SIX

Karland was awoken by Rast in the dim early morning light filtering through a rough window. He stretched and grimaced. This was the second day that he had not had any training from Rast or Aldwyn, and in theory he should have been happy. Instead, he found that he missed it.

He rose and decided to wake up by going through the basic motions Rast had taught him, stretching and loosening muscles, getting blood flowing. His space was limited, but he persevered, and was rewarded by an approving look from Rast.

Feeling more awake, he dressed and followed Rast outside. Aldwyn was muttering at the lack of tea, which seemed to affect him badly in the mornings. He stumbled blearily after them, cursing softly in ancient languages. Part of his ire was at being told by Rast point blank that his chest was not coming with them through the Pass; after the first minute of arguing, he was told firmly that he either carried it himself, or left it here. Danial promised to hide it well in his cabin, and Aldwyn reluctantly agreed.

The party trooped out of the gate with their packs loaded on their backs, carrying enough food for two weeks if they hunted as well. Grukust was heavily wrapped, hiding his face in a huge cloak with a deep hood, and the morning sentry made no remark. At the gate, Danial gestured up the trail.

'Take the right fork. Once you're through the Pass take the right again towards the valley, but if you value your lives, I'd be stayin' away. The other camp we had lay southeast. Everyone there is dead now. Be careful in these woods, but be sure to stay away from the slopes borderin' em – mostly the orcs live in holes in the mountains. Time was when they never came out. The deeper in the trees you are, less likely they will see you, but the more likely other things will. An' beware *Jetzibabah*, if she is real.' He shook his head. 'I still think you shouldn't go. 'Tis easy to get lost in these woods.'

'We have no choice,' said Aldwyn, his face pale but resolute. Karland jangled with nerves, and Xhera was very quiet, her small face scared. Grukust hefted his pack, trying to find a compromise with his huge axe.

'Farewell,' said Rast, clasping hands. 'And remember our warnings, too.'

Danial nodded and moved back inside as the party started off. The clearing was shrouded in mist, trees ghostly at the edges. The stumps dotted around the camp made it feel like a graveyard. Not a cheerful thought, Karland decided.

They walked along a trail growing over with the recent disuse. The woods stretched silent and dank to either side of them. They were probably wildly beautiful in sunshine, but right now they felt ominous.

Travel was slow for several hours before they stopped for food and rest. Grukust was wary of the trees, clearly used to the open plains, and Aldwyn looked miserable. Forced to walk, he clutched his pendant and muttered as mist wetted his fine white hair. After a short while he looked a little bedraggled, and Karland was reminded that he was, in fact, quite old. Being spry only made up for a certain amount of sleeping on cold ground.

Rast kept a wary eye out, telling them all to speak only in low tones, make no loud noises, and move carefully. As a result their progress was slower even than the night before, but eventually they arrived at the fork. The other trail was wider, looking more recently used. Taking it would have made their travel easier, but their concern was who – or what – had kept it clear.

It was past noon before they found their way to the foot of the Pass. The peak to the left was sharply defined, as if it had been sliced vertically in half to look a little like a vast stone spire. The one to the right was heavy and majestic, if not quite as steep. *Iril Ehtë* and *Iril Paúr*, Rast named them; the Spear and the Fist.

The slopes looming to either side descended steeply to a lower, flatter meeting point high above the forest roof. The trees here were mainly coniferous and sparsely climbed the steep slopes on either side to link the woods here with the larger denser forest of the Dimnesdair. The pass itself was a narrow trail barely wide enough for two to walk abreast and dangerously littered with large boulders and scree, making each step uncertain. The trail wound backwards and forwards sharply, slowing any movement. It must have taken logging crews hours to bring trees through here, and the inclines to each side were steep enough that only a mountain goat would find them easily passable.

The climb up to the mouth of the pass was likewise steep, and before long they were all covered in sweat. The sun was shining through the clouds, and the day had turned muggy. Aldwyn in particular was gasping hard; Rast reached over and took his pack, and Grukust helped the old man when he needed it most, but it was hot and tiring work.

Karland wondered how much ironwood sold for. Nothing seemed worth the effort it must take to retrieve it. The pass alone would be difficult for any creatures within to traverse, let alone the steep and dangerous trails either side – good news for the plains towns and loggers in Feller's camp, although Rast had speculated that orcs probably had their own tunnels out of the mountains.

Xhera clearly had more stamina than he did. He struggled to keep pace anyway, puffing wildly. His training with Rast had improved his strength and coordination, but years of work on a farm and a lighter frame gave her an advantage. He was relieved when Rast called a halt next to a large boulder in the middle of the pass, where they could see both the forest beyond and the woods behind.

'This is a good place to rest,' he said. 'If we lunch here, we won't be outlined against the sky. This will be our last chance to rest before we enter the true body of the Dimnesdair.'

The huge forest loomed dark and sinister beyond the pass, conifers gradually accepting the company of bigger trees. Bordered by steep slopes of rock, it stretched away as far as they could see, seeming to dip slightly off to the right in the far distance. Here and there truly giant trees thrust their way up head and shoulder above their fellows, growing more numerous to the south and west.

'There lies the Dimnesvale, and somewhere within, the Pit of Kharkis,' said Rast. 'That is our destination.'

Grukust busied himself with a small fire. Aldwyn sank gratefully onto a rock, panting. Karland looked at him in concern. What good would it do them if they arrived at the valley with him ill – or worse? They were relying on him to find their goal, after all.

'Here,' said Karland, handing a water skin to his old friend. Aldwyn looked at him gratefully and drank deeply, only pausing to pant again as if not knowing which he was more desperate to do. Finally he handed the much-depleted water skin back to Karland.

'Haha. I'm not as… young as I was,' he gasped. He looked at the Karland fondly. 'You have stuck with me through all this… my boy. Changed your whole life! Whatever happens, I am inordinately… proud of you, and, ah, I feel you have a part to play yet in all this. You are not destined to be a footnote in the annals of history.' He smiled genuinely at Karland as he got his breath back. Karland was worried for his friend; Aldwyn was struggling.

'In many ways, I have missed a lot of my life,' continued the old man, a hint of regret in his voice. 'You have a father, but I never had a son. Perhaps… I can think of you as a grandson.'

'I'd like that,' said Karland, touched. 'You have taught me so much, and understand me better than my family ever have. I miss them, but my place is here with you. We will see this through together. Find the key, save the world, huh?'

His mentor grinned at his flippant attitude, his breathing less laboured.

'Indeed. But for now, go and get Xhera. We have a few things we can cover before we leave here. You are both behind in your studies.'

'And then we can spare time for some training,' broke in the voice of Rast. 'Both of you. Memory may linger, but the body will fast forget if you do not practice.'

Karland sighed. It looked like this would not be quite the rest he had hoped.

'Youth recovers quickly,' was Aldwyn's smug remark at his morose look.

CR   SO

While Grukust put a small pot on to cook stew with some of their rations, Xhera and Karland were taught concepts of lateral thinking and logical thought. Aldwyn gave them several examples to apply the theories to, and Karland was pleased to see that he was more or less level with Xhera in his answers. He sometimes still worried that she would make him look like an idiot.

Rast took over, setting Xhera some movements to do to keep her supple and strong. He said that they could, in time, be applied to fighting larger opponents. While she practiced, Karland had the dubious honour of training directly with Rast.

'You need to improve your leg mobility,' remarked Rast. 'You sit for long hours every day on the cart so your back and legs will tighten in time. You will have pain and loss of flexibility. Xhera is graceful and balanced. You need work.' Karland scowled in annoyance as Rast beckoned him over to a spot free of everything except dirt and showed him three kicks, one snapping in front, one to the side, and one behind, and made him do them one after the other, then in reverse, fast, on each leg. After the third time around Karland was puffing as hard as he had earlier, and had fallen twice.

'As I told you once before, I would suggest you rarely try a fancy kick,' Rast said. 'They are very good training, and in the right place at the right time can be devastating, but they are slower than punches and weapons for the most part – and more obvious. Worse, they can put you off balance.'

'So what's the point then?' asked Karland, breathing hard. He stopped kicking.

'Training. Discipline. Being able to do it makes you that much more dangerous and unpredictable. It develops flexibility and leg strength, gives stamina, speed, surer balance and footing. And when you are well trained enough, you will be able to use it to great effect. Anything else?'

Karland shook his head, subdued and panting.

'Then let us continue. This is a spinning reverse side kick.' He spun around in place, his big leg and foot snapping out to the side with devastating power and stopping dead.

'It is like a back kick but your hip stays horizontal as you kick, and it teaches you to shift your footing quickly and surely, or you will...' Karland tried and his other leg shot out from under him and he wobbled and fell '...overbalance.'

Rast held a huge hand out to help Karland up, slapping dirt off him.

'Again.'

Karland kicked as instructed until his legs began to ache. Rast only spoke once again in that time. 'Do not let your leg go loose! You will damage your knee. Always keep it tight. You are using your whole body to strike with the end point.' He moved in front of the boy. 'Kick at me, and *hit* me with it. I will block you. You must train impacts as well.'

Karland did so, and yelped after the first hard kick; the big man only used his arms and legs to block, but it was like kicking an oak. A few minutes later, Rast waved at him to stop.

'Good. We have further to walk today so we will stop here, but you understand the basics. I want you to practice this every day, ten times each kick, in addition to your other exercises. If you can, find something to strike.'

'I don't see *you* practicing every day,' retorted Karland, stung by the instructions and feeling exhausted. *The basics?* His legs ached, and how Rast expected him to walk more today was beyond him. He wasn't even sure he could walk tomorrow.

Rast didn't show any annoyance at his tone. 'Every day I practice, when you are usually still asleep. I also use my whole body to lift weight every few days to keep strong – you have seen me do as much. If you train with me, you will find you can do all this in time as well. It is conditioning, and there is no shortcut to it. Do it, boy. It will keep you alive, and if you want to learn to fight there is no getting around it.' His glance softened. 'You did well, and we have a little longer to rest plus a downhill trail. Aldwyn is right. You are young and will recover faster than you think.'

Karland staggered over to sit next to Xhera, slumped tiredly on her pack. She shook her head.

'You can't kick very high.'

'Yes, yes, fine. I know *you* can,' he answered testily.

'Just an observation,' she said, poking him in the ribs. 'You're stronger and better than I am with your hands, and you know some weapons as well. I can't help being flexible.'

He grunted and rolled over. 'Let me rest,' he groaned.

ଔ   ଓ

Their ease was interrupted by Grukust's announcement that food was ready, a thick, hot stew of dried meat and vegetables with some grains mixed in. Once finished, Aldwyn set another tea over the embers of the fire. Finally he spoke.

'Well. I can't put this off any longer. We had best go in to the Dimnesdair, and find a secure place to camp before dark.'

'Agreed,' said Rast. 'We have rested longer than I intended. I am concerned about you, my friend.' He gauged Aldwyn's condition. The old man seemed much better now, but he was unsure how long it would be again before they had to rest.

'I am merely unused to all this,' said Aldwyn. 'If we moderate our pace, perhaps I will find it somewhat more bearable.'

Rast sighed. He was concerned that this quest was too much for the old man. 'We will move at your pace where possible, Aldwyn, but we must stay hidden. We are in great danger the moment we move out of this pass.'

The old man nodded. 'I am ready. Like it or not, we are here and it must be done. All is for nothing if we do not find the source of the troubles in the lands. I cannot imagine what help the pendant will bring, or what this 'hollow in the mountains' is.' His face was weary, not just with physical exhaustion but with worry.

'I am with you, old friend,' said Rast. He smiled encouragingly. 'We all are.'

Grukust patted Aldwyn heavily on the arm.

'I with you too, Aldwyn,' he grinned, his tusks gleaming near-white in the sun. 'This valley regret day honoured Aldwyn come!' He chuckled, and Rast couldn't help but smile. The ork was proving a loyal friend.

They took the trail down carefully. It was far steeper than the other side, with few safe paths. Finally they warily entered the trees. The trees were actually fairly pleasant in the sunlight, although there was a menacing feel to them, as if malicious eyes watched. The trail bore roughly southwards and they travelled for hours, making reasonable time. The forest grew imperceptibly darker as clouds gathered and the sun began to go down; night would come early here as the mountains cast their umbra.

ର   ๙

Karland's legs began to ache again. He forced them onward, remembering Rast's firm words. *It comes down to a choice*, he told himself severely. Either he did not flag, grew strong, and learned to fight, or he and his friends may one day die. His mind flashed back to Xhera, pale after Rast rescued them both from the bandits, and suddenly he welcomed the pain in his legs. *No one would ever do that again!* He gritted his teeth and pushed on.

They finally reached the second fork in the late afternoon, the left-hand trail barely more than a faint forest path, although once it had been as wide as the right. Already the forest was reclaiming it.

'Left leads to the abandoned logger's encampment. Do we follow the left path and camp? Or do we search for another site?' said Rast.

Aldwyn shook his head, tired and uncaring. Grukust shrugged. A sweet voice spoke from the side.

'Oh, I wouldn't take that path if I were you.'

They spun, Grukust cursing and wrenching at his huge axe, Rast crouched like a coiled spring; none of them had sensed the newcomer. They found a woman facing them, half hidden behind a tree. She was neither young nor old, although her hair was almost white and her skin nearly glowed it was so pale. She stepped out and smiled, and her face then seemed younger, although a very fine network of wrinkles appeared. Clearly not albino, her eyes were almost black. Karland noticed her feet were bare, and dusted with mud and green juice from crushed plants.

Rast spoke cautiously, weighing up this odd-looking woman.

'Why not?'

'It leads to a camp that is no more,' she said. Her voice was slightly singsong, and curiously liquid. It was totally at odds with her appearance, deep one minute and higher the next. 'Everyone dead. Everyone gone. Beasts dance among the bones. Now no one visits any more. Except you.' She smiled, and it was oddly seductive. Karland thought she was very strange.

'Who are you?' asked Rast. 'And why are you out here alone?'

'Why, I am Letizya,' she trilled, and made as if to curtsy, perhaps a mannerism long forgotten. 'And these woods are my home. Should I not ask what *you* do here?'

Aldwyn stared through his spectacles. 'Hmm, well now. You have a point, young lady.'

His words sent her into bubbling laughter. 'Young! Why, thank you. It may seem that I have lived forever from tales, but that is not true, of course. Not yet.' She giggled and smiled mysteriously. 'Why are you here? And look, with a big ork!' Her eyes flashed and her nose wrinkled, but her tone was level as she also glanced at Rast. Karland could not read the meaning behind the gaze.

'We seek... something... that we think lies within the valley yonder.' Rast waved west.

She laughed again softly. 'Even I do not venture there, my fine strapping man. I am left alone here in these woods... my home is safe. But that place is fell, even for me. It would mean your deaths to go there.'

A thought occurred to Karland. 'Um... are you the witch of the woods?'

Xhera glared at him, and Aldwyn shot a look that plainly told him to shut up, but she seemed to take no offence. She pierced him with a keen glance, and after a few seconds smiled and made a rueful moue with her lips.

'I suppose you could say that. I am *Babar-Jagǐnj* to some, *Jetžibaba* to others. Others still mangle it to *Letzibya* or *Latisha,* but I am and always have been simply Letizya.'

'There have been tales of a woods witch in here for generations,' said Rast. 'Yet you do not seem so old. Are you not bothered by the orcs... or other things here?'

'Perhaps I am older than I look,' she laughed. She danced lithely from foot to foot. 'Or perhaps not. Tales grow with each telling, warrior, and as to the dangers... I have been here long enough that I know how to avoid their attention. They do not bother me often.'

'And when they do?' asked Rast.

She smiled spitefully. 'They do not do so again.'

Rast regarded her warily. 'We thank you for your advice, Letizya. We should not keep you; the hour is late, we must find a camp soon, and I am sure you should return home as well.'

The woman laughed, genuinely amused. 'You are unlikely to find a safe camp near here, deary. Goodness no. There are a few safe spots, but far away, and these woods are not as safe as they were. You *might* be lucky.' Her eyes flashed again. 'You might not. But I can offer you a place for the night, perhaps some food. It grows lonely here, and it is good to have company.'

'You would invite an armed party to your home?' asked Rast sceptically.

She smiled and nodded. 'I am a good judge of men. And I am not defenceless. I can give you your last safe haven before you reach the valley. It is your choice to accept, or not.' Her words broke off as a booming bellow echoed through the trees from a distance. She eyed them intently.

Rast looked at the others. Aldwyn was nearly passing out on his feet with weariness, and Xhera and Karland were looking around at the forest in alarm. 'Come then,' he said, determining to be wary of this strange woman. 'Is your house far?'

'Not far, no. Not far,' she said. She pointed off west, directly off the road. 'No trails. No signs; but I will guide you. Follow me.' She stepped off into the gloom, pale as a beacon. She was unmindful of the rough ground and spiky brambles, seeming to avoid them without trying. She ghosted ahead, peering back from time to time to make sure they followed.

'An interesting etymology to her name, mm,' said Aldwyn distractedly as they followed.

Xhera shot Karland a questioning look. He whispered 'It means the meaning of a word, sort of.'

She asked Aldwyn, 'Why?'

'Well, aha, *Babar* means old woman, and *Jagĭnj* can mean either fear or hunger in Old Banistari depending on interpretation. She must have ranged far and wide in these woods, to all the corners of the lands! *Jetžibaba* is closer to modern Banistari. I, mm, guess it means a weird old woman, and I would say the other names are corruptions of that. Either she took the name Letizya as a modernisation, mm, or the original was a close match to her name. Hard… mm. To say.'

He was starting to mumble, and Karland stooped under his shoulder to give him some help. Aldwyn smiled down myopically over his glasses. 'You are a good boy with a good heart, Karland. Never let anyone tell you differently.'

It was a little less than half an hour later than they came across a clearing, with Letizya at the edge, waving her hands in front of her. As they came up, she turned and smiled.

'My home,' she said, waving at a ramshackle hut that seemed part of the forest itself. Bordering the trees, it was at one end of the clearing with a high, thick log fence around the rear that was almost overgrown. The clearing itself seemed to be almost a garden. Karland saw many herb plants he recognised, many more he did not, and other plants that looked decidedly odd. They all grew together in a wild tangle.

'You are not bothered by orcs or other creatures?' asked Karland.

She paused, her glinting eyes boring into him for several seconds. 'They avoid my garden, and I can tell when people come looking, oh yes. I have my ways of hiding it. Are you hungry?'

He nodded. Letizya whirled, and opened the door. She was gone a few seconds, and then reappeared, beckoning them in.

They entered through the door, which had a large skin over it to keep breezes out when open. The interior showed the hut to be bigger than expected, although it was not vast. To the right was a large table strewn with objects. Further along from it a stone fireplace came out from the wall into the room, allowing the hanging for a large pot on a rod over the fire pit. The hearthstone was round, and paving was set around it in a circle before dissolving into a random paving pattern to line the floor throughout the room. It was surrounded by three large pieces of slate on a loose frame, presumably to stop the spitting embers sending out a spark to catch. The room was cluttered and not very clean. At the other end were two more hangings with the smaller on the left wall and the larger on the back wall. The small one was only partially drawn and showed a small alcove with a bed on the floor. Karland guessed the other was a kitchen of some sort.

'Sit, sit,' Letizya trilled, grabbing an empty bucket and sweeping all the debris off the table. She hefted it all, moving quickly to the large hanging. She half pulled it back and stood, watching, until they were all seated, then whipped through it. Karland caught a glimpse of pans and a large pot, and he heard clanking noises as she started preparing food.

They were at the table talking in low tired tones for a long while to the sounds of food being prepared. The fire was glowing, giving some heat, and it sent out a strange sweet heavy smell. Karland guessed it was the scent of some of her herbs. He suddenly realised that he still held his bag, and left the others talking to place it near the door. As he bent to place it he glanced up and froze as a large shadow shuffled across the crack in the shutter at the back of the house. There was hardly any light left, but the inside of the hut was dark apart from the low light from the fire.

Heart in his mouth, he dropped his pack and crept to the shutter. He peered out, and saw a large-framed, gaunt and stooped figure bending slowly to pick up some heavy logs. There was no apparent effort, but it never varied the speed with which it moved. Little more than a silhouette, it could once have been a large, robust man, but now what features he could see hung in folds. The remaining strands of hair were few and the head was shiny beneath it. He was loosely dressed in old rags, and he caught the glint of a milky eye as the figure suddenly stopped dead and turned, horribly slowly, to stare at the window where Karland was.

Karland jerked backwards, gasping, and then jumped and nearly yelled when a big hand dropped on his shoulder. Another hand dropped over his mouth to choke it off, and then came away.

'What is it?' said Rast quietly.

Karland quickly whispered what he had seen. Rast moved him gently aside and bent to peer out of the gap. He shook his head after a few seconds. There was nothing there but a rough pile of logs in the small yard.

Letizya's voice broke in sharply. She stood frowning at them both at the entrance to the kitchen and her voice was less mellifluous than usual.

'What is it?'

'I saw someone in the yard,' said Karland. 'Just a shape, really, but he was big. Do you know him?'

She looked at him intently for a few moments, and then her face relaxed. 'Oh! Yes. I have an old… friend who helps me with heavy menial tasks,' she said. 'He doesn't like to be seen.' She looked at Karland, almost fondly. 'You must have made a noise or something. You will not see him again.' She smiled. 'Do not be alarmed.'

Karland nodded, a little taken aback, as she vanished again. A last glance showed nothing but an empty yard. They moved back to the table and sat, the others looking at him curiously. Rast shook his head and jerked his eyes at the kitchen.

Shortly afterwards Letizya entered with a pot and put it on the fire, building it up with a depleted pile of logs. Before long hot flames licked at the pot. She sat there humming to herself for twenty minutes until she seemed happy and lifted the pot carefully to the table, showing little effort with the heavy iron receptacle. A smell came off it that was nutritious if not that appetizing as the pale woman spooned it out into bowls, starting with herself. She tasted it quickly, presumably to prove that it was safe, then filled the rest, but when she came to Karland the pot was empty.

'Oh my.' She seemed put out. 'Wait right there, and I will get some more.' She bustled off into the kitchen, pushing through the hanging flap of skin. Pots clanked, and then went quiet. There was the creak of a door.

Aldwyn sipped at his spoon and made a face.

'She seems eager to please,' he said glumly. 'A shame that her culinary skills aren't, mm, as honed as the stories of goodwomen cooking up a storm with nothing at all would have you believe, eh?' He peered sadly at his spoon, and sighed. 'It goes to show, hmm, that stories cannot be counted on. A lot of old women who live alone are counted as witches. Greatly exaggerated of course. Ha, um, I think any 'witch' worth her salt would cook up something better than this!' He chuckled until the next mouthful, and grimaced again.

Rast tasted his. 'Well, it's safe enough, I think,' he said quietly. 'She's a strange one, but harmless enough so far. It's better than nothing at all.' He gestured. 'Be polite. Eat.'

Xhera looked mutinous but choked several spoonfuls down. Grukust poured half the bowl into his mouth in an attempt to get it over with, then nearly sprayed it across the room at the taste. Karland choked with laughter, but his twisting stomach reminded him of his hunger, and he could hear muttering from the kitchen. He was eyeing his host's bowl speculatively when she finally came back from the kitchen with a steaming bowl. 'There. Worth the wait!'

As she set it down in front of him, the black eyes regarded him closely.

'You *are* a hungry one, aren't you,' she whispered intently, pleased. His stomach rumbled. She smiled again. 'Eat.'

She sat and began sipping her stew without haste or expression. Her attention was divided warily between Rast, Grukust, and Karland wolfing his food. He barely noticed.

'You're a growing boy. Oh, I know about that.' She chuckled. 'Have more.'

The stew was salty and faintly greasy, with a strange aftertaste, but it was hot. Karland filled his belly, much hungrier than he had realised. The others didn't seem as hungry, and he grinned at his extra portion. She smiled at him again and he smiled back, anxious to please her.

'Thanks,' he said between bites. She nodded, and turned her attention back to her food, glancing again at the intimidating forms at the other end of the small table. In the small room the ork and the big man loomed oppressively.

After they had eaten, she gestured to the floor beside the table. 'There should be room here to rest. It is a bit cosy, but then you're used to that,' she chuckled. 'I have an alcove over there. If you hear me stir in the night, don't fret, dears. I don't sleep much or deeply. An advantage of not being so young now, I think.'

As one the eyes of the party turned to Aldwyn, who sniffed and looked away, muttering imprecations.

'Of course, there are always exceptions to the rule,' said Rast blandly. Grukust snorted in amusement as Karland grinned.

'I hope you not disturbed by snoring, lady.'

She smiled thinly. 'If I am, I shall go outside for a breath of fresh air and some peace and quiet. You've had a hard day. Perhaps you should sleep now. You all look very tired.' Her dark eyes were sympathetic.

Karland had been about to say he was fine, but yawned instead. Even Rast looked tired as he spoke.

'Our thanks, Letizya. You have made our journey easier.' He smiled slightly.

'It is nice to have visitors!' she answered almost coyly.

They settled themselves to sleep, and she moved off to her alcove, bundling herself in skins. Her breathing deepened quickly and she slept. The others packed themselves on the floor tightly around the table and lay down. Aldwyn fell into a deep soundless sleep, and Grukust stopped moving as soon as his head hit his pack. Xhera likewise almost collapsed, and although Rast sat to watch as usual his breathing deepened quickly as well.

It took Karland a lot longer to drop off. Without distractions he could smell a strange odour, earthy yet indefinable. It was very faint however, and he fell asleep dreaming of earthen tunnels and faceless men.

ଔ   ଓ

The next morning Karland woke very late. The others were stirring, and Rast was sitting at the table, spinning a coin. Sunlight streamed in through cracks in the grubby shutters of glassless windows. He greeted them with a troubled look on his face.

'You have finally awoken! I could not rouse any of you. I had to fight my way out of slumber myself, and that is strange. I awoke last night when I sensed our host stir, doubtless thinking us all fast asleep. She left the hut and I followed her from the clearing, but lost her in the woods.' He frowned. 'Her woodcraft is very good. I could not sense where she went, or find any tracks. I was worried she would give us away to the orcs, but not long afterwards she returned and went through to her enclosure at the back. I barely had warning enough to lie back down. The woman moves like the wind, old or no.'

'I had weird dreams,' said Karland. 'As if I was in thick sludge, and could not fight free.'

'Mine were similar,' said Aldwyn tiredly, 'but it was quicksand. I felt a great evil around me, mm.'

'I had the same,' said Xhera.

'And I,' grunted Grukust.

'I think it's this forest,' said Xhera glumly. 'It weighs on my mind. All around the mire that held me were creeping horrors, giant spiders, all sorts of horrible things. But I couldn't wake up.'

'We are awake now,' said Rast. 'And it is time we left. I do not know where our host is, but remember – however strange she appears, she has not harmed us. Now, get your things.'

Karland moved over to his pack, feeling slightly lightheaded and a little odd. He would be pleased when they left this strange forest. Dreams were darker here. The atmosphere was foreboding, and the gloom of the hut was not helping.

Eager to leave, they collected their gear and made ready. Karland had developed a slight headache, only just noticeable but enough to be annoying, and the rest didn't look much better after their night – apart from Rast, as usual. Aldwyn had complained about the lack of tea until Grukust had pointedly reminded him that they didn't know if she even had a well for water, and he stopped, sulking.

A voice broke in. 'Oh, but you must leave, dears? That is a pity. It was so nice to have company last night.' She moved into view and flashed her oddly seductive smile at Karland. 'Come back soon! And stay away from that nasty valley.'

'Farewell,' said Rast, 'and thank you for the shelter, and the food. It was very… filling.'

Her eyes rested on him and darted to Grukust for a second. 'Welcome,' she said, her dark eyes unreadable.

They left the clearing, and when Karland looked back she was gone, only the small hut and a thin stream of smoke coming from the low chimney showing evidence of life. He saw no sign of the mysterious helper. Shrugging, he turned to follow Aldwyn.

They moved back out to the trail and followed it southwest. Noon came and went uneventfully. There was little noise in these trees, and the day was overcast. Everyone was a little irritable, and very tired; they did not move as fast as Rast would have liked, and so they stopped to find a camp early, pulling off the track and moving north until they found a good clearing, close-knit and sheltered from prying eyes. Rast pronounced it defensible and fairly safe.

Karland felt ill now, his stomach roiling. Aldwyn had said that he felt sick as well, but Karland felt progressively worse, while the old man eventually lapsed into weary silence and appeared to feel better. As dusk set in and turned to night, they prepared for their first night in the Dimnesdair alone. Karland tried to hide his queasiness and looked forward to lying down to calm the spinning trees around him, refusing to let anyone know he felt bad. He would rather suffer in silence than be treated like a child.

Rast set about starting a basic stew. Despite saying that they would not have a hot meal after Letizya's the night before, he changed his mind – the night was growing cool, and a well hidden fire would lift their spirits. They had come a long way today, he guessed, in a wide loop along the trail – less than half a day further into the forest in a direct line, but the trail was easier than the trees despite their unease at using it.

The rest of the party looked far more tired than Karland would have thought. Rast himself looked tired, and even Grukust was yawning, showing the thick roots of the tusks set in his lower jaw. Karland curled up on his blanket, shivering slightly. Not long afterwards, pressure built and he made an abrupt move for the privacy of the surrounding trees.

Dusk turned to night.

TWENTY-SEVEN

Grukust rummaged through his pack, making sure that all of his items were still there; his *gropak* and his other clan totem were still precious to him, outcast or no.

He had been uncomfortable last night in the house of the forest woman. She was a very strange human, and he hadn't entirely trusted her. She also hadn't denied being a witch. Like barbarians, Orks had dim views on such matters. He shook his head. He knew little of humans beyond his current companions and the barbarians; it seemed that humans could be very different. His own people were less prone to such excess peculiarity.

Sinking down onto his throw next to the fire he grunted and sniffed, taking in the smell of the beginning of the stew. He had not particularly enjoyed the forest woman's offering, and he was less fussy than the humans. After that meal, virtually anything would be a feast.

Rast was stirring the small pot, adding a few herbs and slivers of dried meat to the stew. A piece of potato bobbed to the surface.

He spoke without looking up. 'You don't like the forest.'

Grukust grunted, not wanting to sound weak. 'It very… cannot say it. Tight? Close. Not open. Cannot see easily if danger nearby. It strange more than worry me. I prefer plains.'

Rast smiled faintly. 'Your choice to stay with us heartens me, Grukust. I have some idea of what you gave up in your decision. I know something of your people and trust your honour. Humans think you savages, but who is to judge true refinement? Certainly the boy considers you a friend, and the girl will defend you as quickly as you will her.'

'I like Karland also,' the big Ork declared. The boy was unlike Ork youths, much more frail physically, but he had a core of toughness that was surprising, and a sharp mind. 'And Xhera – she jump to defend me. So small, fragile! But still want to help me.' He shook his head at the memory, unconsciously tracing his jaw. He supposed she was pretty, in a human way, and her fierce loyalty had startled him. 'They...' Grukust trailed off suddenly, looking around. 'Where is Karland?'

Rast looked thoughtful.

'I didn't touch much of the slop that woman served,' he remarked in his deep quiet voice. 'But Karland was hungry and finished his – the entire bowl, and more besides. He's been looking unwell all day, and moved for the forest almost the moment we stopped.'

'Been gone long time,' said Grukust. He looked over at Xhera talking to Aldwyn, who was still looking a little ill.

'I will look for him. He may be sicker than I thought,' said Rast.

Grukust nodded agreement, moving the pot off the fire so the food didn't burn. 'I wait, look after little girl and old man.' He grinned again and glanced at the pot. '*Maybe* leave some food for you.' Rast glanced over at Xhera and Aldwyn, nodded, and vanished into the forest.

Grukust shook his head, still not quite believing such a large human had such grace. Before he had met Rast Tal'Orien, he would have proudly said there was no human he could not defeat in combat. Now he was unsure; his orkish pride wouldn't let him admit it out loud, but he suspected very strongly that the human could kill him with his bare hands. Rast had certainly handled him without difficulty in Punslon, and he exuded an air of dangerous ability.

Grukust had fought some perilous battles in his time, but he had always survived. Thoughtfully he felt his chest, traced the deep score from the long-ago fight with a deadly wyvern when he had been on his *Kapparin-etsa* to earn the right to his runed name. Grukust mused that he might almost choose facing another wyvern than Rast. The idea would be ludicrous to most orks – that a mere human could be so deadly – but Rast was almost as strong as Grukust, and he moved far quicker than a man half his size, with a fluid grace that was, well... inhuman. Grukust respected the human's skill.

The ork chuckled inwardly. Anything that challenged the capable Rast was likely to be fairly overwhelming.

⋯ ⋯

The turd was coiled with that clenched-fisted end that spoke of too much salty meat in the diet recently. No excrement, thought Karland, should look as pugnacious as that. It stared up at him aggressively.

I shouldn't have had that stew, he thought. *I knew it wasn't right.*

The texture had seemed rough, almost weed-like, the salty meat thickly strewn through it unidentifiable and somehow strange. Dismissing this as a trick of the light he had eaten it all, the food oily and uneasy in his stomach. What the pale woman had served the others had not looked much better, and they had not eaten as much as he had, but he had been too hungry to care – as if his hunger had a life of its own.

That morning he had regretted it, feeling queasy. Trying to ignore it he had bidden goodbye to the pale Letizya with the rest, but after the first few leagues every step made him feel worse. Hours later, as they camped after dusk had started its slow fade into the true depth of night, he had realised he needed to have relief in more than one fashion. Now he felt weak, drained, and the release promised in movement was unattained. In fact, he felt worse than ever, and light headedness had set in as if the stew had – in passing through him – removed all vitality in the process.

Karland wiped himself on a handy leaf, and pulled his leggings up. He tried to belt his tunic. It took several tries to pull a simple knot. Frowning, he swayed and pressed his hands to his temples.

What's wrong with me? he thought drowsily. *I must... get back...*

Turning, he realised he couldn't think which direction he had come from; he started to head towards where he guessed the camp to be and then stopped, puzzled, unsure of what he had been doing.

His mind started to wander and he realised in a detached manner that he was losing all control and care of his body. His limbs had their own ideas, and turned him slowly to the right. Gaining more control with each step, they took him further into the forest. Briefly Karland hoped someone would find him, stop him, take him to the camp and help him, but in the passing of a few more steps he forgot everything.

Time turned into a drunken stumble that passed as if for another. The forest twisted and skewed in his vision. Lurching from tree to tree in a daze his thoughts dissipated, elongating and stretching into a pale ribbon of thought-moths that flew heedless into the approaching vast dark shade of stupor that beckoned.

Karland could have been stumbling for minutes, hours, days – he had no recollection, during the brief times his thoughts resurfaced, of how long he had been moving or where he was. He vaguely knew only that it was a moonlit night, in a forest dark and deep, but was too dazed to think of the dangers rife within this wild part of the world. The only constant was the motion of exhausted limbs no longer his and a growing fear in his gut that spoke through the stupor to tell him that he was heading somewhere that held a purpose for him.

Time passed.

Eventually he stumbled into the clearing that they had left so many hours before. The hut looked as ramshackle as ever in the rising light; a coil of heavy smoke lazed out of the chimney, not rising and billowing as before, but roiling heavily, hanging suspended in the air.

As he approached the door creaked and slowly opened. The dirty hanging caught the uneven top of the door and pulled to the right, and then dropped and fell to move limpidly. A pale form stepped out, feet bare and dusted with dirt, the near-white hair pulled loosely back to cascade down the spine. The almost unearthly glow of Letizya's skin made her seem a beacon to Karland as he stumbled to a swaying halt at her feet. She looked at him through her fine wrinkles and then smiled happily.

'I sensed you as soon as you stepped onto my land,' she said in that unnerving calm voice. 'You travelled *shaded* from others. I knew you would come safely to me.'

She beckoned him inside and he followed like a zombie, shambling and swaying behind her. Letizya directed him over to stand by the rough pile of furs near the fire, and then whispered softly and made a slicing gesture with her hand. Karland collapsed as if he were a puppet whose strings had been cut, barely aware of the ache of overused muscles. His mind began to clear, and he sensed his weariness and realised that soon he would be wandering in his dreams once more, unaware of time around him. The floor was hard under one buttock, having fallen on the very edge of the furs, one leg splayed out slightly to the side and the other folded. He arched back slightly over the mound of furs, his back pillowed and head lolled to the side.

The forest woman stood, looking at him in the gloom. Something in her eyes and manner made his mind call for urgent attention, trying to get him to move again. He put enormous effort into the attempt. One finger twitched and then subsided. She noticed and smiled, speaking in that deep melody so out of keeping with her appearance.

'Never fear. You'll be asleep soon. I broke the *obi-ah*, but you won't be moving for a while,' she purred.

The smell from the fire was heavy and herbal, and the flames were tinged with green as they danced reflections in Karland's eyes. The hut's interior was as gloomy as ever, the fire the only light.

'You'll take a while to recover, and I'm afraid you will be sick for a time. The others got the usual stew, and wasn't it nice? But your stew was... special.' She crossed to look down on him, a strange hunger in her eyes. Breathing heavily through her nose, her chest rising and falling, she stared down at his recumbent form.

She suddenly hissed, her liquid tones adding a strange depth to it. 'The big man... that disgusting ork... the old man with so little time left, the little girl, pah! Useless. I would have dealt with them, but... the ork didn't trust. I could feel it. And I didn't like that man. There was death about him. Best he left. Best they *all* left.'

She laughed at something, cocking her head as if amused.

'These woods are not so terrible, but the Dimnesvale will take them. It is a powerful place. Even if they guessed you here, my garden is protected. They will not find this house again.' She paused and crouched next to him. 'And it's time I had another pretty around here. The last one was no longer of use to me – dour men, chopping wood, old before their time! Bah! You have a good figure, there's muscle there. I wouldn't say you are the most beautiful manling I ever saw, but you have a way about you that I like. It will be a nice change. I have chores that need doing... and needs to be attended to.'

Despite the dirt, there was a strange, feral allure to her, and a scent that was almost animal but not unpleasant. Chuckling, she rose.

'Oh yes... needs.' Her hands ran down her sides, caressed the dirty clothes there, following the figure. 'I'm all alone here, and I'm not so old as to be displeasing, am I?' She twirled almost girlishly. 'These delights are all to come, my pet. We shall see how strong you are... and how long you are of use. But for now you will sleep.'

She turned to the fire, incanted softly, made a pass with her hands and threw a handful of something on it. An initial flare produced a heavy bluish smoke which poured slowly sideways out of the fire under her caresses; no longer rising up the chimney, it began filling the room. The smell was the same as the night they had stayed, but far more pungent.

Karland's eyes grew heavier. The smoke didn't make him want to cough, but it filled his lungs and gentled them just short of stifling. Letizya stroked the smoke, almost like she would a cat, and it writhed past her fingers. Apparently unaffected, she hummed a disquieting melody in her fluid voice. The smoke seemed to curl around him like a translucent velvet fist, squeezing the consciousness gently from him. The room dimmed and began to grow black, fading drowsily from sight.

The voice of his learned friend came back, lecturing in a dry tone.

'Components and spirits, elementals, forces of nature, drugs, symbols. These are the

paraphernalia of the so-called witch. She seeks power from spirits and invocation...'

Forest Witch, thought Karland. *Souls in the smoke.*

The voice in his head droned on sonorously, slowing down as he became wrapped in strands of sleep.

'Anyone well versed in any art is not to be dismissed lightly. You should be wary of all you meet – it is rare that one truly knows what another may be capable of. Remember, too, that it is not so much the practitioner's goal which matters as how it is sought. Witchcraft is just a way of trying to change the world, as a knife is a way of cutting. It all depends on how and what it cuts, the intent behind it, and this can be abused as easily as any discipline...'

The last thing he heard was the bewitching hum from the enchantress, rising and falling through the smoke.

೧   ೭

Rast slipped through the woods, eyes flicking to catch signs of Karland. Stepping lightly and quietly, he was aware of everything around him, a shadow flickering from tree to tree. He moved carefully, knowing predators might prowl in the shadows.

Karland's trail was easy to pick up. In his rush the boy had trampled flowers, bent undergrowth and snapped twigs. Luckily the woods here were not too densely packed with smaller vegetation, so it wasn't hard going. Looking at the signs of a desperate rush, a small spark of concerned amusement touched Rast. Although they could not afford illness now, having tasted that awful stew he couldn't blame the boy.

Not too far from where they had camped he found where Karland had stopped. With a detached eyed he viewed the scene, searching for signs of the boy, worried he might have passed out or walked in the wrong direction. After a cursory search, he found a trail leading off almost at right angles to where they had camped. There was something odd about it, but it proved that at least the boy was moving. Although a skilled woodsman and tracker, it was dark in the trees. Rast knelt to examine it, trying to pin down what was wrong – something here was alerting his senses to danger.

It took a half-footprint in soft dirt in a clearer moonlit patch for Rast to figure out that Karland was not moving well. The trail left out of the area was obvious and lurched, showing damage to both clothes and brush. Shortly he came across a thicket of brambles, noting threads on a few and what looked like blood on the tips of some of the thorns in the bright moonlight. The boy would have some deep scratches – it looked as if he had stumbled through them on a straight path, uncaring.

Rast paused, considering. He was already a good twenty minutes away from the camp. Karland's trail weaved and bobbed, seeming to head roughly back towards the Pass. He could not tell how far ahead the boy was, but chasing meant leaving the others unguarded.

Grukust could be trusted to take care of Xhera and Aldwyn, Rast knew. He was loyal, honourable, and a very capable combatant with the keen senses of a tribal ork. Rast hoped he would stay where he was and wait for his return, but if Grukust decided to follow he would likely wait for daylight.

His mind made up, he placed his trust in the ork and began following the trail again. As the night wore on, he cursed the fact that he couldn't move quickly; in the shadows it was almost impossible to track. Luckily the sky was brightly lit by the waxing moon which filtered down through the trees and occasionally stabbed in silver shafts onto the mossy floor, but his eyesight was only human. He knew there would already be clues going unnoticed, and dreaded any clearings where he might have to hunt for the trail again.

It was evident after another hour that the trail was still going relatively straight, but he kept his pace slow. It was still heading northeast, and this puzzled him deeply, concern foremost in his thoughts. Why would the boy be moving to the Pass again? There were no signs of his being taken against his will; Karland seemed to be moving on his own.

He came to a large clearing and sighed, knowing he would have to begin hunting on the other side for the trail again if it wasn't still dead ahead. As he was about to put a foot down to step out, he froze, senses ranging around him. Something was out there, and it was not small.

His muscles relaxed and he centred himself, ready to react to whatever was out there. A soft sound to his right and the sense of a presence flicked his eyes slightly in that direction, where his peripheral vision could work more efficiently against the dark than his direct sight, registering movement instead of form. A slight movement warned him and he pivoted around, ready, and crouched slightly, hands lifting.

A low rumble sounded, and the ambient light caught in two green lamps. He sensed rather than saw the crouched body of a big forest cat. It stared at him in curiosity. Rast didn't move except to growl low in his throat, and tense slightly, ready. The cat seemed to realise that this large human was far from easy prey and would not be taken unawares. It growled softly and kept its eyes fixed on him. He returned the look with a soft focus, trying not to stare directly at the eyes in challenge. He wasn't afraid, and the cat knew it. He got the impression it was curious more than anything else with the possibility of ambush from the rear gone. Forest cats were cautious and inquisitive, but they were powerful creatures – a hungry one would easily kill a man. This one was large.

Very slowly, he straightened and backed away a little.

'Neither of us wants this,' he said softly in a calm tone. 'I don't have time or inclination to fight.'

The woods tiger growled, unsure, the tone telling it that the shape in front was not a threat, as it had first appeared. This human was not holding a weapon, and yet the big cat sensed he was dangerous. It drew up slightly from the defensive crouch it had adopted, and licked its lips, glancing away to the side of Rast casually whilst not taking its eyes fully from him.

He half turned towards the clearing, tense, and spoke again in the same calming tone. 'I must follow this trail. I wish you good hunting, my friend.'

The cat looked back to him when he spoke, and there was a breathless pause. Then it shook its head as if to relieve tension and made a soft yawping sound. Eyes blinked once and the woods tiger turned, seeming to flow back towards the nearby bushes. He was aware of the ears cocked and the ready tension in the cat, still unwilling to drop its guard against this potential foe. Doing likewise, he turned to the clearing and moved into it, his grace matching the cat's. A few minutes of hunting around was enough to re-establish the trail directly on the other side, all the while keeping his senses attuned for the approach of the cat - or any other nocturnal hunters.

Satisfied he had the right track again, he prepared to follow it. He looked around one last time, and caught a momentary gleam of green eyes on the other side of the clearing. They blinked out and he saw faint movement which suggested the cat was moving off another way. Relieved, he silently wished it well and turned to the trail again.

Time grew ever more critical – the big cat had served to reinforce that these were wild and unfriendly woods. The boy had started out before full night, so he may have avoided the more dangerous nocturnal predators until now. It was to be hoped.

Many hours into the night the big man estimated he had covered nearly half the distance to where they had started out that afternoon. He had started to have suspicions about where Karland was heading. The forest woman had seemed wary of them, although she had been polite enough and fed them willingly, but she had seemed quite taken with Karland. At the time Rast had hardly noticed;

memories of the stay were hazy for them all.

The moon rolled overhead and Rast moved to the rhythm of tracking. He considered Letizya. She was a strange one, seemingly at home in the forest and appearing oddly untroubled by the denizens in it. The rich liquid voice would have been suited to a court noble in tone and manner, but something was not right. Tones of maturity and complexity were at odds with childish words and her half-dishevelled state. Her pale skin and hair and large dark eyes were all out of place and added to the difficulty in guessing her age. It was impossible to tell if she was young or old, only fine wrinkles giving away the fact she wasn't in her teens, and there was a subtle allure about her which was at odds with her half-dirty, half-regal appearance.

She put Rast on edge. Perhaps many men would have found her attractive; to Rast, it spoke of something eldritch. Perhaps there was something to the stories of her being a witch. Her faint timidity had lulled them.

None of this explained why Karland appeared to be making a beeline for her clearing. He was surprised that he hadn't already come across the boy collapsed somewhere on the trail. At his present pace he would reach Letizya's hut in another few hours. Rast wondered how Karland had kept going this long. He didn't relish the thought of carrying the boy back through the night, leaving them both vulnerable to attack. Better they rest somewhere until daylight once together.

Caught up in his thoughts, Rast almost failed to detect the sudden movement to his side. Undergrowth suddenly crashed aside as a huge form leapt, roaring and wielding a thick bulk.

Only his supreme reflexes saved him; at the last instant Rast stopped his forwards movement and hurled himself backwards. Throwing his arms up and back, he felt the roughness of the forest floor on his palms as his momentum carried his legs over his head and he sprang back onto his feet. There was a whoosh as the mass the enormous form was swinging missed him by inches halfway through the flip, and then he was moving, dodging backwards to try and get some space and see what had attacked him.

A frustrated bellow answered his continued survival, overtopping the echoes from a crash as the weapon smashed into a tree. The form lumbered forwards and in streaks of moonlight Rast saw enough to guess that the creature was at least ten feet tall and immensely built. It was dragging what appeared to be a huge tree limb, perhaps seven feet long and as thick round as Rast's waist. One strike with that in those hands and bones would be snapped, organs ruptured, flesh torn.

Enough of the figure was silhouetted to show him it was probably an ogre, and likely to be hungry. It was certainly angry, and it had gained enough ground with its far longer strides to strike again.

The crude club swung around at Rast's head height, and it was deceptively quick. Rast dropped into a low crouch at the last second. The club shot overhead and struck another tree with a crack like thunder. Rast was already moving, springing forwards behind the club. He took three quick steps and leapt. Unable to see as well as his foe he had to guess at his strikes; as he sprang he turned his hips to the left, pulling his left leg up under him and snapping the other leg out sideways. He slammed his heel and all his considerable weight into the ogre, delivering a devastating strike to - he hoped - the lower ribs, just under the arm crossed over them from the club's passage. A pained bellow rewarded him, and the ogre took a slight step backwards.

Rast knew he was at a severe disadvantage. Ogres were the largest of the goblinoids, relatively slow and not very bright, but they were incredibly strong, and could see clearly in the dark. They were reputedly on the brink of permanent anger with everything, fighting easily when they met and bellowing in a rudimentary language. Rast was definitely not a favourite for anything other than a meal and its ire was raising by the second.

He didn't waste time. Landing lightly, he took several swift running steps around the ogre to get behind it. The ogre swung with him and fouled the club in the underbrush. Instead of swinging vertically to try and crush Rast, the ogre gave a guttural rumble of anger and dropped the weapon, bringing hands with palms far bigger than a human head to bear. Rast danced back, slipping under a grabbing hand, and darted for a clear spot lit to his left. Without the club, the ogre's reach and combat style had changed, and he needed room.

The moonlight was bright enough to aid him, and Rast sprinted out, the lumbering goblinoid hindered by trees and brush. He stopped and turned, breathing deeply into his lower lungs, poised on the balls of his feet and hands ready. He watched as the creature thrashed its way into the moonlight. It paused suspiciously when it found him calmly watching.

Rast's head was probably level with its belly, making it easily eleven feet tall. The ogre had a skull hanging from its neck on some sort of thong that sat just below the chest and swung slightly, bouncing off the paunch. It looked like a boar skull.

He noticed the monster was moving as if the spot he had struck was a little tender. Hopefully his kick had cracked a rib, but it had not stopped the ogre's attack.

The moment of surprise passed, and the ogre moved forwards in a half-run, seeing Rast as clearly now as it had in the shadowed woods. Rast had evened some of the disadvantage in the fight as best he could, and he was thankful the moon was so bright and the sky had little cloud.

In the space of ten seconds the attacker reached him. Roaring, it leaned back on the last step and swung an arm straight down, the fist clenched to slam this human into the ground.

The huge hand dented nothing but dirt, and the creature howled in pain as Rast shoulder charged its knee from the side, hitting with enough force to buckle the entire leg.

The ogre roared in agony and staggered as something tore in its inner knee, dropping its hands for balance. While the ogre was crouched, the neck and back were in reach; Rast circled and leapt, almost running up its back.

He threw his left hand over its great ragged left ear and shot a thundering full body hook into its right temple. It was like hitting an oak tree, but Rast could split thick boards with his callused hands. His rock-hard fist slammed into the huge head with all the power that his mighty body could generate, snapping it to the side just as the ogre had drawn itself erect.

Its centre of balance gone, the ogre staggered sideways, stunned by the power of the blow. Rast pulled back and slammed his elbow into the side of the thick neck below the ear just as the creature tried to shake its head. The blow didn't connect properly but it distracted the ogre. Shaking its head and moaning, the huge creature managed to stand fully upright.

Rast lost his grip on the ear, clapping his hands on the shoulders to prevent himself from falling. The ogre's long right arm reached up slowly, the creature slightly dazed. He saw the twisted leather thong holding the skull around the base of the neck and grabbed for it as he felt thick fingers brush his shoulder.

A second later, he had the thong in his hands. He dropped his weight, pulling hard on the leather loop, the leather strap digging deep into the ogre's throat.

Leaning back, he slipped one leg through into the heat and rasp under the creature's buttocks. Not letting himself think of the horrible proximity, he wrapped his other leg around the outside of a vast leg, hooking his feet. He knotted his arms, prayed the leather strip would hold, tensed his shoulders and used his strong lower back to *pull*.

Trying to regain balance, the ogre scrabbled ineffectually at the leather that was biting into the flesh of its throat, the fingers too large to grip the relatively slender strip. In agony Rast held the pressure as it slumped weakly to its knees, choking horribly. His back cried out from the tension but he didn't relax until the ogre fell forwards, the great arms limp.

Breathing hard he stood up. His arms, shoulders, back and legs ached from the effort. Stretching them out, he walked around the fallen mound of flesh.

Out in the light the ogre had hardly improved. The moon revealed a rather lumpy face, heavy browed. The nose was a slightly flattened and twisted affair slashing down the face, speaking of a heavy breakage in the distant past, and the huge, dark, deep set eyes that had glared balefully from the depths of his sockets were now closed. Crooked fangs similar to Grukust's tusks but much larger in proportion poked out of the corners of its mouth, one glistening wetly in the moonlight, with a collection of ragged chipped teeth in between. Unlike their plains cousins, he knew, ogres ate mostly meat. There was little hair to be seen except unruly tufts on the top of the head, and the skin of the ogre was as thick as that of a *rinok*. The head itself hunched slightly into the shoulders, which were huge and sloped.

It wore a filthy loincloth and had found a doublet or similar garment somewhere, which was rolled and rammed up above the elbow on one arm like a cloth armlet. The stocky body was solid with muscle, and the bulging stomach hung low over the top of the loincloth. Very long heavy arms reached down to fists like small boulders with long nails. Rast considered the terrible damage he would have sustained had even one caught him, and silently thanked his training and the luck that helped him avoid the ambush.

He heard a low whuffing sound over the diminishing thumping of his heart, long and steady. Moving to where the moonlight spilled over the side of the ogre, he saw the huge lungs were working, expanding the ribs slowly. It would recover.

He loped back to the scene of the ambush and cast around to find the trail again before the ogre awoke. Despite his fatigue, a growing sense of urgency called him on. Now he hurried on, finding the trail and moving down it. Dawn was approaching, and he had the feeling time was running out for Karland.

It was light when he finally reached the perimeter of Letizya's clearing. He paused and scanned the area warily; the trail ended here. He could quite clearly see the spot where the trees draped over the abode, the fenced yard, and where the herbs grew in a wild confusion, but of the hut itself there was no sign.

It had vanished.

TWENTY-EIGHT

K arland awoke slowly, the pain of sore muscles and numerous scratches pulsing through a hot and heavy headache. He summoned the strength to open one eye and realised he was lying on his side on the filthy floor in a corner of the hut with hands and feet bound, totally naked. Daylight streamed in through cracks in the shutters. There was an acrid smell, along with the earthy odour he had noticed before.

Some of what Letizya had said came back to him, and he shivered. Trying to rid his mouth of the taste of stale vomit, he fought the wooziness and hunched up onto his knees. Shuffling to the nearest wall he used it to sit upright. Weakly, shaking with thirst and hunger, Karland tried to work out how he could escape.

Gradually he became aware of quiet, deep rhythmic breathing. Too tired and awkward to get to his feet, he guessed Letizya was enjoying far better rest than he had. Exhausted, his mind wandered and he dozed awkwardly again for about twenty minutes before shaking himself awake.

I'm not sure how the hells I got into this, he thought, *but I'm the only one who can get myself out.*

Thinking of his friends brought a feeling of despair welling up within him. The others would have no idea of where he had gone, and if the forest woman was right wouldn't be able to find him.

'Sod this,' he muttered. With great effort he forced himself upright, wincing, and hopped forward, bracing his hands on the table. Maybe there was a knife to cut the rope and get out before the woman woke up.

Stiffness and bound hands made him clumsy, and he caught a wooden bowl with a wrist as he shifted his weight. The bowl fell off the edge of the table, making a hollow thump on the floor. Frozen in horror at his mistake, he heard the deep breathing stop and looked up to see the forest woman blinking sleep from her eyes and sitting up, her hair wild and spiky.

'Ahhh my pretty, no no no,' she admonished, her voice still heavy with sleep.

Stretching, she stood up. 'I didn't leave anything nasty out for you to find. I thought you would sleep longer, pet – your will must be *much* stronger than I thought. Well, I shall just have to bind you to me sooner, and then I won't have to worry about you finding things you shouldn't.' She smiled at him mysteriously.

'Let me go,' said Karland, trying to move himself so he was less exposed. He didn't like the sound of *binding*.

'No,' she mused, 'I don't think so. You are a fascinating young man. I have been lonely for a long time, and I need many things done here for as long as you can. There are other reasons too, but all you need concern yourself with is what I want.'

She moved forwards, amused by his attempts to hide vulnerable areas.

'Ah, the shyness of youth. I think I should see if you *want* to bond me.'

Reaching up she smoothed her rough dress down her curves, showing a figure in stark relief through the medium fabric. Karland realised she had erect nipples, and that her curves were very womanly under the dress, despite the shabbiness of the fabric. Her gaze on him, she breathed deeply, shaking her head so that the long pale hair collected and dropped more naturally. Her dark eyes were hypnotic, and the faint odour in the hut was helping rouse him. Karland felt a strange attraction to this woman, at odds with a feeling of unease. Against his wishes, he felt his crotch stir with the eerie promise of what she was offering; as before, she both attracted and repelled him.

Noticing his problem, and pleased that she had had the desired result, she gave a throaty laugh. Karland stared at her, trying to remember how cold it had been during their journey to Darost, before Rast had shown him how to set up his blankets. He tried to recreate the feeling, willing his desire down, refusing to let this witch woman twist him to her will. The warmth of the hut, her presence, and the strange atmosphere were not making it easy.

'You are ready for binding, and I am rested enough. I don't think I can trust you to not run away, and it will be tiring keeping you here. Your waking this soon has shown me there is more strength in you than I thought.'

'Why you are doing this to me?' he asked, feeling panic rise. 'What about your friend?'

Her eyes flashed. 'You're special enough, my young pretty. More than my last pretty, who wasn't so pretty as you, even at first.' She smiled then, in malice. 'And as for my old pretty… part of him was in the stew I gave you. He was woven with bindings, and all I had to do was feed him fresh to the next pretty I wanted to return to me.'

Karland felt his gorge rise as she continued.

'He was getting older, useless. Falling apart. The woodsmen have become harder to entice! The call made you… less noticeable… to trouble as you came. I set a fire with his bones in it, and used the *obi-ah* to call you. And now you are mine.'

The import of what she'd said struck him fully and he felt his stomach contract. Whirling and dropping to the floor, he retched, bringing up spit and bile. There was nothing in his stomach to come out, but he couldn't stop and it was agonising.

Letizya started laughing, her peals ringing out in liquid spite.

'You will please me far more, my new pet. And the first thing you will do when I bind you is clean this place and yourself of your filthy vomit. The second is to spear me until I scream for you to stop.' Her eyes gleamed with lust. The thought revolted Karland almost as much as hearing what he had eaten.

'Never,' he croaked with false bravado. 'I will never do your bidding. Try and bind me, witch, and one of us will die.' He shook with fear and anger, his nakedness and trusses forgotten.

'You cannot harm me,' Letizya shot back. 'Even if you escaped, one step outside into my garden and you would be lost until madness took you. Nothing living may set foot in my garden without my permission and pass through sane. Come, now. Pleasure and some small work are not a bad fate.'

'You will take my mind, use my body at your leisure and then serve me up to some other traveller!' He backed away, nearly falling.

Letizya purred. 'I will enjoy making you biddable. Foolish boy; I have lived here longer than you can conceive. I will be here when you are dust. I will be *ever-living!*'

She stepped forward and Karland scooped a heavy bowl off the table in bound hands and awkwardly threw it at her face. She shrieked and ducked. It missed her head by a finger's width and when she straightened fury roughened her voice.

'It is *past* time for your binding,' she hissed. Stepping forward quickly she grabbed him with alarmingly strong fingers. Karland yanked his arm away from her grasp, eliciting another hiss of irritation. He pushed a chair into her way, and backed off. Letizya glared at him and then made several passes with her hand. She muttered what sounded like meaningless syllables, and the hut darkened imperceptibly. Karland felt a soundless oppression building and the air began to feel like treacle. His body slowed as he moved despite the increasing effort his panic awarded him. Finally he stopped.

The forest woman laughed in triumph. 'I will burn your essence from your flesh and use it to return my years. *I will mark you mine until you rot.*' She cupped her hands in front of her, fingers extended like claws, and murmured. The ropes around his wrists and ankles fell from him. With some effort evident in her face, she gestured to the side, and Karland found himself moving nearer the fire, shuffling slowly. Screaming silently inside, he turned to face it, feeling the heat beating on him, coming to a halt with his feet shoulder width apart and his arms held out slightly to the sides. All he could move were his eyes.

From the side, Letizya advanced with a cup of woad and a dabbing brush, looking paler than usual. 'Direct intervention is very tiring,' she breathed in annoyance as she began drawing sigils on his naked body with deft dabs, pausing now and again to wipe a trickle clear. Her tongue protruded as she painted, and she looked strangely like a windswept dirty little girl as she concentrated. The brush swept over his face, trailing swirls that linked over his brows. Curls arched over his eyes and curved round underneath to join over the bridge of his nose, and still the brush swept on. He wondered what he looked like amongst the patterns and symbols, lines sweeping down over his jugular veins onto his chest.

Carefully, around each of his vital areas, she drew whorls and over it a symbol, each different. Temples, heart, lungs, stomach – the brush marched on, dipping now and again to replenish the woad mix. The brush reached his navel, and then Letizya looked up.

'This won't do,' she said. Her fingers lightly stroked, and Karland cursed as his body betrayed him. 'That's better,' she purred. 'It doesn't work properly without all the right places inscribed.'

If he had been able to he would have jumped at the touch of the cool dye on the delicate and warm parts of his anatomy, but he remained immobile. He realised that the forest witch was tiring fast, that it cost her by the second to keep her hold on the strange force which bound him.

She completed the front and moved to his back. The blue symbols on the front had dried and he could only imagine what he looked like. Finally she finished.

'Let me tell you what will happen, pretty. Part of this ceremony is your male release – a gift of your body. At the same time, I will take your soul.' She stepped around, wan but triumphant. Looking him up and down, she spoke again. 'There are two ways I can do this, pretty. I can draw your spirit from here with a kiss,' and she placed a finger to his lips, 'or here,' and her hand dropped to encircle his penis.

'From *here* it is pleasurable for you. Even as you lose your spirit, the pain is accompanied by so much pleasure you don't struggle at all – the last pleasure, the most pleasure you will ever have. I sometimes permit a pretty this. But from *here*,' and once more she touched his mouth, 'It hurts, like an unending breath you can't take ever again, even as you convulse and give your seed into my hand.' Her eyes gleamed at him. 'Either way your body will gift me its release, but you annoy me, my pet, and I want you to regret it as I make you mine. You will give *me* pleasure, for a long time to come, but your last experience will be of endless agony.'

Karland's heart hammered inside his chest as Letizya stepped back and picked out ingredients from those littering the shelf near the fireplace. Casting these into the fire, she whispered faint words and a green aura tinged the flames. Immediately pulling a pestle and mortar over, she feverishly threw more ingredients into it and ground them together. She reached over and uncorked a dark vial. Pouring the steaming liquid in, she continued muttering, and then suddenly thrust her hand with the pestle in it over into the leaping fire to catch a flame. With a loud pop, the fumes ignited and a small fireball uncurled as they combusted. It looked ragged and tinged with a sickly green.

Pulling her reddened hand back, she ignored it and carried on murmuring. Reaching over to the cluttered table, she picked up a small pot and a twisted piece of wood that looked somehow odd. Pouring the mixture into the pot, Letizya began to wave the stick in a precise pattern over it. The steam seemed to follow the pattern that the tip of the wood described, and something in return seemed to move from the tip into the fluid, making the air shimmer.

Karland desperately hoped that he wasn't going to be fed it. His heart was beating wildly as he desperately tried to break free of the strange hold, and a frantic wail had begun in his head. This couldn't be real - the whole night had been so surreal he must have gone to sleep and had nightmares from the food.

I'm going to die, he thought. *Going to going to going to*

The smell from the pot sickened him, and he felt with near hysteria that if she fed it to him he would go mad, gibbering his last moments into oblivion. He thought of Xhera, his friends, his family. They would never know his soul was gone, taken to feed her youth until the day she found a new *pretty*. It would be a living death.

He, Karland, would be ended.

The pot was lifted slowly as Letizya completed her enchantment, drawing it tight around him. She was crooning to herself in a sing-song voice now. The cup came up before Karland's eyes. For a few seconds he waited in horror for it to be forced into his mouth, and then she set her own lips to it and drank slowly, shuddering. Finishing, she wiped her lips, which were a sickly poisonous green from the potion, and smiled faintly. In confusion he saw the exhaustion there, and a brief hope erupted that she would collapse before she could finish. She moved forwards and the strength left in her step vanquished that hope.

'Now you will see,' she breathed, the stench of the potion rife on her tongue. There was something alien on her breath. He wasn't sure what, but it smelt marshy, fetid, and utterly unnatural. 'Where I draw a kiss, the spirit comes forth.'

She licked her lips, and ran her hand down to encircle his genitals. The other hand slipped behind his head and she leaned forwards, her other hand already manipulating him, ready to kiss him deeply when the moment came. He saw his death in her eyes.

She was inches from his mouth when there was a heavy thump from the roof of the hut, soft but solid. The witch let him go and turned towards the source of the noise.

'What was that?' she gasped. 'Nothing could have entered my garden! I would have felt it! *No one* could have passed beyond it to here!' Her voice rose to a shriek at the end.

There was a sound again from the wooden roof. Silence hung for a fraction of a second and then the roof let out a tremendous crack, sagging heavily. Another breathless moment later and it imploded inwards violently. Shards of wood rebounded off floor and walls, accompanied by snapping and the wooden crack of planks colliding.

Letizya shrieked in horror and fell backwards, knocking her shelf of ingredients over and scattering them across the floor. Through the middle of the destruction dropped a huge form in a cloak. It landed lightly on its feet, knees flexing and one fist slamming into the dirt floor to help absorb the impact. Sunlight streamed in after it, and limned it in a rough circle of golden light.

'Greetings,' said Rast softly.

ଓ   ଥ

Rast flicked his eyes across the scene in front of him impassively, noting the strange immobility of Karland, his nakedness and the unexplained whorls of symbols crossing his body, and the shocked look in the eyes of the forest woman sprawled gracelessly over her components. She spoke, her voice almost a whisper.

'How did you get across my Garden?' The raw tones were full of fear and disbelief. Ignoring her question, he looked at Karland.

'What is going on here, boy?'

Karland didn't answer, and seconds later collapsed as the woman slashed a hand in his direction. She snatched a curious dagger from inside her skirts, a slim, straight obsidian-black blade with two edges coming to a curved point. The hilt was an odd affair curved in the semblance of twisted wood.

Letizya leaped up, springing at him. Her arm moved quicker than he thought possible, almost too fast to follow. Rast was already leaning backwards. The blade sliced into his trailing cloak and left a hole that looked like the fabric had been cut by a red-hot razor. Smoke drifted up from the blackened edges.

Even as she struck Rast brought his foot up hard, slamming it into her stomach. She gasped in pain but somehow shrugged off the powerful blow and reversed the knife's direction. Rast caught her slim wrist with his right hand, clamping down hard before it reached his chest. The pressure from his grip should have broken her bones, but instead she bared her teeth at him and struggled, forcing the knife further; she was unbelievably strong, impossibly so.

He gritted his teeth with effort. The blade slowed, and then he twisted her arm up, jerking it to the side. As she fell toward the floor he wedged his left knee on her elbow and jerked upwards. The arm snapped like a twig, the bone tearing through her forearm in a ragged spike, and she screamed in agony. The knife fell from nerveless fingers and clattered on the stone floor. The forest woman swung a clawed hand at Rast's eyes with her other arm, taking him by surprise. He turned his face and took a deep scratch down his cheekbone. As he brought up his arm to block another strike, he saw her instead point her open hand at the fallen knife, snarling something.

His eyes widened as the knife twitched towards her open palm and he kicked the witch in the sternum with all his power. His much smaller opponent was hurled backwards across the room to strike the wall brutally, but still she did not fall.

Her crippled right arm was twisted and useless, dripping blood, and many of her ribs were obviously broken; her head had cracked against the wall hard enough to knock a strong man unconscious. Yet still she stood, slumped, dazed and struggling for breath. As she panted harshly, her eyes glared with hatred.

What is she?

Looking down, Rast saw the knife near his feet, the evil-looking black blade glinting with malice. He lifted his foot and brought it down hard on the blade, crossways. It offered more solid resistance than he expected, and he stamped again, harder.

It snapped suddenly, cracking more like stone than steel. From the two halves there was a flash and a red haze blasted out of the broken ends in a shimmering flare.

'*NO!*' screamed Letizya in anger and despair. She levered herself upright. Tears brimmed in her eyes and she stumbled towards him, weeping. 'Do you know what you have *done*?' she sobbed, raising her left hand in a fist, then dropping it. Rast watched warily, but she seemed defeated. Over her shoulder Karland shakily pulled himself to his hands and stood slowly.

'Please,' wheezed Letizya piteously. She coughed up blood and spat it on the floor. Snot ran down her lip as she wept through her strangely hypnotic eyes. Rast felt repelled by the strange creature, but found it hard to look away. She seemed so harmless now, but his instincts cried warning.

'One kiss...' As she moved for his face, Karland yelled from behind her.

'*NO!*'

Rast saw the green stain on her lips and tore himself free of the strange compulsion. He swept his fist around in a blur, catching her in the temple. The witch was smashed off her feet, sent hurtling away to land in a heap near the door to the hut. She lay there for a second, twitching, and then to their astonishment jumped up with a wail of despair and hatred that should have been beyond her damaged lungs. With unnatural vitality and a speed that defied belief she flung the door open and, limping, vanished through it, slamming it behind her. The house was abruptly silent.

TWENTY-NINE

K arland heard Rast sprint to the door and fling it open. Apparently she was already gone, as it shut softly a few seconds later. He groggily lifted his head as his strength gradually returned and looked up to find Rast watching him worriedly, blood running down his cheek.

'Are you unharmed?' he asked.

Karland felt numb. It was too much to deal with. He replied in a flat tone.

'I'm all right. I'm tired. I want my clothes.'

'Rest. I will find them.'

Rast searched for Karland's tunic and breeches, but found no sign of them. However, there was a small chest filled with a jumble of clothes for men and boys. He spread a selection out for Karland and told him to choose.

'We'll worry about all those markings when we get to a stream,' he said.

As Karland slowly began dressing, Rast explored the hut. Karland watched him move to Letizya's bed, pulling the blankets and a thick straw filled mattress crawling with lice out of the alcove to reveal a solid wooden door built into the floor. Cautiously he opened it and peered in, then lit a sputtering candle in the fire's embers and descended.

Karland finished dressing. With the hiding of the markings he also felt calmer and more human. He realised his new knife was gone, along with his belt, but it hardly seemed to matter anymore.

Rast reappeared from the alcove floor, his face much grimmer than usual. He replaced the door and the bedding, and didn't say a word about what he had seen. When Karland opened his mouth, Rast shook his head.

'Later. How do you feel, boy?'

'Better. I thought I was going to die.' His voice shook, shame washing through him. 'Rast? Thank you.'

Rast gripped his shoulder firmly and smiled. 'You are safe now.' He looked around the dim hut. 'Come, it is past time we left. I'll help you onto the roof, and we can depart. Whatever fell powers lie beyond the door, we can bypass them this way.'

Rast boosted Karland easily through the hole and pulled himself up lithely. The clearing around the hut seemed very faintly translucent, with a pale haze running to the very edge of the trees.

'It looks as if the old stories of the forest witch are true. I wonder how long she has truly lived here.' remarked Rast. Karland offered no reply; he suspected it had been for a long, long time.

Overhanging the hut were several branches from the surrounding trees. Rast crouched underneath one and said, 'Climb on my back and hold on tight.'

He waited until Karland was securely on, and then leaped straight up. His calloused hands clapped onto the branch above them and he pulled them up onto it. Karland held on tightly as Rast got a knee under himself and stood, balancing on the swaying limb. Reaching the trunk he climbed to a higher branch around the tree and edged out along it. Karland was nervous with heights, and he thought they must be twenty five feet above the ground. He looked forward and saw another branch at least ten feet away.

'Wait, are you-', he began and then yelped as Rast launched himself across the gap, hands reaching. They closed on it and he swung down, his grip slipping for a few feet. Rast tightened his grip with a grunt and they stopped.

They progressed this way until they were well beyond the clearing perimeter, and then Rast climbed down and let Karland off his back.

'Lucky the hut was near enough this edge of the clearing for trees to overlook it,' he said. He looked down. His rough hands had skin missing and were bleeding in several places. Karland winced.

'How did you know there was something wrong?'

'Look.' Rast pointed.

Karland turned. The clearing looked peaceful in the morning sunlight, but there was no sign of the hut. Where he knew it must be was just a clear partially shaded patch of grass and tangled herbs bordered by waving trees. He looked up at Rast in astonishment.

'She is powerful,' said Rast. 'I was wary of the empty clearing.'

'She said anything stepping into the clearing would be lost to madness.'

Rast grunted. 'Whatever that means. We'd best get moving; it's a fair way back. How do you feel?'

'Tired. And I'm hungry.' Karland's face twisted miserably. 'Not for meat.'

Rast nodded. 'Come. I will help you. We should be safer in daylight.'

෬   ౭౦

It was mid-afternoon when they reached the camp. They had stopped at a stream to slake their thirst and Karland had taken the opportunity to wash as much of the woad off as he could and clean himself up. After hours of walking without food Rast had eventually carried him part of the way.

Grukust looked up at their arrival, watching curiously as they approached. 'Where you been?' he grunted. 'We thinking to come find you.'

Any answer was forestalled by Xhera, who erupted from where she was sitting and flew to Karland. She flung her arms around him and squeezed fiercely. 'Where have you *been*?' she demanded. She glared at Karland, relief warring with annoyance. He was finding it hard to focus, although he was glad to see her. 'And where did you get these new clothes? Why is your face blue-'

Rast broke in softly. 'Be gentle, Xhera. Get Karland some food. He is hungry and exhausted.'

Xhera nodded and took Karland's hand, and then looked closer and pulled up his sleeve. Faint blue coils and symbols flowed down the inside of it where the woad hadn't finished washing off. It would take days before the rest abraded off to leave his skin totally clear again. She looked up at him, questions plain in her eyes, but was interrupted as Aldwyn moved over. His initial smile dropped away and he frowned. Pushing his spectacles up his nose with a middle finger, he grabbed Karland's arm, his fingers digging in.

'Take your shirt off,' he instructed in a sharp voice. Karland reluctantly removed it, shivering a little. The shame and terror of his night was still close.

Xhera gasped as she saw his body covered in lines of the faint residue. Grukust grunted in surprise. The markings swept over his whole torso and continued down under his breeches.

'What is going on?' Xhera said. 'What is all that?'

'Ritual markings,' said Aldwyn in answer, his tone grim. 'Used in dark rites.' He looked at Karland questioningly. 'Do you know what these are?' he asked, peering over his spectacles seriously.

'I know what they are *for*,' Karland said bleakly.

Rast broke the silence. 'Xhera. Karland is starving. What do we have?'

'Bread, cheese, dried meat-'

'Just the bread and cheese, I think,' interjected Rast swiftly, looking at Karland's suddenly ashen face.

'I want to know what happened,' declared Xhera, looking upset. Karland still wouldn't look at her.

Rast look at him and took in his pallor. 'After we eat. Karland will tell us what he can.' He nodded, his hunger overriding his reluctance to talk. Grukust spoke quietly to Rast as Karland ate, avoiding Xhera's curious glances. He now understood her reaction after the men had tried to rape her. He felt dirty, shamed; he didn't want people to know what had happened.

With dusk approaching, Rast built the fire up again ready for the evening. Aldwyn passed out mugs of steaming tea, the green leaves lurking in the bottom and a vegetable-orange solid smell rising pleasantly from the cup.

Finally, Karland spoke. Haltingly at first, he explained as much as he could remember, trying to stay matter of fact. He was proud that he managed to mostly control his voice. The hot tea seeming to help him calm a little. Xhera gasped several times, and when he finished there was silence again for a few moments.

'The Ever-Living Woman,' breathed Aldwyn. 'A very old tale. I cannot believe it is true.'

'She was more than she seemed,' agreed Rast. 'Much faster and stronger than she should have been. I maimed her badly and she barely slowed; she should have died. Before we left I found… something. Under her house. A crypt with an altar. A nameless terror lurked there in tunnels in the earth, stuffed with bones and the stench of death, ragged, rotted. Some were ancient. The very walls were splashed with blood and symbols. I have never felt something so *evil*. I think she has lived a very long time, killing untold men, women, children, eating their flesh. Sacrifices, pledges to a dark power.'

Eating their flesh. The words roiled around in Karland's head. He saw Xhera look at him as he teetered.

'Karland?'

'I'm fine,' he said vaguely, and then staggered up and moved for the edge of the trees as fast as he could. He almost made it before his stomach rejected all his food and he heaved it up violently. He shuddered, wracked by reflex, until there was nothing left. The heaving was making him feel sicker, and he struggled to contain it. Gradually he realised Xhera was there, holding his hair back and trying to soothe him.

Minutes passed, and finally he seemed clearer, cleaner. He wiped his mouth and smiled at Xhera gratefully. She smiled through her worry and handed him his cup. He rinsed out his mouth and leaned on her as they made their way back to the fire.

'Are you all right?' asked Rast. Karland nodded. Hard though it had been he was glad he had told them.

'Karland should feel no shame. Even Grukust might have been scared too,' Grukust whispered conspiratorially. 'Nasty witch.' He looked at Rast. 'Maybe you tell us what happen to you, eh, why you take so long?' He threw his head back and poured the tea into it, forgetting there were leaves in the bottom, and started coughing as they stuck in his wide throat. Aldwyn cackled. Karland smiled in amusement for the first time, glad to be back with his friends.

Grukust spluttered, glaring at them, and then abruptly he grinned. He spat the remaining leaves out, picking a sodden bit of greenery off the side of a tusk where he could see it from the corner of his eye.

Rast told them briefly about tracking Karland. 'Whatever she did, Karland wasn't bothered by anything in the forest. I met a woods tiger and an ogre, but he passed them by.'

'Did you kill them?' asked Xhera, her eyes wide.

Rast shook his head. 'The cat and I left each other alone. The Ogre I left unconscious.' There was no boast or hint of the battle it must have been; he spoke simple fact.

Grukust bellowed with laughter, making them jump. 'Unarmed human defeat Ogre. Ha, it never live *this* down.' He thumped his thick chest with his right fist at Rast in a gesture of respect for his prowess.

Rast smiled faintly then stood. Karland felt his eyes drooping. 'Grukust, can you watch for an hour? I will join you then. We must rest; I want to be far from here tomorrow. The witch is still alive and roaming these woods. This will be our last fire.'

Karland shivered as he stood. 'Would you, um… would you sleep nearer?' he asked Xhera quietly, avoiding her eyes. 'Just for tonight, I mean.'

'Of course,' she said. He lay down and rolled himself up. She huddled up to him in her blanket. As he was falling asleep, she whispered in his ear, tartness in her tone.

'So… you found her attractive?'

Karland mumbled, half asleep. 'Repulsive… seductive… hypnotic. Xhera? I'm too tired to argue.' He couldn't stay awake any longer, even though she was still whispering, and drifted away on her voice.

'You *had* to be all right. I can't bear to lose you. You are my best friend.'

You are my best friend too, he thought, but he did not know if he had spoken the words.

THIRTY

Karland was woken early by Rast. He reluctantly started his morning exercises, feeling weak, but his focus grew as he went through them. When Rast stopped him Karland realised he had been at it for nearly an hour.

As they ate Rast told them they would avoid the road now. There was too high a risk that they would meet orcs or worse the deeper they got into the forest. They walked through the trees, picking the easiest way through in silence after leaving the safe little campsite. A foreboding feeling was stealing over them all the further they moved into the Dimnesdair, and the day started light if grey, with tiny spots of rain coming and going as they had packed.

Their campsite had not been too deep into the forest from the Pass. Danial had said he thought the orcs lived mainly on the slopes of the Iril Eneth to the east and did not often venture into the trees, but he could not say for certain. Only the hardier and more experienced timber cutters had handled the ironwoods this far into the Dimnesdair, and they were now dead.

They moved southwest, hoping that if they stayed this side of the trail – which seemed to wend the same direction – that they would avoid detection. Karland walked quietly, wrapped in his thoughts. His stomach still twisted slightly when his mind returned to the night before, and he tried to distract himself by thinking about their destination. He knew he was being quieter than usual, but if there was one positive from his experience it was that he was less afraid of what lay ahead.

Xhera moved alongside him, smiling up at him and trying to comfort him, and he appreciated it. His kinship with her had deepened further, both of them knowing what it was to be totally in another's power. From time to time he glanced back worriedly at Aldwyn, who was sweating profusely. The air was getting more hot and humid as they travelled. The old man trudged along with his jaw thrust out stubbornly, concentrating on his steps, muttering incomprehensible things. Behind Aldwyn he could see the ork bringing up the rear, his green skin shining with sweat. He clearly still neither liked nor trusted the woods, and his huge axe was ready in his hands.

The travel continued for hours. Rast seemed to do nearly twice the travelling of the rest, fading in and out at the fore and sometimes holding up his hand for them to stop in the silence until he was satisfied. The small group stopped for lunch near a small stream and refilled their flasks, speaking in low tones. After a short rest, they hurried on.

Rast cautioned them he had begun to see signs of larger forest dwellers – and other tracks. Orcs *had* come this way, heading east, but not for some time. A little after noon, he held up his hand and they stopped. Aldwyn began to ask a question, and Rast shook his head, pointing at his ear. They listened intently.

There was a faint noise from somewhere in front of them. It echoed and oscillated, but it was hard to define. It came and went, bestial and multi-voiced with cracks, roars and shrieks. They waited for a while after the echoes died and then moved on. Karland realised there were still in fact some things left to fear as Xhera clutched his arm only slightly more than he clutched hers.

Something huge crashed through the trees to their far right minutes later, making huffing noises and snorting, but it did not come near them. Not long afterwards they came to a wide trail through the forest that had possibly been left by whatever the thing had been. Trees leaned away from it as if brushed by something immense, and a few had been uprooted and appeared to have been eaten. They crossed the trail hurriedly and carried on.

They noticed different trees and plants beginning to spring up here and there amongst the conifers and broad-leafed trees that they were travelling under. Occasionally they would pass a massive trunk that ten or more men could not link arms around – one of the monstrous trees they had seen from afar.

They walked the edge of a thicket with strange, broadly curved leaves lining the floor with a large purple trunk behind them. As they passed, Aldwyn glanced at it and then grabbed Xhera by her pack, stopping her foot from falling on the leafy edges lying on the floor. She grunted in surprise.

'What is it?' Rast whispered to the old man.

'It, mm, looks like a Trapdoor Pitcher,' the old man said in low tones. Rast raised his eyebrows and Aldwyn rolled his eyes.

'Did you see the Garden of Traps? In the Sanctum? The misted one? Some of the flowers there eat flesh. They are mostly quite small. One type is shaped like a bell, deep and wide. Some are a partially buried trap. When insects touch the slippery leaves, the woven roots under them snap vertical. It, ah, catapults the unfortunate insect into the mouth of the pitcher, which goes down under the earth. It's full of a powerfully sticky digestive that drowns and consumes prey. It is, aha, impossible to climb out. Even rats have been found in the larger ones.' Xhera gulped and backed away rapidly.

Karland looked at the plant, and then at the scholar. 'Are you telling me that these things come in human sizes?' He immediately imagined falling in and drowning slowly to be digested, and shuddered.

Aldwyn peered at the arrangement of leaves and the pitcher. 'Remarkable,' he said. 'It appears so. I have never seen one so big. The pitcher must end ten or more feet under the soil! I did not think they grew in such dry areas. We do *not* wish to end up in that; we must take care.'

Rast turned to the others.

'Take note,' he said in his deep low voice. 'This forest is becoming more hazardous the further we go towards the Dimnesvale. These things must spread from the valley itself. We must be wary, even here. Watch where you tread!'

They turned back to the trail, skirting the waiting plant. Aldwyn shook his head as he passed it, looking at it keenly. 'Remarkable.'

ʘ   ċ

It was after noon the next day when Rast stopped. Grukust lifted his nose and sniffed. He hurried past the others to the big man. 'Rast?' he asked quietly.

Rast frowned. 'I'm not sure. I think I smell smoke.'

'There more than smoke. I smell… wood. Flesh. Blood.' The big ork's face was grim. 'There is death ahead.'

'I will scout.' Rast vanished into the trees like a wraith.

The others moved cautiously after him, moving slowly. Grukust's eyes were gleaming, and his expression was fierce, almost lustful. He gripped his axe tightly, his prodigious muscles twitching. Karland wondered if it was the nearness of death or the smell of blood that excited his companion.

They came abruptly to the edge of the trees. There was no thinning out – they simply stopped. Healthy living trunks had been torn bodily from the earth, split in two, splintered, their heartwood drying in the air. Others leaned drunkenly, and jagged stumps dotted the floor. Some of them were in flames while others were blackened and charred, being too wet to stay alight. The devastation was immeasurable, and the trees were the least of it. They stared in utter disbelief at the countless bodies strewn around the raw smoking clearing.

Rast was crouched in front of them, peering out. Even as they reached him, he stood and moved into the open.

323

'There is nothing alive here,' he said flatly.

They followed him out into the middle of the clearing, staring around them. For more than five hundred feet in all directions the forest had been totally levelled. Where it wasn't soaked in blood, the earth was blackened in long streaks, and there were terrible rents and gouges in it.

The carnage was sickening. Charred, horrible remains were flung everywhere, some bodies whole, others in pieces. A faint odour persisted beneath the overpowering stench of burned flesh, blood and smoke. There were hundreds of dead orcs, and Karland thought he could see the remains of what must be a few ogres as well. They had been savagely torn to shreds by some incredible force, broken by tremendous blows. A large grey arm lay here, limply trailing torn tendons, while there lay a portion of torso with stark ribs jutting from the bared innards. Further away were two rough lines of heaped bodies, partially blackened and burned. Between them there was nothing but the remnants of black ash stirring in the breeze. Weapons were still clutched in clawed hands, some twisted and broken.

All in all, there must have been nearly seven or eight hundred, Karland guessed. The death was overwhelming. After he fought the orcs at The Croft, and they found the piled bodies of the band the orks had slaughtered, he believed he had grown used to death, but nothing had prepared him for this.

'What *happened* here?' whispered Xhera, her hand over her mouth. Aldwyn was speechless, but his wide eyes echoed the horror in her voice.

Grukust shook his head. 'Something kill them all. Tear them apart.' His voice sounded awed, almost, but there was something unidentifiable in it as well. 'Maybe magic. I never see anything like this.' His axe dangled loosely in his hand, forgotten.

'Here,' called Rast grimly from the side. They picked their way through the dead, skirting a large grey corpse missing a head and one arm that must have been twelve feet or more tall, and looked at where he pointed, mute.

The red of Meyar showed on cloth worn by a broken and burned corpse lying with one hand outstretched. Others lay nearby. As they looked around, they realised that many of these bodies were human.

'This makes no sense,' said Aldwyn in a quiet voice. 'It is one thing to attack Eordeland, but to march with these creatures as allies?'

'It makes little difference now,' said Rast harshly. 'Something powerful beyond anything I have ever seen killed everything here. That must have been what we heard. I have never seen the like. What can have done this, old man?'

Aldwyn sighed. 'Let me think on it a while.' He looked around, and then closed his eyes. 'Can we leave here?

Grukust nodded. 'This not battle. This *joukklomurha*. This… this *masca*.' Aldwyn didn't even try to correct him. Xhera refused to look around her. Karland sympathised. Somehow the death kept dragging his eyes back as if they were magnetised to it.

'Whatever did this has been gone for several hours,' said Rast. 'I do not like this. What lies in wait for us in these woods?' He beckoned them, pointing to the far side of the clearing. 'Come. This carrion will attract scavengers, and worse. The fires will burn a long time, I think, so let us hasten and hope they hide our trail.' He moved quickly towards the canopy. Xhera raised her cloak edge to breathe through, blocking out some of the smell. Karland and Aldwyn did likewise. Grukust snorted loudly several times, trying to clear the smell from his nose.

Two hours later they stopped to rest. Aldwyn promptly collapsed, gasping, and drank huge mouthfuls of water. He seemed to be suffering badly. Xhera encouraged him to eat some food. She also tried to get Karland to exchange his dried meat for her bread and cheese. With a wan smile, he shook his head. He could not afford to be picky, so he concentrated on the fact that the meat was only beef. After a false start, he found he could stomach it as long as he didn't think of Letizya.

He speculated idly what had caused such utter destruction. Had the crashing passage of something gigantic that they had heard before been the same creature, narrowly missing them?

I wonder if blood and guts and death will have no meaning one day, he thought. *There has been so much.* He didn't like the idea of not caring anymore; it somehow felt like he would lose his humanity.

Xhera was dozing. She could fall asleep within a minute, a skill Karland would give much to learn. He moved over to Rast, who stood gazing into the bushes around him. Grukust was also alert, his axe beside him on the ground, the head on his pack.

'What is it, Karland?' asked Rast, his eyes not leaving his surrounds.

'Do you stop caring about death eventually?' asked Karland. 'I mean, you said you get used to killing. But all those dead creatures, and men, back there… what happens when that stops bothering you? Are you the same person?'

Rast looked at Karland. 'Is that what is worrying you? That you will become someone else?'

Karland nodded. Rast shook his head.

'What we saw back there was shocking to us all. You do get used to death, to killing. You learn to disassociate yourself from it all. But you can still stay *yourself*. For me, it comes from remembering that every one of those dead once thought and spoke as I do. Many find it easy to objectify their enemy, but that leads to atrocities. Death you can learn to ignore, and thinking of who they were is what keeps me from coldness. Just do not let it prevent you committing; I may regret taking life but I will never hesitate to strike. Hesitation means death, means losing. You only get one chance at life.'

'Orks love battle,' broke in Grukust. 'We love fight. Kill. The power victory give. But I also stay myself. Stay... Ork. Killing weak, defenceless, young... there no honour or sense there. Ork who only care about killing lose what it is to be ork. They become *murha*. That ork Rast beat, Niruk, he in danger of that, and if he lose himself he will be judged, maybe outcast or slain. They same as *Goruc'cha* – kill for love of killing, without honour. Maybe *urch* love what we saw. That not fight. That slaughter.'

Karland felt relieved. 'I just... I don't know. I was shocked by the carnage back there, but not as much as I thought I should be. Even Xhera was not as upset as she was in The Croft. It worried me.'

Rast smiled slightly.

'Tell me: how did you feel when you killed that first orc during the battle?'

Karland thought back, remembering the terror, the suddenness with which it all happened. 'Frightened. My heart was pounding. Then when I realised I had killed it, and survived... I felt strong, so happy I felt like laughing. Then I looked down at it and saw its open guts, the eyes, the look on its face. The... the dead faces of my friends. I knew it had to be done, I kept saying that it was only an orc. But I killed something that was alive. I didn't like it, even to save my life.'

Rast nodded, scanning the trees again. 'You are in no danger of losing yourself to death. But killing an orc is different from killing a man. Men are often misguided, self-serving, sometimes evil. Orcs have no mercy in them, no compassion, no honour. They are foul creatures.'

'If there one thing I love killing, it *urch*,' muttered Grukust.

Karland glanced at him. 'Why do you hate them so much?'

'We not like talk about it,' Grukust said shortly. He was silent for a moment, then sighed. 'Once, long ago, there a lot more ork. Legend say we live in roots of world. Ogres live there too, all our kind. Then something happen. Something – change. Many of our people die. Others left not the same, made twisted, evil, hating. Lose proud ork body, proud ork mind. Become foul killer, warped, eater of kin, *fallen*. They breed too fast, see better in dark, *hate*. One day not enough true ork left.' He looked unhappy. 'We flee before we all die, and find new life on plain, move with herds.

'We always strong. Hard life make us stronger. One night, *Goruc'cha urch*, they come out, find us. We not expect them; they kill nearly all ork children. But they not prepared for how strong tribes are and we kill many many. Nearly all. It great victory, but *Uruks* nearly gone. It take great age for us recover, and children very precious to us. And that only first war – now just us left on plains.' His voice dropped to a snarl. '*Herjaa ta vihaka!* We *never* forget.' His dark eyes reflected a pure hatred.

'But… how did all that happen?' Karland asked, his mouth open. 'The change?'

'Don't know.' Grukust shrugged, the ire fading from his voice. 'But it the curse of my people.'

'A lot of things on this world have happened without reason,' said Aldwyn from behind him. His voice was tired, serious. 'Many things exist that should not. Records don't go back far enough to say why… mm. But there are theories that something happened long ago that changed many things in this world.' He did not elaborate, and instead turned to Rast. 'We must continue. I am hoping we will reach the Dimnesvale before we camp. This journey is… hard for me.'

Rast looked at him closely, and then clapped a gentle hand on his friend's shoulder. 'Let us go. We will find a secure spot there,' he agreed.

The party travelled on for several more hours. They saw more strange plants and signs of life as they went, but moved with care, and were not bothered. Once strange baying howls echoed through the forest, like nothing they had ever heard before. Later they moved carefully around a clearing that was hung with white webs as thick as ropes, seeing no sign of their creator. A few large bundles hung silent and still high in the trees around the edges. Xhera clutched Karland's arm as they skirted it. She was terrified of spiders. He whispered encouragement to her and hurried along; meeting one the size of a cart was not on his agenda either.

Finally, as dusk dimmed the skies the trees thinned. They came to bare rocky ground not far from a deep drop, falling thousands of feet into a wide valley of shadows. The far side was more than fifteen miles distant, almost lost in the fading light. It swept left and right in front of them, curving out of sight in both directions. In the middle to the right peaks jutted up from the valley floor. The sun was setting behind clouds directly in front of them, the sky grey but tinged with red. A darker bank of them drifted slowly north, in contrast to the smaller white puffs that moved with more speed in front of them. A single glimpse of three sun rays touched down through a gap in the clouds, sparkling off something below, and was then gone.

'Beautiful,' said Karland. There didn't seem much else to say. It was overwhelmingly impressive.

'Well. It's bigger than I expected,' said Aldwyn, frowning and pushing his spectacles up. 'Not so much a valley, mm, as a canyon.'

'Whatever you call it, tomorrow we must find a way down… if there is one.' Rast's voice was bland. 'You should consider where in that place we might find what we seek, scholar. We must plan our entry, search, and leave as fast as we can. Only luck has so far allowed us to escape notice – and our danger will increase a hundredfold once we are in the valley if even half the stories are true.'

As if to punctuate his words, a faint whisper of that unearthly baying drifted through the night air again. They could not tell if it came from the valley, or the trees around them.

᎒ᴿ   ᴔ

Troubled by the unknown calls, as if something was hunting, Rast moved south along the edge of the canyon. He found a large boulder that overhung a rocky ledge and only had one path along the side. The other was blocked, and in front of them the wall sloped away gently for ten feet before plummeting out of sight. Most importantly, it hid them from the forest behind and was fairly defensible. The senses he had relied on for his whole life were telling him that the forest was not a good place to be tonight, especially this close to the valley. The witch woman no doubt could ward her clearing well, and their second campsite had been nearer the Pass, but here was truly wild.

Despite his word, Rast set up a small fire. The blessing of the huge overhang was that the heat from a fire would reflect on them all even as it was well hidden from prying eyes; he doubted anything would scale three thousand feet to investigate a pinprick of a fire from the valley floor. The wind sliding along the valley walls caught the smoke, scattering it.

They slept fitfully, the forest coming more alive than they had heard it before. Rast and Grukust took watches and for the first time Karland and Xhera found themselves on watch too. Like most people they usually slept twice a night, rising to talk or relax before sleeping again; it was a natural nocturnal rhythm. But now more than once they were shaken awake at odd times, their grumbles ignored, and they sat together for several hours.

Karland watched Rast curiously. Rather than lie down to sleep, he sat deep in the shadows, presumably watching them. He wondered idly how he would be rested if he didn't sleep. Faint noises drifted up from the valley below.

The next morning, the sun broke early through the wisps of cloud low over the horizon, shining over the rock sheltering the party. Everyone blinked awake to find Rast sitting in the sun, except Aldwyn; the wind was thankfully snatching his snores from his lips. The dawn was brilliant and beautiful, and Karland closed his eyes to slits. His cheek had slipped off his pack during the night, and was resting on smooth rock, small gritty sand rasping on his face.

The valley below them was unveiling slowly as the sun rose, the shadow from their wall swiftly retreating towards them. It revealed a misty expanse of jungle which ran to swamp, and then became a dark and long lake on the eastern side to their south. What looked like a sandy beach ran along the edges of the swamp, touching the forest at points, and further back to the north it stretched away like some sort of miniature desert up to the low beginnings of the rocky peaks. West of the peaks was a strange arrangement of small gorges or canyons, looking for all the world as if they were gargantuan claw marks, weaving and crisscrossing like a maze. Far to the north on their right were bigger peaks that seemed to be smoking slightly, and deeper shadows.

'Those may be volcanoes,' said Aldwyn. 'That would explain the somewhat tropical atmosphere down there. It must be very hot. Volcanism could heat the ground below half the valley. There must be dozens of different ecosystems down there; having so many different ecologies together is very unusual. Before now I would have said, aha, impossible.'

Further south, as it curved away, it looked cooler. More mist hung over boggy land, and the woods fell away to grass and earth. Rast moved to the edge and stood, apparently not bothered by the drop, looking along the cliffs to try and spy a route down. The soles of Karland's feet tingled sympathetically just watching him.

They were eating breakfast when there was a low rumble behind the rock, accompanied by a crackling noise. Rast rose to his feet like a cat, motioning the others to stay still. He moved to the edge and peered up the short slope before returning.

'A giant creature is moving through the trees. I do not know its like. It is covered in short grey hairs, and bigger than a house with a nose like a snake. It was moving slowly, and did not appear to be hunting.'

'Aha. Some form of forest elephant, perhaps,' mused Aldwyn. 'I thought they only existed in Matalaga. It won't hunt us – they eat plants and wood. That must have been the crashing noise we heard yesterday. Bigger than a house, you say?'

'I would say it was forty feet high. It was level with some of the treetops.'

'Really? Well, that is *far* bigger than usual,' muttered Aldwyn. 'This place seems full of strange creatures. Generally over time a species will grow and grow without cease, but there does seem to be an excess here. I think we should definitely avoid it. The smaller ones bred in Kharkistan are still quite a bit bigger than a *rinok*. They are used in war and are nearly unstoppable. Very strong, and bad tempered if you annoy them.'

A short time later, they were packed and ready to leave. Rast checked carefully to ensure that there was nothing nearby, and then they climbed back up to the level of the forest and struck out south along the wall.

'I saw several places where there may be paths down,' he said. 'I don't know if we can all make it though.' He looked worried and glanced at Aldwyn.

'I will help Aldwyn,' grunted Grukust.

'Who's going to help *me*?' muttered Karland imperceptibly. The thought of trying to climb down the cliff was worrying him. Climbing a tree was one thing, but a drop like this paralysed him. Xhera was skipping along the edge as if rooted to the cliff top, paying no attention, but he was hanging back as far as he could. There was an awful allure about the edge, which warred with his anxiety. He didn't say anything; he didn't think he would be able to explain why he felt an urge to jump off despite his fright.

They came to the first area Rast thought there was a path down. A narrow path dropped along the wall, looking promising, but then petered out and dropped to nothing. Karland took one look at it and then backpedalled frantically.

Xhera noticed. 'Are you all right?' she whispered. He shook his head. She peered over, making his nerves screech, and then looked at him.

'I don't like heights,' he said sheepishly.

'Well, who does?' she asked.

'I *really* don't like heights,' he muttered.

'That could be an issue,' she admitted.

Rast beckoned them onwards. The sun climbed higher, making the trek hot and sweaty work, and they knew it would be even worse in the valley, if Aldwyn was correct. Miles of careful travel further on they found something more promising. A long dip hundreds of feet down towards the edge ended in a high rock wall with a deep, narrow crack canting down at a severe – but potentially passable – angle. Rast moved out to the edge and peered over again. He studied the bottom of the cliff carefully, and then came back.

'This could be good,' he said. 'There are high rocks at the bottom of this crack. I think there was a slide here once. It will not be easy, but I think we can do it if we are careful and use our rope sensibly.' He patted his pack, where the expensive rope he had bought in Punslon lay.

'I will go first to see if it is passable. Wait here. It is best we get this right now than rush.' He removed his pack and cloak, then his tunic, and slung the rope around his shoulders. His torso glistening with sweat, the hair on his chest failing to hide the rippling pectorals, and all of his muscles stood out sharply as the bright light cast defining shadows. He climbed down to the bottom of the curved slope, followed by the others. It was almost like a half-bowl of scree, the underlying soil perhaps having been washed down the crack by rainfall. Karland watched him look into the crack, and then start in, and glanced around. He didn't like feeling so exposed, but all they could do was wait.

೧ ೧

Rast peered downwards. This was definitely not something that could be walked. It would be a heavy mixture of climbing and scrambling, but the walls were dotted with good holds for hands and feet, and there seemed to be quite a few thick-stemmed shrubs as well. He had grown up climbing sheer cliffs in his home, and would find this no issue. He was mainly worried about Aldwyn, who was not as strong or healthy as the others, and Karland, whom he had noticed eyeing the cliff warily. Hopefully the crack would not be too unpleasant for the boy. It was far less exposed than the cliff face.

He started down, constantly assessing the descent. It was not as bad as he had thought, but climbing back up would be far harder. They would have to deal with that when they came to it.

For more than an hour Rast descended carefully. He found one section that was smooth and dropped away nearly a hundred feet before a wide slab broke the descent and holds were available again. Hoping that it was the only one, he found a small tree ten feet up that was solidly attached in a soil-filled pocket crevice, limned in sunlight. It was strongly wound around a rocky outcrop, and he gingerly hung his full weight off it. When it stayed solid, he threw and tugged as hard as he could, but apart from a slight bounce, it held. Satisfied, he tied the rope securely in a double figure of eight, slipped a securing knot on the loose end, and payed himself down the rope. He could chimney either up or down this part if required, with his back braced and his legs extended, but the others would find it hard.

Reaching the slab at the bottom, he left the rope trailing and moved downwards. It was easier going from here, and not too long afterwards he arrived at the upper point of the rock fall, which led down hundreds of feet to a pile of large boulders. He turned and looked up the forbidding cliffs, and then glanced across the valley. Faint cries reached him, the sounds of the valley's denizens. The lake to his left was calm apart from the occasional large ripple. In the far distance he thought he saw a herd of the forest elephants. There must be a much easier way down, then, but he hazarded a guess that it was at the southern end of the valley.

After a short rest he began the ascent. This would take him twice as long as the descent, if he was lucky, but the bottom of the crack was just wide enough for a very cramped camp. He was relieved. Once in the valley proper it was unlikely they would easily find anywhere safe, if legends were true. At least they would have a secure camp to start from.

൭ ൫

Rast had been gone for some time when Karland saw Grukust raise his head. They had moved down the slope to the beginning of the crack, and were sitting in the shade cast by the high rocks. When Xhera began to ask him what was wrong, he held up a hand.

'Shh,' he said quietly. He crept up the slope, trying to be careful on the rocks. His large body glinted with sweat as it passed into the sun, his huge axe on his back. With hardly a clatter he made it to the top and lay flat, peering over. He remained motionless for several minutes, and then slithered backwards and picked his way back down. His lower lip twitched back from his right tusk.

'*Urch* up there,' he said. 'Think something else, too. Smell something bad.' Karland looked around. There was no other escape than the crack.

Suddenly a cacophony of shrieks and cries erupted from the trees above them, punctuated by deep horrifying snarls. Grukust snatched up Rast's belongings and shoved Aldwyn towards the crack.

'Go, go!' he shouted, the noise above covering his words. Karland and Xhera ran for the rift, Aldwyn stumbling along after them. Whatever was going on up there, it sounded like the orcs were being torn apart.

Karland pulled Aldwyn up when he stumbled and they reached the crack moments later. Grukust went into the crack feet first, his axe on his back. He beckoned Aldwyn in and shouldered his pack too, leaving the old man unencumbered. Xhera motioned Karland into the crack, but he shoved her in instead, frantically looking over his shoulder for the menace above. The cries had cut off abruptly with a last horrible scream. She dropped in with a curse that was cut off. He backed into the crack, and as he entered and started climbing down he thought he saw something – or things – at the lip of the bowl.

They climbed down in as much silence as they could, Karland glancing up continuously. Not a minute after entering it, the light at the top was blocked by something large. Karland fancied he saw a glint of an eye. He froze. After a few seconds, the dark something moved away. He breathed out and continued, finding the climb actually not as frightening as he had dreaded. It was not like hanging off a cliff, and for once his heart was pounding from fear for a different reason.

Two thirds of the way down, they came to a halt; Grukust had reached the roped drop. He paused and helped Aldwyn to the ledge next to him as Karland caught them up. Aldwyn looked at the rope, and then shook his head.

'I cannot hold that to the end.'

Without a word, Grukust unslung his axe and dropped a loop of his pack around the head before tying it through his belt so it hung below him. Ignoring the scholar's protests, he swung Aldwyn onto his back and made ready to swing down. Rast's soft voice interrupted him from below as he reappeared.

'Grukust? What is going on? The way is clear, but you should have waited.'

Karland peered down into the gloom. 'Orcs,' he called. 'And worse. Something was tearing them apart, and followed us to the crack.'

'We are lucky we stopped here,' said Aldwyn. 'We might have run into either of them if we had continued south.'

Rast nodded pragmatically. 'We had best move,' he said. 'This is the worst bit – it becomes easier after this. Grukust, bring him down – I'll unhook your axe. We have a place to camp at the bottom to eat and plan our next steps.'

THIRTY-ONE

They ate lunch in the shade of the crack, which was just wide enough for all of them. It was very hot down here, the air in the distance to the north shimmering with heat over the sands that stretched away for miles. Strange cries echoed through the valley. The jungle to the west seemed still, but it was anything but silent. The lake in front of them and to the south looked cool, dark and inviting. Karland morbidly wondered what dread creatures lurked beneath. Occasionally large ripples swept across the surface, suggesting movement beneath the water. Above them and to the northwest, great birds soared on the thermals rising from the cliffs.

Xhera and Grukust sat quietly, the ork's lips occasionally twitching as he brooded. Aldwyn was staring out, pensive. He still had given them no real direction, so finally Rast broke the silence.

'Where do we go, Aldwyn?'

The old man put down a chunk of bread, half eaten, and sighed.

'Little is known of this valley. It has long been regarded as a place of danger. There are tales of an Emperor called Kharkis, the founder of what we today call Kharkistan. More than four thousand years ago he drove a vast army here in search of a legendary power. Whether he thought it would grant him riches or something greater is, mm, unknown. There is a great chasm in the northern end lined with volcanoes now called the Pit of Kharkis. With great loss of life they marched to the Pit... and into the arms of a nameless dread. None of them ever returned.' He shook his head. 'The stories say that they numbered in the hundreds of thousands. What chance have we?'

'Perhaps more,' said Rast firmly. 'You cannot hide a quarter of a million men. We may be able to slip through where they failed. So is that our destination?'

'The only place that has any mention of mysterious powers, of something lying hidden, is the Pit of Kharkis.' The old man trembled. Karland couldn't blame him.

'Figures,' he muttered.

Rast shot him a look. 'It could have been worse, lad. We could have descended at the other end of the valley and had another fifty miles to travel through swamp and jungle.'

'So that must be where this powerful thing lies,' said Xhera. 'This Emperor Kharkis may have wanted it for the same reasons we do.'

'That would make sense,' admitted Aldwyn. 'It is written in the most ancient texts that he was at the end of a long reign as Emperor, and much of his power had been lost. He was the most powerful warlord this world has known. It is the only place this hidden power can be.' Aldwyn looked nervous at the prospect of journeying there. 'The danger is great, Rast. We may not survive this attempt.'

'What is important is that we try,' said Rast. 'We did not survive this far only to turn back here.'

Grukust nodded in agreement. 'We with you, Aldwyn. You not need to fear.'

'Find the key, save the world,' whispered Karland to himself. It was no longer funny.

❧　☙

They finished lunch and packed their things. Rast retrieved his rope and carefully re-coiled it, checking for any signs of fraying. He didn't bother to replace his tunic, although he slung his lightest cloak over his shoulders for shade. The air down here was humid, and with the sun blazing in full force it felt like another climate altogether. The others also lightened their clothing, except Grukust, who had not deviated from his single wide baldric and leggings. His feet were so rough that he could step on brambles without much effect, and he sweated profusely to compensate for the heat in the manner of orks.

They scrambled down a slope of soil and scree before clambering down a pile of rough, large boulders. It was hard going, but they managed it without mishap.

Finally, one after the other they set foot on the sandy scree at the base of the fall and looked around. There was little nearby but the tail end of a marshy section bordering the lake. The true swamp lay far around the lake to the west – this was muddy, but dried rapidly to cracked earth and then the beginnings of sand. Further west before the true swamp the sand touched the water to form a long beach strewn with dark rock formations that stretched north, deeper into the small dunes.

Rast pointed them northeast towards the base of the cliff, hoping to skirt many potential dangers. They quickly found that the marsh deepened right up to the rocky wall. It did not look passable, and any attempts to swim it were dashed by the signs of quite a few writhing snakes.

Aldwyn muttered in carrying tones that they looked like relatives of several poisonous varieties that he was aware of, and turned west. Karland was thankful after he saw the bulk of a snake thicker than his waist winding its slow way past them in the muddy water. It might have been seventy feet in length, and wrestling with it while drowning in mud didn't seem like a particularly good idea.

Grukust called that he could see a firmer patch, and moved ahead, testing the ground gingerly. One foot sank deep in after the fourth step. Rast grabbed his arm and helped him out of it. The ork nodded thanks, and then dropped his equipment, axe included, and turned around, moving fast for the rocks.

He clambered around them and vanished. Just as Karland wondered if the ork had had enough and was leaving, he reappeared with a stick a little shorter than he was, and almost straight, looking like a sapling stripped of leaves and branches. Moving back to the fore, he waved it at Rast.

'This help,' he grinned. Rast nodded.

Testing the footing with the stick, Grukust found a relatively firm way through a shallower part of the swamp. They progressed carefully until Xhera cried out just as they reached halfway to the sandy shore.

Following her pointing finger, they saw strange humps jutting in pairs above the mud, watching them solemnly. They vanished one by one to reappear a second later. It wasn't until they raised further to follow their progress that Karland realised they were the protruding eyes of large and strange-looking horned frogs.

They swam jerkily alongside, watching the company. None of them came close, although a few found firm land and clambered out to watch them. They were about the size of a medium dog, no higher than mid-thigh at biggest, and extremely rotund. They offered no aggressive behaviour, and seemed more curious than anything else. Wide mouths that made them look shocked when open, along with double chins and their rounded bellies, made Karland think of big slimy melons with fat legs. It was an amusing image.

One hopped half-heartedly and stuck its backside in the face of another crouched in the mud. The offended recipient flailed wildly with fat limbs in outrage, prompting a shriek of laughter from Xhera, who was fascinated with them.

'Not everything here is filled with antipathy for all other life, it seems,' mused Rast, smiling slightly at their antics.

Aldwyn laughed. 'I think they are perhaps relatives of the, mm, spineshank frog of Matalaga that I have read of. They have those horns, though. Very odd! I wonder if they are for defence or, aha, mating rituals. Perhaps they have changed beyond the need for the defences of the other frog.' He appeared to be thinking to himself.

'What defences?' asked Karland curiously, eyeing the frogs and laughing. They were so fat and pompous-looking! There might have been thirty of them, but even so he couldn't think of them as a threat, or see what defence they could muster against a predator.

Aldwyn blinked. 'They convulse and break bones in their feet and ribs.'

'They do *what*?'

'Well, then they drive the sharp fractured ends through their skin and into an attacker-'

'Their *own skin*?'

'Um. Yes.' Aldwyn adjusted his spectacles and looked at the frogs closely. 'Maybe these are just poisonous,' he added lamely. 'Or agile swimmers.'

He watched several of them floating like giant green bubbles, bumping into each other and pushing each other mindlessly underwater in a thrashing panic, and frowned. Xhera was giggling incessantly.

Grukust was looking at them sceptically. 'You not serious, old man. Nothing do that. It stupid.'

'It is recorded, actually,' replied Aldwyn haughtily, 'by an *almost* unimpeachable source.'

Grukust stared at him suspiciously, and then moved off, muttering in his own language.

'What?' asked Aldwyn, mystified. Karland laughed again.

CR   SO

Eventually they either passed from the frog's territory, or the fat, haughty-looking things tired of them; they disappeared quite suddenly. Shortly after that, they began to leave the marshland. The mud became gritty, and then they were trekking over sand which stuck to the mud on their feet in a very annoying fashion.

They halted for a brief rest on dry ground. To the north the sands stretched out for over thirty miles, shimmering with heat. It seemed to collect the rays of the sun like some kind of mini-desert; although relatively small, it offered as parched a death as any larger sands. They hadn't seen any bodies of water north, and only a few west, none a tenth of the size of the great lake behind them. The sun beat down through the still air. High in the cloudless sky above them, another form circled on spread wings.

The surrounds were quiet, thought Rast. Not peaceful so much as… watchful.

They were almost a hundred feet from the shore of the lake on the sandy beach bordering the little desert. Immediately to the north one of the dark rock clusters reared, silent in the heat. It looked as if it was the result of volcanic activity, but was heavily eroded. Rast said that if sand blew hard enough in wind, it would eat even rock away after a while.

'While we are here, should we fill up from the lake?' asked Aldwyn. Rast looked at the tiny desert before them and nodded.

'Perhaps, but we should boil the water.'

The company moved for the shore, the water washing lightly and placidly at the edges. They were nearly halfway when Rast stopped, senses alert. Grukust hefted his axe.

He peered at the lapping water not sixty feet away. Nothing moved along the shore as far as he could see. The only breaks in the shoreline were several large tree trunks washed up onto the sand in the distance. The sun sparkled in the quiet water.

Aldwyn frowned. 'What is-'

The edge of the lake erupted in foam and spray as something enormous lunged from the waters, impatient that its prey had moved no closer. Aldwyn shrieked and fell over. Rast dragged him bodily to his feet before an amphibious reptile that must have exceeded forty feet in length.

The long fat body was slung low between short, thick legs that came out to the side, with webbed and clawed feet. The back was armour plated, with a twin row of flat bony plates down the centre. Curved spines jutted from chin and eye ridges, and several rows of dark vertical scales ran between the plates in the back from head to tail tip, growing longer as they went. Long tapered jaws with ragged conical teeth gaped wide in front of emotionless yellow eyes. Rast had seen these before, but never like this.

'Crocodile!' he shouted. 'Back! Get back!'

Grukust tore the axe from his back, snarling. Its initial lunge was short, and now it hissed open throated at them. The hiss was very deep, like a loud exhalation, and unnerving. It spoke of hunger and death.

Rast held its eye and waved his hand. 'Get to the rocks behind you. Climb them! I will distract it.' His body was tensed.

'I stand with you,' growled Grukust, hefting his axe. Rast saw Karland grab Aldwyn's hand.

'Come on!' he shouted to Xhera, who was staring at the crocodilian in shock. She blinked and took Aldwyn's other hand. All three ran for the rocks and began to scramble to the top.

The creature lunged again, the maw slamming shut with a crack. Rast and Grukust scrambled back. With sudden and unnerving speed the great reptile sped forward, jaws wide. They split up, Rast darting left and Grukust right. The beast hesitated before snapping at Rast.

Grukust darted in and swung his axe, which merely bounced off the armour plating despite the edge and his great strength. The beast hissed low in anger again, and then rumbled in rage as the axe bit deeper into its side on a truer strike. As it swung to the pest biting into its armour, Rast's right hand slipped down to his waist and withdrew a long, slim, slightly curved single-bladed knife with no cross guard, one of the *shirkas* he had bought in Punslon.

He sprinted in from the right and slammed the blade as hard as he could into a depression behind its eye. He leapt back, knowing crocodiles had a soft spot behind their eyes.

Either it was not like normal cockindrills or the knife was not long enough. The head scythed sideways to snap at him. Rast pulled his legs up under him in a desperate jump, and the snout shot underneath. He fell on the top jaw and managed to hook an arm over it. Instinctively he slammed his other arm around the bottom jaw and held on as hard as he could, adding his legs to the grip. The beast shook its head wildly, unable to open its jaws.

He caught a glimpse of Grukust on the base of the thrashing tail swinging his axe around his body in an arc. It swept up behind him and hung glittering in the bright light for an instant, and then swept downwards with all the power in his rock-hard body.

The axe bit deeply into the beast's back. Shuddering violently, it moaned and jerked its head so hard Rast lost his grip and was thrown backwards. Grukust cursed harshly; the axe head had been turned from a true hit by a thick bony plate, although it had sheared through part of it.

Freed again, the head snapped at Rast. He ducked, slamming his closest fist into its emotionless slitted eye, extracting a hiss of pain. The head jerked away reflexively. Rast caught a brief glimpse of Grukust rearing back on top of the giant amphibian, his axe in two hands above his head for another mighty chop into the armoured hide. As he swung downwards, the giant crocodilian suddenly rolled, throwing Grukust sideways.

As the ork was mid-air the crocodilian's whipping tail slammed into him with bone-breaking force. He flew headlong, limp, blood trailing. His axe whirred away in a glittering arc, and thumped into the sand twenty or more feet away. Rast couldn't tell if he was still alive.

The beast had rolled back to its feet and lunged for Rast. He threw himself to the side as the gaping mouth shot in again. A ragged tooth scored the outside of his thigh deeply, causing a dark gush of blood, just as the huge jaws cracked shut on the trailing edge of his cloak. Without hesitation, the *shirka* in his hand sliced up to cut the tie, and he swirled out from under it. The giant reptile threw its head back, tasting blood, and the jaws snapped shut on its prize. It shook its head powerfully. The crocodilian was so intent on the morsel in its mouth that it didn't see Rast until it was too late; he sprang at the head, his bleeding leg nearly buckling, and sank the slightly curved blade up to his knuckles in the glaring yellow eye as it contracted to focus on him.

The huge reptile went berserk, jack-knifing its entire body in agony. A low hissing moan came from it, and its jaws clashed over and over, the cloak a ragged mess on its teeth. Sand sprayed in a wide arc as the tailed dashed it high into the air. Rast narrowly avoided being crushed, leaping backwards and rolling. He fetched up against the rocks, bleeding heavily. The gash on his leg was deep, but ran along the muscle rather than across it. He clamped a hand over it. Assuming he didn't bleed to death, it should heal well.

The creature in front of him was in a frenzy, all thoughts of food gone. It hauled itself bodily towards the water, mouth still gaping wide but this time in pain. It bellowed again as it hit the water and the cold shock washed into the eye socket, filling the jellied remains of the eyeball with icy fire. Thrashing deeper, it moved quickly out and was lost to view.

Rast pulled himself to his feet, grabbing a shred of his cloak, and tied his leg tightly. Then he stumbled to the inert form of the ork. Grukust was breathing, but had blood running down his temple, and it looked like a few of his ribs were cracked.

He had no time to do more. The rumbling hissing returned, multiplied threefold. He looked up to see several more crocodilians leaving the water nearby, attracted by the commotion. Crocodiles did not usually attack far from water, but these were very aggressive. Desperately, he tried to lift Grukust, but knew he could not move him fast enough. He cast about for Grukust's axe, but it was lying fifty feet away. He would not reach it in time. Rast looked up.

From the top of the rock, Aldwyn, Karland and Xhera were watching in horror. Rast's only refuge was the rock they were on, and it seemed unlikely he would reach safety. Certainly he would have to leave Grukust here.

Rast crouched in front of Grukust, feeling the blood begin to flow from his leg again as the cloak remnant tore. His *shirka* was lost somewhere in the sand during the battle with his last foe. Rast's hand moved towards the small of his back, drawing his second *shirka* even as he despaired that his charges would be left on their own in this place if he fell.

The biggest crocodilian snapped at another one that had got too close, its head and jaws longer than Rast was tall. It was even bigger than the first one that had attacked them. As it scrambled forwards Rast tensed, focusing on its strike. Another was right behind it, and he could see the third moving in from his left in his peripheral vision. Time had run out. This was one fight he could not win.

A roaring shriek and a gust of wind that made him stagger heavily was the only warning he got as the huge reptile to his left was suddenly yanked backwards violently. Seconds later a bellow that deafened him erupted, and the whole thirty-foot long reptile was flung across his vision, knocking the other two into a hissing snapping mass on the sand. He whirled to his left, his leg giving way. Dropping to his hands and one knee, he confronted something that could not possibly exist.

An iridescent creature that dwarfed the reptiles attacking him crouched on the sand, snarling in challenge. He blinked. It was a shining reddish-gold, and was a true titan; a horned head that must have been twenty or more feet in length was held low above the sand, stretched forth on a long, slender, but powerful-looking neck. The snout was long and tapered, and held a vast array of sharp teeth, longer than swords. At the front, long dagger-like canines rose above the rest, two at the bottom and two longer at the top. The teeth had more in common with a tiger's than of the ragged conical arrangement in the mouths of the long-snouted crocodilians attacking him. Closely-placed nostrils expanded and contracted on the top of the snout as the gargantuan creature breathed. Behind this, slightly to the sides but far more binocular than a normal reptile were two golden eyes that actually glowed brightly with a red hue from deep inside. For the first time, he understood what the phrase 'burning gaze' really meant. The pupils were a concave diamond shape, and locked threateningly on the huge amphibian reptiles.

Behind the head was an equally tremendous body. Lithe and powerful, a deep chest sharply narrowed to a slim belly. Vast pinions carried wings that were curved to the side in threat. They were similar to those of bats, although they were equipped with large claws at the joint and sprang from the back behind the shoulders. The membrane allowed some light through but looked thick and pliant, the veins within visible as dark burgundy ropes. Powerful forelegs ended in paws the size of logging carts which were dug deep into the sand. They had the look almost of hands rather than mere claws, as if they had benefits of both, and three large, long digits tipped with long sharp talons curved from the front of each hand-like foot, a fourth spread back at an opposing angle.

Further back, the spine humped up before dropping away to powerful looking hindquarters, with three-toed feet and a huge sharp spur further up the leg, like a feline dew claw. A tail descended, thick and sturdy at the base but becoming delicately tapered, ending in a flattened diamond shape. It coiled away, the end lashing angrily. The underside of the immense being had brilliant white scales that changed abruptly to red on the upper flanks. The largest was bigger than a shield, and they all reflected light as if they were pearlescent. It was a truly breathtaking sight.

It must be well past two hundred feet long, thought Rast light-headedly as he struggled to haul Grukust's limp form behind the nearest rock. Steam seemed to drift from the nostrils, and then, impossibly, a flame that was visible even in the sunlight jetted out with another roar. Rast blinked, wondering if he had seen correctly.

The colossal creature was fierce and proud, a true predator. It snarled in challenge, answered by a triple hiss. The creatures were not familiar with the intruder, and their numbers made them bold. Fiercely territorial, they ignored Rast and attacked the new threat.

As they weaved towards it, mouths gaping dangerously, it reared up with a full-throated roar, wings flapping and sweeping sand high into the air. Two reached it at the same time, one snapping high at the throat, and one trying to snag a wing. The first received a mighty backhand blow from one of the forearms as it lifted its head. The thirty-foot long reptile wheeled away end over end, its thick neck broken. At the same time, the other claw slammed down on the second crocodilian's head, impaling the skull to the sand. The stocky legs scrabbled in death, the amphibian voiding its bowels messily on the sand.

The largest arrived as the second died, and launched itself at the muscular forelimb. The outsized jaws slammed shut with devastating impact, the ragged teeth digging in. The creature hissed in fury, and to the party's astonishment lifted its arm – and the entire reptile – into the air. It was immensely strong; the last crocodilian must have been nearly fifty feet in length and probably weighed a third of its opponent. The giant creature glared at the foe latched onto its forearm and then snapped its head down into the underbelly, the dagger-like canines scything through the thick armour, flesh, and bone like fabric. The teeth met as the reptile opened its mouth in silent agony. It spasmed, its internals in shreds, and died.

Rast looked up and saw Karland peering over the rocky lip above him, and gestured at him to hide. The boy vanished, pulling the others with him. Rast carefully peered around his shelter to be met with an unsettling sight.

The impossible beast was crouched with a fifty-foot corpse hanging limp in its jaws, its long tail curled around its body and the head raised on the long neck. Blood ran down the dangling head and tail. It looked strangely like a cat with a dead mouse, but its bright gaze was fixed firmly on the rocks where the party hid. The eyes darted to Rast despite his care, and the creature blinked and then deliberately dropped its head to lay the dead crocodilian on the sand. Pacing one fore claw on the dead body, it bit deeper and tore the entire mouthful free, most of the guts and chest cavity. It threw its head back on its long neck, hurling the mouthful to the back of its throat, and swallowed it. A large tongue flicked out to catch some of the runnels of blood. It was delicately forked at the end but rapidly thickened towards the base.

Rast froze. His gaze dropped to the foreleg – or was it an arm? – that had been bitten, and saw to his amazement the scales were barely marked.

There was no way they could fight this foe. Nothing mortal could harm it.

It padded softly over to the rocks, the armoured scales clattering slightly. The vast creature moved like a great cat, too, stepping lightly and with controlled grace despite its vast bulk, leaving prints fifteen feet long in the sand. Its head obscured the bright sunlight, casting the top of the rock into shadow. He looked up to find himself being regarded intently by blazing red-gold eyes that froze him in place, above a snout higher than he was tall.

Rast was looking at a dragon.

ɔ஧   ஦

Karland could not move. The intensity of the glare drove out all thought but overwhelming fear. It was a truly primal reaction, a defenceless creature faced with a supreme predator, and he waited to die. Next to him, Xhera whimpered, but could not move either. He did not know what had happened to Rast and Grukust – for all he knew, they were already dead.

The silence stretched out, and the head moved forward, sniffing, and then whuffed a heavy exhalation over them, hot and musky. Then he heard the last thing that he had ever expected.

'Greetings, ah, honoured *Nāginī,*' quavered Aldwyn's voice, shaking in fear.

'*Hajinamastë maitumhē kenkyo xiàng nìmen,* um, *vinamra anatpūr vaka ō mukaeru badhī.*' Of all of them, the old man had summed up the courage to act. Karland caught Aldwyn's bow in his peripheral vision and wondered how the scholar had the strength of will to even think, let alone move.

There was a terrible further second, and then the dragon blinked. The head drew back, and to his eternal shock, it spoke.

'*Nì wā jiàngèrsu zhōngo Nāgārì dā wén bōlatè?*' it rumbled, an almost human expression of surprise crossing its face. The words were almost liquid, and vibrated through the rock. There were tones in there that no human could hope to reproduce.

'Um, *Bahen shāoka sukuna.*' He coughed, and added under his breath. 'I think.'

The dragon snorted.

'And very badly, human. *Very* badly. But that you speak it at all is… astonishing. Men have not spoken my people's tongue for many ages.' Its voice was still liquid, imparting an extremely archaic and flowing sound to the Darum they all spoke. With the smouldering gaze removed, Karland found he could move. He tried not to look directly at the creature's hypnotic eyes for fear its will would overwhelm him again.

He turned his head to find Aldwyn peering over his spectacles at the dragon, clasping his hands nervously. Xhera was staring at the enormous being in wonder, and he understood. It was a beautiful creature, seeming to make everything around it a little more dull and drab, as if its very vitality shone through its skin.

'*Nāgìnī.*' Aldwyn spoke again. 'You have our deepest thanks for saving our lives. We would have likely perished without you.'

The dragon cocked its head inquiringly. 'What are mortals doing in a place such as this? You are unlikely to survive the perils that dwell within this divide. It grows more perilous as you count your years. And you address me correctly; I would know how you come by such knowledge.'

Aldwyn nodded. 'Yes, of course. But may we climb down and tend to our friends? I fear they may die without attention, if they still live.' The words sent a spike of panic down Karland's spine. He had forgotten about Rast and Grukust! A gasp from Xhera told him that he wasn't the only one.

'Their hearts beat yet,' said the dragon without moving its head. Karland marvelled at senses so fine that it could hear even that. 'You may descend. Tend to your friends, and then I would talk.'

Aldwyn bowed in reply, and allowed Karland and Xhera to help him down the side of the rock. It was high, and Karland marvelled at how they had climbed it so fast without thinking before.

It is amazing, he thought, *what incentive can do.*

Reaching the bottom, they found Rast sitting with his back to the rock, Grukust made comfortable beside him but still not conscious. He was looking up at the dragon with a strange expression on his face. As they started for him, he turned his head and smiled weakly. His hands were clamped hard around his thigh. Red leaked through them slowly, and his leg was darkly crusted and drying.

The sand around him was spattered with blood; he had lost a great deal. Xhera squeaked in dismay, and Aldwyn drew in a sharp breath. Karland was shocked. Rast had always seemed so untouchable. Now he sat, pale and still, concentrating hard to slow his heart rate and blood loss.

Aldwyn dived into his bag, and pulled out a large leather roll. Karland had seen it before, although he hadn't realised Aldwyn had brought it with them. The old man unrolled it on the sand and snapped a finger at Karland.

'Get the pot, quickly. Fill it with water. We must boil it. I have comfrey and yarrow here, but it will need to be applied as a poultice.' He peered at Rast, who returned a wan look. 'I will need to clean the wound.'

Rast nodded. 'I am in the first stages of shock, my friend. I don't think I will feel it. But hurry. I have… lost a lot of blood. The artery is intact.'

Aldwyn looked at his eyes and nodded. He opened a small thick bottle with a tied wax plug which was full of a dark purplish-yellow liquid. Turning the wound to face upwards, he poured a small amount down its length, deep inside. Rast breathed in sharply but made no other noise. Hurriedly, Aldwyn unslung his water skin and squirted some into the wound, mixing with the tincture. He waited, and then used more water to flush the wound clean. Looking at it with a professional eye, he pursed his lips.

'It follows the muscle fibres and should heal clean. It will be stiff for some time; the wound is deep. If it was left untreated, infection or blood loss could kill you.'

'Thank you for that,' breathed Rast, his lips tight. His eyes drifted closed as he concentrated on controlling his breathing again.

'Karland! I need that water now,' barked Aldwyn.

Karland looked up in despair. 'I cannot light the fire! I am trying.'

A vast shadow blotted out the light. 'Allow me to help,' said the dragon. 'Place the pot securely in the sand and stand well back.' Karland did so, and the head dipped, the eyes focusing on the small pot. Gigantic lungs drew a sharp breath in, causing a gust of air, and then the mouth closed slightly. The throat contracted as muscles narrowed the airways, and a small jet of flame came out, swiftly narrowing and focused into a hot point. It played over the sand and the side of the pot, rapidly heating it.

After several seconds the side glowed slightly red, and the sand underneath it began to slag slightly. As they all looked on in astonishment, the water steamed quickly and began to bubble, and the flame died.

The dragon regarded its work critically. 'That should suffice,' it said over the crackle of glassed silicon. Aldwyn shook his head in wonder.

'The legends are true,' he whispered.

Karland blinked, and then realised the water was hot. Running over, he used a gingerly wrapped hand to pick up the pot. The ground was uncomfortably heated under his boots, and he skipped quickly back to his friends. Aldwyn quickly crumbled plenty of yarrow into it, and added a small amount of comfrey.

'Tincture of, mm, iodine, will help kill an infection, but it must be washed clean. Hot water with yarrow should be packed in the wound if it is this deep… comfrey will help bones and flesh knit, but you must use it carefully. Too much can cause damage to the liver,' he instructed Karland as he prepared it. 'I wish I had five-flower with me, ah, for the shock.' Karland thought that the old man was largely talking for the benefit of the others.

The steeped herbs were applied as a poultice. Rast was recovering surprisingly quickly, regulating his breathing and body. The big man watched without comment, though it must have hurt increasingly as the shock wore off.

Xhera was having less trouble looking at the gaping wound than Karland. He could see dark red muscle fibre, slimy and bloody, and it made his own leg hurt in sympathy.

The dragon had watched all of this with interest. 'Mortals are so fragile,' it said. 'Yet you survive. You are fascinating.' Karland wasn't sure what to reply to that.

While they waited for the herbs to have an effect, Aldwyn checked Grukust. The ork seemed to be all right apart from an ugly bruise to the side of his face and several bruised ribs.

'Nothing broken,' Aldwyn muttered. After he had applied comfrey to the affected ribs, there was not much he could do but make Grukust comfortable and hope he would wake soon. He had saved some of the comfrey and yarrow in the hot water for when – if – that happened, and swiftly added a variety of other herbs to it. Karland busied himself hunting for the dropped weapons as Xhera sat with the two injured, her expression worried.

Shortly afterwards Aldwyn carefully removed the poultice from Rast's wound and cleaned it. 'We must stitch this,' he said, pulling an odd thick curved needle and a spool of catgut from the pack. Rast lay calmly while Xhera pushed the edges of the wound together and Aldwyn deftly stitched it, ensuring it was not too tight. 'Don't burst these,' he said, peering over his spectacles at Rast. Rast smiled wanly. Aldwyn pressed the wound lightly with his hands, concentrating on the touch and whispering for long minutes.

As he cleaned up and rolled his medical kit up, the dragon, which had been crouched patiently watching the proceedings, stretched like a colossal cat and shook its body with a clatter, then turned its intense gaze back on the party.

'If you are finished tending your friends, little mortals, I believe it is time for you to answer my question. Why are you here?'

THIRTY-TWO

K arland shook Xhera, who was frozen in fear in the bright gaze. 'How do we stop this fright?' he hissed to Aldwyn, trying not to look up.

'Do not look directly into her eyes,' the old man replied, echoing his suspicions. 'At least for now. The gaze of a dragon is powerful.' Karland nodded, and turned Xhera's face away. She drew in a shuddering gasp. Abruptly, he turned his head back to Aldwyn in astonishment.

'*Her?*'

'Well, yes, boy. She is a female dragon. That is why I addressed her as *Nāginī*. If you speak to her, make sure you use that term. It is a sign of great respect.'

'But how did you know she was a- a lady?' whispered Karland.

'Is it not obvious?' asked the dragon, sounding taken aback. Karland gulped; her hearing was unbelievable. She lay coiled thirty feet away, and her head was at least another thirty feet in the air. 'We often have an unwitting effect on lesser races. Do not look directly into my eyes. The dragonfear is strongest then.' She yawned widely, showing a dark red throat and a mouth that could engulf the entire group with room to spare. Her forked tongue curled up, fully mobile. She continued to the scholar, 'And I am still awaiting your tale, human.'

Aldwyn bowed hastily. 'My name is Aldwyn Varelin, *Nāginī*. The wounded man is Rast Tal'Orien. The boy is Karland, the girl is Xhera, and the ork is Grukust. I believe dark times are coming, and have studied long to find a solution. Whilst in Eordeland, our town was attacked by many foul orcs-'

'*Ghàichū*,' murmured the dragon in disgust.

'Indeed. We followed their trail after they were defeated, looking for information. The nations are in uproar, human realms are on the brink of war, and fell creatures stalk our lands. We hoped to find answers in the Pit of Kharkis.'

The dragon laughed a little cruelly, her teeth flashing silver-white in the sunlight.

'Fools. You mean the chasm to the north? I tell you now you waste your journey. There is no secret power there to save you. Heed my words.'

'So Kharkis was wrong,' Aldwyn said despondently. 'This power does *not* lie in the Pit.'

'All that you will find in that dark place is death, human,' rumbled the giant creature. 'This valley is but a pale imitation of the horrors within your… *Pit*.' She dropped her head slightly, looking at them through slitted eyes. 'It is dangerous for even a Dragon to be here. This valley is filled with dire things that feed on each other. It should not exist as it does. It is unnatural and I like not the feel of this place. The presence of great evil has warped it further; many of the creatures here hate natural beings, of which my kind are the pinnacle, with all their fibre, their perverted hunger. They can sense our power, our vitality. Some lesser dragon kind have even died here.' There was some arrogance in her voice, an overwhelming assurance of her own powers. 'What was this passage in your book?'

Aldwyn sat up straighter, as he often did whilst dictating information. '*Tá cumhachtaí móra fuasgail ag eochair, laistigh de logh ucht an sliabth,*' he said. 'It was written by Sarthos millennia ago in Ancient Ignathian. *Great powers unlocked by key, within deep hollow of the mountain lies,* mm.'

'So you follow prophecy here?' asked the dragon, her eyes opening a little more. 'What is this key?'

'We don't know, but we think it has something to do with this.'

Aldwyn fumbled the pendant out. The dragon had no difficulty focusing on the tiny characters; her burning eyes were as sharp as her ears.

She rumbled in surprise, and her eyes widened, pupils dilating to circles from their previous diamond shape. 'This is *Naga-tō!* An ancient script of the tongue of *Zhōngo Nāgāra*, the language of my people, in *human* hand!' The full force of her gaze swung on the old man, and he cowered away. Karland and Xhera cringed instinctively.

The dragon took pity on them and slitted her eyes again, the glow dimming. 'I recognise that script, if not the hand that wrote it,' she said reflectively. 'It explains much.' Her head rose again, her eyes opening wider. 'I know what you seek, mortal. Long ago my kind were given into their keeping the greatest power a mortal can possess. It does not lie here. It lies deep within a holy place in those you call the Arkon Mountains, inside our most sacred peak of Drakeholm Soaring.'

'I know that name!' cried Aldwyn. His face twisted in misery and realisation. 'Stupid! Stupid! I was terribly wrong.' He sighed heavily. When he spoke again, his voice was filled with anguish. 'The phrase... it could be interpreted as 'the hollow *within* the mountains'. Or even *a* mountain. Curse my purblind bones! This place, Drakeholm Soaring... I have heard of it in connection with a legend called *The Hall of Wyrms*. Men give it many different names, but it is the highest peak in those mountains – and in Anaria.' He lapsed into brooding silence, and then turned a troubled countenance to the others.

'I have nearly got us all killed, many times, and for nothing,' he said quietly. 'We have wasted so much time! I should never have come on this quest. I am a fool.' He glanced at Rast resting against the rock, and Grukust, still not awake, and his expression spoke volumes.

Karland tried to find words for his friend. *He* knew it wasn't Aldwyn's fault. They would still be in Darost, probably at the mercy of assassins, if not for him. Aldwyn had done more than anyone to try to avert the disaster that was creeping upon them all. He opened his mouth, and was forestalled by Xhera.

'Don't be silly, Aldwyn,' she said fondly. 'You are the one who made us all see what was going on. If not for you leading us here, we would never have known about this power, or the pendant, and would never have met this dragon – ah, *Nāginī.*' She hesitated nervously, seeing if the dragon had taken offense. The vast creature returned an unreadable gaze through her still-slitted eyes. Her presence was becoming gradually more bearable.

Karland added his support. 'You are the most important person on this quest, Aldwyn. The rest of us are only here to help you see it through. If you want someone useless, well. That's me, really. I've not been exactly important on this quest.' He recalled Letizya morosely. 'A burden, if anything.'

Aldwyn looked at them gratefully but shook his head. 'That, my boy, is, ah, where you are wrong.' He paused, his face grave. 'You are bound up in this too at least as much as I... It may be that you will both be equally as important as me, mm.'

A soft call from Rast interrupted him. It seemed Grukust was stirring. They all clustered around the big ork. He was smacking his lips slightly, a frown of pain on his face. His eyes opened, and half-focused slowly, questions plain on his face. Blinking, he looked at them, and then put a big hand to his head.

'*Ahei.* What happen? Am not dead?' He turned his head carefully and saw Rast sitting nearby, pale but smiling slightly. He tried to sit up, taking a deep breath, and winced in pain. '*Ah!*'

'Careful, my friend,' said Aldwyn. 'You have serious concussion. Several of your ribs are also damaged, though not broken I think. That giant crocodile caught you solidly with its tail. I am amazed you survived.'

Grukust groaned. 'I remember big lizard. Don't remember what happen after. I not *feel* like I survive. Feel sick.'

Aldwyn nodded. 'That will be concussion. Now you are awake, I can give you something to help you. Karland, Xhera – make sure he is comfortable and relaxed. He needs rest.' He vanished off to find his bag. Grukust tried to focus on the other two. Karland felt his face split into a huge grin.

'I'm so glad you are awake!' said Xhera, relief in her voice, and she hugged him carefully around his neck. Karland slapped his shoulder, and Grukust tried to smile back.

He shook his head carefully. 'Why we all not eaten up?'

'Rast wounded that creature, and it fled,' said Karland, 'but it hurt his leg. He could not carry you away in time. More came, and I thought we were all dead.'

'So?'

'Well, we had some help.' Karland nodded in the other direction from Rast. Grukust turned painfully and found an enormous face framing a mouth as wide as a cave, rimmed with teeth longer than his axe was tall and regarding him with a blazing gaze that stripped him to his soul.

'*Yaaaargh!*' he yelled, trying to scramble backwards, the agony in his ribs forgotten. His hand scrabbled for his axe, but before he could lift it Karland grabbed the haft, and Xhera gently took his bruised face.

'*Nononono*! It is all right,' she said intently. 'This dragon saved us. She killed all of the creatures!' She cast a glare at Karland.

'It was amazing!' Karland chimed in. 'She just… slew them. I have never heard of a battle like it.'

'Dragon?' asked Grukust, his heart still pounding from his fright. Karland sneaked a look at her. The vast face held a reptilian interest, perhaps even faint amusement at his reaction.

'Dragon,' Grukust muttered to himself, and clutched his head. 'I have headache. Maybe I not woken up yet.' He groaned. 'Maybe I dead and this one of the hells.'

Aldwyn returned, glaring at the youngsters. 'Well, so much for keeping him, mm, *relaxed*,' he said severely. He held out a water skin. 'Drink this,' he instructed. Grukust eyed it suspiciously, trying to focus on it, and the old man sighed. 'It's a mixture of herbs,' he said. 'Comfrey, yarrow, Jonaswort, jinkigo, liquorice, ginger, a few others. They should help with pain, swelling and sickness, even with your physiology. Now, are you going to drink it? Or do I have to ask our new friend to help?'

Grukust glowered at Aldwyn, and then tried to snatch the skin from him. His hand missed the grab; it appeared he was seeing slightly double. On the second attempt he caught it, and drank it swiftly, making a face at the mixture of tastes. Karland and Xhera helped prop him against the rock next to Rast, where he sat with his eyes closed, waiting for the herbs to take effect.

Rast spoke, his voice tired but firm. '*Nāgìnī*. May I ask why you saved us? I thought that dragons were not interested in the affairs of mortals.'

The dragon smiled, her lips pulling back from her sharp teeth. 'I am not usually, human. I have been uneasy. The world... does not feel as it once did. I took to the skies to stretch my wings, and see why I could not rest easily. You are correct when you say your world is in turmoil, nations and nature alike. It is evident from above. I have seen many such groups of *Ghàichū* journeying here – many of those foul things live here, hidden in their holes. I observed you descending into this valley and start north, and I wondered what could make mortals do something so stupid. Then I saw you attacked. I was curious.' She looked over at the carcasses of the amphibians before continuing.

'There is a host of the fallen creatures gathering in the east of this forest, on the slopes of the mountains and in the trees. Many tens of thousands upon thousands, perhaps as many as fifty. Also humans, to my surprise. Your people in particular are ever strange to me. Of all the races, your behaviour is the hardest to predict or understand; I believed you hated orcs.' She snorted, heated air washing out of her huge nostrils.

'Two turns ago I spied you moving towards this valley. Foolish mortals, how little you realised. You would have run into the arms of a group at least a thousand strong, and not all of them *Ghàichū*.' Her tone grew puzzled. 'I saw... an *Edhélū*, I think. A *Chīkyū noko hàizi*, perhaps a prisoner. Filthy *Ghàichū*, *bōtodà èdú kēli'ēiva!* I destroyed them all, but it was already gone. It troubles me. There should be none this side of the mountains.'

'*Edhél?* An Elf, here?' asked Rast, bewilderment plain on his face. She nodded.

'It was you we heard!' cried Karland. 'You attacked them all?' Now he understood what creature could destroy a thousand orcs so quickly. He was suddenly fervently grateful she had been curious enough to talk to them first.

The dragon chuckled, the first time that they had heard her show humour. 'They were no threat to me, and I took them unawares. The Elves have always respected us, so I decided to lend aid. I do not know why it fled.'

She paused for a long moment, and then fixed her gaze on Aldwyn again. When she spoke, her voice was grave.

'Your words were correct, little human. The world is changing. Things that have always been are no longer. Things that never were, now are. There *is* great evil here in this place and it has warped much of what lies surrounding it, augmenting its hunger, changing other life as it itself has been changed… but it is not what you seek.'

'What could be worse than the things in this valley?' asked Xhera. Karland nodded.

'Much,' hissed the dragon unsettlingly. 'But I can give a name to the source of the change. It twists and warps, perverts and alters, and stems from four Demons not of this world. They are cold, dark, deadly, soulless, these Lords of Chaos. They have no connection to any world; born in the void between stars, children of the Abyss, they are cold, dark, empty and alone and draw strength from Outer Chaos. These demons have warped many worlds, and came here long ago, but were forced to hide from my greater kin. They have no true names, but we call them *Suŏbhī nō Qūzhújiànvansaka.*'

Karland shrugged, tired of all these words he didn't understand. 'But what does it mean?' he asked, looking at Aldwyn.

His friend was staring at his feet, his face ashen. He spoke one word, dimly remembered as the nightmare to end all nightmares. The monster, the demon, the devil that all others were afraid of. The death of everything.

'Darkling.'

ɑ   ɛ

Karland didn't know what to say. He recalled old stories, about a demon other demons feared, a cold destroyer not of this world. Rast had an unreadable look on his rugged face. Xhera whispered next to him, 'The world eater.'

Grukust muttered, '*Ragnarökkr.* Demon of legend that swallow sun, break plains apart, crumble mountains into ash. Now we fight myth? My head hurt too much for this.' He lapsed into a brooding silence.

The dragon spoke again. 'Even more curious. It seems I was right to aid you. How strange! Mortals questing for that which a dragon seeks. I must find my kin and tell them of what is to come, but I think I should talk with you more first. You, the human with the white hair-'

'Aldwyn,' he muttered.

'-Aldwyn. You are learned for one of your race – impressively so. I would speak more with you on your findings. But that can come later; you should leave here. With two wounded companions you will not climb the east wall again, I think. There is a narrow slope behind the swamps in the southern end.' She reached a decision. 'I will see you there safely, and we will talk as we travel. There is much here I would know before I see my brothers and sisters.'

Aldwyn bowed. '*Nāgìnī*. You do us much honour.'

'Indeed. But it benefits us both,' she replied. 'We know little of the mortal world. My kin would likely disagree, but I think mortals can be valuable. You live complex, fast and disorderly lives in large groups – an excellent measure for marking the progress of chaos, in my experience. I will eat and your friends may rest. Then we will leave.' She turned away, expecting no discussion, and padded over to the massive corpse of her last victim. Settling down to feed, she began tearing the creature apart.

The popping, snapping sounds and the noises of flesh and sinew being torn were unpleasant. Karland valiantly ignored it, but he could see Xhera looked a little green.

'How do you feel?' Aldwyn asked his patients.

Grukust nodded carefully. His breathing was easier, although Karland knew it would be some time before he felt no discomfort.

Rast smiled grimly. 'I need nourishment, but I should be fine. I am just very tired.' Karland held out the two long curved *shirkas*. Rast smiled his thanks and slid them back into the hidden sheaths that followed his waist front and rear, cutting edge out.

'I will bind your leg for travel,' said Aldwyn.

After Rast's leg had been dressed the party made ready. Karland couldn't wait to get out of this valley now that they knew their goal did not lie here.

The dragon turned back to them, her tongue pulling the last shreds of flesh and armoured hide from between her teeth. The remains of two of the consumed reptiles lay behind her next to the third.

'I feel better,' she announced. 'As we are to travel together a way, let us know each other. Aldwyn I know of. You are the human Rast Tal'Orien. The ork is Grukust, and the younglings are Karland and Xhera.' She sat on her hindquarters, her head some seventy feet in the air, and put a huge fore claw to her chest.

'I am named Györnàeldàr.' The word was wrought with subtle tones; Karland knew he could never pronounce it as it should be said. They bowed to her.

'You honour us with your name, *Nāgìnī*,' said Rast.

The dragon laughed. 'I have not encountered your kind for many of your centuries, yet now in one small group I finally meet learned and polite members of my races. You certainly are not the base animals some of my brethren name you.' Karland blinked. 'Know that I will consider the debt you owe me paid when you have answered all of my questions to my satisfaction.' She gestured south, along the shore of the lake toward the swamp. 'Come.'

They set out, their new companion loping along lithely beside them. It must have been frustrating in the extreme for her to move so slowly, but she padded gently along with reptile patience. Karland was fascinated with her movement. She was so large he expected her to shake the ground beside them, but instead her tread was light and he barely felt it. *She must weigh less than she looks,* he thought. Looking ahead to the trees, he wondered if she would simply smash a path through them, or go around. He couldn't see how she would move between trees.

Rast's leg seemed less stiff than Karland expected. As they moved he saw that the logs they had seen on the shore were more of the giant creatures, basking in the sunlight. He wondered what lived further out in the lake; nothing good, he was willing to bet.

They travelled for some time, pausing briefly to rest. The sand began to change colour slightly, and nearer the lake gave way to mud at the beginnings of the swamp. Further back, the damp edges of the jungle loomed, ominous. The large trees were hung with creepers and were very different to those in the forest above. Aldwyn said the heat and moisture of the valley encouraged tropical growth.

As they moved along the stretch of sand near the trees, heading south, the dragon cocked her head and held out a forelimb to halt them.

'Something comes,' she rumbled.

Listening hard, the humans heard faint crashing, as of many creatures running through the jungle. Strangely, they seemed to fade or run parallel to them, instead of getting closer. They barely detected a rising rustling noise before a horde of ant-like insects the size of a human hand erupted from the low trees in their thousands. They were dark in colour, with blind white eyes, oversized jagged mandibles, and spiny legs. They moved in a carpet, covering a wide area with their formation. Along the edges scouts moved, feelers waving to test the surrounds.

They crossed the sand in front of the party, moving towards the lake, until one of them found the tail of a smaller crocodilian. A column swerved and descended on it. At first it seemed impervious to the swarm, but then several found their way into its mouth, biting its tongue, with more clustering around its eyes. It snapped in anger, and then whipping its tail in pain it scattered them, crushing many, and ran for the water's edge, its body held up between its stumpy legs and its head waggling. Submerged, the hangers-on quickly drowned. The amphibian reptile surfaced, watching the living carpet at the water's edge.

Without a victim, it began questing again. The insects appeared to be on the march, most of them moving out onto the sand to the north. A column moved towards the party, sensing something.

A huge inhalation was all the warning the mortals got before a mass of searing yellow flame exploded out from the dragon, charring thousands of the insects in an instant. The survivors swarmed back and north again, away from the deadly heat. As they began to cross the sandy region, the ground seemed to open and a mass of vast humps broke over them, consuming many in wide mouthfuls. It looked like a writhing mass of giant worms.

Aldwyn's voice was weak. 'I say.'

'Let us leave here quickly,' said Rast. 'This place is fell and strange.'

They had to cross the jungle to avoid the wide mouth of a river that flowed from the jungle edge, dividing sand and swamp, and here they were lucky. The mass of insects had consumed any creatures in their path, leaving nothing but bones and shreds. The jungle was quiet, everything else having fled, and so they moved unassailed through the dim trees, the canopy much thicker than that above.

Karland watched, fascinated, as Györnàeldàr weaved through the trees – in here she moved like a snake on legs, flexible and quick. They came to the river, narrower here amongst the trees, and their companion obliged by uprooting a wide, dead trunk that was leaning on a living neighbour, and laying it over the rushing waters. They saw no living creatures, but many of the strange pitcher plants were evident. There were also occasional giant red blooms that looked like sweet-smelling sticky berries, and gaping ovals on stalks with fronds hanging over the jungle floor.

Decomposing animals warned them off the sticky-looking plants, which Aldwyn named Sundews. It was clear that anything trying to take the sweet nectar became trapped, doomed to a slow digestion. The giant ovals were a mystery until Aldwyn noted their similarity to Matalagan Wasp-Traps. When Györnàeldàr poked one experimentally, it snapped shut and coiled upwards as if it had just taken prey passing underneath. Vines that would wrap around an unwary foot lined the floor, with hidden, unpleasant-looking grooved black spines lying flush on them, ready to snap out. Many had been torn up and apparently eaten. It was clear that even with predators avoiding their behemoth companion, this jungle held plenty of dangers, and likely dozens they had not yet seen.

They broke thankfully from the thick strip of trees as light faded, and moved out onto grassy hummocks surrounded by a swamp to the south. There they made their camp that night, the dragon coiled around the perimeter as an impenetrable wall. Her head lay inside and she spoke to Aldwyn long into the night. The scholar was ecstatic to realise that the dragon was far more learned than he was and to share what he had learned. He removed his notebook from his bag, a summary of his studies, and they pored over it long into the night. He had no problem reading it; with the advent of night, her eyes lit their entire campsite.

Györnàeldàr seemed both interested in and troubled with his findings. They spoke away from the others in mixtures of older languages for hours, Aldwyn taking notes. Eventually Karland lay down to sleep, ignoring the rumbling conversation. Aldwyn was even happier than when he had spoken to Night, and he was nearly stammering in his haste to question her.

The next morning they readied themselves early, Aldwyn's snores echoing through the campsite. Rast asked if anything had approached during the night.

'Many things came near,' she replied, 'scavengers and hunters both, but they did not approach too closely. Perhaps my protection is not required, however. Nothing living could withstand the assault my hearing bore last night.' Her gaze flicked to Aldwyn, who was blinking and looking around.

Karland hid a grin. He would not have guessed their somewhat alien companion had a sense of humour.

'Eh? What? What?' Aldwyn asked, straightening with a look of genuine bafflement. Grukust laughed and then winced.

'Pack your bag,' said Rast, straight-faced. Xhera giggled.

The day was better paced than the last one. With rest and firm level ground, Grukust and Rast seemed much improved. They camped again that night, the next morning moving over the grassland towards the western cliff face, where a relatively small strip of solid land bordered the bogs which became the lake edge. Wide paths worn in the grass here spoke of the passage of beasts great and small. Once Xhera spied what looked like a horse in the distance, and cried out in delight, but Györnàeldàr looked closely at it and sniffed, and then dismissed it as a flesh-eater.

Xhera was not convinced that anything looking like a horse ate flesh. Karland distracted her by talking about the wonders of the last few days, and they walked together for some time. Eventually Xhera asked how he was. Karland knew she was talking about Letizya.

'I'm fine,' he said, surprised that it was true. He hadn't thought of her in days, and his dislike of meat had faded. 'How about you?'

She smiled back at him wanly. 'I have been far too worried about creatures to think about Hoge much. It seems so long ago.'

They camped that night and the next on the rolling grassland stretching between the bogs and the cliffs. Both times the dragon coiled around them. At one point she raised her head in the dusk to stare at a herd of the creatures Xhera had thought were horses gathering a couple of hundred feet away. Karland had a good look at them. They were smaller than a horse, although they had hooves, but spiny hocks and flashing canines dispelled the illusion of a true equine. Yellow slitted irises gazed hungrily, and when one threw its head back and a strange snorting snarl came out, it drove the point home. Emboldened by numbers, thirty of them stood around the dragon, their hunger battling their fear.

She fixed them with a level gaze, and then blew a long blasting arc of flame at them. It was a fat yellow-orange flame, but it was still hot enough to set several manes on fire. Frantically rolling, the strange herd erupted in an odd hybrid of whinnies and yelps, and fled. They did not return.

She stared after them. 'Beasts here are fey. They fear me less than they should.'

That night Aldwyn described what had happened recently to them. At several points he whispered to the great creature, who gazed at the rest of the party with interest, her burning eyes now a comfort as much as terrifying. She discussed matters with the scholar deep into the night, at times with an almost human expression of concern. Eventually, she said, 'You have convinced me that that these changes for mortals may not mean that we remain untouched. Now I must convince my people. I will stay with you until you are free from this valley. I fear that you will not survive if I do not. If I needed convincing further that balance is lost, I need only look here.'

She blinked, casting the camp into fleeting darkness, and then turned her gaze to Rast. 'Rast Tal'Orien. Aldwyn has told me many tales, that you are considered extremely dangerous among mortals, skilled in the arts of battle and killing. I saw for myself how you fought the water-beast, hindered only by your companions. Once you gain the lip of this valley, you and the ork must keep them safe. You must leave these woods as fast as you can – the creatures to the east of the forest are many and I could not protect you. It is better if you slip past unseen, unknown. I shall distract them as I pass and hope that it is enough for you to escape.'

Rast nodded. 'It will have to be enough. Györnàeldàr, I thank you for all that you have done.' He bowed fluidly, his leg still a little stiff.

Grukust nodded. 'Do not worry, dragon. We keep them safe after you gone.' He saluted her, banging his chest with his fist. His initial fear and anger had changed into a great respect for her strength.

She stared at them a moment, and then her scaled lips quirked up, baring her teeth in what Karland hoped was a smile. 'I consider my debt paid,' she said in her liquid tones. 'I have gained valuable insights. Truly mortals have an...

interesting way of thinking about things. Perhaps it is because your lives are so short. Sleep now. Tomorrow will bring us out of this place.'

હ   ૬૦

They rose later the next morning as a result of the late-night discussion. They saw little in the way of beasts as they moved south, everything avoiding them. Not long after noon, they finally reached the end of the swamp, which curved to the left. Across the narrowed valley was a gently inclined path through the low cliffs, just wide enough for a forest elephant.

A small herd of the massive creatures was wading through the marshland, too big for the crocodilians to attack. They moved slowly through the muddy waters, their trunks bubbling the mud up for some unknown purpose. Györnàeldàr eyed them. Since she had feasted on the crocodiles Karland had not seen her eat anything apart from soils and some rocks, swallowed whole after careful sniffing. Karland had no idea why she did this, and was not about to question her.

Aldwyn had less reservations and asked her why as an active creature she did not have to eat often – something about conservation of energy. The dragon had replied that she gorged once every few human days, consuming flesh and bone. They descended into a more technical discussion that left Aldwyn scribbling notes in his book and muttering to himself when they stopped to rest.

Finally, with a sense of great relief, they broached the lip of the valley. Rast reminded them that this forest was still dangerous for them, but out of the oppressive heat and danger of the valley below, Karland was greatly cheered.

He was soon brought down to earth when Györnàeldàr said it was time for her to leave. Since those first moments when he was frozen in fear awaiting death his perception had radically altered. He found he was going to miss her, and it appeared he was not the only one. Aldwyn especially looked downcast.

'She is the wisest being I have ever met,' he had confided to Karland the day before. 'I feel like a child beside her. Such a wonderful, mm, mind! She forgets nothing. I have learned much that even our Library does not hold, I think.'

Now Karland looked at the trees and shivered, former memories of Letizya returning. He hoped they did not encounter her.

'Watch for me on the lower slopes of Drakeholm Soaring,' the dragon said. 'Well below the snowline, on the southwest slopes, there is a small plateau with a great circle of rocks against the mountain's side. At the back lies a great rock, riven in twain. There is the entrance to our sacred place, where this great power of mortals lies. There is a path up to it made by wingless mortals ages past who made offerings there to our people, as if we were gods.' She sounded amused. 'I will meet you there in half the cycle of the moon. That should be long enough for you to journey to Drakeholm Soaring, if you hurry. I must meet with my kin and discuss what we spoke of – if I can find them. Bring your pendant and we shall see if your key can be found. I will gain the attention of the horde to the east so you may slip past. Stay to the west! There is evil yet in these woods.'

They bowed, Xhera attempting a curtsy. Grukust thumped his big fist on his chest.

'Farewell, mortals. We may meet again soon,' she said, and turned. Padding away from them, she sprang upwards over the treetops. Her dark pinions caught the air, and with a few powerful sweeps, she was lost to view.

THIRTY-THREE

With the dragon gone, the forest seemed almost preternaturally quiet. Her low passage over the trees left a ripple of hush spreading in her wake as everything her shadow touched instinctively froze in fear. Rast took his bearings and then beckoned them into the forest.

He spoke in a low tone. 'We must be swift, and silent. If this army is as big as she said, we are in real danger of discovery. We will make for the Pass through the woods to the west of the main trails. If we must flee, do not hesitate. I will do what I can to delay any pursuers.' Karland glanced worriedly at Aldwyn, hoping his friend could stand the pace.

'Is your leg work properly?' asked Grukust.

Rast grimaced. 'It will have to suffice. What of your ribs?'

'Better.' The big ork grinned. 'Maybe Aldwyn know something about healing after all.'

'I should say so, too,' sniffed the scholar. 'After all my years in Morland with the Daktarim!' Karland smiled. Aldwyn had been teaching him the basics of real healing for a year and more and he still had little more than a basic grasp; the old man had told him little about the years of study on the southeast coast amongst the dark skinned folk there. The Daktarim were held without peer in the arts of healing, using skills far beyond mere herbs.

Not long after they entered the trees, they heard a very faint roaring to the northeast, accompanied by screams and shrieks. It seemed that Györnàeldàr had bearded the host and drawn their attention. The cries echoed for some time before quietening down.

The party moved as fast as it could through the trees. They heard echoes in the woods but they encountered nothing. Here, closer to this army, the forest had a feeling of quiescence in it that it had lacked on their journey in.

Towards dusk, their luck changed and they found the fresh trail of one of the great forest elephants. Grukust suggested that they find a hidden camp to spend the night and follow it the next morning. It seemed to travel in the right direction and would provide them a quick and fairly well-hidden route back towards the Pass.

Rast nodded, and eventually found a heavy thicket of bushes clumped around several large trees. He carefully wormed his way into the middle, and discovered a small area which would suffice as a very cramped campsite for the night. Tired and tense, they lay down to sleep quickly.

Karland woke with a start during the night. It was strangely quiet. He saw Grukust starting alert with his axe, and raised himself on his elbows. He nearly gasped in surprise when Rast's huge shadow melted noiselessly from the surrounds. Grukust nodded, and Rast stood listening. Then he knelt next to Karland.

'Go back to sleep,' he said in very low tones, not whispering; the harsh noise would carry further than a murmur in this stillness. 'Something has passed us by.'

Karland nodded and lay his head back down, then started up as realisation occurred. Rast held his fingers to his lips warningly. Karland bit down on the whisper and glanced at Aldwyn's still form again, then looked at Rast, concern on his face. The old man was not snoring, not moving.

A ghost of a smile flashed over what he could see of Rast's face. Relieved, he settled down to sleep, and was lost in dreams again.

He awoke to a quick shake in the dim light of a pre-dawn. Grukust grinned at him through tusks that were cream in the low light, and moved on to Xhera. He shook Aldwyn awake with a big hand over his mouth. Aldwyn snorted and sputtered as he floundered towards consciousness, but the noise was muted.

Karland wondered how they had stopped his snores. Rast muttered to him, 'We fixed a small pointed stone to him so he didn't turn to his back.' Karland nodded, the sudden urge to laugh bubbling up inside him.

Anxiously, they moved on quickly. The dawn chorus was slowly awakening. They had a brief period in the lull to make haste along the trampled trail they had found the night before. The day began heavily overcast, which did nothing to improve mood.

It was mid-morning on the third day when they ran out of luck. The elephant trail turned west, towards the northern end of the Dimnesvale. Rast struck out north through the trees, and their progress slowed as the undergrowth thickened.

Forced nearer the main trail, they were crossing a small stream when Rast stopped mid-stride and whirled. Almost in the same instant grating yells and screeches erupted, and a band of orcs charged from the trees. Karland cursed the ill chance as he ran towards Xhera.

Rast leapt at the first orc and ducked under its ragged blade, spinning past it. The orc swung around to follow him and so did not see the axe that hit it in under the arm, folding it with a coughing cry.

Rast sprang into the air, spinning horizontally over two stooped orcs, one cutting at where he had been and the other stabbing with a spear. He landed on his bad leg, wincing, and rotated, the other leg sweeping them from their feet with a clatter. They dropped with a shout, and he fell elbow first onto the face of one, locking his legs around the neck of the other and twisting hard. With a wet crack, its neck broke, and he was up again. If his leg still hurt, he gave no further sign. He deflected three short sword thrusts with his bare hands and then brutally trapped and broke the arm as he disarmed the orc. Whirling in place, he nearly beheaded another orc with the sword he had just taken. Leaving it halfway through the creature's neck as it collapsed, he slammed a jab, then a cross and then an uppercut into the one he had maimed. The blows were faster than the orc could follow. Its jaw unhinged, it dropped limply.

Grukust was in the middle of a spinning figure of eight, his axe head flashing around him like the blades of eternity. Several orcs fell crippled or dead to his assault as he impartially lopped off whatever was closest, head, hand or leg. Lacking Rast's poise and finesse, he instead taught them the fierce merits of brute strength and skill. One orc pushed its comrade onto the tines, fouling Grukust's swing, and turned towards Rast.

It pulled out a long balanced knife with a rough-looking blade and threw it with all of its strength at Rast's unprotected back as he faced four of its kin. Grukust punched another orc in the face with the haft as he lunged forwards, roaring incoherently.

Rast twisted in one motion, somehow sensing the blade, and his hand unerringly found the hilt as he snatched it from the air. Continuing the momentum, he followed the blade around and sank it into the chest of the orc nearest him. It gasped at the unexpected attack, dark blood foaming from its mouth as he punctured its lung. In almost the same motion, he reversed and threw, the knife whipping from its victim and leaving his fingers in one movement.

Grukust leapt forward, his axe high, and then watched in astonishment as the orc fell backwards in front of him, rigid, with the knife standing cleanly from its left eye socket. It landed over into the stream, its lank hair waving in the current, the knife standing almost straight up. There was oddly little blood.

The big ork looked astounded at the unexpected removal of his victim.

Karland watched Rast's dance of death with a feeling akin to delight underneath his nervousness. He did not feel ready to fight, whatever Rast had taught him. The huge man was mesmerising. Fluid, fast and powerful, he flowed between his opponents, killing and maiming with ease. A ruin of shattered limbs, broken bones, and dying orcs littered the ground where he had danced. Karland realised there would be no quarter given here. They could not afford to be given away to the host east of them.

In rage, Grukust tore through the group of three orcs facing him, looking dangerously close to going berserk. The twin blades dealt dismemberment and death with each blow, and he handled them lightly. None of the foe could stand before him, and the remaining three turned to flee only to find Rast waiting for them, having killed the rest.

Two of them lunged at the human in desperation, a ragged sword and a dark stained knife lancing for him. The third fled, heading for the trees. Rast swayed out of the path of the sword, striking the forearm of the orc. The sword dropped from nerveless fingers. He rotated, his leg flashing out and striking the other orc just below the sternum with brutal force. There was a sharp crack, and the creature flew backwards straight towards Grukust, who was waiting with his axe back akin to a boy waiting with a stick to hit a flying rock.

He swung the huge axe and hit the orc hard. The unfortunate creature folded around the blade and then fell soundlessly in two lumps, a spray of thick dark blood curving through the air. Even as the halved orc hit the floor, Rast had hooked an arm backwards around the neck of the other, and twisted as he dropped to one knee. The orc flipped in mid-air, landing on its back, its neck popping in Rast's powerful grip. The limbs jerked and it went limp.

Rast stayed kneeling for a second, and then saw the last orc almost out of sight. He sprang up and ran after it. Grukust ran after him, his axe in both hands. They vanished into the trees. Karland waited expectantly, listening for a death cry. He nervously scanned the bodies, not all of which were yet dead, but none of which were in any shape to attack. Nothing else moved in the woods. He counted fourteen of the foul creatures.

Movement in the trees made him grip the knife he had taken from the witch's hut tightly. He relaxed when he saw it was Rast and Grukust. Their faces were grim.

'Did you catch him?' he asked, knowing the answer already. They shook their heads.

'My leg is not fully healed,' said Rast grimly. 'He was too quick among the trees. This bodes ill, more than I thought; I have not heard of orcs out in the day before. There was no sun, but they hate any daylight. If they hunt in the day, then we are out of time and options once that orc reaches its kin. Our only hope now is to run for the Pass – and hope we reach it before they do.'

ଓ ନ

They pressed on hurriedly, Rast limping slightly. He spoke quietly so they could all hear.

'It will take some time for an army that large to come through the trees and traverse the Pass. I know not what their purpose is, but I do not doubt that some will come for us. An orc horde this big has not been known for millennia. Without warning, they could destroy everything clear to the western coast. We flee for the Pass not only for our own lives but those of many others.'

Aldwyn shook his head, breathing hard, his tunic stained with sweat. 'Armies of orcs... and men. I wish... I had been... wrong.'

The pace was punishing. The only concession to stealth was the continuation of their route through the trees, avoiding the road and stopping only to fill their water skins in a small stream and twice for Aldwyn to catch his breath. The old man was having real trouble keeping the harsh pace. Karland was worried. He didn't want his old friend to kill himself like this, but there was no alternative.

Noon came and went, and still they pressed north. They stopped again at dusk to eat and rest, Rast plainly keen to continue. Once refreshed, he urged them onward. There would be no sleep this night. Aldwyn got to his feet, looking exhausted, and Karland shook his head in worry as Grukust picked up the scholar's pack.

'If you must, Aldwyn, lean on me,' he whispered. The old man nodded, grateful, but too tired to even reply.

They hurried on as moon rose over the forest, Rast stopping from time to time to listen. In the night, the forest was much quieter. The first few times he heard nothing, but eventually he heard something that gave him pause.

'They are searching,' he said. 'We must hasten.'

Aldwyn was beyond exhaustion now. Even with Karland's help, he was on the verge of collapse. Grukust reached a decision, dropping Aldwyn's pack and unlooping his axe. Handing it to Karland with a strong admonition not to drop it, he hoisted the unprotesting scholar up onto his back, as he had in the crack in the Dimnesvale wall.

Karland found the axe heavy and cumbersome, but discovered a way to sling it over his shoulder while he scrambled through the trees, rubbery-legged. Xhera picked up the pack, pale with exhaustion but her face set stoically.

Rast led them out through the trees to the trail, to Karland's relief. He did not want to venture too near Letizya's clearing, and speed was now their only ally with the orcs actively searching; he only hoped that their luck held through the Pass. Far away, faint echoing howls crept forth again.

They made better time on the trail, Aldwyn bouncing uncomfortably on Grukust's broad back. The ork didn't seem to be much slowed by the extra weight, although he grunted from time to time when Aldwyn squeezed his bruised ribs without meaning to. Karland staggered along, horrible visions of tripping and taking his own arm off on the huge axe flitting through his head as they hurried along the moonlit trail. Switching the axe from shoulder to shoulder in a semi-trance, he barely noticed the turn off to the abandoned ironwood logging camp as they passed.

Their fortune held, and they met nothing. The night seemed to go on forever, a wearying race against unseen foes stretching into a dark forest frozen in time – and then suddenly, blessedly, it changed.

Numb and weary, they finally came within sight of the Pass, a pale winding snake that wended its way between the mismatched peaks of Iril Paúr and Iril Ech. The moon was not overly bright tonight, scattering its light through a haze, but it was enough for Grukust's night vision.

They slowed as they entered the Pass. The path rose steeply, and taxed muscles screamed with exhaustion. Rast's leg was showing dark spots of blood through the bandage, and Grukust had to force breaths deeper than before. Karland and Xhera stumbled onward and upward, almost reaching a standstill at times as the inertia of their forward momentum battled gravity on the slope. The path felt eternal, the night unending.

Finally the party reached the apex, stopping at the rock that they had rested at before. Rast sat with his leg up in front of him on another rock, gently kneading the swollen tissue then re-bandaging it to compress the wound. Grukust, lowering his burden, nearly dropped Aldwyn as he twisted and hissed in pain. Karland simply dropped where he stood, and regretted it instantly as a pointed stone bruised his left buttock sharply.

After only half an hour they moved on. The downward slope was welcome for tired legs. Rast pushed them as fast as they could move; it was a miracle that none of them fell on the dangerous path down. Dawn was breaking as they came in sight of Feller's camp, torches on the walls glowing above the low early morning mist rolling around their ankles. Karland's relief at seeing the human settlement was palpable.

A cry went up from the fort walls as the party moved swiftly to the south gates where they were grudgingly admitted. The watchman that met them was very nervous, seeming to think Grukust was an orc from the Dimnesdair. Before he could say something possibly fatal, Rast spoke.

'We need to see Danial. A host of orcs is heading this way out of the Pass. There is little time.'

The watchman blinked in confusion. 'What? He is sleeping-'

'*Wake him.*'

Another man spoke up. He was young and skinny with the markings of a Corporal of the Punslon Guard, and his face held a faint sneer. 'And who are you? Why should we believe you?'

Rast shook his head. 'We do not have time for this. Trust my words and leave, or stay and die. Did you listen? An army of orcs that will kill and defile unchecked if unleashed follows us. You must all leave here, today. Punslon and the plains tribes at the least must be warned.'

'A likely story,' scoffed the guardsman as his nervous colleague hurried away. 'Even if there are orcs, who stirred 'em up, eh?"

'Don't be a fool,' said Aldwyn sharply. 'Fifty thousand orcs would come this way sooner or later. We face *war*. It will take time for them to bring that many through the Pass, but come they will, and they have ogres and men with them. You must flee.'

'Really. And I should believe some old vagabond?' snapped the man.

'What is wrong with you?' said Karland in exasperation. 'Didn't you hear what he said?'

'I don't trust no-one who comes from the woods,' said the watchman sourly. 'Mebbe this orc you br-'

'*Mebbe* you should take your face for a shit,' broke in Danial's voice, mercifully cutting the guard off before Grukust was insulted. 'I saw them goin' into the woods days gone, and warned them of the dangers. That they come out tellin' of worse ain't exactly a shock to the system. But if someone tells *me* there's fifty thousand orcs comin', I pifin' well *listen*.'

The young guardsman bristled, and Danial shook a callused fist threateningly. He was roughened from years hauling heavy timber and looked quite ready to use his big fists as punctuation. The man backed down, scowling, and Danial said, 'Go and rouse everyone. *Everyone.* You might not think this is serious, laddio, but the rest of us ain't so stupid.'

The guard left sullenly and Karland nearly laughed, tired as he was. Danial watched him go.

'*Idiot,*' he muttered, and turned to Rast. Despite his scowling demeanour, he grinned suddenly. 'Well! Ain't sure I expected to see any o' you again! Did you find what you were lookin' for?'

'It was not there,' said Aldwyn wearily.

Grukust grinned tuskily. 'You nearly not see us again. Valley even more danger than you say!'

Danial glanced at them all, taking in their exhaustion and wounds. 'I ain't sure I care to know what you found in there. Can you spare time to rest?'

'They were far behind and may not have even left the Dimnesdair,' said Rast. 'We can rest a few hours. Ready your people to leave. This army must have been gathering for some time. For what purpose I cannot say, but there are too many for a raid. This feels like war. They bring ogres… and there are men with them. Meyari. I am greatly troubled.'

Danial looked astonished. '*Men?*'

Aldwyn suddenly cursed, shaking his head. 'We are *fools*. We asked how Meyar could sustain a war with Eordeland, Eyotsburg, any of the lands. This is how. And if they strike unexpectedly, with orc allies using human tactics-'

'Entire realms could be decimated,' said Rast. 'One ogre alone is trouble enough; may the gods have mercy on us if they learn to fight in formations. Danial – we thank you for tending our horses. Can they be made ready while we rest?'

'Right quickly. I wish you brung better news, friend, but rather I hear about it from you than find out from the orcs, haha.' He grimaced. 'Mebbe it's time men left these woods.'

Karland looked around at the grim-faced people and agreed. No one should live so near the horrors the other side of the Pass.

'There is somethin' else you should know. There was people here askin' after you. Oh, they used no names, but they described you mighty fine. An old man with eye lenses, a warrior, a youngster. They din't say nothin' about no mighty ork or a girl, and I weren't about to tell them; I din't trust them at all. I sent them packin' with some gobbledegook. They left for Punslon, but that don't mean they din't talk to no one else. I'd steer clear of town, I were you.'

'Oh, we intend to,' agreed Rast. 'Can you get word there? If the horde does cross the Pass, they may strike northeast to Eordeland, north into the plains, or west. If they move towards Novin they will raze Punslon to the ground.'

'I'll warn 'em meself,' said Danial grimly. 'I thought about what you said before. This place holds memories for me, but they ain't good – the best ones are in my own head. If I die, Sara and Tam ain't livin' on *anywhere*. These woods get darker by the month, and it sounds black as all midnight in the arse of a Morlander to me right now. I'm gettin' out of here and any who stay are welcome to their deaths. I'll warn Punslon as I pass through, and get Geraldt to follow me if I have to burn grandad's inn down. Here, you rest up. I'm goin' to make sure that moron did what I told him, and sort your horses.' He nodded to them and left the cabin.

Thankfully, the party spread themselves over the floor of the cabin. After the nights in the Dimnesdair it seemed safe and luxurious. Despite the morning light waxing through the dirty window, they fell asleep quickly, their flight having drained them heavily.

୧ ଛ

Karland woke, sticky-eyed and groggy. The light coming in the window was strong; it must be nearly noon. He glanced around to see the others still in slumber, although he didn't need to look for Aldwyn, who sounded as if he had decided to saw through the wall of the cabin in his sleep. Xhera's face was elfin and pretty in repose despite a smattering of dirt from the travel.

He sat up to find Rast standing quietly near the window. He had a fresh bandage on, and his leg looked much better. He turned his head as Karland stood and stretched.

'Don't you *ever* sleep?' Karland asked, yawning.

Rast smiled slightly. 'In my own fashion.' He pointed to the table, where food lay. 'Eat while I wake the others. I have let you sleep as long as I dare, but we must leave here soon. I fear the horde will follow us fast. Now they are discovered, they must cross the Iril Pass before they can be trapped there. Our journey lies north toward the Arkon mountains and Drakeholm Soaring. Once on the plains I hope the orcs will have other concerns than a few travellers, and I wish to avoid the orks too if I can.'

Karland nodded wholeheartedly. The others woke as he chewed hungrily at the plain bread and meat. For once Aldwyn, usually the most irritable, woke with surprising optimism and vigour given their recent trek. He stretched, his old joints popping.

'Why are you so cheerful?' Xhera asked him as she gnawed at some bread. The old man smiled.

'Well! We are free of that dreadful place. I honestly thought we would die there. And we met a wonderful creature – so intelligent, so knowledgeable! I learned so much. I wonder if we can, hmm, elect her to the Universalia Communia.' Karland nearly choked at the thought of trying to get either the dragon or the scholars to accept *that*.

'That would certainly be… interesting,' Xhera managed, eyeing Karland's coughing fit. Grukust slammed a huge hand on his back in an attempt to help. Karland nearly swallowed the whole chunk of bread in his mouth. Aldwyn didn't notice.

'For the first time, we know where we are going, what we are doing. The answers lie at Drakeholm Soaring. Györnàeldàr taught me much, and we are not alone in seeing what is happening; there is also Night, and there must be, ah, others. So there is some hope yet.' He beamed at them all, and then his face fell. 'Ah. There is no cheese? No cheese. Hmm.' He sighed and shrugged. 'Finding this key, this power, is the first step towards perhaps regaining some semblance of balance. For the first time, I feel that the most important work of my life has meaning, will be of benefit.' His beaming face seemed to have some inner peace for the first time since Karland had known him. He smiled fondly at the old man.

An outburst of raised voices a little way away brought them all back to the present. They exited the cabin. Rast led them through the strangely quiet camp towards the north gate, where the stables lay.

Karland and Xhera were sent to refill the water skins. Rejoining their friends, they found a large crowd nearly two hundred strong in a knot at the gate. There was a general uproar; few were as steadfast as Danial in making their lives here, instead preferring to stay in seasons, but most looked in agreement with the long-time woodcutters.

At the centre were several large men, one of them Danial, facing the Corporal from earlier who appeared to be the highest ranking guard here. From what Danial had said, time at the camp was considered the lowest duty of the Punslon guards, but the little man had still assumed airs from the post. The Corporal was shouting orders at the folk around him, who looked more likely to punch him in the face than obey him. Danial's rough voice cut through his sneering tones like a trunk falling across a stream.

'Well, you listen here, Corporal rat-bastard. We're all leavin', and you can stay and argue with the orcs all you like. You're here to protect us, not oversee us, see, and we are headin' for Punslon. Good luck, matey.' He punctuated it with a hard poke to the chest, and the little man flushed with rage. His hand flailed for his weapon, his men trying to stop him, and one of Danial's colleagues laughed.

'*I wulnt,*' he said, lifting the axe haft he was leaning on. 'I reckon I knows how to use this better than you do your little pig-sticker. Come with or stay and die, but I seen too many men go missin' these parts in recent times. I ain't goin' to die here for nothin'. Those traders in Punslon want the pifin' trees, they can come and talk to orcs about it. I seen 'em here before. Fifty or fifty thousand, these woods ain't safe no more.'

'Anyone else agree with this little snot merchant here?' shouted Danial. The crowd shouted back, the vast majority demanding they leave now. The big man caught sight of his guests and smiled.

'Only needed an excuse,' he called. 'Rest of us are tired of worry, turns out. Took a lot less than I thought it would. Upshot is, Corporal Pustule here can stay. We are goin'.' He looked to the crowd. 'Best go pack now, you lot. By nightfall, this here camp will be home to nowt but mud and insects.' He looked meaningfully at the Corporal, and several people laughed amidst a general chorus of agreement. The crowd broke up, moving for their homes. Karland grinned at the look on the Corporal's face, and Xhera laughed aloud.

'You may not have until then,' Rast said quietly as he approached. 'Orcs hunted us in the day, although it was heavy with cloud. They will not move through the pass in this sunlight but I wager they have their own tunnels through. You may be lucky.'

Danial nodded, and walked with them as they moved for the stables. Stryke and Hjarta looked well groomed, and Rast thanked him. Against his protests, he pressed another small pouch of money on him.

'You will need it, if you are leaving,' said Rast. He smiled warmly. 'You have been a true friend. Thank you. Where will you go?'

Danial shrugged. 'There many trees in Eordeland?'

'Quite a few, my friend. Inns too. Good luck, to you and Geraldt.' Rast clasped hands with him. Danial bade farewell to them all, not hesitating when it came to the big ork. Grukust grinned at him.

'May your axe be ever sharp, human.'

Danial grinned back. Karland had seen him eying the war axe with professional interest.

They led the horses out and mounted. Aldwyn handed the reins to Karland with a flourish. 'Your turn, my boy. I need to rest.' He looked much refreshed, but the rigours of the last few days had told on him. He still had dark circles under his eyes.

Rast moved for the trail at a trot. He was still wary, and did not like the fact that they had been followed to the camp, so planned to skirt northeast to avoid Ork territory and then west along the roads into the foothills of the Arkons.

Aldwyn believed it would be easiest approaching from the Dwarven settlement of Deep Delving, where they could restock.

It was a pleasant ride in the sunshine, easing their hearts after the last few days of tension and fear. Grukust loped tirelessly next to the cart, and Xhera and Aldwyn chatted brightly over his books. She had taken them from the small chest and laid them out, asking him questions while he leaned back and checked them carefully. Karland grinned to himself. Aldwyn had taught them both much about a wide array of subjects he never knew existed, from healing to tactics, politics, and more esoteric things.

He held up one book. 'Of all these, this is the treasure beyond compare.' Aldwyn looked very proud. 'My journal. The only book I took into the Dimnesdair. It holds observations, notes, thoughts, details of our quest. This is the latest volume, mm, of many.' He beamed. 'But *this* one holds information about Dragons that no one else has. The Academia Esoterica will be green with envy when I publish this.' His eyes were bright behind his spectacles, and Karland chuckled.

'Despite the danger, life is good,' said the old man reflectively. 'For the past decade I have lived with a growing fear. Then I came to fear not just for my life but the world. Today I feel that we may not fail yet!' He picked up his pack and rummaged in it, pulling out a red apple, fresh and shiny.

'So we have a chance to make things right?' asked Karland, one eye on the road.

'That's right, mm, my boy.' Karland watched him take a bite, talking in a more muffled voice. 'We have come further than I hoped we would, and seen things unseen by others. We have gained a powerful ally. This is the first step, aha, to turning the tide. What was it you said? 'Find the key, save the w-''

He stopped abruptly, a choking sound coming from his throat. Karland turned, half amused, thinking to thump him on the back to dislodge a bite of apple. To his horror, there was a thick black arrow sticking out from his friend's throat, piercing the airway and exiting next to the spine. The blade was cruelly barbed and broad; thin streams of blood ran down from the two wounds. Aldwyn looked astonished, trying to breathe in. Pieces of half chewed apple falling from his mouth, he tried to form words, and then he fell over backwards, clawing at the arrow, his thin chest heaving and what breath he got rattling wetly. He landed on the books he so loved, missing Xhera by inches.

Karland dropped the reins and dived for his friend, screaming, '*RAST!*' even as Xhera shrieked in horror. Another arrow sliced through the air where he had been sitting, but he barely noticed it. 'Nononono!' he said desperately, trying to deny what he saw before him. 'We need you. *I* need you! *Aldwyn!*'

Aldwyn's mouth opened and closed, his rheumy eyes staring in pain and fright at his friend; then he convulsed and died, Karland his last sight. His hands lost their rigidity and fell limply. His mouth was fixed open, lined with blood, and his eyes lost their vitality.

Karland stared at him, his face twisted in denial and loss. Tears welled up, prickling hotly in his eye, blurring his vision. His throat was constricted so hard it physically hurt, and a low moan was forcing its way through it. Next to him he could hear the shocked sobs of Xhera and thud of another arrow into the side of the cart, a world away. His friend lay, spectacles askew, gone forever.

He was just talking to me.

He grabbed a cooling hand and looked up desperately, searching for Rast, for some miracle that could undo what had just been done. The huge man whirled Stryke to the right and whipped his hand forward from his waist. The hidden *shirka* left the sheath in a spinning blur, ending up standing from the throat of a bowman who had thought himself well hidden. Choking, he staggered out of the bushes, red blood pumping down his front where the blade had struck the artery, and collapsed. Karland howled; it was a fitting death in kind.

There was a chorus of shouts from the trees and men erupted from the bushes. They held their weapons low or behind them, and had the look of professional soldiers. Another arrow winged towards Rast, but he threw himself to the other side, coming off Stryke and landing on his feet. As the arrow shot over the saddle, he sprang forward under Stryke's belly, sprinting full speed at the attackers.

Grukust roared in fury, tearing the axe from his back, and swung to engage the threat. Three reached Rast and struck with swords simultaneously. He should not have survived, but he somehow whirled through unscathed and struck back.

One fell with his comrade's sword through his ribs. Another, weaponless, snatched at his knife even as Rast chopped the wrist, then gripped and tucked it. The man's leg came out to base himself, and Rast bent forward and stomped viciously on the outside of the knee, a snarl on his grim face for the first time. It broke loudly, the leg at ninety degrees sideways, and the man screamed as he dropped to the floor, landing on it hard and passing out. Even as Rast stamped, his leg curved back up and he turned and hooked his heel around the face of the third attacker. The man fell backwards, dazed, and Rast leapt after him, landing his full weight through his knees on his chest. There was a chorus of ghastly snaps as his ribs buckled and snapped, and bright blood squirted from nose and mouth.

His emotions dulling in shock, Karland saw Grukust reach a knot of four men who were heading for the cart. They turned to meet him, trying to surround him, but they were not prepared for the ferocity of the attack. The axe hummed in an arc faster than they expected, and they leapt back to avoid decapitation, then jumped in.

They were probably not used to fighting someone as strong as the ork, however, and he was a master of his weapon. He tightened his core and pulled downwards, rolling his arms over. The axe curved sharply down and then back, this time at leg height. The nearest man had his sword raised, and the axe caught him square on the thigh, slicing through and breaking the femur. Grukust's phenomenal strength virtually tore the leg from the man, rupturing the artery and sending him into his comrade. Shuddering with the release of blood and gasping from shock, he lay twitching, his face greying rapidly. The other two attackers stumbled around the unexpected impediment and were met by the ork's enraged glare, and his axe.

Karland could see he was fully berserk now, foam flying from his mouth, and his face was a terrible sight. One of the men quailed, and then lurched backwards and dodged around the ork as the other stabbed at him. Grukust swayed to the side, the sword laying his shoulder open in a deep slice, and heaved the axe upwards. The man was already moving backwards and the axe caught him in the crotch, shearing up through flesh and arteries in a deep gouge that missed the pelvis.

He flopped backwards oddly, his stomach muscles severed and his guts sliding free. The last man was pushing his dying comrade aside, awash in red blood. He could not see clearly, the spray having caught him across the eyes. As he wiped them he just had time to start screaming as the heavy axe blade fell across his head above the eyes, crushing his forehead and tearing the entire top of his skull off. He spasmed, the remnants of his brains spattered down his back and running from the emptying bowl.

Grukust howled in triumph, looking for more to kill, and saw the knot around Rast, who was ducking and spinning as they slashed at him. Stryke was with him, lashing out. Many were down, and even as the ork ran towards them, Rast trapped another arm and used the elbow to slam the owner full length into a tree, smashing his face. He slammed his free foot into another's face, launching him backwards, and then shifting his grip, he raised his powerful arm and smashed his elbow down across the wounded man's collarbone. It snapped, the jagged end plunging deep into his thorax, and Rast let go of the now-useless limb and hit his open palm hard against the chest as he pressed the back of the shoulder in. The man jerked as the end of his own splintered bone tore into his lung, and he fell, coughing blood violently, each cough ripping the end deeper.

Numb, Karland watched the one left facing him chopped down, knowing Rast could not move in time. Xhera gasped as Rast clapped his hands over the flat of the blade as it descended, arresting its fall. The young man's eyes bulged in astonishment and he pulled down hard, but the blade did not move. Rast's piercing blue eyes bore into him, as they stood locked for a second.

Grukust's axe caught the man at the base of the neck, chopping downwards into the body and almost halving him. He wrenched the axe back up, blood arcing over him. The ork looked like a nightmare come alive, his tusks, face, and torso running with gore in rivulets of red on green skin.

The body fell, limp, and Rast was left holding a sword immobile by the blade. Two more men broke and ran for the trees. After a moment the one recovering groggily from the kick to the face whirled and followed. Behind them, the second bowman rose up again, no longer foiled by the close combatants. Rast's second *shirka* whirred flashing towards him even as he drew and took him in an eye socket. His arrow flew high and was lost among the trees.

Roaring incoherently, Grukust powered after the three fleeing men. He was beaten to the dazed one by Stryke. The horse wasted no time in furiously stamping the man into the forest floor, and the ork disappeared into the trees after the other two.

Rast was left facing two men, lean and forbidding. He glanced backwards and hesitated, and Karland followed his look to see a man with a drawn sword drawing near and another with a skewed leg hopped towards them. Rast would not reach them in time.

THIRTY-FOUR

I gnoring the approaching bandits, Karland held his knife in white-knuckled hands, a deep hot core of molten fury inside him growing by the second and threatening to overwhelm his reason. He knelt next to his friend again, and looked at his still face. An expression of surprise, shock, and terror was imprinted on it. Xhera was holding Aldwyn's other hand, sobbing bitterly.

Karland could not bear to see his friend like that. A ringing started in his ears, and he gently removed the spectacles, somehow unbroken, and placed them to the side. Using his fingers to close the open eyes he ran them down the face, feeling the weathered texture of his friend's features, the bristle of his eyebrows, relaxing the muscles and composing him. Aldwyn could be the most dignified person he knew, he thought distantly. It was only right that it was returned at the last.

He gently replaced Aldwyn's spectacles. The ringing in his ears was growing, and his breathing was tight in his chest. Xhera looked up at him tearfully, stroking Aldwyn's gnarled hand, and something unbearable gave inside him.

He turned and dropped down to meet the nearest approaching man, glad for a demon to fight. The ringing was there, the fury, but they were locked away behind cold doors. He stared at the attacker with contempt.

The man grinned when he saw Karland's smaller blade. He wasn't much bigger, but he obviously had military training. Karland noted the fact almost casually, and stood loosely, waiting.

The man lunged with his sword, the point slicing for Karland's throat. Karland blocked, slashing it out of the way with the knife held along his forearm. The man's eyes reflected surprise – he hadn't expected that. He slashed this time, and Karland leaned slightly back, not going over the centre of balance, and let the blade pass. The instinct Rast was building was awakening. Always before, he made mistakes, panicked, failed. Now in this cold calm everything seemed obvious.

The attacker moved in warily, flicking the blade up then stabbing. Karland ignored the misdirection, watching his opponent's face. He moved out of the blade's path, stabbing with his own knife. He missed the hand of his foe by a mere inch, and the man recoiled in reflex, then lunged at Karland's eyes. Karland nearly stumbled trying to evade the blade, and the man was on him. Just as fast, he was dancing back, cursing, a thin red line up one thigh. Karland had recovered balance quickly and moved fast, slicing upwards and catching the man a lucky strike almost without meaning to.

They circled each other warily. Karland wanted to hurt him, to kill him, but he knew little more than defence. The man had no such limits and would not misjudge Karland again. He raised the sword, the tip unwavering. Behind him Karland saw the other man hopping, his leg twisted badly at the knee. He reached the cart, Hjarta shifting nervously at the noises and watching them all carefully, and leaned against the nearside wheel for balance, watching with a cruel smile.

Distracted, Karland was almost spitted as the man in front of him lunged, encouraged by cries from his comrade. He began trying to circle again, to drive Karland around and expose his back to the wounded man. Karland was becoming desperate, and tried unsuccessfully to close. With his fear, natural movements slowed, and his calm receded.

None of them were prepared for the empty but sturdy wooden chest which crashed into the shoulders of his foe and sent him stumbling forwards, to a yell from his comrade. Almost of its own volition, Karland's knife entered his chest, sliding between the ribs with deceptive ease. Karland felt the heart beat weakly along the blade he held. The man gasped and dropped his sword; blood dripped down Karland's hand. The man's own arm raised weakly to touch the boy's hand, and then he slid off the blade, his mouth opening and closing like a fish trying to breathe.

Karland caught a split-second glimpse of Xhera's pale and tear streaked face. As he tried to comprehend what he had done, there was another scream.

Hjarta, frightened by the sudden movement of the chest being hurled, had nervously lunged forward a few feet. The man leaning on the wheel fell, the wheel trapping and twisting his badly hurt leg. At his agonised scream, Hjarta flattened his ears and danced further. The man's other leg fell between the spokes and hoisted him up, the rim of the wheel shattering the shin of the damaged leg while the spokes trapped and snapped both the bones in his other shin against the cart.

Xhera lunged for the reins, a horrified look on her face. Bringing the shaking dray to a halt she peered over the edge at the unconscious man. Karland ran over and pulled him free, dragging him carefully to a tree and propping him upright next to the cart. He was sickened by the man's injuries. They would leave him a cripple at best, but he wanted, needed, *demanded* answers. The man moaned piteously, coming to, and Karland stood back.

He looked around for Aldwyn, needing his healing knowledge, and then bit his lip in agony at the loss that flooded through him. Blinking back tears, he looked for Rast instead. The big man was away at the edges of the trees, fighting two men at once. Something about this battle was different from Rast's usual fights; as he watched, Karland realised that both the men his friend faced were also experts in advanced combat. For the first time, he watched men trained in similar styles battle each other, and it was a truly awe inspiring sight.

There was less sheer brutality, and much more finesse. The violence was there, but tempered to avoid mistakes. Rast blocked cleanly and efficiently, with no big movements, his style different against two armed opponents.

There was a flurry of motion, and one of them was empty handed. Karland could not quite tell what had happened, all three of them lunging and striking at lightning speed, but he saw the short sword flip end over end to slap into the dirt. With the sword gone the weaponless man engaged at close quarters, trying to grapple so the other could stab his foe.

Rast dodged a slice and the unarmed man leaped on his back, trying to choke him. Karland blinked as his friend somehow shucked out from the grip and turned. His leg scythed up over the sword and chopped down at the man holding it, who swayed backwards. The man grappling with him clapped a big hand over Rast's neck in preparation for a lock. Rast grabbed his wrist, stepped both feet through under the extended arm, and flipped him right over his head, straight into the path of the returning swordsman.

The sword fouled by his comrade, the second man had no defence as Rast leapt in one fluid motion, both feet driving into his chest. Off balance, he was blasted backwards. Rast landed on the unarmed man, and whipped around on top of him. He didn't stop moving, and it was hard to see what was going on. He seemed to have him pinned by a knee on the sternum, and the man was desperately defending, his hands flickering. Rast shifted and suddenly the struggling attacker had a massive forearm locked across his own. Rast jerked upwards and with a sharp snap the radius tore through the skin. The man yelled and Rast used the distraction to thunder blow after blow to the man's face and throat, smashing his head into the forest floor. He quickly stopped moving; Karland couldn't tell if he was dead or not.

The last foe got to his feet, seeming to have trouble breathing. Karland held his breath; the man moved like Rast did. He slid forwards, hands up and ready.

Rast crouched, then shot his leg out in a powerful kick. The man raised his leg to block, and Rast's iron shin connected hard. Again he struck, and again. The two circled, and then came suddenly together. The man dropped to a knee, his bruised leg buckling slightly, and then slammed his shoulder into Rast's waist as he tried to take his legs.

Rast tucked the man's head under his armpit and hooked his legs. They toppled backwards, the man on top struggling furiously. In an incredibly powerful move Rast wrenched hard backwards. His foe shuddered, jerking wildly before going limp.

After a few seconds, Rast pushed the body away, rolling lightly to his feet.

ଔ ଓ

A single glance told Rast that the youngsters were all right, Karland guarding a man that appeared to have survived. He was propped against a tree, staring at the boy, a sneer of triumph showing through a face twisted in pain. He hoped the boy didn't do anything rash. These were no mere bandits. The last two he had fought especially had been highly skilled, and the attack had been well co-ordinated. He wanted to know who had sent them. Seeing the still form in the back of the cart, with Xhera slumped over it, his jaw muscles tightened. As a last scream of terror echoed through the trees, he smiled grimly. Someone would pay dearly for this.

ଔ ଓ

Karland turned his gaze back to the man near his feet and found him watching, his face distorted in pain but his eyes alert. He wanted to shout, to strike, to stab him, but it was a distant emotion held behind the fact that he had just killed another person. He could still feel the other man's heartbeat as it shuddered up his knife.

'Why?' he asked instead, quietly. 'Why did you do this?'

The man looked at him dully, and then chuckled harshly. 'I can't believe a shitty little group like you killed us all.' He coughed. 'You have something we were sent to get.'

'Well, you failed,' said Karland fiercely. 'You failed! You did nothing but murder an old man, and I hope you freeze in hell for that.'

— 379 —

The man laughed hard, only stopping when he started choking.

'We *failed*?' he gasped. 'The old man was the prime target. He holds the ke-' he broke off before he said more than he had intended, grinning, and then winced as a fresh wave of agony shot up from his shattered legs. 'Give it up, boy,' he said through clenched teeth. 'You'll get no more from me.' His eyes bored into Karland hatefully.

Karland clenched his fist until the knuckles went white. A scream of terror drifted faintly from the tree line where Grukust had vanished. 'We'll see how much you say when we hand you over to the ork,' he said quietly. The man paled slightly.

As if summoned, Grukust burst from the trees nearby, fury on his face. He was obviously still in the throes of *baresark*, barely holding on to reason. His axe dripped with gore, and he was sprayed in it. A deep cut on his shoulder oozed, as did a shallower one on his other forearm, but he didn't seem to realise it. His tusks ran red with fresh blood where he had torn the last man's throat out.

Catching sight of Karland with the wounded assassin and Xhera next to the still form of the scholar, the banked fury exploded again in his eyes. Roaring, he charged into the clearing. Karland held out his hands, running in front of the injured man, but Grukust bowled him over like an infant. A shout came from Rast, far to the side. The big man sprinted towards the berserk ork, but would never reach him in time. The captured assassin screamed in terror as he saw his doom.

His broken legs useless, he flipped onto his stomach and tried desperately to crawl away. Grukust caught him in a few more strides and roared in triumph as he leapt, the axe flashing up. The descending blade caught him in the spine and ribs with a meaty *chock*, crushing his chest as it cleaved through vertebrae, ribs, heart, and lungs. So powerful was the blow from the giant ork that it lodged in the underside of the man's sternum. Grukust howled in rage and tore his axe upwards. The limp body came with it, flopping weirdly, hooked on the beard of the axe. The legs hung at unnatural angles and the dead man's chin was dark with blood from his ruined lungs, vomited in a last spasm. The eyes were frozen, starting from his face in horror.

The enraged ork hauled the corpse fully over his head before he brought the axe down in another blow that sank deep into the earth. The ork jerked the weapon this way and that, seeking to free it. The dead man was in serious danger of being completely torn in half. Not until Rast's iron forearm closed around Grukust's neck, cutting off the blood to his brain, did he stop.

After a few seconds Grukust's struggles weakened, and his axe slipped from his grasp. Karland knew it was too late. He could not be happy at the man's death, however deserved. Rast let the ork go as he calmed and moved to the ripped torso, his face bleak.

'He had no chance to give us information,' he said, his voice flat in anger. 'Fool, fool. You have denied us a greater vengeance.'

Grukust stood, snarling, his eyes glaring around him as he regained his breath and his reason. Xhera called to him, her voice thick with tears.

'Grukust. Grukust, he's gone. Aldwyn is gone. There is nothing more we can do.'

The ork stared at her, and then stared at Aldwyn. He threw his head back and howled in impotent fury, a sound that went on and on. Finally he dropped to his knees where he stood, slumping forward and breathing hard. After a moment he spoke.

'Rast. I am sorry. When *baresark* take me I not able to think right, see what happen. Aldwyn my friend. When I see that man alive, I revenge Aldwyn because I fail him. I promise to protect him, and I fail.'

Karland's throat was painful, but he could not blame his companion. He understood how he felt. Rast sighed and shook his head.

'I understand berserkers. I know you lose reason. It is done, my friend. I cannot blame you. I just wish you had managed to regain control sooner.' He looked at the old man's body sadly. 'You failed him no more than I. I knew full well assassins were tracking us; they failed once in Darost. We were not cautious enough after the Dimnesdair. I thought them to be in Punslon now. We walked straight into their arms… and now we are no closer to knowing who was behind this.'

Karland wanted to tell the big man that this was no one's fault, but he didn't know what to say. He felt totally drained. A tangential thought prodded his weary mind from the side.

'Is that it? Have we failed?' The thought troubled him. He knew Aldwyn would have wanted them to carry on, although he couldn't imagine doing it without his mentor.

'No, Karland. Aldwyn knew he might not finish his work. He also knew he could rely on us, his closest friends, to do so. His was the knowledge – but we can still bear that knowledge for him.'

Karland's eyes widened. *Aldwyn's journal.*

'He has the key,' he whispered, and then repeated it louder. 'He has the key! That assassin *did* tell me something. That was what he nearly said! 'He holds the key'. *That* is what they have been after. His master sent him to retrieve something. That pendant may be more than a guide… and everything Aldwyn studied he put in his journal!'

'Well done, boy,' said Rast. He looked around. 'We must leave this place. Aldwyn is gone, but we must continue. We must bury him, and move on.'

'Just like that?' cried Xhera, as Karland cried, 'Bury him here?' He felt wrong, leaving Aldwyn so far from his library, on his own in the middle of strange woods.

'Yes,' said Rast looking at them both. 'One day, perhaps, we can return for him… if we all live. But we must continue this quest without him, and we are running out of time.'

Karland looked over at his mentor for long minutes, and the silence stretched. He thought about the memories he had, the emptiness inside; there would be no more. It was as if he had lost his own grandfather. Things Aldwyn had taught him flashed past, and he understood now that the old man had been doing more than being kind to a boy who didn't fit his own life. He had been preparing Karland – and Xhera – to be able to understand, even perhaps continue, the long work of his life.

'Not *here*,' he said in a voice that brooked no argument. 'Not with… these.'

Rast nodded. 'These will lie here and rot. Let us find a fitting place nearby. But we can leave no markers, no tributes. I will not have his body defiled by men or orcs.'

Grukust went scouting for a resting place while Rast checked the bodies. He returned eventually with several swords, knives and sheaths, both bows and quivers, his *shirkas*, and several T-shaped pendants.

Karland and Xhera sat at the back of the cart, not wanting to leave Aldwyn alone. The sunlight shone down on his still face, glinting on his glasses. He almost looked like he was sleeping.

Rast's face was set in a dark scowl. 'These were not just any trained men,' he said, holding up one of the pendants, 'They are an elite unit of the Church of Terome. Teromants, men dedicated to that bleak God. Meyari men, for the most part.'

Xhera started. 'Everything we find leads back to Meyar!'

Rast pinched the bridge of his nose in a surprisingly familiar gesture to Aldwyn's. 'We must be careful. When these men fail to return there will be more. The church has grown in power for years, but this time I think it has made a mistake involving itself so obviously with Meyari politics. Meyar will pay in time; if the realms of Anaria find out all that has happened I doubt there will even *be* a Meyar.

'All that changes if these orcs join their armies. Entire lands could be lost. What is worse is that there must be thousands of innocent Meyari caught up in this. Whatever happens, many people will die now.' He sounded resigned and dropped the arms in the back of the cart. 'We have found decent weapons. Karland, I will train you in sword and knife play, and bowmanship. Pick your weapons. Xhera, we will drill more with knives. I fear the draw is too great for you to use these bows.'

Grukust reappeared, breathing heavily and covered in sweat. 'I found glade,' he said quietly. 'It peaceful. Full of nature. Small stream. I think he like it. I already dug grave.'

Rast nodded and clapped him on the shoulder, noting the ork's prized axe had dirt on it. He realised how much the ork had respected the old man – no warrior would normally do that to his weapon. It would cost him hours of cleaning and attention. He clicked his tongue and called, and Stryke trotted over.

Rast pointed at Hjarta. '*Hastus verin*, Stryke,' he said softly. He undid his big cloak and laid it next to Aldwyn, snapped the shaft and withdrew the arrow, and then gently lifted his friend's body onto it.

'We will each take a corner, and bear him to his rest,' he said.

No one spoke. Karland and Xhera took the front, sliding him forwards. Karland could not believe what was happening. The anger, the shock, the loss, it was all receding, leaving him detached and numb. Grukust and Rast each took a back corner, holding it over the edge of the cart. Grukust pointed with his free hand, and they started off.

They walked through the trees in silence for several minutes, and then came out in a pretty, diminutive glade. A tiny stream, hardly more than a rivulet, was running through it, tinkling with leaping reflections. At one end was a hoary old oak with a grave several feet deep in the grass at its base. Earth and a section of root lay to one side.

They held Aldwyn as Rast dropped in. Lifting the scholar gently down to him, Rast laid him to rest with his hands crossed on his chest. Grukust passed him down a carved charm to place in his hands – the ork symbol for protection.

'*Gropak,*' he said in answer to their questioning looks.

Rast nodded. He placed it in the long delicate fingers, carefully straightened the spectacles one final time, and then climbed out of the waist-deep hole. Grukust must have worked furiously to clear it so quickly.

They stood, heads bowed. Karland didn't want this moment to approach. He did not want to say goodbye to his friend, but nothing he could do could stop it coming. A lump was forming in his throat.

'Goodbye, old friend,' said Rast softly. 'Rest in the peace of the gods.'

'I swear that I will finish what you started, Aldwyn,' said Karland, his eyes shining with tears and his voice rough. 'I *swear* it. *We will find the key.*' His throat hurt with the pain inside him.

'And save the world,' whispered Xhera next to him. Her voice strengthened. 'Dear Aldwyn: if we win, it will ever be your victory.' Her lip quivered, and then she turned and threw her arms around Karland, sobbing. Karland had no words, and brushed her hair gently.

Grukust said nothing, but bumped his fist gently on his chest in respect for the fallen.

After a minute, Rast turned to them. 'We must mourn properly later. Grukust, I will finish this. Take them back to the cart and make ready.' The big ork nodded, and they turned to go.

Karland looked back for one final time as they entered the trees, Xhera sobbing bitterly beside him. He saw Rast bowed next to the grave in the bright little clearing, and he smiled sadly. Aldwyn *would* have liked it, *um, ah.* Grukust was right.

кк оо

Karland was sitting impatiently on the cart when Rast finally appeared, his hands and clothes covered with soil. He wanted to leave this place, like a physical itch. Rast led them along the path, and so they left that sad place behind. Less than an hour later they broke from the trees to find the Reldenhort Plains once more stretching away in front of them. The road split, curving west to Punslon and northeast to Eordeland. They turned northeast, following the line of the trees bordering the Iril Eneth. Once on the road, they made faster headway, the cart rattling along at a good pace.

Karland almost felt like they were racing from the memories of the day, and concentrated on the cool breeze on his face. Clouds had begun to drift, casting patches of shadow over the grasslands to their north. They saw no travellers that day. Weary from loss, sleep came quickly.

The next morning their conversation was muted. Xhera burst into tears again as she moved to put a kettle on for Aldwyn's tea, and Karland felt lost without the world-shaking snores that he was used to. He wondered if he would have been able to sleep without them had he not been so tired.

The day was slightly overcast – warm, with the sun a white mess behind the clouds. They continued on the great road, stopping for a listless lunch. Xhera took the reins after they started out again, and Karland slumped in the back, staring at a spot of dried blood from his old friend's mortal wound. He reached out and touched it carefully, his mind wandering. For the first time in a while he wondered how his family were. He hoped they were well, and that no more attacks had occurred. Life was more fragile than he had realised. Karland didn't want to lose anyone else.

He remembered the journal and the questions it might answer, and opened the chest carefully. Gingerly removing it, he sat looking at the cover for a time, replaying moments with his friend in his head. Aldwyn had never let anyone else near his precious collection of thoughts. Finally, he shook his head and sighed, and opened it.

On the first page of the thick journal was the heading, *Thoughts and calculations of Aldwyn Varelin – Tome Eighteen*. This last was scratched out, and replaced with *Twenty*, which was also scratched out, and finally just with the excited words '*Draco Noblis*'.

He almost grinned. That was Aldwyn, through and through.

Eighteen? Twenty? He shook his head. Underneath it all in newer script was a note that caught his eye. He saw his own name underlined, and stopped to read.

'*Karland, my boy,*' he read. '*If you are reading this, you possess my journal, which means I have likely left you. For that I am truly sorry, and hope it does not pain you too much. You have been like the grandson that I never had, and more beside; an energetic inspiration, a student, a friend.*

'*There is something you must know and I may not have had the opportunity to tell you in life. You must continue what we started; I believe the very world depends on it. Trust Rast with your life, as I have, and look after Xhera. The world needs you both.*

'*There is something hinted at, some kind of breach in reality that happened long ago which lets chaos into the universe. If it exists, it could destroy everything. There are writings of this scattered throughout ancient texts, of a choice that may have to be made, and I trust you two as no others to continue my work and stand at the end for good or ill; chaos and dissolution, or balance and redemption. Beware evil and chaos! But beware also sometimes the guise of Order.*

'*I know not what this key is or what this power may be, but you must find a way to use it, to prevent this dread future coming to pass... if you can. It may be no one can stop it, and this has been a fool's quest from the outset. I have tried to prepare you both in our limited time. I have given you groundings in skills you may need in times to come, a wide understanding of concepts, and hopefully the importance of lateral thinking. I feel you will both change this world. Of this one point I am positive.*

'I hope that I died easily. I have long been terrified of my own death... cowardly, I know, so when I tell you that my concern for the world surpasses even that, you may understand the dangers we all face. Use the knowledge I have collected. Use it wisely. Heed Rast... and may GAL be with you.

'With the love of a grandfather-in-spirit, and the respect of a friend... I give you all that I have.

'Aldwyn.'

A tear ran down Karland's cheek, and he sat looking at his friend's excitable writing, his mind far away.

ↄ҃   ৪০

Karland sat silently for some time, rocking with the cart. The painful lump had returned to his throat, warring with a strange mix of sadness, and the urge to laugh out loud at his old friend's scribbling and dread at the great things alluded to in his journal. Wondering about the reference to GAL – a god? – his mind drifted back to the conversation he had overheard months ago between Aldwyn and Rast. The sky darkened, and he was finally brought out of his reverie by a spot of rain hitting the pages, left open and forgotten on his lap. The ink of the word *Twenty* ran slightly, and he hunched over and blotted it hastily with a sleeve before placing the book safely in the chest again. He scrambled for the headboard with their cloaks and put Xhera's around her shoulders, holding out his hands for the reins. She smiled at him in gratitude.

They rode for hours, at first in spitting drops and then in a full downpour which seemed well suited to their mood. It was as if the heavens had decided to mourn their lost companion with them, and unleashed all the water that the skies above the plains held. The world was a dark place, and any of them – all of them – might fall before they reached their goal. The mountain was still distant, and the world was full of danger.

They rode on into the gloom, hearts heavy. Rast sat in his saddle nearby, solid and safe, and Grukust loped alongside them, his mouth open and welcoming the cleansing rain.

THIRTY-FIVE

The rain continued until dusk. The road was awash with mud, and the white noise of the drops hitting the ground was lulling, making Xhera drowsy. Rast rode at the fore, ever alert, and Grukust ran tirelessly next to the cart. Dusk arrived with little in the way of darkening; the rain clouds were heavier than ever, and there was little wind. The rain sliced down, cold and thin. Welcomed at first as a fitting match for her mood, Xhera eventually grew to loathe it. Karland's breath misted in the air. His hands were white and numb on the reins as Xhera hunched in the back, trying to escape the cold drumming under a hastily-pulled out sheet that covered their belongings. Thankfully both their cloaks, gifts from his father, were well-waxed. She hated being cold and wet.

Everyone was glad when Rast pulled off the road to settle down for a campsite. There was no fire for cheer, as Grukust's *rinok paska* fuel was finished. The rain finally became a light pattering that continued unabated.

Rast left Grukust on guard and sat down next to them.

'How are you both?'

Xhera shook her head sadly and looked at her friend. Aldwyn's loss had hurt Karland deeply. She was still having trouble coming to terms with the brutality of what had happened.

Karland was silent for a minute, and then said, 'All I can think about is what that man said.' His jaw clenched. 'I wish I had killed him myself.'

'There is a difference between revenge and justice,' said Rast. 'Aldwyn always knew we would take up the burden if he fell, and he knew that we were one step closer to finding answers. This was the happiest I have seen him in years, and although it was not the death I would have chosen for him, he died quickly. He died with that happiness, in the company of his closest friends. Set your heart at ease.'

'I cannot,' whispered Karland. 'I saw the pain and terror in his eyes.'

Xhera felt like crying. She had also seen Aldwyn's confused terror as he died.

'No doubt. But in his heart would have been comfort that you were with him. You were his legacy, and his friend. He is dead, but we had the honour of knowing him, being a part of these times. They may be dark, but they are defining the world, for good or ill, and his was a great part. It is not so very bleak… we still have each other, and we will hold his memory close. Justice will be done. I *will* find the one who ordered his death. Believe that, if nothing else.'

He stretched under his heavy cloak – the last one he owned – and changed the subject. 'Both of you showed courage. Karland, your training saved your life. You did well.'

'I was lucky,' said Karland morosely.

'Luck is a fickle ally, but it is there to be used if you can see it,' said Rast. 'All warriors depend on a degree of luck. Skill and training fill in the rest. Do not lessen your achievements, either of you. Against two trained and armed warriors, with greater reach and weapons, you survived. You are both learning. Use what you have to hand, at the right moment. Commit. Do not hesitate.' He eyed the boy. 'Do you regret killing that man?'

'Yes.'

Xhera knew he did. When he was not mourning Aldwyn, he was numbly talking about how he had felt the man die on his blade.

'Do not,' said Rast sharply. 'It saved Xhera's life, and your own.'

'Who were they?' asked Xhera. 'You said something about a church?'

'They were soldiers from Meyar. Teromants, soldiers of Terome led by two Meyari assassins. It is probable that they will try again, but for now we are free.'

Karland stared at his feet, and then looked up at them both. 'I will continue his quest. I will finish what was started. I swore it, and I meant it. I will train hard… I will study hard. Perhaps I could have saved him if I had also learned with the Mors.'

Xhera doubted that anything could have saved him, but his words inspired her. 'He was a link to my past,' she said quietly. 'I have so few. I want to continue his work, chronicle his life. Everyone should know how wise he was… how much he gave.'

Rast nodded in approval. 'If you both stay true to those goals, it will be a fitting immortality for him. He is owed that. But now – unwrap a sword and knife, and I will teach you basic foot and blade work. You too, Xhera. It is time we added attack to defence.'

'Shouldn't we be using – I don't know, wooden swords or something?' asked Xhera doubtfully. She didn't want to cut herself.

'Not really. I want you to learn to *respect* this blade. You will not hit yourself with it more than once! You must know its balance, its edges, the feeling in your hand, to teach your wrist how to lock correctly for it. You must become conditioned, learn the basics. Use a live sword and you will gain them fast along with the importance of cleaning and sharpening the same blade. You will practice live and spar sheathed.'

They moved away from the packs, and he set them to drills, showing them how to move. His sword hissed through the air as if it was part of him. Xhera irritably wondered if there were any weapons the big man wasn't an expert in.

After half an hour, both wrists and forearms were aching; Rast made them do the exercises with each arm. Exhausted, they stood, waiting for him to finish. Instead, he set them to sparring after fitting the sheaths, using what they had just learned. Xhera was gasping and shaking by the time they stumbled back to the fire. Both had fallen over more than once and had numerous scrapes.

Rast eyed them over. 'Good. But you must remember that everything you do is based in your feet. The arm does not swing the sword. The whole body moves it as another limb. And where do you think you are going?'

Karland looked up hopefully as he paused in the act of slumping down onto his pack. 'Erm-'

'You must yet learn how to care for a tempered blade. If it is touched by skin or blood, wipe it – preferably oil it. Skin oils will damage forged metals. *Always* clean a blade after battle. Here, use this oiled rag. Then we hone the edge – it will take a while, but you need to feel your way. Sharpen the blade like so.' He demonstrated.

Xhera grinned at the worried look on Karland's face. She had spent many hours sharpening knives for her sister's kitchen. She tried to help with some of Hendal's teaching. 'You can sharpen a blade on anything that would dull it. Remember, grind with rough, strop with smooth, and keep the angle constant.' He shot her a look and sat down.

Xhera ran the stone down the blade, feeling the grain, the edge, the angle. Karland looked pleased, managing for once not to cut himself. Rast looked at the swords after they were finished.

'Well done, boy,' he said. Karland beamed. 'You have proved you can dull something by sharpening it. Lessen the angle of the stone. Don't rush. It takes repetition, stropping and *little* pressure. Better with light oil, or if not that, patience.' He looked at her swords and nodded with approval. 'This is good, Xhera.' She smiled as Rast collected the swords. Karland looked downcast. 'It will come with practice. Time for sleep. I hope to find the Arkon foothills the day after tomorrow. There is a dwarven city in the low mountains, and we need supplies and directions.'

He relieved Grukust on watch as they unrolled their blankets. The ork came and dropped next to them, looking annoyed.

'I forget cut wood for new *gropak*,' he said distractedly with a slight frown.

'*Gropak?*' asked Xhera.

The ork nodded. 'Make with wood from Rowan tree. We carve Urukin symbol for protection on it. It keep us safe. We give as special gift, or swap them. When Uruk and Uruk-i join, they give to each other as sign that protect each other, love each other. Very sacred.'

Xhera smiled. 'That is very romantic,' she said. 'I didn't know orks were so sweet.' Grukust shifted, uncomfortable. Karland smiled then and leaned forward, eyes narrowed.

'You gave it to Aldwyn!'

Xhera felt a pang, and laid her hand on Grukust's warm arm.

'Yes. It too late,' and the ork's face turned down, 'but it maybe keep him safe until friends get him again. He deserve to rest away from woods.'

Swallowing a lump in her throat, she hugged him hard, and he muttered but did not look displeased.

'So how will you make another one? There is no wood here,' asked Karland.

The big ork shrugged. 'Maybe when we get in Arkon foothills I find tree. Until then, I have to just making sure I kill anything that attack me.' His grin returned. Xhera smiled gratefully at the attempts at humour. Grukust had a true heart under his impassive green exterior.

They lay down to rest, and Xhera listened to the light pattering of returning rain. It seemed like it would never end.

☙   ☣

Rast woke them early the next morning. The world was fresh and wet, and although overcast, the clouds looked thin and frayed; the sun would be fighting for its place today. The rain had finally stopped in the night, and the horses were cropping the wet grass with abandon. The cart was dry under the oiled cover, although the box and footboard were still damp.

They loaded up after a quick meal and got under way. Karland gazed around him as he drove. To the south and east the Iril Eneth had receded, and the much higher Arkons were beginning to loom to the north. Their morning was uneventful and dull. The wind picked up a little, and the occasional ray of sunshine pierced the clouds.

They camped again that night and set off early, another long subdued day stretching out before them interminably, and another.

At mid-afternoon the next day Rast reined back alongside the cart. 'There is a large camp ahead,' he said. 'They look to be Travellers – I can see more than one wagon.'

'Travellers?' asked Karland. 'Like gypsies?' He could see a knot of brightly coloured wagons.

'Not quite,' said Rast. 'Between Meyar and Eordeland lie the cold Nassmoors, north of the Arkons. Nomad families that call themselves Travellers often journey from there through all the realms, following the road. This camp might be a good place to rest. Travellers are welcoming of guests.'

Rast hailed them as they got closer. Men peered around the wagons, and the baying of large dogs was heard. Karland was surprised by the genuine smiles they received. Most people were wary of strangers, especially these days.

Calling, 'Come!' to the others, Rast wheeled off the road and cantered to the edge of the circle. Dismounting, he stayed Stryke, and then stepped forward to bow before a man in a bright red shirt with dark hair, a goatee beard, and dark eyes with a mischievous glint in them. His ears held gold rings, and his hair was pulled back in a pony tail, as was most of the men's here. The women had their hair loose or in braids, and like the man greeting them were predominantly dark haired.

'You are welcome to our Circle, strangers,' he said heartily. 'I am Geb. For a pittance, will you join us at bread?'

Rast nodded, smiling. 'Well met, *Hastan*. We thank you for your hospitality. What will your pittance be?' The words sounded like ritual.

'That can be decided after eating,' the man said, his eyes twinkling. Karland felt uneasy, but a glance at Rast told him that his fears were unfounded.

Xhera's eyes were fixed on the bright clothes and wagons. Geb followed her eyes and grinned.

'We roll with the road, and it is ever rolling, never ending. We trade many things for many things, and enjoy the world as it is in its glory – something, sadly, city folk do not. There is happiness in everything, if you but know where to find it.' He flourished a courtly bow and the girl giggled at his flamboyance.

Karland half-turned to ask Aldwyn about them, and was pierced with sadness. He missed his friend and his annoyingly complete knowledge about almost everything; his perfect memory for detail lost in time.

Geb caught the look and his face dropped some cheer.

'Come! We cannot have sadness here. Our Circle is a place for lightheartedness and rest. Come in and tell us your stories. If they are good enough, then perhaps your pittance is earned before the meal.' He held out his hand, gesturing them past. The other Travellers were smiling. Karland found himself smiling back, and dismounted, helping Xhera down. Rast gave his customary warning about Stryke. They walked into the Circle to find a fire burning merrily, with nearly thirty men, women and children around it. There were no weapons in sight, and everyone looked content. A large pot was bubbling on a giant iron tripod.

Rast said, 'Do not worry, Karland. These are Nassmoor Travellers. No land is really theirs – they travel them all. Even the orks tolerate them for trade. Ignore stories of tinkers stealing your pots. Novinian tinkers, maybe, but not Travellers. They will not lie or cheat –although they can bend the truth better than most! – but they are a good people who believe in seeing the good things in the world.'

'There are no weapons, though – what happens if they are attacked? No one's life is totally happy,' said Karland, feeling a little annoyed at the omnipresent cheerfulness.

'Oh, they have weapons, and large dogs, too, but only for defence. They are peaceful, on the whole. You can trust Nassmoors with your possessions and life. What they take from you is to cover what you take in turn from them… and it is not always something material.'

Geb had heard much of this, and he smiled.

'More or less true. Karland, is it? We do not steal babies or pots and pans. We will, however, play with the first and repair the latter.' He grinned, and then turned to Grukust. 'Look everyone! We have an *Ork!*' He sounded genuinely excited. After a moment trying to decide if he was being mocked, Grukust nodded instead. A chorus of calls and welcomes came from the gathering. Many had food on their laps, and did not rise, but smiles were very much in evidence.

It is like coming home, thought Karland. The look on Xhera's face said the same thing.

They sat at the fire, and were handed bowls. Karland saw Rast talking to Geb, the man's smiling face growing serious. Grukust found himself a little swamped by curious men, women and children. The women seemed especially curious about him – they were a diminutive people, and his impressive frame drew them. Karland and Xhera also found themselves chatting and laughing with youngsters ranging in age from ten to sixteen as naturally as if they had grown up with them. They forgot their woes, and relaxed for the first time in days, listening to jokes and stories of the Traveller's recent travels. It seemed that they had come from

Peakston, a town to the east in Eordeland near the Iril Eneth, and were wandering towards either western Banistari or Novin as the whim took them.

It was a very pleasant meal, and the whole party felt their hearts lightened. Even Rast smiled more than they had seen for some time. The Travellers were simply pleasant to be near, and they all seemed guileless. A number of the girls gazed at Karland, sending him into a stammering, blushing fit when they tried to ask him whether Xhera was his sister or not. They seemed to find it a game, laughing and whispering to each other. He was not entirely sure if their interest was serious and eventually ended up sandwiched nervously with two giggling and leaning on him.

Xhera looked unsure whether to be annoyed or amused at his predicament. Grukust however bellowed with laughter until the women, chuckling with mirth, did the same to him, the ones to each side dropping a hand on his knees and gazing endearingly into his huge dark eyes. He looked so astonished – and somehow trapped – that Karland and Xhera howled with laughter, tears running down their faces, the tensions of the last few days removed in the release of emotion.

Rast and Geb watched for a time and then Geb clapped his hands. The laughter was swiftly muffled as the Travellers turned to their leader. Geb bowed fluidly, and said, 'My apologies, Traveller clan… sincerely. But I must share bad news.' Smiles faded and the people looked serious; this was obviously something that happened rarely.

Geb continued, 'These people have twofold news that saddens me. They lost a companion but a few days ago to violence, so if you see them sad, lift their hearts! And more importantly for us… forgive me, but for now we cannot Travel west.'

Cries broke out. Karland heard one say they should travel as they wished. Geb raised his hands.

'I know, our hearts roll west for now, but it seems grim legend follows these four. Rast Tal'Orien tells me that thousands of *orocs* are gathering for war. We must move another way, or risk losing the roads forever.'

Whispers broke out, faces now solemn. Geb smiled. 'Raise your hearts, O my people! For it seems to me that we have not spied the Elven Forests for many a year. Perhaps we may travel west in time, but through the edges of the Léohtsholt.' Murmurs sprang up, and smiles returned. A few people laughed.

'How lucky Peakston, to see us again so soon!' someone called, laughter in their voice, and the gathering grinned and chuckled.

Geb called again. 'Also, I have decided their pittance.' The people watched, waiting. Something in their leader's voice said it would be interesting.

'Rast Tal'Orien has requested the loan of a lute. He wishes to give a short tribute to the one they lost.' Sympathetic eyes turned to them all. Karland felt the returning lump in his throat, and Xhera's eyes began to overflow. Grukust solemnly looked at Karland and wiggled his eyebrows quizzically. Karland shrugged.

A lute?

One was brought, incongruously painted with purple flowers, and given to Rast. It looked like a toy in his grasp. He bowed to Geb, tested the tuning, and then sat quietly, his scarred hands holding the instrument delicately. A moment later, his fingers touched the strings, and clean, sorrowful tones rang out in minor chords.

Karland was astonished. He had never dreamed that Rast knew anything apart from fighting. Xhera's mouth was open, and Grukust was watching with interest; Karland remembered Aldwyn saying their culture's music was mainly percussive. Rast's fingers danced over the strings, sometimes touching a wrong note – but gently, more as someone exercising a long-unused skill than someone unable to play. It did not mar the emotion in the music.

He lifted his face, and began to sing. His deep voice was pleasant and clear, though without training, and provided a base for the more intricate playing to weave through. He sang a threnody for Aldwyn: his love for books, for knowledge, and for his friends. His unsurpassed knowledge of so many subjects; his frailty, which made Xhera sob openly, garnering her sympathetic hugs. His passion for strange things, his speaking with Dragons. Rast added the occasional *um, mm, ah*, which made those who had known him smile. When he added a description of his snoring, accompanied by a discordant rasping across the strings, Karland burst out laughing, as did everyone listening. The last chord was major and the message was clear: celebrate their friend's life, and make their victory his victory. The song hadn't been perfect, but it was honest, and captured his mentor.

The camp sat silent for a moment and then Xhera ran through it to throw her arms around Rast. The big man put a hand on the small of her back, and laughed softly. As if a spell was lifted, the whole camp joined in the merriment.

Geb smiled, and called, 'Our thanks, friend Rast! I wish we had known this man Aldwyn. You gave us more than a pittance, this day!'

They slept soundly that night, feeling secure. The night was warm enough, so the free people joined their guests outside around the fire for comfort. They sang and played music and danced happily, lifting the hearts of their guests.

As people began to drift towards their blankets, many quieter conversations were struck up. Karland and Xhera found time to relax, and read some of the books Aldwyn had left. Karland flipped to the last few pages of the journal and found a section entitled *Notes on Dragons*. He read page after page, marvelling at how much Aldwyn had gleaned both from his time talking to Györnàeldàr and his prior studies. A lot of it went over his head, but the rest was fascinating reading.

Xhera settled down with Aldwyn's notes on his precious Book of Sarthos, second only to his journal. Her small face was determined, and her lips moved in constant perplexity as she read the notes, especially any references to a 'hollow in the mountains'. After the fifth time Karland interrupted her to read out a fascinating fact, she shushed him in exasperation.

'I'll read it myself later.'

Karland wisely left her to her studies, realising she was working on their journey.

Grukust was already asleep near the fire. The huge hounds they kept for guard alternated between watching with the men and draping their huge frames familiarly over feebly complaining Travellers to snuffle in slumber. They seemed to like Grukust's musky smell, and heaped themselves around him.

Rast was out somewhere with the men on watch. As both he and Xhera yawned and prepared for rest, Karland wondered when he would ever catch the big man actually sleeping. He slept soundly for the first time in many days – a real rest, rather than recovery from exhaustion.

They woke gradually to the bustle of the camp in the once-again grey of a new morning. Many of the Travellers were still sleeping, but others were up and packing; Geb's proclamation had been taken seriously. After a hearty breakfast, Karland and the others took leave of the Travellers. The people refused to accept their thanks, saying instead they were in their debt. The Nassmoors considered it a great honour that they had opened themselves so willingly.

Each Traveller insisted on shaking hands or kissing goodbye. Grukust turned a darker green at the amount of women kissing him on the cheek, which produced much laughter. Eventually the goodbyes were done, and the horses were ready. Geb bowed, surrounded by all the clan. As they all called and waved he shouted above the noise.

'Go in peace, and may you keep some from our Circle.'

'May your Circle ever roll on the Road,' replied Rast formally. They moved to the road. Karland looked back to see the people break over the camp like ants, making ready for travel. He shook his head.

'What strange people! But so pleasant and honest. Why do they ask strangers in? It seems dangerous.'

Rast shrugged. 'They see the world differently. They are a free people with no real land – or every land, depending on your view. They believe that everyone has something worthwhile to them, a story if you will, and seek to find it so that they are the richer for it. They can never meet everyone in the world, but they seem to be trying. I respect them greatly. They mean no harm, and are talented musicians and storytellers with wild and free feet. The worst thing you can do to a Traveller is lock them up; they have to follow their hearts on the road. That is why when *Hastan* Geb said they could not go west, they were so upset.'

'What does *Hastan* mean?' asked Karland.

'Who cares?' interrupted Xhera. 'You play the *lute!* Rast, it was wonderful. Why didn't you tell us?'

Grukust nodded. 'It was very good play,' he approved.

Rast smiled. '*Hastan* is Geb's title as leader. It means little unless you speak the convoluted language of the Travellers, which I do not. And as to the lute… you never asked.' His smile faded. 'But I hope that it was a fitting tribute to Aldwyn. I played it as I knew him, though I made much of it up, and I cannot play as well as I once did.'

Karland looked at the big man, and shook his head at another depth unveiled. 'It was more than fitting, Rast.'

Grukust grunted agreement and Xhera smiled. 'I somehow feel a little less sad for it. Thank you, Rast.'

Rast nodded. 'He was a good friend, for many, many years,' he said softly. Karland had forgotten that Rast had known Aldwyn far longer than any of them.

They arrived at a large fork after midday. North lay the Arkons and the turning to Darost while east was Eordeland – specifically Sudland, the southern city of Irilview, and presumably Peakston.

They turned north, and moved along the road. Karland began talking to Xhera about his good memories of Aldwyn, and then somehow found himself trying to explain his theory of the two platters when travelling open country. Xhera looked at him as if he was mad, but Grukust looked around.

'What? What plate?' he snapped.

Karland tried to explain further, and said, 'Maybe it doesn't work if you walk. You might need to be on the cart.'

Grukust pulled himself aboard without further ado, causing it to rock on its leather straps. Xhera yelped as it swayed, and there was a startled grunt from poor Hjarta, who suddenly found himself pulling a few hundred pounds extra. Grukust sat, watching one side, then the other carefully. Eventually he rubbed his eyes and then glared at Karland.

'I not like it. Everything spinning. Why you tell me this?'

Karland blinked in surprise and Xhera hid muffled laughter. Rast glanced back with a smile. It dropped from his face as he reined in and stood, looking back to the south east.

'What?' asked Grukust, dropping off the cart to Hjarta's relief.

'There,' pointed Rast. 'It seems there is no longer any question that we are pursued.'

Behind them was a dark spot on the horizon, barely visible in the overcast light. It could not be a small party. Karland felt a sinking feeling in his stomach.

'Is that all of them?'

Rast shook his head. 'No. A fraction, but more than I expected. They must have good trackers; I had hoped that they would assume we had struck north across the plains. I can only hope that Geb and his people started east in time.'

Xhera gasped in horror. The thought of the cheerful Travellers butchered made Karland feel ill.

'They may be safe,' said Rast. 'They went east, and were not long behind us. These come north, and at some pace. They cannot risk being caught in the bright sunshine if they have orcs and ogres with them. Come – we must hurry to the foothills. If we can reach the dwarves, we will be safe. No nation in their right mind would challenge them, let alone a handful of orcs. Dwarves hate orcs nearly as much as Urukin do.'

Grukust grunted in disbelief.

They fled north into the afternoon, moving as fast as the little dray could manage, close to Grukust's top speed. Several hours later dusk was falling, and they rested the horses.

'No camp tonight,' said Rast. 'We must push on to the beginnings of the foothills. Once there we can hope to lose them, but out here on the plains we are easily seen by sharp eyes and they will move faster at night.'

He dismounted and worked to hitch Stryke to the wagon alongside Hjarta. 'We need more speed.' Stryke whickered, glaring at him ungraciously, but submitted.

'Again?' groaned Xhera. 'We are always pursued. When will it end?'

'When we lose them, or they catch us,' responded Rast grimly. He finished his makeshift trace. 'Let us go.'

Karland felt anger mix with his fear as they travelled through the night. He was tired of being chased, tired of these creatures, and tired of this quest. So far all they had achieved was to lose Aldwyn. Every few hours they stopped to rest and he switched with Xhera to snatch some sleep. He found it annoying that Grukust and Rast seemed to have their usual untapped wells of energy. The clouds cleared but there was little moon.

They rested for a few hours and watered Hjarta around midnight before pressing on. The next day was tense, grey, and hurried as they followed the road at the maximum their valiant dray could manage.

Eventually Rast directed them west and they rode towards a growing darkness which began to blot out the sky: the Arkon mountains.

Some time before dawn, Karland was staring ahead, his eyes dry and his hands numb. Sleep was not very restful on the swaying cart. Rast pulled alongside the cart, talking, and eventually leaned over and pulled the dray to a stop. Karland realised he had been speaking to him.

'Mmmm. Sorry.' He rubbed his eyes.

'We are here,' said Rast. 'We have been in the lower foothills for an hour now. The road will be slower from here, but we can rest a good few hours in these hills after dawn. The sun is rising and the sky is clear, so those following will have to go to ground in the outskirts of these hills while the sun is high. Tomorrow is another day, and it will not be many more before we are to meet the Dragon on the slopes of her Drakeholm Soaring. We may rest when we enter the dwarven city of Deep Delving.'

'Where is the city? Is it far?' asked Karland, looking around. The hills were still dark and there was no sign of a city.

'A little way yet, and under our feet mostly. The dwarves delve deep, and suffer intruders rarely.'

'What are they like?' He swung his head at a suspiciously heavy snore from the rear of the cart. His dainty passenger sat with her head lolling back, snorting.

'They are a literal, direct, often strange race. For all their brusqueness, they are very hard to read or judge. But they are greatly feared in battle, and marvellous craftsmen of metal, stone, and wood. They have more patience than other races, and greater endurance than even the orks.' He lowered his voice. 'They are also nearly their match in strength and are more than a match in skill for most warriors of near any race.' His voice rose again. 'They are tough. They can survive wounds which would kill most, and are long lived. You'll see when we get there. Just be aware – dwarves brook no nonsense. Their tempers are not quicksilver, like an ork's. Grukust snarls one minute and laughs the next. A dwarf's temper is slow to burn, but will do so for hundreds of years.'

As the sun came up, Rast pulled over into a small flat clearing in the brush.

'Two hours,' he said as he swung down. 'I believe they are orcs behind us but if there are men as well we will have trouble sooner. We press on to Deep Delving in two hours.'

Karland slid down, and set up his blanket. He had barely touched his head to his pack before Rast was shaking him awake again. Groggy and muttering, he blearily climbed into the cart. Xhera had taken up the reins, having had more rest than him in the run of the night. They set off again, following the winding road over the tops of the foothills and into the edges of the true mountains.

Finally they had to stop again, and sleep. Deep Delving was still another day and night's journey, and Rast was worried about the orcs, but they all desperately needed rest. After six hours of meagre sleep, they pressed on, hurrying Hjarta as much as they could.

Many hours later, after a swift rest for lunch from their dwindling supplies, they came in sight of a deep cleft in the rocks and paused to look around. The road ended at its foot, and Karland wondered where the entrance to the city was.

A gravelly cough sounded, and he looked left to be faced with a figure standing next to a rocky outcrop, both hands resting on the haft of a single-bladed heavy war axe carved with runes head-down on the ground. His heavy beard was braided to his waist in a brown and pepper bush. A few inches under five feet tall, built like a powerful but thick-set human with dense muscle, he glowered from under bristling brows.

They had found the dwarves.

ର   ฆ

The dwarf tilted his head back and regarded them all critically. 'Move no further, strangers. This is our land. Where are you bound?' He had a strange accent that sounded quite unlike anything else Karland had heard.

Rast slid off his horse and bowed politely. After a second's hesitation, the dwarf bowed back. Grukust thumped his chest, and the dwarf nodded. 'Strangers are unwelcome in these times. Our borders are closed. Why are you here?' The question was blunt.

'We journey to a mountain. Drakeholm Soaring, it is called by some,' said Rast. He looked up at the massive peak rising majestically behind the mountain they were at the foot of. The dwarf raised a bushy eyebrow and stroked his thick beard. Karland idly noticed it was tucked into his belt, which had an impressively-wrought buckle.

'I know that name,' he said reflectively, glancing up at it. '*Hámark Zegíln Ybirnâdur-Svífa*, we call it. It is the highest mountain in Anaria. Even we do not delve its roots. What seek you there?'

'A hollow within the mountain,' said Rast. 'We are told that within lies a power that can help our peoples. War is coming to many lands – surely you have noticed the unrest in Anaria?'

'We noticed,' said the dwarf. 'And we wish none of it. *Khazâ-dí Djûpur* is closed to outsiders.'

'What about the trade?' asked Rast.

The dwarf laughed sourly. 'That will be missed, 'tis true, but we have more riches below than you *Jörû langtskréf* would see in a hundred years. We will survive. I am set on patrol here to turn back any that approach our gates.' He jerked a thick thumb behind him. Karland peered at the blank rock face behind him, looking for it.

'You are out here alone?' he asked, surprised. The dwarf put thick fingers in his mouth and whistled shrilly. In a clatter of steel and rock, four more dwarves appeared from the rocks, eyeing the newcomers with a mixture of interest and mistrust. They carried an assortment of axes, except one who favoured a squat maul.

'A full squad,' remarked Rast.

'These hills are not safe,' replied the dwarf. 'Not in these times.'

'They are about to become even less so,' said Rast. 'We fled from an army of orcs in the Dimnesdair. There may be fifty thousand of them all told, and at least some of that number pursue us here. We sought refuge.'

'I doubt there are twenty thousand orcs gathered in all Anaria,' said the dwarf flatly. 'You will find no refuge here. We have encountered fell things of late, and false people. We no longer hold trust with the outside world.'

'All we ask are supplies,' said Rast reasonably, 'somewhere to rest, leave our horses secure, and directions to Drakeholm Soaring. Surely you can allow us access to Tradesholding?'

The dwarves looked at each other.

'You have not been here for a time,' said another one with dark umber hair and a beard braided in two to his waist. '*Stavdûrbrénaeid* is no longer a trading post. Dark things move in the hills and the mountains grow wild. Go away, human. Leave us be.'

'And what you do when hills crawling with *Goruc'cha*?' growled Grukust, looming over them. The dwarves pierced him with gimlet stares and loosened their weapons. Rast put a warning hand on the ork's shoulder.

'We will deal with them. Orcs would be foolish to come here.'

'You may be lucky,' said Rast softly. 'Perhaps they will strike at humans or the Urukin instead. But then, they are no more fond of you than they are of their… untainted kin.' Grukust rumbled alarmingly, and Karland saw Rast's fingers bite deeper into his shoulder. He hoped the ork didn't do anything violent. 'But even the mighty dwarves should be concerned at a gathering of that number. On my honour, a host has gathered, tens of thousands strong. They will soon leave the Dimnesdair, if they have not already. They bring with them ogres, beasts, even false humans. Wicked alliances have been forged. This affects us all. Will you turn us away still?'

The dwarves looked at them with taciturn expressions. Hard to read behind the beards, their stubbornness was palpable to Karland. Eventually one shook his head and his heart fell. If the dwarves did not help them, he suspected they would not survive much longer.

'We have our own troubles. Dwarves have gone missing, been killed. We trust no one now. If what you say is true, all lands could be in danger, but our gates are strong, and our walls are thick. No enemy has ever breached them. None can force the city from the world above.'

'If the world above is lost to them, one day you will find there is nothing left for you under the mountains either,' said Rast. Karland silently urged these stubborn beings to relent. 'You assure our deaths if you deny us. Will you not at least keep our horses safe? They cannot climb with us. Can you not even point us to Drakeholm Soaring?'

The dwarves' implacable faces did not change. One pointed further up the opposite slope. 'In ages past some would come to climb, and pay homage to the Dragons.' He sounded disgusted. Karland remembered Aldwyn saying the idea of dragons was not welcomed by dwarves. They were jealous of riches in the hands of others. 'There is a trail there which leads into the mountains. If you are lucky it will still be there. It will lead you near the place you seek, if you survive.'

Rast shrugged. 'That at least is something. Perhaps we can forage. What is your name?'

'I am Jari.'

'I am Rast Tal'Orien. I have visited Tradesholding before, and have met many times with Regin.'

'I know your name,' said the dwarf, raising his eyebrows. 'You are known as a foe of evil men and creatures, and a friend of Regin. But I cannot go against the word of our King, even for you.' He sighed and to Karland's relief their demeanour changed slightly. 'I will send word to ask if an exception might be made but I would not expect a favourable answer.'

Karland glanced at Xhera, who was as quiet as ever. She looked tired and frightened. The dwarf signalled to one of the others, his stubby fingers flickering remarkably quickly. The other nodded and vanished around the rock.

'How long might it take?' said Rast, his face bleak. The dwarf shrugged, and turned back to the east.

'We are not the only patrol but we must continue on our way nonetheless. Wait here. Someone should return in time. Do not think you go unseen.'

Karland muttered to himself. Time for a dwarf was clearly different than for a human. They measured their span in hundreds of years and had the patience of the rocks they worked.

Rast shook his head. 'I told you, we are pursued by many foes.'

'If we find them, they will be dealt with,' was the response. The four dwarves moved off in the direction of the foothills, their tread sure and solid. They vanished into the rocks, and Rast motioned the others to rest.

'All we can do is wait,' he said. 'The hospitality of the dwarves has lessened much since last I was here, as has their ability to listen.'

'Isn't five quite small for a squad?' asked Karland sceptically.

Rast smiled slightly. 'Dwarves are probably the best close fighters, pound for pound, of any race,' he said. 'Five dwarves might easily be a match for a squad of fifteen or twenty humans, but I fear that they will not find so few if they encounter our foes.'

Grukust grunted. He obviously held his own opinions on the skill of dwarves.

They sat for an hour, which stretched into two. Even Rast began to show signs of impatience, and Karland grew more and more agitated by the delay. Their pursuers could not be far behind, and so far had shown no difficulty in following; the only blessing was that with the sunlight, they would have gone to ground.

Finally Rast lifted his head and stood. Seconds later, a gravelly voice said, 'Rast Tal'Orien.'

Karland looked around curiously to see a tall dwarf, well over five feet. He wore heavy chain mail and a rounded helm with a short nose guard, and carried two short throwing axes on his waist. On his back was a larger axe that looked startlingly similar to Grukust's apart from only having one blade; the other side held a hooked spike. He was accompanied by the other dwarf, who nodded at them all and then jogged past on the trail of his kin.

'Regin!' said Rast, smiling. The Dwarf glowered at him then cracked a smile, his eyes crinkling and strong yellow square teeth breaking through his black beard. He crossed to the human and clasped his hand and then looked over all of them, his eyes lingering on the ork.

'That is Dwarf-forged,' he said, eying Grukust's axe with approval.

Grukust nodded. 'Best weapon I ever have. Maybe best weapon in all tribes.' He grinned, his tusks ivory in the sunshine.

The dwarf laughed, his voice low and rasping. 'I believe you, ork. I wish I could say you were all welcome here, but,' he grimaced, 'you are not. That I speak to you at all is on the sufferance of King Thekk.'

'I am glad to see you, my friend. I was beginning to despair,' said Rast. 'You find us in desperate straits. We are pursued and I have much to tell you. I tried to tell the patrol that our foes are powerful and many, but they would not listen.'

'We do not listen to outsiders much these days,' Regin admitted. 'Come. I will vouch for you all, and secure you in *Stavdûrbrénaeid*. It is all but empty these days, and the way is shut. If orcs follow you, they will receive a welcome at hammer's end.' He beckoned them with him, and descended towards the sheer rock face some way behind him. Before they reached it, he veered left towards the dark crack. It looked wide enough to fit the cart, but it ended a few feet in.

He held up his hand to stop them, and moved forward. Placing his hand on the rock, he intoned a few words in his own language, and then placed his runed axe horizontally on the wall with his other hand. It seemed to shine briefly, and then a door was outlined where there had been none before. Xhera gasped. Karland could not tell when it had appeared; suddenly, it had always been there.

Rast noticed their surprise. 'Dwarves are cunning artificers,' he said. 'This is a lesser door to an open-air town. The ones to their city are far better hidden.'

The door swung open slightly, ponderously. Regin fitted both hands around the edge and pulled hard. Slowly, gaining speed, it swung back to slam with a dull booming thud against the edge of the crack.

'Hurry,' he said. 'I must close this again.' They led the horses in, seeing a light at the other end of a short tunnel, as he started it swinging shut again. Karland tried to see what vast hinges moved it, or how it was weighted to allow one person to operate it, but in the gloom there was no way to tell. It closed with a crunch, leaving them in almost total darkness.

Regin grunted in satisfaction. 'Done,' he said, and led them towards the light. They emerged to find a deep, sheer-sided hollow. A small town wrought of stone lay within its centre.

'Welcome to Tradesholding.'

THIRTY-SIX

They settled the horses in the empty stable, and followed Regin to a nearby house. Everything was silent and still – they were they only living people in the town. Even that felt claustrophobic; hemmed in by the high walls, it was almost like being underground. Grukust shivered and Karland remembered his people had forsaken their tunnels millennia ago for the plains. He was not comfortable with enclosed spaces.

After Regin had settled them, he asked what supplies they needed, and then sighed. 'I will try to procure them. It may take days, though, and much persuasion, even for gold. I can care for your horses when you leave. If – when – you return, they will be ready. Now tell me why you are here, and why you are pursued. The message from the patrol was somewhat confusing.'

Rast told him a great deal more than Karland had expected him to, beginning with the Council of Twelve and the assassins in Darost. He then told him of the orcs in Eordeland and their alliance with Meyar, at which Regin spat.

'Meyar,' he rumbled, grinding his teeth. 'Ever have they been a thorn in our side, demanding goods and weapons for little payment, and then trying to take what they will not buy with mercenaries. They are one reason we have closed our borders. But even I never thought they would tryst with orcs.'

Rast described the attack on The Croft, their chasing of the survivors, the capture by the orks, and their escape. Regin looked at Grukust in approval. 'Earned that axe, lad, I'd say,' he remarked. 'Champion of the tribes, eh? Glad to see at least one ork has honour and sense over bloodlust.' Grukust nodded bleakly. Rast outlined the events in the Dimnesdair, and then finished on their conversation with the dragon. Karland realised the big man trusted this dwarf greatly.

Regin looked astonished. 'You actually spoke to a Dragon?' he said, shaking his head. 'Are they as treacherous as the tales say? I have seen only one, from afar. I have not heard of one speaking to another race in my lifetime.'

'No. She was honourable, and I trust her. She saved us more than once,' said Rast quietly. 'Times are changing, my friend.'

Regin nodded. 'That cannot be argued.' He squinted, thinking. 'So. There is a path – that much is true. I have not travelled it, but it was used by others once. It rounds our mountain here and enters a small valley betwixt the two, then follows the great slopes mayhap two thousand feet up and finishes below the snowline in a great circle of rocks... or so it is said. It is not likely to be a safe path now. Many years have passed since it was travelled. As to a hollow in the mountain... even we have not delved below that peak. *Jörmunrdrasill,* we call it.'

The name pricked Karland's ears. 'I thought that was a myth of some kind of enormous tree?' he asked. He was sure Aldwyn had mentioned it.

The Dwarf looked at him oddly. 'Myth?' he asked. 'You humans are strange. It is no *tree.* What else is white and reaches into sky, higher than all else, with roots that grasp the foundation of this world?' He shook his head. 'And within those roots... something slumbers, something better left undisturbed. We can feel it.'

'Györnàeldàr called it the Sacred Place of the Dragons,' Xhera spoke up.

Regin barked a laugh. 'Dwarves have delved too deep before, and awoken foul banes,' he said. 'We have not done that here, and do not intend to. You do not know what this key is, or what you seek? Bah! I wish you luck in your quest. It sounds like a fool's errand to me. So – now you must finish your tale, Rast. You escaped that dark place, I can see that.'

'Not unscathed,' said Rast. 'We lost the one who had the knowledge of our quest. Assassins had tracked us, and we were ambushed. Men of Meyar, allied with the orcs and men who seek us. But what I tell you now is dire, and you would do well to listen to me.'

Regin shrugged. 'Never have I known you to exaggerate.'

'Your mind may change, Regin.' Rast smiled wryly. 'There are fifty thousand orcs massing in the Dimnesdair; men, ogres, and fell beasts gather with them. We believe they plan an alliance with the armies of Meyar to make war on Eordeland. Now they are discovered, they must leave that place or risk being trapped at the Iril Pass. We know not how many of them hunt us, but they did not seem few.'

Regin's mouth snapped shut. 'Fifty thousand, you say?' He stroked his beard, and abruptly sat forward in his chair. 'Fifty *thousand?* Our greatest war against the *Rühk-villazhü* was against a host of thirty thousand and it was a millennia ago. Allied with men, ogres... they could sweep away entire nations. You are *certain?*' Rast nodded. Regin blew out through his beard. 'I am sorely troubled by this. I will speak to Thekk. This is woeful news indeed.'

'Your patrol did not seem to believe me,' said Rast.

Regin waved his hand dismissively. 'Young fools,' he said. 'None of them past a hundred and fifty. What do they know?'

Karland's eyes widened. He glanced at Xhera, who shook her head. *A hundred and fifty years old is young?*

The Dwarf rose. 'I will go now and return with enough supplies to make you comfortable. There is hay for the horses enough, but be prepared – you may not see me for some time after that. Rest, and await my return.' He left abruptly, and closed the door.

'You told him everything,' said Karland in surprise.

Rast nodded. 'Dwarves appreciate the detail in things,' he said. 'And Regin is trustworthy. He is a longbeard, and will not conscience falsehood.' He stretched. 'Our immediate danger is over. Although it will be difficult to wait, we must use the time to recover and prepare. Our journey has been hard, and I fear it will get harder yet.'

CR   SO

Five anxious days passed. The days were mostly sunny, meaning that their enemies could only move at night. Nevertheless, the sense of urgency increased. Karland spent his time sleeping, reading, and learning the ways of combat with various weapons and bare hands from Rast. Now he had time to rest, his melancholy over Aldwyn returned, and he often wondered how his family were. Xhera was even quieter than usual, although she sometimes spoke to him about her sister and for the first time said she missed the farm.

Their deadline with the Dragon came. In agitation Karland explored the town with Xhera, but found no other entrances than the tunnel. The Dwarves crafted too well for his eyes.

The sixth day dawned with the threat of heavy rain, and clouds so thick that the small town was shrouded in gloom. Sometime after noon Regin finally reappeared. His weathered face was troubled, and he hurried in and sat down without greeting.

'Good, you are all here. I beg your forgiveness that matters have taken this long,' he began without further ado. 'Thekk did not at first wish to listen. I found my people… unwilling… to give me supplies for outsiders, even for gold. Then the first patrol went missing.' His eyes were dark, as if he had not slept much. 'We waited for them a full day, and then sent another. They also failed to return.

I spoke again of your warnings, and this time Thekk was troubled enough to listen. He sent out one hundred dwarves, a full battle group, and the remains of the patrols were found. They did not die well.

'They found no foe, but the entire city is in uproar. Orcs have never been this canny before and I cannot believe the patrols could have been slain without shedding their share of blood. There is something strange about this, but whatever it is we will avenge our people. Curse these treacherous vermin! Another battle group will be going out again today. Thekk has told them that they are not to return without finding the foul ones that did this.

'If you are still set on leaving today may be the best time, but I would be wary of the trail up. By now it is likely spied out and foes may lie in wait. Take instead the south slope; it is a harder climb through the trees, but you have a greater chance of moving unseen. Pray that your Dragon awaits you! Your supplies are ready with enough to see you on the mountain for two weeks and your horses will be cared for. I have left wo-'

He broke off at the sound of heavy feet. The door burst open and the first dwarf apart from Regin that they had seen in days stood there, breathing heavily. He was pale from loss of blood from a deep wound in his side and he pressed hard on it with a stained cloth.

'We are beset,' he gasped. 'Near two thousand orcs with men – and ogres! We do not understand how they came to our gates unseen. We battle at the second gate, but they have cut the battle group off! We must assemble on the western slope before they fall.' The concern was terribly real in his eyes: Dwarves had few marriages or young, and each lost was a tragedy.

Regin whirled. 'I must go,' he rasped. 'Loni will see you to the gate.' The wounded dwarf nodded. Regin clasped Rast's hand, and nodded to the others. 'Good luck,' he said, and then he was gone.

'Let us go,' said Loni. 'You must hurry. Will it take long to make ready?'

Rast shook his head. 'Karland, Xhera: pack those books away. They stay here with the horses. Carry only what you need. Xhera, do you carry the pendant?' She nodded, and grasped it through her tunic. He glanced back to Loni.

'Five minutes.'

Loni nodded, then looked more closely at Grukust's axe. 'I recognise this work. How did you come by it?'

'Won it by arms,' said the big Ork. 'Good fight. Dwarf annoyed when beaten but honourable. It gain more honour on plains.'

The dwarf nodded, impressed. 'You must have defeated a mighty dwarf for it. This is a great prize, worthy of a fine warrior. It has runes of edge-keeping on it.

Mikill-Kbönödil, it is named. You should not need to hone it; it was crafted by Onar, one of the greatest of our smiths.'

The ork shook his head. 'I never needed sharpen it. Always wonder why.'

Rast returned. 'We are ready. We just need the supplies.'

Loni led them outside. Rast carried the chest of books to the stable, and found neat packs there. Everyone picked one and moved with the dwarf to the tunnel. Loni moved slowly and painfully, still very pale.

'Let me bind your wound, at least,' said Karland.

The dwarf shook his head. 'There are healers enough in our halls. You must go before the fight spills around the base of the mountain.' He led them through the tunnel and placed his hand on the rock. There was no spell this time – he merely pushed, and the door began to swing. Peering through the crack, they saw the small vale, empty. He pushed harder, and they slipped through the door.

Loni pointed up the slope the other dwarf had previously indicated. 'That way lies the mountain you seek. Follow the path over that crest and you will reach it on the other side of our own. It looms above us even here.'

Drakeholm Soaring lived up to its name, rising behind the mountain they stood at the base of, the peak vanishing into the clouds. It seemed strangely out of place, so much larger than the others around it, although they too were larger than many of the Iril Eneth.

Loni placed his hands on the door. 'Good luck. May you find what you seek… and may your axes be ever-sharp.' He pulled, and the door swung shut with a hollow crunching thud.

Rast led them swiftly up the slope, trying to get around cover as fast as possible. They could hear faint blood-curdling sounds from the western slope of the mountain. Screams and cries and guttural screeches, punctuated by the grim chants of dwarves and the occasional bellow of an ogre, drifted around the curve of the mountain. The battle sounded fierce but the outcome was inevitable; it only remained to be seen if the dwarves triumphed quickly enough to save their people that were cut off.

They moved quickly up the slope indicated. The grass and sporadic trees gave way to young pines, and other conifers started springing up as they travelled. There was a definite pathway here, barely more than a trail worn into a groove which widened out and led northwest.

Some time later they reached the apex of the curve in a low pass over a ridge. Karland glanced behind them and bit off a curse.

'What is it?' asked Rast, coming to him. Karland motioned downwards. A dark knot of creatures poured around the rocks far below, flowing past the vale they had emerged from, led by several lone figures. A small group had clearly broken away from the battle and was moving fast for their slope. It was hard to see exact details but they were clearly not dwarves.

'*Move!*' barked Rast. 'This could be a well-laid trap. If we are lucky, they have not seen us yet. When I change direction, follow me. We must not be herded into the arms of the enemy.'

He moved out along the downward slope at a run, dipping along the trail into a deep valley. On the other side, the path curved off up to the right, running around the base of the vast mountain and rising upwards out of sight. They charged down the slope to the valley floor, moving as fast as they safely could. An hour later, they were nearly up the other slope, the trail the only clear path.

Rast looked back. There was no sign of the pursuers. Without a word he wheeled left off the road, directly up the slope of the mountain in front of him. Above them, the peak stretched away out of sight into the clouds. To the east a single shaft of sunlight speared down, lost among the mountains. Rast led them carefully up the steepening slope and spoke in low tones.

'They knew we must come this way. I wonder if the whole battle was meant to flush us out. With luck they will not realise we left the road.'

Behind them a howling drifted on the wind, and faint shrieks and calls were heard as the hunters gained the lip of the valley between the two mountains.

Rast's face was grim. 'I cannot see the dragon anywhere. If we have missed her, we are doomed. I only hope that we reach the circle of rocks in time to hide, or lose those behind us.' He did not sound hopeful and no one had the breath to respond.

They moved on steadily up the slope of Drakeholm Soaring, the vast peak looming above them impervious to the drama unfolding at its foot.

THIRTY-SEVEN

The sounds of their pursuers echoed through the trees surrounding the mountain. Grukust helped the children up the slope for hours, through the treacherous scree and brush at the mountain's foot. The sun was dipping steadily to their left, breaking through the clouds more and more; it would be a clear night.

He used his superior weight and strength to break a trail. His orkish endurance made it easier for the younger humans to make good time, but he knew that one mistake at this scrambling pace would spell disaster. He hoped Rast could find this meeting place. There was nothing to do but keep going and hope they would gain some kind of sanctuary on the mountain that loomed above them.

Rast moved over the ground lithely, eyes darting and senses alert, often ranging off to the side. Sometimes he vanished from view and caught up from the rear. Once or twice they found him waiting for them ahead.

'How does he… do it?' gasped Xhera. 'He must be doing… twice the distance… we are.'

'Training… conditioning… stubbornness… not right in the head, who… knows,' puffed Karland. Grukust grinned to himself. The big human's endurance was almost orkish.

The sounds behind them were still faint, but he was under no illusions; they had finally been followed off the path. Grukust knew his trail-breaking made them far easier to track.

Not far ahead, the ground began to rise out of the greenery that surrounded them. Grukust shouldered his way through a small thicket of stunted evergreens and broke out into a small plateau. The clearing was reasonably level although covered in a rough stony gravel underfoot, but it was easier to move on than the slope.

Karland and Xhera stumbled out after him. Clear, level ground nearly threw them off balance when it abruptly appeared after hours of the slope. They paused, panting, and rubbed sore legs.

'Must keep moving,' grunted Grukust, breathing deeply and regularly in reply to the oxygen debt. He was heavily scratched and bruised but ignored it. They needed to find shelter. He looked around. 'Where Rast gone?' He hadn't seen him for some time.

'He could have gone ahead again,' said Xhera tentatively.

'Not matter. We must go,' said Grukust firmly. 'Rast look after himself, but Grukust was given care of you.' Part of him angrily demanded he face their pursuers with honour, but he needed to keep them safe.

The young ones staggered into motion again, following Grukust to the other side of the clearing. It began to rise before the tree line, and glancing back he could see they were already high above the foothills they had travelled. All around them the plains stretched into the distance, the road a sliver winding through it. He turned back and carried on, and had almost reached the trees when a quiet voice behind them spoke and made the children jump.

'We must hurry. They are not far behind and have found our trail.'

Rast slid past them noiselessly. He had donned his remaining cloak before moving into the woods, the dark grey cloth melded into the woodland colours around him. There were several new rents in it, and a few more smatterings of dirt, but he didn't appear to be wounded.

Grukust cast an eye back as he walked beneath the trees. 'How many?'

'Hard to say. I found orcs running as advance scouts,' Rast answered. He motioned them onward, and hardly twenty minutes later and hundreds of feet further upslope they heard a brief echoing roar of many-voiced anger far behind them.

'Think they found scouts,' remarked Grukust with a dark chuckle, climbing steadily.

'We must move quickly,' said Rast. 'There are perhaps forty orcs and men with an ogre and another creature. It looked akin to a Dire Wolf and can no doubt scent us. They want us badly.'

'*Haar'luc pasklia,*' Grukust cursed in a snarl. 'Curse all men who run with that foul meat!'

'There was also something else.' Rast's face was troubled.

'What?' Grukust demanded. Anything that worried Rast was something he did not want to meet.

'I'm not sure,' said Rast. 'I only sensed it. There was something familiar... whatever it is, it is more than at home in these woods. I was almost detected.'

The slope steepened and they found themselves moving further to the right, following a shallower cut running upwards. They were not very far up the mountain and Grukust was unsure how far up this riven rock was.

For nearly another hour, the party moved up the increasingly steep slope. The wind picked up the higher they went, and the cover of the trees became more sporadic. An inquisitive bear cast an eye over them from a distance, but the occasional sounds of the following band kept it cautious, and it quickly moved off in search of a less crowded area.

The sun sank towards the horizon, despite the fact that they were travelling around the curving slope towards it. The mountain ascending for many thousands of feet yet. As they broke from another treeline Grukust found he had to help Xhera and Karland more than once – the younger humans were nearly spent, lacking the stamina of their larger companions. The pursuit was very close now, seeming to have split up into several bands.

'If they are close enough to be heard so clearly, then there are those amongst them that are much closer,' Rast cautioned them all quietly. 'Scouts could be on us before we realise. We must throw them off our trail.'

He headed off to the left, forsaking the spiral they had been following and heading for a steep face that went up to a gently sloping top nearly fifty feet up.

'Grukust, can you climb this?'

'Yes,' grunted the Ork, eyeing the ascent. 'Grukust is not a rock-rabbit, but he can get to top.'

'Get them both up,' said Rast. 'I will create a false trail and return. We do not have long, but this face is not as fierce as it seems and it is less chancy than becoming trapped here. If they believe we have gone further along this cut, we may buy enough time to find the trail up again.' He tossed the coiled rope to the ork, then turned and stomped his way further up the cut, moving with a strangely graceless gait that seemed unlike him. He slammed his feet here and there, brushing plants aside, and dislodging stones every so often. As he disappeared around a boulder Grukust realised he was making it look like many had passed.

'Karland,' barked Grukust as the boy stood there staring upwards. He headed for the face where Xhera was already climbing and ignored Karland's shiver. He knew the boy hated heights, but it was this or death.

The going was slow and steady, and they didn't seem to be making good headway. Grukust was worried; the hunters could see them at any point now. He could see the last part up ahead was sheer, and wondered if they would make it at all.

Abruptly he made a decision. 'Keep climbing,' he called quietly, and ascended as fast as he was able, moving recklessly and using his great strength to haul himself up. His breath was bursting from between his tusks and several times his hands or feet slipped, but he made it to the top whilst the humans were still carefully climbing at halfway.

Not waiting to get his breath properly, he opened his pack and uncoiled the rope. He quickly tied a knot in the bottom and then a loop, and then another knot, so that the rope would dangle with a solid loop right at the end.

He fed it down until it slapped the cliff next to Xhera. He didn't dare call down to her, and prayed she would grab it quickly. Xhera started and nearly slipped when the rope fell next to her. Karland, despite his dislike of heights, frantically lunged for her with his left hand and nearly fell himself. He caught her hand and pulled, and she shook off her fear and slipped her foot into the loop of the rope.

Grukust stood taller, hoping he wouldn't show against the mountain for all to see, and pulled hand over hand. Xhera was light and came up easily, fending off the rock face with her free foot and one hand. Nearing the top, the ork slowed, and she slowly and carefully put her hand out to the edge and held on tightly. Grukust leaned down and lifted her easily. Xhera gulped and, leaning forwards, threw her arms around his neck. He braced one big hand on her back, stepped away from the edge, and let her down with a gentleness that would have surprised anyone who thought they knew orks. Then he hurried back to the ledge, hoping Karland was near the top. Peering down, he cursed. The sun was sinking and the shadows were getting longer, making it easy to notice unusual movement on the mountainside.

Karland hadn't moved an inch from his last location.

03 80

Karland had nearly fallen when he had lunged for Xhera, and had scraped his right palm raw. He managed to get his other hand up, but was trembling with reaction, and when he tried to move his feet slipped. Nearly weeping with fright, he felt tingling shivers sweep through his soles.

Now he could not move up or down, and he was tiring fast. He finally got both feet back on rock, but there he froze, his arms shaking and his knuckles white. His senses were screaming that they were running out of time; at any moment he expected the pursuers to burst from the trees and cut him from the cliff face with arrows.

The rope slapping next to him penetrated Karland's fear, and he slowly looked over, hands in a death grip. It took a few seconds to realise here was a way out, considerably longer to manage to summon the courage to unclench a cramped hand from the cliff face and grab the rope desperately. From there it was easier to slip one foot in the loop and hang on tightly. The rope hardly moved as his full weight moved onto it – Grukust might as well have been carved from stone. As soon as Karland was fully on the ork began hauling with all his strength.

Karland felt himself rising at an astounding rate, spinning as he rose. He was too tired to do much to stop himself hitting the wall. When he tried, he skinned his hand raw again. He gyrated and bumped to the top, wondering if he would have the strength to climb over.

Grukust gave him no time to try. The ork jerked his arms straight up with the last few feet to go, launching him upwards, and shot his arm out to grab Karland by the front of his tunic. As soon as the big hand closed on his clothes, Karland felt the ork throw them both backwards from the edge. Karland's loud squawk of surprise was cut off by the movement. They landed next to Xhera with a soft thump, and Grukust immediately moved a hand over Karland's mouth.

Using a finger in a human gesture of quiet the ork raised it to his lips. Pushing them both firmly down flat he slowly pulled the end of the rope back from the edge. Karland turned around on his elbows and squirmed to the lip, peering over as cautiously next to Xhera. Grukust joined them a second later, his large nostrils flaring.

They had been not a moment too soon. Breathlessly they watched a dark shape move out from the trees and cross lightly halfway to the rock. Karland hoped desperately that this scout had missed their ascent as the slender figure below moved forward, intent up on the ground, a large ornate bow held in his left hand and a quiver of arrows on his back.

This did not seem to be an orc. He wore an oddly organic-looking dark grey cloak, which blended as well with the rocks around him as it had with the shadows of the trees. The hood was drawn back enough to allow for peripheral vision, and strange-looking dark armour was visible underneath. The slim form moved as lightly as a dancer over the loose scree, but the movements seemed to carry with them an odd dissonance.

Crouching, a hand flicked out very quickly to touch something, perhaps an overturned stone. The head jerked up in a swift curve, and then cast around, taking in the surroundings entirely, the hood falling back. The movements spoke of a grace that was inhuman, and with slow disbelief Karland realised they must be looking upon an elf. The sharply upswept ears were not easy to see, but the movements and features were plain.

Karland's first instinct was to stand and call to the elf to hide, that he was in danger from the orcs that must be only minutes away, but Grukust held him down. Understanding grew; something was not right here. The elf would surely not be unaware of the hunters so close behind him. And how did a single elf come to be here?

The elf moved in some ways like Rast, Karland thought, but whereas Rast was a finely controlled balance of power and stealth, this elf flowed like a natural spring. It was the difference between a cat stalking and water running over soft land.

The form below seemed to sense something and they drew back slightly as the elf dropped his hood back. Fair hair glowed, but there seemed to be some shadow still upon his face. He looked up the trail, and then appeared to spy something near the bottom of the rock face where they had climbed. Clearly there was something in both locations that drew his attention, and Karland's alarm grew as he wondered if the elf had seen evidence of their climb. Elven senses were legendary; if he had puzzled out their ruse they were trapped. They couldn't move up the slope without being seen, and once they were pinpointed they would be trapped. There weren't even any rocks here big enough to drop on the form below.

As the elf reached the bottom of the cliff, he froze as something knocked off a tree behind him. The elf's head whipped around, snakelike, to follow the sound. Suddenly Karland saw a huge form to the elf's right sprint around the small boulder marking the beginning of the cut.

Despair welled up in him; there was simply not enough time for Rast to reach the elf. Despite the lack of noise, at the first movement from Rast the elf whirled with inhuman speed and grace, his hand blurring to his quiver. Before they could even register it, an arrow had been nocked and sent flying towards the incoming human.

Elves were famed as extremely skilled archers. With sharper senses than all other races and centuries to perfect the art they could see a target clearly, register its speed and angle, and send an arrow on its way with deadly accuracy faster than most other beings could even react. Tales of them splitting their own arrows abounded. The arrow reached the hurtling form before Karland could even register its release.

It slashed into Rast's running form... and bounced off to the side. Karland blinked and it took him a split second to realise it had not, in fact bounced off. Rast had apparently swept it out of the air with the back of his hand an instant before it struck him.

The elf appeared equally astonished. By all rights, this shot should have struck the running human through the throat and killed him instantly. He could clearly not believe what he had seen.

The frozen second the shock awarded Rast was not wasted. His left hand up to ward off any more attacks, he reached the elf as the inhumanly fast hand darted for another arrow. The elf nocked it, but as it released the bow was slapped sideways by Rast's other hand. The arrow skipped off the rock face and pinwheeled off into the trees down the slope as Rast shot an arm straight out at the elf's throat, fingers stiff.

The elf threw himself backwards, hands planting as his feet flipping up to strike Rast. Rast leaned back slightly and the soft boots whipped in front of his face. Even as the elf flipped back to his feet, his hands moving in a blur as he struck back at the big man, Rast moved forward. A dagger flashed in the slim hand and then spun off even faster than it had appeared. With a shiver Karland realised that Rast was at least as fast as the elf.

The elf aimed several frantic blows at Rast within a mere second after the loss of the knife which were deflected or absorbed. The blows became more desperate, and suddenly the elf reeled backwards, his delicate nose smashed bloodily across his face. Rast's arm was straight out, almost fully extended but slightly bent. Neither the watchers nor the elf had even seen it move, the arm deflecting a strike slightly up and to the side and then connecting in one movement.

The scout realised he was in trouble through his pain and turned blindly to escape. As he whipped around into a sprint, Rast's huge hand shot out and grabbed the hood of the cloak. The elf was already moving so fast his feet simply lifted up in front of him. Karland heard a gasp from Xhera as a faint choking noise reached them.

Rast hauled the elf up by the cloak and slammed an elbow into the side of the struggling being's head with a solid crack. The elf's wiry strength was no match for the enormous human and with the strike the elf collapsed.

His struggles became disoriented and Rast heaved him up and swam a massive forearm over his throat. Locking the palm around his other bicep, he passed his other arm and hand up behind his head. His shoulders and upper back bunched as he tightened his arms and jerked down hard three times. On the third, they heard a very faint crack, and the elf's arms flopped weirdly, all grace gone.

Shocked, Karland watched Rast lower the dead elf. Even in death he appeared beautiful. He understood why Rast had killed him; they would never evade an elf tracking them, but he could not understand why it had been. Rast had talked much of the Elves, saying they were gifted fighters and the longest lived of mortals. Yet they were always known as gentle, a goodly and carefree folk. Elves were closest to the natural harmony of nature and the world they lived in.

Rast knelt next to the elf, gazing intently at the delicate face. With the elf dead and still, the watchers could see that the shadow on his face was lifted somewhat, the remainder due to looping scars on the cheeks and lips. They were faint at this distance, but dreadful, marring the beauty of the fact and lending a sinister aspect to it.

After a moment Rast pulled the hood over the still face, and bowed his head, reflecting a deep sorrow. A few seconds later, he sprang up and crossed swiftly to the discarded bow. Picking it up, he moved to where he had knocked the original arrow aside and retrieved that as well, and then, returning to his fallen foe, replaced that in the quiver. He picked up the dagger and re-sheathed it on its former owner, bent over the ground where they had fought and randomly turned a few rocks, then hefted the still form over his shoulders.

'What is he *doing*?' whispered Xhera. Her face was very pale.

Grukust explained quietly that he was taking the body to try and trick their enemies into thinking that the elf had been tracking elsewhere leading away from them. Rast disappeared into the trees and was gone some minutes; the three on the outcrop took the chance to look around and see how they would carry on moving. It seemed that with care, they could move in the encroaching shadows and travel up to a wider area that looked like it could be a rough path around the mountain.

The fight had started and been over in under a minute, but already both moons were beginning their climb into the sky, and dusk was nearer. Though the sky was light the sun had moved behind the mountain.

A large form re-emerged from the trees. After checking that the base of the rock face was clear, Rast began a swift climb. Grukust unlimbered the rope again, but when he dangled it Rast shook his head and carried on climbing. Smooth and tireless, he used his legs more than his arms and found holds the others had not even seen. It was hardly a minute before he appeared next to them, a thin line of red evident on the back of his left hand from the arrow. Rast saw the incredulity in their faces.

'I was lucky,' he said quietly. He shook streaks of blood off the hand. 'We must move. Elves can see in the dark better than any of us and at night they can almost track the heat from our passing.' His voice sounded very tired, even if he did not look it. 'If there is another, we could still be tracked for long minutes yet.' He shook his head, sounding distressed, as they started to move. 'I cannot believe that elf was in league with Teromens – with *orcs*. And so eager to kill! I could feel his bloodlust, and his face was ritually scarred.' The disbelief was evident in his voice, and he looked wan. 'I have never heard of this. It is ill.'

Grukust grunted. 'Nothing says only *urch* fallen,' he remarked sourly. 'Dark times, many changed from what once were. Look, Rast: now more *Goruc'cha* in world than true ork. One day perhaps no orks left. Why not same with Elves?'

'I always thought they would remain incorruptible,' sighed Rast. 'They are old and powerful, and closest to the world of all the races. There are not many; the loss of a single elf is grievous. I carried him to a place where the rocks had fallen in a slide – even an elf can mis-step, although I doubt many would believe that he died so simply. There is but some small hope they will think his death accidental. I was lucky that I distracted him, and there is a slim chance it will be believed. If it works, it will have gained us precious time to find that which we seek. We are nearing the snow line and the riven rock cannot be too far. If we do not find it before dark, Grukust, you should take the lead. Your eyes fare better than mine when the light has gone.'

The ork nodded. 'Maybe two, three hours more of light on other side. Dark will help. Even Elf cannot track in dark like in day.'

'No, but they see in the dark better even than you, my friend. Now we know who directs the orcs. To find them aligned changes things.' His tone held something approaching despair. In no stories that Karland had ever heard was an elf evil. Rast was right. It changed everything.

'He was so beautiful,' Xhera whispered. 'How could Rast kill him?' She still looked horrified. Although he understood how she felt, Karland felt impatient.

'He would have killed us without thinking about it. You heard Rast. Don't give him a hard time, either – you can see how he feels about this.'

Reluctantly she nodded.

They continued to follow the open cleft, which evened out and grew more horizontal. As it rounded the face of the mountain, the sun once more bathed them in light from lower on the horizon, the sky tinged a reddish pink. After nearly two hours of climbing with no signs of imminent pursuit, they reached a path along the edge of a cliff. To the right was the rough end of a trail; it seemed likely that this was where they could have emerged had they not left the road. To the left was a steep slope running upwards, turning to run up the side of a cliff. It seemed to be a natural pathway, and was wide enough for two abreast, bordered by a sheer drop into abyssal depths.

Cautiously, they started up. This was their last chance to find the ring of stones in the light. If it was not there, they would try and hide as best they could and wait out their pursuit. Györnàeldàr had said she would meet them, but they were nearly two days past the appointed time. If they did not manage to survive the night, she would find only corpses.

Rast helped Karland and Xhera up the scree-strewn slope, aware that they were past the limits of their strength. Karland stayed near the wall and was relieved when Grukust sighed heavily as he reached the top corner, which turned sharply left back into the face of the mountain, and rumbled, 'I think we found ring.'

Spurred on he used his last burst of energy to reach the corner and found a shorter, gentler slope rising northeast to two massive mismatched boulders, a gap the width of two men lying head to toe between them. Almost opposite was a huge split rock that dwarfed the others; a great crack ran its height. It sat slightly further into the rough circle than the others, which formed an arc to either side ending in the boulders in front of them. The circle was more of an oval, easily several hundred feet across at the widest point.

Karland moved quickly away from the sheer edge behind him, repressing the light-headed feeling from being too near drops that he had battled much of the day, and tiredly used his hands to help him up the slope. The others joined him, and they moved between the boulders and across the circle to stand in front of the riven rock. He dropped in exhaustion, Xhera beside him. Rast moved up to look at the massive rock, but could see nothing to suggest that there was a path into the mountain. Grukust looked around him, irritable.

'What now?'

Rast shrugged. 'I do not know. We were charged to journey here. I was not expecting close pursuit, especially by orcs in daylight. Perhaps we have lost them, but if there is even one more elf with them, our chances are slim. An elf *must* have been what the dragon saw in the Dimnesdair. If they trap us here, we are lost. I do not know why it was so important to bring the pendant here.' He looked at Xhera, who was lying with her head on her pack.

'Isn't the dragon coming?' said Karland.

Rast shrugged. 'She may be looking for us, or have given up and left by now. This has been a hope and a dream from the start. I wish Aldwyn were here to tell us more - that old man knew far more than we ever realised. We have followed all the signs to this place, but I see no entrance – only a dead end. '

He motioned them down.

'Get some rest. If we are tracked, here we will make our stand.'

Barely half an hour later, they heard the first sounds of pursuit echoing up from below. The orcs were making no effort at stealth, the enemy approaching slowly up the same narrow slope they had used, wary of the drop into the shadowed abyss. The stone circle, a little way below the snowline, was now the lowest point with any real daylight left.

'They have found us,' Rast said. 'All we can do now is fight.'

Grukust cursed savagely in orkish, his bloodlust rising. To come so far and still fail infuriated him. Karland knew he would kill all he could before he fell, at any cost. Rast calmly cleared his belongings and unburdened himself, breathing deeply into his stomach and sides, closing his eyes and listening. His stillness unnerved Karland and Xhera more than Grukust's incipient berserk rage.

Karland wondered how many Rast would kill before he too died. There could be no escape for any of them. Apart from the entrance the terrain was impassable or dropped away into deadly depths.

'So, it ends here,' he whispered to himself, a sick feeling in the pit of his stomach. 'We've failed.'

Rast moved forwards, an air of readiness about him, and spoke softly to Karland and Xhera. 'Be ready. If they break through us you will have to fight, tired as you are. I pray that all I have taught you is enough.'

He beckoned Grukust with him, and they moved to the top of the cliffside slope where only a few could come at them at once. Grukust pointed to a rounded rock as high as his waist, worn by the elements. Rast looked at it intently and then nodded.

Karland licked dry lips. If they could send it careening down the slope they could hopefully thin the ranks of their attackers, many of whom would be struggling with the sunlight. He turned to Xhera. She looked tired; tired from the climb, tired of pursuit, tired of being afraid. He wasn't sure if he could even lift his sword when the battle began.

'I wish...' he began, and had to clear his throat. He tried again, with a broken smile. 'I wish we weren't here.'

She turned to look at him and her eyes trembled with tears. 'Karland...' she said. 'Always before, we could run, could hide. I'm so scared.' He could see her lip trembling.

'Me too,' he whispered. 'But I promised I would protect you.' It felt empty now.

She suddenly threw her arms around his neck. 'You're my best friend,' she whispered fiercely, and then let go.

Rast and Grukust suddenly tensed and heaved. Karland guessed the enemy was rounding the corner far below. They heard the bouncing clacking of the rock, and then Grukust shouted in anger as the sound stopped abruptly.

Both he and Rast retreated from the corner hurriedly as the same rock flew back up and smashed into the wall.

'Ogre,' said Rast bitterly. 'We would accomplish nothing fighting it on the slope. It would hurl us to our deaths. I suspect it may simply throw rocks until we are lifeless… or the rest surround us.'

Karland's eyes met Xhera's, wide with fright. He turned his head slowly, and looked at the others. Rast stood staring at the slope, but Grukust was staring into space, an unreadable expression in his huge dark eyes. He turned his head to Rast.

'Ogre is the problem,' he said. 'We kill ogre, we have chance.'

Savage cries interrupted him. A knot of orcs poured suddenly into the circle, eyes slitted against the light, with a group of men close behind.

Rast and Grukust leaped to meet them. Rast flowed among them, breaking limbs and necks, sliding away from cuts like a shadow, provoking screeches of frustration that turned to death gargles. Grukust's axe hummed around him in a blur as he hewed necks and limbs. They were gods of carnage, and the orcs and men facing them quailed at the onslaught, then broke and fell back. Rast fought three men and an orc over on the left as Grukust killed his last foe. Karland cried a warning as a huge grey hand clamped over the rock at the edge of the circle, dragging up the ogre's body. Its brutish face creased as it bellowed, catching sight of them through narrowed eyes.

It rounded the rock, closely followed by those who had fallen back, wary of the ogre. Stepping into the opening of the circle it stopped, lifting a large rock in its other hand. Men and orcs poured around its legs.

As it drew its hand back, Grukust, far to the right, shouted, '*Urukin vah varsi, Ogrin! Urukin vah varsi! Hai! Hai!*'

The ogre looked around and with an orkish curse of fury the huge ork swung his mighty axe in an arc around and then up over his body, letting go at the apex. He put his full massive strength into the throw, sending the large axe spinning end over end with all his might. Men and orcs ducked in fear, but it flew high.

A second later, one crescent of the axe slammed the ogre full in the face with a sickening crack. The huge creature screamed in a spray of bloody agony through a smashed mouth, the bones of its thick skull shattered and split; the rock it was holding fell from its hand, crushing a man beside it. Humans and orcs alike stared in disbelief. Although Grukust was now weaponless, the mighty strike had literally stopped the huge creature dead.

The dying ogre stumbled backwards, crushing more men standing behind it. With a groan, blood pouring from its cleaved skull, the giant tumbled backwards down the slope sweeping clustered orcs and humans with it, sending screaming bodies flying out into space and crushing others beneath it. It ended up on its back mere feet from the sheer edge and died, shuddering violently and choking on its own blood.

Their enemies drew back in dismay. Rast used the opportunity to kill his last opponent quickly, and Karland's hopes soared as he moved back towards them, the ring clear. Then up the slope came a strange deep baying, and the cries of men and orcs leaping out of the way. It was a sound they had heard before, in the Dimnesdair.

Furious snarls erupted, coming closer. Grukust, far to the right and nearest the slope, turned his head to regard his companions. In that second, Karland felt like everything was moving in molasses, slow but inexorable. In the Ork's dark eyes were compassion for his friends, and resignation.

'To be your friend has been my honour.'

The words drifted through the air as the ork thumped his big fist against his chest deliberately, holding their eyes, and then Karland saw the fires of fury ignite in them as he gave in to his rage. His full berserk fury rising, Grukust swung around and charged forward towards the gap between the stones.

He was mere feet from it when a nightmare bounded over the top of the slope. It was nearly four feet at the shoulder and heavier than any of them, with an armoured head and neck, heavily muscled shoulders, overlong teeth, and glinting amber eyes.

Karland had only a second for the sight to sink in. The tales of intelligent bloodthirsty demons that could tear through entire groups of armed men without slowing were real.

'Gar-wolf,' Rast said bleakly.

꿈   꿈

It crested the lip, its primary thought to meet its teeth in a soft throat. There was barely enough time for it to see the forms directly ahead before it snarled in shock.

With a roar to match its snarl, Grukust hit the unprepared gar-wolf so powerfully that the deadly teeth reflexively snapping for his throat instead met in his shoulder. As he drove the bigger creature backwards he gave himself totally to the fight, all thoughts except killing now gone, pain distant lightning lacing a red mist. Locking his massive arms around the creature's ribs to prevent it gaining room to tear his arm off, he clasped it tightly. Jerking his muscled neck back, he sank his own tusks into the gar-wolf's throat, ripping at the flesh beneath the fur as he used his powerful legs to drive it backwards.

The gar-wolf howled in shock around his shoulder. It now only had two legs on the ground, and could not brace itself properly. Growling through its teeth, tasting the ork's blood, it tensed to force him to the floor and tear him apart, but it was too late. Grukust, with a growl of triumph, drove it off balance and down the short slope with all the unbelievable strength in his powerful body. He ignored the agony-laced red pain and knew only that this was just another foe, its blood upon his lips. He had killed a wyvern. He would kill this beast.

He was Grukust, champion of the tribes.

C3   80

Rast and the children ran to the short slope, watching helplessly as Grukust gained momentum, orcs and men scrambling from their path, past the dead ogre and to the sheer edge. With a yelp of terror the gar-wolf's legs slipped, and they stumbled in a thrash of limbs, Grukust wrapped around it like a furious green limpet.

For a second they hung on the very edge of the drop. Rast caught a glimpse of Grukust's face, pale but roaring in triumph, his shredded arm hanging by tendons from the powerful bite of the gar-wolf, and then they fell from sight. There was a moment of shocked silence broken only by a howl of fear which cut off suddenly, and then Xhera screamed.

'*NO!*'

Rast saluted his friend silently even as he dragged the youngsters back from the slope. He knew Grukust could not have survived. There were still many more attackers, and now they were three. His sacrifice had done much to thin their attackers; perhaps it would be enough.

Barely had they set their backs against the riven rock than the remaining attackers poured back over the lip of the slope, coming between the rocks to stand fifty feet away in a spreading arc.

None of the orcs were as big as Grukust. They were warped, stunted imitations of the proud warrior, squinting in the fading light. The men wore the red and grey of Meyar. All seemed eager for the kill, although reluctant to approach through the mounds of dead bodies scattered in the circle, a testament to the fate of those that faced Rast. More poured into the circle, and he knew that when there were enough - or if they had archers - they would simply overwhelm them.

They did not attack. Rast's heart sank as he saw why, and he heard exclamations from the children. Another elf stepped delicately through the ranks which parted for her. She moved to the front, a slender sword sheathed at her side the only visible weapon. Her hair, so blonde as to be almost white, was swept back with a dark band, and she wore similar curious dark armour to the other elf. Her perfect, pale face held none of the peace usual to the Elves; her eyes glittered with malice, and she had an air of madness about her. Yet when she spoke, her voice was as gentle and melodic as any of her kind.

'Humans,' she said. 'Cease this pointless fighting. You know well what we seek.' Her arm raised and pointed at Karland and Xhera.

'Give me the pendant, and you may go free.'

'Since when does an elf lie?' Rast said sadly, backing up towards Karland and Xhera. 'Since when does an elf ally with their greatest foes and forsake her bond to this earth?'

She hissed suddenly, and her face twisted into something alien. 'I offer you a chance, then. Give me the pendant and your corpses shall not be defiled.'

Goblins and orcs snarled and laughed in anticipation. Men grinned as Rast opened his mouth, but before he could answer, the elf suddenly whirled with shocking reflexes and crouched to leap.

A roar that virtually flattened them all to the ground blasted down from above, and the scene lit up as brightly as noon. The springing outline of the elf was visible for an instant in a tightly controlled jet of incandescent fire; then it was gone, leaving only a shadow upon the ground where she had been.

There was a frozen moment, and then with a sound like someone tearing the world in half a shape beyond huge ripped overhead, darkening the scene where there had been searing light moments before. Wheeling abruptly, impossibly, the shape pivoted in the air and slammed its wings forwards to slow itself, dropping fifty feet to the earth with feet and claws extended.

The wingbeat sent orcs and men tumbling back down the slope into the dead ogre. Several fell screaming over the lip of the rock where Grukust had fallen and the rest broke and fled back down the steep path.

The impact of the landing knocked Karland and Xhera flat, Rast dropping to one knee. Rock under the huge feet cracked and crumbled, and earth and dust was thrown up around them. Over the cries of terror from the fleeing attackers, a huge voice rumbled.

'I see, little humans, that you could use my help.'

Two hundred and fifty feet of giant dragon lay curled around them in a protective circle, an iridescent red-gold in the last of the dying light.

Györnàeldàr had arrived.

THIRTY-EIGHT

With the arrival of the dragon, Karland felt the relief mirrored in the eyes of his companions. The dragon reported their pursuers still fleeing. Rast moved down to the edge in search of Grukust, but could see nothing in the shadowed chasm; Karland saw his shoulders drop in a sigh.

Turning, Rast levered the axe handle to free it from the face of the ogre, putting his whole body into it. A testament to Grukust's strength, the throw had split the top jaw and cleaved through the nose and part of the left eye socket, cracking the thick bone open and embedding the axe almost to the brainpan. Karland would not have thought such a blow possible from such distance.

The axe finally came free with a wet creaking. Shaking the blood from it, Rast cleaned the crescents on the cloak of one of the fallen. Returning to the others, he shook his head at their questioning stares, and said only, 'I will not leave his mighty weapon lying on a mountainside. I will return it to Darus one day, along with the tale of Grukust's bravery. It is fitting he should have his brother's axe.'

Karland bit his lip, feeling his nose and eyes sting, and Xhera quietly began gathering her things, tears streaming down her cheeks. It felt as if Grukust were still there, his brutish presence hiding his sly humour and friendship. A mixture of numbness and disbelief vied with his emotions; he wasn't sure how much more he could take after losing both Grukust and Aldwyn. The ork had been so full of vitality that it didn't seem possible he could have been lost.

Sensing their distress, their huge companion pulled herself from her contemplation of the gigantic split boulder. Lowering her scaled head, she spoke.

'I am sorry for the loss of your companion. I was many miles away when I saw your plight, searching the mountains for you. I could not arrive in time. He was brave.' She paused. 'Where is Aldwyn Varelin?'

Rast shook his head despairingly.

'He also fell, nearly two weeks gone. Assassins took him. We are all that is left of his quest.'

Györnàeldàr snorted quietly.

'That is news I am sorry to hear,' she rumbled softly. 'He understood much. It is meet that you continue his work though; it is more important than you may know.' She moved over to the rock. 'And so you shall. Take heed, mortals. None living but you have ever seen this sight. Stand away, for I cannot vouch for your safety.'

Györnàeldàr spread her forelimbs as wide as she could, placing one massive claw on each half of the giant rock. She rumbled, her attention focused on the boulder, her tail lashing. The humans moved hurriedly away. A low murmur seemed to arise in the air, and her rumble deepened until it was less heard and more felt through the feet as she hunched her shoulders with effort.

Slowly, the huge rocky halves moved, and then abruptly closed together with a crunch, startling the humans. The strain evident, the dragon held the rock together a few moments longer, rumbling in her own language. With a start, Karland realised it was now impossible to see where the join in the rock was. It appeared whole.

Györnàeldàr stirred, extending her wings back for balance, and dug her hindquarters deep in to the ground. With a shudder of effort and a long twist of her powerful body she turned the now more or less circular boulder to the side, lifting as she went. Her feet gouged deep into the rocks and soil beneath her as she struggled with a chunk of rock which outweighed her many times over. For a few moments nothing happened as a rumbling groan broke from her, yet ever so slowly her enormous strength won out. Flapping her wings hard for momentum and using her long tail to gain extra leverage on the ground, she slowly moved the rock to reveal a massive hole in the base of the cliff – a tunnel leading down into the mountain. The rock had been plugging the hole almost perfectly, but Karland could have sworn that when the rock was split there was only bare rock behind it.

The opening looked big enough even for her, and it was obvious why the dragon's place of rest was undisturbed. None but the most powerful of dragons could gain entry.

'Come,' said the dragon. She shook herself with an armoured clatter, and moved into the tunnel. They passed through down into the darkness which gradually increased until the only light remaining was the banked glow from her eyes, and a moment later their hastily lit lamp.

Wearily, the party travelled on foot down the wide tunnel, which sloped uniformly at a gentle angle – except for the roof, which dipped and rose so that Györnàeldàr's spines scraped it at intervals, even forcing her to drop to her stomach and slither underneath with sinewy grace a few times. She moved deliberately, casting her eyes around to illuminate the tunnel for them and rumbling to herself from time to time. Her furled wings were short of the walls, and as the tunnel widened, the humans moved up alongside her.

Karland stumbled on blearily. He was careful not to look directly at her face. In the pitch black her blazing eyes were bright enough to ruin night vision. After a time, Györnàeldàr rumbled in anticipation.

'I sense space ahead. We are near.'

Karland wondered why the tunnel was sometimes a tight fit if other dragons had once journeyed this way, and glanced at Györnàeldàr as he walked, having to tilt his head back even to see above her spurred elbow. Not watching where he put his feet, his foot hit a loose rock and he nearly rolled his ankle, a painful sprain prevented only by Rast's quick reflexes. Fingers like iron caught his bicep in a grip that made him gasp but kept him on his feet. He nodded in thanks to Rast, who nodded back, expressionless, and moved on.

Györnàeldàr noticed and snorted in draconic laughter which would have been muffled if she hadn't been so large. It sounded like distant thunder.

He guessed they had travelled miles. Further on he sensed the echoless quality of stilled air that was somehow different from a tunnel. The gloom ahead began to brighten imperceptibly until they realised they needed the lamp no longer. Finally the tunnel widened and heightened quickly into a mouth, and they stepped out into stillness. He stared in astonishment.

The cavern could have held cities. The ceiling rose to shadows thousands of feet up; the cave itself must have been over a mile long at the narrowest point and stretched off perhaps ten times that into the dimly lit distance. The air was dry and earthy. It was as if the entire inside of the mountain was simply hollow. The sensation of emptiness was staggering.

The source of the glow came from clusters of stones holding crystals which shone with a peculiar white-blue-green light. Close enough to daylight for comfort, it gave everything a cool hue. There were so many that they formed an ambient glow, some reaching a hundred feet or more up the wall. As the further reaches of the cave faded from sight they began to resemble stars. It was a profound sight, like seeing the night sky in a great dark still lake.

Xhera whispered to Karland, 'I wonder what holds the roof up?'

He immediately wished she hadn't. The fact that literally nothing had propped up the hundreds of millions of tons of rock above them for millennia made him feel nervous.

'What are these?' Xhera asked Györnàeldàr, waving her hand vaguely at the nearest glowing cluster.

'This place is precious to us,' Györnàeldàr said, whuffing her large nostrils. 'We set these to shine for as long as a dragon might live – our beloved night hid underground.'

'Do you hoard treasure here?' asked Karland.

Györnàeldàr hissed in quiet laughter. 'Often have I heard that Dragons desire treasures of men and dwarves,' she said in amusement. 'What would we do with them? We met here in ages gone. Dragon kind do not meet often in numbers, or lightly. But this place is holy to us; here, we are closer to one of the Dreamers of the World.'

'Dreamers?' breathed Xhera, her eyes alight.

'Yes,' said Györnàeldàr. 'All of us are part of this world's dream. Every action by any living creature is merely a way of changing the Dream a little... even simply observing it. But herein lies sleeping one of the Dreamers of this World, who weighs heavy on reality – a conduit of the power that draws from the dark strands of the Universe itself.

'There is an abyss at the other end of the cave that is said to be a source of the Dream. This cave has been unused for thousands of your years. While I lay in slumber, we were apparently tasked with safeguarding something of great importance here. This is the place you humans insultingly term *The Hall of Wyrms*.'

Karland nodded, recognising the legend from Aldwyn's notes.

Her breath sang between her huge teeth in scorn. 'Rather call it a place of Dream's Making, of Dragon Lore. Knowledge and power are to be found here, but not for mere mortals. My kind hoard treasures, this I cannot deny, but these places, the lore they contain... *they* are our treasures, not your meaningless metals. And look, does this not outshine by far your jewels and gold?'

Looking at the underground night she shook herself, her scales clattering and her ire seeping away.

'It also holds what you seek, this power we were given to safekeep. I do not know where or what it may be but I should find it without difficulty.'

Rast frowned. 'You said this was given to your safekeeping – is there no dragon here to guard it?'

'Do not doubt that it is protected,' said Györnàeldàr, sounding amused. 'Your sorcerers and elves are not the only ones who have power.'

Her tone was pleased, almost smug, and Karland remembered the old tales of the vast pride of dragons. They were the oldest and most powerful of all races, so he supposed they had reason.

Györnàeldàr extended her wings out and then her spine, like an enormous cat.

Her great claws opened out as she stretched, digging into rock with a rumbling screech and the odd spark, leaving gouges in the solid stone floor as an unmeant reminder of her power. Xhera looked at the cracked and torn runnels and shivered.

Unnoticing, the dragon shook herself out with an armoured clatter. 'Wait here,' she instructed. Her haunches bunched and she sprang into the air, reaching almost a hundred feet before her lifted wings slapped the air down with a crack. It was an incredible sight. Her wings lofted her further, and the backdrafts blew the human's hair haywire, swaying them on their feet.

Xhera's eyes never left the giant form gliding steadily into the cavern. 'How can such a large creature do that?' she said in disbelief.

'Aldwyn speaks of it in *A Note on Dragons*,' said Karland. 'He said dragons are not mortal flesh and bone like us.' The dragon swooped like an overlarge swallow to investigate something, even from here making a distant sound like the air being ripped in half, and then spiralled up on beating wings once more. It was evident she revelled in the feeling of flight.

'They are flesh and blood, yet... different, stronger. They have something to their bones and flesh, maybe...I don't know. It was very technical. I just don't think that they are the same as other creatures. When I was younger, my father told me many stories of mighty dragon slayers, but they are probably just stories. I cannot imagine anyone fighting a dragon, not really. Aldwyn wrote that they are 'immortal and immutable'.'

He smiled sadly at the memory of his old friend. 'They were the first and oldest living things, and they challenge the world around them like no other creature can. They never die unless killed. There is nothing else like them on this world, he said. I'm only glad he met her before he died.'

Knowing the scale of Györnàeldàr, the sheer weight and power of her presence, Karland felt again an awed sense of surrealism. Up close it was so overpowering you could almost ignore it, unless those bright eyes had their searing gaze fixed on you. Then you could be frozen with fear, speak truths without meaning to, even offer yourself up to die if you were sufficiently weak-willed. As if this was not enough, they were said to have powers beyond the physical. A powerful enough being *might* injure a dragon, perhaps even kill a younger one – as had happened at the outset of the Drake Years, where the hubris of a human king who slew a young dragon caused kingdoms to be laid waste – but Györnàeldàr was old, large and cunning, a queen of her kind.

The distant bird-like Györnàeldàr suddenly wheeled and flew back quickly, landing far enough away that the backpedal of her wings to settle her didn't blow the humans off their feet. She touched down lightly.

'There is nothing here but a stone archway, behind that slope of fallen rock,' she said, pointing back to her right with a fore claw, her right wing lifting and curling out of the way unconsciously. 'I searched for signs of my kin, but it appears this Hall has long been unused.'

Karland realised that this place was tantamount to a temple of sorts for her, one that had essentially been abandoned. She seemed a little sad.

'I'm sorry,' he said.

The dragon looked down at him. 'We meet from time to time elsewhere. You might call it a Drakemoot.' She smiled – a frightening sight since many of her teeth were as long as he was tall. 'Do not be disheartened by my melancholy, little mortal. Although the most sacred place in which we once gathered, this place is now abandoned to preserve a trust – but it is not the only place we have.' She lowered her head and whuffed a hot dry breath over him. He imagined rather than saw a suggestion of a glow in her throat, and felt a little heat. Her breath was musky but not as unpleasant as he had imagined it might be.

They moved off to their left along the cave wall, the dragon walking with them out of courtesy. For nearly an hour they travelled, moving several miles into the cavern. Finally they rounded the edges of the slope of rubble that Györnàeldàr had indicated. A large section of the wall had broken off in ages past, crumbling and sliding far out into the cavern.

As they cleared it, they could see the arch at the far edge. It was set perpendicular to the wall on a smooth stone platform with rounded steps. Boulders and rubble continued further out onto the cavern floor to either side of the portal.

It looked as if the edges of the slide had fallen over the arch and the dais it was on, yet the absence of debris on both suggested the rock had somehow been prevented from falling onto and in front of either side of the stone doorway, almost as if it had hit an upturned dome. The archway itself hinted at having been grown rather than hewn. Even from here, hundreds of feet away, it contained a dim liquid blue glow which seemed to Karland to come somehow from *elsewhere*. It rippled, speaking of silver-metal currents beneath the translucent surface. He noticed that the glow only appeared when they were in a direct line in front of the arch; too far to either side, and the arch was simply empty.

'From the air, that light was not visible,' said Györnàeldàr thoughtfully. 'This must be the artefact that you seek.'

Rast stopped. 'Well, we are here,' he said, 'and with little idea of what we must do next. *Nāginī, w*hat of the tunnel that we entered by? We should be wary. If we used it to enter, so might others.'

'No creature would dare enter a Dragon's lair,' hissed Györnàeldàr. 'Especially when a Dragon lies within. Should anything be foolish enough to pass within you may be assured that I will deal with it.'

'I meant no offense, *Nāginī*,' remarked Rast, inclining his head. 'I am simply a cautious man.'

Despite the reassurance, as they started towards the portal again Karland's unease began to increase. Barely two hundred feet from the goal of their journey, an increasing dread without discernible source struck him.

'What is happening?' mumbled Xhera.

Györnàeldàr slowed, senses probing. She suddenly reared on hindquarters to full height, snorting in alarm over the dry hiss of scales. Her head towering over them, she cast her burning gaze around the vast cave. The far reaches were shadowed despite the ever-present glow from the crystals fading back to the intensity of a starlit night. The top of the cave was still lost thousands of feet up in blackness, but the weaving head swept the merciless gaze to all points in an attempt to find what had disturbed her.

'We are no longer alone,' she rumbled.

☙ ❧

Karland looked around, his vague sense of dread growing. The cavern seemed to chill, the air feeling pressured; the cavern seemed dimmer. The encroaching darkness seemed ominous.

Györnàeldàr hissed, her eyes sweeping shadows forming near the wall to their left over a thousand feet away. Her wings snapped out menacingly. Curving them out to their full span, she dropped back to all fours with sinewy grace and slithered sideways from the party, gaining room and whipping her tail in agitation. All of her huge length was tensed and she appeared – impossibly – somewhat frightened.

'What could scare a dragon?' whispered Xhera fearfully, her teeth chattering in her own fear. Rast shook his head. Karland felt as scared as Xhera. He could not imagine anything more deadly.

'*That*,' Györnàeldàr hissed, her inner fires no longer banked. He followed her gaze.

A vague shape was forming on the nearest wall, as if fading through the rock.

The shadows collected across the wall before their eyes and faded into a blackness from which no light escaped. The pressure in the air increased, a humming discord in their minds which was more felt than heard. It vibrated through their minds and bodies with an awful tolling, dropping rapidly into the mental subsonic below perception. The ambient light seemed to weaken and dim with its descent.

Karland felt as if the sheer presence of the darkness would make his mind buckle like an eggshell under a heavy palm. Frantically he struggled not to go lose his grip on his mind, sure if he did he would go insane with loathing. Thoughts became erratic. Xhera looked panicked, reason fleeing, and even Rast was pale. A sheen of sweat dotted the big man's brow as his stubborn will fought the mental pressure, and he swallowed convulsively and supported Xhera as her knees buckled.

The scale of the shadow was such that it took several moments to realise it was becoming humanoid, but so vast as to dwarf Györnàeldàr. Smoking red eyes coalesced hundreds of feet over the floor, dull and burning; they lit nothing, sucking light into their burning pits. A suggestion of curved horns and a sense of a ragged pit of a mouth below them danced in their thoughts. Karland's eyes could not see the full shape clearly but his mind sketched the image from a more primordial sense. The outline seemed to be constantly shifting, as if it was only vaguely defined.

In a voice that seemed to be pulled from the dark places around and within them, from a source somehow *outside*, the form spoke into their minds.

-*Give me the Key.*-

Karland moved back, his face slack. The awful power of the words reached him and he strove with all his might to hold sway over his screaming instincts. His will was drowning in the shadow that loomed. He barely noticed Rast standing rigid, stark fear in his eyes and all his immense willpower battling the sheer, overbearing presence.

It smothered every action, rendering Karland barely able to breathe. The demon before them was everything men had ever feared in the darkness, everything that spoke of not just death, but utter annihilation.

Movement caught his eye, pulling him out of his terror. Györnàeldàr crouched, lashing her tail, hot light spilling between her teeth as her fires flared in hatred.

'Vile one!' she spat at the shape. 'Darkling of the Abyss! I know of you. You should not be here!'

-*I go where I will,*- replied the shape, taking a long step forwards and to the side, towards the portal, the thud of the indistinct foot speaking of immense weight and sending a shiver through the rock. The shape turned towards them, the stone arch slightly behind it, effectively stopping them moving past into the rest of the cavern. There was nowhere to go but back towards the tunnel mouth. A long sharp patch of darkness stabbed in front of the archway, blocking it, and Karland dimly realised it was a twin-tined tail nearly as long as the dragon.

The shape took an enormous step further over, and the dragon gathered herself. Rast's hand fell on Karland's shoulder. As he shook off some of the feeling Karland saw the fear on Györnàeldàr's scaled face as she prepared all her considerable powers to strike the demon. He distantly understood that for the first time in living memory a dragon faced a foe and was overmatched.

'*Leave this place,*' she hissed.

The murky red burn watched her coldly.

-Who will compel me, Wyrmling?-

The words numbed Karland again as she roared at the insult, eyes blazing, and crouched low to spring, tail lashing. Time slowed, stretching out. It seemed to the spark of cognizance left to Karland that the dragon and the shadowed demon became an unmoving tapestry.

Then Györnàeldàr stilled, even her tail pausing, cocking her huge head. The burning scrutiny stayed on her as she took a deep breath and streamed a brilliant line of defiant dragonfire out between them. Even the Darkling narrowed its eyes. She snapped her toothy jaws and bit off the sun-bright flame, her tension lessened and a look of strange reptilian peace suffusing her face as an almost imperceptible shaking pervaded the cavern.

'I am but a part of the great Dream, and you are beyond the Dream. I have not the power to hold you.' The words were a bitter admission.

-You belong to the Dream,- acknowledged the Darkling, *-but I am the unceasing Nightmare.-*

The demon stepped forward, shrouded in despair.

THIRTY-NINE

As the demon of shadow stepped towards them, a thunder transmitted through the very rock shook the entire cavern. It erupted from far behind the dark being, which turned at the commotion. In a scene impossible to behold, what appeared to be the whole far end of the huge cavern floor exploded upwards.

Györnàeldàr whirled and threw talons the size of wagons out, grabbing the humans none too gently. She leapt towards the wall, powered by her hind legs and aided by her wings, landing hard. The spell of the demon lessened; the awful presence was no longer fully focused on them. As she placed them on the floor as gently as she was able, a feeling of tingling freedom began to push back the frozen dread. The demon seemed frozen in place.

Debris blanketed the far lights, casting the end of the cavern into darkness and dust.

Staring in incredulity, Karland watched as two titanic beams opened in the darkness, sending a lancing light through the smothered air. The bright beam of Györnàeldàr's eyes was a spark to bonfire in comparison. It was as if the sun had risen underground.

In disbelief, he realised that the twinned brilliance was a pair of eyes. The light cut through the falling rock and lit the cavern as bright as day, masking the pale glow, and the shadowy being seemed to lessen in its glare. A taloned forefoot many times bigger than the Darkling slammed down through the leading edge of the destruction like an avalanche, causing the cave to tremble again end to end. The being beyond seemed to glow in a way that went beyond sight.

The dust and rocks still falling from hundreds of feet up unexpectedly blew aside, a beat from a wing wide enough to shelter half a city sweeping it in a lazy movement. The debris impacted into the wall like a puff of sand, and then the wide front of air from the beat swept over them all.

The demon was unaffected, as if the air had simply passed through its substance, but the humans reeled with the impact. The dragon folded her wings down to stay stable and crouched low. Bruised and battered, Karland stared as the glare lessened with the narrowing of immense eyes. Shining in a strange ethereal way, the form somewhat resembled Györnàeldàr in shape, but was vast and unearthly beyond all imagining. Filling the entire end of the cavern, the body alone seemed to be well over a league in length. He caught glimpses of jagged scales that were neither flesh nor rock, iridescent with colours.

'What is it?' he screamed to Györnàeldàr. She turned to look at him, her eyes so wide he felt the stare tangibly and had to squint and cover his face.

'You are blessed, human, beyond all mortals and your capacity to understand,' she shouted through the tumult. 'He is one of the *Próarkhe*, the Great Dragons, a Dreamer of the World. He is of the same stuff as the very bones of Kuln, a maker of life, and He has sensed the desecration of this place!'

'Does its power match the demon?' Xhera shouted hoarsely, moving to Karland's side, holding her ribs and wincing with the sentence.

'Listen, mortal, and take heed! He is a god of this world! He overmatches this demon born in the void between stars, and He is *angry*!' Her voice rose in a deafening shriek of triumph at the end.

Shaking off the last effects of horror, Karland watched in awe as the giant form approached. A few quake-inducing steps brought it very close. The vast wings could not stretch out without hitting the walls in the cavern, and the eyes were bigger than the Darkling's entire head. A wrenching boom seemed to vibrate through everything around them.

LEAVE!

The voice came, a part of the world itself, felt through every atom of those listening, directed at the demon. It took a step backwards, wilting in the overwhelming light of those eyes, and Karland felt the awful compulsion in the words.

YOU ARE NOT PART OF OUR DREAM, came the voice of the Greater Dragon. YOUR PRESENCE IS A HUNGER IN THE STOMACH OF THE WORLD, EMPTINESS OF THE DARK. LONG HAVE WE SOUGHT YOU TO CAST YOU OUT. YOU DO NOT BELONG.

The Darkling threw out its arms, like tiny sticks compared to the mountain before it, and hissed like the atmosphere burning off a planet. Streamers of shadow flew and writhed off its indistinct body towards the magnificent being that faced it, a pulsating dark beginning to grow around the strings. The air grew thin and chill. Rock stressed and fractured under the Darkling's feet, cooling so suddenly that it broke in strange chaotic patterns.

The colossal Dragon rumbled in fury, the sound throbbing through the floor of the cave. The great mouth dropped open and Karland could see a light that made the sun look tamed. He hid his eyes too late, afterimages purple in his vision. Xhera covered her face and even Györnàeldàr squinted. Before the raw energy the dark tentacles fell and vanished into wisps. When she spoke her voice held horror.

'This confrontation was not meant to ever be,' she choked. 'Such power! They will destroy the entire spine of mountains around us!'

YOU CANNOT INTERFERE. I WILL NOT ALLOW IT.

The great maw dropped further open and the glow inside grew incandescent, spilling around teeth higher than church spires. The light inside was as Györnàeldàr's fire, yet not; something in it was alive, as if pounding blood had combusted into star fire.

The pulsating living flame suddenly burst forth in a controlled plume, and the darkness and cold vanished as if it had never been. The focused burst, large enough to engulf the Darkling, played over the cracked rock where it had stood moments before. As the living plasma erupted in a line, the demon flowed sideways with surprising speed to evade the flame and spat sibilantly in alien anger. Chaotic scrapings like red polygonal lines skittered aimlessly across Karland's mind, like jewelled spider legs on slate.

Suddenly the Darkling was accelerating towards the humans, determined to take what it came for. An angry roar erupted from Györnàeldàr, deafening Karland anew. The Darkling was too close for the massive Dragon to interfere without destroying them.

Her tail lashed in anger and she sprang over their heads at the approaching form, tail whipping barely above their stunned faces. Two hundred and fifty feet of enraged dragon flew at the face of the demon. Lashing out with claw, flame and every power she possessed, she slammed into the demon's indistinct right shoulder and throat with thundering force, sending it reeling against the wall. Stressed rock crumbled and shattered under the combined impact; even as the demon coalesced slightly to strike back, dragonfire roared directly into its face as she delivered her hottest fire with all her might, pouring all of her energies into it.

With a pained shriek which drilled through their skulls and set their minds hammering, the gigantic demon flickered like a candle-flame of shadow under the assault. Part of her fire licked the wall, the searing heat flashing layers of rock into vapour around white-hot slag.

The Darkling twisted, lashing out. A strangely empty note tolled coldly through Karland in backlash. Györnàeldàr, tearing at the demon, roared in agony. Almost negligently, the Darkling cast Györnàeldàr free with a sweep of one of its limbs, sending her hurtling end over end to crash into the floor of the cavern hundreds of feet away. The dragon landed heavily on her back, sending a shockwave through the floor.

Her attack saved them. The demon turned to find the furious Great Dragon looming. Pressing its back against the wall, the darkness composing it began to dissolve into its original component shadows on the rocky face as the Darkling fled. Within seconds it had finally disappeared with a dry hissing wail which started low and rose, echoing from and then dispersing back into all the dark places around them, growing fainter as the shadows moved apart and faded.

There was an abrupt silence.

Györnàeldàr rumbled in distress and rolled to her side, her energy spent. The stony floor under her was cracked and shattered where her full weight had impacted it, and her left front claw, arm and shoulder were white with frost, the scales cracked and dented. The armoured meat of her shoulder was open wide, white glinting in its depths, and blazingly red blood ran from the shockingly deep wound. Where it pooled on the floor a faint sizzling arose from the stone.

One wing was obviously broken in many places, and the other waved weakly, slapping at the floor in pain as her flanks heaved. With great effort, she turned her head towards the Great Dragon, and Karland stared in shock as Xhera gasped. Part of her face was also damaged, one eye closed and her jaw white-rimmed. She shook her head groggily, and another low rumble of agony rolled out from her.

The light dimmed as the Great Dragon closed his mouth and lidded his eyes, the glare diminishing to twin piercing slits. The cavern shook lightly as he moved carefully closer. His immense head moved down sinuously to look at Györnàeldàr.

LITTLE SISTER, came the voice through their bodies, the cavern only vibrating slightly now, YOU ARE WORTHY AND COURAGEOUS.

'Lord,' came Györnàeldàr's weak voice, unsteady with a snarl of pain at the end. She spoke in the oddly inflected tonal language of dragons. She shook her snout, coughing thunderously. Blood ran from one nostril. When she could resume speech, her voice was weaker still, but she spoke Darum.

'Please, I beg of you... end my suffering. These wounds will not close... I sense it. There is a strange feel to them.' Her scales clattered as she shivered.

The titanic snout dipped lower, hundreds of feet across.

PEACE, came the answer. ITS POWER IS DRAWN FROM THE COLD BETWEEN THE STARS. IT COULD NOT END ME, BUT YOU WERE ALMOST LOST. YOU HAVE FELT THE EMPTINESS OF SPACE, THE BLEAKNESS AND COLD OF THE ABYSS, THE RAW POWERS OF

CHAOS. YET IT IS NOT YOUR TIME.

Györnàeldàr tried to move without strength.

'I am crippled, and will never know the freedom of the sky again. Rather would I die than live eternity like this.'

I HAD A DREAM, smiled the great drake, AND IN IT YOU WERE WHOLE.

His mouth opened and before any of them could react she was engulfed in a blinding sheet of translucent living dragonfire. Karland shouted in horror.

The flame played for only a few seconds; it winked out, leaving more purplish after images. Blinking them away, to his astonishment he saw that somehow Györnàeldàr still lay breathing deeply. She had no frost on her, and her bruised and dented scales were smooth and bright. Her shoulder was healed, the scales only showing a line of darker iridescence where once there had been a deep, pouring slice opened up, and both her eyes were open and gleaming. Her wings were straight and strong, and gingerly she extended them, along with her forelegs.

A look of reptilian ecstasy came over her face. Stunned, the humans looked at each other in question.

'I am not even stiff!' called Györnàeldàr in wonder. She sounded amazed. Carefully she rolled to her feet, her strength returned. 'I feel as if I was never wounded.' Turning to her great kin, she bowed her head to the floor, her wings flat out to either side in deepest honour. 'I can never repay you, Lord.' Her voice was choked with emotion.

Karland saw that even where the floor had broken under her, the rock was flawless as it always had been, with no sign of the damage they knew had been there.

Györnàeldàr followed his gaze and smiled, her teeth glinting sharply in the ambient glow of the Greater Dragon.

'What he Dreams, is,' she said simply.

THERE ARE LIMITS EVEN TO A DREAM, LITTLE SISTER, came the gentle but permeating voice. I AM PLEASED IT WAS POSSIBLE TO DREAM YOU WHOLE ONCE MORE.

Rast moved forward. His usually complacent face was awed, but his voice was troubled. 'Great One – we were given a trust, and do not know what we do now. Our time grows meagre. I beg of you – if you can guide us, please help.'

MORTAL MAN, IN AGES GONE THIS PORTAL WAS GIVEN TO ME TO GUARD. IT CONTAINS KNOWLEDGE THAT CAN BE USED TO HELP OR HINDER THE BALANCE OF THE UNIVERSE. IF BALANCE IS LOST MY DREAM WILL END. I WILL SLUMBER FOREVER ALONE IN

DARKNESS. THE PENDANT YOU HOLD ALLOWS ACCESS TO THIS PORTAL. IT IS BUT ONE WAY TO ACCESS WHAT LIES BEYOND, BUT THE PORTAL IS THE KEY TO UNLOCKING THE KNOWLEDGE HELD WITHIN.

He towered, blotting out the roof, the rest of the cavern. He was the world, his scales iridescent and metallic, seeming to change hue and glow with a faint white light as they watched. The smallest of them would have covered a barn door twice over.

I AM TROUBLED. FOR THE FIRST TIME, A DARKLING HAS REVEALED ITSELF TO ONE OF MY KIND. IT WOULD NOT HAVE UNLESS DESPERATE – OR HOLDING VICTORY IN ITS GRASP. THE END BEGINS.

'Come,' thundered a voice behind the staring humans, and they turned to see Györnàeldàr, who had moved over without them noticing. 'The portal lies nearby and we are safe now. My Lord will watch over us.'

Rast shook his head wearily. 'We must all rest,' he said. 'Karland and Xhera are beyond exhaustion. Today has drained what little we had.' Karland couldn't argue. With the excitement over he felt like he would collapse. Xhera was wincing at her ribs, and Rast moved to check them without waiting for a reply. 'Sprained, I think' he grunted. 'Lucky – no breaks. I'll look properly later.'

Xhera's face flashed scarlet. 'I don't think so,' she retorted.

Rast shrugged and Karland tried not to think about her without her tunic.

Györnàeldàr snorted. 'Human, for you to rest for a mere few of your hours means little to me. It will make no difference. I am surprised you are all unscathed; much longer near that abyss-spawned creature and your minds would have been shredded into irrevocable madness. Only the presence of one of the *Próarkhe* saved us.'

Rast looked around. 'We will move to the archway, then, and rest there.'

Anywhere, thought Karland. He wasn't sure if he was holding Xhera up or she him.

The dragon turned towards the arch. Tiredly and painfully he followed, avoiding rock where some of the wall had collapsed from the emergence of the lesser god. He stumbled to a halt with Xhera at the bottom of the dais.

'We will rest here,' said Rast, fatigue evident in his voice. The events of the day and the past hour had taken their heavy toll on them all. The flight up the mountain, the battle, the emotional losses, and the mind-bending terror of the Darkling had taken the last of Karland's strength. Too tired even to succumb to nightmares he unrolled his sleeping blankets and collapsed.

His last vision was Rast settling himself cross legged, breathing deeply. Watched by Györnàeldàr and lit gently by the glow from the slitted eyes of a living mountain, Karland closed his eyes and slept.

∞   ∞

Xhera opened her eyes, vaguely remembered horrors receding from her mind. She felt much better. Though her eyes were gummed with sleep, she nevertheless felt able to cope with the rush of events from yesterday, despite the pang whenever she thought of Grukust. Rolling over she noticed the still form of Rast standing and staring at the portal.

She could not recall ever having seen Rast sleep. The big man was alert when she went to sleep, and already up when she awoke. He looked as ready as ever, his face expressionless; whatever emotions he might feel at recent events were hidden.

Xhera rose stiffly, her muscles protesting, and moved to Karland. A slight snore drifted from him.

'Let him sleep.' Rast looked at her and then glanced back to the portal. 'You slept for near seven hours. In that time I have studied this archway. I do not know what this glow is or what we should do next. Our companion has not elucidated much.' He looked at Györnàeldàr, crouched to the side. She seemed frozen in place, her eyes hooded and contemplative. A nictating membrane flickered over her dimmed eyes occasionally. Xhera supposed that to her, hours were but a fleeting moment.

She watched her for a while, the light sparkling red-gold off the shield-sized scales, abruptly changing to the scaled near-white underbelly which was as armoured as the top. That piercing gleam shot from the lids, augmenting the glow of the star-lights in the cavern. Then she realised with a jolt that the colossal being that had faced the Darkling had vanished, the only evidence of its existence the healed form of the huge dragon next to them.

'I do not know when he left, but I still feel his presence here. He is awake and watchful,' commented Rast, seeing her glance around. 'His presence aided us much in our rest, I think.'

She said nothing, but understood – a feeling of peace and awe was still there, slightly muted. For some minutes she stood in silence, studying the archway. This was the culmination of the journey they had undertaken; that Aldwyn, then Grukust had given their lives for.

A sleepy yawn made them turn. Karland sat up, half his hair sticking up like rough straw. He blinked blearily at them both. In the first moment of amusement since before the loss of Grukust, Xhera grinned at Rast. Karland was not a morning person. He did look quite cute at the moment, though. She found him comforting, and at times she found herself idly tracing the features of his slightly long homely face when he wasn't looking.

They broke fast. Györnàeldàr's nostrils twitched at the smell of the unwrapped food, but she otherwise did not move or speak until they packed their gear.

She opened her eyes wider and gazed curiously at Rast. 'You know secrets known to few mortals, Rast Tal'Orien,' the dragon remarked thoughtfully, her burning gaze shielded by hooded lids. 'I have not heard of any but the elves passing into *dônaethar*.'

Rast shrugged. 'I learned much from them. A human can gain much rest from a few simple hours if you know how, though it is not the same as the sleeplessness of elves. We are very different.'

'*That* is why you never sleep!' said Karland in triumph. 'You never told us!' His tone was accusatory. Rast shrugged, a small smile on his face.

'You never asked.'

Ignoring the look of outrage on Karland's face, Xhera turned to collect the rest of her pack, smiling to herself.

଼ ଼

The portal was ten feet high and a third that in width. The stone it was made of was a medium grey with a smooth grain, more rugged than marble but with that strange organic quality to it.

Slightly uneven with a rounded rectangular shape, the arch looked quite ordinary for the most part. There was a suggestion of an unfamiliar plant woven in stone up the plinths, looking as if it had more grown there than been carved. The bottom of the left plinth held markings that could have been runes surrounding a depression.

'Why did the demon demand the pendant?' asked Rast, looking at Györnàeldàr. 'What knowledge within this portal is so important?'

Györnàeldàr sighed.

'That was no ordinary foe,' she said in a subdued voice, crouched low so she was close to the humans. 'I have only before heard our legends of such Demons. Never have I met such strength!' She brooded for long minutes. 'The Demon is totally alien, not of the Dream, so my Lord cannot command it. He could

⊣ 442 ⊢

destroy it, perhaps – at great cost – but such a battle would lay waste to much of the world. I am thankful it was not yet willing to face His power.'

'What do these Demons want? How can we fight such a creature?'

'You cannot,' hissed Györnàeldàr. 'Your scholar knew more than you realise. These Darklings wish only to turn this world to chaos and despair, as they have many others. One was enough to destroy us all by its very presence; four could ruin this entire world. Even the gods are wary of them.' Her tail flicked side to side, like a huge cat. She glanced at the portal again. 'I do not know what awaits you within. Knowledge to hold the balance of this world, perhaps.'

'Do we just step through?' asked Rast as they approached the arch.

'I do not know. This gate is for mortals.'

'Aldwyn called the pendant the key,' said Karland thoughtfully.

Xhera looked carefully at the stone, and then had a flicker of insight. She removed the pendant and fitted it perfectly into the hole surrounded by runes with a click. There was a white flash, and streamers of light reached towards them. The translucence stretched to infinity, slowly twisting hypnotically.

'Well done,' said Rast. Karland squeezed her hand.

Xhera swallowed nervously and nodded. 'Let's go.'

She took a deep breath as they passed through the arch. The blue seemed to freeze everything, time itself stopping. She had time to realise she wasn't breathing, and then with a surge of tingling ice-cold power that swept through their entire bodies they were sucked into the endless tunnel, and into blackness.

FORTY

K arland floated through the blackness. He was disembodied and felt at peace, though his thoughts were strangely sluggish. With nothing to focus on he drifted, the pains and weariness at bay.

Gradually, pinpricks of light began to manifest, and as they grew a blue marble came into focus. It was wreathed in white swirls, and had patches of white, green, brown and yellow. Just as he realised this was his world, he found himself standing on a featureless plain of cracked earth. He could feel it under his feet, hot and dry, although he still appeared to have no form. Mountains reared, wine-purple, in the distance. They were massive, most of them far bigger than mountains should be.

All was peaceful. The light suggested it was nearing nightfall, and indeed part of the sky was giving over to stars, although the other half retained some of day's colour. The heavens stretched over him like a dome, and the light faded from the sky, leaving only reflected ambience to see with, the precursor to true dusk and nightfall.

Time passed.

A sense of wrong slowly pervaded, and his gaze was drawn up towards the sky. A green glint winked. Somehow he realised that he would not normally be able to see this, but Karland accepted this as if in a dream. The glint gave the impression of being an unfathomable distance away, but he sensed it was getting closer.

His stomach plummeted and somehow he knew that should it arrive something terrible would happen. Fear twisted its way up from the depths of his guts.

As he sensed this the mountains before him seemed to shudder, and a minute later he felt the earth jump under his feet in shockwaves. Gradually, parts of the mountains vanished in upheaval, and other parts appeared to grow. The change was far enough away to appear very slow, but soon the entire topology of the range in front of him had changed dramatically.

For the first time in his trance Karland felt a thrill as he realised suddenly that the mountains themselves were moving. A faint miasma seemed to hover around them, a range-wide cloud of dust and rock reaching high into the air, buffeted and thinning all the time. As the air cleared much of the range resolved into vast creatures, huge beyond all comprehension. Their very emergence had destroyed and reshaped the world in front of him, and he sensed it happening all around the planet.

As they stretched their strange heads towards the sky a low singing howl reached his ears, and he realised that these were the Great Dragons. Thousands upon thousands of feet in length, leagues long, they shook their titanic wings, their eyes glowing and stabbing towards the heavens. Karland felt that his heart would burst with the mystery and beauty of the sight. His mind numbed slightly and withdrew into calm to preserve his sanity at the view in front of him. The thoughts of the Dragons brushed him, allowing him an understanding of events far beyond him. Their calls pierced him, their distress and anger evident; a testament to a very great wrong done, a great injustice in the grand scheme of the universe.

The Dragons began to glow brighter and brighter, and Karland felt himself fractured. With vision beyond understanding he saw the source of the glint more clearly. An immense tumbling rock trailing green gases that were escaping from geysers of tinged ice shot through emptiness with staggering speed. Sometimes a particularly large jet would explode out from the rock, venting in an enormous spurt out to the side and catching the sunlight.

Through them, he understood that the gas jets were hundreds, perhaps thousands of miles in length, and were producing the green glints that announced the death of his world. This single rock was many times greater than the size of all the mountains combined in the range he had seen before the Great Dragons had emerged, and moving faster than he could comprehend. If it impacted on Kuln it would strike with so much force it would rip the crust of the earth open, stabbing downwards into the fiery heart of the planet and annihilating everything in the greatest cataclysm imaginable as it cracked the world to its core.

The seas would boil and vaporise quicker than thought, life die in an instant. Even the Great Dragons might not survive the death of their world; it would exist only in tattered chunks of broken rock in the cold dark between the stars. Kuln would be unrecognisable as the glowing jewel it had been.

Somehow, some untold force had levered against the fabric of the universe at a critical moment and ripped an entire moon from its orbit around a nearby world – an ancient and majestic moon larger than some planets.

Hurled through all barriers in its path, it wreaked havoc as it moved out of the natural order of things. Smashed, burned and broken by gravity and heat by other celestial bodies in its journey through the solar system and then by passing too close to its star, it was slung out in a slingshot path that accelerated it towards the orbit of Kuln. The battered fragment that had survived the journey was set on a curved, inevitable trajectory that ended at this planet, guided to collision against infinitesimal odds. There was a sense of dread following its wake as if ill will was carried with it.

At the same time Karland was aware of the plain on which he stood. Gouts of flame so intense they were like slices of the sun began to erupt from the mouths of the Great Dragons in their distress, jetting miles into the air. The roars of the flames reached him a moment later and minutes after that a wash of heat, gentle at this distance, broke over him. Moments later, the agitated leviathans gathered themselves and leaped into the air. They travelled several miles straight upwards before their wings even took a beat downwards. It was an utterly inconceivable sight; beings so huge as to be impossible sent their miles-long bodies straight up, cracking the very mountains they leapt from.

In seconds the Dragons were vanished into the starry abyss above, having torn through the atmosphere into the space around the world. They left a vast front of wind expanding out that travelled hundreds of miles across the land in a gale. Karland's consciousness went with them, spinning in their wake until he could see them arrayed in empty space, looking tiny against their home world.

Here in the empty blackness they didn't flap their wings. The vanes were spread wide as if hovering and their gazes all focused on the green mass growing nearer at frightening speed. The chill of space and the lack of any air did not faze the Dragons; they still seemed to be communicating, and without any apparent means of changing their orientation they somehow all turned towards the oncoming mass of rock.

Karland felt a low thrumming, although he could hear nothing. The absence of noise was almost painful, but his being registered a building of power which emanated in some fashion from the scores of Dragons formed in front of him. Against the mass of the planet they seemed to no longer be moving at all.

One by one, they began to glow, dimly at first. Then they accelerated, trailing small streamers of light. The Dragons surged towards the oncoming moon fragment, wings sweeping back to lie lower against their bodies, rolling and twisting like stooping birds in flight. Karland knew without being told that these creatures were somehow twisting the natural order of things to do what they were doing – they could fly as fast as the light itself. He could not see how they were moving with nothing to push against and no air to breathe.

He found himself travelling with them in a roiling mass of multi-hued bodies spinning around each other in what he could only think of as graceful flight. There was a sense of anger and desperation there, and he could not see how even these titans could affect the path of the monstrous rock.

The Dragons slowed as they approached the spinning colossus, which was also tumbling slowly forward. As they curved out from its path in separate directions like petals unfolding from a flower he realised that they were looping in great arcs, matching its path to travel parallel to the spinning rock.

Karland could no longer see his world. They had travelled far from it, and only a blue-tinged star shining steadily nearby, bigger than the others, suggested the direction from which they had come.

The fragment of rock dwarfed the Dragons. The moon had lost much of its mass through collisions and the terrible forces exerted by its star, but what was left was still enough to decimate his world a thousand times over. He knew without understanding how that the fragment remaining was still half the size of Kuln's own moon. There was a dark, sinister feel to the rock, as of something hidden and unsettling. However wrong the force that had sent this moon from its natural course, it seemed a more evil chill followed it, deeper than the cold airless space it moved through.

The Dragons felt it too, and their upset was plainly felt. They banked in towards the tumbling rock, several moving to alight but foiled by the motion. One Dragon darted in and mistimed its approach, and the spinning rock clipped him in a silent explosion of rubble, gas and dust. The Dragon was smashed sideways with incredible force, flung far out into space away from the group around the rock. It happened almost too quickly to see, and all that was left was a trail of huge pieces of rubble and tapering streamers of green and brown-grey.

Time seemed to freeze, and the Dragons roared in silent fury. Karland felt intense sorrow at such a shattering loss – the Dragon had been like a fly swatted by a man. Nothing could hope to survive such a devastating blow.

A piercing gleam shone from the direction the Dragon had been thrown, growing in an explosion of light. Moments later a glowing form shot back in from the darkness, blazing in fury and shining so brightly that Karland could not look directly at it. The Dragon seemed unharmed, although something in the way it moved suggested it was in much pain from the impact. It seemed a miracle that it had survived – the mountain of rock that had smashed into the Dragon was mostly gone, the remainder a jagged ruin trailing the last evidence of the impact.

The Dragon that had been struck moved closer in again and slowly started to spin around the rock. Faster and faster the Dragon spiralled. The other Dragons peeled from the main group one by one and began doing the same thing at different intervals, until the group was spinning with the tumbling form.

The Dragons were now spiralling around the rock like streamers running around a maypole, matching the turning of the juggernaut. As one they moved in to land on the rocky face. Their claws slammed fifty, a hundred feet into the fabric of the moon, holding them firmly in place.

Karland's view drifted with them until he was standing on the moon surface, the sensation the same as when he had alighted on the plain on Kuln. He was relatively close to the Dragon that had been struck, and he could see a shining liquid, like luminescent gold, trickling slowly between scale plates on the side and shoulder. They drifted off its body in a trail of hot shimmering globes as big as a house and hung above him, drifting slowly away in the lack of gravity. One wing trailed out slightly as if it pained the great being.

The blue unwavering star spinning in and out of view ahead of the asteroid was bigger and brighter now. Karland felt that time was growing short, and wondered what even these creatures could do.

As one, the Dragons spread their wings out fully, curving them forwards slightly. Rearing their heads back a little, a throbbing hum could be felt all through the rock surface. Each Dragon was many hundreds of miles from the next, spread over the rock evenly, yet Karland was somehow aware of them all; whatever sight gave him this dream enabled him to experience it without questioning his usual senses.

The hum grew more and more powerful, dropping and rising alternately. The Dragons increased in glow with the level of the vibration. The colossal serpents sang noiselessly, detectable by the trembling of the rock underneath them. It grew until Karland was sure the whole moon was vibrating with it.

Suddenly the Dragons increased their voices and as one lowered their heads, their jaws dropping open. There was a pause where even the humming seemed to dim, and then incandescent plasma burst from each mouth in a great stream. This close to, the fire was like a living thing, hotter than the sun and potent with powers unseen and unknown. It stabbed down into the massive asteroid in scores of places like needles made of starfire. The humming swelled and multiplied exponentially, magnified by the power piercing the asteroid to its core. Karland felt his grip on his mind slipping.

The surface of the moon fractured as lines shot out from each point of fire, travelling thousands of miles in an instant. The lines met, forming a net of fire as if the moon was made of dark plates on a core of molten rock. Each Dragon threw its head back and roared silently, glowing brightly. The humming, throbbing vibration reached a shriek and faded.

Impossibly, the moon began to separate along the lines of fire. The Dragons pulled the immense chunks of rock they held tightly until each was a tiny radiant dot on a gigantic asteroid of its own, jagged on one side with the other faces as smooth as if polished.

Slowly, ever so slowly, the fragments moved from their path of destruction. One by one they curved from heading towards the planet, which had grown large in the sky, and in a gentle arc began to move towards the sun. The rocks accelerated even as Karland watched, and gradually vanished into the corona of light.

Finally there was only one large piece left tumbling on the same path as the original, nowhere near as big as the others but still massive next to the countless smaller fragments left in the wake of the Dragons' work. Karland moved with it, deprived of any other surface to stand on. The feeling of wrong was thicker and colder here, as if the trail of space behind this last piece was somehow darker.

It flew past Kuln's moon, followed by the last small pieces. Some smashed into the moon in soundless pinpricks of light, but the majority carrying on towards Kuln. The planet was looming large now, and this remnant was still large enough to wreak havoc and perhaps doom the planet.

Just as Karland began to believe that all that had gone before had been in vain, a last Dragon arced in and turned in front of the fragment. Karland saw it was the one that had been wounded by the tumbling moon. Raising claws and wings, it slowed, allowing the fragment to catch up to it. Alighting gently on the surface, it relaxed and showed a deep concentration, its body glowing brighter.

The rock decelerated. The smaller fragments struck the rear or swept around it to fall to a fiery death in the atmosphere.

As the Great Dragon slowed the massive piece a little over halfway between the moon and the planet, the last vestiges of the dust flew past. A cold horrifying darkness erupted twisting from behind the asteroid, spinning out like a tornado. Karland screamed as his feeble mind registered a shrieking flapping of night-hidden wings, ragged red maws and whipping tails; despair and hatred, and the cold unfeeling countenance of the space between the stars. This close to the planet most of the stars were no longer visible, yet, blacker than black, it was even visible against the starless darkness of space.

The Dragon roared in silent fury, realising that this was the true intent behind events. He was unable to prevent the presences from reaching his world without allowing the still-moving fragment to impact.

Quicker than thought the four-fold feelings of horror had vanished into the jewelled body hanging over the sky, out of reach of the immense flame that shot after them in vain. Darkness bloomed from a spot on the atmosphere, sweeping out like a spreading inkblot until it covered a huge area as abruptly as a dark heartbeat, and then suddenly was gone. No trace was left that they had even been there.

The Dragon glowed brighter as it brought the huge rock to a final stop, forced to complete its task. Karland was again brushed with colossal thoughts that imparted insight.

This fragment of rock was too dangerous to leave moving uncontrolled in the sky above its world. Somehow those presences were bound to this rock. The Great Dragons had felt something amiss from the moment they detected the moon torn from the ordained order of universe, and unnatural as it was it could not be predicted. The Dragons were a powerful force within universe and could have tried many defences. As virtually no other creature could, the behemoths understood the concepts of cause and effect within space and time and despite their fury could find no other options.

If they had used their energies to open a rift in the cosmos that would allow so large an object as the shattered moon to pass through, there was only a slim chance it would work. There were also other risks involved in opening a wyrm-hole so close to a living world. They might have even attempted to move Kuln itself, but even if they had succeeded the Great Dragons might not have been able to restore their world to its rightful place before it became lifeless. If they had instead tried to forcefully move the entire incoming planetoid the stresses could have been too great. It could have split and rained destruction and fire down over all Kuln.

Thus they had moved a heavenly body nearly a quarter of the diameter of their world in the only way remaining. The fragments would be left close enough within the gravity well of the star in the centre of their solar system to drift in and be consumed with no more threat to their home.

This last piece had hidden the source of the wrongness they had felt. Some alien force had held it together when they had broken the rest of the rock, long enough to hide the presences from the distracted Dragons. On their escape they entered a virgin world unchallenged and with enough time to hide themselves far away from its guardians. The alien power that had been impressed upon this last piece of rock had attuned it to them, however, and the last Great Dragon pulled it close into the world in the hope it could be used to recall or thwart those that had so abused it.

With one last gout of flame into space, the Dragon turned the rock ponderously and accelerated it until the fragment was circling the planet. It would not be greatly affected by either the planet or the other moon at this point in space, and would be a constant reminder. The Great Dragon hung in vacuum with wings partially furled, a radiant dot next to a green leviathan, awaiting the return of its fellows.

Through his detached numbness Karland felt a curious buzzing in his thoughts. He stood on the new moon orbiting the planet and felt the anger and upset of the other Great Dragons as they returned too late from their tasks, aware of the arrival of *something* on their home world. The moon glowing emerald beneath him had an ill-omened feel that went beyond mere rock.

His mind finally began to buckle under the strain of his visions, unable to cope with concepts and experiences no human was meant to ever encounter. Karland's numbness increased; whatever protective barrier seemed to be present for this vision, it was acting to preserve his mind. Something had meant him to see this event, which he guessed had happened in the unimaginable past.

His thoughts began drifting and the memories of what he had experienced began to dim, his consciousness forgetting what it could not contain safely. The dream state lessened and through the encroaching blackness he started remembering some of who he was, events from his life. His last conscious thought was to hope that the others were all right, and then there was - blessedly - nothing.

FORTY-ONE

The dark was shattered by a flash of returning vision. Rast stood alone in a hall that stretched off to either side into the distance. Pillars to either side of the hall were spaced at regular intervals and he couldn't tell if there were walls beyond them; his eyes slid off the spaces between pillars as if they couldn't quite register what they saw. Flashes of alien images, of towers crumbling in ruins, of an ancient red sun all flickered through his mind. Discomfited, he looked down.

His feet were set upon cold flagstones of differing sizes. They stretched into the distance. Turning, he saw the same featureless hallway. At the back of his mind, a voice clamoured to be heard, nagging him to wonder how he came to be here. He had no answers. Instead he picked a direction and started walking. The dry cold hallway gave off an insidious feel of disquiet.

After what felt like hours in the unchanging hallscape he stopped. It was pointless to wander, and he knew he wasn't actually moving in a straight line, whatever his eyes told him. Rast concentrated on the pillars, ignoring the slippage of his vision when it rested between them, and realised that the hallway imperceptibly bent to the right. His mouth unconsciously thinned in a grim line. Suspicion flared up that this mysterious place was a giant circle. There was no point in walking it until he was dust, so he sat to think, falling into a state of meditation.

As he sat his mind emptied. The voice softly whispered again and with nothing else there, he focused. Time slowed, and sweat beaded his brow as his mind fought to regain its innate iron control, to break through the barriers that wrapped it.

Suddenly his eyes snapped open. Rast knew who he was, what had happened. A trace of worry shot through him at the thought of getting back to the Hall of Wyrms, but he rose swiftly with no sign of stiffness and pressed on stoically. Time seemed to pass again as Rast moved on.

Reaching a decision, he shook off his mindless lethargy and stopped before the next door. Cautiously, he opened it a crack. A gloomy room was all he could see, full of covered shapes that seemed familiar. Dust was thick everywhere and there was no obvious outlet to the room, so he shut the door and moved on.

He forced his focus onto the next portal. Moving to the door opposite, he opened it a crack again. A piercing light shone out, and he sensed a never-ending litany of dutiful pain. Shutting the door quickly against the unceasing throbbing in his head, he backed away from it.

It felt like all the times in his life that he had forced himself through agony to better himself, the years of focus on working through pain, feeling like his heart would burst, pushing himself until his limits were reached – then surpassed. Whatever was in there, it did not seem like a place to be for no reason.

'What is this place?' he muttered to himself. The volume of his voice surprised him. The hallway was deathly silent apart from the impression of a low keening wind from outside, unnoticed until he spoke and the words broke through it. It made him think of the wails of the defeated, and he shivered.

He nearly walked past the next door. It had a feeling around it that made him tense – a feeling of danger. He cracked the door the merest width to peer in, ready to defend himself.

Rast barely had a chance to register the moving darkness before the door was ripped from his grasp. He leapt back and to the side as a howling mass poured out through the door, dark and somewhat formless. There was no solid recognition of a single foe here, but he sensed familiarity with old battles. Vaguely outlined, there were hands and claws and tails and wings on sinewy forms, muscled forms, all manner of shape and size. The only constant was the eyes; they gleamed out wickedly from each one, focused on him in hatred.

Rast immediately attacked, sensing the danger. As he had his whole life, he committed, cut, struck to be the victor.

His hand shot out and grabbed the nearest form by the throat as he lifted his opposite leg and smashed it in a kick through the face of another creature. The shape felt insubstantial in his hand but there was a grip, as if he was holding solid, heavy wool. His blows, however, seemed to hurt it as any real foe would suffer.

As his leg came back down he moved his weight to it and twisted, slamming his other elbow into the side of its head once, twice. The eyes dimmed in unconsciousness or death – he didn't know – and he dropped the form as the rest of his assailants swarmed him.

As he had so many times before, Rast became the fight. The pure song of a true warrior sang in him, and his lips drew back slightly in a grin. He accepted weak blows, blocked others. Most were avoided in a dance, and the energy of still others he used to damage his opponents.

Ducking a claw that might have ripped his head off, he came back up in a powerful uppercut that took the creature off its feet. Another form dodged his next palm strike, its hands raised protectively next to its face, and he realised that some of these beings were versed in fighting techniques. Its hands jabbed in towards his face, and he stepped back, chin tucked down, and swept his right leg around in a powerful roundhouse to collapse the knee, a crippling strike. The creature dropped to be trampled by its fellows.

By now the creatures had moved to surround him, and he had nowhere to retreat. It was a bad situation to be in – even the most gifted fighter would not last long against multiple attacks from all sides. But there was nothing but the fight, and without companions to protect or any other considerations he gave himself up to it completely.

It was as easy as it had been his whole life, dropping into the flow of battle without thinking, his body directed by a perfect symphony of mind, training and instinct. This was what he lived for, was trained for, had been born for.

More figures came through the door to join the throng, and he knew he could not defeat them all, yet smiled grimly. The fight was everything; pure, a beating throb in his being, the living drum of the warrior. The only reason they were not dragging him down already was that they were not working together, or even seemingly aware of each other. Despite his prowess and the genius of his combat, each attacked him as if alone. They got in each other's way, frowning at the unexplained resistance to get to him as if they couldn't even see each other.

On the heels of this Rast realised that he was not tiring, and the sense of displacement returned. Distracted, he didn't move from a strike quickly enough and felt his side open in a shallow cut up his ribs. Angry at himself, he retaliated. Spinning in place, he deflected another incoming strike and then struck backwards with his left foot, slamming his sole into the face of the attacker that had hurt him with sickening impact. The attacker hurtled backwards, flipping end over end to vanish in the gloom between the doors.

Fast, strong, and deadly, he had a lifetime of training behind him. Almost every strike was powerful enough to stun, maim or even kill if it landed cleanly. Regaining his momentum, Rast laughed. He could fight forever, although he knew eventually he would make a mistake… and it would only take one serious error for him to fall.

Taking advantage of the space, he threw a hard cross into the man-shaped thing before him, and then grabbed one shoulder while he slammed his opposite hand into the other. The figure pivoted around on the spot, and Rast locked his arm around its throat, grabbing his own neck and shoulder and hunching his upper back – not ideal, but he wanted his other hand free. With no chance of hooking his heels in, he relied on his opponent being dazed to retain his grip for long enough. Within seconds it paid off as the creatures before him waded in to strike at him, tearing into the body of their unseen companion instead without seeming to notice.

Keeping an eye behind him, he threw his other elbow back into the throat of another shape, slamming his leg out in kicks to damage others, trying to drive them back. Although he felt he could keep this up indefinitely, the shapes were not tiring either and it would be a war of attrition as the damage mounted up. Too, those defeated or out of the fight were steadily being replaced from the open doorway.

So was this his destiny? To fight forever, or until he died? *Could* he die in this place between worlds? Suddenly the prospect of living for the fight seemed less appealing if it were for the rest of time. He reached a decision; shrugging off the blows it cost him, he planted his foot out and used his silent captive as a prop. Rast lifted his thigh and scythed his other huge leg in a circle at head height, knocking or warding several opponents away, and then in the same movement let his grip go and put his foot on the back of the badly damaged – and probably dead – form he held.

In an explosive movement he kicked as hard as he could, tilting his pelvis with the kick for extra power, slamming the broken form through its fellows and clearing a gap. Without a second's hesitation, he sprinted after it and ended up close to the doorway, his upper arms bleeding from strikes that had landed. The creatures surged around him and he was forced to stop, the door out of reach. The figures were packed closely here and Rast didn't think that trick would work again.

Instead he exploded into a flurry of motion, hammering knees, elbows and fists into the forms around him, spinning and weaving with no room to kick. Throwing forms past him gave him valuable seconds, and he focused on a large figure that looked vaguely like a fat man with horns and stubby wings.

Feinting towards its face, he stepped out and swung his entire body in the hardest punch he could, burying his massive arm almost to the elbow in what was hopefully its gut. As it sagged he leaned in and hoisted it onto his shoulders, grunting heavily; his healed leg ached and nearly buckled. Ignoring the strikes that he could no longer block he jerked the figure up so he held it above his head, arms trembling. A punch closed his left eye, and a raking claw sliced deep into his back.

Growling in anger, he threw the form forward as hard as he could, stumbling with the momentum. The figure did not fly far, but it was far enough; it swept several attackers away and smashed into the door heavily, ramming it shut and cutting off the flow of enemies.

The move left him very vulnerable. Rast fought for his life, protecting his vitals and throwing punches and elbows everywhere. When he could, he jabbed stiffened fingers into eyes, and thumped solid shins into groins. Not every figure reacted in pain as he expected, but he kept fighting.

This would not end well. The door was closed but the hall was still filled with foes, and Rast could not see a way to defeat them all before he fell. Once he went down he would never get back up.

Something nagged at him and as he lent his instincts control, he considered it distractedly. He did not love killing, but committed to it without hesitation when he had to. Yet here – despite his intuition – the creatures had not attacked him until he struck. Every instinct he had screamed that they were going to attack, but none had until he did so.

A foot shot in at head height and he deftly avoided it just in time. Countering the next moves he grabbed the shape's head and jerked it down to meet his rising knee. As the form dropped Rast stared, for a second too long. His focus lessened, and a wicked blow hit him in his left kidney, making him grunt in pain. Those attacks had seemed very familiar... as did most of them, now he considered it.

The familiarity of his enemies and their attacks troubled him, and suddenly he made a decision. Whatever the consequences, he entrusted himself to his new suspicion. A last kick blew through the arms of the form to his left and into its sternum, folding it in half and breaking bones. He dived through the gap, rolling over as hands grasped at him and ending up back lightly on his feet. Without pause he moved swiftly away, temporarily outside the press; warily, he backed away from the array of forms which moved forward intently, matching his moves.

Finally understanding, he lowered his defences in defiance of every instinct and screaming nerve demanding he use his body to fight, and let them take him.

They bowled him over. A mouth closed painfully, sharply, on his left arm and something solid connected hard with his right ribs, shocking his liver. As he tried to protect his head and neck through the crippling pain he had a brief second to wonder if he had made the most costly mistake of his life, and then the figures drew back. He looked up, trying to focus.

Leering faces shot in, slavering, but none contacted him. His breath whistling through clenched teeth, arms held tightly at his sides, he stared grimly at them, his good eye steady. It seemed that his decision not to fight had reflected into the horde about him, for though their eyes glared in hatred, they no longer attacked. As before, there was the feeling of imminent attack, of bitter hatred, but nothing happened.

'I have fought all of you... before,' he said, willing the pain in his middle to lessen. The forms remained implacable as he struggled to sit up. 'I think you... are enemies I have defeated... in battle. *I will not fight you... again.*' He drew a deep breath, and spoke resolutely.

'Leave me alone.'

Slowly, the forms began to dissipate like mist. Within a minute they had evaporated, the only evidence of their existence the wounds he carried.

Rast sat there for a while, letting the pain of his wounds recede. This place seemed to reflect aspects of him and he had now had his fill of finding it out firsthand. Foremost among his thoughts was the need to escape this endless hallway.

Eventually he felt well enough to move on. His midsection ached, and his wounds were clotted. His eye had started to lose some of the swelling, although he did not doubt it would be splendidly bruised.

'I need to leave this place,' he remarked deliberately as he reached the next door. Confident now that his thoughts were linked to the doors, he carefully opened it. Another wooden door was in its place, the other side of the frame, inches from the first.

Rast swore softly then slammed his foot hard into the middle of it. From the feeling, it might as well have been a large block of granite. He didn't think that what was there was really a door. Shutting the first door he calmed himself and considered carefully before moving on to the next door. This time he focused on why he was here and what he needed to leave. He stared at the door in challenge, and then reached for the handle.

Rast opened the plain wooden door and stepped through the doorway into a chamber which fanned out from the door he had stepped through in a gentle curve to either side. The floor in front of him was flat and appeared to be rough white marble flecked with gold, catching the light when he moved. The light itself was from two steadily-glowing braziers set to the edges of the room, outputting a far more ambient light than they should. Twenty feet in front of him the floor rose up in thirty chiselled steps to a wide landing, twice the width of the floor below; at the top of this chamber stood a tall being, hard to make out in the glow. To the left side of it was a smooth archway with a large keystone, made of the same material as everything else in the chamber. Rast could not see through the archway, but could detect a faint light. To the right side was another archway, similar in appearance, but dark and shadowed.

The being stepped forward and came into sharper focus, as if moving away from the arches allowed Rast to see it. Rast raised his eyebrows in surprise.

The figure appeared to be an elf.

Yet it seemed different from the elves he knew. Rast had – as very few humans also had – spent some time amongst them, in his case to learn their fighting techniques. Whatever you visited the elves for, if you stayed for long you both absorbed some of their culture and learned to discern more readily than most between them. This looked like no elf he had ever seen. The robed figure seemed even less human, if possible, than the elves he knew.

He was taller, lither, with sharper features. When he moved it was in a sinuous controlled fashion that suggested he was not connected together in the same way as humans, or even the comparatively fluid grace of elves. In some indefinable way this elf seemed faintly *other,* making other elves seem as graceless and clumsy as humans. For all that, the being was beautiful in an odd way and seemed to glow faintly with a power that radiated from it. The robes were a mixture of dark purple with a metallic pink sheen from certain angles that looked like no fabric on earth.

Rast began to suspect that this was a high elf, an *Ældarín,* one of the nearly mythical figures that even the elves were reticent about; most others knew nothing at all. The being lifted a hand in greeting.

'So, you have found your way here,' it said in melodious tones. 'Well done, mortal. And you are fully aware!' It seemed surprised. 'I am impressed, truly. It takes brain and will as well as brawn to surpass learned limitations and move to where you need to be... and not lose yourself, as almost all others entering here have.'

He gestured liquidly around him. 'This is a place removed from the fourth dimension of reality. You are here because you dared the unknown and braved the *Talénthese,* the Portal, the Key to Knowing that is hidden in the place sacred to dragons and watched over by one who is distant kin to me. This portal gives answers – that is its purpose. Those who must understand themselves may end up here in the Hall of Ages, as you have. For your courage and your hard choice to seek an answer rather than lose yourself in the fight – as would be so easy for you – you are given a decision to make. A gift, if you will.'

The elf smiled at Rast, his features alien but gentle.

'This is a choice, human. A decision for the here and now. One arch leads to all that which you never had but part of you has desired, as all those who choose one path must sometimes ponder the others they might have walked. Through this you could be the lover, the husband, the classical lutist, the farmer. You might never leave your loved ones, never see all those you care for die in violence. It holds your innermost desires in the stillness of your heart. You can see the peace through it, yes?'

Rast could not read the tones of the elven lord. He warily considered the archway and realised the gentle golden light pervading it reminded him of sunlight and gentler days. He nodded, feeling a little homesick.

'I can see your yearning, human. Your life has been hard; there must be things you miss very much, have always wanted.' The elf's eyes were sympathetic. 'It is not for me to judge or persuade, however. I am merely revealing a choice. For there is another archway and this contains perhaps not what you fear... but what you must give up that life for.'

Rast looked at the other archway, which was simply a dark hole filled with glints. As a few of them vanished and reappeared in pairs, he realised that they were the gleaming eyes of unnumbered ranks of creatures, enemies all. He could feel the slow malice behind them, the eagerness to destroy from foes past and present, perhaps future – an unending struggle. The hallway was the merest trace of what this portal offered him. He turned back to the elf.

'I think I understand,' he said. 'One way lies happiness. The other way lies death. You want to see what I will choose, given my own free will, maybe a test of worth. This is a question of my loyalty?'

'All mortals die,' the high elf smiled sadly. 'Your duty is without question. I can see it within you. Your loyalty no less, I think. But I cannot deny that you are being asked to choose between death and violence, and happiness and life.'

Rast turned to look at the portals again. His heart sank at the old loss of the long-forgotten memories of a brief, happy youth and what might have been, buried beneath time and scar tissue. To have something more than fighting would complete him.

His heart hardened at the prospect of the struggle and death implicit in the other choice. Death was an old friend, faced and fought beside too often to count, and her soft kiss had no fear for him. Struggle was an old burden; all his training, all the battles, all the losses of his life, learning, loving – living itself. Everything in life was a struggle of some kind, even happiness. Death and struggle were a natural progression and he shied from neither – because woven between them was duty, and a meaning to his life.

The elven lord spoke again.

'Perhaps this is not a question of loyalty or worth, but rather a question of the reasons behind your choice?'

Rast mulled over these words, trying to keep his mind open. Like a door in his mind opening he began to see clearly what had brought him here. With sudden clarity Rast realised that what the high elf said may be true. He thought about what he had chosen, his companions, everything he had ever fought for. The elf waited patiently in this place of no time, and added, 'I am purely objective in this. You must make your own choice, mortal.'

Rast spoke harshly. 'This is no choice. I must choose to fight. To not do so would doom myself and my companions, and worse, perhaps the world if what Aldwyn told me of the times of Chaos is true. I know that this is a futile fight... but I will fight nonetheless.'

The Eldar smiled.

'Not necessarily, human. You had two companions when you entered this realm. Both of them are part of what is to come. Everyone is unique in some way; no one being is completely ordinary, least of all you. Your companions are both given a gift of knowledge; of what was, and an understanding of Beginnings. You have a different role to play. Destiny is a path, not set in stone but merely with a beginning and an end. The path you walk, however, is up to you, although free will means something other than what you humans may think.

'You alone are given a choice where they are not. I beseech you to consider it carefully. See what you are being offered, and let not the clutter of your mind twist the meaning behind it. You are not the first to see this place. You are not the first mortal to gain a choice. But many have been where you are now, even those of my younger kin, and their choices have been neither better nor worse than your own. Many mortals never even find their way here – it takes many qualities to do so.' The high elf paused, seeing Rast's troubled expression, and then smiled. 'I would say you should consider this choice as you have lived your life, mortal – using your head, heart, and being. Think, feel... and know. More I cannot say, but here there is no haste. I will await your decision.' His eyes bored into Rast, and he stepped back.

Rast hardly noticed. He didn't see the point in this, but obviously someone, or something, felt this was important – though in what way he was not sure. He calmed himself and cleared his mind, gradually falling into a state similar to a light trance – a point of focus, of meditation, familiar ground. This was where he found his centre, where he began his descent into the *dônaethar,* a deep trance similar to the resting wakefulness that the elves had instead of sleep. In humans it was more complete, giving him something akin to six hours of deep sleep in an hour or so of meditation, but it required preparation and focus to maintain. He was aware of the world around him and could react relatively fast to stimuli, but it also shut down cognitive processes, removing the ability to think or dream while the brain rested, releasing hormones and healing the body quickly.

That state would be counter-productive now so he held himself empty, a candle in a dark windless void; a black mote in a universe of white. He could hear his beating heart, calm, strong, measured, a constant in his existence. Relaxing into the quiet, distanced from the turmoil of his emotions and thoughts, he considered carefully what the Eldar had asked him to choose.

Should he choose to fight, to die fighting? To cease to exist in battle, to die in the fight as he lived for the fight? Or should he choose to experience something that he only desired in a part of him – the potential to be something other than the unbeatable warrior? He excelled at all forms of fighting, was proficient in almost any weapon, and learned quickly and completely. Rast was as near to a perfect warrior as a man could be, without the complications of ego to hold him back – but without experiencing all the other things in life that he could do, he was potentially missing part of himself.

But then no one person could do or learn everything. There were practical limits as well – to excel at something was to focus entirely upon it, to live it to the detriment of other skills. It was a paradox.

Still... he had no children, no wife. No one to mark his mighty deeds, no one to bear his name forward through time when he was gone. He owned little other than his weapons and his small home, built with his own hands and empty now. However much he may believe he needed none of this, that duty was all that was required... a part of him spoke quietly, telling of the wonders that he might know, reminding him of when he was younger, innocent, and free to choose his paths.

He thought back to the corridor he had walked, each door a depiction of his mind, a compartment of his inner self. He had only won, rather than destroying himself, through using his mind *and* his body; by the realisation of choosing and not the action of choice.

The natural reaction of one with duty, or honour, or revenge, any kind of goal that required adversity, was to fight until the fight was done. Rast had been doing this for so long it was second nature. Despite only ever fighting when necessary, his time in the Hall showed him that sometimes even then it was not the right way. Perhaps the message was that it was not the choice that mattered so much as the reasons for the choice – the path was not as important as the why of stepping onto it.

Rast fought without peer, but most did not realise he was also a peaceful man, balanced in this as most other things; but when he fought, he lived for the fight. Maybe he must be sure he chose to fight selflessly. Not for the love of fighting, not for the duty of doing so, but simply because if he did not, his friends, his charges, and perhaps the world he knew would not be protected. Maybe he should not battle from desire, or because he could and his body dictated it, but because he was *needed* to.

With that came another realisation. The Eldar had not confirmed his suspicions exactly, nor denied them. He had simply stated the facts of mortal life. What if this choice affected nothing… or if it was actually his choice as to how he lived his last years?

SHOULD I choose happiness?

A decision deliberated too much becomes agonising, as few mortals were granted access to see the future. Quite simply, Rast could not know the outcome.

So, how did he *feel* about the choice? Battle did not change his emotions one way or the other. The dark portal was just another fight, albeit with more riding on it. Despite this, there was a small part that was weary at the prospect, and another part that hungered for it. But there was some longing for the other portal, for peace, as well as curiosity… and perhaps excitement.

As he had so many times before, he made his decision. Mind, body and soul all agreed, a triumvirate of balance, and his choice rang true within him.

Rast opened his eyes to find the high elf still standing, waiting.

The being smiled in his alien fashion. 'You have reached a decision, Rast Tal'Orien,' he stated. 'Will you choose to complete yourself and live, or battle on and die?'

Rast nodded. 'I have reached a decision,' he said. 'I choose to go through the portal… of peace. But I choose to go through it to fight.'

The Eldar pierced him with a curious glance. 'Why?'

The question was not entirely unexpected, and reinforced Rast's train of logic. 'I choose it because it will complete a part of me I have not seen in a long time, will make me whole. But I will not forsake my charges, or my friends. I will fight for them with my last breath.'

'An interesting choice,' said the alien being, showing neither approval nor disapproval. 'I do not recall allowing conditions on the path you choose, however.'

'I do not recall conditions being forbidden, either,' said Rast equably. 'I choose peace… as the goal. But I will *fight* for it. You did not mention that death lies for me on both paths, but since I am mortal, it does. So I will choose both paths. I choose for myself and my friends, not simply from a set choice in an alien place for an entire world.'

The Eldar smiled his sharp grin again, his delicate, powerful face splitting cleanly. 'And so I did not, human,' he said. 'You have accepted, I see, two things: that a choice is rarely water or stone only, and that the reason for the choice often means more than the choice itself. Well done.'

As he spoke, the portals vanished, and only a large dark tunnel remained, looking very much like the portal they had all stepped through.

Rast blinked. 'So my choice, and my reasons, were correct?' he said.

The high elf shook his head, but was still smiling. 'Mortal, know this: both portals lead to the same place. There is no right or wrong answer, outside that which you define yourself. But I think you leave here changed. Stronger in some ways, perhaps weaker in others. In a way you may never fully leave here, for as you saw in the Hall of Ages, this place is also within you, as it is within every mortal. Some choose badly. Some never leave at all.' He smiled. 'I think however that, unlike many who have stood before me, you have gained much here. That could make a difference to your life in times to come, and you will find it easier not to lose yourself in the fight. But as to the reason for all this? Perhaps there is none.'

Rast nodded. Initially he thought this had all been for nothing, had been a waste. However he began to understand that everyone - including himself - eventually imposed limits on themselves and stopped evolving. Those limits always needed to be surpassed to progress, this he understood well from his training, but it was humbling to also remember that he was only who he was. His duty and discipline and supreme focus, in fact, may have even been detrimental in some ways to his life.

'It may be no comfort or indeed interest to you, but you have been a... remarkable encounter,' said the Eldar. 'You may also not believe or care about what I will tell you, but know this... even immortals continue to learn and grow within ourselves. Very little is *truly* immutable. May the peace you chose find you, Rast Tal'Orien.'

He moved to the side, out of the opening, and bowed very slightly to Rast. Rast bowed back, briefly wondering how the elf lord knew his name. Dismissing the thought he crossed to the portal without looking back and stepped through it.

Quicker than thought, darkness descended.

FORTY-TWO

X hera opened her eyes, confused. Darkness was fading around her, and she was uncomfortably stiff. Moving slightly, she discovered that she was lying prone on the ground. Something about how she felt disturbed her, but she was not sure exactly what was wrong. She lay in a darkness infused with a silvery sheen, on soft grass thinly veiling hard-packed earth beneath a bush, not far into a small copse.

Even stronger than the feeling of wrongness within her was a feeling of déjà vu. It was powerful but subtle, thrumming through her conscious mind. Unable to remember why it seemed so familiar – or why she could remember nothing of how she got here – she sought to shake the turmoil inside her, pulling herself to her feet and cautiously moving to the edge of the trees. It was plainly deep night, but the silver moon, almost full, was so bright everything was lit nearly like day.

The world seemed strangely large. She was not moving with her usual grace either, and this bothered her. A call to her left made her jump, heart hammering.

'Xhera! I told you to stay where you were.'

The tone was scolding, bossy, but also familiar. With a start Xhera realised it was the voice of Talas – but it sounded so young! She watched her approach in the darkness, barely more than a silhouette. From what she could see her sister looked no more than twelve years old, and with that came the realisation of her change in perspective, the lack of coordination and height finally making sense.

Xhera was young… very young. If her sister was truly twelve, that would make her only five years old. Despite the lack of any other memory, Xhera was sure she should no longer be a child.

Nevertheless, there was Talas, glaring at her. 'I shouldn't have brought you,' she said hotly. 'I'll never find the elf grove with you around! And mother and father will kill me if you get lost.'

Xhera felt her eyes well up, unbidden. She idolised her sister and didn't want to be left alone, or shouted at.

She sniffed. Talas's face softened and she knelt with a sigh and gave her sister a hug. Xhera's little arms clung around her neck and she snuffled into it as Talas rubbed her back.

'Oh, you're not that bad really,' Talas said. 'Just do what I say, please. I would never forgive myself if you got lost. Don't cry, Xhera. I brought you with me, didn't I?'

Xhera nodded into her neck.

'Well, then,' said Talas. Xhera knew that Talas had mostly brought her because she would only have tried to follow anyway, but she was glad. She loved spending time with her grown up, pretty, clever sister.

'Come on,' said Talas, standing. Holding Xhera's hand she walked slowly back towards the woods. Xhera sniffed the last bit of her upset away and toddled along next to her.

'Look, I was only looking at Lunis. It's bright tonight, isn't it? If Jons is right, the fairy grove will appear tonight, and we will watch them dance. And when they are finished, we will get three wishes!'

Talas's voice barely contained her excitement. She loved listening to Jons's stories when the smooth-voiced old man addressed the gathered people of the city in the square on Borningday, regaling them with stories. Their father said that Jons had trained as a Chanter in the great cities of the Banistari Empire. True or not, he could play almost any instrument and had a marvellous voice, with stories that came alive in the telling. He was welcomed in any tavern in the city, and never paid for his bed or board.

The children, of course, took every story as gospel, whereas the older townspeople accepted that some of the stories were either fanciful or parables. The last feast was a week gone. The harvests were in, and Birth was celebrated. Jons had spun many tales, one of which was of a fairy grove in the woods west of the city at the top of the cliffs which appeared on bright summer nights when the green moon was hidden. Xhera and Talas had listened with wide eyes as Jons told of elves, laughing and dancing all night in splendour, light-hearted and fanciful, giving thanks to the stars above them. Finishing the tale with a twinkle in his eyes and his old seamed face grinning as he surveyed his rapt audience, he added that if anyone ever saw them – and managed to not interrupt the dance the whole night through – the elves would grant them three wishes. He added warningly that the wishes were from fairy-folk and should be considered carefully.

Xhera and Talas had heard only *elves* and *wishes*. Talas had spent every waking moment since thinking about the grove and had resolved to find it on the next bright night.

Located on the borders of Eordeland, Morland, and Banistari, the town of Valesgate was prosperous. It sat at the bottom of a deep ravine, next to a clear river which emerged from the depths of the rock. By the time it reached the town, the rapids were thinned and the river broadened and slowed enough for river craft. Behind the town rose the sheer cliff paths to the surrounding countryside where farmers grew their crops. At the other end of the town the ravine opened out, flattening and widening next to the river enough for ample sunlight to get in. The mainstay of the town's food came from here, and the mines nearby produced enough copper and iron to keep the town very financially secure.

Blacksmiths and metalworkers abounded, some of the best in the region moving there to get the purest possible metal to work with, and trade was very good. The local militia kept watchtowers on the surrounding cliffs, and the town and surrounding countryside was considered safe and abundant. Predators steered clear of so much humanity and the inhabitants by and large led a sheltered life. Eventually, after old walls and lower farmsteads, the valley widened out to plains, so the town saw a goodly amount of merchants passing through to and from Morland.

Talas had brought her sister to the top of the road up the western cliffs. The Léohtsholt forest ran the other side of the great North-Eastern Trail for hundreds of miles, and she was sure this was where the grove lay. It meant nearly two hours of climbing and walking, but she was sure she could get there and back in a night without her parents knowing; their father never rose to trade early on a Solaceday. Their house lay nearer the west of the city outskirts, and the area was safe enough for children to have explored thoroughly. The problems occurred when Talas rose not long after her parents went to bed. Xhera begged Talas to take her. Fearing that Xhera would wail if she refused, and worried she would miss the chance, she reluctantly agreed.

Many hours later, it was plain she wished she had not. Xhera was too young to make such an arduous trip, and had to be carried several times. When they finally arrived at the edge of the woods, Xhera had fallen asleep almost straight away. Talas was angry and upset that she might have missed the elves, and worried that so much time had passed. At least the cliff road would be easier going down.

They stood now hand in hand at the edge of the woods, wondering where to begin their search. In a world silently bathed in silver, and with green Xoth nowhere in the sky, the night was still relatively young. There was almost no noise, apart from the wind brushing the leaves of the trees from time to time and the sporadic sounds of nature. Tiny rustling noises of the night denizens came from all around them. The foxes were quiet tonight, their hoarse cries few and far between, and from a little way away floated the soft hooting of an owl.

Xhera was too young and Talas too self-absorbed with finding the fabled grove for either to be frightened. With youthful lack of foresight they gave no thought to how large the woods were, what they might contain, or how easily they might become lost. Even had Talas heard of strange creatures or the sheer size of the Léohtsholt Xhera knew she would have ignored them still.

Xhera saw her take a step forward and tried to follow, but her own legs would not respond. She was suddenly aware of a strange sort of building pressure in her head. Talas turned to ask her why she was not following, but paused with her question dying on her lips. Now she too detected something wrong as all around them the world went utterly silent. Nothing moved; even the air seemed stilled, and the world held its breath.

Trembling, Xhera looked around. Looking up at her sister she could see fright begin to etch itself on to her face. With that came a realisation that her sister's face was very gradually becoming easier to see. All thoughts of the grove were gone. She was thinking now only of how they could return home and hide in their beds.

'Come on,' whispered Talas after they had been standing for a few minutes. She started for the cliff road, pulling Xhera around with her.

They had barely moved when they became aware of the brightening of the sky above and in front of them, centred around a green-white column of light. Both girls stopped moving, watching the light appear to drift very slowly diagonally downward across the great dark bowl of the sky.

Frozen in place and staring in wild-eyed incomprehension, Xhera watched as it grew rapidly, a flaming light swelling in the sky.

'What is it?' she asked.

Talas did not answer. The column of light was growing steadily more painful to look at, outshining the bright silver moonlight and giving everything a greenish tint. Even as they tried to make out what it was, it was suddenly upon them, moving faster than they could follow. A trail of thick black smoke hung in the sky above it, tilting upwards at an angle.

A split second was all they had to register a loud high-pitched whistle, and then a bright flash that rivalled the sun erupted below the edge of the cliff. Instinctively shutting her eyes tight, Xhera saw the shadows of her own protecting arms through her eyelids as she wrapped them around her head.

The ground she had known as solid her entire short life shrugged her off like a dog with a tick. Bucking underneath them, it hurled her backwards to land heavily with no breath to even cry. An unholy cacophony of noise accompanied the shaking ground in the form of grinding rocks and creaking, snapping trees, instantly overwhelmed by a roaring boom that seemed to go on for many seconds and left her head ringing.

Cowering on the ground, she was reduced to primitive terror for long moments. When she finally stirred, Xhera became aware of the night as a wall of noise. Behind them, the tips of many of the taller trees left standing were on fire. Great pieces of trunks were missing, as if large objects had shot through them at an upwards angle and incredible speed. Many trees were leaning drunkenly away from the blast and some had fallen altogether.

The farms to the north and south were awash with cries. Animal noises and shrieks came from the woods and the animals in the surrounding farmsteads. Near the cliff in the distance a tall barn was on fire from halfway up; several other buildings had collapsed, crushing the animals and people within. Talas staggered towards her, eyes streaming.

As she staggered to their feet, unsure whether to trust the ground which seemed strangely waved as it got closer to the edge, Xhera saw a massive column of black smoke tinged with orange rising from a glow and vanishing into the once-more dark sky. As her night vision slowly returned and the moon and fires lit up the destruction around them, Xhera saw the chaotic aftermath.

The cliff edge seemed different. With a start, the buried adult part of Xhera realised that much of it was gone, bitten off in a ragged melted chunk several hundred feet deep in a wide swathe from left to right, dropping down almost to the base a thousand feet below them. Even as they watched, more of the remainder began to slide down into the canyon.

With a whimper Talas started towards where the road down the cliff had been, dragging Xhera like a rag doll. Her hand was so tight that Xhera could no longer feel all her fingers, but she hardly noticed. She was crying in shock, a child's heaving wails, and she followed her sister automatically.

The new edge of the cliff was dangerous, but as they drew closer they found it too hot to get perilously close. The glassy slope was no longer sheer but now at a gradient where they could look down at their home. There they stood silently, Xhera gulping, snot running down her lip, unable to comprehend what they were seeing.

Where their home had been at the base of the cliff there was nothing. A huge crater described its empty arc slightly to the southeast of the centre of the town. All that remained to say that there had been people living here were some ruined shells of buildings – mostly on fire and leaning acutely away from the crater in line with its radius – and the walls in the distance.

The river was almost empty, its egress blocked by partially melted rock and slides. Much of the water had been vaporised, what little remained thick and dark. The crater was nearly a mile across; the evidence of the blast around it at least double that. Against the far canyon wall were remains of many boats, burned and hurled by the blast twenty or thirty feet into the air and smashed ruthlessly against unyielding rock to tumble into piles of matchwood. Further out on the dockside along the river there were mounds of debris and rubble thrown and mixed with detritus from slides.

Nothing living stirred. A shimmer of rising heat and smoke from the superheated rock and the burning fires blocked their view in ripples as wind rushed up the cliffs around them.

Somehow part of Xhera understood what had happened. The meteor had detonated a little before the very base of the cliff, exploding only a few hundred feet before it hit the ground. The largest piece, composed mainly of iron, was ejected into the ground at a hypervelocity, obliterating itself and everything around it in the impact. Just as great were the effects of the rest of the meteor, which released the remainder of its energy in a fireball. The blast wave a mere hundred or so feet above the floor of the gorge destroyed rock, home, and flesh with equal impunity. Further away from the crater, shadows of matter vaporised in an instant were left on structures that withstood the blast. The wall of the cliff and the shape of the canyon back to the road rising up at the point near the meeting of the walls meant that the blast was collected and focused both upwards and back down the canyon. The increased destruction left only the town's outer walls leaning drunkenly outwards at the valley end.

The whole town, packed closely over nearly a square mile, had been eradicated. Entire sections of cliff had collapsed, burying more of what little was left of their once-secure and peaceful home. Propelled at incalculable speeds by the expanding fireball, debris had been shot out in all directions and punched holes in solid structures.

Some had been flung up the melting slope of the cliff over the girls' heads to tear through the tops of the trees half a mile behind them, starting fires and disintegrating what it hit. The rest was thrown high into the air and out into the valley. Many pieces plummeted to earth far into the Léohtsholt and out on the plains beyond the town; many animals and people safe from the blast itself were killed before they knew danger was there.

Xhera knew nothing of this, of how lucky they had been to be missed by the blast and the falling rubble. Everything she had ever known, their entire world, had been obliterated in a green flash – in an instant. Talas was blinking rapidly, squinting around.

'Something is wrong with my eyes.'

Suddenly she whirled screaming and ran back towards the woods, dragging Xhera behind her. Xhera could not keep up, and fell, her hand slipping from her sister's. Talas kept going and did not stop until she careened heavily into a fallen tree. The slam of the fall knocked the breath from her, and she lay as if dead until Xhera had stumbled to her side. Talas finally rose shakily, some sanity restored, and limped hurriedly towards the woods with her little sister in tow.

Xhera realised dimly that her sister could not see very well. Her adult mind realised she must have had her eyes open at the time of the blast, although the fact she could see anything meant she had not looked directly at it. Talas was unable to pick out anything clearly more than a few feet in front of her, and Xhera wondered dully if she realised the true extent of the devastation that had been their home.

Finally, they reached the woods, Xhera guiding Talas as well as she could. Their hearts were still beating in panic and their heads filled only with thoughts of fleeing the madness behind them, the sounds around them only adding to their desire to escape the hell that had erupted in front of their eyes.

Xhera was swept along in the rush, the adult part of her detached and observing. They stumbled through the woods for what felt like hours, unable to think of anything except fleeing. After falling many times Xhera's bruised and cut little legs finally gave out for the last time and she collapsed. Talas fell next to her, weeping. Both of them were covered in blood, dirt, dried tears and snot, their clothes torn. Now that their frantic flight had stopped they began shivering from the cold and in reaction to their shock. Xhera cuddled up to Talas, exhausted. Her sister sat limply, occasionally stroking Xhera's hair and crying silently, her face pale. The beech tree they sat against was not very comfortable, but she was simply too tired to move. Neither girl had any idea where they were, or what to do. The strain caught up with them and without realising it both of them fell asleep, the tears drying on their faces in muddy streaks.

ca   so

Xhera was aware of the woods around her even as she slept. Something within her – the adult observer – was still partially awake. As they slept both of their faces relaxed and the nightmares fell away. Gradually a lilting music crested the bounds of her hearing and crescendoed, rising from the point where the ring of a bell fades to silence and bringing peace. She dreamed of pale lights and fair faces. Chaos receded and soft laughter tinged with sadness filled the air around them.

They awoke slowly, passing gently from rest to alertness like the brush of a feather, and found themselves lying on soft pallets beneath the trees at the edge of a grove. Light cloth wove in and around itself to form a connected town – even a small city – of fabric.

Dirt and twigs seemed reluctant to cling to it. Pale lights hung from branches in trees, and were clustered more brightly around the girls. Not far away, a beautiful chant rose and fell in mourning. Soft laughter was still around them, but it was laced with sorrow. The air was warm, with hints of a summer breeze, and the stars were clear through the leaves.

Forms moved at the edges of the light, gracefully coming forwards. Each of them moved like dancers, stepping lightly and unconsciously with a fluidity quite unlike anyone Xhera had ever seen.

As they neared, pale fair skin, high cheekbones, tilted almond-shaped eyes, and upswept points on the ears became visible. Xhera realised these were not her people at all; these could only be the elves they had sought.

A woman and a man stepped forward lightly. They were ageless, their faces serene and perfectly, impossibly beautiful, showing no blemishes. Straight fine silver-blonde hair was gathered simply back from the temples up in a ponytail, leaving the rest to hang naturally underneath. The woman also had braids hanging from her temples, and wore a white robe of thin fabric folded in intricate layers. The male wore a similar garment split up the front to reveal a tunic patterned lightly with green leaf swirls. The male elf moved to the front and bowed gracefully to them, whilst the female regarded them intently.

'Greetings, children of Man,' said the male in a melodious voice. 'I am Doródon. Please, do not be afraid. Let your hearts be at ease. You are no longer lost, and we are glad to have found you. Lucky it was too since you travelled far from our Grove here. You are safe from harm this night.'

Talas looked around blearily in wonder, struggling to focus. Xhera thought her sight better than last night. Doródon noticed her watching her sister and smiled. His teeth were white and very straight, seemingly slightly flatter than human teeth.

'We did all we could for your eyes, young one. Alaria is our most skilled healer, and she tended you both.' The girls realised that their limbs and faces were clean, and the bruises and scratches were faded and almost gone. As one they looked at the female, who knelt next to them.

'I am sorry, young one,' she said to Talas. 'Your eyes were badly damaged.

You will never see quite as clearly as you once did, but you *will* see.' Talas nodded dumbly, the fact insignificant next to the tragedy of the night.

'What are your names?' asked Alaria gently. The girls replied haltingly, the words coming slowly.

'Talas, Xhera', repeated Doródon, 'you are welcome to our Grove. I only wish it was in more joyful times. Are you of the human dwelling Valesgate, at the bottom of the cliff to the east?'

Both girls nodded, and Talas began to say something, then dissolved into tears. Xhera began crying as well, largely because her sister was. Although too young to comprehend the depth of the tragedy, the adult side of her realised along with Talas that everything they had ever known – Jons, their parents, their friends, the house and streets that were their world – was gone, and they were cast adrift. Alaria cast a concerned glance at Doródon over their heads, and he nodded in return.

'Come,' murmured Alaria, gathering the girls into her robe. They cried as she comforted them, but it did not last long. A sense of peace seemed to flow from her, and gradually the sobs and hiccups died away. After a time, she pulled back and looked at them gravely.

'We will care for you here and make sure you reach your own kind again. You are brave to have survived where many have not. Even we felt the effects of the star that fell.'

Talas sniffed. 'Is that what it was? A star?'

Doródon nodded. 'Not a true star; yet it came from the heavens, and had a taint upon it… an ancient evil. The fragment moved with speed even elven eyes could not follow, but it was likely no more than fifteen ells across. Sometimes these lesser stars fall to earth, but not in my living memory has one caused so much destruction – and I am old.'

The girls stared at him in confusion. Doródon looked barely as old as their father.

Alaria saw their expressions and said gently, 'Elves are longer lived than humans. Doródon is approaching his eighth century of life.'

Doródon smiled slightly at the disbelief on their faces. 'Elves are long-lived, children of Man, but we are not immortal. Only the *Ældarín* are truly ageless. We may be struck down as readily as any race, as we saw to our sorrow this night.' He sighed. 'A few of our brethren were nearer the destruction. Most escaped completely or with only injury, but some did not.'

Alaria changed the subject. 'Talas and Xhera. Not all humans have such lovely names! Please, come with us, and we will give you food and drink to strengthen you for your journey back.' As Talas started with a look of fear, she added, 'Child, you will not be alone. You are in our care.'

They rose and joined Doródon, moving towards the soft singing. Xhera found that her strength had returned somewhat, even though it appeared to still be the same night and dawn was not yet evident. Passing beyond some of the partitions of fabric, she saw a group of elves to their right, separate from the folds of the city.

Within the circle of elves, Xhera saw several still forms, covered in white and surrounded by candles. The elves sat, grief evident on their faces, and sang softly and mournfully, swaying with the music.

Doródon spoke, his voice filled with sorrow. 'Alas. Even elven ears cannot pick out the rush of a falling rock from the heavens, especially when all around them is in uproar. One of our kind might survive a blow that may kill a human, but there is only so much damage that can be borne before life flees. The son of my brother was barely two human centuries old. He had only recently reached his Quickening. The others, too, were my friends. The stars will seem dimmer without their dance beside ours.' Xhera felt a sorrow separate to her own. It was evident how much the loss of an elf meant to the others.

It all seemed dreamlike. The choir of elven voices lent a surreal quality to the walk, and the pale lights and almost-glowing light fabrics of the elves only served to reinforce this.

A minute later they had arrived at their destination, a laced hall filled with gentle conversation. Within, many elves sat cross legged on woven mats in front of low tables. Delicate wooden goblets carved with loving skill sat next to thin wooden plates and small, rotund bowls. Much larger long oval platters with gracefully curved lids sat in the middle of each table. When the lid of one was lifted, they saw it to be heaped with fruits, vegetables, breads, and biscuits. Slender pot-bellied jugs sat next to them for the goblets to be refilled from.

Xhera had never seen wood worked so delicately; the whorls and grain virtually glowed, crafted and polished so that they looked as if they had been grown whole from the trees that made them. The elves ate from their plates with two delicate sticks carved with no less detail. Perhaps six inches long, they wielded them as if part of their hands, gracefully using them to pick up small pieces of food.

'Do not worry,' smiled Alaria. 'We do not expect you to learn the use of *chórel* in one sitting.'

She gestured to the nearest free table, and Doródon moved away, to return with what seemed to be a combination of a fork and a spoon, with shorter tines around a shallow bowl. Handing the girls a napkin that looked like cotton but felt like silk, he set the curious yet somewhat more familiar utensils down in front of each.

'Please. Eat.' He smiled and with Alaria gracefully sank down next to them. Xhera heaped her plate, as did Talas, although her sister paused in distress when she noticed that her hosts took several of the small plates and bowls and placed a small amount of food in each. Alaria smiled at her hesitation.

'Do not worry for our customs. We eat slowly and savour food, and take it piece by piece. Humans are hastier, and eat more quickly. You are young yet, and weary. Do not fear to offend us.'

Xhera, her cheeks already bulging with grapes, watched Talas slowly dip her utensil into what looked like small grains with vegetables and a light oil coating. The first mouthful overrode all caution, and she was soon eating with as much gusto as her younger sister.

As they grew fuller they slowed and their hosts began to talk to them, asking questions and telling them what they could. Talas managed to eventually tell the whole story of how they survived. Alaria and Doródon listened gravely. Xhera only spoke once.

'Will you grant us three wishes? Jons said you would. I only want one wish. I wish the star didn't fall.'

Doródon smiled sadly. 'Alas, Xhera: that we cannot do. Our wishes are the same in this, but there are few we can grant. The stories told by your people are oft-times just myths. This we can promise, however: we will protect you, and heal you, and feed you, and ease your burdens until we can find your people. This I swear.'

They then turned the subject to lighter matters, catching the girls up in delight, talking of how the Grove was a temporary rest for their people and how they had great cities to the west carved skilfully from stone and wood and beautiful to behold; how the very plates they ate from were each lovingly brought forth by an elf who saw them in dead and dying wood, and chose to preserve some of the beauty of the tree, of how insects and other bothers did not trouble their camps, and how carefree and laughing were the elves.

In time they arose, the girls replete and sleepy, and guided them back to their warm pallets beneath the trees. The sky was lightening as the night finally drew to an end, and Xhera sank down gratefully into a thankfully dreamless sleep.

When they awoke, it was past midday. Doródon sat peacefully near them and they saw he now wore tighter fitting clothes in hues of brown and green, lightly patterned as if part of the woodlands. His eyes were shut, but he did not seem fully asleep. Even as they moved, his eyes opened and he smiled at them.

'I hope you are rested,' he said.

Talas started to apologise for waking him, but he waved his hand elegantly. 'Elves do not sleep as humans do,' he smiled. 'Rather, consider that we have a waking dream, a reverie if you will. You did not disturb me.' He rose without effort. 'If you are ready I will take you back to your people. They will be looking for any survivors, and you will be at ease with them. We must also depart from this place soon, and travel west to the city of Gílas'tor.' Talas and Xhera stared at him, the rigours of last night returning. 'I will be with you, children of Man,' he assured them. 'Come. We will make the journey easier for you.'

They walked around the edge of the Grove until they were near an obvious path. As they waited, Alaria walked from the fabric walls with a small grey pony and a white horse. Both looked daintier than those they had seen ridden in and around Valesgate.

'These are elf-bred steeds,' said Alaria, smiling. 'The little one will bear you swift and true. She shall not let you fall.'

Talas and Xhera looked doubtfully at the little pony, which had no bridle or saddle. Beckoning them forward, Alaria helped first Talas then Xhera up. Talas worked her fingers tightly into the mane of the pony, and was rewarded with a snort and a slight shake of the head.

'Not so tight, little Talas,' laughed Alaria. 'She knows her duty.'

Doródon mounted his horse. There was now a slender sword at his hip, and he bore a quiver and bow across his back. 'Come,' he said, turning the horse toward the path.

Alaria raised her hand in farewell. 'Fare thee well, Talas, Xhera,' she said. 'May you come through tragedy safely and find your paths.'

Xhera waved back. Talas nodded, although she did not remove her hands from the mane in front of her. The pony turned and followed Doródon. The gait was incredibly smooth and as the minutes went by Talas relaxed her grip.

The journey that had taken them hours of stumbling the night before was less than an hour in the day on horseback. In mid-afternoon they broke from the trees. The sky in front of them was dark from debris, ash and the remnants of the smoke. The edges of the forest were leaning in, some of the trees bent or broken. Many also showed signs of fire.

Doródon deliberately took them along the treeline, avoiding the road until well past their former home. Several burned-out buildings and farms nearer the edges of the cliff spoke of tuns taken unawares by the blast. A pall of smoke lay on everything, thickening the air as they rode past. Finally in the distance they saw a relatively untouched tun with men around a large barn and most of the buildings intact. The elf headed for the gate and the figure standing there, sensing his search was at an end.

Xhera saw the guardsman as she approached. He was ragged and tired; later, he told them what had happened to him that night. He had been outside his clifftop watchtower, thankfully several towers from the impact site, when the blast had come. The top of the tower had caught fire and crumbled, killing and wounding the guards on duty. The rest woke below and tried to help. The lower part of the tower had been damaged by flying debris and began to give, the wooden supports screaming a warning.

Many of his colleagues had fled for the door, some still valiantly trying to reach their comrades trapped above, but only a few managed to get through before the tower toppled off the cliff it stood on, carrying the terrified screams of all within to the bottom of the cliff a thousand or more feet down. Mortified, they had looked down to the broken rubble, and then in disbelief at the firestorm along the valley where the garrison had been. Since then the remainder of the patrol had moved tiredly and steadily back along the roads, helping those they could, trying to find an officer and a purpose. They could not understand what had happened, and only the hope that something might be left of Valesgate drove them on.

When they had come to the slide where the road had once led a thousand feet and more down to the river and city below, they stopped in tired horror. Nothing was left. Even the fires had burned out now, and there were few survivors from the reports they received from other bands of guards. Many were badly burned, wounded, deafened, or blinded. The city was no more and the nearby mines were closed by a giant slide, trapping watchmen and workers on the night shift alike and dooming them to a slow, starved death.

All that remained were farms surrounding a crater. Some chanced the uncertain new slope to try and rescue any trapped below, and the rest had turned to help where they could here. The cliff-top farmsteads had been partially spared due to the massive rock face, which absorbed and deflected much of the blast, but much was still lost. Unfortunately that deflection had sent much of the energy back out down the valley, and they surmised that the far plains tuns had suffered badly from debris from the blast.

When Xhera had first seen him, the guardsman was leaning on a farmstead gate to the south in the late afternoon, grateful for the refreshing water and fruits offered by the farmer. The patrol had worked long hours to help save his barn from fire and to shore it up when it threatened to collapse. Even so, several cows had died, but the farmer, aware of how much more he would have lost, promised the men fresh meat this night.

As they rode up his eyes fixed on Doródon. The guard realised he was staring at an elf with his mouth open. He closed his mouth and swallowed, then spoke. 'My greetings. I am Corporal Greck Hordane of the City of Valesgate Militia, overseeing rescue of anyone that needs it, in light of... last night.'

Doródon regarded him with sympathy. 'I greet you, Corporal Hordane. I am Doródon. I mourn the losses we shared last night when the star fell from the heavens.' He bowed his head, and Greck likewise bowed his. Doródon continued, 'Luck was with some of your people, however.' He indicated the girls. 'We are withdrawing to our nearest city today; this star falling may be a grave portent of much to come, and we must discuss it. I have come to find your people, so that Talas and Xhera may be cared for.'

Greck looked up at Doródon and nodded. 'They will be well cared for, elf. My thanks. You've brought us some hope; where there are some survivors, there may be more.'

Doródon smiled, and then turned to the girls. 'Live in peace, young ones, and may this night not greatly burden your lives.'

To his surprise, they both hugged him tightly. Unused to such physical shows of emotion, he stiffened briefly, and then his face relaxed and he hugged them back, laughing softly. Laying a hand on their heads, he turned to Greck. 'I must leave. You have my thanks for taking the children in, Greck Hordane.'

He mounted. Looking back to the girls, who had started crying, he raised a slender hand in farewell, and then turned his horse to the woods. The pony followed him, and Xhera watched as he rode into the distance.

Greck turned to the girls. 'Well, I'm Greck,' he said. 'I guess we'll be staying together from now on. I have a friend, a scholar I am going to see who can help me look after you. Would you like some food first?' They nodded silently, and Xhera looked up to see determination in his face. 'Well then,' he said resolutely, starting away from the gate. 'Let's get you some. And then, well. I will look after you. *That* I promise.'

Talas and Xhera both smiled through the last of their tears. Xhera faltered as she followed Greck and Talas to the farm house door. As she fell, Greck turned and caught her. Hoisting her in his arms, he carried her as she laid her head on his shoulder.

'Everything will be all right,' he whispered brokenly as everything faded to blackness. 'Everything will be all right.'

FORTY-THREE

S ontles dreamed as his men carried him. Far from Meyar, they had been travelling for more than a month. He had still had no word from Ventran on the removal of all the Darostim, but it did not matter.

It was time.

Bypassing Eyotsburg as it spanned the foot of the great lake Merimakea, lying hundreds of miles long between the foothills of Nassar and the foothills of Rhe and tipped by the mighty Arkon mountains, they instead crossed the mighty river Relden by boat as it fed out of the lake west towards the sea, and travelled east through the edges of the Reldenhort plains, avoiding Punslon and the tribes. It had been a perilous and secretive crossing, especially for so many men, but there was no time to cross the Nassmoors and travel south around the Arkons; Sontles had been called, and he obeyed with all speed.

His thoughts were full of puzzles, pieces, and blood, like gory cogs meshing together. Since he had forsaken his fellow men and corrupted the church of Terome, he had seen and done glorious, terrible things, but none of them had ever approached his melding with Chaos.

In his youth, he had been a simple accountant, but one day a darker path had been granted to him by a stranger visiting his lord's keep. The shadowed man had seen something dark hidden within him and both destroyed him and renewed him to bring it forth and augment it. All his petty ambitions were nothing compared to what he had gained.

He had chanced upon hidden tablets of platinum in his earlier years, after he had learned control of his new powers. Most humans would have melted them for their incredible wealth, but by this time he was no longer the man he once was.

Sontles had recognised the tablets for what they were. Inscribed in alien lettering, he spent many years deciphering them, and found they were from an ancient race that had worshipped a hungry god. He had become obsessed with obtaining its power, like many before him; but unlike them, he had powers that they had never possessed. That fool Kharkis had been just a man, for all he was an Emperor.

Whispers of even more power had led him to the far western continent, and there he had finally fallen into a black place with winds of chaos blowing around it. No normal human could have survived, and there in the dark he was nearly destroyed, but on finding the chaos and evil in his heart the powers that found him instead whispered to him, filling him with new purpose and even greater promises than the hungry god could offer.

He had become their vessel all those years ago, and now the time had come to release chaos, to prepare for the coming of his masters... to release a bound god. He grinned in the darkness, his fangs protruding as his coffin swayed in the grip of his minions. Cleric of Terome, agent of chaos, defiler of life.

How far he had fallen.

FORTY-FOUR

Floating unmoored in limitless, peaceful black, time ceased to have meaning for Karland. Whispered words of prophecy swam slowly through the murk to alight within his mind. A veiled, threatening deep rasp spoke words of portent and doom. Alongside it chimed a melodious if alien voice speaking the same words, yet this voice spoke of signs and salvation. Together, the words reverberating, the prophecies spoke of deliverance or despair, and neither voice was stronger.

The darkness faded, vibrating still with the words. Karland sat up slowly, raising himself off a rocky floor. They were behind the Portal, which stood silent and dark, lying as if they had stepped through and fallen together in a heap.

His mind rang with the vision of great forms defending their world, and their anger at the ploys of Chaos. The vision was muted somehow, but some parts were clear. He whispered fiercely to himself, and to Aldwyn.

'Find the key, save the world.'

His eyes pricked slightly at the thought of his old friend. He looked at Rast. The huge man looked somehow less grim, more at peace, and he smiled at Karland.

Turning to look at Xhera he saw that she sat, numb. Her face was pale, and tears silently tracked down her cheeks. Shaking off his uncertainty, Karland rose and moved to her side; taking her limp hand, he sat next to her, deeply concerned. After long seconds she finally responded to the pressure of his hand, and spoke without looking at him.

'I know where I came from. I saw my childhood. I saw them all die.'

His heart twisted at her grief. 'Who?' he whispered.

'Everyone but Talas. My family, my friends, my home. It was all gone in an instant.' Her voice trembled and dissolved into racking sobs. Karland patted her shoulder ineffectually, and was taken aback when she threw her arms around him and cried into his neck.

After a time her sobs subsided. As she lifted her face, Karland felt the side of his neck grow cold. He was wet from the ear down, and his tunic was tear-sodden and crumpled from snuffling. Rast moved to his side and laid a big calloused hand gently on Xhera's shoulder. Her lips were quivering too much to speak properly.

'I was young,' she whispered. 'Very young, not six years old. A great falling light in the sky, a star, destroyed my home. All these years, and I never remembered. No wonder Talas never wished to speak of it. I have nothing, no one. I am cast adrift.'

Karland was struck to the core by these words. 'No one?'

Xhera did not respond, too bound up in her grief.

Rast's face showed disappointment. 'Come,' he said. 'We have much to consider.' Swallowing the lump in his throat Karland looked around to Györnàeldàr, crouched patiently at the bottom of the dais.

'Humans! You are returned.' It was a statement tinged with some surprise. 'You stepped through the archway but moments ago.' It felt like it had been days to Karland. 'Did you find the knowledge that you sought?'

There was a silence as each reflected on what they had seen.

'I do not know,' answered Rast finally, removing the pendant with a stony *chock* and collecting his pack and the great axe of Grukust. 'I will need time to consider what I found within.' Karland and Xhera nodded, Karland avoiding Xhera's gaze.

'We should leave,' said Györnàeldàr. 'Your quest is accomplished, though I am not sure to what end. I wish to feel the sky under my wings once more, and I must hunt. I am hungry.'

MORTALS, came the voice of the Great Dragon from all around them as they moved to depart. TAKE HEED OF WHAT YOU LEARNED. OUTER CHAOS IS NOT ALL THAT STIRS – AN ANCIENT HUNGER IS AWAKENING, RAVENOUS, DISTURBED BY THE PRESENCE OF CHAOS TO THE SORROW OF ALL. HEED MY WARNING. IF YOU DO NOT UNRAVEL THE MYSTERIES YOU FOUND WITHIN, THIS WORLD MAY PERISH.

What DID I learn? thought Karland.

Györnàeldàr turned and called loudly in her own language, a farewell to the god that lay dormant but alert within the cavern. Rearing to her full height with her wings outstretched to their greatest extent, she sent a great stream of brilliant flame aloft hundreds of feet above them in respect, ruining his night vision. For long seconds it shot towards the cavern roof before she dropped gracefully back down.

It was not until they were at the tunnel leading upwards out of the cave that Karland realised he had forgotten the lantern, now miles behind them and somewhere near the archway. He fumbled for a minute, wondering how he could somehow not look stupid, and then muttered, 'Shit.'

Rast raised an eyebrow.

'I, um. Left the lantern,' he said, feeling like an idiot. Rast said nothing and shrugged, apparently not too worried. Somehow Karland felt even worse. 'Sorry,' he mumbled.

Xhera however replied tartly. 'How *could* you forget it? It will be fun now, walking in the dark-'

'I didn't ask for your opinion, *thanks,*' Karland snapped, red-faced. He turned his back on her shocked expression and started into the blackness of the tunnel.

Györnàeldàr moved in beside him and opened her eyes wide. 'I can provide enough light for you to find your way out safely,' she said. 'It is of no matter.' Before them the glow lit the rock for many paces. Sighing, Karland started up, thankful that he could at least see where to put his feet.

 C3   80

As Karland walked ahead, embarrassed and upset, Rast moved up alongside Xhera. 'Xhera,' he said in a low voice. 'We should speak.'

'Why?' she asked.

'You wrong Karland, and myself as well,' said Rast.

'How?' she asked. 'Is that why he is being funny with me? He's being stupid. And rude.' She did not bother to keep her voice low. Karland's back stiffened in affront.

Rast shook his head. 'If you insist on acting as if you were a child, you will be treated as such. You may have lost everything you had as a child, but that happened ten years gone. Karland cares for you deeply. Your words were profoundly unjust. You have him, and me. You had Grukust too. Your sister. Aldwyn was another whom I thought meant much to you. Are we all *nothing*?' His steady gaze pinned her, and her face flashed crimson in mortification.

'No!' she said. 'Oh, I did not mean it like that!' She felt tears prickle her eyes again, and felt deeply ashamed. She had been so wrapped in misery she had not given thought to her words. Rast held her gaze, expressionless.

'Sadly, that is how it sounded,' he said. 'I suggest in future you do not treat those who offer you comfort so badly, or you may find little in times to come.' As her face creased and her mouth opened in attempted rebuttal, he forestalled her with a raised hand. 'I will keep you safe to my last breath, Xhera, but I will not accept your excuses. You must learn to deal with the consequences of your actions.'

With that, he increased his pace, leaving her alone with her guilt. She cried silently, following the others alongside the dragon.

ℤ ℥

They emerged from the tunnel into bright morning sunlight that peered through a dappled cloudy sky. It was warm for the altitude. Above them stretched many thousands of feet of rock and snow, all the way up to the peak. Györnàeldàr yawned as she came out of the tunnel. Moving to the side, she stretched her spine out, front claws raking and wings extended.

'It is good to be out of that passageway,' she exclaimed. 'Another few ten thousands of your years, and I would find that a tight fit indeed.' Karland shook his head, still not comprehending the span his large companion had lived for. The dragon waited for them to clear the tunnel and turned back to the rock. Preparing herself, she grasped the huge boulder and drew in a deep breath. Shuddering with the strain, she growled low as she wrestled its stubborn weight over, covering the tunnel. As soon as the rock settled back into place, she spoke in her own language and smote the rock hard with one massive fore claw. With a sound like a crack of lightning, the boulder split down the middle. Karland jumped as the crack reverberated off the rocks around them. Rast whirled, hands raised to his sides and his legs flexed slightly.

Behind the once more riven rock, there seemed only to be a stony face. The two halves settled together firmly into the ancient groove in the floor, wedging each other in. Without the rock in one piece, it would be near impossible to move again.

Rast relaxed. 'We should camp here,' he said. 'It will be a long road down the mountain, and we must be wary of ambush – perhaps not all of our enemies fled far. I would like to rest properly – and there is, too, another reason.' His face was solemn. 'I wish to mark Grukust's fall. This place is holy to dragon kind, but now it will hold meaning for mortals as well. If we live to battle onwards, it is because of his sacrifice.'

'I see no reason not to honour your fallen comrade. I regret I did not arrive sooner,' Györnàeldàr said.

Rast shrugged unhappily. 'Rarely does timing meet the needs of those relying on luck. That we survived at all is due to you, *Nāgìnī*.'

Karland helped him set a small fire up with the last of the kindling and wood that they had left from the night before. They would relax and recuperate after the harrowing days behind them, and tonight pay tribute to their fallen friend. Tomorrow would see them down the mountain and – he guessed – on their way to Darost.

He left Rast setting up and moved to the top of the slope. There were still smears of blood from the body of the ogre left in a pool nearly half way down, the great form lying among the other foes near the edge. The dragon removed the still forms from the ring of stones behind him, pushing them in a heap onto the gentle slope and clearing the sacred place. Sliding along the wall around their camp in the centre of the circle, she moved down the slope and casually swept all the bodies there off the cliff, save that of the huge ogre which she sniffed at then picked up in one taloned fore-claw, rumbling in satisfaction. Just as Karland began to wonder what she was doing, she sprang from the cliff to vanish out of sight around the mountain with her grisly trophy.

After a while Rast moved down towards the precipice and began searching for pale stones, stacking them into a cairn securely back from the edge near to where Grukust had fallen. Without speaking, Karland and Xhera moved to help him, working until the cairn was waist-high, the rocks pale against the darker rock around them. At least their friend would have a tribute here to his heroic sacrifice.

Karland didn't move towards the cliff after it was done. He had no wish to see if Grukust's broken form was in view far below, and was still leery of great heights. Instead, he revelled in the unparallelled view the heights afforded him of the plains. In the distance, Karland could see the dark forms of the Iril Eneth mountain range more than one hundred miles to the southwest, rising from the surrounding edge of the Dimnesdair. Rast said the elves to the east named the woods the Bal-Móralin. Karland remembered the strange forest and valley with a shiver. It had been a long hard trek here, and they had lost much. He still did not know what they should do next.

He turned back to camp, awkwardly avoiding Xhera's gaze. She seemed upset, as if she wanted to speak, but he refused to look at her. Her trivialising of him had hurt him more than he wanted to admit.

The sun was still high when Györnàeldàr returned. There was no evidence of the body or what had happened to it, but Karland saw Xhera shudder as she realised that Györnàeldàr had probably eaten what amounted to a snack. By this time Karland and the others had eaten their own rations of dried fruit and salted meat. They had plenty, although for the trek back across the plains they would need to restock in the foothills.

They gathered their strength for the journey, waiting for nightfall when they could hold vigil for Grukust. Rast unsheathed his *shirkas* and honed the edges, then polished Grukust's axe. Györnàeldàr lay in a semicircle around them. Her huge snout rested on her forelimbs like a gigantic cat, and she closed her eyes, snorting in contentment. The day was cool despite the sun; their altitude and the dappled clouds tempered the heat considerably. Karland almost enjoyed the respite.

◌   ◌

Barely two hours later Györnàeldàr opened her eyes. Tensed and crouched as if to spring, the tip of her tail was lashing again. Karland was beginning to take that as a bad sign.

'Something is wrong,' she muttered, her breath hissing through her teeth. 'I feel a great change coming.' Her head moved to follow a tiny speck that circled a distant peak. Karland couldn't quite see it, but he knew Györnàeldàr could likely see every detail.

'Some of my kin are near,' she said. Karland did not know if this worried or upset her; her tone was cautious. Even as he strained to see it, her ears twitched and her head curved sinuously around on the long neck to look up the slope of Drakeholm Soaring. The party stared. Several distant forms were circling above them, a suggestion of slowly flapping wings at their sides, rising and falling. Györnàeldàr watched them warily, her movements suggesting she was hearing their cries. Karland heard nothing.

A huge form swept to the side, closer but still some distance up. A brief eclipse of the sun and a ragged shadow were both gone in an instant. Györnàeldàr raised her huge head in agitation and roared in challenge, a great cry that bounced off the sheer slopes above them. From a great distance, answering cries came. Somewhere above them was a faint rumble as the volume of the huge beings' voices touched off an avalanche. As the humans watched, the peaks around them gradually filled with circling shapes.

Excited, she flapped her wings, causing them all to move out of range or be thrown tumbling. Half lifting off, she shouted to the nearest form in draconic tongue. The answering call came in the same language, and then the form flapped its wings hard, gaining altitude.

'What is happening?' asked Rast, tension evident in his voice at her unease and the presence of more dragons.

'I do not know,' said Györnàeldàr distractedly. 'The wrongness I have felt before is much stronger, but it is not that which we faced below. It worries at me like a rotting tooth. My people also feel it, and come together. Look! I see more than six of my people, and in one place.' She searched the peaks around them for more. 'I fear something dreadful approaches.'

Even as she spoke, one of the distant forms above began to spiral down towards them. The vast form blotted out the sun as it swept in, and it alighted gently with a scrape of talons on the rocks around them, staring down. Black as the heart of the mountain, the scales broke into a rainbow radiance where sunlight glinted off them. The underbelly was a rich cream colour of armoured interlocking scales. Spines ran in a twin row along its back, and dropped to run either side of the long tail, ending in two flatter spines like the pointed tines of a mace that ran back from the tip. This dragon was like yet unlike Györnàeldàr. It seemed to have a more angular structure to it, but was also bulkier, less slender, and was visibly larger than their companion. Karland guessed it to be in excess of three hundred feet long, and everything about it spoke of dangerous power.

The burning gaze fell from eyes as agate-blue as Györnàeldàr's were red, bright even in daylight. Györnàeldàr bowed her head low, surprise and respect evident in her voice.

'Körànthír.'

The blazing blue eyes bored into them all, the irises rings of sapphire fire. Dismissing the humans, he focused on Györnàeldàr. In a grating voice, the behemoth spoke in dragon tongue. Györnàeldàr responded at length, and as she talked she indicated the humans with her head. The burning gaze swung back to them, fixing them with its intensity. The eyes lidded somewhat, and abruptly the dragon spoke in Darum.

'Mortals. Györnàeldàr bears strange tidings. Long it has been since I found need, or desire, to speak to any of your kind.' The intonation was much more archaic than Györnàeldàr's speech, but clear. 'I awoke in recent times to hear that this place of our people was sought by such as you, even that Györnàeldàr did enquire at the behest of mortal beings. Strange this was to my ears. Long have we been apart from your kind, although ever has she been of curious and empathic nature.' He snorted in what could have been disdain.

Karland realised that, strange though Györnàeldàr might be to him, she was benevolent and gentle in her dealings with them compared to Körànthír. The gigantic dragon obviously cared little for their kind; if anything, there was a note of deep dislike in his voice. Karland's mouth was dry. He could not summon the nerve to speak in the face of Köranthír's general contempt, feeling judged and found wanting.

Rast may have felt the same way, but he showed none of it.

'*Nāgā*,' he said respectfully, bowing as if the dragon's tone held no hostility. 'We were sent here by the combined counsel of the Darostim, the Council of Twelve in Eordeland, and Györnàeldàr herself. The world enters dark times; even the mortal races are beginning to realise that something is wrong. War is imminent everywhere, not just in this land. Something steers this world into chaos. So we seek answers, hearing rumours of an ancient evil that has awoken in the far west.'

Köranthír's eyes hooded in thought. He looked at Györnàeldàr, and then back.

'Darostim? They know much, for mortals.' He looked as if he was struggling with an obvious reluctance to respond to Rast. 'Evil does arise,' he agreed finally, according Rast recognition. 'But though it might seem ancient in aspect to one as short-lived as you, to us, it is but recent. It is not of this world, and its arrival is fresh in my memory. I awoke with anger in my veins, and fear in my heart. My slumber since that time has been uneasy.' He blinked slowly.

'But that is not what has roused us now; Györnàeldàr spoke of what happened below. Something else is wrong with the world. It is an echo of the times of madness, when chaos swept the land and even dragon kind suffered. I travelled with all speed here, and am joined by the nearest of our kin. I am troubled beyond countenance. Of the other Elder Ones, there are no signs.' He pronounced the words with peculiar importance, sounding unsettled. 'Something stirs, an evil more ancient by far than the dark demons of Outer Chaos. One familiar to me.'

Györnàeldàr spoke, her own tone now troubled. 'Of what do you speak, Köranthír? I too feel it, though I am unsure of its source.'

Köranthír spoke one word with a hackle-raising growl.

'*Hyldjúpurgjá.*'

It meant nothing to Karland, but the effect on Györnàeldàr was startling. She hissed in agitation, her tail thumping into the ground with enough force to shatter rock. Her claws dug reflexively into the rock, leaving deep rents. 'The place of ancient evil,' she whispered.

Köranthír nodded. 'What is bound there is not free – for that we can be thankful. But I am not at ease. The earth speaks out in warning.' Györnàeldàr rumbled uncertainly.

Rast took the opportunity to interject. 'What do you speak of? An evil more ancient than the Darklings?'

'And what is '*Hiyeldiyehepurgdya*'?' asked Xhera, mangling it somewhat. Karland hadn't liked the sound of it, or Györnàeldàr's reaction, one bit.

It took some seconds for the dragons to respond. They seemed to have forgotten the humans even existed. Finally Györnàeldàr spoke to Köränthír, who looked displeased but turned his gaze back to them, and began to speak with no little scorn. 'In your limited tongue, *Hyldjúpurgjá* may be taken to mean 'bottomless pit'. The rest of the meaning is lost, but it matters not. What is of more import is that it is where, long ago, a demon was imprisoned.'

'Not a Darkling?' asked Karland.

'No,' replied Köränthír. 'A far more ancient dread. Even the Great Ones do not know truly how it awoke. It may be a lesser god such as they, or a First One akin to us, perhaps somewhere between the two. All that can be told is that it awoke in slime at the dawn of this world, possessed of a terrible hunger. It was here before us all. It may be that it was the First of the First Ones. In time, it saw the advent of life, and gorged upon it. The demon feeds upon the life force as well as the flesh of the body. Much life suffered in agony and died.' His eyes dimmed, he looked inwards to another place, another time in the far distant past.

'I flew the skies when the demon was yet free. It is known as Yosgaloth, *That Which Is Nameless*, the Bane of the Old World. All who fell into its path were devoured. The First Ones learned fear, and fled the demon. Not sentient as are we, yet it craved life and sentience to feed on. But this world could sustain it, even then; it slept often and long.

'An old mortal race, now long dead, learned to temper the demon with sacrifices and summon it to devour their enemies. Even for them, Yosgaloth was ever fickle. Ever have mortals meddled where they should not! Eventually, it came to lair in the depths of the abyss in which it now lies bound, and rarely came forth. The world for the most part was spared its hunger. Indeed, the place in which it lay spawned many horrors in its own right, and the demon even spared the world their threat by feeding on them in languor.'

Karland could not imagine something so ravenous, so frightening that even Dragons feared it. It was unsettling to think the first life to awake fed upon the rest, or worse, some elder god fed on mortals. This was the third creature he had discovered was older and more powerful even than a dragon, and it drove home how frail all their mortal civilisations really were.

'That first race to know of Yosgaloth waged war to find slaves and sacrifices, and over the centuries drove hundreds of thousands of mortals to their deaths to feed their hungry god. The other races rose against them in the greatest battle the ancient world had ever seen. At the peak of the fighting Yosgaloth was summoned, to the sorrow of all... but with the aid of the First Ones – and even the lesser gods – Yosgaloth was finally bound for all time in its lair. Without their god, the race was defeated and cast down, and vanished from this world, which knew a time of peace and respite from the hunger of Yosgaloth. The demon slept for a long age, shackled and quiescent, and the world turned.'

Karland could imagine the battle, but it must have been lost in history. If anywhere had records, it would be The Sanctum. He caught a glimpse of Xhera's fascinated face.

'Some thirty thousand of your years ago, a time of chaos and madness erupted in the universe. A trail of madness blazed through the vastness of the heavens, touching in its passing this world and many upon it. Much changed throughout the universe we knew. Many creatures vanished or died. Others warped, twisting into distorted versions of what they once were. Others changed completely, become unrecognisable. Parts of our own world became alien to us.

'So, too, was the place in which Yosgaloth bound touched, and Yosgaloth itself. We sensed many changes in the world, and strove to understand them. As we did so, the First Ones came to realise that the ancient enemy had also been warped. When the chaos swept through it, the demon awoke, grown overwhelmingly ravenous. No longer content with consuming sentient life from time to time, it was driven to devour *all* life without surcease. At the lip of the pit, we found to our sorrow that there is no longer any reasoning with it. It is angry, mindless, controlled only by its hunger, and more powerful than it ever was. Should it break free, may even the Darklings be wary.'

The rasping voice paused, breaking Karland free of the images he saw in his minds. 'Even now, Yosgaloth hungers and still attempts to escape, to devour all life. It thrashes deep below the earth with its need to feed once more, causing much upheaval in the lands around it. Yet still it lies bound, much diminished. It may be I am the only living creature awake that remembers when it was not so. But my heart is troubled and the very earth cries out in warning. So I came here to confer with the Dreamer, and warn my kin of the true horror we will all face should it ever break free. Even mortals should have some warning. I tell you this in the hope that you may perhaps shed light on my unease.'

He turned abruptly from them, and spoke to Györnàeldàr once more. She bowed her head, and moved to allow him access to the riven rock. With markedly less effort, he held the halves together and melded them even as she had. His powerful back and shoulders tensed, and he rolled the rock away with only a single grunt of effort. Without looking back, the huge black slid sinuously into the entrance, wings folded close to him. It was a much tighter fit that it had been for Györnàeldàr.

With Körànthír no longer there to overawe them, Karland began to feel affront at the insulting way he had dealt with them. Rast quietly asked Györnàeldàr why the huge black disliked mortals so.

Her reply was likewise low. She spoke softly of the time, nearly four and a half thousand years ago, when a human nation had deliberately trapped and killed a young dragon, barely out of the egg, at the demands of their arrogant ruler. Her eyes blazed in anger as she relayed the tale, yet her voice held no accusation; she obviously considered the instigators punished. Karland had never heard of the nation, but the legend of the Drake Years was well known.

Györnàeldàr spoke of the terrible anger of the dragons, and described how every one awake had gathered to exact revenge. The humans had fought back with every means, even gaining help from Dwarves and other races. They managed to injure and even kill several more of the younger dragons, but against the terrible might of the older drakes there was no defence. In a few short years the host had decimated an entire realm, ending an enduring civilisation. For well over one hundred years their anger waxed, and any mortal – bar the elves – unfortunate enough to venture across a dragon was slain.

The dragons had lost four young. Humanity and its allies had lost scores of thousands of men, women and children, and an entire nation was laid waste. Yet it was obvious the dragons considered their loss the greater by far. The slain young were irreplaceable, their immortality taken from them, whereas mortals proliferated and spread like wildfire – especially humanity.

Gradually, they had calmed, and the Drake Years had ended. The dragons had returned to their lairs, leaving a wasteland behind. But since that time, myths and tales had spread across the sea to all the lands. Humanity feared dragons greatly, and dragons henceforth distrusted humans and dwarves before all other mortal races.

Karland understood that Györnàeldàr did not hold blame, aware that within a few short generations all those who committed or remembered the atrocity had died. However, Körànthír and many of the other dragons never forgot the killing of their young, and their loathing of the puny mortals that had dared to strike at their defenceless children remained.

'Körànthír is ancient. He is one of the eldest of our race, and the eldest awake. He has flown under the sun for at least half the lifetime of humanity. You must understand that even five millennia of your years to dragon kind is akin to a brief time in your own lives. We still remember the pain clearly, as if it had just occurred. But some of us realise-'

At a cry from above, Györnàeldàr stopped abruptly and turned her head to the southwest. A distant dot in the sky grew with astonishing speed. Glinting blue, it grew swiftly. A piercing cry became audible from it; the dragon was obviously troubled greatly, and occasionally a spark erupted as it blew jets of flame. A larger shape from above flew out to meet it. Maintaining flight for a few moments, the larger form broke away and bugled to the rest. The call passed from form to form, and the blue dragon stooped and dropped straight for the ring of stones.

Landing with a lashing of wings from which Györnàeldàr quickly shielded the humans, the blue dragon folded them swiftly. Much smaller, it was perhaps one hundred feet from snout to tail, and the deep blue of an ocean in sunlight. Its body was smooth with high ridges rather than spines, and a tail forked near the end. Like all the dragons they had seen, it was mesmerising in its beauty and power. The dragon bugled loudly and excitedly to her, speaking quickly in liquid dragon tongue. Long minutes passed before she turned to them.

'She says that she felt uneasy and journeyed here from the southern coast. She passed high over the Dimnesvale, and was troubled to see many mortals within the valley itself,' Györnàeldàr relayed. 'Thousands, perhaps. They seek a route north and have already lost many. The creatures within must delight that such easy prey has entered their home.'

Köranthír, summoned by the commotion above as he descended, re-emerged snakelike from the tunnel in a hurried clatter of scales as she continued. 'It would appear that their destination is *Hyldjúpurgjá*. This alone would not be enough to worry her so, but alongside the whispers from the very earth, she sensed a growing dark presence with them that frightened her greatly – so she made all speed here.'

'This bottomless pit is in the Dimnesvale?' asked Karland, confused.

The dragon whuffed her breath at him. 'Little human, *Hyldjúpurgjá* is what you name the Pit of Kharkis, at the northern reaches. The place I told you would mean your deaths.'

'It is too much coincidence this happens now. Could they journey to free the demon?' asked Rast.

Köranthír rumbled loudly in harsh laughter. 'No matter if they do, mortal. No living being has the power to break the bindings of Yosgaloth, not even the First Ones. Even dragon kind could not rupture those wards.'

Xhera spoke up for the first time, her voice quiet and her face pale with her thoughts. 'What about that demon we faced? The Darkling. Would that have the power?'

There was a moment's silence. All three dragons stilled. Three bright gazes lit Xhera in consideration, and then Györnàeldàr replied, her tone deeply troubled.

'Yes. I felt it. A Darkling has power enough, although the hand that wielded it would have to be of this world. Who could bear the risk of that power, or would perform that deed? But forced to flee, who can say how that demon might try to thwart us? *It had power enough.*'

CR   SO

Sontles stood on the lip of the Pit, wincing at the sunlight around him. The smog from the low volcanoes to the south dimmed the lethal radiation, and his men had erected a shelter for him. There were many missing; many thousands had fallen to reach here.

He did not care. Their lives were his.

He awaited direction. No mortal had the power to do what his masters wished, but they could not use outer chaos directly here. To undo this ward, a creature of this world would have to wield their power, and he was their vessel. Sontles knew it would not be long. He had felt his master's anger at being thwarted in some way, and now it came.

Gazing into the pit before him he felt the tainted sense of horror rise from it. It was different to his masters. Their power was ultimate chaos, but passionless, cold, dead. This was boiling, hungry and evil, existing only to consume.

Men cried out as dread thrummed through them all. Sontles shivered in ecstacy as his master came, the shadow flowing through his being. The skies dimmed and shadows crept from the rocks to converge on him, pooling and then whipping up around him in a maelstrom of insane whispers. He felt cold power flowing into him, barely controllable. His vision changed, and he could see new layers to the world; the pit before him was bound in energies that would let all pass but one thing.

The hungry god. The nameless one.

No High Elf, no Dragon could penetrate this bubble, but through him, his masters could weaken it. Their power was old Chaos from outside this universe. The bound creature, terrible in its strength, would do the rest.

Filling to the brim, a toneless sound plummeted through him and he vomited forth streamers of darkness from his hands, eyes, mouth, every pore. No man could have withstood the flux of energy, but he was no longer human. Even immortal, as powerful as he had become, the fabric of his being began to dissolve under the chaotic energies.

The bubble thinned. The creature bound within sensed the weakness, thrashing and shrieking deep within his mind, and then suddenly a rent appeared. It was small; even all this power could only pierce the veil in one place, but it was enough.

A sickly light tore through the ragged edges, widening the hole, and the shrieks were suddenly real. The very ground rocked, men tipping screaming into the darkness. Sontles dropped to his knees, feeling himself dying as the powers left him empty and corrupted.

Grabbing the nearest man, he sank his teeth into his throat until they met, severing windpipe and carotids. Blissfully he drank the hot salty torrent, blood spraying his face and clothes, feeling strength return.

If he stayed he was doomed.

'Master!' he cried as the shadows dissolved. 'Aid your servant!' Around him the remaining men shrieked in terror as the writhing horror burst from the pit.

The shadows around him coalesced again, deepening under him, and he fell into them.

-You have done well.-

છ   ѕо

Köranthír roared in fury, and sent a huge column of flame up towards the heavens. The blue dragon screeched in reaction and leapt backwards off the stones it perched on, beating its wings hard. Györnàeldàr herself snarled with a note of dread.

Köranthír sprang straight up, all care forgotten. Karland was getting very tired of the giant creatures bowling him over without meaning to; the stroke flattened them to the floor.

With amazing speed for his gigantic size, Köranthír gained altitude and banked. He sped southwest with terrible purpose, but had barely cleared the edges of the mountain when every dragon suddenly shrieked in hatred, their cries forcing the humans to cover their ears tightly or suffer deafness.

A beam of light stabbed skyward, to the southwest, gone again almost immediately. Köranthír increased his frantic flight and receded quickly to a dot in the sky above the plains. More than two minutes later the earth shivered gently, a fractional rumble coursing through it. Moving quickly to the slope outside the circle, Karland and Xhera flanked Rast as he looked out over the plains before them. Dust was visible rising in the distance from the Iril Eneth, casting the far peaks in a hazy shroud. Transfixed, they watched as another beam of light swung up and around. A sliver at this distance, it was a pale throbbing yellow, a sickly hue.

More than six minutes after the first beam of light had shot over the Iril Eneth, a very faint rumble reached the slopes of Drakeholm Soaring, loud enough even for the humans to register. It was accompanied by a shrill screaming wail that set the heart pounding in dread. Rising and falling, it cut through the faint rumble and spoke of a terrible hunger.

Karland turned away to find that every remaining dragon had alighted on the high boulders forming the ring behind them. There were six of them – the smaller blue, two greens of different size, a spiky gold, one a coppery colour with shifting turquoise patterns in its scales, and one large brilliant white with glinting silver highlights, with Györnàeldàr a seventh in the centre of the ring next to the tunnel lying open and forgotten. None of them were as large as her, and every dragon was unique in form.

They all keened low in upset. Györnàeldàr spoke in Darum, her voice laden with despair.

'The Eater of Life has broken free.'

Karland felt sick as the pit of his stomach dropped. Köranthír had sounded as if he considered this demon as great a threat as the Darkling, and having seen that bleak darkness, he was afraid.

'What of Köranthír?' asked Rast.

Györnàeldàr turned her red gaze to him. 'He is wise and powerful,' she said with a faint note of worry, 'and he is the only living being awake today that remembers Yosgaloth. He will be wary. We must know the extent of the damage. Of all of us, Köranthír is best able to judge and advise. We must wait for his return.'

FORTY-FIVE

It seemed to Karland as if hours had passed before Köranthír returned. Every now and then, faint shrieks rent the air, sometimes having a strange duality to them. The nervousness of the dragons was palpable.

A trill went up from the dragons. Long moments later, the humans could also detect a growing dot in the sky. Köranthír swept in, landing with a clatter of scales in the space the rest hurriedly made. His great head was bowed, and as he folded his wings back he sighed mightily. He spoke in Darum, his antipathy towards the humans seemingly forgotten.

'Yosgaloth is freed.'

The dragons hissed in unison like steam vents on a volcano. They had all feared it was so, but hearing it confirmed removed all hope.

Köranthír continued, 'I saw it emerging from the Pit of Kharkis. Already its thrashings have collapsed the eastern cliffs, and earthquakes have widened the pass 'twixt the mountains and opened new paths. All life within that valley knows it is free and is fleeing. Creatures forgotten by all save us are spreading into the defenceless lands around the vale and pouring through. Yosgaloth has already consumed many creatures within the valley. I would hasten to stem the outpouring of so many dangerous beasts if it were not for the far greater evil that drives them out. I cannot know if Yosgaloth will stay within the valley long, but sooner or later, it will leave, seeking more life to consume. In these times mortals have spread far; it will not want for prey.'

Karland looked at Xhera. She shook her head mutely, not knowing what to say. Rast had no expression; he just stared south. Karland wondered if this was what Aldwyn had predicted; it sounded like the end of everything.

Györnàeldàr spoke up. 'Köranthír, I beg you to heed my warning. More than Yosgaloth threatens us. Yosgaloth will destroy this world if unchallenged, perhaps even then. But should that come to pass, more than the world will be lost. For if this world is also lost to Outer Chaos, then all of creation will fall into darkness and the chaos of the Outer Void. It is strange that I should find myself saying this, but I believe mortals are the key. The *Próarkhe* said as much, and his knowledge comes from the untainted Four of the Twelve Gods themselves.'

Körànthír snorted, then nodded. 'Fear not, my kin. Mortal creatures are undisciplined, young, and untrustworthy, but I cannot deny that they have power in their own way. They are separate from us and our kind, and ever was it so. They come from a life that is not bound to the world's spirit, to this universe, as we are, and so perhaps can affect causality in ways we cannot. Our course is clear. If we do nothing, this world will become barren and lifeless. Even we would fall eventually.'

The smaller blue flared a jet of flame. 'But what may we do against this demon?' it asked in accented Darum.

Körànthír looked around and exhaled from gigantic lungs. 'We must find our people. *All* of them, or as many as can be located. We have multiplied since the old days, and many of us have grown in strength and power; more great drakes are there now! But it required the *Próarkhe* to confine Yosgaloth in ancient times. I do not know if we can hope to imprison it once more before too much is lost to recover. The demon had not yet been corrupted then.

'Summon the *Zhōng Gúorén Huáng dì Nāgāra*. Assemble our people! I will fly as fast as the skies will carry me, and you must do the same. Warn any dwellings of mortals on our way of this threat. Not in long ages have we spoken to mortals directly, but we would be diminished if we failed in this; even they must know of what awaits them, must have the chance to flee. With every feeding, Yosgaloth will grow in strength. When we are assembled, we will seek the aid of our Lord below.'

'I will fly these humans to the great city they call Darost,' said Györnàeldàr. A ripple of astonishment passed through her kin. 'It may be the greatest collection of learned mortals in these realms. Such gatherings of sentience will call to Yosgaloth, and it is in Darost that the scholars await these mortals to unravel the plots of chaos. If the demon reaches that city above all others then what we seek could be lost.'

'Hang on,' said Karland. '*Fly?* Are you mad?' The words came out before he could think, his panic at thinking of the height removing all caution. Rast's hand fell on his shoulder.

'It is the only way,' the big man said softly, although even he looked taken aback.

The dragons ignored them.

'Are you sure of this?' Körànthír asked in astonishment.

Györnàeldàr grinned, her long fangs glinting at the larger dragon. 'What is our pride measured against our existence?' she asked. 'It has not been done before, but much will need to be done that has not been done before if we are to survive.'

Köranthír shook his great head in astonishment. 'Ever were you strange to us, Györnàeldàr. I do not think I could learn your restraint, but I honour your choice. Ensure they arrive safely. If we may drive Yosgaloth to entrapment, then can we call for the *Próarkhe* to help bind it once more. Go! And may the Twelve also watch over you, my sister. Keep a watch to the skies. The *Zhōng Gúorén Huáng dì Nāgāra* will come.'

One by one, the drakes bowed their heads to each other, and leapt from the wall, the humans never failing to be astonished at the grace of such large beings. Dropping like birds from the side of Drakeholm Soaring, they spread to all points of the compass and swiftly vanished.

Last to leave was Köranthír, who looked upon the humans with an unreadable expression. Karland grew uncomfortable under his fiery blue scrutiny, the gut-deep dragon fear ever-present, but then the greatest of the dragons said simply, 'Fare you well, mortals.' Beating his vast wings, he lifted himself into the air, and flew west with great speed.

ଔ   ဢ

A moment of silence was broken by a rumble from Györnàeldàr. She shifted restlessly, feeling the need to be gone. Rast turned to her.

'*Nāginī*. We will need a harness, so that we do not fall.'

The dragon's eyes flared. 'What do you propose?' she asked reluctantly. Rast looked at her shoulders, forward of the massive wings and wing muscles, and then at the rope they had. There was quite obviously not enough to go around more than once – hundreds of feet of heavy rope would be needed.

'I have an idea,' he said, looking at her spines. With some help, and some lifting from her, he secured the rope around three long spines a little way forward from the wings. The rope was tied to one spine at chest height and then crossed back to wind around the second, then again to the third. Rast pulled the rope taut, and then tied it off as tightly as he could. Running it down to waist height, he then threaded it back along again, so they would all three sit inside rope walls. Tying it again, he looped it under the base of her neck to secure it, then cut hand holds and fixed them to each spine between the two rope windings. To each end he tied a noose with a stop knot so they could grip tightly without fear of crushed hands.

Finally he cut the remainder of the rope into three equal lengths and lashed all three at one end to the central spine, to tether them all on tightly in case one slipped through the ropes. Testing it, he tied himself in, and asked the dragon to weave and dart her neck and head. Despite the jerking around and being flung into the ropes, he was satisfied that it was as secure and safe for all three as could be achieved.

He turned to the others. 'Let us go.'

&

Xhera approached Karland as he nervously gathered his pack, and finally took his hand, forcing herself to look into his eyes.

'I am so sorry, Karland,' she said thickly. She was normally so strong, but now she felt like crying. 'I never meant that you are not important to me. Before anyone else, you are whom I hold dear. Please. Don't turn away from me.' Her voice quivered, and she hated it. Karland studied her for a long minute, and then the grin she loved came back to his face and he drew her into a strong hug.

'Silly girl,' he whispered. 'It would take more than an argument for that. I'm sorry too.' She gripped him tightly, and they stood for a long moment. Out of everyone but her sister, she could not bear to lose him.

As they attached themselves to the stay ropes the dragon turned her burning red eyes to them. 'Are you ready, mortals? I will fly slower than is my wont – so that you may see and speak – and I will attempt to fly smoothly, but we must go now. I fly south first – I would see this Bane, and know what we all may face. Köranthír alone should not have knowledge of it, and perhaps the knowledge may help us in Darost.' At Rast's protest, she added pointedly, 'It will add perhaps a few hours to our flight, mortal. I deem it important, and I am flying. You are not.'

&

Györnàeldàr glided lower, watching the curving line of dust.

'I will not pass too close,' she called. 'But I would see this enemy, and gauge its intent.' They had made their way south easily and passed the mountain peaks.

The ride was surprisingly comfortable once the humans had become used to the motion, although Karland was still terrified he might fall.

A clear scar below pointed out the trail of the demon. It was in the Dimnesdair now, not far from the valley's edge. Quickly closing in, she circled round and down to hover above and behind Yosgaloth and he looked over her shoulder at the demon below.

Yosgaloth glinted with slime, its glistening dull brown hide not as slick as a slug, but oozing slightly. Almost four times Györnàeldàr's length and undoubtedly many times her weight, two heads weaved on long necks. They were long and snakelike, slightly translucent, a third of the length of the body or more. A series of ridges ran in rings around the necks, just visible, as if it had swallowed huge, evenly spaced coins. At the end of each the head was a short, curved, almost beak-like leathery hood which overshadowed the mouth.

A single pale eye could be seen on each head above the beak. A sickly pale yellow, having no discernible pupil or iris, they glared forth with a luminance entirely different to the burning gaze of a dragon. Three curved triangular plate-like leathery pointed scales at the rear of the hood suggested the top of the neck. The mouth itself was a wet hole with no teeth, akin to that of a worm but with webbing to each side.

Even as Karland watched one mouth dropped open impossibly wide, nearly wide enough to accommodate Györnàeldàr's body. The neck itself was easily wide enough to swallow a fully-grown *rinok*. In fascination he guessed anything that got eaten would be sucked in whole and moved down the neck with a peristaltic motion.

One head breathed forth a billowing, roiling cloud of light greenish vapour. The mist shot from the mouth and quickly disintegrated a wide swath of trees and many terrified fleeing animals. The cries were terrible, but mercifully silenced as they rotted quickly into slime, which the head lowered to and sucked up with relish.

Disgusted, he looked away from the heads. At the base of each neck were three slits to each side which pulsed rhythmically. These appeared to be breathing tubes or nostrils, moist and unpleasant with clear mucus, and looked wide enough for him to crawl into.

The demon seemed to use the necks as tentacles or limbs as well, helping it drag itself unmindful over all terrain with terrifying speed for its bulk. It moved mainly like a serpent, undulating itself along the ground in a sinuous slither, but it also used its long necks for purchase against trees and rocks. The body was bulky, fatter round than any dragon's, and long, tapering towards two long tails.

That end held a horror just as alien as the heads. The tails ran for a third of its own body length, but the brown skin covering it faded after a little way, stopping as if peeled back to expose lengthy drooping, ragged pink wet tendrils that looked a little like seaweed or loose veins. Karland was not sure what they were exactly, but they looked vile. They hung down in clumps, pulsating with their own movement, and would ripple down to implant themselves in the floor, or whip around trees and rocks to push and pull the body forward with a strength belying their delicate appearance.

They snapped ahead, adhering to anything and everything. Each tail was independent, like the heads, and dug or clutched at the terrain to provide extra purchase, leaving a trail of slime. They were not only for locomotion; they seemed to be very sensitive, detecting the slightest signs of life, wrapping around prey with killing speed and power to drain its life.

He had never seen anything like this snaking body that used four multifunctional limbs, the whole demon moving with terrifying and destructive speed. Seconds later, they saw yet another demonstration of Yosgaloth's power. Frustrated as indistinct prey fled beyond range of its reach and breath, the demon seemed to contract in effort. A lancing beam of light shot from one of the eyes, striking several forms, flashing all organic material it touched to dark vapour and steaming chunks.

Upon seeing the stabbing beam Györnàeldàr cursed in dragon-tongue and wheeled away hurriedly. She was just in time; at the sound, the demon whipped one long neck around and shot a green cloud upwards. It fell far short, blowing away, and the head shrieked in hungry outrage. Its pupil contracted with concentration, and a beam lanced out at the fleeing dragon.

Györnàeldàr wove frantically and dodged out of range. Karland, through his terror, could feel her shaking underneath them, from outrage or fear he did not know. The demon, thwarted in its attack, ignored them further and continued on through the forest. From where they flew, he could see a veritable tidal wave of creatures big and small frantically pouring through the trees to escape. Hunter and quarry ran neck and neck, terrified with the primal need to escape the demon devouring all within reach. Yosgaloth overturned any normal definitions of nature with its presence, turning every living thing within reach into prey. The sight was incredible enough to distract him from vomiting, for which he was thankful.

Some creatures did not get out of range of the killing breath or gaze. Some came within reach of a hungry mouth and still more were trapped and sucked dry of life by the tendrils on the tails. Yosgaloth pulled itself through the forest at considerable speed, but did not run down the fleeing creatures or consume all the trees. The demon's lust for more vital life drove it onward, a wide trail of destruction left in its wake like a scar stretching from the broken lip of the valley.

Györnàeldàr circled, out of lethal range, and then turned to the north. She flew fast. Karland squinted his eyes against the rushing wind and held on tightly to the saddle. Despite airstream, still he could hear the powerful voice of the dragon beneath them.

'I will fly as fast as I can without harm to you, mortals,' she cried. 'I have seen the enemy – and despaired. It is greater than I ever feared possible. Where it will turn I cannot say. We must seek Darost, but it will be a long flight there. Many hours, if you can bear it.'

Long minutes later, they reached the gap. Rast pointed and shouted to Karland and Xhera. 'I fear not all those fleeing are simple forest creatures.'

Below them ran a pack of gar-wolves, silent and fierce. Keeping a wide berth were several other packs of wolves, both grey and dire, and many deer and smaller creatures. Bears lumbered through the brush to one side. Off to the other, the crash of branches announced the passage of a giant crocodile, kin to one of those that had attacked them. Surprisingly agile for its short limbs, it ran head up and wagging, body off the floor. It did not move at a sprint, conserving its energy with reptile efficiency. Similar smashing announced the presence of other flight. A herd of the enormous forest elephants charged into view, scattering all other creatures and smashing even the largest trees out of the way. They and the reptile were quickly lost to view.

'This is ill,' shouted Rast. 'Even should Yosgaloth be halted, many of these creatures were bound in the valley. Who knows what horrors now roam free, or where they will find sanctuary? With them loose, the world will become a far more dangerous place for all - should it survive.'

Xhera shouted back, 'What about Punslon? And the tribes?'

Karland agreed, calling, 'They all need to be warned. Grukust's people should not die like he did!'

'We must not stop long,' said the dragon. 'Much depends on our speed. I will do as you ask, if you make haste.'

Trees swept by underneath, yet as fast as they moved the shrieks and crashes and cries of living things fleeing in dread still caught up with them as Yosgaloth continued its terrible rampage. Rounding Iril Paúr at the Pass, they circled west towards Punslon.

As it came into view, they stared, stunned. Karland gasped in shock; fully a third of the town lay buried under a massive rockslide. The Inn of Cards had been torn nearly in half by quakes, split timber poking out of the rubble. The sign lay flat and mysteriously unbroken on the floor next to the wall under a window covered in dust, and Karland hoped Geraldt had not been inside. The road was cracked and split; of the Town Hall and the richer abodes back in the cleft, there was no sign. A steep incline of rock and earth was all that stood there now.

He saw townspeople crowding the streets, many helping clear the rubble, many more watching with blank expressions. As people in the crowd noticed the huge dragon bearing down on them, screams erupted. The crowd bolted in all directions, most only mindful of themselves. Hundreds of people knocked the young and weak down. Karland shook his head at their flight, amazed that many seemed to care only for themselves.

The dragon hovered, shouting, '*Enough!* I mean you no harm. I bear humans who bring grave news!'

She was largely ignored. Those able to flee had gone to ground inside buildings. Rast pointed her to the open market place, and she flew down, scattering abandoned stalls.

◌   ◌

'Stay here,' Rast instructed the others, and set off in a run for the southern side of the road. Already a few curiosity-driven faces were peering out at the mammoth creature settled impatiently in the large clearing. The cries of the wounded were faintly evident, and there was a large knot of people behind the row of stores.

'Where is the Mayor?' called Rast. Mutely, a man pointed to the huge pile of rubble. 'I must speak with whoever is in charge now then,' Rast said. The man shrugged, disinterested, and turned away. As he did, a woman's voice spoke out from the crowd that had gathered.

'You are calm for someone in the company of a dragon, stranger. You have added to our wounded and injured with your appearance, so I do not welcome you. Who are you, and what do you want?' He looked towards the source of the voice, and saw a woman with streaks of grey in her hair, a proud slightly beaked nose and a seamed face. She must have been in her fifties, and wore expensive clothes which were covered in dirt and blood. There was an air of command about her, and Rast addressed her directly.

'My name is Rast Tal'Orien. She means none of you any harm – on the contrary, we come at great cost to warn you. The quakes are as a result of a great demon that has awakened in the Pit of Kharkis. It has broken free, and comes this way. The screams and quakes you hear and feel mark its progress. You must flee, quickly. Today. Now.'

Her mouth quirked in disdain. 'You appear from nowhere, on a dangerous beast no less, and expect us to believe you our saviour? The tremors have stopped. We are safe now, and have many wounded to care for. I do not trust your motives to make us leave what little we have. No, you are a bearer of ill, I think. I will not help you, nor will I let you take advantage of my people.'

Rast shook his head.

'Even the dragon fears this demon. It will feed on all here if it finds you. Even if it does not, uncounted dire creatures have broken free of the Valley-'

'There have always been earthquakes here,' she interrupted. 'Those noises could easily have been your dragon. I do not think our poor remnants will interest such a demon or any other legendary creatures, should any of them even exist. We deal in reality, not fantasy. I do not know your intentions with these tales, but I will remain here and care for those hurt. We will rebuild. If your demon appears we will hide, but I do not trust you, stranger. Who can say what wickedness rides with you? Leave us be. We have much work to do.'

Rast bit his tongue. Behind her hauteur he could see terrible weariness, shock and anguish.

'I must leave. Consider what I have said. You have wounded here, and children… whole families. I swear to you this message is true. At least hide children now, before the sounds of destruction are too near, and some of you may survive. I go now to the orks with the same message; believe what you will, and may your gods be with you. I can do no more.' Holding her gaze, he bowed slightly and turned to go.

As he left the village, he heard her thoughtful voice cutting through the noise, ordering the evacuation of the old and young. His heart more at ease at her caution, Rast ran back to Györnàeldàr quickly. At least some might be saved, and perhaps the children would live.

Györnàeldàr lifted him high to her back. As soon as he was secure, she sprang into the air, heading north.

໖   ໄ

Karland spotted the camps of the orks long after Györnàeldàr called them out. There must have been nearly twenty thousand; it looked as if the entire nation was coming together. A massive corral held hundreds of the nomadic people's short-furred plains *rinoks*.

Wary of another panic she landed a distance from their camp, yet close enough for their sentries to easily see her. This time they all climbed down.

Karland watched the orks as they approached. Like any creature of Kuln, they felt the instinctive fear that welled up with the sight of a dragon. The full-fledged fear of a dragon was debilitating, but they were fully prepared for battle, and seemed astonished to see three humans approaching from the direction of the dragon.

Rast called out as they neared, his voice loud. He was answered by a great scarred ork who was obviously in command. Head and shoulders above the rest, he looked like a stunted ogre, and was missing an eye. His incredible tusks were as chipped as if he had been chewing rocks, and he was easily the largest ork that Karland had ever seen, bigger even than Grukust.

Seeing the large goblinoids again brought back bittersweet memories of their fallen friend. Karland bit his lip. Rast called out again, his arms held out, palms towards the sentries in obvious lack of threat.

The large ork snorted and shouted back. 'You speak our tongue badly, human. I use Darum instead.' Karland noted the large ork's command of the language was noticeably better than Grukust's had been, although his gigantic tusks were not helping.

Rast shrugged.

'Very well. We have little time. We come to speak with Brukk. I bring tidings of Grukust, and a dire warning of a terror that will shortly sweep these plains of life-'

The big ork interrupted him, a snarl on his lips. 'You bring tidings of Grukust? Where is he? Woe to you if you brought harm to him, human. He is mighty warrior. Do not expect welcome here any ways. Brukk very angry that Grukust side with you. All the tribes felt his anger. You not welcome here. Maybe you should go back.' His lip pulled back over his tusks threateningly, his face unfriendly. Rast stood still, his expression not revealing the frustration Karland felt.

'Welcome or not, I come to warn you. Surely you felt the earth quaking this day? You cannot have missed the cries that I can hear even now, or the portents from the valley beyond the mountains. A great demon has awoken and it will kill you all if you do not flee.'

'We do not fear demons,' grunted the huge warrior. 'Brukk will be told you are here but you might not be happy at response from him.'

Rast unslung the huge axe and held it up for all to see. The twin crescents glistened in the sunlight, runes clear upon each blade.

'Perhaps. But I swore to return this axe to Darus, the brother of Grukust. He died valiantly; he killed many men and *Goruc'cha*, an ogre and a gar-wolf before he fell. Grukust was mighty, and I counted him my friend.'

There was a low guttural murmur at his words, particularly at the ogre and the gar-wolf. To kill two such fierce combatants in battle spoke of strength and courage beyond most, even for one who had earned his name killing a wyvern.

The large ork looked at the axe, and then started to speak. He paused, looked at Rast again, and finally said, 'Wait. Brukk will come.' He turned and left the humans standing. Karland glanced behind them, to Györnàeldàr coiled patient as a stone. He sensed tension despite her lack of movement. Yosgaloth worried her beyond all measure.

Rast turned to him and Xhera. 'Speak not a word,' he warned. 'Whatever is said, we cannot afford to make things worse.'

Half an hour passed. Karland was growing anxious, but dared say nothing under the watchful eyes of the guards, and Xhera was staring at the orcs, especially the women. Eventually, the dragon stretched her neck up and looked over to them, speaking loudly. All those assembled heard her clearly.

'What is this delay? If these greenskins will not believe you, leave them to their fate.' Almost immediately, she raised her head higher, and then said 'Something is happening.'

Seconds later the wide shoulders of Brukk forced their way between the nearest guards, followed by the big ork who had spoken earlier. Brukk's face showed intense dislike, and he looked at Grukust's axe as if he expected to see his nephew's blood on it.

'You are not welcome here, human Tal'Orien,' he said, echoing the words of the big ork. 'Doubly so now you bring this news of my sister's son. Grukust was among the mightiest of orks. I find it strange he fell so easily.'

'Not easily,' retorted Rast. 'You have no liking of us, Brukk, yet believe me when I tell you this. We became trapped, with only two of us to defend these younger ones. Grukust gave in to his rage.' Many orks nodded, understanding. Berserk rages were honoured among them as a pure state. 'He killed countless men and orcs, and then at many paces yet, he flung this axe, and struck the ogre in the face with it, killing it in one blow.'

At this, a harsh murmur did arise. The orks knew the strength of their large cousins, twice their size and more, and knew the power – and luck – that the blow must have taken. Rast continued, his eyes not leaving Brukk, who in turn stared at the human, blinking little.

'The fall of the ogre killed many orcs and men. I counted a dozen fallen before any other had struck even one blow. At the last, a fell gar-wolf set upon us.

Grukust faced it even without his weapon, and cast it from the mountain, along with himself. Even as he fell, he tore at its neck with his tusks. Never have I seen such a mighty deed. He sacrificed himself that we might live, and killed many enemies in the doing.' Karland's eyes pricked at the memory, the last sight of his friend roaring in triumph.

The buzz around them grew. The feats were honourable worthy of legend; a gar-wolf was one of the most feared single creatures among the tribes. Brukk held his hand out to Rast, who passed the great axe over to him. Turning it end over end, Brukk stared at it, perhaps envisioning its last victory. He seemed mesmerised by the play of light, and the humans saw his face soften slightly, turned away as it was from his proud people.

Then the brows beetled once more, and the eyes lifted, but not to them. Turning, he held his hand out, holding the axe horizontal and near the head. Unnoticed, another large ork had stayed back beyond the guards. As he moved forwards, Karland was struck by the similarity in features to Grukust – yet there was also youth in his face. He faced again Grukust's brother.

Darus took the axe, and hefted it. His mouth quirked and his lips quivered. Before he lost control, he swung it above his head and howled, a mixture of sorrow and anger and triumph for his brother's victory. The sound was taken up an octave lower by all the orks around him, in an expanding circle outwards. Quickly, it swelled, until the plains vibrated with it, thousands upon thousands of throats bellowing. Every ork stopped what they were doing. Mid-sentence, mid-stride, they roared Grukust's triumph and honour to the heavens, as was their custom for the mightiest of their warriors. Györnàeldàr, surprisingly, added her voice, accompanied by a long jet of flame into the sky which was visible to many far and wide. Karland's heart raced, and he felt like adding his own voice. He saw Xhera's face streaked with tears.

Darus's howl dwindled, and slowly the roaring faded out to the reaches of the tribe. 'My brother has heard us,' he said in his own tongue, his voice hoarse from the effort. 'He will not come unlooked for to the Great Plain.' He looked at the axe in his hand, and then to Rast.

'Thank you, Rast Tal'Orien,' he said in Darum, his voice thick with emotion. 'I will earn my rune-name with the axe of Grukust. Thank you for bringing it back to us.'

'Perhaps Grukust also left the axe deliberately, in part,' said Rast. 'I know he would have wanted it to come to you – for it not to fall into darkness with him.' Darus nodded, and turned away, his face bleak. Brukk watched him go, and then spoke to Rast sternly.

'Murlok said you spoke of two reasons for coming here, human.' The giant ork rumbled, staring down at Rast, who looked at them both impassively. Before he could speak, a girl's voice broke in.

'Haven't you heard the screams? Seen the light? The ground has been shaking for hours. There is a giant demon coming, and it will consume you all if you are here. You must run!' Xhera said frantically, unable to bite her tongue. Tears still glistened on her cheeks, her anger and distress evident. Brukk's brow drew down thunderously, and then he laughed, loudly and suddenly. Karland cursed inwardly.

'*Run!* You say all the ork tribes, gathered in our greatest strength, should *run?*' Shouting with laughter, he bent double, hands on knees. 'Ah. Girl-human, we will deal with a demon how we deal with all else. The tribes gather here, and soon we are complete. Then we go to war with the accursed *Goruc'cha*. If that means I kill a demon on the way, so be it.'

Rast cut him off. 'This is no laughing matter. Every ork alive would make no difference. This is like no demon you can imagine, Brukk. Legend says it killed Kharkis and over two hundred thousand warriors untold centuries ago. It has consumed even dragon kin.' Brukk's eyes popped at this last statement, and Györnàeldàr bugled in anger in the distance, whether at the memory or Rast's bluntness Karland did not know. 'It feeds on every living thing it comes across, and it will kill you *all.*'

'Your words mean nothing to me, human!' shouted the chieftain. 'Orks run from no one! No demon! No *legends.* We will fight this demon, and perhaps some of us will die. But we will win, as we always do. We are *strong.*' His chest heaved with anger. Karland shook his head despairingly. Xhera's outburst had done more damage than good. The orks would not back down now.

'Then you condemn your women, your children, your people, to death,' said Rast coldly. 'This is not about *honour.* It is about the survival of your *race.* Even if they escape, you will all fall. With all the warriors dead, they will not outlast the coming of winter… or the orc hordes. The barbarians of the Sergoth could help them, but they will also be dead, gone to feed the hunger of the beast that comes. Everything alive is in peril. Will you not listen?'

Brukk spun to Murlok. '*Get this filth out of here now!*' he roared in orkish, spittle flying from his mouth. Ignoring the spray on him, Murlok regarded them thoughtfully, his face unhappy. To Karland it seemed that, like Grukust, his bulk belied his thoughts. The giant reluctantly moved to do as commanded, but even as he dropped a heavy hand on Rast's unresisting shoulder the nearest orks shouted in panic.

Seconds later gales beat and eddied through the camp far and wide, sending orks sprawling at the epicentre. Györnàeldàr hovered above them, beating her wings. Carefully she landed, the orks scurrying out from under her bulk. Even Murlok was little more than an ant in front of her furnace glare. Her gaze flashed around, pinning orks where they stood. Many hooted in fear and covered their faces, or dropped their spears; some broke and ran. Even the proud warriors were no match for the intense fear that washed through them, and it was reinforced by her evident rising anger.

Honour broken, the orks looked upon one of the mightiest of the dragons still walking Kuln, and Brukk stood as frozen as the rest. Györnàeldàr's voice thundered, nearly deafening them all.

'Foolish mortals! This demon will kill you all. If you will not listen to Rast Tal'Orien then you will listen to *me!*'

No one dared move. Karland saw her tail twitch and realised she must be trying not to lash it. If that happened she might kill many warriors without meaning to.

'Yosgaloth comes! Your tribes would be swallowed in an instant, and your souls will be lost along with your honour. You cannot fight it. Even my kind fear the Bane of the Old World, and fly from it. So I tell you once only: *flee!* Yosgaloth is terrible. It is not a matter of honour. The human risks much to bear this news to you and you repay him with tantrums befitting a child! The honour of orks has lessened greatly. Perhaps you slip towards your fallen brethren.' Cries of fury arose at this last, anger cutting through the dragon-fear. Györnàeldàr ignored them.

'If you would wish the orks to be no more, stay. Otherwise leave now, within the hour; scatter across the plains. Go north! Go west! Anywhere but here! Warn all you see! All my kin gather to battle the demon and even that may not be enough. Guard well your tribes, for many fell beasts have escaped the valley beyond the mountains. You may yet face peril, even if the demon does not find you. Pray to your gods that the *Zhōng Gúorén Huáng dì Nāgāra* do not fail.'

Lowering her great head, she spoke to Rast. 'We have delayed too long, mortal. We must leave for Darost. Let these fools die, if that is their wish. I tire of mortals who do not respect our efforts.' She held out her taloned arm, foreclaw palm-up for them to step on, and then raised them to her shoulder.

As Karland secured himself to the dragon's back again, he saw Darus talking to Brukk. Brukk looked troubled, and looked up at them all.

'Wait,' he shouted up. Drawing a deep breath, he growled, the words pulled from him reluctantly. 'Your words are troubling, dragon. If you alone can turn my warriors to faint goblins,' and he glared around at his shamefaced warriors, 'what then would this demon you flee do?' He cast around, desperately seeking a way not to apologise and lower his honour. Karland could not help enjoying his discomfort.

Under the wilting gaze of the dragon, he finally settled for, 'It may be that I was hasty. We will send warriors to warn the barbarians and guard our children. But still we must fight, even if we avoid this demon. A huge army of *Goruc'cha* has gathered from their holes, many thousands upon thousands, and struck northwest. If we do not go to war, it finds us unprepared. Even so, we may fall.'

The dragon rumbled. 'Fine, greenskin. If you must fight, fight them. But leave here now, or your people will find oblivion.'

Rast smiled faintly. 'Strength to your tribe, Brukk. Seek Nilthar and his people in your war; humans can be your allies yet, and the *Goruc'cha* themselves seek to ally with Meyar. Be cautious.'

Karland saw one last view of the stoic Murlok and Darus, his face unreadable, before Györnàeldàr leapt into the air, her wings descending like the coming of doom upon the tribes. They headed northeast, towards Darost, and hope.

FORTY-SIX

Györnàeldàr's wings beat tirelessly. For her passenger's safety she could fly neither too fast nor too high. Karland could not decide whether this was his worst nightmare or the best experience of his life – he was utterly terrified that the ropes would break, sending him tumbling to his death, but his interest in what he could see kept him from total panic.

His hands were numb and white from the grip he held on the rope, unable to feel the rough twists any more, but eventually as his heart rate slowed he found he could let go and flexed them painfully. His forearms were sore and stiff, but this was made up for by the fact that they flew at around two thousand feet and the realms were spread out around them in startling clarity. To their left, the forbidding Arkons loomed, Drakeholm Soaring peaking far above them. To their right, the lower but longer chain of the Iril Eneth roughly parallelled their flight. From this altitude, they could see the great forest of the Léohtsholt stretching along the other side of them in gaps through the higher peaks. Far greater than even the Northing Woods, it ran for hundreds of miles.

The plains were green below them, with the great western road curving alongside and steadily left out in front. Dark shadows moved across them and with a start Karland realised that they were cast by clouds before the sun.

His ears sang form the constant battering roar of the wind, and his skin numbed. He had to slit his eyes against the dry air. It was not as cold as he had expected – in fact, he was nearly sweating. The dragon exuded a dry heat that negated most of the chill of the altitude. Her huge red dorsal scales were smooth beneath him, and he had to keep blinking against drying eyes.

They were covering more than one hundred miles in one hour according to Györnàeldàr. He thought it must be faster than any humans had moved before, though she had mentioned that she could move much faster. In front he could see a small distant dark patch on the horizon, the edge of the Northing Woods bordered by a thin glistening snake off to the side; the river Nass, flowing from the Arkons before it split and flowed east as the Run, and finally the Eaofer as it reached Darost. Seeing it from this height, he could appreciate for how many miles it ran.

'This is incredible!' Xhera shouted back to him, grinning. 'It's so beautiful!'

Karland nodded carefully. He agreed, but the height was not helping him. It was fine when he was concentrating on other things, but looking down was always a mistake. Seeing the tiny speeding dot that was the great dragon's shadow brought home just how far he could fall. Xhera seemed to be having no such issues.

It had taken almost three hours to fly from Drakeholm Soaring to the Pit of Kharkis. This journey was over twice as long, and Karland felt his legs getting stiffer as the time went by. Eventually they passed over the borders of Eordeland. Below, the road to Irilview held a few travellers. There would be far more to the north, on the GreatWay moving to and from Darost. Patrols moved along the border of the realm, alert for intruders. It looked as if Eordeland knew war was coming. Darost gleamed as a dot in the distance, and off to the right, close to the tail end of the Iril Eneth, a smaller pinprick came from Irilview, the third largest city in the realm.

Eordeland was a beautiful place and it made the threat of the demon all the more grave. Unlike the deserts of Banistari and the vast plains of the Reldenhort and Sergoth, the fertile land was littered with farmstead and small towns and villages; the destruction would be horrific if the demon came this way. Karland prayed with all his might that it would not.

He wondered what the people below thought, looking up. Perhaps they mistook them for a very large bird, but the shape would be wrong – some of them must be panicking. There was certainly a lot of activity in many of the guard posts that they swept over when he looked back.

Finally, after nearly five hours of flight, the dragon banked around the great city of Darost. The Sanctum was clearly seen at this height as a perfect circle, symmetrically festooned with spires. Györnàeldàr's head came around to look at them, eyes partially lidded.

'Where should we land, Rast Tal'Orien?' her voice rumbled through the streaming wind.

'You see that huge circular building? Land us between the building and the front gate, if there is room,' he called back.

The dragon eyed the landing zone critically. Below her, guards scurried like ants, frantic at the sight of her predatory form circling their seat of power. 'There is room, just,' she said. 'I shall have to pull in my tail.' She sounded like it was a great favour.

Györnàeldàr banked sharply, and Karland's heart hammered into his throat so fast he thought he would vomit. Instead he astounded himself by laughing, adrenaline coursing through him. Spilling the air from her wings, Györnàeldàr sliced down, and then reared back, beating her wings to land gently. She tried hard not to jam her talons through the cobbles, but there was a crash as her tail demolished a high hedge lining one side of the road.

'My apologies,' she said in the sudden calm, her voice rumbling loudly.

With the blessed ending of the constant roar of wind, the silence was almost loud to them. It was not total, however. Cries of fear and shouts reverberated from all around them. Rast looked around at gates thick with curious onlookers and guards. Behind them, Welcomer and City Guards poured out of the Sanctum, ready to defend it.

'Come on,' said Rast. Karland hurriedly slipped between the ropes. They had to avert a potential disaster; Györnàeldàr was unlikely to appreciate being attacked.

He was glad to be down, although he was terribly stiff. The dragon's back was a worse height for some reason than two thousand feet in the air. He had never been so pleased to be on solid ground again before.

Rast leapt down, waving his arms at the guards approaching from the Sanctum and calling to them in his deep voice.

'Do not attack! She means no harm! Do not attack!'

The guards spotted him, and stopped in surprise. They approached cautiously, wary of the titan, which had made no move to attack them.

One called out, 'Who are you?'

'Rast Tal'Orien,' Rast shouted, causing a mutter among the men. 'I was here some two months ago with Councilman Aldwyn Varelin. I must speak with Captain Dorn Gardenson.'

'Wait,' called the guard. 'We will send for him. Do not move.'

'Well,' muttered Rast, 'You heard the man. We had best not move.'

This produced a huge snort from Györnàeldàr.

'Or *what?*' she said snidely, although she did not shift other than to curl her long tail around her and crouch. The movement caused a stir of panic among the men surrounding her. More and more people were crowding outside the gate. Ready to flee at the first sign of flame, they stared, whispering. Györnàeldàr's pointed ears twitched in irritation, but she otherwise ignored them.

Rast moved a little way from her and waited. He motioned Karland and Xhera to stay near the dragon. Through familiarity they all felt the dragonfear less, but many of the guards were pale and shaking, especially when the search-lamp gaze fell on them.

A commotion caught his attention. He saw the familiar sight of Captain Dorn approaching hurriedly, his usual twin swords replaced by a single drawn sword and a large steel shield, as if he would slay the attacker himself. He held up a hand.

'Captain Gardenson! Over here!'

Dorn, already looking shocked at the presence of a creature straight from the oldest myths, blinked in astonishment. 'Rast Tal'Orien! Do you bring this creature here? What is going on?' He looked nervous. Iron control kept him from showing fear, but his hand was tight upon his hilt.

'It is a long story, Captain, but we have little time. The dragon is a friend, this I swear. She does not wish a fight. We are here with the direst of news.'

'One would consider a dragon dire enough! What passes?'

'Something that concerns not only the Council, but the city, perhaps the whole land. A dark power has awoken in the Iril Eneth southwest of here. It is hungry and moves to consume anything that it encounters. We seek knowledge of it... and bring warning to flee if it approaches.'

Dorn stared. 'You want me to evacuate a whole city because of a possible attack from one creature?'

Györnàeldàr's head rose on her long neck, staring down on the Captain. He took an involuntary step back.

'Foolish mortal. It is terrible! Do not wait for it to reach you. It will be too late. If it comes, you must flee!'

Dorn shook his head. 'I wish it were that easy, dragon. But I must speak with the Council before a decision is made, and give evidence. I cannot evacuate more than half a million people on a supposition. Even then... it is an impossible task.'

She dipped her head to stare at him, and several guards quailed. Many tightened their grips on their weapons, and made them ready. Her eyes narrowed.

'Rast Tal'Orien! Caution these fools to stay back. I will not countenance an attack when I come in peace. I have already given much to warn you mortals.'

'You had best do as she requests, Captain Dorn,' said Rast mildly. 'She is not given to light words.'

'Fall back!' shouted Dorn. 'Do *not* engage the dragon! Pass the word!'

Even as he spoke, one man's courage snapped, and he yelled and hurled his weapon. At the sound, her head came around on her neck, bird-quick. The spear hurtled into her face, and struck point-first before rebounding. She hissed in anger, and stared at the man who had thrown it. Before anyone could react, she had sent a focused burst of flame into him. The man shrieked in agony and collapsed backwards in charred ruin, his sword softened and slumped, clothes and mail blasted from his blackened body. The guards around him shrank back in terror, some fleeing, and those further back readied themselves as the crowd at the gate fled screaming.

'*STOP!*' shouted Dorn. '*The next man to attack will answer to me!*'

There was a pregnant pause underlined by a subsonic rumble of anger. The guards backed away, their faces unsure. Terrified and outraged they looked at the roasted corpse of their comrade, crackling and almost unrecognisable. Rast smelt cooked flesh.

'Another insult, and I leave you to your fate,' Györnàeldàr snapped, flame puffing in bursts between her words. 'I came in peace. Is this how mortals rate their honour?' She was clearly furious, and Rast dreaded her next actions if provoked.

Dorn's face was white, with anger or fear Rast could not tell. 'I will kill the next man to attack without my command myself, dragon. You have my apology.' He deliberately did not look at the dead man.

'We have no time for this,' said Rast. 'Karland and Xhera came with me at great cost to warn you. We have lost many comrades, including Aldwyn Varelin, but we have succeeded in the Council's charge to us. They laid a twofold quest on Aldwyn, and one part at least we have completed. We have sorely missed his wisdom – now we sorely miss his esteem. We must try to convince the Council in his place. If we come within to see the Council, will we see them immediately? And will our friend Györnàeldàr be unprovoked?'

Dorn shook his head. 'This is ill. Councillor Varelin was… a good man.' He sighed. 'I will take you to them now. And you have my word she will be unprovoked.'

Another man ran up, wearing the garb of a Welcomer Captain. Rast realised that this must be Robertus's replacement.

'Captain Jekob,' Dorn greeted him. He murmured into his ear, and then for the first time looked bleakly at the body of the man who had disobeyed him and nearly started a massacre. 'Cordon off the area around the dragon. And somebody clean that up.'

ᙉ   ᙏ

The next few hours were a blur of activity for Karland. He stood again before the Council, hastily assembled in the Bulge. Any hope on their faces faded as Rast recounted the outline of their journey. They knew of the attack on The Croft, but the news of a fifty thousand strong orc army loose on the plains was met with stunned silence, the thought of Meyar bolstered by such numbers alarming. Karland wondered if they had escaped Yosgaloth; if not, that would be one problem solved.

They were saddened to hear of Aldwyn's death. Karland thought he would always feel a deep twinge of sadness when he thought of it, and Brandwyn Tarqas especially took the news hard on the heels of the losses of his other close friend and his nephew. The report on the attitudes of the dwarves dismayed them far more than that of the orks – they relied heavily on arms and trade from Deep Delving. Descriptions of the Hall of Wyrms amazed them – only a few of them even knew the name – but there was a disappointed silence as he finished.

'No weapon, then,' said Augusta Andragostin in dismay.

'No,' said Rast.

'This portal of yours seems nothing but a doorway to illusion and false hope,' Councillor Eremus said sourly. Karland's ire leapt again; he really did not like the woman.

'Each of us was clearly meant to learn something,' said Rast imperturbably. 'We were told the Portal holds power in the form of knowledge. But there is more; we found that everything that has been happening does indeed have one source. Remember, Karland's vision and Györnàeldàr's words speak of four great demons of darkness: Darklings.' Several councillors looked uneasy at the name, but most glanced at each other. Karland glared at them. They would never understand what he had seen, and he seethed with the futility of trying to explain it to them.

'We faced one in the Hall and it was overwhelming in its power. If the visions were true they came to this world to destroy it, but they are unable to truly affect the world except through mortals. This is why unrest has sprung up in so many realms at once.'

'Really? Demons?' said Daffydd Gusta acidly. 'We wanted facts, not child's tales.' Eremus nodded in agreement. Rast held up his hand, forestalling an angry retort from Karland.

'You asked us to find what proof we could. We have done so – at awful cost!

Do not then doubt what we tell you. And do not discount the dragon, or the reason for our haste: the power of one of these demons has been used to unbind a different kind of demon, one which could destroy everything that lives. It is free, now, and we are here to warn you. Everything we have done, that is happening now, means nothing if this threat consumes us. We have seen it with our own eyes, and it is terrible!'

There was a silence. They had hoped for a weapon of great power. Several councillors looked alarmed at the thought of yet another problem, and others looked frightened.

'We have had no reports of demons,' Jamus Holmson said doubtfully.

Ulric looked at him in exasperation. 'Are you an idiot, Jamus? They flew here on a damned *dragon*. I hardly think word of mouth will be quicker. The Darklings are mentioned in some ancient texts, and this Yosgaloth may be too. We made the mistake of scepticism before, and it cost us dearly.'

'That is another thing,' said Councillor Regus, frowning. 'This dragon. What are we to do with her? Yes, yes, fine, we admit that she is not an... unthinking beast. But we cannot sustain her appetite for long, and already we have had riots at her presence. People are terrified. What if someone else works up the courage to attack her, and she decimates the city in retaliation? I think we should remove her, persuade her to leave. The city is in danger while she remains.'

Karland shook his head in angry disbelief. Tired, hurt, and feeling the loss of his mentor and friend, he had lost his nervousness with the men and women that ruled his land yet understood so little. A greater world had opened for him; as The Croft had changed, so now had Eordeland itself, and he could not hold his tongue. None of these people were the powerful beings he had thought. Now he saw only petty arguing.

'The city is in the least danger while she remains. You are *all* missing the point,' he snapped. Xhera gave him a dismayed look which he ignored. '*None* of this matters right now–'

'I beg to differ,' snapped Eremus. 'What right have *you* to instruct us?'

Karland flushed. '*Right? You* sent *us* on a quest, and we completed it – *and* warn you of a demon freed that could destroy this city! *This* is our thanks?'

The Councillor's eyes bulged in affront. 'How *dare* you! Guards, remove thi–'

'Give it over, Eremus' said Ulric wearily, waving the guards back. 'He's right. Your manners are inexcusable. Didn't we have this argument with Councillor Varelin last time *he* tried to warn us? The boy has every right to speak, although he could *also* use a little diplomacy.' He glanced at Karland from below bushy brows, and Karland's face heated again. 'So, this mighty demon, this Yosgaloth.

How do we know that it comes here?'

'We do not,' Rast said bluntly. 'But it can only break free of the Pit of Kharkis in one direction: through the Iril Pass. That puts it on the plains, and it is most likely to go either west, or northeast, following the mountains – where the greatest numbers of prey are. Darost has the largest population in half the continent. This demon is *terrible*. Even Györnàeldàr fears it. She bore us here to warn you - the first of dragon kind to ever do so. Other dragons, many of them, are trying to warn other mortal cities. This danger is so great they will risk receiving attack and hatred to deliver the message even to mortals. The demon threatens us *all*. You must prepare for the events that may come.'

'We cannot sanction the evacuation of five hundred thousand and more people on a supposition!' snapped Councillor Regus. 'There would be chaos. This realm relies on Darost. The impact on the economy, on the military – while at war with Meyar! – and on the entire region would be unthinkable.'

'*If* this demon even exists,' sniffed Eremus.

Mira Lyss shook her head. 'We didn't believe in dragons before, and there is one almost tall enough to see into the windows up here lying outside,' she said. She looked around, considering. 'Advisor Interjectory: I think it is time this Council kept an open mind to heretofore unlikely matters, given the bearers of the news.' Karland felt like crowing; at least *some* of the Council were listening.

'We should involve Györnàeldàr in these discussions,' said Rast. Karland nodded to himself; she was wiser than anyone else in here, that was certain.

'Bring a dragon in to a Council meeting?' protested Councillor Jamus. Mira Lyss said nothing, and Ulric looked thoughtful.

Nessa Contemus was looking at the big man with a small smile on her face, however. Her voice cut through the others, clear and strong.

'How do you propose to do this? Do we hold our meetings in the fields outside Darost?' A few chuckles came, her dry sense of humour and cool tones calming the excitement, and the talk died down.

'What about the chamber at the base of the tower?' said Karland. 'Her head *might* fit through the tower doors, and even if not, her hearing is incredible.' He looked at their expressions. 'Aldwyn called her the most learned being he has ever met. In his notes he lists her as over a *quarter of a million* years old. He said dragons know more lore than any other race.' A snort erupted from Eremus which he ignored. 'You would be fools *not* to listen to her.'

Marcus Andragostin leaned forward. 'What you say may be true, but first the Council must discuss this. It is a lot to swallow. Perhaps we have something in the Combic Libraries that will provide lore on this demon, this Eater of Life.

There may be ways to protect against it. If it exists and has been fought in the past, it may be in the scripts… somewhere.' The others nodded. 'The problem for this evening is: what are we to do with the dragon?'

'She can rest where she is. Only bring us tents, and we will sleep alongside her,' said Rast.

'You would not prefer rooms?' queried Councillor Brókova.

Rast shook his head. 'It will relieve… tension, if we stay with her. Tension on both sides.' That suited Karland; he remembered what had happened last time they had stayed in a room here.

Mira Lyss nodded. 'So. Captain Dorn, Captain Jekob: let it be done. We will meet again tomorrow morning and decide our path.'

∞

They ate quickly, accompanied by Jekob and Dorn. The new Welcomer Captain was young and somber-faced, having taken on a role he did not want from someone he had admired. Little was said; afterwards they returned to their huge friend to tell her the afternoon's work.

'They do not heed you?' asked Györnàeldàr in disbelief. Karland knew how she felt.

Rast shrugged. 'They are cautious. It is the way of Councils to discuss that which will affect the greater number. I pray they end their discussions in time.'

She snorted hotly, watching Welcomers put up three spacious tents for them. They were at least being accorded decent quarters.

Guards had watched in disbelief as Györnàeldàr, given a freshly killed cow at the Council's orders, had rumbled in satisfaction and taken it in one mouthful. She didn't even need to chew. She was polite to the men, giving thanks, but remained distant. Draconic memories were long, and she would not soon forget that she had been attacked after coming in peace with human companions.

As it grew dark, Councillor Tarqas appeared with Councillor Ulric. He held up his hand to the great creature in greeting, reminding Karland a little of Aldwyn, and politely requested permission to approach before sitting with them.

'Things changed rapidly after you left,' said Tarqas. 'We found a large community of Meyar-dissidents, either sympathisers gained through lies or active insurgents working in cells. Darost has seen bloody work these last few months. They are now either in prison or dead, but we are by no means certain that we found them all.' He sighed. 'The Meyari strike force was driven out of Eordeland in tatters. We found atrocities in their wake. Many smaller towns and farmsteads in the heart of east Norland have been utterly destroyed. Bands of orcs, some hundreds strong, have been travelling west from the World's Crest Mountains. The Meyari were protecting orcs! Thanks to you, we know the reason. We have tracked thousands and destroyed them. Our full military reserve patrols Eordeland now.'

Karland's mind flew back to the battle with his town. Many had not been so lucky. He wondered for the first time in a while how his oldest friend was, and hoped that Seom was not one of the dead.

Ulric took up the thread, his face disgusted. 'Politikus Beren vanished, too. Somehow he escaped the lockdown of the city. We are formally at war with Meyar now. It is a sore blow that we have no real answers, although we can prepare better now for what comes.'

Tarqas nodded. 'We have not replaced Draef Novas. Every one of the Universalia Communia that would be capable enough is either dead, or not in the city. Aldwyn would have been the logical choice, but...' he shrugged, smiling sadly. 'I doubt he would have accepted it anyway.' Xhera's sorrowful face caught Karland's eye, and he looked away. He knew Aldwyn would not.

'None of this is the priority,' said Rast bluntly. 'We do not have time for the Council to decide the fate of Eordeland in committee. You must make preparations to flee should the demon come this way. All else can wait.'

'I believe you,' said Tarqas. 'As do others, but we cannot make a hasty decision. Evacuating everyone in this city will cost money, time, and lives. People will invariably panic.'

He was silent for a few minutes, and then spoke again, quietly.

'How did Aldwyn die?'

'Meyari assassins ambushed us and he was struck down by an arrow. The end was quick. They were well trained. I think they were connected to the men that struck here... and they were all Teromens. The Church of Terome is the true power in Meyar now – it must have been planning this a long time. They also knew of his connection to the Darostim, and our goal. So you see, I do not discount the value of the visions. They tell us things that may somehow aid us, and should be heeded if our enemy tried to gain it so desperately. It may be that this is what was meant by 'great power'. Aldwyn used to say knowledge was the greatest power there was.'

'Meyar and Terome have a lot to answer for,' grunted Ulric. 'And now the news of these orcs allied with them, gah! Orcs! It leaves a sour taste in my mouth. We must send emissaries to Eyotsburg pledging them aid – if Meyar takes that island, they can strike south *and* east. Perhaps even Novin and Ignat will ally over this threat.'

'Poor Aldwyn,' said Brandwyn wretchedly. 'He was so frightened of death. I will never stop feeling that I sent him to it, I think.'

Rast shook his head. 'Councillor Tarqas, he had no choice but to go. He was our best hope of unravelling the events we are caught up in. He was scared, but his fear for the world outweighed it. He was a good man… a good friend. To all of us.'

They sat in silence until they were surprised by a rumble from the dragon.

'Aldwyn Varelin was a rare human,' she said. 'He was learned, and he even spoke my tongue. I have never met his like before. I, too, am sorry that he is no more.'

Tarqas smiled faintly. 'Trust Aldwyn to impress a dragon,' he said. 'Whatever others may say, *Nāginī*, know that you are welcome here, and more. You are invited to Council tomorrow. We must know more of this demon.' He quirked his lips. 'I must admit, I am looking forward to seeing some of them cowering in fear.'

'Tomorrow, they will listen,' she promised. 'And I will fly to scout where Yosgaloth roams. With luck, it will not come this way before my people can drive it back to the Pit.'

From your lips to the ears of the gods, thought Karland fervently.

ରଷ୍ଟ   ଷୋ

The next day brought a sight Karland had never dreamed of. Györnàeldàr circled the Dodecagon, settling lightly one garden from the tower doors. There was little room for her; her tail circled the tower under one bridge, and her body filled the garden. Her neck snaked under the next bridge, and she turned her head to look into the Tower Hall, although she declined to try to fit it through the doors for fear of damaging them.

He could see several of the Council were white faced with anxiety – one fiery breath from the dragon would wipe out the leaders of Eordeland in seconds, and they were all trapped in the room. Tarqas was smirking at Eremus, who was being unusually polite and cooperative. Many of them looked astonished at her formal reply to their greeting.

Mira Lyss rose. '*Nāginī*. We ask your help and advice on dealing with this threat Rast tells us of. We are scouring the archives for any mention of this demon. Perhaps there is some knowledge on how we could defeat it-'

Györnàeldàr interrupted. 'Mortals, you are wasting time. Yosgaloth was defeated many scores of thousands of your years ago only by the combined powers of my people, entire armies of mortals, and the *Próarkhe* – the Great Dragons, those you term lesser gods. Even then it could only be locked away. The creature is not entirely of this world.'

'So what can we do?'

'Flee. There is no other choice.' At the mutterings this produced, Györnàeldàr spoke sharply, her voice overriding all others. 'This is not something to be discussed! I, too, must flee. There is no denying the Bane of the Old World. Until my people have gathered to drive it back, there is only one defence. I am old and powerful, but Yosgaloth has destroyed my kin before and is far older. No single creature can face its hunger and live.'

'Then we must prepare,' sighed Mira Lyss, 'and hope that it does not turn this way.'

'Your hope is in vain, mortal. I flew up this morning, and saw the demon from afar. It has turned east. Whether it senses your cities or it is just following the mountains, chance has forsaken you. The demon does not sleep, does not pause. You do not have long. It would have been better had you listened yesterday.' Her words were greeted with silence.

The demon had followed the mountains east. Karland's stomach dropped. He had hoped, prayed that it would turn somewhere else. Maybe it really could sense so many sentient beings together. Karland knew most of the Council had not seriously believed in the demon, or that it would come this way.

Whyll Regus spoke up. 'Has anyone else verified that the demon comes to Darost?'

'Do you doubt my word?' asked Györnàeldàr in astonishment. Mira Lyss held up her hand as Councillor Regus shrank back. Karland didn't blame him, in the blaze of the dragon's glare.

'We are a Council over hundreds of thousands of people in one place, *Nāgìnī*. We believe you, but forgive us for a desire to make sure. We will begin making preparations this morning, and send word to the other cities. Is there any way this thing may pass us by?'

'It is possible. Yosgaloth will sense the elves beyond the mountains, as it will sense me. The older and more powerful the life – and the soul – the greater the need for it to consume. But a great number of humans hoarding lore will prove a temptation whether I stay or go.'

'*Irilview*,' swore Ulric softly. 'If this thing follows the line of the Iril Eneth, it will come upon Irilview unprepared. It is one of the largest cities in the realm. Captain Gardenson!'

Captain Dorn stepped forward. 'Councillor?'

'Send your swiftest riders now. Immediately. All towns and cities in its path must be cleared. Captain Jekob, prepare the people of Darost for evacuation. Women and children are a priority.' Both Captains nodded and ran for the doors. He looked around the rest of the Council. 'Let us pray that Darost is far enough from its path to be spared... and let us pray that we are in time.'

Mira Lyss nodded. '*Nāginī*, Rast also tells us of four great demons, unlike the one approaching. He says that they may be the cause of the unrest in the lands, and that they may eventually present an even greater threat than this Yosgaloth.'

The dragon laughed, her rumble hissing dryly through the chamber. 'He speaks truth. Yosgaloth will consume us all if it can, but on the defeat of the Darklings rests the very fate of reality. The cosmos itself may give way to chaos in time if balance is not restored.' She snorted, a phantom of flame popping briefly, making several councillors jump. It had been close enough to feel heat.

'Listen well, O mortals. The other dragons have warned mortal peoples of the danger and then gone on to find our brethren. I alone have stayed. I alone bore mortals on my back, something never before done.' She cast her gaze around the chamber, and all the Councillors showed the impact of her burning eyes and the weight of the dragonfear. Eremus cowered, moaning.

Györnàeldàr continued. 'That is because, for you, there is more than the threat of Yosgaloth. You are the pinnacle of learning among the shorter-lived mortals. You proliferate and gather lore with such speed that you will one day hold more than any other race; you are strange creatures, you humans. Among all the realms, you are the most able, the most widely learned, the most *likely* to act, yet at the same time the most uncaring, wilfully ignorant, and selfish. But that is not the reason I came here. None of you realise the power and import of the visions imparted by the Portal, but I do.

'I tell you now, you sought a weapon, *and it was given*. *Knowledge* is the greatest power you can possess. What it is, and how you use it, is not for me to say. Because of this, it is vital that this mortal city of Darost *over all others* stands. It is now the only mortal city that knows the truth of the chaos and has the knowledge, the *key*, to preventing the destruction of all creation. That is why you must not fall to the hunger of the demon. You are all that is left between the seething darkness, and the burning light. *Heed my words.*'

It was everything Aldwyn had hinted at and more. The dragon's words held a disturbing ring of truth. Karland watched her with troubled thoughts as, with one last glare around the room, she left with serpentine grace. The sudden removal of forty tons of dragon left sunlight streaming in through the wide double doors. Over the sound of her flapping wings, the Council sat silent. After endless minutes of sober reflection, Mira Lyss rose. She left without a word, and everyone else followed.

Outside the doors the Sanctum gave way to a flurry of frenzied activity that spread outwards into the city. The faintest of noises began to be heard in the distance and Karland knew that Yosgaloth drew nearer.

ଔ   ଓ

The next morning Xhera was caught up in thought. They had come such a long way, and her experiences had sobered her. She was frightened, but through this a solid core of determination lay to continue what Aldwyn had started, as she had promised. Karland was smart and capable, but he lacked direction. She thought maybe between them they could help unravel the mysteries they had uncovered.

Her thoughts were interrupted by his voice.

'Xhera. We are to go to the West Gate with Rast. The dragon is returning from scouting, and I think the news is bad.' His young face was much grimmer than usual, missing the boyish cheerfulness she loved. Her heart fluttered with fear.

On their arrival she learned of the night's tragedy. The Council gathered with Captain Dorn at the west gate to await Györnàeldàr. Word had come from one of the riders sent to warn the nearest city, and it had caught all of them unawares. She listened with mounting dread.

Yosgaloth had moved faster than even the dragon had thought possible. It had come across Irilview in the night and torn down the walls, levelling the city and consuming every soul left within. Only a handful had escaped, and an entire garrison was destroyed. The horror writhed amongst the ruins of one of the fairest cities in Eordeland, seeking out the last trapped people. Distant shrieks could be heard clearly now and the city was in a panic, rumours spreading and people demanding answers. Mira Lyss spoke to the crowd, her voice trembling.

'Our scouts say Irilview has been destroyed. There were forty seven thousand souls in that city and a bare fraction of them escaped this horror. The rest... the rest were consumed.' She swallowed. 'The accounts from the survivors are horrific. Thousands of screaming people, swallowed, dissolved, sucked dry in an instant.'

Whyll Regus moaned. 'This is the end of things. The nameless being has arisen at the end of days to consume the world, just like the prophecies of the Harridin.' He referred to the ancient race that had one lived across the entire western coast of the continent.

Ulric snorted. '*Now* you believe? Pull yourself together, man. Captain Jekob: evacuation is the highest priority. Hurry.' Jekob nodded and left swiftly. Ulric sighed heavily, his big chest falling. 'Once again, I fear we have not listened in time.'

Xhera caught Tarqas's humourless smile.

The shrieks seemed to be growing in intensity. They all kept watch upward to the clear sky, but could not see the dragon. It was an hour before she reappeared, landing in the space cleared for her and addressing the Council.

'I bear grim tidings, humans. The Bane has utterly devoured your southern city. With each soul consumed it grows in strength. I hoped it would set out east to pass around the Iril Eneth, but it has sensed the life within this city. The demon comes north.'

FORTY-SEVEN

D orn's face was grey and slack. 'The Demon has turned towards the city?' he gasped. No one else spoke, but Ulric grunted as if struck.

Györnàeldàr hissed sibilantly. 'Yes.' She swung her head back to Rast, Karland, and Xhera. 'I am sorry, mortals. This will be your end. Yosgaloth will destroy every living being within this city. Your knowledge and lives will be no more – and mayhap this world, in time.' Her tone held genuine regret.

Dorn snapped out of his paralysis and started barking orders to the squads around them to accelerate the evacuation of everyone they could from the rear of the city, starting with the women and children. Karland hoped they could escape in time; he could not believe the number of people reported dead. He couldn't imagine so many in the world. The captain's face showed that there was little hope many would escape, or that there would be any order to the fleeing hordes. There was no time to safely move more than half a million people from Darost, for all the evacuation had begun last night. Against their protests, Dorn nodded for guards to remove the Council. Several squads ignored their protests and bodily hauled them into the city.

'If Darost falls, the knowledge we worked so hard to gain will be lost, and the world plunges into chaos,' said Rast grimly to his huge companion. 'Even if you carry word, or one of us, still we do not have the answers we need.' Karland looked at Xhera's face, pretty for all its paleness. After all they had been through, he could not believe that this was it.

An unreadable look appeared on Györnàeldàr's long face.

'Some might say that chaos is already unleashed, Rast Tal'Orien. But you are correct. The world stands in jeopardy and none will survive here. If the Darklings succeed at the biddings of their masters, the fabric of space and time itself may unravel and the universe will be torn into Outer Chaos.'

A twin shriek rent the air, growing closer. Yosgaloth would not take long to reach the city now. Screams and cries from within the city were constant and the faces of the guards were ashen around them all. Karland felt their doom approaching. Györnàeldàr appeared to reach a decision.

'I am sorry, Rast Tal'Orien, Karland, Xhera,' she said. 'Whatever comes to pass, I name you dragonfriends... *my* friends.' The tone of her voice sent a chill down his spine. 'Time cannot be stilled in its flow, even for me. It grows too short. I bid you farewell... and may *Arkhe* be with you in your quest.'

Karland could not believe it. *She's going to fly away,* he thought. He didn't blame her – why should she perish with them when of all of them she could escape?

Rearing up, she flapped her massive wings, unmindful of the humans who dived for cover in fear or were knocked sprawling. One guard screamed as he toppled in fright off the wall, landing hard on the cobbled ground fifty feet below. They could not tell if he was dead or wounded; he lay unmoving. Many of the surrounding humans recoiled in fear and readied their weapons, shouting. Captain Dorn gripped his sword tightly and stepped back, cautious.

Ignoring them, Györnàeldàr stared over the wall, one foot braced on the top fifty feet above the ground. Looking down, she called one final time to those who had journeyed with her, her gaze burning into them one by one.

'Pray my people come quickly enough, lest all is lost!' Turning her head to stare back out, she shouted in defiance in her own tongue. Karland watched in awe as, proud and beautiful, she tensed, crouching on her huge hind legs and springing forward and upward so powerfully that she cleared the thick wall entirely - all but her tail, which slammed into the stonework, smashing a deep gouge and sending rubble falling onto the humans below. He dodged backwards from the debris, his eyes still on the dragon.

As she leaped, some men shouted in anger and fright, believing her fleeing to leave them to their fates. Others cursed, some in their deep distrust even thinking she would attack. Disparate arrows bounced off her, even a few spears. Repelled by her armoured hide, they fell to dangerously shower those below.

Györnàeldàr ignored them all. Bringing her vast wings down as she began to drop, she lifted her giant frame higher, flattening the humans beneath with the blast. Another man fell shrieking from the wall, catching himself desperately to be helped back by a companion. Györnàeldàr shot out over the wall and the outlying buildings below towards the oncoming demon, straight as an arrow.

'Come on!' yelled Dorn, sprinting for the nearby stairs leading up the wall, Karland and the others at his heels. At the top, they staggered to the crenellations, the children's chests heaving with the strain. White-faced, Karland looked up at Rast, whose face was furrowed with grief.

'She is going to die, isn't she?' he said, quietly.

'Yes,' said Rast softly, his voice woven through with anger and sorrow.

တ   ဘ

In seconds Györnàeldàr reached the halfway point between the giant demon and the city. Dropping, she landed so hard her feet and claws sank deep into the ground. Dust and dirt erupted around her from the landing and Karland could see her tail lashing angrily. With no humans around her to mind, it thrashed side to side, sinuous and powerful.

She glinted an iridescent red in the bright sunlight. Dropping her head, she froze; her flanks heaved as she breathed deeply, over and over again as if preparing for huge exertion. Ignoring the vast demon before her, she sucked an enormous lungful of air, her sides expanding as if she would burst. Abruptly Györnàeldàr threw her head back between her wings to point up above the horizon.

With evident effort, a shuddering, trumpeting cry forth burst forth, a ripple of dust marking its travel, expanding outward from her quicker than the eye could follow.

Cutting through the shrieking of Yosgaloth and all other sounds, seeming to pierce the mind without going via the ears, it was the loudest sound Karland had ever heard. A low throbbing ululation with high oscillating tones, a pure clarion call, it lanced into the heavens. It could be felt in the earth and in the air, deafening the whole city. Guards on the walls clapped hands to their ears at the pressure, some with burst eardrums.

Yet it must have been far louder in the direction she faced, away towards Yosgaloth and the Arkon Mountains. It rang in the air and the ground for a full thirty seconds, and reverberated even after she ceased: a call to fight, a cry for aid, a sound of defiance, the acceptance of death. A call for vengeance, and sorrow... a farewell.

On the walls, the sound wrenched tears from Xhera and Karland as they held their ears. He knew it was a call to aid from her kin who were not there, and a goodbye. Rast was clenching his big fists furiously in impotence as yet another companion sacrificed themselves.

The demon hesitated for a second, clearly puzzled by the unfamiliar noise, and flinching from the volume, but it was not affected as the humans were. Hunger drove it onwards.

It slithered forward, one of its mouths opening in another mind-tearing shriek. Györnàeldàr panted, the effort seeming to have drained her somewhat. Shaking her head, breathing deeply, she lashed her tail once more.

Crouching and spreading her huge wings to curve forward and intimidate, she roared in challenge, her burning gaze lancing in utter abhorrence at the monstrous form that undulated towards her. Her pupils were wide and round in fear. Against its hunger, its unparalleled need to consume, she matched all the hatred her powerful form could generate.

She roared again in dragon-tongue.

'Come, Eater of Life! Bane of the World! You shall not prevail!'

Yosgaloth did not answer in words. It shrieked its twin shriek, each head screaming discordantly and independently of the other. The vast underside rippled as it snaked with great speed over the land, crushing trees, fences, dwellings. The tails lashed, the vast network of pink tendrils latching into the ground. The heads bobbed and writhed, ignoring all else now but the large form before it. So full of life and power, it was an irresistible target for the demon.

෬ ෩

Györnàeldàr did not wait for the lethal stare to strike her. She sprang straight up, and accelerated frantically sideways as a bar of light stabbed out, curving around the demon at astonishing speed. Yosgaloth stopped in its tracks and followed her with its hungry gaze. The heads were agile, following her flight, but the fat body was sluggish to turn.

She was out of reach of its horrible breath and lashing tails. Its protective lids rolled back and the eye on each head focused, unleashing more stabbing beams of sickly yellow light. Györnàeldàr rolled and evaded them both, causing the demon to scream in frustration. For a fraction of a second, the heads were split, one turning to look the other way in anticipation of her coming around the side again, and she banked abruptly and dove at the broad brownish-grey back, talons extended.

Her mouth opened and a lancing flame of incandescent fury stabbed into the spine of the giant demon, even as she slammed into it with stunning force. Dust was thrown high into the air from the thrashing tails and the collision.

Györnàeldàr caught one neck between her huge teeth just behind a head which was gaping and shrieking in pain and anger. Her foreclaws sank deep into the muscular serpentine form beneath her, and she wrenched her powerful neck, trying to tear one head from the demon. Her rear talons were ripping deep furrows into the lower necks and back of the horror, and she was desperately trying to whip her powerful tail to stop the other head coming to bear and stay clear of the grasping tendrils.

Both were sinuous, but Györnàeldàr was the quicker and had searing flame not even solid rock could withstand for long. Her talons were sharp, as were her formidable teeth, and she struck with more powers than just the physical, tapping into the strands of power woven through reality to augment her attacks.

Yosgaloth had no teeth, but its mouths could stretch to engulf her entire head. Its gaze would weaken and kill her, its breath would burn and dissolve her flesh. The ancient demon was three or four times larger than she was, and far heavier and stronger. With all her own terrible strength, capable of tearing apart rock and stone, Györnàeldàr was still not able to cause significant damage to Yosgaloth. A brown ichor ran thickly from the wounds she was causing, but it dried fast.

Flapping wings to gain purchase, the dragon tried desperately to finish the head she gripped, but she was out of time; the other head finally managed to push her tail aside and turn on her. The head between her teeth was blasting furiously with its eye, and shrieking in rage and pain. Wisps of vapour trailed from its mouth, making her eyes sting. She narrowed them, her blazing glance intense, and loosened her teeth enough to breathe her hottest fire on the form she had trapped.

The flames played over the rippling neck of Yosgaloth with the fury of the sun, but power that could slag stone left demon flesh only cracked and smoking. It was obvious that her breath caused the demon the most pain, but like its own power it could only be used sparingly.

The other head flashed in, and she raked a talon out across it, scoring a hit on the eye. It retreated protectively into the head, the hood coming down to cover it. Whatever it was, it did not feel like a normal eye. Damaged but not beaten, the demon shut its eye and opened its mouth instead. The six large breathing slits on the trunk at the base of the neck flared, and she realised it was about to breathe its lethal breath on her. That might not kill her outright, but it would weaken her dangerously.

She let go of the neck with one last rip, and sprang upwards, her weight pushing the demon flat. Most of the attack missed her, but she caught some of the vapour in the face and coughed frantically, spurts of flame spearing out.

Half-blinded, she yawed frantically, trying to gain height. The freed head w with a dangerous hiss toward her, dripping ichor from deep wounds in its neck. The eye swelled and the strange yellow-on-yellow pupil narrowed. A beam shot out and glanced off her shoulder, narrowly missing her wing. It left the scales where it struck blackened and warped, buckling and brittle as she moved. She screeched in pain. Her left forelimb felt numbed and strange.

Swiping at the two faces of the beast, Györnàeldàr managed to gain height and flew upward in a spiral, gaining height rapidly. Trailing black smoke and injured, she found the low cover of the clouds and entered it. Once inside she shook her head to clear her vision, and ducked it under her wing to inspect the damage. She had a long black streak that was charred and lifeless along the shoulder, trailing off under her wing. She shuddered to think what a full strike would do to a wing. It was near where the Darkling had struck her, and it ached much more deeply than the surface mark would suggest.

In addition to that, she had torn a few muscles holding on to Yosgaloth. The creature was unbelievably strong. Never before had she been outmatched in might by a creature of Kuln! She was accustomed to being amongst the most powerful of her race, the most powerful race on the planet. Her deadliest weapons were inflicting only superficial damage. Her strongest magics were deflected by the essence of the demon. The creature was so *other*.

In desperation, she formed another plan of attack. Stretching sore muscles, she soared and looped, allowing herself to feel the loving caress of the air one last time, and then turned her focus back below.

ભ   છ

Karland watched in horror as his friend was savaged by the ancient evil. Every guard stood speechless as the behemoths collided. The thuds and impacts were felt faintly through the earth even inside the city and the size and ferocity of the combatants was almost beyond comprehension. It had quickly dawned on those watching that the giant dragon was fighting to save them all.

One man began shouting encouragement, and it spread. As Györnàeldàr slammed into Yosgaloth's back, a roar went up from the watchers. All had been bewildered by the powerful call she had sent out, which had reverberated in their very bones throughout the city. Now they screamed and shouted, cursing the demon and cheering the dragon, knowing their survival hinged on hers.

Xhera watched with tears in her eyes. 'We must help her!' she implored Rast and Dorn. Rast stood immobile, obviously yearning to help his huge companion. Dorn, so nervous and distrustful moments ago, now looked as if he were losing his family.

'What can we do?' he said, gesturing.

His arm said it all. A two-hundred-and-fifty-foot dragon wrestled a thousand-foot demon with serpentine fury, digging massive furrows in the hard ground, whipping around with great speed. It was impossible to fully define: it was like watching a cat fighting a ferret fighting a bag of snakes in a dustbowl.

Rast appeared to reach a decision. Karland's attention wavered as he spoke.

'Keep Xhera safe. I want you to make for the eastern gates now. Do it. Do not quarrel.' His tone brooked no argument. He turned back to Dorn. 'You do what you must, Captain. I am going out there.'

'The gates are closed!' protested Dorn. He shook his head at Rast's madness.

Rast pointed at the abomination thrashing not a quarter of a mile away.

'You honestly think they will stop *that*?'

Dorn stared at him for a second, and then whirled, shouting orders and sprinting down the stairs full tilt. Rast looked at Karland, nodded, and ran after him. Karland ran straight to the edge again to continue watching, Xhera right beside him. Neither of them were leaving their friends.

Dorn gathered a group of about a hundred men, and shouted for the gate to be opened. The gates swung open on their own, a process Karland always found eerie for such large gates, and Dorn called out to all those around him.

'We ride out to aid our ally. That creature must be stopped! *Who is with us?*'

A fresh roar erupted from over a thousand throats. As Dorn and Rast stepped out, a trickle of soldiers that became a flood poured through the gates. As they started out towards the battle, which was not going well for Györnàeldàr, the dragon disengaged, groggy and in pain. A bar of power from an eye caught her and sent her reeling. Hurt, she pulled away and flew upwards into the clouds.

A murmur of dismay came from the men, and they came to a halt. Yosgaloth swayed under the spot where Györnàeldàr had vanished into the low clouds, hissing and weaving its heads, looking for her.

Nothing.

After a few minutes the vast bulk of Yosgaloth began to move towards the city again. It could not ignore its hunger for long, and it sensed a multitude of intelligent life before it to feast on. Karland searched desperately for the dragon. He could see the gathered men wavering, their courage failing. They were already within reach of the demon's strange eye beams, and they had seen what it did to a dragon. Men would blacken and die instantly with that force on them. Dorn shouted to them to stand firm, standing at the fore with the huge warrior.

Rast moved out from the men to meet the demon. Xhera gasped and Karland felt sick. He knew he would watch his friend die. Rast stood defiantly, drawing its attention. The demon reared up in front of him, only a few hundred yards away, its tails already slapping the ground in anticipation. One head snaked around to regard the morsel from the side in curiosity at the challenge – the first of hundreds of thousands of souls.

Nearly a quarter of Dorn's men broke and ran for the gate. The rest steadied and stood firm. Rast's bravery sobered them, and they prepared to fight an enemy they could not hope to harm – to fight, and die. There was no escape.

Karland cast his gaze upwards again, hoping, straining to see his draconic friend. At first he could see nothing, but then he blinked. A dot appeared. It burst from the clouds, and quickly resolved into a recognisable shape arrowing downwards soundlessly, wings stooped and held close in, plummeting at terminal velocity straight at the unprotected back of the demon.

Györnàeldàr.

CR SO

She sliced down like a peregrine falcon, the wind spilled from her wings. They were tucked tightly in with only the wingtips extended for manoeuvring and her neck was straight as she fixed her entire being on the demon below her. All forty tons of her plummeted at nearly two hundred and forty miles per hour, exploding from the clouds six thousand feet above the ground.

The city was a tiny anthill below her, the demon a writhing shape turning towards the humans. She saw with her dragon eyes the small line of humans who had come from the city. At the front, facing the demon, was that indecipherable human Rast Tal'Orien. Less than an ant before a man, yet he faced the Bane, and she realised at that moment that he and the humans with him came to her aid.

Her heart warmed, and she did not regret facing Yosgaloth.

These humans are worth fighting for.

Her eyes narrowed, and she stared through the screaming wind at her target expanding quickly below her. She allowed herself to revel in the feeling as she sliced through the air. It had taken her barely more than half a minute to fall this far.

Then there were only seconds left, and all else left her mind except striking Yosgaloth with her whole being. With the focus of a supreme predator, and the hatred of a sentient being for the destroyer of all life, she struck.

CR SO

A fraction of a second before the impact, Karland saw the dragon snap her wings out full and bring every talon to bear. With a crack like thunder, they caught the air, straining the membranes to splitting point. She slammed into the back of the demon like a meteor, sending a whiplash along both tails and heads. Yosgaloth was driven into the earth, a huge fountain of dust erupting from the site. Cracks shot outwards in the ground around what the thinning dust showed to be a near thousand-foot diameter crater.

Rast was hurled into the air by the shock of the collision and every guard was sent sprawling. Pieces of stone rained down from the walls of Darost, and many there fell to their deaths, unable to keep their feet. Stress cracks shot up through the stonework. Karland held on, terrified, as the ground continued to tremble. Shrieks and screams came from the shallow crater as the battle was fought with renewed fury.

CB SO

Györnàeldàr seized the advantage. Yosgaloth was stunned by the force of the blow, and appeared to be groggy as it snapped its toothless mouths wildly. Vapour leaked from the corners of the mouths, but no lancing beams of light fell from its unfocused eyes. She tore at the juncture of the necks now, seeking to harm the six flaring breathing apertures. Opening her mouth she sent a piercing line of flame into it, her throat contracting to focus it down as finely as she could. It would have vaporised granite, thousands of degrees at the tip, yet the flesh of the Bane she rode gave grudgingly to it, charring and steaming.

Yosgaloth writhed in sheer agony. Hissing, it bellowed acrid vapours around the ripping talons, and they enveloped her head. Most of it was flash-vaporised in her breath, but enough got into her eyes to disrupt her attack and half blind her. She whipped her tail around one head, pulling it back as hard as she could. It was not enough, and a second breath sizzled into her armoured side. It ate into her scales, burning.

Györnàeldàr was in trouble. The impact had stunned her nearly as much as it had Yosgaloth and she had almost blacked out when she hit. The demon's back was unbroken, although it was deeply scored and bleeding ichor, and she realised that her foe might not even have bones. Her front right limb dangled useless, snapped at the forearm. She was blinded and shaken and the digestive breath was burning her left side like acid.

Györnàeldàr did not let up tearing with all her power at the flesh of the demon, however. Never had she inflicted such damage on something! Yet it did not die. She felt weariness creep up on her; injured, she had weakened, but the demon seemed as strong as ever.

Weaving her head on her neck, she just managed to avoid the gaping mouth of one of the glaring heads snaking around her. It darted around for another try and she opened her mighty jaws. As the gaping maw opened, she unleashed everything she had in her flaming breath.

The flame engulfed the head in front of her, causing the eye to slam shut and the mouth to gape even wider. For the first time Yosgaloth wailed in pain along with the mindless shrieking of its other head. Then they were rolling and snapping at each other, and Györnàeldàr made her mistake.

She held on too long in her attempt to widen the wounds, and the entire bulk of the demon rolled over her, crushing her. She felt several ribs snap, some tearing through her armoured hide from beneath, and the breath whooshed from her huge lungs.

Her fire winked out.

Holding on blearily, she could not react fast enough. With her unmoving, the whipping tails found her and snapped around her. The tendrils latched on to her side, worming their way beneath her scales to her flesh, fastening and burrowing to feast on her. Some found her right wing, shredding the membranes like paper.

She screamed in true agony, throwing her head back and pulling away with all her might. It was not enough. With every pulse of the pink tendrils she weakened; they were far stronger than they looked, and they drained her by the moment. Every breath was like being stabbed to the heart now.

Yosgaloth's left head shrieked at her and too late she turned to snap at the other head. It grabbed her left wing in its mouth and wrenched powerfully. The wing was torn bodily from her, leaving glistening white bone amidst a fountain of blood. She screamed in denial and agony, thrashing with all her might, and managed to tear through the tendrils of one tail with her back claw, freeing her body. Bracing her tail on the ground for leverage she dimly felt it snap under the pressure.

A beam of sickly light lanced into her stomach, and this time it hit true. Her scales buckled and blackened as the blow hammered into her, charring flesh raw. Hot red blood ran from her body in sheets from the ragged rent left.

Blearily turning her gaze, her whole body raw with pain, she saw a dark throat glisten as Yosgaloth swallowed her head.

ଔ   ๛

The demon held the twitching creature firmly. It felt the spark ebbing, knew the end was near. It had been a fight such as the demon had never known, but the demon was weak after hundreds of thousands of years without feeding – and it had forgotten dragons. *Never had any one creature caused it so much pain!* They were the lords of this world, and they were not the same as the other races. Nothing else would have survived such terrible punishment, though it was nearly ended.

But Györnàeldàr was not dead yet.

ଔ   ๛

Fire exploded deep into Yosgaloth's gut as Györnàeldàr spent her last flames down the terrible throat around her. The vaporous juices were eating into her face and eyes; this close they were so concentrated even her scales were dissolving under the assault. So she closed her eyes and poured her soul into her heart's fire. If Yosgaloth was to take her flesh and soul, it would pay dearly for it.

Choking in agony, its other head shrieking like all the demons in the hells, the demon spasmed frantically. Györnàeldàr was hurled from it like a man might throw an infant. She bowled end over end towards the city, the men who had rushed out to aid her scrambling out of the way. Several were smeared to paste by her passage. She fetched up against the weakened wall of the city, causing the entire gate section to collapse on and around her.

Yosgaloth was knotting and writhing like a snake now, sending sprays of dust up the sides of the crater. The men could not even approach closely enough to attack. They would fall and be crushed by the convulsions, and could find no way to harm a creature the dragon could not.

Györnàeldàr could feel her life ebbing. She blinked, seeing a blurry figure in front of her. Through torn lips, she smiled slightly, her fangs broken and bloodied.

'Rast Tal'Orien,' she whispered roughly through a throat raw from acidic fumes.

ଔ   ๛

Rast fell back, drawing any willing men with him to ring the stricken dragon and face the Bane of the Old World. Rast surveyed her terrible wounds in a glance, his face bleak.

Györnàeldàr was barely conscious. Hardly able to see, her face was disfigured and scarred, one eye whitened, a cheekbone shattered and half the flesh gone. He knew the dragon was dying. Her wounds could not be healed and the demon would not be stopped for long.

She spoke his name.

Behind him renewed shrieks rent the air as the writhing horror erupted from the crater. Rast rolled as a beam of light scored the ground. Men dived out of the way, one being caught across the torso and falling out of sight in two pieces. The sickly pale beam shot up the wall, leaving the stone cracked and blackened as if acid had been thrown. It swung over several guards who didn't duck in time. Only one had time to scream in anguish before the area they were struck puffed into blackish vapour. The rest of the bodies fell in steaming chunks, their clothing dissolving and the metal they wore dropping warped and ringing to the stones.

The other head hissed a cloud of vapour which shot through twenty men; their screams barely began before they turned to choking gurgles, their throats dissolving into slime around the noise. Tendons unravelled from their bones and their guts fell through their flesh as they decomposed where they stood. Yosgaloth undulated forward, barely two hundred feet from the city wall, and whipped a tail around. Men dangled screaming as pink tendrils wrapped them and sucked their life from them.

They were all out of time.

Rast hoped Karland and Xhera had heeded him, and would be saved at least.

ᑒ   ᔕ

Karland knew they would never escape in time now. Already weakened by the force of the meteoric attack by the dragon, the section of wall nearby had crumbled when Györnàeldàr fell against it, carrying the stairs down with it. He and Xhera could only look on in despair.

Abruptly the sky darkened, a vast form shimmering into existence overhead. To the onlookers in the city it seemed as if the sky had been eclipsed. The whole city dimmed; suddenly in a great shadow, Yosgaloth froze, dropping men like grains of rice. It stared upwards.

At first no one knew what they were seeing. Slowly it dawned on everyone looking up that there were definable edges to the darkness, which was slightly translucent.

It appeared to be an immense dragon of sorts, but impossibly large. The wings extended over the entire city, as if an entire mountain had taken flight. Nose to tail, the dragon stretched entirely between the great gates, the western to the eastern. The form sparked memories of legends from the dawn of time, its wings seeming to curve to catch the air and slow, the sun limning its edges in a corona, seen through the impossibility as a dull orb.

Karland, astonished, recognised the shape of the great dragon from the cavern – as it appeared did Yosgaloth. The giant demon hesitated a few moments more, and then screeched defiance. It slithered backwards, heads bobbing, its hunger forgotten for the first time. The tails dug into the ground and its eyes focused. Beams stabbed upwards, but seemed to have no effect on the great form.

Karland became aware of a noise that had been slowly building for several minutes, and now it became consciously noticeable. A sound like a deep roaring wave was building, and suddenly one guard shouted, pointing. It was unlikely he heard the noise; his ears streamed blood and he shouted unnaturally loudly. Karland followed his gaze, and then revolved, looking at all points of the compass.

Dots lined the sky. As he turned, he could see more dots growing rapidly in the air from all horizons. Most were coming from the west and he counted more than a hundred, all preceded by flashes of light. With a start of insight, Karland shouted in triumph.

'*Dragons!*'

So great was their speed it was only seconds later that he could make out the form of Köranthír, the huge black leading his kin. They shot straight for Yosgaloth, descending in flights from all directions and raking it with flame and talon.

The demon reared, stabbing skywards with its powerful eyes. Scoring few hits – and those glancing – it hissed in frustration, barely heard over the furious roaring of the dragons.

One of the heads caught a jet of flame straight in the face and eye. It threw up a cloud of acid in defence. A small green dragon barrelled through it, coughing with streaming eyes, and fell hard to crash to the earth in a heap at the end of a furrow. Unsteadily, it shook its head, eyes blazing orange in anger, and hauled itself aloft again for another pass at the ancient enemy.

Flame by flame, the Bane of the Old World was driven backwards, away from the city and its stricken defender. It wove for a gap to attack, but the dragons worked together and did not let up for an instant. Finally it was pushed back into and then past the crater, confused by the overwhelming life it craved but could not reach. Charred, blackened and slashed uncounted times by the continuous assault, the demon was driven westwards at great speed, snapping at its aggressors.

Karland watched them recede, numbed. He was barely aware of the painful grip Xhera had on his right arm. Many men around him were also silent but as many were yelling in victory and release. All stood for long minutes until the battle had retreated into the distance, Yosgaloth driven back from whence it had come.

A large dark form detached from the dragons and flew back. It landed lightly next to Györnàeldàr and dipped its head in sorrow, not far from where he watched. Köranthír rumbled deeply, and the grief evident in his tone carried to all gathered on and around the walls. The shouting and dancing diminished, until everyone within view stood gravely, watching. Xhera was sobbing openly, and Karland couldn't see past his own streaming tears. With the danger averted, it was clear what awful damage Yosgaloth had wreaked on Györnàeldàr.

☙   ❧

Rast stood with his head bowed. He touched her snout, ignoring the pain of her blood as it washed caustically over his hands and feet, hissing hotly on his boots.

The huge dragon lay battered and broken where she had fallen. Deep rents in her abdomen trickled blood; the ground was soaked and hissing as the grass she lay on wilted under her hot life's flow. One wing was completely shredded and the other was a nub of broken bone, thick tendons trailing from the torn flesh. Her right foreleg was bent at a horrible angle, and the talon was crushed. Her tail was snapped and lying useless. The iridescent hue of her scales was vastly diminished, as if her colour was leached with her life. The only thing keeping her red was her own blood.

Where the beams of light had glanced off her armour, the scales were buckled and split, as grey and lifeless as ash. Massive ribs jutted through her skin, broken and torn, and she wept a yellow pus from her entire left side under the brittle greyed scales where the tendrils had attached.

He shook his head dully. Her face was the worst. The flesh was torn over her teeth, and her fangs were bloodied, some broken. Her tongue lolled limply between them, large enough for five men to stand on, and her features were a bloody ruin. One eye gazed blearily out, tinged with yellow and emanating the faintest red glow. The other was a white dissolved mess in a shattered socket missing much of the flesh around it. Horns were missing and her jaw was swollen.

It was astonishing that she still held to life. Any other creature should be dead. Her sides expanded slowly with what must have been hideous pain, and she coughed blood every few minutes, the agony of each spasm obvious to all. It could not be long now, and he tried to give her what comfort he could.

Köranthír glared at the surrounding humans in mistrust, and hissed. Rast held up one hand. In the silence, his voice was clear, if faint.

'Peace, mighty Köranthír. We honour a fallen comrade, who named us dragonfriend, and fought to stave off the darkness that threatens us all.'

A wheezing hiss came from the dying dragon he still touched, and thickly, she spoke many words in dragon tongue. Then, with obvious effort, she switched to Darum.

'They are the key, Köranthír. They will help right the balance. *Believe.*' The last word came out in a gurgle, and she lapsed into silence, flanks heaving. Köranthír bowed and touched his snout to hers, to look into her good eye.

'Sister.' His voice was full of unfathomable grief. 'You are truly mighty. You will fly forever in my heart.'

At that, her face twisted in denial.

'I will never fly again,' she whispered, 'Let me die. Let me find peace from this pain.'

Rast saw dragons dropping silently down out of the sky, dozens of them returning from the west. There were many, but not all of them – the rest must still be hounding Yosgaloth far away. They formed a semicircle around Györnàeldàr's body, some of the smaller dragons alighting on turrets and abandoned sections of the wall. All bowed their snouts to stare down into their kin's eyes in profound respect.

'No other could have held for so long against such a foe,' whispered Köranthír, his powerful voice reverberating like a high wind. 'You are named Soul Eater's Bane, and we will never forget, *Györnàeldàr al Ssúrak kä.*'

NO, said a voice that all within miles felt from their own heads, the ground around them, the very stones. YOU WILL NOT BE FORGOTTEN.

The vast shape hanging above them moved with the slightest flap of wings, restoring bright sunlight to the city and turning gracefully to land without sound or tremor behind the semicircle of dragons, the wings folding in. The great head, hundreds of feet high, bowed down to look at Györnàeldàr. Several dragons flapped sideways, making room respectfully.

LITTLE SISTER, YOU HAVE DONE THE IMPOSSIBLE. YOU

PREVAILED AGAINST THE MIGHTIEST FOE IN THIS WORLD.
THROUGH YOU ALONE DO WE STILL HAVE A CHANCE TO AVERT
CHAOS. FOR SUCH A SACRIFICE, FOR SUCH COURAGE, ALL WILL
HONOUR YOU. COME. FLY WITH ME ONE LAST TIME.

'I cannot, Lord,' Györnàeldàr wept, hot tears coming from her eyes. The
world was dimming, and she couldn't draw breath. Rast saw the fear in her eyes,
felt it pierce his heart.

YOU CAN. I DREAMED IT SO.

Rast moved backwards as fast as he could, and the great drake's mouth
dropped open, cathedral-high, a light brighter than the sun blazing within. It
seemed barely more muted than it had in the cavern and gently expanded
outwards to engulfe the dying dragon, flames playing joyfully over where she lay.

Hearing the words, Rast felt a sense of anguish at the death of Györnàeldàr.
The Great Dragon immolated her dying body in living sunfire, leaving nothing
but a vibrant mound of grass in the rough outline and size of her body. Not even
bones remained.

The lesser god spread its wings and lifted its head, and then wheeled to face
Drakeholm Soaring. There was no wind from the wingbeats that hauled it miles
upwards, and it wavered and dissolved even as it rose. It seemed to Rast that a
faint shimmering shape that reminded him of Györnàeldàr rose with it, wings
curving joyfully in the air. Tears wet his cheeks unnoticed.

Köranthír threw his head back and cried in anguish. All the dragons gave note
to a high eerie keening with a low undertone that sounded like nothing Rast had
ever heard. Steaming tears ran down the faces and necks of every one; the dragons
wept for their fallen sister, at the passing of one of their immortal kin. One by
one, they sprang into the air, slowly beating their way towards Drakeholm
Soaring.

Finally only Köranthír was left, head bowed in mourning, grieving.
Györnàeldàr was gone.

FORTY-EIGHT

Those on the walls around Karland bowed their heads along with the dragon, silent at what they had witnessed. Many bore wounds. Ruptured ears bled and more had bruises from where their footing had been lost. Further back in the city, he could hear guard squads in the uproar trying to recall the evacuation orders. The city was safe, for now, but it was tightly held in the grip of chaos and panic.

On the city edge, the noise faded to a profound silence. Karland stood with Xhera, his arm around her shoulder, tears drying on his face. What he had seen was so beautiful, so heartrending, that he knew he would never find the words to express it. To face annihilation, and then a mystery so profound, all within one day… no mortal that had seen such things would forget them.

The great black approached the walls slowly. Stunned onlookers clearly saw the thick glimmering tears on the dragon's face.

Dragons can cry, Karland heard whispered. *They are like us.*

The reverie was broken by a great silver-sheened dragon which flew in from the west. It circled the city, sending jets of flame into the wind, and then sent a cry down to Köránthír. The greatest of the dragons lifted his proud head and called back. The silver, strangely smoothed in form, swept lower and hovered above him. They spoke in dragon tongue for a few minutes, and then with another cry, the silver banked and flew higher, back west out across the plains towards the Arkon mountains.

Köránthír regarded Rast, standing tall in front of the ranks of men that had dared to face a demon, and then his head rose up and right to regard Karland and Xhera solemnly with his burning blue gaze.

Something in his demeanour was changed. He snaked over to the wall next to the remains of the gate, in front of the mound, and looking down on them, offered an upturned foreclaw on the top of the wall.

'Come, children of man,' he rumbled with a hiss. 'Let me reunite you with your companion, whose bravery is worthy of Dragons.'

With a glance at Xhera Karland carefully clambered onto the huge hand-like claw. They were lowered gently to Rast. Many had gathered to watch, realising that these three were integral to all that had happened.

Still more people came through the shattered gates, to stand wordlessly behind them. Köranthír glanced again at the mound where Györnàeldàr had lain and then spoke, his powerful voice penetrating into the city.

'Mortals all, listen well. My kin have brought word. Yosgaloth makes for the mountains you call *Arkon,* harried and burned. We try to drive it back to the Pit but I fear it may slither into the darkness under those high peaks. Even dragon kind dare not follow it into those deep lairs; in there we would be trapped, consumed, lost.

'The Bane is weak after so long held captive, but will slowly gather its strength again. My sister was mighty indeed to hold that abomination for so long alone!' This last came with a ring of triumph and pride in his voice. 'Already it has consumed one of your cities along with many smaller towns… and many creatures. Every soul consumed means it is more powerful. It will grow in strength. In the end even we will not be able to hold it back – but for now, it will hide itself deep in the bones of the earth. We will have to deal with it eventually, but for the moment the demon is routed. It may not stir again for many of your years when it runs to ground; it has fed after a long fast of eons, but mark me well, O men. One day it *will* return and we must be ready.' His gaze swept the crowd proudly. 'Until then, the *Zhōng Gúorén Huáng dì Nāgāra* will stand watch.' He looked back to the three weary humans in front of him.

'Dragonfriends, you should know that Our Lord has afforded Györnàeldàr an honour like none other. She is not gone from this world – not entirely. Her body was broken past repair, but her soul is strong. The *Próarkhe* could not heal her because He was not truly here, and would never reach her in time. The damage was too great, her soul slipping away. He preserved what he could.

'The enemy now has a monument to its defeat above, high on the slopes of Drakeholm Soaring beyond the reach of mortals. Our Lord Dreamed her spirit into a hidden placid valley we have loved to rest in, in ages gone. Györnàeldàr loved it more than most, and found much peace there in her time. She becomes a part of this world, to perhaps outlast all of us.'

Xhera burst into tears as Karland gripped her hand tightly. That Györnàeldàr still lived in even some small way… it lightened his heart. He whispered, 'How is this even possible, Köranthír?'

'Much is possible to the Ones who Dream the world,' was the answer.

The crowd moved closer, despite the dragonfear they must have felt. 'We want to honour the dragon too,' shouted someone.

Köränthír blinked in surprise. He was long unused to mortals, and had obviously not thought that any besides these three would care about his sister.

'Weren't for her, we'd be et now,' someone else called. The crowd agreed, and their voices swelled and rose, shouting to be heard. Then three peals from a trumpet rang out, silencing them, and five squads of guards, City and Welcomer both, pushed a path through the throng and lined it at attention.

Into the gap came the Council of Twelve, hastily assembled and brought through a city in uproar to meet the eldest dragon still walking the earth. Their faces were bleak. On the way much had been said of events by Captain Dorn.

They stood, regarding the huge creature, and then Mira Lyss stepped forward, and bowed low. The dragon waited, unsure of what she wanted. The Arbitrator to the Council of Twelve took a deep breath, and spoke loudly for all to hear.

'Mighty Köränthír, Lord of the Sky; Györnàeldàr did us much honour. She bore mortals here. She warned us of both Darklings and Yosgaloth. In the end, she defended us all with her life.

'We are only humans. Doubtless you have cause to mistrust us, for I know our kind have not always been at peace with dragons. But in our own small way, we will honour her too.' She held his gaze, and Karland saw her jaw tremble with the effort of battling the fear. 'Let it be known that from this day, all dragon kind are welcomed in our land and in our city. We have much lore, and now realise the extent of your own... so we freely share with you as we do with all other races that love learning. Come back in a year, O Köränthír, and you will find not only welcome and rest but a statue to Györnàeldàr's sacrifice... a reminder to all of the courage of a Dragon.'

There was an astounded silence and then, to Karland's astonishment, Köränthír spread his vast wings to the side, and bowed to the mortals in front of him, the only dragon to have ever done so.

Rast knelt on one knee in return, and Karland and Xhera did likewise. Others followed: the Council of Twelve, the guards, the men lining the walls. The crowd dropped in a wave, back to and through the gate, and the ripple spread into the city itself. Köränthír raised his head, and gazed out over them all.

'Never did I think that I would find worth in mortal men,' he said in wondering tones for all to hear. 'Never did I think you to be worthy of the respect of my kin. When I lost my son to human avarice, I was stricken with grief. I killed all mortals I saw, and for many years my kind realised not that you bore no malice for the greater part. It was but some few mortals alone that deserved the blame.'

Karland's heart skipped a beat in shock.

The Drake Years were begun over Köränthír's own son!

'I now realise that Györnàeldàr saw more clearly than I. You have more worth than I thought possible. I understand now, perhaps, your place in the coming battle. The *Zhōng Gúorén Huáng dì Nāgāra* will ever be your friends from this day forth, people of Darost.'

His great black head, so different to that of his lost sister, rose and looked out west. 'The End of things is near – and of the End, this is only the beginning. Watch to the skies.' As if to put action to words, he unfurled his wings. Darkness fell across them. 'We will meet again, mortals, ere the end. The darkness spreads.'

Leaping powerfully into the air, his downbeat pulled him higher. Karland watched him spiral up, and then finally the black dot sped west towards his people holding a foe at bay.

Slowly, the people gathered moved apart, no one speaking above a murmur. In ones and twos, they gradually moved back inside the city. Every face was drawn, exhausted, and thoughtful. Today they had stood on the brink of destruction, and their deliverance would be held in the legends of men.

Karland stood once more with his arm around Xhera's shoulders. They stared out at the dimmed mountains to the west, the sound of the city coming back to life gradually rising behind them. For now, they were not part of it. For now, Karland's thoughts were on his lost friends: the people of The Croft. Captain Robertus. Aldwyn. Grukust. Györnàeldàr.

All of them as they had been were now just memories; they would be moments lost in time when he was gone. He had grown up quickly and experienced much heartache, and now as he stood there he realised that this was his fight too, to the bitter end. What he fought for was his friends, his family, his honour, his very world.

Rast's blood-burned and reddened hand dropped lightly onto his shoulders, the huge man saying nothing. He grimly stared out with them, his thoughts a mystery. Karland looked up at him, and then down at Xhera. She gave him a small smile.

As he looked back out over the wreckage and scarred land, smoke and dust high in the air dimming the bright sunlight, he knew in his heart that Köränthír was right.

The darkness was spreading.

Here ends Book One

The Balance is shifting. Our world is slipping into chaos. I can see how it will end; in darkness and despair. For nearly ten millennia, we have been at peace, as much as any can. Empires and lands have risen and fallen, as is the manner of these things. But now the world changes.

Slowly, like rot, war is spreading. Chaos is beginning to overwhelm our world. Strange creatures stir, and many are consumed by the promise of power as the Gods watch and do nothing. A great and ancient Evil awakes in the far west, tainting the hearts of those drawn to misdeeds. I fear for the fate of all races, weakened by war and distrust. The Evil gathers its strength, and I fear too: all shall fall into darkness. All shall fall to despair.

The eclipse of light has begun. The Darkness spreads...

- Personal excerpt, Unknown

About the Author

Chris lives in the UK and is the author of the World of Kuln series, as well as other diverse stories, and also writes articles and books in non-fiction and business. He moonlights as a TEDx and conference speaker, coach, and consultant for executives and organisations in complexity, agility, resilience, and human learning. He has too many hobbies – which include scuba diving, climbing, martial arts, gaming, reading, working out, photography, composing music, and generally learning anything and everything he can – and leads a very active lifestyle as a strong mental and physical health advocate. He reads almost constantly. For him, life is about learning and doing. His brain is... busy.

Chris is atypically autistic (ASD 1/2, with likely dyscalculia and occasional dyspraxia), and has differences in sensory and emotional input, as well as increased sensitivity in all of them, and annoyingly persistent imposter syndrome, so he sees different patterns and linkages in the world. He is very imperfect. A lot of his dreams end up in his books.

Lightning Source UK Ltd.
Milton Keynes UK
UKHW012000280322
400734UK00003B/30/J